And in the Morning

AND IN THE MORNING

Elizabeth Darrell

THE
LEISURE
CIRCLE

ACKNOWLEDGEMENT:
The publishers wish to thank Mrs Nicolete Gray and The
Society of Authors on behalf of the Laurence Binyon Estate.

This edition specially produced for
The Leisure Circle Limited
by Century Hutchinson Ltd,
Brookmount House, 62–65 Chandos Place,
London WC2N 4NW

Set by Avocet Ltd

Printed in Great Britain by
Anchor Brendon Ltd, Tiptree, Essex

They shall grow not old, as we that are left grow old:
Age shall not weary them, nor the years condemn.
At the going down of the sun and in the morning
We will remember them.

Laurence Binyon:
Extract from FOR THE FALLEN (September 1914)

Chapter One

TO CHRIS SHERIDAN, the Dorset village of Tarrant Royal was beautiful at any season: whether it was dappled with primroses during spring lambing; sleeping beneath summer heat and heavy with the scent of wild roses; mysterious in the autumn valley mists that shimmered cobwebs with diamond drops; or vivid with holly and full of the cry of the hunt.

Tarrant Hall, his family home, stood on a rise above the village. It was a beautiful square house of grey stone, crenellated and covered with ivy, set in extensive landscaped grounds. He spent very little time there, which was probably why he valued his infrequent visits so greatly. To a man who regarded the whole world with the familiarity with which most people know just their home town, a few days amidst the picturesque cluster of thatched cottages in the heart of Dorset that was a whole world in itself was a keenly enjoyable occasion.

However, at six o'clock this evening, two days before the Christmas of 1939, as he passed along the lanes leading to the village from Greater Tarrant station, the crisp, frosty stillness of the valley for once failed to invigorate and refresh him. There was an ache in his breast, and the past seemed closer than it had for some time. It was caused by more than the feel of the khaki he had never thought to wear again; by more than the sound of the old wartime songs of over twenty years ago that the troops had been singing at Waterloo Station; by more even than this Christian festival by which all optimists always predicted wars would be over. It was something to do with the peacefulness of a village where he had been born, and which had seen the dramas of his youth. In the darkness, he could well imagine it to be another time, another war.

Leaning back in his seat, Chris gazed at the stars, crystal-bright in the clear air, and thought of Rex, who had found affinity with the sky, and had roared up into it one day in 1918, never to come down. For a moment, he could clearly visualise

1

his brother's merry face with its happy-go-lucky smile and broad, friendly wink. Then the vision faded, leaving only a rash of twinkling stars, and the ghostly memory of the sound of Rex's old motorbike, running along the lane beside the car.

Frampton slowed the Daimler as it approached Brigadier Tarlestock on his white thoroughbred, crossing the lane from the track down from Longbarrow Hill. The brigadier negotiated the swing gate into the copse, which gave him a short cut to the mansion he had paid a fortune to have built just off the new main road to Dorchester. It was a monstrosity of a place that resembled a miniature Rhineland castle, and the villagers hated it. The old boy himself was a likeable eccentric, and the inhabitants of Tarrant Royal had eventually accepted their military madman, whilst privately begging Chris never to fell the stretch of copse on the Sheridan estate that obscured the view of the house.

The car edged past the rump of the white gelding as it nosed through the gate, and Chris raised a hand in response to the brigadier's greeting. Next minute, horse and rider had vanished into the darkness, leaving Chris with his thoughts of times gone by. How many times had his older brother Roland covered this well-loved countryside on the creatures with which he had had a greater rapport than with his fellows? Lost in that war with Rex, Roland's spirit also seemed to be there that evening, mingling with half-forgotten names, vague memories; the ghost of the boy Chris. Twenty years or more had passed since then; years packed with achievement, activity and fulfilment. Yet, tonight the past was suddenly so fresh in his mind it was almost unbearable.

He leant forward swiftly. 'Stop here, Frampton. By the church gate.'

Chill rose from the ground as he stepped out, and the sad rapture of the dying day was all around him, in the scents of field and hedgerow, in the frosty air, and the woodsmoke coming from cottage chimneys. In the distance he heard the bark of a dog fox, disturbed by the brigadier's progress through the copse, and, nearer to him, the uneasy quacking of Ron Browning's ducks by the pond.

The gate squeaked as he pushed it open. He made his way down the moss-covered path to a grave in the distant corner of the churchyard. The headstone was simple for the same reason that the resting place was unobtrusive. Chris had insisted on both because he had been so afraid of the sacrilege that might be committed by those determined on sensationalism. There had been some disturbing scenes when news of the secret burial had

2

leaked out. Flowers had been stolen from the grave, but others had replaced them tenfold. A procession of sightseers and photographers had invaded the village and trampled sacred ground around the old church, until the villagers had organised a relay of vigilante guards to augment Constable Peters and his dog, Bess. Today, few people remembered the drama that had captured the imagination of the entire country in 1918.

Reaching the grave, Chris squatted down beside it, and ran his hand gently over the stone at its head as he paid homage. With his lips forming the silent words that had become part of the ritual, he reached into his pocket for matches. Light flared as he struck one, enabling him to see the words he had chosen all those years ago.

LAURA SHERIDAN
Killed by enemy action May 1918
Loving and beloved wife of Rex
Brilliance lasts but a short while
The afterglow remains forever

The match burned down to his fingers. He dropped it automatically, too absorbed to feel the pain. Laura, who had given herself so totally to Rex she could not have lived without him. Laura, with hair as red as her husband's, and a temperament as vivid as her beauty. Laura, a girl full of passions and longings and laughter. Laura, whom Chris could not entirely forget twenty-one years later.

Tarrant Hall was usually lit from top to bottom, a welcoming sight for night visitors. Tonight it was dark, all the windows clad with the compulsory black curtains that had turned the whole of Britain into an isle of mourning with the suggestion of funeral drapes. His spirits grew heavier as he said goodnight to his chauffeur and trod the gravelled drive to where the main door stood open, allowing a glimpse into the dim, panelled hall.

'Hallo, Robson,' he said to the ageing butler, who stood ready to take his cap and greatcoat.

'Good evening, Sir Christopher,' came the warm but dignified greeting from the servant, who characteristically refrained from displaying surprise at the sight of his employer in military uniform. 'Did you have a comfortable journey from London, sir?'

'Reasonably. The trains are packed with troops, which sobers one – especially at this time of year.'

Shrugging out of the heavy khaki coat, Chris looked around

with pleasure and aesthetic appreciation. Lovingly polished wood panelling gleamed in the light from logs crackling in the great open fireplace; showy arrangements of amber, rust, and yellow chrysanthemums stood on the antique dresser and tallboys; and in the spacious stairwell stood a fifteen-foot fir tree, dressed with silver strands, tiny lanterns and brightly wrapped packages.

For a moment, Chris found his throat constricting. It all looked so normal, so peaceful, so human. Yet the inhumanity of war had begun again and increased. Death, torture, hate and greed stalked the streets of Poland right now. So many people he knew and respected had vanished from there without trace. Standing in his present freedom, Chris felt the anguish of all those European people with whom the ghosts of the past had taken up permanent residence.

A sudden rush of running feet accompanied by laughter broke into his thoughts, and drew his gaze upward through the stairwell. Robson appeared at his elbow with an explanation.

'Miss Patricia came over for luncheon, sir. She has been helping Miss Vesta to put up holly and mistletoe, in addition to rehearsing a concert, I understand. A somewhat lively entertainment, judging from the sounds emanating from the music room earlier on.'

Chris smiled at him. 'A necessary evil of yuletide festivities, I fear. So much for my hope that they had become too self-consciously adult for such things.' Even as he said them, he felt regret for the words. Would there ever be a Christmas like this again? Giving a faint sigh, he asked after Mrs Robson, who was a permanent invalid.

'My wife is fair, sir,' came the resigned judgement from a man whose long, thin face rarely betrayed great depths of expression. 'I can't say more than that without being guilty of false optimism. But Her Ladyship has been a tower of strength.'

'She always is in times of stress,' agreed Chris. 'Where shall I find her?'

'In the drawing room, Sir Christopher. I understand she has withdrawn from the ... er ... concert rehearsals to drink a glass of madeira.'

Chris headed for the drawing room deep in thought. When Marion took to madeira it was usually a sign that she was upset. It was hardly the best time for him to walk in dressed as he was, but she would have to know the truth. Better not to wait for the right moment – was there ever a right moment for ill tidings? – and to keep their pact never to hide things from each other.

His wife was sitting near the fire in a room of elegant

4

proportions, filled with furniture and ornaments which reflected his own aesthetic and cosmopolitan tastes. Marion had placed bowls of preserved autumn leaves about the room, and a large jug filled with the dark green and scarlet glory of holly sat in the wide hearth. She seemed to be staring at this. A glass of madeira stood untouched on the table beside her. As Chris entered, the three family retrievers jumped up immediately and came forward, tails swinging, then slowed to halt uncertainly. One even growled softly, until the unmistakable scent of the man they accepted as an infrequent but welcome visitor overpowered the alien sight and aroma of the khaki uniform. They surrounded him in apologetic delight, and Chris absently fondled their golden heads as he gazed across at Marion. She took the evidence of his new status badly. Getting to her feet in obvious shock, the colour drained from her face, and she stared as if at a ghost – a ghost from over twenty years ago – her dark eyes full of fears.

'It isn't what you think,' he explained swiftly. 'The uniform is merely expedient at a time when all men young enough are going to be wearing one of some kind or another. There is no question of active service.'

'That's what they said last time, and look what happened.'

He had prepared his answer to that one in advance. 'Last time I was an eighteen-year-old subaltern, during a period when the supply of live ones had run out. They've given me a much higher rank now, and I'm a damned sight less green than I was.' Pushing the dogs gently aside, he crossed to her. 'I'm sorry if it came as too much of a blow.'

She wore an unconvinced expression. 'Couldn't you have written, telephoned?' she appealed. 'Just walking in like this . . .'

'Would it have altered the fact?' he asked gently.

'Oh, Chris, it arouses too many memories.'

'What do you think it does to me?'

For a long moment she struggled with her unusual lack of control, holding aloof from this man in khaki she could not easily accept. Then she put out her warm hands to take his cold ones.

'Forgive me. It wasn't much of a welcome for you, was it?'

He smiled with relief. 'Well, I'm not surprised. Even the dogs took exception to my new suit until they realised it was the same old me inside it.'

Back on an even keel now, Marion said lightly, 'You look ridiculously young to be a colonel. Does this mean David will have to salute you now?'

'Theoretically, yes. But the day I start receiving any kind of

5

recognition from my son will signal a new stage in the curious relationship we have.' He walked across to pour himself a glass of vodka, a taste he had acquired during his many visits to Poland and Russia. 'Is he being granted Christmas leave?'

'Yes. Isn't it lovely?' Her voice was warm now with enthusiasm for her adored boy. Then, as he returned to the fire with his glass, she added persuasively, 'Be nice to him, Chris.'

'I'm never sure what that request means,' he observed, settling in a chair facing her. 'Are you asking me to spend a lot of time with him, or to keep out of his way as much as possible? I'm certain *he* would regard the latter as infinitely preferable.'

'And he'll continue to do so, unless you make an effort to thwart his indifference,' she told him.

Looking at her with resignation, he sipped his vodka, then sighed. 'My dear, it is twelve years too late, and you are the only one who is unhappy about the situation. David *enjoys* his metaphorical self-bastardisation. It gives him a source of justification whenever he falls short of the high standards he sets himself.'

'What do you enjoy about it?' she challenged.

His hand reached out to stroke the head of one of the dogs at his knee. The warmth of the fire, the beauty of his home surroundings, the relaxation of just sitting with a drink in his hand after the past seven weeks were all he wanted right now. Marion was good to look at – a little plumper these days, perhaps, but glowing with health and quietly attractive in a blue wool dress. Chris liked her in blue, and he also liked her hair arranged as a soft, brown frame for her face, as it was now. After almost two months apart, he had looked forward to the short break over Christmas in her undemanding company. They had started off wrong. Why did she now have to embark on this thorny subject?

'I don't *enjoy* any aspect of a relationship you cannot seem to leave in peace,' he told her heavily. 'Conversely, I don't *abhor* the situation. I simply accept it, and instead pursue roads that lead somewhere. David is twenty-four. Old enough, I would have thought, to see the ridiculous affront to which he has been a martyr over the past twelve years for what it really is. If he can't, I certainly do not intend to hang onto his coat-tails all through Christmas. It is the season of goodwill toward men, even one's father. He adores you. Isn't that enough?'

'Not when you constantly criticise him,' she countered.

'He is a young man of immense personality and intelligence. I just deplore the fact that he constantly overplays the first, and

6

insults the second by living in the fantasy that he is a reincarnation of Rex, when he is a very poor imitation.'

Marion flushed. '*Anyone* has to be a poor imitation of Rex. David knows that. But can't you see that being the nephew of a legendary aviator puts a terrible onus on him when flying?'

'That's his excuse for everything.'

Marion sighed. 'I do wish you'd try to understand him more. You're so much younger than the average father of men his age, you should be closer to him, not miles apart.'

Chris put down his empty glass. 'And he is so much older than most men with a father my age. Perhaps he should make an effort to understand me.'

With a shake of her head, she said, 'The only person I know who comes anywhere near to understanding *you* is Bill Chandler, and that's only because he's a doctor who specialises in unravelling the human mind.'

'You make me sound like some Archimedian sibling who creates universal bafflement,' he protested mildly. 'Am I really so unfathomable?'

'No,' she relented with a smile. 'Not when it comes to the aspects of life we ordinary mortals indulge in. Then, my dear, you are dangerously transparent.'

'Now you make me sound like a silly old buffer.'

Laughing lightly, Marion left her chair in a swift movement to kneel beside him, catching his hands in hers. 'You are neither silly nor old. At forty-three, it is positively unfair to look every bit as handsome as your son, especially when you seem as unaware of the fact as you always have been. It's one of the things I love about you.'

He glanced up at the clock, then back to her very obviously. 'I believe I have time to hear of the others.'

Her eyes glowed as she whispered, 'Kiss me, Chris. I didn't give you a chance when you came in, did I?'

The pleasure of her body, round and soft in his arms, drove away the tension of his arrival, and the irritation engendered by the discussion about their son. This was what he needed to drive away the pressures and horrors of the past weeks. He lingered over the kiss, enjoying the pleasure of a slowly rising desire within him that had been slumbering too long.

Lifting his mouth from hers, he said, 'I suggest we continue this upstairs.'

'We can't,' she whispered with regret. 'Tessa and Bill are coming to dinner, and we'll be rushed to bathe and change, as it is.'

7

He leant back with a sigh. 'Time. Time! Everything today is governed by hands and pendulums. The Greeks had a much better arrangement for...'

'The Greeks, my dear, had a better arrangement for everything, according to you,' she interrupted, getting up and holding out her hands to him. 'If their civilisation was so perfect, why did it ever end?'

Allowing himself to be coaxed to his feet, he cocked an eyebrow at her. 'You don't really want me to answer that, do you?'

'No, no,' she assured him with a laugh. 'We would be here all night, and I wouldn't understand half you said.'

At that point, the door burst open and two young girls came in, like dual harbingers of Christmas. Rosy cheeked, with sparkling expressions, dressed in reds and greens with touches of frosty white, his daughter and her closest friend were lovely to see. But the two youthful faces, so different in type and shape, altered rapidly when they saw him. Vesta rushed forward to kiss him with gusto.

'Daddy! How absolutely marvellous you look! Turn around!' She seized his arm and pulled him clockwise so that she could fully appreciate the smartly cut uniform. Then she swung him back to face her, still full of enthusiasm. 'When did you join up? Mummy, doesn't he look astonishingly romantic? Just like those old photographs up in the storeroom.' Rounding on her friend, she demanded, 'Pat, isn't he simply the *ultimate*?'

Chris was surprised to see that the girl had grown incredibly still. The rosy bloom of her healthy young complexion deepened to a pronounced flush.

'You look... different, Uncle Chris,' she said in a strange tone. 'Are they sending you to France?'

'Good heavens, no. It was simply that they felt things would run smoother if youngsters in uniform received orders from a senior officer, rather than from a civilian,' he explained, finding the story easier the second time of telling. His life was going to be one big deceit in the days to come. It was important to lie with assurance right from the start.

But Vesta saw him dressed in the traditional garb of heroes. She was an idealist destined to be hurt by the truth of war, he felt; shattered by the degrading shame of being part of it. He extricated himself from her gently.

'I wish you would express yourself verbally with as much finesse and intuition as you do on canvas,' he complained. 'Although your paintings tend also to be somewhat inconclusive in statement, at times.'

8

She wrinkled her nose at him. 'It's no good putting on that donnish pose with me. I saw through that years ago, Daddy dear. In the storeroom with those old pictures of you with Uncle Roland and Uncle Rex are some of *your* canvases. They're just as vague and romantic as you say mine are.'

He frowned. 'Good Lord, are they? Small wonder they are hidden away in that room.'

'Vesta, when did you go in there?' Marion asked sharply enough to draw everyone's gaze to her face. 'There's nothing of yours amongst those things.'

'Shouldn't I have done?' asked their daughter curiously. 'It's not locked. We've been in there several times, haven't we, Pat?'

'For what reason?'

'Looking for props for our concerts. We came across all that old stuff several years ago. I'm sorry, Mummy. We weren't prying, honestly.'

'Why didn't you mention it?'

The girl looked uneasily at Chris, then at Pat Chandler. 'I suppose I had a feeling it might upset you. We found it all fascinating, didn't we?'

Pat nodded. 'Looking at old photographs always is. There were some there of my parents that I'd never seen before – and a gorgeous one of my Uncle Mike with Rex in RFC uniform. They both look so dashing and saucy. I wish I had known them. The village looks so different, too,' she went on hastily, seeing Marion's expression. 'Nicer, I think, and much more rural. The Brig's ghastly Rhine castle wasn't even a twinkle in his eye then.' She turned to Chris, her usual calm having returned, to pour oil on troubled waters, as she had on other occasions. 'Fishy Whitemore is spreading it around that you'll be forced to raze the copse to provide timber for the war effort, and Tarlestock Towers will be a blot on the horizon for miles around.'

He smiled at her. '"Fishy" Whitemore and "the Brig"? The expressions of youth today!'

She smiled back. 'What about the copse? Will it have to go?'

'Over my dead body,' he told her vigorously, then realised his choice of phrase could have been better, under the circumstances. Walking to the door, he added, 'But *I* shall have to go now, or your parents will arrive for dinner before I'm dressed.'

'Can't you stay like that, Daddy?' Vesta appealed. 'You do look so handsome.'

Looking back over his shoulder, he said, 'Before many months are out, you'll be sick to death of uniforms, my dear girl. You'll probably be wearing one yourself.'

*

9

The two girls dressed for dinner in Vesta's room, a familiar routine for lifelong friends, and one that was always accompanied by non-stop chatter. They had attended the same exclusive school, but there was nothing identical about them, despite the narrow training. A year ago, at eighteen, Vesta had exchanged the ordered life of a boarding school for the daughters of the wealthy for the unconventional Bohemian chaos of life as an art student. Pat, a year her junior, had only that summer put away her school uniform and joyously joined her mother in the running of their farm, which maintained a flock of pedigree sheep.

Vesta lived in the realms of romanticism. The introverted urge to hide the fact, revealed in her painting, had led her to adopt the traits of the more exaggerated of her fellow students, which were foreign to her true character. Pat, on the other hand, found the simplicity and uncompromising routine of farming suited her commonsense approach to life perfectly. Where Vesta saw mystic, unobtainable beauty in autumn hillsides wreathed in mist, Pat saw only hazards to animals that strayed and fell in the obscuring greyness. When Vesta delighted in the rural beauty of lush meadows filled with fat spring lambs, Pat saw only lush grazing and fat profits.

In appearance, they were also vastly different. Vesta had inherited her mother's brown hair and eyes, but was tall like the Sheridans, and had the beautiful smile that identified her as Chris's daughter. Pat, too, favoured her mother, with hair so dark it was almost black, unusual silvery green eyes, and a figure very rounded in all the right places. Vesta's willowy shape was a constant source of envy to her, and they were discussing it as they dressed.

'I wish I could wear something like that, Vee,' Pat said, as she watched Vesta step into an expensive gypsy-style creation of orange chiffon sewn with heavy silver fringing. 'Even if I could squeeze into it, I'd look like a Christmas cracker that had failed to go "bang" when it was pulled.'

Vesta laughed as she smoothed the material over her narrow hips, then picked up the long matching chiffon scarf to wind around her head as a bandeau with floating ends.

'You don't know how good it is to talk to a person who is normal for a change. Some of the girls at the school are *the end*. They're so cocooned in the chrysalis of "art, darling" they drive me to drink. Literally! One night I deliberately guzzled gin until I passed out. *They* said it was an essential experience to open the mind to the depths of understanding and representationalism, which is necessary to any artist. All it did to me was give me a

10

foul headache next day and bring on "the curse" a week early.'

'Why do you do it, Vee?' Pat asked quietly.

Vesta turned, hands to her head, busy with the fastening of the bandeau. 'Do what?'

'Behave like an idiot just because you're studying art? It's not a bit like the real you, and, if you're not enjoying it, why do it?'

Feeling suddenly false, Vesta left the chiffon dangling round her left ear, and dropped heavily onto the bed with a sigh.' I wish I was full of courage like you, Pat.'

'Me? Full of courage? What a peculiar thing to say!'

'But you are,' Vesta insisted warmly. 'You love farming, working the land, drenching sheep, driving tractors, and going around in old clothes and gumboots in all weathers. It's men's work, really, but you don't care what people say.'

Pat's round healthy face registered surprise. 'Do people say things?'

'You know they do. David, for one.'

Pat shrugged. 'Oh, *him*. A fat lot I care for his opinions. In his view, girls were created merely for his entertainment. He finds no other point to their existence. I can't see anything "courageous" in defying your brother.'

Wanting to pursue the subject, Vesta said impatiently, 'I'm not joking. You have courage enough to show the world what you truly think and feel, and apparently don't worry about anyone's opinion. I do.' She made a face at the other girl. 'If you want to know the real reason I moved from the comfort of our town apartment, to a ghastly bare room full of draughts and the most putrid smells, it was because one of our scruffiest male students saw me going indoors with Daddy, and put it around that I had a rich lover who was corrupting the clarity of my perception of the truth of existence.'

To her annoyance, Pat flopped onto her back on the other bed, convulsed with laughter. As she watched her friend rolling from side to side with mirth, Vesta saw the ridiculousness of what she had said, and her annoyance increased. The world of art students, bare attics, Bohemian *poseurs*, the need to conform to the defiance of conformity, and the fear of being the victim of cruel mass ridicule, was impossible to explain in the world of a Dorset village. At Tarrant Royal, the way she lived in London would be ridiculed just as cruelly by others with their own rigid rules. Yet she felt that Pat would always be herself, no matter what her surroundings. That was what she had meant about having courage.

Vesta admitted that she was timid in other ways. Always having shied from revealing her most private feelings, she was possessed with a need to speak of them through brushes and colours. A talent she had inherited from her father, it was more developed in her, and had earned her a place in a distinguished school. Yet she was unhappy, and oppressed by the teaching. Constantly criticised for concentrating on inconsequential detail to the detriment of the picture as a whole, she found herself unable to paint well. Her canvases lacked imagination, were too full of vivid colour, and totally out of character. Sensing that she was expressing a mixture of everyone else's opinions, which she merely signed with her own name, she often longed for the holidays at Tarrant Hall, when she was free to sit with easel and paints, putting her real self onto canvas. Then she painted gentle images in pastel tones, creating pictures full of soft hints and half-awakened emotions. There was only one person she would show these pictures to, because he really understood what she was trying to say. Unfortunately, he was rarely at home when she was.

Now she had foolishly deprived herself of the pleasure of living at their London apartment with him. She had moved into a freezing, smelly garret over an Italian restaurant with another girl, and lived a lie the whole time instead of half the time. Seeing her dearest and closest friend choking with laughter over this evidence of her weakness made her hit out in retaliation.

'You wouldn't guffaw like that if someone imagined Daddy was *your* lover. You'd be thrilled.'

Pat sobered immediately, and sat up wearing a wary expression. 'What do you mean?'

'You've had a pash on him for ages! I guessed you had when you took one of those photographs from the storeroom two summers ago – the one of him with Uncle Roland and Uncle Rex just before 1914.' Seeing her friend's stricken look, she relented. 'Don't be daft, Pat. I don't mind. He's so frightfully good-looking, and so much younger than most girls' fathers, nearly all my class at school were crazy about him.'

Pat still looked stricken. 'You don't think he suspects, do you? Oh God, Vee, I'd *die*.'

Vesta shook her head. 'Daddy is so divinely unaware of a thing called "passion" he wouldn't even suspect Mummy of having designs on him, much less a child like you.'

Ignoring the jibe at her year's less experience of life, Pat said slowly, 'That's one of the silliest things you've said this evening. Uncle Chris fathered David when he was only eighteen and a schoolboy. You were born when he was no more than twenty-four, and the twins were miscarried by Aunt Marion when he was twenty-five. I'd say he was hardly unaware of passion.'

Vesta flushed. She never liked Pat's frank attitude toward something that was practically taboo in her own family, and that had caused the trouble between her father and brother. 'Well, he's forty-three now, and thinks of nothing but his work. Don't worry. He certainly wasn't aware that he had knocked you for six tonight by appearing in uniform.' Looking hard at the other girl, she went on, 'It did knock you for six, didn't it?'

Pat nodded slowly. 'He looked so sensational I just couldn't equate him with your father, somehow. Funny how uniform makes a man take on an aura of unfamiliarity, as if you were somehow seeing all the qualities he has previously hidden from you.' She looked beseechingly at Vesta. 'But it isn't just that he's so terrifically good-looking. He's the most marvellous person, Vee. I know it's a forbidden subject in your house, but I've been brought up on the facts. Mummy and Daddy admire him tremendously, and so do I, for what he went through and overcame. If I had been in your shoes, I'd have told a whole battalion of scruffy male students that he was my father, and gone on to say that their pathetic ideas on drinking gin to gain essential experience of life are an insult to men like him.'

Vesta took in the ardour of her tone, the brightness of her cheeks and eyes, and formed a dismaying conclusion. 'Pat, you haven't *really fallen* for him, have you?'

The courageous honesty with which she had just been endowed by her friend seemed to desert Pat now, for she got to her feet with too much speed and said heartily, 'Good heavens, no! It would be incest, or something, wouldn't it?'

'He's not your real uncle,' Vesta pointed out, still dismayed. 'It's only because our parents have been friends since before we were born that we call them "aunt" and "uncle".' Addressing Pat's back as her friend applied a brush too vigorously to her short black curls, Vesta went on, 'David looks disgustingly like Daddy. Why don't you fall for him?'

'Because I always feel like knocking *him* for six, instead,' came the smart reply. 'I'm sorry to inform you, Vesta Sheridan, that I detest your beastly brother.'

This brought a laugh from Vesta, as she moved back to the dressing table to finish tying the bandeau. 'Since you've been telling each other the same thing for years, I've given up all hope of having you for a sister-in-law.' Her glance met Pat's in the mirror. 'I don't really want you as a stepmother, either.'

Pat's hands stilled as she stared back. 'Love is the most wretched thing, Vee. It hurts like nothing else I can think of. Have you been in love yet? *Really* in love, I mean. Not some

13

immature pash over a schoolboy or the art master.'

Vesta shook her head, which dislodged the bandeau around her hair. 'Oh hell, I think I'll give this up,' she swore, tugging the chiffon undone, and ruffling her shoulder-length hair into an untidy mass again.

'Let me do it,' offered Pat, putting her hairbrush down and taking the length of orange material from her. 'Gosh, I wish I could get away with something as swanky as this. Keep still!' With the tip of her tongue protruding as she concentrated on the task in hand, she went on, 'Could you imagine me in anything stylish? Good old plain Jane, that's me. If I could only lose a few pounds it might help, but I get so hungry I eat like mad. This suspender belt is killing me, but I daren't leave it off. I'd look like the ghosts of Christmas past, present and future all rolled into one.' She sighed. 'By the time this one is over, I'll have eaten so many mince pies even this monstrosity won't keep it all in.'

Vesta giggled. 'Mummy always holds you up as an example when I refuse bacon and eggs for breakfast. She calls you "a lovely bonny girl".'

'Ugh,' groaned Pat. 'Next to being dubbed "ever so nice", that's the final death knell to any girl's hopes.'

'Daddy thinks you're "ever so nice",' Vesta ventured gently.

Pat's expression sobered as she said faintly, 'Does he?'

'You don't realise what a compliment that is. He can talk to people for absolute hours and not be able to tell you a thing about their looks afterward.'

The bandeau successfully fastened, and with perfume lavishly dabbed behind their ears, they prepared to go downstairs. As they left the bedroom, Pat said heavily, 'I think animals have a much better system. They spend the minimum time doing the necessary, then produce the next generation with dutiful regularity, without getting involved in emotions. Let's face it, one ram is much like any other to a ewe.'

They walked along the wide corridor towards the head of the stairs. 'Perhaps "doing the necessary" is so ghastly it's better not to be emotional over it,' suggested Vesta.

'Mares make a frightful row while it's going on,' mused Pat. 'I've never decided whether they're squealing in delight or pain. Horses make the whole thing seem rather harrowing and disgusting.' She cast a glance at Vesta. 'Do you know any girls who've done it?'

'The girl I live with has,' she said, finding relief at being able to tell her oldest friend something she could repeat to no one else. 'I walked in one evening after going to the cinema, and a man was there with her. I mean, actually doing it behind the curtain

14

where the beds are. I could tell by his grunts, and the squeaking of the bed springs. It was frightful!'

'*Vee*,' gasped Pat. 'Whatever did you do?'

'Bolted. It was the only thing I could do. I stayed at our place for the night, but I slipped out early and made Sandy promise not to let on to Daddy that I'd been there. Somehow, I couldn't face *him* and invent an excuse. I'd have felt like curling up.'

'What did the girl say to you when you went back?' asked Pat avidly, as they started down the stairs.

'Offered to fix up someone for me. "An essential experience" she called it.'

'Like the gin? I suspect it would also give you a foul headache the next day,' commented Pat dryly, 'but it wouldn't bring on "the curse" a week early. More likely to drive it away for nine months.'

They descended the rest of the way in thoughtful silence then, as they crossed the hall past the lofty Christmas tree, Vesta said, 'She seemed to find it more than enjoyable.'

'That sort of girl would,' stated Pat. Then she looked at Vesta with laughter brimming in her eyes. 'I don't think I'd be very good at it, somehow. By the time I took off this suspender belt, he'd have grown tired of waiting and fallen asleep.'

Laughing with the pleasure of being together again, they walked in to find that Pat's parents had arrived. Vesta greeted them warmly, kissing the assured attractive woman she called "Aunt Tessa", and being enclosed in a bear-like hug by the silver-haired neurologist she had known all her life as "Uncle Bill". Receiving the usual smacking avuncular kiss on her cheek, she wondered briefly what such a greeting would do to poor Pat if her own father were as hearty as Bill Chandler. She looked across at him, now extremely handsome in the usual dinner jacket, and tried to see him through her friend's eyes. As his daughter, all she could see was an attractive blond man with a brilliant brain, who was gentle, artistic, humorous, and constantly perplexed by anyone with less intelligence than himself.

'Wow! That's some outfit, my girl,' exclaimed Uncle Bill in his inimitable manner. He, like his wife, had never lost the Australian accent. It sometimes seemed strange that Pat, with her cultured voice, could be a child of theirs.

'Do you really like it?' Vesta asked eagerly.

'I'll say... and then some! What a colour!'

Vesta turned to Pat's mother. 'What do you think, Aunt Tessa? You have such good taste.'

She smiled. 'I know Christmas is a time for universal

15

goodwill, but that compliment is pushing it a little too far, dear. I spend most days in clothes the rag-and-bone man would turn away. But, for what it's worth, I think you look extremely *soignée.*'

'But much too thin,' put in her mother characteristically. 'I don't think she eats enough... and why she had to go off and live in a damp room in Bayswater, when we have a comfortable apartment near the school, I cannot think.'

'Independence, Marion,' advised Bill Chandler. 'It's what all youngsters think they want until things go wrong. Then they complain that everyone has stopped being interested in their affairs.'

'What do you think of Vee's frock, Uncle Chris?' asked Pat in wistful tones, her eyes large and full of silvery lights.

'Are you asking what I think of the frock itself, or of my daughter inside it?' he queried quietly, causing her colour to rise slightly. 'If the former, I have to say that there appears to be very little of it for the amount I paid; if the latter, my only comment is one of wonder that she feels obliged to dress in such startling garb in order to be an artist. I manage it without donning bright orange and sporting the headdress of a Red Indian squaw.'

They all laughed, and Vesta wrinkled her nose at him affectionately. 'I asked you to come with me to choose your birthday present to me, but you blanched at the thought and dived into a pile of books, if you remember.'

'I should think so! Can you imagine anything worse, Bill, than sitting in a large store, surrounded by females oohing and aahing at each other in puce and purple?'

'It sounds like one hell of an interesting afternoon,' came the irrepressible answer. 'Lucky dog to be given the opportunity! My womenfolk lullop about in mud-splashed raincoats and gumboots most of the time, then cut along to Dorchester, without telling me, whenever they want to glam up.'

'God knows what that expression means, but Tessa always appears delightfully free of mud whenever I see her... and young Pat is always very nice to look at.'

Vesta caught her friend's anguished eye, and said under her breath, 'Don't take it to heart. From Daddy, that's praise indeed.'

'Shut up!' hissed Pat fiercely, and walked away to study an arrangement of tall candles and Christmas roses with great intensity.

Watching her, while conversation went on around her between the four older people, Vesta found herself troubled by her friend's behaviour. Could Pat be "in love" with her father?

16

How awful if she was! Was it possible to love someone who hardly noticed one in return? Pat had said love hurt. In what way? There were plenty of poems, novels and films, all obsessed with love, but what was it? Suppose it never happened to her; suppose she went through life never discovering what everyone else seemed to find so easily and so often. Her fellow students were forever pairing up, parting, forming new pairs. A lot of them went all the way with each other, Vesta knew, yet when she studied them they looked no different. Boys had tried it on with her, of course, and she had always been annoyed and upset. Had it been because none of them had ever appealed to her? If she found herself in love with one, would she want to go all the way with him? Surely she would look different afterwards.

Somehow, she hoped and expected the mysterious state of love to be something tremendous, like hearing all the bells in the world ringing at once, or feeling as if one were in a lift that was not stopping at any floor on the way down. Was that how Pat felt when she looked at her father? And – horrifying thought – did her friend long to go all the way with him? The heat of embarrassment over such thoughts flooded through her, and she looked again at the girl studying the flower arrangement. A pretty girl, in a blue silk dinner dress, with short dark curls and very nice eyes. She looked little different from when they had last met, two months ago. Where were the signs that she was 'in love'? Coming to the conclusion that Pat was just being dramatic, Vesta then remembered her friend's face on seeing her father so unexpectedly in uniform. That *had* hurt, she now acknowledged. Was love only painful and never joyous? She was nineteen and had not yet found out.

Her attention was drawn to her parents by the sounds of discord. She caught Uncle Bill's wink of understanding, and smiled back at him.

'Surely we can wait a little longer for him,' her mother begged. 'He promised to be here in time for dinner.'

'Then he miscalculated,' came the mild response. 'It's not always possible to be where one has promised at the required time.'

'You seldom are, Chris,' joked Bill Chandler.

'The trains are all crowded with troops,' Vesta's father continued in the same tone. 'He has probably had to wait for the next one.'

'He isn't coming by train, Chris. I did tell you that earlier.'

'Did you? In that case, I'm definitely not waiting any longer for my dinner. If David is driving here in whatever contraption he has presently acquired under the nomenclature of "motor car", it could be midnight before he arrives. Robson has indicated that dinner is ready to be served, so let's go in and eat whatever Cook's culinary skill has provided.'

It was a very good meal, despite the fact that the two sets of parents could not finish discussing the war. It had been a fact for three months and nothing seemed to be happening, except in Europe, Vesta thought impatiently. Some terrible events had taken place there, she admitted, but this was Christmas, and she thought they were all being unnecessarily gloomy. At the school, no one showed much interest in the war, and she personally thought all the preparations against attack a bit melodramatic. It was not as if there would be any fighting in England. It had all started in Poland and would probably end there. The Poles were always being invaded and integrated into other empires and cultures. Why make such a fuss this time?

David had not arrived when they left the table and went into the sitting room for coffee. The two men stayed to smoke and talk about the things they would not discuss in general company, and Vesta noticed that her mother gave only half her attention to what they were all discussing. It was always the same. David was notorious for lateness, and for making casual promises he instantly forgot. Yet her mother never ceased to expect him on time, and to believe he had suffered some terrible accident when he was not. Finally, Vesta could stand the situation no longer. She crossed the room to sit on the arm of her mother's chair.

'Don't worry,' she urged with a smile. 'It's just David being David. I expect they all decided to have a drink together first.'

'Why hasn't he telephoned, in that case?'

'When did David ever telephone to explain where he was?' Seeing that her mother was really upset, she patted her hand. 'It isn't that he doesn't care, you know. Truly, it isn't. It simply never occurs to him that you will worry. Daddy is just the same. I expect most men are.'

'I expect they are,' agreed her mother, with a smile that belied the surprising mistiness of her eyes. 'It's just that . . .'

'Yes?'

'It's just that this Christmas is so important. There may never be another like it.'

There it was again, this gloom of the older generation. 'Oh dear, you really do have a fit of the blues,' Vesta said. 'Is it because Daddy came home in uniform tonight? He won't have to fight, surely. He's much too clever, and far too valuable in that obscure government department of his. As for David, he's got nine lives.'

18

Her mother's normally calm face was full of strange shadows as she looked up. 'They said that about your Uncle Rex... But his lives finally ran out.'

'Only because he was doing something almost impossible that earned him the VC,' Vesta declared, worried by the conversation, and wishing her brother would arrive to put an end to it.

'Besides, the aircraft they flew then fell apart more often than not. We've got the Spitfire now.'

'Yes, we've got the Spitfire now,' agreed her mother with a sigh.

'Cheer up, Mummy,' she said encouragingly. 'If this Christmas is so important to you, you must enjoy every moment of it. And that includes Uncle Bill's frightful conjuring tricks.'

That reference to an annual event that was a standing joke between the two families brought a smile to her mother's face, and Vesta made it broaden by confiding that there was an item in the concert she and Pat had devised that was a sketch about a conjuror whose tricks never worked.

At that point, she heard voices in the hall, and got up in swift relief. 'That sounds like David arriving now. I didn't hear his car on the gravel, so perhaps he did come by train after all, and couldn't get a taxi from the station. I'll go and explain about dinner, and stop him from walking in on Daddy and Uncle Bill. We don't want to start Christmas off with too much of a bang, do we?'

Hurrying into the hall, she found Robson talking to someone outside. It could not be David after all. 'Who is it, Robson?' she asked, anxiety sharpening her voice.

The butler turned immediately. 'A gentleman in the services. A friend of Mr David's, I understand.'

Anxiety turned to fear. Had something happened to her brother? Going to the door, she saw a figure in air-force blue standing in the faint pool of light outside.

'Won't you come in?' she invited. 'Where is David?'

The man came hesitantly indoors, shaking rain from his uniform. He appeared to be very wet indeed, and worried about the mess he was making with his muddy shoes on the beautifully polished wood-block floor. He took off his cap swiftly as he looked across at her.

'Forgive me, please. The weather outside it is very bad. I must introduce. Felix Makoski of the Polish Air Force.' He snapped his heels smartly together, and bowed briefly from the waist. 'I am honoured to present myself at the home of an English family, but it is a most unmannered situation. David has

19

generously invite me to spend Christmas here. We had an assignation at the Greater Tarrant railway station for twenty hundred hours. I wait one hour, then I think he has go ahead of me. I ask the direction of Tarrant Hall, but I have walk here to find he has not arrive. Please to tell me what I must now do.'

Just then, the door of the dining room opened as the two men strolled out, still deep in conversation. Vesta called to her father and explained the presence of a dripping young man in their hall. From then on, the matter was taken out of her hands. Her father walked forward smiling, and burst into a flood of what she took to be Polish. The visitor was completely overwhelmed by the approach, and stared in something approaching shock for a few moments at this Englishman, who could speak a language only a few Western Europeans bothered to learn. Then they were shaking hands, and Robson was being told to take Flight Lieutenant Makoski to one of the guest rooms, and to inform Cook to prepare a tray to take up, as soon as their visitor had had a bath and changed into dry clothes.

As she watched the thin, lively face, saw the delight in eyes so dark they were almost black, took in the close-cropped black curls, and listened to a rich voice saying words she could not understand, Vesta seemed to hear all the bells in the world ringing at once, and felt as if she were in a lift that would not stop at any floor on the way down.

Chapter Two

HE WAS going into another steep dive at 400 mph, and it was proving difficult to pull out, this time. There was cloud everywhere. It was impossible to see how close to the ground he was. Reaching desperately for his oxygen mask, which was not there, he saw suddenly it was too late. He hit the earth with a great smack that set his body jerking violently, before lying still. Someone began hitting his face quite smartly. So he was still alive! Surely there was no need to whack him into unconsciousness. A shot in the arm would do it better.

'David. David! *Wake up!*'

He opened his eyes warily, certain his head had been cracked open. It hurt abominably, and felt as if it had been split asunder from the forehead to the back of the neck. How could he still be alive after a crash like that? A girl's face swam above him. They had carted him off to hospital in the blood waggon, then. Good, he could do with a spell in bed surrounded by pretty nurses.

'David, for heaven's sake,' said the girl in exasperation. 'Do I have to drag you out of bed?'

He gave a grin. At least, he hoped it was a grin, and not too much like a leer. 'No need for that, sweetheart, just jump in here and leave the rest to me.'

The slap on his left cheek stung even more, and he thought gloomily that it was typical of his luck to encounter the matron instead of a young probationer.

'Just my bit of fun,' he murmured, peering at the blurred face, and thinking she was young to be a matron. Then he realised he knew her. 'Pat! Good God, I never thought you'd visit me on my deathbed.'

'You're right, I wouldn't,' came the tart answer. 'I'm only here now because you're in such hot water at home I felt I had to do something about it. But don't think it's out of any consideration for *you*. It's because I don't want their Christmas spoiled. Uncle Chris is after your blood, and Aunt Marion is convinced your dead body is lying somewhere it will never be found.'

'It darn nearly was.' By swivelling his eyeballs he could see an old wardrobe, a washstand containing a chipped bowl and jug in a cheap design of puce roses and emerald green leaves, a worn armchair with a darn in one of the arms, a rag rug with a sinister red stain in one corner, and a chamber pot proclaiming itself to be a present from Blackpool. Definitely not a hospital ward, he decided. Then he noticed his uniform neatly laid across a straight-backed chair beside the bed, shoes and socks in regimental style beneath it. He could not possibly have undressed himself. He was never that tidy. Who had done it? Pat? Her face looked a lot clearer now, which was a pity, because it wore an expression of acute annoyance. It was not the sort of thing a chap wanted to see on the sort of morning this was proving to be.

'What's a nice girl like you doing in a strange room with a man of my reputation?' he ventured, even though his head was still thumping badly.

'Not in the least what girls usually do, I expect?' she replied prosaically. 'If I was certain you were just drunk, I'd pull you out of that bed, and throw jugs of cold water over you until you promised to do just as I say. But it's possible you could have knocked yourself out in the crash, and have done some slight injury to your head. I'm giving you the benefit of the doubt. The landlord's wife is bringing up a gallon of black coffee, and there's a doctor on the way.'

Both propositions sounded attractive, because it meant he could stop in bed, lumpy though it was. So there had been a crash. He knew he could not have dreamt it all. He looked up at Pat pathetically.

'I assure you I have hurt myself. My head feels like... like...'

'Like it does after drinking too much?' she suggested dryly. 'Don't push your luck too far. You were definitely tight. The landlord told me they all heard you singing a very vulgar song fifty yards away, before you drove into the side of the barn. No one was surprised that you missed the sharp turn over the bridge and went straight on. Count your lucky stars you didn't go off the bridge and end up in the river. Aunt Marion's fears would have been reality.'

He was beginning to get hold of himself now, and frowned. 'Was she really worried?'

'Of course she was, idiot!' came the angry retort. 'I

22

telephoned just now to tell her you'd had a bit of a smash-up but were all right. I made it sound as if you'd got concussion and didn't know where you were. They're sending the car for you. If I were you, I'd stick to the concussion idea. Uncle Chris is hopping mad. Not because of your non-appearance – he's used to that – but because that Polish pilot friend of yours turned up for Christmas.'

Memory returned and his heart sank. 'Oh Lord, a fine time we'll all have now!'

'Whose fault is that?' she snapped. 'Honestly, David, couldn't you have behaved yourself just once?'

'Now, look,' he began, trying to sit up and finding the room spinning around. 'Aaah, I think I have got concussion,' he groaned. 'I feel really dicky, Pat.'

'A hangover, I expect,' was her unsympathetic opinion.

Lying back on the pillows, he said, 'I know a hangover when I have one. This is far worse.'

Softening her approach, she asked, 'You're not pulling a fast one, are you?'

He managed a grin. 'Not on a girl like you, old dear. It wouldn't work, would it?'

'Well, I suppose you must have hit that wall with a hefty smack.' She seemed quite concerned. 'I wish that doctor would hurry. They should have called one right away, but you were so plainly inebriated, they just pulled you out of the car, and put you to bed in their cheapest room until you sobered up. You've only got yourself to blame.'

'That's where you came in,' he muttered, feeling very sick now, and wondering whether to tell her to leave before he was.

'Do you remember what happened?'

Concentrating made the nausea recede, so he kept on doing so. 'Those chaps who weren't granted leave looked a bit forlorn, so we decided to cheer them up before we left. They took exception to our high spirits and retaliated. One thing led to another, and I eventually realised it was getting late. I think there were rather more than two in my car when I set off. One of them was meeting his sister in Salisbury. She had a couple of friends with her, so we took them in somewhere for a quick one to celebrate the festive season.' He winced as a particularly sharp pain shot through his head.

'There was this socking great bunch of mistletoe hanging there, and it seemed a shame to waste it. As it was dark by that time, and pouring with rain, I very gallantly offered to take one of the girls home. She lived on a farm way out to the west of Greater Tarrant. Her people invited me for a drink, so I went, just to be chummy. Unfortunately, her boyfriend had been waiting a long time to take her off to the local hop, and didn't seem all that keen on me right from the start. I left pretty soon afterwards. From then on everything seems rather vague, except that I recall feeling a whole lot worse than I should have done, and suspecting that the boyfriend had slipped me a Mickey Finn. I seemed to be driving through a maze of narrow lanes, without having a clue where I was.'

There was a knock on the door, and a thin, tired-looking woman came in with a wooden tray that had a splinter missing from the side. It held an aluminium teapot, and a yellow cup and saucer. She gave Pat a snooty look.

'I hope you can pay for all this, young woman.'

'I should think most people could,' Pat replied in superior tones. 'It's not exactly the Ritz, is it? I hope that cup is clean.'

'Don't you be cheeky with me,' snapped the landlord's wife. 'So-called gentry! You're nothing but a lot of ruffians, if you ask me.'

'I didn't,' countered Pat calmly. 'Send the doctor up when he comes, and let me know when Sir Christopher's driver arrives with the Daimler. Thank you, that'll be all.'

The woman went, and David could not resist saying, 'You're damned cool, Pat.'

'Good job someone is.'

'I'm sorry,' he repented. 'I never thought about Mother getting in a state.'

'You never do think, that's your trouble. Why didn't you telephone?'

He put his hand to his head. 'Isn't it obvious? Where is this place, by the way? Yes, and how do you come to be here and so full of the facts?'

She held out the yellow cup, filled with steaming coffee from the teapot. 'You'd better drink this now she's brought it. Are you decent under the bedclothes?'

His hand moved down and encountered underpants. 'In the area that matters, yes.'

'I'll help you to sit up, in that case.'

He got upright very gingerly, still convinced it was not a normal hangover that chiselled away at his brain. 'You haven't answered my question.'

She sat in the darned armchair watching him drink the coffee. 'This ghastly place is called the Crook and Fleece. I think the latter should be spelled FLEAS. The landlord is probably the crook. It's an inn halfway between two villages

24

called Cringe and Fawcett. Sounds like a firm of Dickensian solicitors, doesn't it?'

'Mmm, it does, rather,' he agreed, through sips of coffee.

'You obviously wandered off course somewhat last night. Luckily for you, one of our shepherds had been to visit relatives at Cringe last night, and recognised your car when he passed it on the way in this morning. He couldn't wait to spill the beans to Cook when he came in for his mug of tea on arrival. I overheard him, telephoned the people here, and came over. The landlord wasn't very happy. I got him out of bed.'

'What time did you telephone?' he asked, fascinated by all she was saying.

'Six a.m.'

'*What?*'

'I always get up then, David. We run a farm, in case you've forgotten.'

He gazed at her. Pink, healthy cheeks, shining dark curls, yellow jumper over plump breasts, jodphurs, good quality boots. She looked alert, full of life, and good enough to eat. How did she do it?

'Do your people know you've come?'

She shook her head. 'I left a message for Mummy with Dobbs. It seemed better to come alone, and tell whatever lies were necessary. Parents tend to tell the truth, and make the situation a jolly sight worse.'

He held out the cup. 'Can I have some more? It tastes distinctly odd, but I'm sure it's doing some good.'

She came to him with the cup refilled, but he delayed taking it for a moment. 'It's very nice of you to do what you've done.'

'It wasn't for your sake.'

'So you said. Thanks a lot, all the same.'

'That's all right,' she said diffidently, thrusting the cup forward. 'We'll cook up a story that'll save your bacon and put Christmas back on its feet again. *You'll* have to sort out your Polish friend, however. He's not my responsibility.'

'Oh God, poor devil,' he exclaimed, remembering. 'What happened?'

'He walked all the way from Greater Tarrant. In the pouring rain,' she emphasised heavily. 'Vee said he was dripping water all over the parquet, and then was engulfed in embarrassment when Uncle Chris walked out, broke into a flood of Polish, shook his hand like an old friend, and organised a bath and dinner for the poor man.'

'Naturally,' David said with the usual bitterness. 'My father will enjoy Christmas now he has someone to dazzle with his brilliance, in addition to a just cause to censure me.'

She was silent for a moment or two, while he drank his second cup of what he concluded was tea with vague overtones of coffee. Then she attacked him with surprising heat.

'You really are one of the beastliest people I've ever known.'

It caught him off guard, and he frowned at her over the top of the cup.

'Most girls think I'm the cat's whiskers.'

'I'm the only girl in the world who knows what you're really like. Even Vee is influenced by sisterly indulgence. I know the truth, and see you without blinkers.'

'Well, well,' he drawled, wishing the thunder in his head would ease. 'You have come into the open, haven't you? Still, it's always been apparent you prefer older men. A sort of father figure.'

Her colour flared. 'What's that supposed to mean?'

'If you don't know, you *are* wearing blinkers, old girl.'

Moving round, and grabbing one of the brass knobs at the foot of the bed, she cried, 'He's worth ten of you! Ever since Gabby Payne told you about that old scandal when you were twelve, you've treated your father unforgivably. Yet, from the age of sixteen – or before, for all I know – you've been indulging in the very thing you condemn him for. You're hypocritical, and insufferably pious.'

'I don't go off leaving a girl holding a baby, though,' he interjected with barbed accuracy.

This halted her for a moment or two, but he was a captive, and she made the most of her opportunity. 'That's because your Uncle Rex never did. Isn't that whom you idolise and try to emulate – the great "Sherry" Sheridan, who won the VC, DSO, MC *and* the Croix de Guerre with his flying exploits, and who won all the girls with his breezy attraction? Don't you fancy yourself as some kind of pre-destined hero because you are the nephew of one of aviation's greatest aces? Bearing the family name, joining the RAF and chasing every girl in sight isn't enough to put you up there with him, David.' Her voice began to wobble with emotion. 'Ask anyone who knew him, and you'll be told that, apart from his great courage, he was one of the nicest men you could ever meet. You're not!'

It hurt very deeply, especially coming from a girl whom he had always regarded almost as another sister. Lifelong friendship did not give her the right to preach to him, however.

'You bouncy little prig!' he said furiously. 'You're scarcely out of gymslips, and think you understand what makes the world go round. If I wasn't feeling so damned ill, I'd take down those breeches and give you a hearty tanning.'

'Your answer to anything you don't like is to hit out,' she retaliated, 'instead of trying to come to terms with it.'

'And you just go around dispensing worldly wisdom, of course,' he said sarcastically. 'What makes you think you know all the answers at eighteen?'

'In this instance, because I'm in a unique position. As the people who were most closely involved, my parents have given me unbiased accounts of what really happened. As I've grown up with you, and know you better than most people, I can give unemotional judgements on you all.'

'All except one,' he interspersed swiftly. 'Own up, Pat. Isn't he the reason for all your hostility towards me? Wake up, you little fool. There are hundreds of virile young men looking for girls like you to cuddle before they die. If you're determined to worship someone to the point of making yourself look ridiculous, choose some poor devil your own age. Before long, there won't be many of them left. They'll all be blown to bits.'

The doctor was annoyed at being called out early in the morning on Christmas Eve to a privileged youngster, who had got himself tight and driven an expensive scarlet two-seater into the side of a barn. When he arrived to find his patient had a pert, pretty girl with him in the bedroom, he was more than annoyed. Ordering Pat out, he proceeded to read a sermon on the evils of drink and fornication, both of which he personally enjoyed, while he tested for broken bones. As he took in the details of the strong muscular body, handsome features, eyes of intense blue, and blond, springy hair with a hint of gold in it, he relented and recalled his own youth.

'You could have killed yourself, you bloody young fool,' he said in kindly manner. Then, nodding at the RAF uniform beside the bed, he continued, 'You'll have plenty of opportunities of doing that for your country before long. Don't take risks just for the fun of it. You were lucky,' he declared, straightening up and polishing his spectacles. 'Nothing wrong except slight concussion. Your powers of focusing, at present, are slightly better than a Christmas goose, and quite a lot worse than a mole. When they get you home, go straight to bed. Alone, mind! That applies to the entire festive season. No stimulants whatever – in a bottle, or a transparent negligée.' Packing his thermometer away in his bag, he asked, 'Do they still wear nonsense like that, these days?'

David grinned at him. 'Yes, but not for long, if I can help it.'

27

'Mmm,' the man mused. 'Keep this pace up, and you won't live to enjoy things like that. Still, I'm not your father, thank God. It's up to him to tell you all that.'

His father did, and in no uncertain terms. Even though David was forced to admit that he was decent enough to give the dressing-down in private, and that the main reason for it was because his mother had been worried and upset, the incident merely widened the gap between their understanding of each other. David stood silently throughout the coldly angry verbal punishment. He always made a point of displaying indifference to his father's opinion of him. When the interview ended with a concerned enquiry on how he was feeling, David merely said, 'Fine, thanks.'

His father nodded briefly, and said, 'Good. Now, perhaps, we can get on with celebrating Christmas in the way your mother wishes.'

Keeping quiet about the doctor's advice, he spent the next hour with his mother, putting presents on the tree. At that point, he remembered that his own gifts for the family were still in the boot of his car. Frampton had to be sent back to the Crook and Fleece to collect them, and David could guess what the man said under his breath.

'I've got something rather special for you this year,' he promised his mother, handing her some square packages wrapped in scarlet paper.

'It can't be more special than having you here,' she said warmly, as she clasped his hands around the parcels. 'Darling, don't tell me yet when you have to report back. I shall start ticking off the days, and spoil the time that you are here. Let me know on your last morning.'

'All right,' he murmured, wondering if she realised he only had seventy-two hours. He had better make the most of them for her sake.

After they had finished, he suggested a walk with the dogs along Longbarrow Hill, where his sister and Felix Makoski had gone earlier, to see the village and the view over Dorset.

'We'll probably meet up with them, and we can all come back for coffee together,' he said. 'Come on, let's get our thick coats and gumboots on. Race you to the old barn!'

Her face lit with pleasure as she laughingly allowed him to propel her into the outer hall, where bad-weather clothing was kept, along with the riding boots and stocks.

'That old joke, David! Fancy a strapping young man of twenty-four remembering the things he said as a small boy.'

He grinned. 'If I ever stop remembering, you have my

permission to give me a good hiding. Like you used to.'

'I *never* gave you a hiding, you dreadful boy,' she cried. 'There was never any need. You were always so well-behaved.'

'Not any longer, Mother dear,' he teased, kissing her soundly on the cheek.

It brought a surprising response. Turning to him with eyes grown glassy, she said,' You will take care, won't you? Don't try to be too brave.'

'I'm no fool,' he responded lightly. 'There are enough heroes in this family already. England will become sick of the name Sheridan if I try to add to the number.'

'I mean it, David,' she insisted earnestly. 'So many were lost last time. Nearly everyone I knew. It seemed that no one would be left at the end of it all ... And this one has only just begun.'

'It'll be over before long. We've got air power now. There's no longer any need for us to be forced to wallow in mud or carry out bayonet charges "over the top".' He took hold of her arms in the thick tweed coat and shook her gently. 'Hey, what is all this? I thought we were going to indulge in festive frolics.'

Her smooth, pleasantly pretty face retained its shadowed expression. 'I'm sorry. I suppose it began all wrong yesterday. That Polish boy arriving, exiled from his country and his family, both of which are being oppressed by our old enemy. My heart ached for his mother. Then, when you didn't come, I suppose it dawned on me that I might lose you one day.'

Swift, loving remorse swept over him, so he took her in a bear hug, saying, 'I *do* deserve a good hiding for being so thoughtless. You won't lose me, I promise. Haven't I always been here – even when others deserted you?'

She pulled free, and searched his face with her clear brown eyes. 'One day, you'll be able to understand what happened, and why we all did what we did. Things are not always as clear-cut and simple as they appear.'

'I've challenged any number of people to deny that he pushed off, and left you to cope with the results of his selfishness, and they can't,' he said harshly. 'I'll never forgive him for what he made you suffer. And I'll never understand how you can.'

'I pray you won't learn the way he did.' She gripped his hand. 'He arrived home in uniform last night. It was a dreadful shock. He assured me that he won't be expected to fight, but they sent him last time against all recommendations. Tell me truthfully, David, will he have to go to France?'

Sighing heavily as his resentment against his father increased, he shook his head. 'They'd never risk losing a man like him. He's far too valuable where he is.'

'That's what Vesta said.'

'Then believe her. Apart from his importance as an international figure, his eyesight is so bad it would put him into a noncombatant category, even without the fact of his deformed hand.'

'Why put him in uniform, then?'

'For convenience, I expect. He's young enough to fight, and wearing khaki saves him from criticism. Ever the handsome hero,' he quoted sourly. 'Now can we go for that walk?'

As they made their way over Longbarrow Hill, the dogs racing madly back and forth, he told her about Felix Makoski.

'A lot of young Polish fliers got out when they saw the situation was hopeless, even though it meant leaving their families to face occupation by the enemy. It must have been a heart-breaking decision to make. Some of them had young brides with infants, but they felt they would help them more by coming here to continue the fight. Of course, there's a core of resistance fighters in Poland, but they are limited in effectiveness by lack of weapons. We try to help, but it's difficult to get stuff to them because the distance is beyond the range of most of our aircraft, and most of it is over enemy-occupied territory where the flak is...' David broke off, realising it was the wrong subject to discuss with her. For a brief moment, he wished he could talk things over with his father, who knew Poland and the rest of Europe well, and whose views he would welcome. Felix had had a long animated conversation with him – in Polish, of course – and no doubt thought Sir Christopher Sheridan a father in a million. He was, but the one in a million David would sooner not have had.

'I met Felix a couple of weeks ago at a base a few miles from us, where I was picked up after I had ditched... *hitched* a lift to see a pal,' he amended smoothly, feeling it was better not to reveal that he had been forced to bale out after testing a machine that consistently went into a dive on turning. 'We got into conversation, and I felt sorry for the poor blighter when I heard his story. His people are wealthy – *were* wealthy, I suppose I should say. His father was a count, who was killed right at the start. His mother and two sisters went into hiding in a church, but were dragged out, after being betrayed by a peasant who hoped to be spared.' He looked down at his mother apologetically. 'I'm sorry, I can't really tell you about him without being depressing.'

'Go on,' she said quietly. 'I can take it, you know. I was just being ridiculous a few minutes ago.'

'Felix's mother was shot, and the two sisters were... well,

30

they were treated pretty badly by the soldiers. Felix doesn't know where they are now. When he told me all this, I thought how lucky I was to live in a country surrounded by sea, and to be going home to spend a first-rate Christmas with my family.' He looked away over the rolling countryside, suddenly strangely diffident. 'When a chap equates a story like that with his own life, the element of shock comes home to him. Suppose it was you and Vee hiding in our village church.' He glanced back at her. 'I invited him here for Christmas because it seemed the least I could do.' He added reluctantly, 'I thought it might help him to talk to Father. There can't be that number of Englishmen who know Poland well, and who can speak of it in the native tongue.'

An arm was suddenly linked into his, and his mother's face was full of love and pride. 'My son is one of the nicest men in the world.'

'Pat doesn't think so,' he said smartly. 'She told me this morning I was one of the beastliest people she knew.'

This brought a laugh from her. 'She would not have gone to all that trouble over you if she really thought that. You're like a brother to her, and Vesta would probably have said the same to you if she had gone out to fetch you. They both adore you.' The upturned face took on an elusive expression. 'Is there any other girl who adores you, David?'

'Hundreds,' came his prompt affirmation.

'Any one, in particular?'

He grinned. 'No, Mother, and for being inquisitive, you can run to meet your daughter, who has just appeared about a hundred yards ahead. Come on.'

Seizing her hand in his strong clasp, he set off at a gallop. She was laughing and breathless by the time they met up with the couple returning along the top of the hill. Vesta seemed rather breathless herself, and the crisp air had put an extra bloom on her cheeks.

'Have you run amok?' she cried. 'The dogs are going crazy with excitement, and Mummy's exhausted, you beast.'

'There you are, another girl who thinks I'm beastly,' he complained. 'For that, you can run too. You look rather cold.' So saying, he seized his sister's hands and galloped madly off, whooping loudly, and thinking of Felix Makoski's sisters being raped by a succession of bestial soldiers. 'Merry Christmas! Merry Christmas!' he yelled at the top of his voice, as Vesta shrieked with laughter, and protests that he was going too fast.

'Stop it! Stop it! Mercy, I beg of you,' she gasped.

He came to a halt and held her steady whilst she regained her breath. Then he caught himself saying, 'I love you, Vee.'

She looked back at him curiously. 'And I love you, David, what's the matter?'

'I don't know. I have a feeling that it will never be like this again.'

'Of course it will,' she said softly. 'You've just got the blues. It must be that bump on the head.'

'I expect it is,' he agreed. 'But everyone seems edgy. Pat went for me this morning, Father read the Riot Act, and Mother thinks she's back in 1914, just because he came home in military uniform last night. You're the only one who seems pleased with herself. It wouldn't be anything to do with Felix, would it?'

She put out the tip of her tongue.

'Oh, fine,' he grumbled. 'Abuse from you now, and right after I've confessed a slight fondness for you.'

Grabbing the end of his old college scarf, she flicked it neatly over his head, then pulled it free of his neck to run off with it. He set off in pursuit, with great growls of aggression that made her shriek with further laughter. Felix and their mother had begun walking together back towards the house, so they fell in behind, and told each other the news of their respective lives since they had last met several months ago.

The morning was chill, with a fresh breeze hinting at frost, but the air was so clear it was possible to see for miles. Perfect flying weather. As they fell silent for a while, David imagined his Uncle Rex taking off from this same hill, in an old biplane he had bought and rebuilt after its owner had crashed it and killed himself. It must have been quite a sight for the villagers to look up and see old Branwell Sheridan's middle son gliding overhead in a machine that was a novelty, in those days. What would his famous uncle think of the way aircraft were designed and flown today, he wondered. Could he have ever imagined a machine like the Spitfire, even in his wildest dreams?

'Penny for them,' said Vesta.

He focused on her again. 'I was wondering whether you've bought me a decent present this year, for a change.'

'Hateful boy! I've a good mind not to give it to you, now.'

Flicking her lightly with the ends of his scarf, he said, 'Do you think you could find something to wrap up for Felix? I've got hold of a Polish book – I hope to God it's not a rude one – and some thick socks. It gets cold at twenty-eight thousand feet, so it won't matter if he's got stacks of them already. But it would be nice to put something on the tree from the family, don't you think?'

Her eyes shone with unusual brightness. 'As a matter of fact, I've already done it.'

He grinned. 'It's not one of your frightful paintings, is it?'

'No, it's not, you wretch. I've wrapped *that* up for you.'

'I might have guessed. Why don't you...' He broke off abruptly, as the world suddenly swung upside down, righted itself, then spun round with dizzying speed. He grabbed his sister and stopped dead.

'What's wrong? she asked in concern.

'Eh?' He felt deathly cold, and very sick. 'A giddy turn, that's all. It's the high-altitude flying. Makes the system a bit dicky.'

'Are you all right now?'

'Yes, I'm fine,' he lied, wondering how he would reach the house. Maybe the doctor had been right, and he should have gone to bed. That would have worried his mother even more, and he only had two days left. He would have to try and rest without making it obvious.

It happened twice more before they arrived home, and Vesta began to show real concern. 'Surely you don't go around like this all the time, just because of the flying? I've never noticed it before.'

'It's today's low temperature,' he lied further, finding it hard to keep her face in focus. 'I'll be all right when we get indoors. Keep it to yourself, or Mother'll start fussing.'

But it was not due to any words from his sister that his condition became obvious. Two steps inside the sitting room, he blacked out, and collapsed onto the carpet.

The lovely seventeenth-century church was filled to capacity for the service that night. The stained glass windows glowed richly in the light from massed candles. Branches of holly and fir trimmed the narrow sills. Near the altar a low lantern illuminated a nativity scene, constructed every year by children from the village school. There had been a small dispute this year because the boys, influenced by fathers and older brothers, had desperately wanted to dress the Three Kings in uniforms. Miss Barker had been hard put to reconcile them to tradition. Since a large number in the congregation wore khaki or blue, it appeared to make nonsense of her lecture on Christmas being a time of peace and goodwill.

Yet, both were there as men and women who knew and loved this green rolling area of Dorset stood shoulder to shoulder in the narrow pews of ancient wood, singing the familiar hymns and carols with calm confidence that what was happening in Europe could never be repeated on their island home. Tarrant

Royal had lost its young men before; it prepared to do so again now. But the village would not go under. Such losses only strengthened the fabric of rural life, the bonds that existed between people determined to remain free.

The villagers displayed more than determination that year. Peace existed already in the valley near the cliffs of the southwest coast, but a new type of goodwill was extended now towards erring children, disapproving parents, quarrelsome neighbours, petulant lovers, and long-standing enemies. Beneath the surface of normality, folk felt that now was the time for forgiveness – before it was too late. Tarrant Royal had never been as united in praise as on that night.

In the Sheridan pew, Vesta sat almost bursting with emotion. The church had never looked so beautiful, the old organ had never filled the ancient stones with such triumphant chords, and the voices of yeomen had never moved her so deeply with their lusty vocal praise. The Christmas message had never seemed so poignant. The glowing candles echoed the glow within her.

Beside her sat Felix Makoski, so close they were almost touching. He was totally absorbed in his first experience of an English church service. But Vesta was totally absorbed in studying him: finding delight in every expression of his narrow, vital face; the sound of his strong, young voice as he sang verses in a language foreign to him, to tunes he seemed to know. She was excited by the masculine smell of his uniform and of his hair oil. It was different from the familiar scents of her father and David. This fascinating foreign young man touched all her senses in a way that was breathtakingly new. It was the first time she had heard a baritone voice caress words as his did, had seen eyes contain such mysterious beckoning lights, had felt a person's proximity with such tingling, yearning awareness. She had never before felt such a desperate longing to be with anyone, to hold his attention, earn his approval; to keep him to herself as something too precious to share.

Her mother had told her what David had related of the tragedy in the life of this twenty-two-year-old, and Vesta felt near to tears during the short sermon on how the message of Christmas should start within each family, within each community, and within each nation, until the whole world was embraced with love. Felix's hand lay on his knee as he listened, and the desire to put hers over the long, slender fingers was so strong it was almost a pain. He must feel so bereft, so alone, so vengeful. If only she could console him, make him aware that there were those who would punish what had been done, and ensure that his people would be free to live again in peace, as they did here. They knelt to pray, and his upper arm brushed hers as he crossed himself. She heard nothing of the prayers, thinking only of someone whose existence she had been unaware of all these years as he had lived a life parallel to, but oh so different from, her own. Because Vesta's father had always been deeply involved in world affairs, he had insisted that both she and David spoke the local language when on youthful holidays in France, Bavaria and Switzerland. As a result, they spoke fluent French, German, and limited Italian. But, as their mother did not really enjoy foreign travel, and made the estate an excuse to remain where she was happiest, the brother and sister had not travelled as widely as they could have done. They had, of course, met many foreign visitors brought by their father to Tarrant Hall or the London apartment, but they had been too young to join the adults except for tea. More recently Vesta had been immersed in her artistic career, and David had been home only for spasmodic leave. He never went to the London apartment, because their father used it most of the time. In consequence, the vast intimate knowledge their father had of the world and its peoples was not shared by them. Poland, a country he had visited a great deal in recent years, for reasons Vesta had not bothered to enquire, was as unknown as its language to the younger Sheridans. Now, she found herself avid to learn all she could about Felix's country. She had approached her father on this subject just before dinner that evening, but he had only laughed.

'Tell you about Poland?' he had echoed. 'In ten minutes, just before the gong goes for dinner! My dear girl, all I could impart in that space of time you can discover for yourself, by opening my atlas on the realignment of Slavia and Eastern Europe after the Treaty of Versailles. That will give you latitude and longitude, plus its relationships with its neighbours before Hitler invaded.'

So she sat that midnight beside a young man who had suddenly and deeply altered her life, knowing little about him, except that she did not want him to leave it again. If only she could talk to him in his own language. If only she knew and understood those places he regarded as home. If only she could reach him through that barrier of distance and incomprehensible words, as her father did.

The prayers she had not heard ended, and they stood up from the hand-embroidered hassocks. In doing so, Felix accidentally knocked her purse from the chair. He bent swiftly to retrieve it, handing it to her with a little bow.

'Pardon. I am clumsy.'

His smile smote her anew, knowing the deep sadness he must be feeling inside. What courage he had. How proud of him his family must have been. Where were those two poor girls now? Even David, who was not often given to demonstrations of brotherly affection, had plainly been touched by the thought of what Felix must be suffering. Felix was so courteous and gentle, he must be filled with revulsion at what was happening all over his homeland. It was that thought, plus the fact that the church path was slippery with frost, that gave Vesta the courage to slip her arm through his after they had said goodnight to the Rector, and as they prepared to walk back up the hill to Tarrant Hall.

Her parents left the path to cross to a far corner of the churchyard, where an unobtrusive grave lay. Vesta did not go with them this time, but stayed with Felix, holding his arm, and shivering more because of her daring than from the frosty chill of this clear night, brilliant with stars.

'They won't be long,' she explained. 'My aunt is buried over there, and they always put a candle at her feet at Christmas. There, see, they have just lit it. I think it's Daddy's idea, really. He does it for Uncle Rex.' She glanced up at him in the darkness. 'Have you ever heard of someone called "Sherry" Sheridan?'

'Naturally, I have heard of such a man. Any man who flies must know of him. This is your uncle?'

'Yes.'

'Then I feel sorry for your brother.'

'Sorry for David? Why?' she asked in surprise.

'The world will expect so much of him. It is always so.'

Sensing there was more behind the remark than his casual tone suggested, she wondered if he felt the burden of responsibility for avenging his family too much. To console him, she held his arm tighter, saying, 'That's silly. Each person lives a separate life. It's his to do with as he thinks fit. I don't think anyone should take on the responsibility of what the world expects of him. Why should he?'

His teeth showed white as he smiled down at her. 'You are very quaint. This is a correct word? I think you have not seen much of life yet, and that is very nice for now, when young girls are too often being despoiled. I find it very charming.' His own arm tightened against hers. 'But today every young man has to do what the world expects of him. His life does no longer belong to him.'

Her parents joined them, and they all set off along the narrow lane, which sparkled with frost in the beam of the powerful torch her father carried. They said little during that short uphill walk. The lingering memory of the church service, and the wonderful, breathless peace of the night making speech unnecessary as they climbed, arms linked, toward the lights of the house. David had been put to bed, with orders to stay there until morning, when he could come down for Christmas breakfast, on condition that he let Bill Chandler look him over when the family arrived for lunch. It was a pity he had had to miss the service, the ritual glass of hot punch and mince pie at home, but, since it meant Vesta had Felix more to herself, she felt guilty gladness over the situation.

Robson had maintained a roaring fire in the small sitting room that they used for cosier occasions, such as this, and the two women went to it as soon as they had taken off their coats, and had received the butler's assurance that the invalid was sleeping soundly, after waking long enough to consume two bowls of soup, and a chicken leg with a plateful of brown bread and butter.

'I don't think there's much wrong with him,' said her father, when Vesta commented that it sounded pretty typical of David. 'If he had taken it easy at the start, all would have been well. Here you are, my dear,' he went on, handing a glass of hot punch to her mother, then to her, and finally to Felix. Then he looked around at them all. 'Christmas Day is only an hour or so old, and there'll be no end of toasts before it has ended, but I'd like to make one now which is more of a dedication, before we follow the pattern that is beloved by the Sheridan family.' He lifted his glass. 'I salute all those, wherever in the world they happen to be, who are denied the precious gift of closeness with those they love tonight, whether they celebrate this Christian festival or not.' He looked at Felix, adding, '*Boze Cos Polske.*'

Vesta caught herself repeating the alien words, as she gazed at the pale face of a stranger who found he was unexpectedly amongst friends. Her heart contracted when she saw he was on the verge of tears, and she said quickly, in a voice two tones higher than normal, 'This punch of Daddy's is quite potent, Felix. Don't drink it too quickly.'

Felix sipped obediently, his dark eyes regarding her with gratitude over the top of the glass. He seemed more in control of himself as they discussed the service, and how ironic it was that at times of stress even the most ungodly felt a need for reassurance in a church. Soon, however, they stirred from the deep armchairs, made sleepy by the cosy firelit atmosphere.

37

Her parents said goodnight, and made their way upstairs, leaving Vesta admiring the tree in the hall with Felix.

'Do you have this custom?' she asked, hoping to prolong the magical sensation of being alone with him for a few moments.

'In many ways we are like this,' he said softly, with a sweet, sad smile that seemed to suggest he also found the moment magical. 'But with us there is snow. Very much snow. And the church has the Blessed Virgin who, through her agony, produced the Christ this night. It is a time for much adoration and thought. I think we are not as jolly as you, but I find this an honour to share with you and your family an English Christmas. Such kindness I had not thought to be possible.'

Feeling more and more bewitched, she said faintly, 'Daddy has always advocated friendship between the peoples of the world. He says lack of understanding of customs and cultures leads to unnecessary animosity.'

He pursed his lips. 'Sir Christopher is a most unexpected man. I have been much surprised by his knowing of my land and people. David did not explain this me.'

She smiled, wondering how it would feel to run her fingers through his dark, curly hair, so glossy in the firelight. 'Oh, that's David all over. He never explains anything.'

Moving closer, he said softly, 'There is one thing he has explain about your customs, and I must fulfil it or be dishonoured, I think.'

She was drawn against him by arms of surprising strength, and was entirely unprepared for the demanding pressure of his mouth on hers, as he held her expertly immobile for a kiss that was stunning in its audacity and overwhelming in its surprise. She had been kissed by boys. Never by a man. There was a world of difference, she discovered.

Releasing her slowly, he looked down into her face. 'It is correct that beneath this mistletoe a man must kiss a girl when it is Christmas Day, or she will feel insulted? David has said me right?'

Damn David! Praise be to David! Weak, shaken, swept with a sense of shameful excitement, she managed to say, 'Yes, he is right.'

His smile intensified the pain that had started in the pit of her stomach until it reached her thighs. 'Then I have to say I am glad of this custom. It is very nice.'

Very nice? *Very nice!* It had changed her whole life! She was in love with Felix Makoski.

*

Bill Chandler spent ten minutes in the bedroom with David, then echoed the words of the doctor who had examined him at the inn. Slight concussion, but nothing worse. Don't drink, and take things steady, was his advice. This time it had to be observed, because everyone made sure the patient did as he was told. Because of it, Felix had to take his place in the concert devised by Vesta and Pat. It was all the more hilarious because he had no idea what he was supposed to be doing, and had to be prompted vocally whilst being pushed and pulled to the required spot to say his lines, parrot-fashion. In this merry mood, they progressed to the usual display of acutely unclever conjuring tricks by Bill Chandler, whose sleight of hand was non-existent, and caused a great many rude comments from his uproarious audience.

Chris watched and participated in slightly abstracted mood. He had a lot on his mind, and much as he valued his family and friends, his home, and the peaceful normality of Christmas, he could not forget that the world was again at war, which was certain to snatch up his children. He had meant the words of reassurance to Marion regarding his own safety, but had made no attempt to feed her sugary lies where their son was concerned. As a fighter pilot, David's life would be very much at risk in the coming conflict. Fortunately, it appeared not to have occurred to Marion that women would almost certainly play a greater part in this war. Young girls like Vesta and Pat would be in uniform and fighting before the issue was settled, he knew. The impression that nothing much was happening might be fooling a great many British people, but Chris knew far more than most, and he was deeply worried.

The marriage he and Marion had determinedly rebuilt after 1918 had worked very well. They had made a pact of complete honesty with each other, but Chris had only honoured that pact when asked direct questions. Since his wife never delved deeply into the nature of his work – partly through mutual understanding of their differing worlds, but mostly through lack of interest – he had been able to keep from her the truth of what he had been doing over the past few months. Whilst supposedly in Switzerland for talks on neutrality, he had instead witnessed first-hand the surrender of Warsaw, which had signalled the loss of Poland, then had flown over the border into Russia, as interpreter to a delegation instructed to persuade the Soviets to renounce their friendship pact with Germany. Since the pact had resulted in their gaining for themselves a large part of Poland, the Russians had taken no heed of the warning that Hitler would disregard the nonaggression pact as soon as it suited him.

Chris had seen no need to tell Marion of the horrors he had witnessed in Poland. She had had more than her share of sorrow and despair, and was now comparatively serene in her true métier as landowner's wife and 'first lady' of Tarrant Royal. With the aid of their manager, Clive Hudson, she ran the profitable estate Chris had inherited due to the death of his two older brothers: and ran it very well. A countrywoman at heart, Marion was never really happy acting as hostess to international guests. Chris brought them to Tarrant Hall less and less frequently, entertaining them instead, bachelor-style, in the London apartment. Mutual respect and understanding had been the solid foundation of a marriage deeply scarred and almost broken by the events of 1914–18. Chris was now grateful for his wife's lack of interest in his professional life. It would make his new rôle much easier.

Looking across at her now, he was filled with warm affection. Gentle, acquiescent, her marital loyalty made as few demands on him as his did on her. She had her beloved rural life, and she had her children. The miscarriage of twins a year after Vesta had been born had been a double tragedy for her, for it had ensured that she could conceive no more. She had been deeply saddened by the loss, but, had she produced those two, they would now be seventeen and standing in line to risk sacrifice. A blessing in disguise, perhaps.

His gaze moved to Tessa and Bill Chandler, their oldest and dearest friends, and the only part of their past to survive into the present: the lively, straightforward woman who had run the estate so profitably during those other war years, and who now owned one of the largest flocks of pedigree sheep in the south of England; and the man, now in his early sixties, to whom Chris knew he owed everything. Bill had retired from the army as a colonel ten years ago, but he had already offered his services to the military neurology centre, and had been accepted as a senior consultant. As the man who knew Chris better than anyone else in the world, he had accepted the public reason for donning uniform again with the nonchalance of a man who knows it to be a lie, but who acknowledges the need for it. Bill would have a good idea of the uses for men with a brain as devious as Chris's in the coming conflict.

It was reflection on those uses that prevented Chris from giving his undivided attention to the party atmosphere around him. They had told him so little, but that was the nature of the work. The less each of them knew, the better. Chris Sheridan was an accomplished linguist, experienced in international cultural affairs, acquainted with important foreign personalities, familiar with most of Europe, and possessed of a brilliant brain, but he wondered whether subterfuge was one of his strong points. Would he be able to live a double life without anyone suspecting?

He was worried about his ability to uphold their faith in him. He was also worried about Felix Makoski. For the son of a Polish count, he was remarkably unfamiliar with places he should know well, and he rode a horse like a peasant.

Chapter Three

THERE APPEARED to be a stalemate in France. The troops on the spot were afraid it would mean a repeat of the hideous trench warfare of the other war; those at home believed the Germans had taken fright over the immensity of what they had started, and would probably agree to a face-saving armistice before the worst happened. Those with a deeper knowledge of the complexities behind the conflict waited fearfully for the holocaust that was sure to come. Could Britain possibly survive this time? Hardly recovered from the last war, how could one small island and its far-flung empire take on the might of a united Europe, plus a Far-Eastern oppressor waiting in the wings for the right moment to launch its own bid for the world?

In Britain, the most stringent measures had been taken. Road signs, place names and all directional information had been removed from towns and villages; from shop fronts, railway stations and buses. Garrison towns, ports and busy industrial cities had been evacuated of children, who now crowded village schools to the extent that alternate half-day schooling had had to be introduced. Public shelter for those caught in the streets or at work during air raids were erected near to those places regarded as prime targets for German air attack. Smaller underground shelters were dug in private gardens, to ensure all citizens a modicum of protection in their own homes. Everyone had been issued with a gas mask, which had to be carried at all times. Very young children had their fears of the masks banished by being given those with the face of Mickey Mouse. Tiny babies had to be enclosed in a cover down to their feet, and mothers were instructed on how to pump air into the contraption so that the baby could breathe. Gas, that terrible weapon that had been used to such deadly effect between 1914 and 1918, was the dread of everyone, and the suffocating rubber masks increased that dread in an anxious public.

Britain was now dark. Every house, factory, public building and shop had black curtains at the doors and windows; street lights were off 'for the duration'. Cars, buses and lorries had covers over their headlamps, which gave out no more than a criss-cross of light to warn of their approach; buses and trains were lit within by dim, green lights which gave passengers' cheeks and lips a sickly, purple hue. Important public buildings were protected by piled sandbags; the Channel coast was protected by concrete blocks, and miles of barbed wire along beaches and promenades; and the general public was protected by the formation of the Home Guard – a formidable force of men too old for, or exempt from military service. Food rationing had begun, and with it propaganda on the nutritious qualities of foods formerly regarded with disdain, but which could be produced cheaply and plentifully at home. Church bells had been silenced, so that they could be used more effectively to announce an invasion by enemy forces; and air-raid sirens had been placed in positions that would allow their warning to be heard and heeded.

The first weeks of 1940 seemed slightly unreal to the waiting Britons, but they had hints of the horror to come from stories of those arriving from countries overrun by the Germans. These refugees from oppression arrived in all manner of ways, having travelled tortuous routes; sometimes escaping over one border, only to find that country swiftly falling victim too, and being forced to head for another. They arrived in varying condition of health and desperation. Some had brought their wealth with them; others were destitute. Men and women of all nationalities, tongues and beliefs escaped from the mainland of Europe because they believed France would fall, and that only the narrow barrier of water would stop the sweeping enemy advance.

Public sympathy for these people was nevertheless overlaid with suspicion in official circles. A vast network of agents had already been set up in Europe, and government and military alike had no doubts that the enemy would do the same in Britain. Foreign nationals already resident, plus those flooding in from Scandinavia or the Mediterranean ports, were subjected to rigorous questioning before being allowed to mingle freely. Those who did not satisfy their interrogators were interned; those who did were considered for espionage purposes. Men whose knowledge of languages, cultures and European countries was wide were loaned by their various employers to this end. Chris Sheridan was amongst them.

In a large isolated country house near the capital, agents

were trained to work in areas already occupied or threatened by the enemy. This very secret establishment brought together a strange assortment of experts, each one concentrating on an individual skill, knowing very little about the others he passed in the corridors as he went about the place. The administrative staff knew, however, that under that one roof were linguists, athletes, engineers, explorers, mountaineers, explosives experts, doctors, artists, safe-breakers, photographers, radio technicians, forgers and thieves.

In this establishment Chris played a rôle he loathed. As head of the section dealing with languages, identities, and general knowledge, it was his responsibility to ensure that agents were word-perfect in any language they might need, totally familiar with the false identity given to them, and well able to move around the area to which they were going, without making vital mistakes. However, it was not so much this, but the other part of the job that Chris found abhorrent. It was completely against his nature and all he had worked for during those years since 1918. Only because he knew it to be vital did he force himself to carry out what he was obliged to do.

Prior to clearance, each agent had to pass the final test of absolute reliability. In addition to bombarding men and women with questions on their false identity, background and geographical knowledge, often in a language not their own, for hour after hour until they grew dull and confused, it was essential to simulate the danger to which they would be exposed. Whilst they might be perfectly calm in daytime classes, held deep in the safety of the English countryside, they could well panic when faced with brutal enemy policemen. In consequence, without warning, these trainees would be woken in the night by men in German uniforms and dragged none too gently to a cell-like room, where they faced a barrage of blinding lights and interrogation so close to hostile reality it was an excellent test of stamina and wits. For men with a sadistic streak, it was an enjoyable game. Chris found it revived memories of his own past, and he often woke in the night following such a session bathed in the sweat of hovering nightmares.

There was another problem connected with the work. When a civilian with a knighthood is given the instant rank of lieutenant colonel and a position of command in a new unit, there are invariably regular army officers who resent it. When the civilian is younger, better looking, wealthier, more intelligent, and on first-name terms with the war lords, they resent it even further. And when the civilian is known to have

44

spent most of the previous war in a mental ward, resentment is too mild a word to describe their feelings. Lieutenant Colonel John Frith had hated Chris from the word go, and had allowed his feelings to colour his professional behaviour. In peacetime it would be no more than foolish; in a time of war it could be dangerous.

John Frith was on the permanent staff of the establishment. He lived on the premises, was very good at his job, and had put the army before his wife, family and God. The army *was* his God, and nothing shook his conviction that the military solution to all problems was the right one. Knowledgeable and experienced in the field, it was his final recommendation that sent agents out on assignments. This meant he always sat in on the mock interrogations. He appeared to find satisfaction in watching people being reduced to exhausted, confused creatures fighting for their lives, in an exercise that grew all too real after hours and hours of cruel questioning designed to trap them into making mistakes.

Chris's gentle nature made these times into almost as much of an ordeal for him as it was for the victim. It was bad enough when the agent was male. When females were under test, Chris found the business of cross-questioning and browbeating particularly harrowing. It would be untrue to say that John Frith enjoyed it more with women, but he certainly made no differentiation between the sexes. He was right, the work was too dangerous to let personal elements creep in, but it was his extreme callousness towards one French girl that resulted in the first major confrontation, after a series of minor skirmishes, between the two men.

At around four in the morning, after he had mercilessly bombarded her with questions on the French railway system, the names of top German officials in charge of rolling stock and troop movements by rail, followed by further testing in French and German on her false background and the layout of cities and the university she was supposed to have attended, the girl could take no more, and burst into tears after making an error in her replies to Chris.

John Frith got up from his chair, apparently as fresh as when he had sat in it three hours before, and said harshly, 'Go back to school! You have just condemned all your fellows to death.'

Still crying, she left the bare, stuffy office numb with exhaustion, shame and despair. Chris turned in a rare rage to the heavily built, aggressive man with steely eyes.

'One mistake. That's all she made.'

'It could have cost her her life.'

'She has been here more than three hours. It's very hot, we are all sweating and befuddled, and she looked ill.'

'That's no excuse.'

'Dammit, man, she can't be any older than my daughter.'

'That's no excuse, either.'

'It should make you more understanding.'

'It won't make the Gestapo more understanding. That slip could have cost her her life. More importantly, it could have cost the collapse of an entire network. She is expendable. A group that has been painstakingly set up and works well is not.'

Chris eased the khaki shirt from his wet back. The man was right. It was his attitude he condemned.

'I'll allow you have the responsibility of deciding whether or not an agent is safe to send into the field. I'll also allow that on that decision rests the lives of many others who will be linked with each agent. Fail them, by all means, but do it humanely. I suspect that this all becomes too deadly in your mind, Frith. You are not the Gestapo. Do remember that.'

The other man stood in his path as he tried to leave, arms folded across his shirt, an expression of acute dislike on his fleshy face.

'You're a new boy at this kind of thing, aren't you?'

'Aren't you?' countered Chris.

'Not in the least. I know all about you, Sheridan, but you plainly have not been filled in on my background, which doesn't include benefit from the old boy network. I saw service in the last little dust-up. All four years of it. Got my commission in 1915, then served in Flanders and Russia. Since it ended, I've been all over the place. Shanghai, Hong Kong, Africa, Ceylon, Malta. There's not much about soldiering I don't know, believe me.'

'I do believe you,' Chris assured him tightly. 'But surely this establishment is a far cry from trench warfare and the outposts of the Empire. Frank Moore led me to believe there had been no precedent.'

'Really?' came the sneer. 'Since I'm not on chatting terms with Lord Moore, I wouldn't know. Is he another of you arty-tarty lads who go into orgasm over half a cracked Roman pissing pot, or a painting of a bloke with a human torso and a goat's arse, who is playing a whistle pipe to a group of naked boys?'

'I suspect you mean is he also a connoisseur of the arts,' Chris responded in chilly tones. 'I take it you are not.'

'Not on your life. Most of it is bloody nonsense, if you want my opinion.'

46

'I appear to have got it,' Chris snapped. 'Now we have established that you are the type of man to call a spade a spade, one who cannot resist the opportunity to reel off the details of a long career that appears to have taught you little but unimaginative brutality, I'd be pleased if you would step out of my way and let me get some sleep. My work makes greater demands on the mind than yours appears to do.'

His words enraged Frith further. 'There may be a use for men like you here, Sheridan, but when it boils down to basics, it's men in the fighting lines who win wars, not those who go off their nuts at the first sign of battle because their artistic sensibilities are shocked.'

Chris looked him up and down with disdain. 'It's your brand of outlook that creates wars, Frith. If more people con-centrated on arts instead of arms, my two brothers would still be alive, and I would never have been blown up at Gallipoli.' Stepping past the man, he opened the door. 'That was why I went off my nut, incidentally.'

The relationship between them worsened. It was not long before Chris spoke of it to Lord Moore, the man for whom he had acted as advisor and interpreter for many years. Chris's fluency in so many languages, his ability to translate at high speed, and his impeccable background had led to his being the natural choice for talks of a highly delicate nature between heads of state who did not share a common language. Being one of a select band of men who could translate the words of every delegate at a multi-national conference meant that Lord Moore had used Chris exclusively, instead of being obliged to entrust confidential and high-powered information to a group of interpreters each specialising in one language. The result was that Chris had an extremely good understanding of inter-national diplomacy, and a personal acquaintance with many of the world's leading figures. He was trusted, and respected as a man dedicated to world peace. Small wonder he felt unhappy over the whole business of espionage. He had expressed his unwillingness for any part of it at the outset, and had been talked into it. Now he spoke of his feelings again, to the man who was a friend as well as a close associate.

'Frank, I'm not cut out for this,' he complained, as he sat in the dignified office drinking coffee from a Royal Worcester cup and saucer. 'You forced uniform onto me just before Christmas, saying that it would make my work easier. But I'm not an aggressive man, and donning khaki hasn't changed my basic personality. I was no good at being a soldier last time.'

'You won an MC for an attack on a machine-gun post at Gallipoli.'

Chris sighed. 'It was not an attack, as you'd be aware if you had been there. I was the only live subaltern left, and they wanted a figurehead. Even though I was classed as non-combatant because of my bad sight, it was me or nothing. I didn't attack, Frank. I was pretty damn scared, I can tell you. All I had to do was get up out of the trench, and go up a cliffside so that the others would follow. They needed someone to go first, that's all. Why didn't they give medals to all those who were left alive at the end? They all did the same as I did.'

Frank Moore smiled. 'Methinks he doth protest too much.' He put his cup and saucer on the table and sat regarding Chris with his fingertips together, a familiar gesture. 'I'm not asking you to take up arms and perform in the field yourself, my dear fellow. And you are eminently cut out for this, despite your protestations. Aggressive types like John Frifth doubtless enjoy the mental torture of their fellows. You remain clear-headed and unemotional.'

'That I don't,' Chris contradicted immediately. 'I get very het up over the whole business.'

'Nonsense! A less sanguine man than you I have never met.'

Chris got to his feet and moved about the rich, red and blue carpet restlessly. 'My God, have you really learned so little about me during these past years? I said just now I was not an aggressive person, but that doesn't mean I never have strong feelings. Damn it all, some of those poor devils I am badgering almost senseless are women. What are we coming to when we use them for such dangerous, abominable work? You know very well what will happen to them if they are caught. And they know we will disclaim all knowledge of them.'

Frank Moore continued to contemplate him impassively. 'You're a romantic, Chris, that's your trouble. An idealist and an old-fashioned "gentleman". This war isn't going to be in the least like the last one. The trenches of Flanders put paid to the romance of Uhlans and Hussars galloping gallantly to excruciating but honourable death, at a time mutually agreed by opposing generals who wished to partake of breakfast before a battle. Hitler has put paid to any notion of "fair play" warfare. Your brother Rex and his cavaliers of the air have been replaced by men dedicated to killing by any possible means, because they now have an enemy who is utterly ruthless. Young David will be a killer, not a cavalier. Warfare at sea has become more dirty because the killer ships lurk *beneath* the waves to strike unseen. In the field, battles will be fought at long distance. Soldiers will not see the faces of those they are murdering. A tossed grenade, a long-range gun, a long line of invulnerable tanks will dispose of human life in advance. The infantry will merely trample on anonymous corpses as they follow behind. Women are already involved, Chris. You saw and heard of atrocities committed in Poland as we left. The women you "badger almost senseless" are burning to avenge their sisters. They cannot wait to strike at those who butchered, raped and humiliated their friends and loved ones. They welcome your interrogation. The more merciless you are, the better they are pleased. It means they will wreak revenge more thoroughly.'

He waved a hand at the chair Chris had vacated. 'Do sit down again, my dear fellow. Your greatest fault has been your failure to understand human nature. Speak to you of Greek classics, the peasant dialects of Outer Mongolia, or the distinguishing brushwork of Van Gogh, and you feel quite at ease. But I'll wager you have no instinctive understanding of the man who delivers your letters, or of the girl behind the counter at the florist where you order a bouquet for your wife.' As Chris sat again, he continued. 'During our long association I've never been aware of any sexual sidelines, yet you are separated from Marion for long periods on end. Perhaps you should find yourself a woman to relax with in the coming months. No man can work as intensely as you and not release stress and strain in the accepted manner.'

Chris suddenly found his sense of humour. 'You begin to sound like Bill Chandler. He has always believed there is no better remedy for anything than a woman, preferably a redhead. In his youth, I believe he must have known one who was highly promiscuous, and has been reflecting his own experience in his medical advice ever since.'

'You shouldn't have any trouble. Half my own staff have been waiting for the chance to soothe your brow, and to bring out the satin sheets they have been saving for such an occasion. All the same, I beg you not to select one of them, or one of the agents to whom you feel you are being brutal. They work better without romantic involvements.'

Chris gave an incredulous laugh. 'I do believe you're serious.'

'I am. I'm deadly serious, Chris. You have been at this work a mere three months, and came here today hoping to be relieved of it. I am under pressure from another quarter to lend you for another purpose. Men of your unique qualities are more precious than diamonds right now. If you don't give your talents to this essential work, you will be defeating all you have aimed for throughout our years of association. If we lose this war, there never will be peace. Hitler is an idealist, like you. But he is also a madman, who thinks to gain his ideal by killing all those who do not share his enthusiasm for it. Is that what you want? You must continue to help those who, like yourself, have unique qualities we have to use in a time of desperation. If the pressure is already telling on you, it will grow insupportable if you have no light relief. Find yourself a woman, Chris. A discreet, reliable female. Bill Chandler's prescription is very sound.'

Getting to his feet again, Chris found disturbing memories filling him with guilt. 'I have a discreet, reliable wife,' he said firmly. 'I'll try to get down to Dorset this weekend.'

Frank Moore shook his head regretfully. 'Sorry, but I need you at Guidons. If all goes well, and the weather is right on Friday night, two very important people are due to arrive in this country with top secret information. They know you from the past, and have requested that you be there at the meeting.'

So Chris did not get to Dorset that weekend, nor the next three, and he continued to work at the secret establishment, as more and more networks were set up in all parts of the world. But he had occasional quiet periods when he could return to the apartment, which he had agreed could also be used as overnight accommodation for those special guests of Lord Moore who did not particularly wish to use their club or a well-known hotel for reasons of security. His personal assistant, Alexander Matherson, was an MA with a promising career ahead. The fact that he had only one lung made him ineligible for call-up, for which Chris was very grateful. Sandy was invaluable. He knew how to run affairs perfectly, reminded Chris of things he constantly forgot, and dealt personally with anything trivial. A bachelor, Sandy had a pair of adjoining rooms within the apartment, and Chris's cook/housekeeper, Mrs James, also lived on the premises. The middle-aged widow had found the arrangement necessary over the years, due to her employer's erratic way of life, which had him arriving or departing at short notice, requiring meals at irregular hours, and entertaining any number of guests of all nationalities who ate all manner of unusual foods. A lesser woman would have been defeated. Mrs James thrived on excitement.

When Chris let himself into his apartment one late-March evening, he was therefore confidently looking forward to a good meal, a quiet relaxing atmosphere, and a full night's sleep in a comfortable bed. He looked around with pleasure at the beige and gold decor, the heavy leather furniture, and the large paintings in thick, gilded frames that enhanced the walls. Sandy took his cap and greatcoat as he gazed with pleasure at the place he saw too little of.

'The hallmark of a good home is not that one never wants to leave, but that it gives the same pleasure each time one returns,' Chris commented with a smile. 'How are you, Sandy?'

'Very fit, sir, thank you. It's nice to have you at home. Shall you be here long?'

'It depends,' he replied vaguely, still enjoying the normality of being surrounded by beautiful things. 'Pity about those black hangings at the windows. Suggestive of a funeral parlour, wouldn't you say?'

Sandy grinned. 'They do tend to add a sombre touch. Somehow one doesn't notice them as much at the butcher's shop, or the tobacconist on the corner, as one does here.'

'I suppose not. God, I'm tired. I hope Mrs James hasn't prepared a banquet to compensate for the days I've been absent. I doubt I could do justice to it.'

He walked across to the cabinet and poured himself a glass of vodka, as his assistant said, 'I understand dinner will be quite light. After you telephoned your pending arrival, Mrs James confided to me that she has been studying the new recipes being distributed, and has been awaiting an opportunity to try one out. Her banquets will be a thing of the past, I fear, now meat is being rationed.'

'Is it?' Chris asked in surprise. 'I wonder what the Chandlers will do with all their spring lambs.'

'All surplus supplies will be stored, I should imagine,' came the reply. Then, as Chris handed him a tot of whisky, added, 'Thank you, sir. If it goes on long enough, I suppose this stuff will be rationed.'

Settling himself in one of the large armchairs, Chris gave him a straight look. 'It's going to last a long time, Sandy, believe me. You only have to hear what refugees are saying to realise we are up against a man who will never stop until he has conquered the world, or until he and his fanatical followers have all been killed. However, enough of that. Bring me up to date with all that has happened in my absence. Nothing in the nature of an emergency, I take it, since you haven't been in touch with Lord Moore on that number I gave you.'

His companion took up a file from the nearby desk before settling in the other chair by the fire, and stretching his gangling legs out beneath the marquetry table where he had set down his glass. The light from the flames danced on his round fair-complexioned face, and lit his light brown hair with a golden sheen. Chris reflected, not for the first time, that he had a better relationship with this youngster than with his own son. If the boy David had not been told about his past by an old man of the village with more tongue than wits, would the close companionship of those first years after the war have continued into adulthood, or would the facts from any lips have turned David against him? Sudden sadness touched him. In the 'last little dust-up', as John Frith had called it, the chances of survival had been very slim. He couldn't bear to think that David might not live to forgive him.

'. . . and he wrote, at some length, in appreciation of your paper on the subject,' Sandy was saying.

'Kind of him,' Chris murmured, completely at sea over who had been kind enough to write to him at length.

'The parcels of books you ordered arrived. Would you believe it, on a horse-drawn waggon,' came the amused comment. 'The chap who brought the parcels to the door said it was for the war effort, and further informed me that Craigie and Wilkinson had handed over their entire fleet of delivery vans to the military. Quite a few firms are doing it.'

'I'm glad to hear that,' said Chris, the strain of the past weeks fast overtaking him, making him sleepy. 'My brother Roland would approve of keeping horses here and sending vans to war. He always hated the use of horses for battle.'

'He was an accomplished horseman, wasn't he?'

'He was also one of the most peaceable men you could wish to meet. His collection of letters, which I had published, were hailed as a brilliant outcry against war in the years after 1918. Now, copies are being removed from the shelves of bookshops and lending libraries, condemned as pacifist propaganda.'

'You should have sent a copy to Adolf Hitler, sir,' Sandy joked gently.

'Maybe I should. That's assuming he reads books other than his own.' Determined to concentrate on the matters in hand, he sat up in his chair, asking, 'What else, Sandy?'

The young man detailed several other pieces of information, then said, 'I sent the usual telegram to your son on his birthday, and arranged for flowers to be delivered to Lady Sheridan on hers. They telephoned from Cartier to enquire whether you would be collecting the piece you chose for Her Ladyship when you went in prior to Christmas. Knowing you were likely to be tied up all through that weekend, I instructed them to have it sent to Tarrant Hall.'

'Oh, Lord,' said Chris. 'I should have remembered to telephone. Why didn't you remind me of the date?'

Sandy's expression was carefully neutral. 'You told me to contact you only in an emergency, Sir Christopher.'

He sighed. 'So I did. I had better ring my wife this evening to apologise. She is very concerned over David, and I sincerely intended to keep in touch more frequently, under the circumstances.'

'Lady Sheridan telephoned several times over the last few weeks, and I told her you were at important meetings. I think she is aware that you have a great deal to do.'

'We all have a great deal to do, Sandy, but it is essential to maintain family ties at times like these. One can feel immensely alone without them,' he finished, an echo of remembered terror touching his voice.

'Vesta came on two separate occasions.' The young man grinned. 'The first time, I suspect she was hoping for a decent tea. Mrs James produced muffins, egg sandwiches, and a jolly fine cherry cake, which your daughter tucked into despite being disappointed that you weren't here. The second time, last Wednesday, as a matter of fact, she brought a friend with her. They didn't stay for tea. I had a feeling the chap was relieved, for some reason. Afraid you might not give your approval, perhaps, because he was a foreigner.'

'The friend was a man?'

'Yes. A Polish pilot who had spent Christmas with you, I was told. Vesta seemed on very good terms with him.'

'Did she?' Chris realised there was something else he had forgotten because he had been so busy. He had fully intended to make enquiries about Felix Makoski. If Vesta was now on very good terms with him, it was essential that he should do so.

It was springtime and she was in love. In the London parks flowers and trees were blooming, despite the grim reminders of trenches and shelters built to give protection against attack, and the mass of barrage balloons floating overhead like great, grey weeds on elongated wire stalks. On a day of vivid blue skies filled with a dotting of fluffy white clouds, Vesta could think only of the coming evening as she stood before her easel. She had not seen David since Christmas, but she nevertheless wished he had not decided to turn her tête-à-tête into a foursome. She longed fiercely to have Felix to herself.

Since Christmas she had met Felix regularly. She could clearly remember the unbelieving thrill with which she received his first letter. She now compared life with the cinema. Day-to-day existence was like a black-and-white film; when Felix was there it burst into glorious technicolour. At Christmas he had been very correct, and probably conscious of somehow being a 'charity case'. But as their relationship had progressed, Vesta had seen him change from a courteous, somewhat bewildered refugee from violence, to a passionate, courageous young man. He held her in thrall to his ethnic magnetism. Heart and soul his, Vesta could scarcely believe he returned her wild devotion. Yet his kisses and ardent declarations suggested that he was ruled by longings as difficult to deny as her own. For almost four months she had fought them. Now, surrender beckoned ecstatically, despite parental teaching and instinctive fears.

In letters to her mother she casually mentioned Felix; in letters to David she did the same. She had taken her love to her father's apartment, somehow feeling that there she would be able to put her emotions in perspective. After all, Sir Christopher Sheridan was constantly in the company of foreigners, and had a far more liberal view of international friendship than most. He would more easily accept a young man with alien religion and culture as a partner for her than her mother, who loved her voluntary exile in a Dorset village, and who based her views on that tiny rural community. However, Sandy had offered the usual excuses of important meetings, heavy commitments and unexpected delays, and she had turned down the offer of tea for herself and Felix. Her need for parental approval frustrated, she had been angry that her father was not there when she wanted him. Forgetting the times she had been filled with pride on presenting to her friends an astonishingly young and handsome man who made them all weak at the knees, she now resented the fact that he was not the kind of ageing father who presided over home and family with old-fashioned protective wisdom. Was David right in his assertion that their father was supremely selfish, pursuing his brilliant career with little concern for his family? For the rest of that particular day she had been inclined to believe it, but in the night hours she was filled with remorse in case he really was sent to France, as Pat feared, and did not return. Felix had often spoken of the things he had seen before leaving Poland, and dark wakefulness in a lodging she shared with a girl she did not really care for made it seem too frighteningly real. Suppose such things ever touched her own family?

Turning into her pillow night after night, Vesta tried to stifle her longing for Felix. When it refused to be stifled, she told herself that he could not be compared with anyone else she had met. His manners were impeccable, his courtesy fascinating. That European élan beloved by females, but considered by most Englishmen to be showy nonsense, was evident in him,

54

and he treated her with something verging on reverence, which she had never encountered in an English boy. It was only natural, she told herself, that his Eastern European blood should make him passionate, and that the tragedy of his recent past should drive him to try to forget for a while with a girl from a family that had taken pity on him. Felix was reaching out for consolation. When his kisses became demanding and his hands unruly, it was only because he was carried away by the need to obliterate those scenes of terror from his heart and mind. He had confessed to her that he never slept without nightmares marching through his brain. When he was with her, he said, it was possible to feel human again, forget that he had lost all that was near and dear to him. It was purely because she wanted to ease his unhappiness that she let him kiss her with such hunger, hold her so close against his body, touch her breasts. She could not be grouped with those girls she knew who let any man do it because they considered such things as essential to an art student as a good set of brushes. It was not cheap, or in any way disgusting. Felix loved her the way she loved him. There was no reason why she should allow a sense of shame to spoil the most wonderful, irresistible experience of her life.

She had not mentioned these things in her letters to Pat, although she had confessed to being in love and finding it changed life completely. Privately, Vesta was horrified to think of Pat feeling for her father what she, herself, felt for Felix, and could not believe her friend serious in her claim. She wrote, also, that this heavenly state inspired her artistically, so that she was painting better than she had ever done. Unfortunately, her tutors did not agree. Her pictures were criticised for being too pretty and whimsical, lacking authority, and too concerned with small detail to the detriment of the main subject, which needed stronger colour and more vigorous brushwork. In vain she told them she felt she was expressing herself more freely than before. Unimpressed, they insisted that she was there to be shown how to be an artist, not to express her immature thoughts on canvas willy-nilly. If it was her aim to become an illustrator of fairytale books, now was her time to pester publishers, rather than waste time and her father's money on further lessons. Nevertheless she continued to turn still life, landscapes, studies in light and shade, interiors and portraits into misty dream-like impressions that charmed and fulfilled her, whilst enraging her tutors.

Fellow students joined in the criticism, indulging in the cruel frankness that parades in the disguise of artistic discernment, anxious to display their own talent as vastly superior.

Vesta was too happy to let it bother her. She now viewed their Bohemian posing in the same light Pat had seen it in at Christmas. She also laughed at their pompous pronouncements, their earnest discussions full of opinions that blinded speakers and listeners with their inexplicable profundity. She alone knew the secret of existence, she felt, and put it onto canvas because she was unable to express it any other way. The school might censure her style, but she knew her father would praise it. His own paintings, mostly done in his youth, contained that same quality of mystery; of truth just out of sight along a twisting pathway, round a corner, or over the brow of a hill. As a child, Vesta had called them 'through the looking glass' pictures, because she had always longed to climb into them to explore further. Time and again she wished her father was at home more often, for he had always encouraged her to paint instinctively, and would support her now.

After another day of criticism she gladly abandoned her brushes, rushed to her lodging to change into a dinner dress of deep blue and saffron Burmese silk, then left for the restaurant that had been designated by David as the meeting place. She took a bus because she had spent most of her allowance on the dress, and as she sat in the eerie green light, unable to watch the passing scene because the windows were all painted over for blackout purposes, she was conscious of being studied by the other passengers, most of whom were in uniform. She felt there was no justification for their critical stares. The war still seemed unreal, despite the sinister changes all around. The enemy was far distant, halfway across Europe; the French and British armies were united between them and the English Channel. Why should she not go out to dinner with the man she loved, and wear something pretty to please him?

An s-shaped arrangement of screens at the entrance to the restaurant ensured that no light escaped when the door opened, and Vesta was initially blinded by brightness as the head waiter asked whom she was joining and led the way to a table in a secluded corner. To her dismay she found David and his partner had already arrived, so Felix could do no more to convey his delight at seeing her than kiss her hand formally. Weak with the thrill of being near him again, she was afraid to say anything to him in case her voice gave her away. David looked at her curiously as he kissed her cheek, then went on to introduce her to Cherry Fortnum, a blonde feline girl with very red lips, eyes that were large and full of assessment, and a figure of which nothing was left to the imagination by a clinging dress of silver satin. Vesta immediately felt gawky, inexperienced and overdressed. She also felt very jealous. Felix appeared to be on good terms with her. How long had they been there together?

David put in a brotherly foot immediately by saying, 'Good Lord, Vee, that frock is a bit *outré*, isn't it?'

'I think it's very swanky,' Cherry commented in purring tones. 'It's essentially Bohemian, and the sort of thing artists are expected to wear, Davey.'

Vesta shuddered at the ghastly diminutive, but David followed his tactlessness with more. 'I've never understood why. Just because a person paints pictures, I see no justification for prancing around in purple dustsheets or copies of Ali Baba's outfit so that everyone knows. I don't go everywhere in a flying jacket and fur-lined boots, do I?'

'You don't need to, you wear a uniform,' Vesta flung at him.

'Fair enough, bad example. A motor mechanic doesn't walk the streets in greasy overalls, or a butcher turn up at the theatre in his blue and white striped apron.'

Felix took her hand under the table and began stroking it with his thumb in a way that made her colour rise as her thoughts ran away. 'I think Vesta looks of the most charming,' he said. 'Of course, she must display her artistic talent in every direction.'

David grinned and held up his hands in surrender. 'All right, all right. I see I'm outnumbered three to one. Let's order before the place gets too full. I don't know about the rest of you, but I'm starving.'

After that the evening grew better, and Vesta found herself quite liking the girl David had with him, despite her conviction there was no real fondness between them. Her brother worked his way through a succession of such girls without becoming emotionally involved with them, and she had often wondered whether he would ever meet someone who meant more to him than flying. Looking covertly at Felix, she felt her brother had no idea what he was missing by not being in love. All the same, there was an air of maturity and experience about Cherry Fortnum, who could not be more than twenty, that made Vesta very thoughtful, especially when she caught Felix eyeing the daringly low neckline of the girl's evening frock. Did that kind of girl appeal to him too? Surely not. He was too deep and intense a personality.

Near the end of their meal voices were suddenly raised at the bar. A group of naval officers had just entered with a disturbing item of news, and the entire restaurant was soon in uproar. The Germans were on the move again. Denmark and Norway had been occupied. The enemy was coming nearer. Inexorably nearer.

The two men with them reacted violently, albeit in different ways. Felix was almost stunned. 'It is like a poison, this Germans. Everywhere it spreads, and kills as it moves. Can no one stop it?'

'Yes, by George, we can,' vowed David, his eyes bright with excitement. 'The nearer they come, the easier it'll be for our aircraft to reach 'em and give cover for our boys on the ground. That was the trouble last time. The power of an air force was realised too late, and then the machines the poor devils had to take up were hardly suited to the task. It's different now. The Huns haven't discovered the stuff we're made of yet. Just let us get at 'em.'

'They bombed us on the ground, destroyed our aircraft before we could get into the air,' Felix told him stonily. 'They are so big, so strong. You have no experience of what they are.'

'We soon will,' promised David sharply. 'Don't underestimate us, old chap. People who do always eat their words.'

'I, for one, am going to eat my chicken,' pronounced Cherry. 'We came out to enjoy ourselves. Let's not start discussing the war. It's so tedious. Don't you agree, Vesta?'

Watching Felix, and aching with compassion, she replied, 'I feel it's a subject we don't really understand yet, so don't let's talk about it tonight.' Turning to her brother, she pleaded, 'David, this is supposed to be a relaxed occasion. Must you hold forth on the love of your life right now?'

He frowned. 'But you must see the seriousness of this news. You'll soon be jolly glad of the RAF.'

'Especially of the nephew of "Sherry" Sheridan,' put in Cherry, coquettishly, causing David to look at her with a mixture of curiosity and annoyance.

'Who the devil told you that?'

'A little bird, darling,' came the teasing reply. 'One with higher rank than yours.'

'Oh, indeed,' he said crisply. 'Don't be fooled by rank. It doesn't always mean the little bird is superior in *everything*.'

'Whatever do you mean?' she asked wide-eyed.

'You'll find out soon ... on the dance floor. Come on, let's stretch our legs.' He gave one of his dazzling smiles as he pulled her to her feet, and led her through the tables to the tiny area where people were dancing.

Alone with Felix at last, Vesta found he was unable to shake off the mood brought on by the news, and she could only sit holding his hand, agonising, while he voiced his despair, his conviction that he would never see his homeland again. His vow that he would give his life to wreak vengeance on the race that was now terrorising the world made her afraid. She could not bear to lose him.

David and his girl appeared to have cast aside depression whilst dancing cheek to cheek, and returned full of laughter and teasing. Vesta wished them both far away, and sat through the following two hours feeling Felix's unhappiness as her own. Finally, David offered to take Vesta back to her lodging in his MG.

'I've had eight in her before now,' he explained with a grin, 'so four will be easy.'

'Well...' Vesta hedged, wondering what Felix would do on reaching her place. Would he go on with the other two, completing the disaster of the evening?

'That is most kind of you,' he put in, making the decision for her. 'If the ladies will fetch their coats, off we shall start.'

Before they picked up their coats, the two girls went into the ladies' room together. As they powdered their noses in front of the long mirror, Vesta found herself excusing Felix's black mood.

'News like that must hit him very hard. His father was killed early on, during the general massacre of the aristocracy. He was a Polish count.'

'Weren't they all, sweetie?' came the amused response.

Her hand holding the pink velour puff stilled in mid-air. 'Pardon?'

'My dear Vesta, when were you born?' The large eyes looked her over candidly. 'They all spin the same tale. Who's to disprove it? It compensates for their feeling of national humiliation. I don't blame them, and your Felix is a real dish.'

Feeling anger rise in her, Vesta said hotly, 'I don't think you understand. Felix saw his mother dragged from a church and shot. Then his sisters were taken off by a group of drunken soldiers. You can guess what happened to them.'

'The same thing that'll happen to us if the Jerries ever reach England,' said the girl, with a sudden touch of savagery. 'If I'm going to be violated by drunken soldiers, I intend to ensure I've had my fun with some lovely men first. You'll do the same, if you've any sense. That Polish boy is ripe for consolation, and you appear to be dotty about him. For heaven's sake, give him what he needs. Who cares if he is the son of a count, or not? Men all look the same when it comes to bare flesh, don't they?'

The two girls squeezed into the other seat in the car. Felix perched on the back of it with his legs each side of them. David drove recklessly through the dark streets to Vesta's room in Bayswater. The total blackout was their ally. Any policeman about would be unaware of the number in a car intended for two, so they reached their destination undetected. To Vesta's relief, Felix also climbed from the car, said polite farewells, and stood beside her as David gave her a brotherly hug, told her to be good, then roared off, probably to some discreet hotel with Cherry. If he had not already planned it, she would be sure to put the idea into his head, Vesta felt.

As the roar of the car faded into the distance, it suddenly seemed very quiet there on the pavement. There was no moon to relieve the blackness. Swept by unusual nervousness, and knowing she could not bear to let Felix walk off in his present mood, Vesta said awkwardly, 'Would you like to come up? I could make some coffee.' Afraid of a refusal, she added quickly, 'It's all right, Deirdre's out. We'd be on our own. We could talk. About anything you like.'

She almost held her breath until he said, 'Yes ... I think, yes.'

It was a large, very untidy room, that held the aroma of kippers Deirdre must have had for supper. Clothes had been scattered everywhere as the girl had searched for articles that suited her mood, and the curtain that shut off the sleeping area was still drawn back to reveal two beds. Vesta's was comparatively neat, with the patchwork quilt her mother had made thrown over it. The other was a tangle of sheets, underwear and the goathair cover that still smelt of the foreign bazaar where it had been bought. Seeing the sordid aspect of the place as never before, Vesta swiftly crossed to swish the curtain shut. The small pile of shillings they kept for the meter had plainly been taken to finance Deirdre's evening out, and she had to search in her purse for a coin to ensure the electric fire and the lights would stay on while Felix was there. Wishing fervently that she still lived in the apartment in Belgravia, which was comfortable, elegant and more suited to someone of Felix's background, she put the shilling in the meter, plugged in the fire, then turned to say, 'I'll make the coffee.'

She never formed the sentence. Felix was standing just inside the door with his head tilted back, his eyes closed, and tears streaming down his cheeks. Vesta had never known a man to cry. She found it one of the most shocking things she had ever seen. For a moment or two she was rooted to the spot, having no idea what to do. Then instinct took over. Going to him, she seized his arm and led him to the ancient *chaise longue* that was covered with a Victorian shawl, treating him with infinite

60

gentleness in her awe. Seated on the shabby velvet, he fought for control of himself, wiping the wetness from his cheeks with a clenched fist, and murmuring thickly, 'Excuse... excuse. I could not help it.'

Unable to stop herself, Vesta put up a trembling hand to touch his dark curls, in the way a mother would comfort a child. 'Please don't,' she whispered. 'I can't bear it.'

The dark fiery eyes now swimming with tears gazed back at her in desperation. 'It is the loneliness. You cannot understand. My family, my country... I can do nothing. *Nothing*. Soon they will be here. It will begin again. You have been so kind, but you cannot understand what it is like for me. You cannot.'

Swept by a fatal combination of emotions, Vesta strained forward and laid her cheek against his wet one, as her hand slid from his hair to cradle the back of his neck.

'I try... But all I can do is love you.' Having put it into words, at last, she had to convince him of her sincerity. 'I love you, Felix,' she breathed against his ear. 'It happened the minute I saw you standing in the hall, drenched and dripping water all over the parquet. It happened as quickly as that.'

In a flash, the situation changed completely. With a sigh verging on a moan, he seized her in a vice-like hold, and began kissing her so fiercely her head swam. His wet lips and wet cheeks brought to the surface all those basic desires she had tried to ignore since meeting him. Surrender filled her mind and body until the ache to be possessed was uncontainable. His feverish hands were at the fastenings of her dress, her throbbing breasts were bursting to be free for him. Naked to the waist, she lay moaning with the fire of his hands on her skin, and such was the agony of unfulfilment, she kicked and wriggled her way free of the long dress and petticoat, making it simple for him to remove the last impediment to total nakedness. Almost melting with the anticipation of his soft caressing fingers on her stomach and thighs, she was shocked out of her mood when he fell heavily upon her, forced her legs apart, and began inflicting such pain deep inside her she cried out with it. Pain, and still more pain, until the moment became a nightmare from which she was powerless to escape. Then he gave an explosive grunt, she felt hotness inside her, and he rolled away, stood up, and shuffled across to flop into a chair near the fire.

It was terribly quiet, save for his heavy breathing. The flat had turned very cold, even though the fire was still on. She was in agony, outside and within. Humiliation and shame put ice in her veins to set her shaking uncontrollably. Her body felt as if it was slowly breaking apart, and she was sobbing silently. What, in heaven's name, had happened to *love*?

For two days Vesta did not attend classes. Unable to eat, she felt sick and ill, and at her wits' end. Over and over again she could hear Pat's voice saying, 'It wouldn't bring "the curse" a week early. More likely to drive it away for nine months.' Whatever would she do if it did? How could she ever face her family? Frightened and ashamed, she sat in the tawdry room huddled into a rug, feeling totally abandoned. She now regarded her body as a loathsome thing that had betrayed her. There was no one to whom she could turn. Her fellow students would ridicule her, confirm what she suspected. They did it openly and enjoyably. Vesta Sheridan must be a freak, an unnatural woman, because she had found it painful, disgusting and shocking. Afterwards she had gone to pieces, flinched away from Felix when he approached her, sent him away angry and contemptuous of her. Completely mortified, she now hated herself. There must be something wrong with her, something that made her unlike other women. If they felt as she had they would never do it a second time, never get married and condemn themselves to such a ritual for life.

Felix's attitude supported her belief. He was naturally gentle and courteous, certainly not a person to do what he had done if it was meant to be brutal. The fact that he had been so angry with her surely proved he could not have expected it to have been a painful thing, could not have known it would hurt so much. His lack of patience with her distress could only have been caused by his inability to understand why she behaved as she did, after something normal people apparently enjoyed. Knowing she would die rather than face him again, yet bereft at losing the wonder of him, she huddled in a daze of misery, feeling dreadfully alone.

On the third day her misery was partially relieved by the evidence that she was not pregnant, and she was driven to go for a walk to ease the normal growing stomach ache. Wrapping herself carelessly against the treacherous April wind in an old coat and woollen hat, she marched along oblivious of where she was heading, or of whom she passed. The two days without food took their toll. She was about to cross a wide road, when severe giddiness caused her to grab at someone beside her to keep from falling.

'Are you all right, miss?' asked a man's voice kindly.

Loosing her clutch on the policeman's sleeve, she said faintly, 'Yes, thank you. I felt giddy for a moment, that's all.'

'Well, I'll just see you safely across to the other side,' he went on, 'then, if I was you, I'd get back home.' Taking her arm he led her over to the other pavement, then gave her a stern look. 'You're to get indoors as soon as you can, miss. You still look very pale. What's more, you aren't carrying your gas mask. I won't take your name this time, but someone else might if you wander around for long.'

She tried to smile. 'You've been very kind. I'll remember the gas mask in future.'

'Good afternoon, constable. Is something amiss?' asked a quiet voice to her right, and she spun round so fast the giddiness returned.

'Daddy!'

He put out his hands to steady her. 'Are you all right? Not in any trouble, are you?'

Suddenly too emotional to speak, she could do no more than shake her head, then stand with his arm around her for support while he explained who he was to the policeman, said he would take his daughter home, then began leading her to his car, which had drawn up beside the curb several yards away. Her father had never been a person to indulge in idle chat, but whether it was this trait or consideration for her that kept him quiet through the journey, she could not decide. The silence allowed her an opportunity to collect her thoughts, and to think up plausible answers for the questions he would surely ask when they reached the apartment, which was where he appeared to be heading. Instead of frantically inventing excuses for herself, all she could think of as she sat beside him in the chauffeur-driven car was that he had done what Felix had done, and had been forced to marry her mother as the result of it.

Sandy was well-trained and diplomatic. He took their coats, went off to tell Mrs James to bring tea, and did not come back. Vesta felt even more of a mess in the familiar plush surroundings of the family apartment, and sat hunched on the edge of the chair, warming herself by the fire. Her father came to sit in the chair next to hers, and held his hands out toward the flames.

'Tea won't be long. Mrs James will make it an extra special one now she knows you're here. I hope you're hungry.'

She shook her head. 'Not very, I'm afraid.'

'Ah me, that means I'll have to eat most of it myself to avoid offending her.' He leant back in relaxation. 'Always treat your cook with the utmost flattery, for she can make your life perfection or purgatory.'

Silence fell as she stared at the fire, seeing the leaping flames as symbolic of the hot fire Felix had spilled into her resisting body. When her father spoke next it made her jump. But he posed no more than a gentle question.

'Giving class a miss today?'

She shrugged, murmuring, 'You know how it is. Sometimes ideas just don't turn out right.'

'Yes, I know too well, which is why I never became the world's next Matisse.'

The tea tray was brought in by Mrs James, and while she said her usual few words about not returning to live at the apartment, Vesta studied her father as if he were a stranger. That old scandal David had taken so badly had never bothered her before. It had seemed almost romantic to an adolescent schoolgirl, with Pat breathing admiration and hero worship over photographs of a boy officer who looked very like Rupert Brooke. All the while it had seemed like a gilded novel of love and war, Vesta had enjoyed the sighs and envy of her friends. Now such things had been reduced to naked bodies, raw pain, and brutal abandonment in a chilly room smelling of kippers, the father she had loved had turned into a disgusting poseur. He was even worse than Felix because he had made her mother pregnant, then walked out on her when David was born.

'Are you going to pour the tea?' he asked with a smile.

She did so with clumsy hands, wishing she had never gone for a walk that day. Then she passed the buttered toast to him, taking several fingers to put on her own plate so that he would not comment on her lack of appetite.

'I'm sorry I haven't seen much of you lately,' he said. 'I've been phenomenally busy. I even forgot your mother's birthday.'

She forced a smile. 'What's unusual about that? You always forget it.'

He cast her a look under furrowed brows. 'You always remind me. What happened this year?'

'I've been phenomenally busy myself,' she declared theatrically.

'With Felix Makoski?'

That shook her badly. How did he know about Felix? Could anyone have said anything to him about what they had done? No, there was no person who knew.

'What do you mean?'

He smiled, dispersing her fear. 'You know how things get round. Sandy said you had brought him here one day, and then your mother told me on the telephone yesterday that David had mentioned meeting you both earlier this week for a dinner-dance. I formed conclusions. People love to gossip. Why do you think they have put up all those posters warning that "careless talk costs lives"? Not that news of your friendship with young Makoski is a vital secret.' He pursed his lips. 'It isn't, is it?'

'Good heavens, no. Besides, I hardly know him.' She hoped that was the end of the subject, but it turned out to be the end of something else.

'I'm glad our paths accidentally crossed today,' her father went on. 'It saves me the onerous task of writing you a letter concerning that fellow. There's no doubt he has been through something of an ordeal, due to the occupation of his country and his forced escape to freedom, but I feel I should warn you that he turns out to be rather less than he makes out.'

'Go on, Daddy,' she heard herself say.

'People I've spoken to about him confirm that he's a courageous pilot, and a great patriot, but he told a few lies about his background. His father is a teacher of English at a high school – still is, as far as anyone knows. His mother died soon after he was born. He was her only child. Two years ago, Felix Makoski married a young girl of his home town. Their son was born five months later. His wife and baby are still in Poland with the girl's parents.'

Chapter Four

THEY ALL sat around in the sunshine like schoolboy cricketers clustering around the pavilion, waiting for their turn to bat. Many of them had been schoolboys only several months before, but even the older ones exhibited the breezy confidence of youth, with the keen eyes and throwaway style of speaking that identified them as fighter pilots as much as the clothes they wore. As they waited, they indulged in various forms of occupation, or dozed full-length on the grass, occasionally belying their comotose state by inserting a pertinent comment into a conversation going on above them. Sometimes this brought a laugh, sometimes a well-aimed cushion, sometimes a full-scale attack on the speaker's person by youngsters keyed up for action. The serious-minded read books or played chess, the lewd thumbed through girlie magazines, the musical played the mouth organ, the amateur philosophers debated endlessly. Beneath it all, each and every one was like a coiled spring waiting for the telephone to ring with the message that would set them all running for their aircraft.

None was more inwardly tense than David as he lolled in an old basket chair, swinging his gauntlets relentlessly to and fro. The testing time had finally come, and he was afraid. France had fallen. The defeated armies had been brought from Dunkirk at the start of June, in a rescue operation that would surely rank in history with the evacuation of Gallipoli. The Germans were just across the English Channel, poised to cross it and occupy the island they had not conquered last time. Before they could do so, it was essential to gain superiority in the air, and everything hung on the destruction of the RAF. The men of the Royal Air Force had a few rude words to say about that idea. David had added a few choice ones of his own, but it was pure bravado on his part. More than words were expected from him now.

From as far back as he could remember, there had only been

one thing he had wanted to be, only one thing that had interested him. From the age of constructive thought, his Uncle Rex had been David's great hero. Rex 'Sherry' Sheridan was a legendary giant of aviation, a wartime ace whose unconventional battle tactics had been adopted by those who now followed in his image, and his exploits still thrilled youngsters who read of them in histories of the Royal Flying Corps. Winner of innumerable awards for gallantry, including the Victoria Cross for a near-impossible mission from which he had never returned, his mysterious departure from the world at twenty-four was as legendary as his career as a pilot. Reckless, happy-go-lucky, loyal in friendship, and fatally attractive to women, 'Sherry' Sheridan was regarded as a god by those concerned with aviation in any form. Small wonder his young nephew had dreamed of emulating him.

But when his young nephew passed the age of dreams, he discovered chill reality. The kinship that had undoubtedly worked in his favour in many instances then revealed its drawbacks. *'Sherry' Sheridan was my uncle*, was a phrase that began to heap pressures on him. He stopped saying it, but by then it was too late. It dogged him wherever he went. Introductions brought the inevitable, *'No relation to THE Sheridan, I suppose?'* Before David had climbed into his first cockpit, he had been prematurely accredited with brilliance at a skill he had not yet learned. At Cranwell there had been no doubt in anyone's mind who would pass out top. His uncle's reputation had caused David to be surrounded by social climbers, and shunned by inverted snobs. He was ruled by the obligation to honour the continuation of the legend. His boyhood dreams of becoming a carbon copy of 'Sherry' Sheridan turned into the nightmare of discovering that the world already believed him to be so.

Thanking God from the bottom of his heart for a natural aptitude for flying, all he had had to do was flout the rules now and again and add a touch of recklessness to persuade watchers here was another giant in the making. Pure hard work and endless hours of desperate study had just, but only just, gained him the expected top marks at Cranwell. The rest had been easy. A fast car, a bevy of fast girls, and an extrovert life completed the pose. For a while he had breathed again, and his career had certainly been boosted by possessing that famous name. Now it had changed. It had been one thing to emulate the qualities of another man. It would be quite another to emulate his courage. If he failed the coming test, he would be letting down his squadron, those in higher command who had been influenced by his kinship, and the members of his family. But, most of all, he would be letting down a man he could only vaguely remember as a very tall, jolly man in uniform, with red hair and a kind voice. That meeting must have taken place very shortly before his uncle had disappeared for ever, and was a memory David cherished. If he disgraced that memory, how could he go on?

The telephone rang. David's nerves jumped. His stomach tightened, and his heart thudded so heavily he thought he must be visibly shaking from it. Silence had fallen, all heads had turned to where the nearest man had picked up the receiver, an American called Enright.

Features settling back to normal, the man looked up and drawled, 'Relax, guys. Which one of you bums parked a red MG in the space reserved for the SIO, as if we didn't know? He's jumping like a cricket on a hot griddle over it.' Replacing the receiver, he went on. 'There's a couple MEs shunting up and down the Channel, but they're too far away and minding their own business. Go back to sleep. Mom'll tell us when to go out to play.'

David swallowed nervously. His throat had grown unbearably dry. They had been up on two occasions to intercept enemy aircraft entering their sector, but either Control had mistaken the direction, or the Germans had changed course, for there had been no sign of them. Other squadrons had been in the thick of it for some time, and stories of daring and endeavour were legion. When would their turn come? When would he have the chance to prove himself? Or fail. Or die without ever knowing the answer.

The telephone rang again. Enright snatched up the receiver anxiously. His freckled face creased into a delighted smile. 'Scramble! *Scramble!* Sweet dozens of 'em, all coming straight for us,' he yelled, flinging the receiver back in the vague direction of the stand, and charging through them towards the waiting Spitfires like a wounded buffalo.

David raced with the rest to where the machines were lined up ready for takeoff. With a roar, the engines were started by the watching ground crews before the pilots reached them. The sound of twelve engines set David's blood rushing through his veins so fast he felt giddy. His legs were weak with excitement and fear. Struggling into his parachute, he climbed into the cockpit, and strapped himself in with shaking hands. There was a bang on the side of the fuselage to signify that all was ready, the chocks were pulled away, and he gave the 'thumbs up' sign.

'Dear God, please help me,' he prayed softly, as he taxied into the wind. 'Don't let me fail him now.'

They were off, climbing and circling to make formation. The squadron leader's voice came over the R/T with instructions of altitude and direction, followed by a few reminders on basic tactics, and a warning to watch every direction at once, especially the rear, even when chasing a kill. There was a cloudless sky, and David experienced the thrill he always felt once he had left the ground. He knew of nothing to compare with this feeling of power, of utter freedom. It grew rapidly colder, and the clothes he had found so stifling on the ground were now barely sufficient to keep him warm. Higher still, and he turned on the oxygen, feeling the benefit immediately. He checked the instruments. All normal. Putting out a gloved hand, he switched on the gun sight, turned the safety catch to 'Fire', and offered up another prayer – this time that it would not prove to be another false alarm. His throat was so constricted he had difficulty in replying to his commander's verbal check that everyone was fully operational.

At twenty-five thousand feet they levelled out and began searching for their victims. Looking down, David could see the south-east coast of England, and in the hazy distance, separated by a gash of blue water, the outline of France. Swivelling his head to left and right, he could see only blue sky and his colleagues flying alongside. The young former bank clerk on his left made a vulgar gesture, indicating what he thought of the men who had sent them up on another wild goose chase, and David grinned his agreement. Comradeship came easier to him in the air than on the ground. He supposed it was because they were all equal up there – just one man in one aircraft – and it did not matter if the name was Sheridan or Smith, because the squadron expected equal performance from each member with no time for assessment.

Then an excited voice shouted through the headphones, 'Tally-ho! Tally-ho! Bandits in sight, low to starboard.'

There they were. A mass of black dots in a clear, cobalt sky, moving relentlessly over the coast of England.

'Christ, there must be at least a hundred of the bloody things!' David swore involuntarily, then jumped as his squadron leader's voice crackled over the R/T.

'Too right, Davey lad. That makes eight and a third each. Or eight for the rest of us, and twelve for you. Everyone happy with that arrangement?'

'Suits me fine.'

'All right by me.'

'He's welcome to 'em.'

'He can have my eight as well. I shan't argue.'

Voices came from squadron members in clipped or deceptively lazy tones, until Chuck Enright came in with, 'Yeah, go to it, *Sherry*. We can't wait to see how it should be done.'

The American had never lost any opportunity to rile the man he saw as the epitome of upper-class privilege and arrogance, and persisted in using that famous nickname even after having been asked not to by David. The use of it now brought back all his fears, and he felt desperately sick.

'Approach in formation, then you can all do as you bloody well like – so long as you turn up in time for tea,' came the calm voice of their leader. 'Remember, don't let them get behind you. Here goes, lads.'

Peeling away from the squadron, the leader headed for the German formation as the gap between them narrowed fast. The rest kept close behind him, still as a group. As David concentrated on keeping his position, he forgot about the nausea that had filled him. It was all happening so fast now, there was no time for introspection. The last coherent thought he had before all hell broke loose was the uncanny feeling that his uncle was watching and encouraging him, as if he knew all would be well.

That day's experience was something he would never forget. One moment there was peace in the heavens, save for the sound of his own engine; the next he was lost in a hellish confusion of zooming dark metal shapes intent on destruction. The noise was a deafening mixture of engines under stress, chattering guns, men's voices pounding his ears with warning shouts, high-pitched cries of triumph, screams of pain. What had been a beautiful summer sky with a clear-cut corner of England below, turned into a nightmare of diving attacking machines, some with streams of gleaming tracer bullets issuing from their wingers, others with streams of smoke and flames pouring from the place where the pilot had been the moment before. He had swift glimpses of men he must try to kill, as they flashed past intent on killing him; and suffered moments of terror when a collision seemed inevitable. He hauled desperately on the control column, diving, climbing, banking; all the time afraid of the man on his tail. The cobalt summer sky turned to grey, black and orange as aircraft began to fall and spiral helplessly, leaving trails of smoke to mingle with the grey puffs of anti-aircraft shells from the guns on the ground, and the white contrails of battling machines at great height.

His neck ached from constant swivelling of his head; his eyes ached from the bewildering kaleidoscope of images; his ears ached from the inhuman sounds coming from those of his comrades who were dying in agony. Breathing had become a frenzied gasping; thinking had become a thing of the past. Time and again he jabbed his gun button when an enemy aircraft came into his sights, but he never knew whether or not his fire did any real damage, due to the criss-cross pattern of the battle. After what seemed half a lifetime had passed, he spotted a Messerschmitt streaking off after the young banker who had flown on his own port wing. The Spitfire had smoke coming from its tail, but its attacker was intent on blowing it completely to pieces. David realised that here was the perfect opportunity to jump on the German's tail.

Peeling away, he latched onto the enemy, racing up behind him to plaster his machine with bullets in a prolonged burst from his guns, holding the button down with cold calculation. His calm was shattered when the aircraft exploded with a tremendous roar almost under his nose, and threw out a shower of smoke, flames, metal and pilot. David's Spitfire rocked as it caught the edge of the explosion, and he murmured, 'Dear God, I've killed a man. I've killed a man.'

Stunned and shaken by the reality of something that had been no more than bravado talk amongst other youngsters like himself, he was jerked back to action by a sight that filled him with the urge to kill again. As he was banking prior to returning to the main mêlée, he was horrified to see another Messerschmitt streak across to where his colleague had jumped from his burning machine and shred the parachute with machine-gun fire, so that the dangling man dropped like a stone through the fifteen thousand feet that separated him from the earth. The killer circled lower, then pushed up the nose of his machine, well satisfied with his handiwork, and ready to attack again. At that point David had only one thought in mind.

'Sherry' Sheridan's most famous tactic was to fly headlong at his adversary, firing all the time, holding his course until he broke his opponent's nerve, forcing him to turn away in a manoeuvre that signalled his end. Machines had been a lot slower then but, nevertheless, as the ME climbed, David pushed down the nose of his Spitfire, diving headlong on a collision course. Calm, confident, and feeling he was accompanied in the cockpit by the spirit of his gallant uncle, he knew he would not veer or pull out until the other man was spiralling earthwards.

71

They closed dangerously quickly, but David knew he could not allow a man who would shoot down a pilot who had baled out the chance to do it again. On equal terms, all was fair, but a man's parachute was equivalent to a white flag of surrender. Violation of that was unacceptable.

All he could see was the dark nose of the other aircraft, and he watched it like a hawk for the slightest sign of deviation as he poured bullets into it. It came on suicidally, apparently as determined as he not to veer. Then it appeared to shudder, to hang motionless for a moment, then arch over in a death roll before plunging earthward, its port wing breaking in two beneath the strain. David was flooded with immense exhilaration. Killing this man had been a savage pleasure. He had deserved to die.

'Come back, David, all is forgiven,' said a voice in his ear, and he pulled out of his euphoric dive to discover it was all over. Above him there were only Spitfires; below was a veritable mushroom field of drifting parachutes. The 'Garden of England' was now marred by a scattering of fires where crashed aircraft had hit houses, shops, orchards, or open fields. Civilians had died down there as a result of the battle, but how many more would have died if the bombers had been allowed to operate unhindered? He looked at his watch. Forty-five minutes had passed since the enemy had been sighted. It had seemed like an eternity. Now he felt immeasurably tired, yet his heart sang a sweet song. The test had come, and he had met it honourably. Not only could he fly, he could fight. The memory and reputation of his gallant uncle would not be sullied by him. Even if he was killed tomorrow, he had done what everyone expected of him.

They returned to base one by one, some badly mauled, others with smoke beginning to drift from their machines. Chuck Enright and a young Welshman called Mears executed belly flops, sliding across the grass like wild geese landing unexpectedly on a frozen waterway. The fire engines and crash waggons raced out to meet them only to be greeted with very rude gestures from the pilots emerging, white-faced but grinning. Everyone began talking at once: reaction after tension. Some rattled on in high-pitched voices about what they had seen and done, others recounted slowly and sadly how they had watched the end of two of their friends and colleagues.

Someone slapped David on the back as he stood quietly for a moment taking in the fact that he was safely back on the ground after the greatest test of his life, so far.

'Lucky dog. But we all knew we could rely on you. I watched

72

you get that bugger who shot up Peter after he'd baled out. It was the coolest thing I've ever seen.' The speaker turned to the others crowding round them and asked enthusiastically, 'Did you see the way he charged headlong at that ME's nose, blazing away for all he was worth? I thought there was going to be a bloody almighty collision.'

'Didn't you get another one, too, David?' asked the squadron leader. 'It was pretty confused, but I thought I spotted you on the tail of the bastard who knocked out Peter's machine.'

'That's right,' David agreed exuberantly. 'Two of them for one of ours. That's the odds they'll get from this squadron.'

'All in favour signify in the usual way,' cried someone, and a roar of agreement rose from the group of weary, relieved, over-excited youngsters who had faced instant agonising death and returned. *This time.* All they wanted now was a shower, a change of clothes, a hearty meal, and either a girl or a booze-up to stop them thinking about next time. First, however, they had to report 'kills' to the Station Intelligence Officer – a man universally disliked for his lack of humour, miserliness, and determination to do everything by the book. Since this was their first real engagement with the enemy, they had no idea how he would deal with the vital job of notifying losses and victories to the relevant department. They soon found out.

Pedantic in the extreme, James Robbie found it necessary to extract every detail of every man's story, then question it minutely to satisfy himself that their claims were genuine. Several had brought down ME fighters, one vowed he had damaged a bomber so severely it had crashed into a field near Folkestone. There were reports of five of the enemy turning tail and going back over the Channel pouring smoke. The SIO would not allow any of these to be counted in the tally. Unless the enemy machine was seen to crash it would be disregarded. Loud grumbles and muttered imprecations greeted that announcement, and a young New Zealander called Garfield said explosively, 'You can't duff the pair bagged by David. We all saw them fall to bits.'

'*One*,' put in a drawling voice that made heads turn.

'Eh?' queried the Kiwi.

'Sheridan bagged one,' corrected Chuck Enright. 'I got the other.'

'Rot!' exclaimed a public schoolboy by the name of Charters. 'One of them blew up practically underneath him. The other was blasted in a nose-to-nose confrontation that was like knights jousting. Christ, I should know. I was only a few hundred feet away, gawping in disbelief.'

Feeling some of his sense of well-being starting to fade, David asked quietly, 'Which one are you claiming?'

From his lounging position against the door jamb the sandy haired American replied, 'I poured three rounds into that sod just before he gunned Peter dangling from his parachute. Why d'you think he did it, if not as last-shot revenge before going down? When you performed your Royal Flying Corps stunt he was already doomed. I'd all but sheared off his port wing.' He jerked himself upright and gave a mocking smile. 'OK, so you got one. Don't try to be the greatest ace of this war yet. There's time, pal. There's time.'

James Robbie looked up impatiently from his methodical lists. 'Make up your minds. Who is claiming the success?'

'I am,' put in Enright forcibly. 'Anyone care to argue?'

A slightly built boy of eighteen said diffidently, 'I did see Chuck punishing the hell out of one, raking its wings with enough bursts to cause serious damage, but I got distracted and didn't see what happened to it.'

Several others admitted that they had seen the American hot on the heels of a Messerschmitt, but no one could definitely identify it as the same one David had challenged so recklessly. Finally, the squadron leader had to conclude the uncomfortable situation by asking Enright if he was certain of his claim. When he said he was, James Robbie was told to credit him with it. As they were all trooping from the hut towards the trucks waiting to take them across to the Mess, he came alongside David saying, 'Sorry about that. It's bound to happen in a scrap of that kind. Three or four of us might have a go at a Jerry before he goes down.' He gave a warm smile. 'It doesn't matter who gets 'em so long as one of us does.'

It appeared to matter to Chuck Enright. The following morning while they were sitting around at Dispersal after a hearty breakfast, the American suddenly said, 'Jesus, I don't believe it!'

A couple of heads turned his way, looking at him over the top of newspapers similar to the one he was reading. 'Is it that story about the vicar and the cleaning lady?' asked one.

Getting to his feet, Enright walked across to David and flung the newspaper into his lap. 'When a guy has to resort to that he's either a creep or afraid. Right now, I'd say you're both.'

Wary, and thick-headed after drinking the night before, David picked up the folded sheets. The paper carried a brief report of the three raids over the Kent coast the day before, giving the British public a sugar-coated pill to boost their

74

morale. Several lines at the end of the item leapt up at him.

... The daily total of enemy aircraft shot down by various squadrons of the RAF was eleven, two of these by Flight Lieutenant David Sheridan, nephew of the Great War flying hero Rex 'Sherry' Sheridan. While we have men like him in the skies above Britain, we need not fear the Luftwaffe.

David looked up to meet the stony gaze of the other man. He made no attempt to say he had no idea who had given that information. Enright would never believe him. He would continue to think what he wanted to think. However, it no longer mattered what others thought. Yesterday he had proved to himself that he possessed the right qualities to emulate his uncle, if life dictated that he should.

As July progressed into a hot August, German determination to knock the RAF from the skies hardened in direct proportion to the Allied pilots' determination to stay there. But determination is not always enough. The men and women of the flying force took more mental and physical punishment than the human body should be asked to withstand, as the grim battle for Britain went on and on. The Luftwaffe, rattled by the apparently unflagging resistance of the fighter squadrons which repeatedly rose up to meet them when they crossed the Channel, decided to destroy the RAF on the ground. Day after day the bomb-laden Junkers and Dorniers headed for the coastal airfields of England, from Suffolk right round to Dorset, in a campaign to smash operations centres, kill essential ground staff, blow standing aircraft apart, and make such a mess of runways they would be impossible to use. They achieved all those aims, but the one they failed to realise was the demoralisation of the desperate defenders of an island that had been free too long to accept conquest.

The merciless attacks went on day after day, almost hour by hour. The blue summer sky over south-east England seemed to be constantly full of the thunderous roar of heavily laden bombers, the zooming, screaming whine of fighters, the pounding of ack-ack guns on the ground, sending up shells to explode into the mêlée. The green coastal belt below was full of the wail of sirens, the subterranean shuddering of falling bombs, the urgent bells of racing ambulances and fire engines; of whistles, screams and prayers. Newspapers did their best to hide the evidence of looming defeat by concentrating on individual stories of courage and success that rose above the growing devastation that could no longer be hidden from the people of Britain. The BBC stuck faithfully to its policy of presenting the truth, however bad, in its news bulletins, but compensated with a wealth of programmes designed to encourage and sustain morale. Songs like 'There'll Always Be an England', 'We'll Meet Again', 'I'll Be Seeing You' and 'Run, Rabbit, Run' were broadcast frequently to a public that went around whistling or singing them in factories, fields and air-raid shelters. Comedy shows were full of Hitler jokes, and defiant caustic messages to Goering about his hopes of spending a seaside holiday in Margate that year. The bravado catch phrases, the propagandist humour, the suggestion that there was really nothing to worry about, sustained the spirits of people who were nearer to going under than they had ever been before.

Although there was a general air of incredible resilience, grief, fear, loss of homes and possessions, lack of sleep, the constant sounds and sights of air raids, and the sense that as Europe had fallen, so must they, put such stresses and strains on ordinary men and women they often broke under the weight of it all. For those in uniform it was doubly bad. In the air, or at their essential work on the ground, they were bound by a common bond of brotherhood; but once off duty, personalities changed, vices came to the fore, jealousies reached extreme limits. A man who had yesterday risked his own life to drag another from a burning aircraft in danger of exploding, could rush at him today with murder in his soul, merely because he had sat in a favourite chair or was reading the last available newspaper. A WAAF who had lent a friend her last lipstick for a dance the night before, could scream and call her a painted tart when she failed to return it next morning.

In David's squadron things were no different. Up in the skies of that glorious late summer they all did incredible things to help or protect each other; on the ground, tempers grew dangerously short, personalities clashed constantly, small things began to matter too much. In the Officers' Mess they all drank too much in order to sleep, and inebriated men soon quarrelled with fists as well as tongues. Those who could not let off steam with a WAAF or a girl from the village, indulged in wild horseplay that too soon turned to savagery.

David drank heavily like the others, but he did most of it in the local pub, with a young schoolteacher who had accompanied a group of London evacuees to the safety of the country.

'Fat lot of safety there is here,' she told him one evening, holding back her tears. 'One of my kids was killed yesterday in that raid. They're getting up a petition in the village to send to Mr Churchill, asking why the Jerries are being allowed to get this far. They might be after the airfields, but civilians are being killed by planes falling all over the place. Why can't you go up before they get here, and fight over the sea where people won't get hurt?'

Taking a pull at his beer, David replied tightly, 'I'll tell the squadron, Maisie. They had no idea they were hurting people by shooting down the enemy. I'll tell them not to do it in future.'

Staring at him aggressively, she said,' What's up with you tonight?'

'Nothing,' he snapped, slamming the tankard onto the counter. 'Nothing's wrong with me. I'm not one of the poor bastards who stopped in their burning aircraft this afternoon in order to clear a built-up area, then found they'd left it too late to jump. They burned to a cinder, Maisie. I don't suppose their mothers are too happy tonight, either.'

Shaken, she stammered, 'I'm sorry... I didn't mean... It's just that it was one of *my kids*. I've never felt so angry in my life. Why did they send us to a place near an airfield?'

'Don't worry, it won't be there much longer,' he told her.

Two days later, after a day in which the squadron went up five times to fight off massive waves of bombers striking airfields all along the coast, they returned as the sun went down to find nothing but an area of desolation which had once been their base. The field looked like an archeological dig, the Mess and hangars were nothing but piles of rubble, small pieces of reserve aircraft were scattered far and wide, the fuel and ammunition dumps were raging infernos. They all circled, looking down. It affected them in strange ways, judging by the comments coming over the R/T.

'I never really liked the place. Too far from a cinema.'

'That's what comes of striking a match too near the fuel dumps.'

'My sister just sent me one of her awful cakes. Got a good excuse for not eating it now.'

'Oh God, poor Bonzo! I didn't have time to take him for his usual run.'

'I promised to ring and find out if the baby had arrived. Betty'll be livid because I don't.'

All David could think of was what had happened to his MG.

A harassed controller instructed them to divert to a small club airfield on Longbarrow Hill in Dorset, and David realised he would be landing only a few miles from his home. In that, he was one of the lucky ones. Three members of the squadron had lost fuel due to damage to their tanks, and would never make it. They had to land where they could. All along the Channel coast it was the same. Severe damage had been caused to so many airfields, squadrons were being diverted to small private flying clubs, or any large area of downland suitable for emergency use. Those too short of fuel or too damaged to reach their destination were finding it difficult to land because many fields had concrete blocks, barbed wire or rusty wreckage scattered over them, to prevent enemy invasion aircraft from landing there. That evening the air over Kent, Sussex, Hampshire and Dorset was blue with RAF oaths.

As David went in to land on the pocket-handkerchief field of the club where he had learned to fly, he could see Tarrant Hall and the extensive grounds surrounding it at the far end of Longbarrow Hill. He wondered what his mother would make of the sight and sound of five Spitfires swooping low over the Sheridan estate. Knowing she lived in a fever of anxiety over his safety, he had consistently resisted her plea for him to telephone her after each heavy raid to put her mind at rest. She would soon hear if anything happened to him, he had said, and he was now glad of that maxim. As he climbed wearily and blearily from the cockpit with the sun dipping behind the distant hills, he was glad she had no idea he was so near. Even for his mother, he could not stay awake that evening.

Tired though he was, as his propeller stilled and four other shattered men walked with him over the grass towards the tiny clubhouse he knew so well, the overwhelming peace of the place made him stop to savour it while the others walked silently on. Softly rolling emerald hills were dotted with sheep and echoed with their soft baaing call. The evening was sweet with the smell of late-summer grass, the faraway song of birds who found the sky given back to them, the heavy enchantment of skies changing from gold, to rose, then to hazy mauve. Up on the hill he had known from the time he had begun to walk, it was so quiet. To his horror he began to cry. Not abandoned sobbing, but with slow tears that inched their way across his cheeks as an involuntary result of immense sadness. He had seen his friends die, he had killed enemies and watched them fry in flaming cockpits, he had forced down fear and urged his unwilling body to further effort. Throughout that screaming horror he had remained outwardly calm. This utter peace now broke him apart.

A mobile field kitchen and two cooks arrived at nine in the

evening to prepare a hot meal for them. The five pilots were dead to the world, snoring in unison on chair cushions spread on the floor. The cooks made themselves a pot of tea and bully-beef sandwiches, then joined them in sleep. For David, however, sleep brought only a series of nightmares in which German bombers with a new, sinister, silent engine glided over Tarrant Hall to drop bombs on the house and all those in it. The noise of the explosions and screams of his family sounded like sheep baaing, another new device the Germans had invented to frighten the British. Through it all came the voice of a girl saying, *Why can't you fight over the sea, where people won't get hurt?*

The following morning they heard that the Germans had bombed London during the night, an act that injected the British people with fresh stamina, and renewed determination to resist invasion to the last man. Airfields and shipping were military targets, but dear old London was sacred. Adolf would not win by trying to destroy the heart of Britain. Every bomb he dropped on London would double their hatred and treble their unity.

David's hopes of getting across to Tarrant Hall for a few hours were dashed. Despite the damage and destruction inflicted on their bases over the last few days, the RAF saw this bombing of the capital as a sign of desperation by the Germans. A switch of tactics designed to break the morale of the civilian population suggested that enemy confidence was cracking, that they were sensing the cost of winning air supremacy was proving too great. Command was wavering across the Channel, doubts were piling too high. Now was the time to hit them, and hit them hard. Yet how could a nation do that with a handful of youngsters, whose self-control was snapping, whose courage had already been pushed too far, and whose bodies were physically incapable of performing what they were ordered to do? Even more to the point, how could it be done in broken aircraft based at ruined airfields? No one knew how, but it was done, all the same. Every available man in every available machine was launched into the sky as August blazed into September, and the first anniversary of the start of the war passed almost unnoticed.

Life for David became an endless succession of days that frequently began at 4.30 a.m. with the telephone ringing the order to scramble. An hour or so of wheeling, diving, dealing out death and dodging it, then back for breakfast. In the middle of wolfing ham and eggs, the telephone would ring again. Another return, sweating and dull-witted, to gulp down pints of sweet tea and munch biscuits before the bell shrilled again. Taking off, coming in to land, firing guns, checking instruments, opening and closing the hood, taking in oxygen, ears ringing with screams and voices, noise and flames. Death! Back in the chair outside Dispersal on a sunny afternoon – the sort of afternoon when Englishmen played cricket on every village green, and girls donned their best frocks, shady hats, and Evening in Paris perfume. Girls... what are girls? Forgotten what they look like. Eyelids droop, thoughts wander, limbs feel leaden. Bells ring. Stomach starts to churn, teeth clench so tightly they almost crumble, hands start shaking, legs feel wooden. Inner voices say, *Don't go!* But the engine starts to roar again, thumbs go up, the ground starts to fall away fast. What is waiting up there this time? Who cares? *Who bloody cares?*

The squadron grew smaller. When it was down to just five, some schoolboys arrived, with clean eager faces and uneducated accents. What was the RAF coming to? Never mind, so long as they could fly. They could not. Back to five again. More schoolboys arrived, watching David with bright, worshipping eyes. *Aren't you 'Sherry' Sheridan's son? Nephew? Oh well, it's much the same, and you're now as famous as him. How many is it you've got?* Five veterans who flew like aces, but only one with a famous uncle. It made all the difference. Three of them did not care. Chuck Enright did.

Dislike turned to hatred, hatred to enmity. Small things grew unbearable. An unpopular record deliberately played again and again by the American ended up being smashed by David. Letters were taken from his pigeonhole and put into others, prompting a search through all the mail to find them. David 'accidentally' knocked over a chessboard which had been left by Enright with a game at a vital stage to be resumed later. The American was cheated of that victory. Enright read aloud a paragraph from his newspaper concerning the award of a DFC to an American pilot, and sneeringly commented that no one in his squadron had a chance of a medal unless he had an uncle with the VC, a father with a title, and lots of friends in all the right places. David flew at him, fastening his hands round the other man's throat, and had to be pulled off by his comrades. An hour later, the American almost certainly saved David's life by shooting down an ME that had fastened onto his tail unnoticed.

That evening, they again set about each other, this time over the reluctance of the United States to come into the war. The squadron leader had them both on the carpet, and with uncharacteristic loss of temper told them to stop behaving like spoiled children, and to remember there was a war going on. How could they forget? That morning at nine their commander was shot down in flames over Bournemouth pier. David was promoted to replace him. Death was so commonplace now it did not prevent him from feeling immensely proud over his new appointment. His uncle had led a unique squadron over Flanders, he would make his as immortal.

It was not the easiest job in the world. There was a great deal of paperwork to add to the testing frequency of the sorties. On his first day in command, his Spitfire, which had become as much a part of him as an arm or leg, was so badly riddled with bullets that he had to bale out and leave his aircraft to crash into the Solent. Drifting down into the garden of an isolated manor on Hayling Island, he was held at bay by two elderly ladies brandishing an air rifle and an antique cavalry sword, who assured him they would attack if he attempted to move before the local policeman was fetched. He arrived back at the airfield extremely drunk, having been plied with homemade damson wine by his captors when they were satisfied he was not a German. Taking a patched-up aircraft as a replacement, he was again badly mauled the next day, in person this time, as well as mechanically. Bleeding profusely from a slight head wound, and fighting the urge to go to sleep, he came in to land forgetting to lower his wheels, and careered across the field on the belly of his machine. No one took much notice. It was a common occurrence these days. They were all so tired, it was a wonder they did not put out a mat saying 'Welcome, Adolf' and go home to bed. They probably would have done so if they had been capable of cohesive thought.

Another hot day! Men gathered at Dispersal; Spitfires lined up on a pot-holed airfield. Ground crew operating from camouflaged tents pitched in front of the ruins of the old hangars and workshops. Telephone ringing. *Scramble!* Racing for the machines. God, it seems harder to run these days. Must be getting old ...

Airborne, David listened to the information given by Control, then spoke into the R/T. 'All right, lads, stop climbing. They're coming in fast and very low – skimming the waves, in fact – and they're almost here. Radar didn't pick 'em up. They'll be sitting ducks, so make the most of it.'

'They've come for a paddle,' joked a cheery voice with a touch of hysteria in it. 'Must've heard how good our beaches are.'

'Good? Hell!' drawled Enright's voice in David's ear. 'You wanna see California.'

'I'd rather see Dorothy Lamour,' said another, following that with a series of sexy pants to emphasise his admiration.

'You'll have to make do with Jerry and his gang,' put in David sharply. 'There they are – angels nought – right ahead.'

The sea was a true navy blue that day, and the beaches along the coast looked like golden sickles between it and the jumble of seaside shops that had once sold sticky pink rock, floppy hats, rude postcards, and buckets and spades. Down there, there used to be donkey rides and Punch and Judy shows, sand castles, chocolate machines and swings. Now there was barbed wire, anti-tank blocks, mines, submarine nets. All that was in David's head as he said, 'Each man for himself. Go to it, and don't take no for an answer!'

He pushed down the nose of his plane and screamed towards the leading German bomber, intending to scatter the enemy's formation and make attack easier. They began firing back almost immediately, but he hung on until the last minute for better effect. Then he jammed his finger on the firing button and felt the satisfaction of seeing his prolonged burst go home, shattering the turret and killing the man inside. Flattening out, he prepared to bank, then realised something was wrong. One of his guns was still firing, spitting out bullets non-stop, completely out of his control. Trying to take in what was happening, he was already into the right bank when another aircraft executed a tight turn to avoid colliding with him, and therefore became raked with fire from his runaway gun. There was a brief moment of continuing flight before the other aircraft disintegrated in an explosion of smoke and flames, fragments of wreckage scattering everywhere, dropping to start small fires amidst the empty beach shops and boarded-up ice-cream stalls. Flames licked the wooden shacks hungrily.

'Christ, that was Chuck! You bloody shot down Chuck!' screamed a voice in David's ears, as his gun rattled inexorably on. .

He flew low over the sea, parallel with the coast, and all he could think of was the Sorcerer's Apprentice, who could not stop the relentless flow of water. All he could see were the RAF roundels on the wings of Chuck Enright's Spitfire in the seconds before it had blown up.

By the time the magazine had emptied, it was too late to go back to the fight. Tucker, the chief mechanic, came up to him as soon as his machine rolled to a stop.

'Anything wrong, sir?'

'One of the bloody guns,' he said in his normal conversational tone. 'It wouldn't stop firing. Get it put right,
quick!'

James Robbie came out of the Dispersal hut as he
approached, screwing up his eyes against the brilliance of the
sun.

'Trouble, David?'

'Bloody gun wouldn't stop.' He looked around furiously.
'Where the hell is the tea?'

'It'll be here in a jiff. They'll have seen you come in. Pacing
around like that won't bring it here any quicker, so why don't
you sit down?'

'I have been sitting down,' he flared. 'That's what we do in
Spitfires, you know.'

The heavy urn of tea was brought cross from the Mess, and
David took a mugful gratefully. He could not face the doorstep
sandwiches, or the currant buns. For some reason or other, he
did not feel as hungry as usual. The squadron began returning
half an hour later. Apart from a new pilot, who limped in to
make a creditable landing with his flaps still up and half his tail
missing, they all came back whole, for once. All except Chuck
Enright.

Tramping across the field with dragging steps and grey faces,
they made a bee-line for the tea and sandwiches. Their voices
were unusually quiet as they gave their reports to Robbie. One
bomber was a 'definite' and two fighters had been so badly
damaged they must be considered probables.

'Chuck bought it,' someone said, at last. 'Just blew up. Bits
of him must be scattered all over Bognor beach by now.'

It was curious how they all sat in the chairs by the tea urn,
and David was the only one on the side near the telephone.
Well, he was the squadron commander. Not yet ten o'clock.
When would the next call come? The growing heat of the sun
made him drowsy, so he let his lids droop. Funny how sleeping
in the daytime was so hard to do. Instead of welcoming
darkness there was a hideous red glare from the uncompromising sun. Groping for his gloves, he picked up one to put
over his eyes, but the redness remained. Still he did not sleep.
From a few yards away came the sound of soft voices as the
others talked amongst themselves. Dick was not playing his
mouth organ, for once; Freddie and Lance were not recklessly
gambling away their pay on a crooked game of cards, as they
usually did. Randy Chilworth, dubbed as such for obvious
reasons, was still trying to teach his little stray terrier to beg for
a sandwich, but without the usual authority in his commands.

The morning advanced slowly. All remained quiet. Were the Germans trying something new, like flying across the Channel backwards to fool radar and the Observer Corps into believing they were really heading for home? His mouth formed a faint smile. What a clever idea! Why had no one thought of it before? He must patent it and send it to the Air Ministry. Somewhere on the far side of the field a radio was on, and Vera Lynn was singing a sentimental ballad. She really got to a chap's guts, had him longing for the feel and smell of a girl in his arms. How long since he had had a girl in his arms? Too long. Still, they were all much the same. He had never found the one and only girl, someone he would give his heart and soul to, as the songs proclaimed. Come to that, he had never made a real friend of a chap. At school, at Cranwell, everywhere he had been, there had never been a shortage of companions, a lack of a wild group to laugh and drink with; or an absence of someone with whom to share a room, an adventure, a crazy spree. Yet there had never been a person he counted his brother, his lifelong chum. Why? To pass the time, he tried to think of all the boys he had known at school, so that he could work out why he had never become their close friend. Then he mentally listed the others on his course at Cranwell, carrying out the same exercise. It produced an astonishing answer. They had expected certain things of a chap called Sheridan, and close friendship might have disillusioned them.

The telephone rang. Someone answered it. James Robbie's voice called sharply, 'Scramble, David!'

As he ran, he pondered why being called Sheridan mattered so much. Would life have been different if he had been called Ponsonby or Humphries? Would he have fallen in love and have a wife and children by now? Would his mother be less possessive? Would he have had brothers, as his father had done, and been shattered by their deaths? Reaching the Spitfire, he was accosted by a man whose face he seemed to know.

'Gun's all right now, sir,' said the man.

'Thanks.' He climbed into the cockpit and fastened his straps. The engine was already running sweetly, so he put his thumb up to those controlling the chocks. They dragged them away and stood clear. He stared across the field where the grassy surface seemed to quiver with the heat rising from it, then found he could not move. His hands were glued to the control column; his head was fixed in one position, staring at the gun sight. His feet were stuck to the floor of the cockpit. It had turned arctic cold, yet his body was swamped with sweat.

All at once, he began to shake, starting with his teeth and working right down to his legs. The shaking increased until he was shuddering convulsively, yet his body appeared to be paralysed as he continued to stare at the gun sight. Chuck Enright's face stared back at him. Men appeared at his side. Voices said things at him. But he was in a freezing, twitching purgatory from which there was no escape. The squadron took off, leaving him on the ground.

Chapter Five

THE BATTLE of Britain had been won. German plans for the invasion of England were cancelled due to their failure to destroy the RAF. Of those men and women who had kept going against overwhelming odds, Winston Churchill said, 'Never in the field of human conflict has so much been owed by so many to so few.' The words went down in history; many of the few went down in flames. Britain had been saved, but at what cost?

David stood at the window of his bedroom at Tarrant Hall looking out at the rural scene. The hedges were full of Old Man's Beard and blackberries, the trees were a glory of gold, russet and red, and storm thrushes were singing in the topmost branches as if it might be the last song they ever produced. The air hinted at the smell of distant rain, the breeze was freshening. At the airfield they would all be sitting around discussing details of their sexual conquests last night, or making plans to drive the ten miles to see the film that was currently showing at the Troxy – variously known as the bughutch, the fleapit or the smooching house. They would all be laughing together, happy and confident.

Glancing down once again at the official letter that had arrived for him that morning, he fought the urge to crush it in his hands and fling it from the window into that mocking peacefulness outside. The station medical officer had grounded him for forty-eight hours after he had been forcibly dragged from the cockpit that day. Hours of sleep and quiet solitude had made him feel a new man. Yet, when he had climbed into his Spitfire once more, he had lost all control of movement and begun the shakes. After the squadron had left him on the ground for the third time, command had been given to another man, and he had been sent on sick leave. His promotion had lasted exactly seven days. The notification this morning that he was to be awarded the DFC for his gallant action on two separate days during August was the final straw. He could almost hear Chuck Enright saying, 'Well, wouldn't you know it – a gong for "Sherry" Sheridan's nephew! Or was it because "Daddy" put a word in the right quarter?'

He had been home a week. They all thought he was on normal leave, and luckily there had been no time to tell them of his promotion to squadron leader before it was reversed. Strictly speaking, it had not been reversed, just not confirmed. There was no suggestion of unworthiness or disgrace about it. It was just that to be a leader of any kind, one had to lead, not stay on the ground when the rest took off. It was plain commonsense.

A light tap on the door heralded his mother. He made no attempt to turn around as he heard her moving about the room. It was the one Rex Sheridan had counted his own. The boy David had wanted no other. The furniture was different – Tarrant Hall had been used as a convalescent home for officers during the Great War – but the layout had been meticulously copied, and the essence of that red-haired young hero had seemed to be still there in the large room with polished wood floor, and windows facing the village and Longbarrow Hill. Rex would have insisted on a view of the hill from which he used to launch his old biplane. That view had been the basis of all David's boyhood dreams.

'This old quilt really ought to be replaced, but it's so difficult to get things now. Nice things, I mean. I could make a new patchwork one, but what was suitable for a boy won't necessarily please a man of twenty-five.' She came up beside him. 'Darling, what is it?'

He continued to look from the window towards Longbarrow Hill. 'We made an emergency landing up there one evening. On the club field. Five Spitfires. Can you imagine it? I expect you heard us go over. The club telephone was out of order, so I couldn't tell you one of them was mine. Just as well, really. We all went straight off to sleep, and didn't even hear the cooks arrive to give us a hot meal.'

'Aren't you pleased about the medal?' Her hand fell on his arm. 'I can't help being proud of you, David. As proud as any mother with a brave son.'

Rounding on her, he said, 'I'm no braver than any of them. We were all the same. We did it instinctively, knowing it was kill or be killed. No one can tell what it's like up there except those who have done it. How can some brass hat at the Air Ministry decide that one did more than the rest? It's obvious they didn't put all the names in a hat and draw out the lucky

87

winner, because it's too much of a coincidence that his name should be Sheridan.'

Her calm, unlined face gazed back at him, apparently unperturbed by his outburst. 'Don't undervalue yourself, David. The people who make these awards do so on the recommendation of the man on the spot.'

'The man on the spot in this case is dead,' he told her. 'Are you saying that my name didn't influence the decision?'

'Why should it?'

He screwed the envelope he was holding into a ball, and threw it onto the floor with an angry movement. 'Oh, come on, Mother, don't be naïve.'

She moved slowly away from him, and sat on a chair covered with a Jacobean print. 'Listen to this, if you will. Your Uncle Roland won the MC in the trenches around Ypres where heroism was commonplace, your father won the MC at Gallipoli where courage was the essential ingredient for survival. Your Uncle Rex won a whole list of medals for gallantry in the air amongst others who were all doing incredible feats. No one ever questioned their personal worth, and it certainly had nothing to do with being called Sheridan. The name had scandalous overtones, at that time.'

'Now it has heroic overtones – three times over. You've just enforced my point, Mother.'

She studied him for a moment, her clear brown eyes shadowed with perplexity. 'Tell me the truth, David, as you have always done when I asked for it. Didn't you do those things mentioned in the citation?'

He sighed and perched on the broad window-ledge. 'Yes, of course I did them. I was really chuffed, and the whole squadron had a booze-up on the strength of it. We'd lost a lot of chaps, and my personal tally of Jerries cheered us all up.'

'Then what is all this about?' came the probing question. 'For three months I've been sick with worry. No one can tell what it is like for a woman at time of war, save another woman,' she went on, using her own form of his earlier words. 'For three months I have heard the sound of engines overhead, seen little black dots battling way up high, and watched some fall like bright shooting-stars... And I've never known if I was watching my own son fall. The radio and newspapers have told of terrible slaughter and superhuman efforts by all involved. Day after day RAF stations have been bombed and attacked, with tragic losses, but I have accepted your instruction to believe that no news is good news. Now you've come back to me for a few short weeks, thinner and showing signs of strain, but whole, thank God, and you're behaving like a stranger. Vesta looks positively ill, and has withdrawn further into herself than before, and I've heard no word of your father for five weeks, at a time when London is being bombed nightly. When you rang to say you had four weeks' leave, I was overjoyed. You mean the whole world to me. You always have. Please, darling, don't shut me out like this.'

He sat on that windowsill looking helplessly at her. Ever since he had learned the truth about the past, he had gone all out to compensate her for what his father had done. The bond between them was mutual and strong, weakening him now.

'I'm not shutting you out,' he said gently. 'I'm just trying not to add to your worries.'

'By not confiding in me that is just what you are doing. I believed there was nothing we couldn't say to each other, David.'

Looking down at his linked hands for a moment or two, he frowned. 'I shot down a chap from my own squadron two weeks ago.'

It was plain she was deeply shocked. 'David . . . How terrible! Was he a close friend?'

He met her gaze. 'No, I disliked him intensely. My gun was faulty and wouldn't stop firing. He flew right across my path. I hit him. His machine blew up. It was all over in seconds.'

'Now you are holding yourself to blame.'

'No, I'm not. Truly,' he insisted, seeing her disbelief. 'Things like that happen in a scrap. Chaps sometimes collide because they can't pull out in time, or they catch another machine with a wing-tip as they veer. Accidents are bound to occur. There have even been a couple of occasions when friendly aircraft have been deliberately attacked due to mistaken identity.'

Getting to her feet, his mother crossed to stand in front of him. 'You have just given me a lengthy explanation of what is *not* bothering you. Are you now prepared to tell me what is?'

'I can't fly any more.' It was out; a bald statement she did not understand.

'They're refusing to let you go up because of this man you say you killed? It was an accident,' she cried.

He took her hands in his, shaking them gently from side to side in a gesture of affection. 'I didn't say I was forbidden to fly. I said I can't.'

'Explain, please.'

'I get in the cockpit and can't move. That's all there is to it.'

'You're exhausted,' she protested.

'No, Mother, they gave me two days' rest. I tried three more times. Same thing happened. They had to lift me out bodily. *I can't fly any more*. These four weeks are really sick leave. It's given to chaps who've lost their nerve. If they're allowed to remain on a station it undermines the morale of the others, especially the very young ones.'

Putting up her right hand, she smoothed his hair very lightly, as she had when he was a small boy. 'You speak as if you were an old man. I don't believe for one moment that you have lost your nerve, and it's only because you're so tired that you believe it.'

'I don't,' he contradicted immediately. 'I'm not afraid to go up again. If I could just take off, I'd be perfectly all right. But I get in that cockpit and . . . and . . .' He got to his feet and pushed past her to stand with his hand gripping his hair despairingly. 'All I can see is Enright's face framed in the gun sight.' When she said nothing, he swung round to face her once more. 'If I could put the machine in motion, I would. Flying is my life. It's all I've ever wanted to do. You know that. I'm not afraid. I don't feel to blame. I'm not grieving over his loss, I'm no more exhausted than any other pilot. I'm also a damn good flier. *Why can't I fly?*'

She looked at him with compassion. 'I'm only your mother, darling, I can't answer a question like that. All I can do is give you maternal advice. Go and see Bill Chandler.'

He stiffened. 'You're not serious.'

'I'm perfectly serious, David. He's a neurologist dealing with cases much worse than yours. He saved your father's life and sanity after Gallipoli.'

He stiffened further. 'I'm not off my rocker, if that's what you think. Don't compare me with Father, who went stark staring mad.'

Paling slightly at his words, she remained controlled enough to say in even tones, 'I shall be very happy if you never fly again. It means you'll spend the rest of the war safely tucked away in an office behind a desk. I'm selfish enough to prefer a live son who has lost his nerve to a dead hero. I saw too many of those during the last war.'

As they stood facing each other, he trying to work out what she was really saying, there came the sound of a car drawing up on the gravel outside the front entrance. Then, through the open bedroom window, floated the echo of Robson's greeting.

'Sir Christopher, what an unexpected pleasure! Lady Sheridan had been considerably worried over the air raids on London.'

His mother was off immediately. David heard her footsteps

90

on the staircase as she hurried down it. All he needed to complete his mood was the presence of his father. Acting quickly, he changed into a pullover and a pair of old jodhpurs, pulled on his riding boots, and took the back stairs to the stables. They had kept the horses because they were necessary to the running of the estate, and old Tom Ferney came in each morning and evening to look after them. Taking a saddle from the wall, David selected a grey called Boss, and was soon leading it out into the yard where he mounted, and trotted through the gate into the lane, raising his hand to Clive Hudson, their estate manager, in casual greeting. Deliberately turning his back on Longbarrow Hill, he took the track that met the main route through Tarrant Royal to Tarrant Maundle. By crossing it, he could climb through the copse, break through just north of the brigadier's tasteless attempt at a Rhineland castle, then have a long canter over Wey Hill.

During the short length of road he must travel to reach the staggered crossing of tracks leading to various farms and fields, he met people he had known all his life. They greeted him with friendly respect, because he was a popular figure with the local community. Today, he was reluctant to stop and talk. It was his first outing since starting his leave, and there was an eagerness to question him in those who had heard he was up at the Hall. Of course they had heard he was home. In a small village nothing went unrecorded. How soon would it be before they decided he was as barmy as his father had been? If his mother thought it, so too would everyone else.

Spotting Elsie Meadows coming towards him on a bicycle, he quickened the animal's pace to gain the upward track before she could reach him. He had had a hot flirtation with her two summers ago, and the fire had apparently never died in her. But goggling eyes and breathy invitations were not what he wanted right now. As he entered the dimness of the copse, he wondered if that was the root cause of his problem. The last time he had slept with a girl had been on the night he had met Vesta and Felix Makoski for a dinner-dance. All he had managed since then was a grope and cuddle. There had been no time, or he had been too tired.

As the horse picked its way through the trees, crunching the dry fallen leaves beneath its hooves, he thought about the young Polish pilot. He would be happy now. Although the foreign squadrons had initially been kept inoperational through the language difficulties that made them a risk in battle, the shortage of men and aircraft had forced the ban to be lifted a few weeks ago. Earning a reputation as maniacs in the air, they were nevertheless fearless, vengeful, and absolutely invaluable to the decimated force. The RAF was desperately short of aircraft but, even if a miraculous gift of machines was offered, they were equally short of men to fly them. The training was lengthy, and often youngsters were shot down on their first sortie. There was instant death, but no instant pilot.

Breaking through the trees he skirted Tarlestock Towers, noticing how dark the sky had turned to the west. A downpour was on its way, for certain. The squadron would all be keeping their eyes on it. Rain meant little prospect of flying, and sitting around at Dispersal all day with the windows steaming up and the air getting thicker and thicker with smoke. Rain meant the Germans probably would not come that day. Rain meant they would all still be alive when darkness fell. Yet they hated it, hated the postponement of the inevitable. Each and every one of them yearned to take off and go to meet their fate.

If I could just take off I'd be perfectly all right.

I shall be very happy if you never fly again. It means you'll spend the rest of the war safely tucked away in an office behind a desk. I'm selfish enough to prefer a live son who has lost his nerve to a dead hero.

I'm not afraid to go up again. If I could just take off . . .

Go and see Bill Chandler. He's dealing with cases much worse than yours.

By now he was riding along the level top of Wey Hill, and found himself reining in at one of the many vantage points that gave a view across three counties on a clear day. It was hazy to the east, where autumn sunshine was retreating before oncoming rain, and the succession of ridges to the west were standing out clearly in the darkening atmosphere. He swung his leg over his horse wearily, and went to sit beneath the lone tree, leaning back against the trunk as he gazed out at a scene he had known since childhood.

Below, in the valley, lay Tarrant Royal and the rival village of Tarrant Maundle. Most of the inhabitants were simple Dorset folk, tough, hardworking, and symbolic of Britain's yeoman stock. The rivalry between the two hamlets was mostly of the friendly or sporting variety, although there had occasionally been enmity between families, inspiring one instance of a 'Romeo and Juliet' marriage which had fortunately ended in no worse tragedy than the newlyweds moving away to Cornwall and the two sets of parents never speaking to each other.

The greatest battle between Royal and Maundle men took

92

place on the cricket pitch, the annual match for the cup having been fought out for over forty-five years. Although it was almost fully that long ago that the incident had occurred, men still argued over whether a Maundle stalwart should have been counted out when the blacksmith's dog caught the ball just inside the boundary. Royal men, to that day, maintained that the dog had been nominated official substitute for Amos Kite when the man had hurt his wrist in a fall on the slippery grass.

Another perennial topic of village conversation was the cricketing prowess of Rex Sheridan, who had cavaliered his way through many a merry unorthodox innings, delighting old gaffers, thrilling lovelorn maidens, and filling his opponents with admiring despair. David had participated in the annual match ever since he had been counted old enough to do so. He was a good all-round sportsman, and had played for his school, for Cranwell, and even for The Gentlemen versus The Players on one occasion. He always contributed a solid innings to any match, including the inter-village one, and no one had expected him to copy his uncle on the sports field. True, he had had the local lasses shrieking their support and clustering around him in admiration, and he always earned respect from the members of both teams. But one only had to look at past team photographs to see that Branwell Sheridan's red-haired second son, in cream flannels, with a school tie knotted around his waist, and a Cambridge blazer slung across his shoulders, had a panache second to none.

From that thought it was easy for David to recall photographs of his uncle in RFC uniform and his famous 'scarf', displaying that same panache on an airfield. Misery formed a ball inside him. His mother had put into words what he was refusing to face. Suppose this terrible business continued. Suppose he spent the rest of the war behind a desk. Suppose he never flew ever again. All his dreams, all his ambitions would be gone. Irrevocably gone. For two short months he had been and done all the world had expected of him. Even more important, he had done what he expected of himself. Throughout those two months he had sensed the spirit of the legendary 'Sherry' Sheridan had been with him, encouraging, praising, full of approval. What had gone wrong? He knew he was not afraid; he knew Enright's death had been a tragic accident, for which he did not hold himself responsible. The gun had been faulty. The mechanic had confirmed that. What happened when he climbed into a cockpit was beyond his understanding, and out of his control. The first time he had been totally unprepared. Now, he felt it coming on before he climbed into the machine. It was as if he was expecting it to happen for evermore. Why?

Staring out at the green rolling countryside, the sheep grazing peacefully, the golden harvest gathered into stooks, the clusters of colour-washed cottages with thatched roofs lining the lanes, he felt the cool rain-laden breeze touching his tanned cheeks to chill him. How would he bear the prospect of seeing out the war behind a desk? How would he bear the sight of others flying into that freedom of the skies he might never know again? How would he bear the sidelong looks, the whispers behind hands, the forced jollity in his presence? How would he cope with being the suspected coward in a family of heroes? Tilting his head back, he stared up at the dark, racing clouds that had obscured the sun, and prayed as he had never prayed before, promising impossible saintliness in return for an end to this ridiculous affliction. In truth, he was uncertain whether his prayers were to the Almighty or to his Uncle Rex, so desperate was he for understanding and help.

It was indicative of his absorption that he was unaware of anyone approaching until a female voice said, 'So you've surfaced at last!'

Jerking his head round nervously, he saw Pat dismounting from her mare, a broad smile of welcome on her round face which was as deeply tanned as his own from working the land. Cursing the intrusion of this girl, in particular, he scrambled to his feet as she approached him looking the picture of health and contentment.

'When I came over on Tuesday you were asleep, and I had the unworthy suspicion that you were deliberately avoiding me by pretending. Now I feel guilty. Those bags under your eyes are real enough, and so is that grey complexion. You look terrible!'

Since he had pretended to be asleep during her visit, and because he sensed Pat would be more forcedly jolly than anyone if she knew the truth about him, he retaliated quickly.

'You look fatter. Go on like that and you'll resemble a ball on legs.'

She put out the tip of her tongue, then laughed as she reached him. 'Now we've exchanged civilities, give me all the news. Aunt Marion rang Mummy this morning to tell her about the DFC. Congrats! Go on like that and you'll soon have as many as your famous nunks.'

She could hardly have said a worse thing to him right then, and he hit back. 'You'll be pleased with the news that Father has just arrived home, risen unscathed and unscarred from the blitz like the phoenix.'

Her cheeks grew rapidly rosy, and her smile vanished. 'That's a rotten thing to say!'

'I've just reassured you he's safe. What's rotten about that?'

'It was the way you said it. Becoming a hero hasn't made you any nicer.'

'I'm not a hero,' he denied swiftly.

'You've just been given a medal.'

'That doesn't mean a thing. Anyway, the requisite quality of a hero is to be brave, not nice.'

'"Sherry" Sheridan was both.'

It was a thrust that caused him more pain than she could guess. In his present state, it was more than he could take, and he strode quickly across to where his horse was pleasantly grazing.

She came after him and seized his arm so that he could not mount. 'David, I'm sorry. It came out before I thought.' She tried a faint smile on him. 'You don't have the monopoly of rotten things to say, it seems.'

Before anything more could happen they were engulfed in sheeting rain, made more forceful by a strong breeze accompanying it. With unspoken mutual decision, they speedily mounted and made a dash for a red tin open byre some hundred yards away, where hay tumbled from the stack to provide cosy shelter. Jumping from their saddles, they stood breathless, pushing back wet hair to gaze out at a hilltop that was now almost obscured by lowering cloud.

'I saw that coming before I set out, but thought I'd get there before it began,' Pat said, surveying the scene.

'Where were you heading?'

'To the Hall. To tell you how pleased we were about the DFC.' She turned to him. 'You're the nearest to a brother I have ever had, and I was fearfully bucked about it when I heard.'

Disconcerted by her honesty, he said dismissively, 'It wasn't for a deed of valour, you know, just for shooting down a few Germans. We were all doing it. That's what we went up for.'

The silvery green of her eyes contrasted strongly with the brown of her face as she gazed at him in that half-light. 'Perhaps it was for going up in the first place. That's a deed of valour, in my opinion.'

The sickness of failure swamped him again as he considered that he might never do so in the future, and he stared at the rain, lost in his own thoughts. He was brought back to the present by a strange sound, which he gradually realised was Pat's teeth chattering.

'Good Lord, girl, you sound like a horse clattering across a cobbled yard. Get that wet jumper off! I'll give you my shirt. It's still dry under this heavy pullover.' He began stripping off the thick, knitted garment, then found she was making no attempt to remove hers. 'Come on, you're shaking with the cold.'

'I can't undress here.'

'Rot! You won't be naked. I take it you've got the usual on underneath.' When she still hesitated, he grinned. 'I've seen girls in their scanties before, you know.'

She pulled a face. 'Trouble is, mine aren't all that scanty.' That brought a laugh from him. 'All right, if it'll help I'll turn my back.' Doing so, he unbuttoned the silk shirt, pulled it free of his breeches, slipped it off and held it out to her. 'I've kept it warm for you.' It was taken from his hand, and he added as he tugged on the wet pullover once more, 'I don't know why you're making all the fuss. I've seen you and Vee cavorting about in vests and knickers umpteen times.'

'Not since we passed the age of ten, you haven't.'

'You just claimed you thought of me as your brother.'

'I do. All right, you can turn back now.'

He laughed again at the sight of her. 'I wish I had a camera.' A reluctant return smile touched her lips, but it was not echoed in her eyes. 'In the films girls always look alluring in the hero's shirt. Why don't I?'

'You've got too much else on. In the films they've got bare legs. The hero isn't looking at his shirt, take my word for it. Besides, the girl is usually some glamorous floosie, not his little sister.'

After a moment or two of silently watching the rain, she asked diffidently, 'Is it absolutely essential to be some glamorous floosie before a man notices a girl?'

The atmosphere in the cool rain-beseiged hut on an isolated hill encouraged a truce between them, and his own present pessimism caused him to say, in genuine affection, 'Not essential, but preferable. There are exceptions, however, when being sensational makes no difference.' Hesitating for a moment, he went on with what he felt ought to be said, 'Pat, he's twenty-five years older than you, married to Mother, and so involved in his brilliant career that Greta Garbo could sit on his lap and he wouldn't notice her. That's the plain truth, nothing to do with my feelings for him. Find yourself a nice young farmer to adore, even if he's not as good-looking.'

Instead of flaring up in defence, the feeling that they could be the only two people in the world up there on that misty hill must have overtaken her, also. With cheeks a fiery red she turned away to say, 'It's more than his looks. I know you don't agree, but I think he's the most terrific person. For anyone to endure what he did and survive takes incredible courage. To go on from there to build up a reputation like his is the evidence of great strength of character.'

'OK. Believe all that. Admire him, respect him, use him as a shining example to follow, if it makes you happy. Just don't imagine you've fallen in love with him. It's no more than a schoolgirl pash you'll grow out of. There are lots of *young* heroes in the making. Concentrate on turning into a glamorous floosie for one of them.'

Still staring at the rain, she asked, 'Have you ever loved anyone, David?'

'A girl, do you mean? Hundreds.'

'I mean really love. Enough to die for them.'

'Good Lord, no! I shouldn't think any girl would make me feel that way.'

She glanced back at him then, and said softly, 'Poor David.'

Riled for a reason he did not fully understand, he launched into a 'big-brother' lecture.

'You girls dream up a lot of romantic nonsense, then add to it by reading magazine love stories that suggest it's all true. Believe me, Pat, as far as chaps are concerned, the whole business is pretty basic. I'm not saying they don't eventually find a girl they want to stick with and have a home and family, but as for *dying* for them, you've been reading the wrong kind of fiction.'

'Romeo died for love of Juliet. That's not the wrong kind of fiction.'

'It's fiction, nevertheless.'

'Your father would have died for Laura. He almost did.'

Angry, he snapped, 'He was married to Mother at the time, and Laura was married to his brother. I have another word for that, and it isn't anything like *love.*'

'If you had a brother, wouldn't you try to save his wife from danger?' She put her hand on his arm. 'Don't be angry, David. We were getting on so well.'

He looked down at her impatiently. A plump country girl in jodhpurs that strained at the seams, and his shirt that hung off her shoulders so that she had to keep pulling it up, yet she dreamed of knights in shining armour. Where was the man

97

who would be prepared to die for Pat Chandler? Brotherly affection touched him swiftly.

'Keep your dreams intact for as long as possible, old girl. There aren't that number of them about these days.'

Still looking pensive, she asked, 'Do you hope to find a girl to settle down with and have a family?'

'I'd rather find a glamorous floosie.'

Giving a little nod, she said, 'I thought so. It's just as well. Aunt Marion prefers it that way.'

'What has Mother to do with it?' he asked, puzzled.

Her frank eyes looked straight at him, as she said above the sound of rain beating on the tin roof, 'If she ever has to let you go, it will be to the world's most perfect girl, or not at all . . . And we all know the perfect girl doesn't exist.'

When Chris walked into Tarrant Hall that day, he appreciated his home probably more than he had ever done before. He had not managed a visit for some months, and its unchanged elegance touched his aesthetic soul with gentle familiarity. He sighed as he handed cap and gloves to the butler.

'After London it's hard to believe places like Tarrant Royal still exist, Robson. Everywhere one goes there are piles of rubble and skeletal buildings. Most of Whitehall is buried under sandbags, the parks are filled with air-raid shelters, and people are sleeping in the Underground stations night after night, despite being forbidden to do so. Danger and devastation are increasing, yet the worse it gets, the stronger the people grow.' He smiled faintly. 'We are a curious race, showing our passionate feelings for what we have only when someone tries to take it from us.'

'The London apartment, sir?'

'Still standing.'

'Her Ladyship has been extremely concerned, due to the fact that each time she telephoned this week she did not appear to be able to make the connection.'

'I understand the exchange received a direct hit. I've been unable to make calls myself,' he said calmly. 'How is Mrs Robson?'

'Much the same, Sir Christopher, although she did brighten a little after Mr David visited her yesterday. He is home on leave, and not before time by the look of him. It is very distressing to see young gentlemen worn out and ill from constant danger and stress. We all hope, sir, that four weeks at home will put him back on his feet.'

Chris's heart sank as his hopes of a few days of peace

vanished. With David in the house, Marion would be working hard to bring them together, which invariably only served to make their son all the more resistant to it. At that point he spotted her coming round the bend in the staircase, and walked to the foot of it to greet her.

'Chris! I have been so worried,' she declared. 'Why didn't you telephone to say you were coming?'

'I only had a few minutes to catch the train when I reached the station.' Kissing her fondly, he put his arm along her back to coax her into the sitting room. 'For a worried woman, you look wonderfully calm and attractive. Have I seen that green dress before?'

'Apparently not, even though I've worn it often during the past two years,' she said reproachfully. 'I suppose I should feel flattered that you have finally noticed it.' Coming to a halt just inside the room, she put her hand on his arm. 'No word from you for five weeks. Didn't it occur to you that I would be worried with all those raids on London?'

What could he say? That he had not been in London but at an address in the country, where he had been helping to train spies and saboteurs; and at several highly secret conferences at Guidons, with foreign statesmen who had been smuggled out of Europe?

'If there was any justification for your fears, you'd soon hear,' he offered for want of a better way out.

She moved away in irritation. 'You men really are the limit! I was given the same advice by David. "They'll soon notify you if I'm dead" is what it amounts to.' Swinging round to confront him from several yards away, she said, 'This war is not exclusively yours, you know. Like it or not, we women are in it too.'

Sighing as his initial feelings of homecoming pleasure began sinking beneath the weight of warring responsibilities, he said, 'We simply try to minimise your involvement, my dear.' He was surprised at the extent of her agitation. When David was at home she normally glowed with well-being. During their marriage he had frequently been away for months at a time, so she should be used to his absence. Why was she so upset? It was not like her.

'You can't minimise it, Chris!' She put out her hands in an impatient gesture. 'You have always been the same. That astonishing brain of yours that can absorb thirty languages, untangle complications with speed and ease, and retain facts, sights and sounds with perfect clarity, can't grasp the simple details of day-to-day existence. Telling me I would soon receive

99

notification of bad news does *not* stop me worrying about you all. Every news bulletin about the devastation of London makes me afraid for your safety. Every sight of an aircraft falling in flames over there at the coast makes me fearful that David is in one of them. You are in London knowing whether or not you have been buried under rubble; David is in his Spitfire knowing he's all right. I'm here knowing nothing. How long does it take, Chris, between death and the arrival of the telegram? At what point after an air raid or a dog fight can I tell myself "I have had no notification, therefore today I am not a widow or minus a son." At what point can I say that?'

He crossed swiftly to seize her limply hanging hands and enclose them in his. 'You should know the answer. You've been through it all once before.'

'Exactly.' She drew her hands away from his. 'Once was enough.'

'Once was enough for all of us,' he said quietly.

She continued her theme as if he had not spoken. 'Laura once told me she could never make Rex understand why she pursued her career so determinedly against his wishes. It was because she saw other women gathering around the casualty lists each day, then walking away in tears, or knowing they had a reprieve until the same time on the morrow. She vowed she wasn't strong enough to endure that, so she simply escaped into pretence in the theatre. It was the only way she could keep going, Chris.'

Immediately the memory of Laura Sheridan's vivid pointed face, wicked green eyes, and curls the same glowing red as Rex's filled his mind to bring a sadness that had never entirely vanished. It was as if he had seen her only yesterday.

'I have no such escape.'

He focused on his wife once more. 'I thought you loved your home and the life you lead here.'

She looked at him for so long in silence, he felt even more at a loss. What had he said to prompt such a challenge bordering on aggression? She had always been so happy on this estate, and with village concerns. Surely she had no hankering to be an actress. That could not be what she was trying to tell him. When she finally spoke, it was in weary tones.

'I should never have expected you to understand ... But you might make the effort to get in touch more often, even if poor Sandy has to do the job for you.'

'Point taken,' he said carefully. 'I am sorry about the past few weeks, but I've ...'

'... been phenomenally busy,' she finished for him. 'I'm sure you have, Chris, and I'm also sure it is all vitally important. It always is.'

Robson entered with a tray containing a pot of coffee and several cups and saucers, plus a plate of biscuits. He set it on the coffee table, then straightened up to look across at Chris.

'Cook sends her regrets, sir. She was unable to get your ginger snaps this week. Mr Anderson imparted the information that there is a shortage of them now, due to the fact that ginger has to be brought from the Indies, and there is no room on the ships. He further indicated that they could be purchased on the black market for two shillings and sixpence the packet, but he was assured you would not support the practice, no matter how fond of the biscuit you might be.'

'Good heavens!' was Chris's mildly astonished response to a speech concerning something as mundane as ginger snaps. Were they important enough to warrant trading illegally at exorbitant prices?

'Er, no, certainly not, Robson,' he hastened to add as the man stood there, plainly expecting some kind of response from him.

Satisfied, Robson left. Marion began pouring coffee, while Chris finally sought the comfortable chair he had hoped for on arrival. Taking the cup and saucer from her, he sipped the coffee gratefully as he looked around the room. His two homes were markedly different, yet each reflected his appreciation of the arts. In London, the decor and furnishings were masculine in style; here, Marion had used a combination of feminine flair and country elegance to make a home that was both comfortable and pleasing to the eye. It was good to be here. It was good to munch *petit beurre* biscuits and drink fine-quality coffee in the soft Dorsetshire setting. It was good to rest his tired brain.

All through that long, hot summer Chris had sweltered in closed rooms, tutoring, interrogating, sleeping when he could, eating hardly at all because he was always too tired. His early crossing of swords with John Frith had not made life any easier. The man was highly suspicious of him, because of what he and the family represented, and because he had friends in every nation's government or aristocracy, had worked with the League of Nations and other organisations dedicated to peace, and had determinedly published a book by his late brother, Roland Sheridan, which was so unashamedly pacifist in content it had been removed from library and bookshop shelves at the outbreak of hostilities a year before. Chris felt that his adversary was watching him like a hawk, and would use the slightest excuse to have him dismissed from the establishment under damning conditions, if he could possibly contrive it.

The granting of seven days' leave had been a godsend, and he had hastened to Tarrant Royal at the earliest opportunity. Marion was right, however. He had always been so absorbed in his work, he forgot that life went on elsewhere, and things changed for those around him. He had come home to something that no longer existed. His restful wife was distressed and therefore quarrelsome, his stranger-son had been challenging death hour by hour in the skies over the coast, and his sensitive artistic daughter had made no contact with him since the day he had seen her from his car and taken her home for tea. The servants were worried about biscuits that could now only be bought on the black market. It was a lot to take in after weeks of intense concentration on work that would affect men's lives, the fate of nations, and possibly the future of the whole world. He was so tired, his brain that could cope with enormous complexities could not seem to appreciate a woman's anxiety for her family, and the fact that ginger had to be brought from the Indies for biscuits.

Then there was Laura. He had not thought of her for weeks, yet he could now see her beautiful face so clearly, he could hardly believe it was twenty-two years ago that he had held her in his arms and said a final goodbye.

'Chris, you're not falling asleep, are you?' Marion asked sharply. 'After all this time away, surely you can give me more than five minutes of your time before closing your eyes.'

He opened them, banishing the vision of Laura, and sat up. 'It's the peacefulness of this place,' he explained apologetically. 'Another cup of coffee might help.' While she poured coffee, he poured oil on troubled waters. 'You have such a wonderful air of quietude that I envy. Tessa has it, too. Don't ever change, Marion. We all depend on you to provide a haven.'

She offered him the Spode cup and saucer, saying, 'I'm not a stretch of still water, Chris, I'm a person with feelings. Does it ever occur to you that *I* need someone on whom to lean, occasionally?'

The oil had not done the trick, he realised. Putting the coffee on the table beside him, he frowned. 'I admit your charge that I'm too distant from day-to-day living, but you've accepted that as part of our marriage for the last twenty-odd years. It's one of the contributary factors to its success. Why does it bother you so much suddenly?'

Her aggression crumbled into pleading eagerness as she

clasped her hands tightly and leant forward. 'David is in trouble.'

It was the very last thing he wanted to hear. 'Serious trouble?'

'Very serious.'

'Is it a girl?'

She stared at him uncomprehending. 'A girl?'

Thank God for that, he thought. The poor devil would not be forced into a marriage he did not want. On the other hand, it might have made him understand the realities behind such a situation. 'Is it money or the law?' he asked then.

'Chris!'

He watched his coffee growing cold as he reminded her that she had claimed their son was in serious trouble. What was he to think?

'I know he has been wild, at times, but only because he felt obliged to imitate Rex,' she said.

'Rot!' It came out sharply, and she bridled.

'For heaven's sake, Chris, he's your son!'

He said something he had never put into words before. 'I fathered him, but he's *your* son, Marion. He always has been.'

'That was the way you wanted it, if you remember,' she said in a voice that trembled. 'Vesta was the result of your attempt to put things right. You have never wanted fatherhood, Chris.'

Realising with a shock that they were on the verge of a quarrel, he put in sharply, 'What about the twins? Have you also a theory on what I was trying to do then?'

Getting to her feet, she looked down at him with the echo of that double loss on her face. 'You had been to a world peace convention. Even you need to satisfy certain basic desires, now and then, and it was a perfect summer evening when you returned after six months' absence. I remember it as the most wonderful night of our marriage. When you have time to include such things in your timetable, you can be a breathtaking lover, Chris.' She sighed. 'But you were never as anguished as I when I miscarried.'

'How could I be? I have never been a mother.'

'Neither have you been a father.'

He stood up slowly. Normally an equable man, he found his present anger unwelcome. 'I'm prepared to allow that for the first three years of David's life your accusation is valid. Neither of us has ever forgotten, nor has the village. My son hates me for it, although he was too young to know about and suffer from my absence. When we agreed to abandon the idea of divorce, I set out to discover my son. I wanted him to achieve

103

all I had been denied. I wanted him to live the life Roland and Rex had had snatched from them. I gave him a heritage dearly bought, Marion, and worked hard towards making a world that was safe, free and never likely to subject him to what we all suffered. When he turned his back on academic or artistic pursuits and eagerly sought diametrically opposite goals, I accepted his right to his own life, and gave him every opportunity to follow his chosen star. With Vesta to provide you with the valued mother-daughter relationship, I grew to know and love my son.'

He turned away from her doubting expression and walked to the window, where rain was beginning to beat against the glass. 'I hardly knew my father. He was never there with us, as you know, and I suppose I looked on Roland with the sort of respect I would have given to him. When he killed himself and left us three in debt I didn't hate him. Because there had never been love, there could not be hate. With David, it's different. The strength of his feeling now is a reflection of how much he must have loved me before an old fool in the village told him some bald facts he was too immature to understand.' He turned to look across the room at her. 'I have a brilliant brain. It has brought me some golden rewards and some terrible penalties; it means I am at ease with complex things and bewildered by simple ones. I am satisfied by challenges to the mind and fulfilled by aesthetic perfection – probably to a greater extent than most men. Do you believe that therefore makes me incapable of human love? Do you believe I was not deeply hurt the day David burst in and told me, white-faced, that he would never forgive me for what I had done? Of course your love for him is greater than mine, but he is my son, and my compensation for the loss of two beloved brothers. Only because David is a male Sheridan with life before him can I accept the deaths of those other two.'

'And Laura?' she prompted on a breath.

He angled his head to the window again, and watched the rain running like a cascade down the panes. 'You and I have built a good marriage over the years, and love has been gentle between us. But neither of us has pretended that it will ever be like it once was with someone else. I thought that had been our strength.'

He heard the rustle of her dress as she came to him, but he continued to gaze at the rain, running like Europe's tears.

'Chris, why haven't you said all this before?'

'I didn't realise it was necessary.' He reached for her hand with the one mutilated by shell blast all those years before, and

104

and held it to his cheek. 'Our youth was too violent, and our emotions are too afraid.'

As she moved to lean against him, he circled her with his arm. They stood silently together watching the downpour turn the garden outside into a vision of dripping trees and sodden brown earth, until he said softly, 'Those borders have been the same for as long as I can remember. It seems incredible that I once came here and thought I'd never seen it before.'

She tilted her face up to him. 'I want you to ask Bill to speak to David.'

A quick bolt of alarm shot through him. 'The trouble you mentioned is that kind of trouble? He's been wounded?'

'No, Chris, no,' she assured him quickly. 'Nothing like that. But I think Bill Chandler is the only one who could help him.'

'It's a mental problem?'

Breaking away from him she said, 'I'm not sure. Bill would soon tell, wouldn't he?'

Still concerned, he probed further. 'Robson said he was here on leave. Is it sick leave?'

In quick anxious sentences she told him of the notification of the DFC which had thrown David into such a strange mood she had forced the truth from him that morning. Chris was relieved. It did not sound like serious trouble to him, just understandable reaction to the shock of killing one of his own comrades.

'Surely the RAF is sorting him out.'

'I think their doctors are all too busy with casualties to go into anything like this, and are hoping a month at home will do the trick.'

'It probably will,' he said confidently. 'A man can only do so much without a rest. His body is simply telling him that time has come.'

'Please ask Bill to have a chat with him,' she persisted. 'If nothing else, it will set David's mind at rest. I can't bear to see him like this.'

He sank down on the window seat, urging her down beside him. 'If the boy is worried, he'll seek Bill out himself. If Bill should suddenly approach him, David will know you've betrayed his confidence... And if he should ever suspect you've told me, he would never forgive you. Leave him to sort it out himself, my dear. In this instance, you'll help him best by ignoring what he said.'

'How can I?' she cried.

'Because you love him,' he replied, drawing her against him to kiss her temple. 'We are all selfish enough to come here, even in these terrible times, and expect to find you as sweet and calm as always. If you ever go to pieces, my dear, we shall all be lost.' Glancing across at the small table holding the tray, he went on, 'Do you think we could now have some fresh coffee and relax for a while together?'

At that point the door burst open, and Pat poked her head into the room. She caught sight of them and blushed. 'Oh, sorry. I was looking for Vee to cadge some dry clothes from her. David and I got absolutely drenched on Wey Hill, and Vee isn't in her room.' She came a little further round the door. 'Hallo, Uncle Chris. I knew you were home because David saw you arrive.'

Chris then knew why his son had gone off to Wey Hill. Getting to his feet, he went across to the girl. 'Hallo, Pat. Is that David's shirt you have on? It certainly enhances the "drowned rat" look.' He laughed heartily. 'I wish I had a camera handy. Where is David now?'

Giving him what seemed amazingly like an agonised look, Pat mumbled, 'He's seeing to the horses,' then stumbled off up the stairs without a word.

At the point of turning back into the sitting room again, Chris stopped when David entered by the side door from the stables, hair plastered to his head and clothes dripping wet. There was only the slightest hesitation before he continued on his way to the stairs, saying tightly, 'Hallo, Father.'

As he passed, Chris said, 'I hear you chaps in Fighter Command have been busy.'

'That's right.' He continued to the foot of the stairs.

'Your mother has just told me about the DFC. Well done!'

Cold blue eyes were turned on him. 'Thanks... But I know your views on medals.'

He tried again. 'You're confusing it with posthumous medals. I believe I have expressed views on those. Yours is different.'

'Because my name is Sheridan? Well, it'll be another to add to the family collection.' With that, David took the stairs two at a time and vanished from sight.

Before Chris could move, the door from the garden room opened and Vesta appeared, stopping dead when she saw him as if he were a ghost. She looked painfully thin, and lacking the liveliness she used to possess. He was shocked.

'My dear girl, are you all right?' He moved forward, but she replied in clipped tones, 'I didn't know you were home.'

'I only arrived half an hour ago. Haven't had a chance to seek you out.'

But she walked past him and began running up the stairs. 'I saw Pat come in wet through. She'll want a dry frock, or something.'

Within seconds he was standing alone again, staring at the staircase. He shared a warm, generous relationship with his artistic daughter, yet she had just looked at him the way David had done for the past fourteen years. As if he had done something unforgivable.

Chapter Six

PAT STAYED for lunch. There were two chickens with brussels sprouts, carrots and potatoes from the vegetable garden, and the usual bowl of home-grown fruit to follow. Chris received another apology from Cook through Robson for the absence of his favourite Bavarian cheese. Mr Anderson from the village shop had reported that even if it could be obtained now, which it could not, he would not allow enemy foodstuffs to sully his shelves while his twin sons were at sea escorting vital convoys at risk to their lives. Not that he believed, for one moment, that Sir Christopher would wish to eat such unpatriotic cheese.

Sir Christopher kept to himself the fact that not only would he eat and enjoy it, given the chance, but that he had been drinking Rhine wine and Chianti from his London cellar without the faintest feelings of treachery. He had also listened to records of Wagner, Puccini and Richard Strauss whenever he had had a long enough period of solitude to enjoy them. If old Jock Anderson held such narrow views, would other people have a case against him for eating Bavarian cheese, or perhaps for drinking from Venetian glasses? The thought led him to glance around the room. Finnish carvings, Hungarian ceramics, Italian paintings. Should he remove them all in case he was suspected of unpatriotic sympathies? What would John Frith think? Would he vote Sir Christopher Sheridan a security risk because he admired the beautiful things produced by their present enemies?

'You're quiet, Uncle Chris,' said Pat suddenly.

He smiled at her. 'I was reflecting on how much the nations of the world have to give each other if only they would stop taking.'

'That theme is an ideal,' claimed Marion. 'It's unrealistic.'

'Only because people never give it a chance. They all prefer to say what you've just said.' He looked deliberately at his daughter. 'Do you agree with me, Vesta?'

Keeping her attention on her plate, she said, 'Ideals are like bubbles. They burst leaving people with soapsuds all over their eager, upturned faces.'

He pursed his lips thoughtfully. 'Cynicism overriding idealism? That's not like you.'

'Isn't it?'

That was as far as he got, because Marion said, 'Is that all you're going to eat, Vesta? Cook told me you didn't have breakfast.'

Their daughter looked up swiftly. 'All that propaganda about "careless talk costs lives", yet our servants go around telling all.'

'In this instance, I'd say it was angled at saving a life,' put in Chris mildly. 'If you get much thinner you'll vanish entirely.'

'I was actually thinking of doing that,' came the immediate comment. 'If you'll all excuse me, I have rather a lot of things to do.' She left the table hurriedly, and went out to cross the hall then mount the staircase.

'I don't understand her lately,' complained Marion with a sigh. 'She has always been dreamy and too reserved – until she gets with you, Pat – but lately she's become positively secretive. And she hardly eats a thing.'

'I eat too much,' confessed Pat gloomily. 'I don't even benefit from rationing, like people in towns and cities. We grow more than enough on the farm.'

'You work hard on the land,' Chris pointed out, half his mind on Vesta's strange behaviour. Recalling the last occasion they had met, when she had been in tow with a policeman, he wondered if she was in some kind of trouble which she was afraid to confess.

'I think I'd be the same if I was at art school like Vee,' Pat went on frankly. 'I just enjoy food. That meal was delicious, Aunt Marion.'

Marion made a face. 'One would never think so. My husband was more intent on international idealism, my daughter toyed with half a carrot and a slice of chicken, and my son devoured everything with such urgency he couldn't possibly have tasted it.'

'That's probably habit now,' put in Pat gaily. 'He's expecting to take off again at any minute.'

There was an obvious silence, during which Marion's distressed gaze at their son, plus David's massacre of an apple while he refused to meet her eyes, plainly told Pat she had somehow said the wrong thing. Chris felt sorry for her, and gave a smile.

'Thank goodness you came to lunch, Pat. You have preserved Marion's faith in the human race by eating heartily and thoroughly enjoying it. The rest of us are a source of great disappointment to her.'

Seizing the opportunity to change the subject, the girl said, 'I hope you won't be a disappointment to Mummy. She wants you all to come over on Sunday, and it'll be some beano. Daddy's coming for the weekend. We haven't seen him for absolute weeks.'

'Oh, that's splendid,' said Marion with a delight that was not lost on David. 'It'll be good to have both families complete and together again.'

'I shan't be able to make it, I'm afraid,' said David, having reduced the apple to pulp. 'I promised a chap from the squadron I'd visit his mother on her birthday, which happens to be on Sunday. I can't let him down.'

'You didn't say anything about it before,' Marion charged.

'We didn't have another invitation before.'

'You'll still be here, won't you, Uncle Chris?' Pat asked eagerly.

He nodded. 'Wouldn't miss it. I saw your father around two months ago in London. He looked very well. He said he'd come across a chap at the hospital who was an expert at magic, so I suspect we might see some new tricks at the weekend.'

Pat groaned. 'I wish he was as good at conjuring as he is at sorting people out. If he had to cure his patients by waving a wand and saying "abracabra" they'd all still be out of their minds.'

'I think I'll skip coffee,' David said suddenly, getting to his feet. 'I have some letters to write before the post is collected. See you around, Pat.'

'I really ought to be getting back, too,' she said. 'The rain has stopped now.'

Left alone with Marion and the after-luncheon coffee, Chris could hold off sleep no longer. When he awoke in the armchair, Marion had gone, and the clock showed him it was well past mid-afternoon. A watery sun was breaking through to close the day, and he sat on, still heavy with the need for prolonged sleep in a bed, looking from the French windows onto gardens that had changed little since his childhood. The gardens had not changed; everything else had. Wars did that. The last one had seized up a dreamy academic of eighteen, torn him apart with claws of pain, loss and terror, then thrown him down again to learn to survive. It had been a slow process, but he had won through.

Now the whole thing had begun again. Today Marion had shown him that the marriage he had believed to be sound had something eating away at the core; David had emphasised the estrangement that barred him from confiding in his father, who could have given advice from personal experience; and Vesta had inexplicably turned her back on a bond he had thought unbreakable. What hope was there for the world when families were at war with each other?

Suddenly sick at heart, he thought of all those years he had spent working for world peace; all the charming and cultivated people he knew in various parts of the globe whom he was now expected to treat as his enemies. Eating Bavarian cheese was even regarded as an act of treachery. What a waste of his life! His work had proved totally unproductive; his attempts at marriage had apparently been a failure; his children had no need of him. At the end of that other war he had stopped painting, given up writing poetry, abandoned all thought of renewing the pursuit of an academic career, and firmly set out to help stabilise the world, as well as his life with a wife and son. It had been a mammoth task, which had taken all his time and left him with none for living, he realised now.

He also remembered that summer night when the twins had been conceived. Returning to Tarrant Royal after six months of world travel and intensive discussions, the enchantment of green valleys, pretty thatched cottages, cream-flannelled men playing cricket on the village green, and the distant late sound of the nightingales had aroused him unbearably. He had walked through the churchyard to that grave in the far corner, and stood there feeling very near to her. When he had made love to Marion that night it had been, in a way he knew Laura would have understood, a tribute to her.

A breathtaking lover, Marion had said earlier. He was forty-four and, today, felt love had said its final farewell to him long ago. The things that had taken its place were now one by one being denied him: international friendship, travel, a sense of achievement; the hope of ensuring his brothers' deaths had not been in vain; a calm, satisfying relationship with his wife; the pleasure of watching his children develop their talents to the full. Even his favourite cheese and biscuits were things of the past. What was left? What was the point of going on? They might just as well have left him in that blazing sea at Gallipoli. A wry smile touched his lips and he got wearily to his feet. Bill Chandler would have a good old-fashioned Australian oath to counter that kind of thinking. Nevertheless, Chris wondered if his friend ever questioned, these days, if it was worth trying to save the minds of young soldiers. They would probably lose them again in the next war, twenty years hence.

The garden was cool and full of the pleasant smell of wet earth. All the paths had faint steam rising from them, and Chris allowed himself to lapse into the realms of fantasy as he imagined the Swan of Tuonela, the mysterious legendary creature of Finland. The pale late-afternoon sunshine had the quality of the Northern Lights, and his inner eye saw the places he knew so well in that hazy garden on a hill. He walked for a while, his hands in the pockets of his grey flannels, the first hint of evening chill penetrating his Cashmere pullover, and as he walked he experienced an echo of that summer night when he had been a 'breathtaking lover'. Could such enchantment last more than a few short hours? Rex had found it with Laura. If they had lived, would it still be there between them? Perhaps it was like Bill's conjuring tricks and needed real magic to make it work. There was little enough evidence of that in his life, these days.

Turning a corner, he came across someone standing by the weather vane. They were both startled for a moment, then she turned away. He called to her sharply.

'Don't go, Vesta. I'd like to talk to you.'

She stood while he took the few steps to reach her, but there was no smile for him, no evidence of warmth. He came straight to the point. 'It's plain you are plagued with the need to be alone, for some reason, and I would normally respect that. Since we are here together, however, I think you should tell me where my loving daughter has gone. She appears to have been replaced by a stranger.'

'It's six months since we met, that's all.'

'That's neither an explanation nor an excuse,' he said.

She looked almost trapped as she cried, 'You go away for ages, then come back and expect to catch up on all that has happened, when, for us, it was all over long ago. You're always the same.'

'That makes me one up on my family. They all appear to be different suddenly.' Silence developed between them until he asked, 'Are you going to tell me what I've done to cause you to look at me the way David does?'

She drew back from him, saying, 'If you don't even know what it is, how would you ever understand?'

Completely bewildered, and growing more and more hurt by the way she was rejecting him, he tried again. 'If I have failed you in some way, I'm dreadfully sorry. I love you very much, you know that, but I have been phenomenally busy since

112

Christmas, with very little spare time for my family. When the new term begins, why don't you move back into the apartment where we'll have more time together, perhaps go to the galleries and theatres as we used to do. Some are still open.'

'I'm not going back to the school,' she told him abruptly. 'I've realised that I'm not cut out to be an artist. All that misty romantic nonsense is immature, and the other students are so busy trying to be clever they don't realise how stupid they are. Their conversation is nothing more than strings of empty words; their way of life is basically crude. I can't spend day after day putting babbling brooks and fairytale glens onto canvas. Real life isn't like that, is it?'

Fighting to accept that this bitter accusing girl was his gentle daughter, he said, 'Real life is how you personally live it, Vesta. It can be heaven or hell.'

'How would you know?' she demanded with the selfishness of youth. 'You're always so busy working you see nothing of what is going on around you, like the ostrich with its head in the sand.'

He grew very angry then. 'Don't speak to me in that manner! I have encouraged and supported you in your desire to be an artist. I have always praised your talent when you have had doubts. I secured you a place in one of the best schools in the country, and I have made it possible for you to live in comfort while you followed your chosen path. I have always given you the freedom to develop your own personality without imposing repressive parental demands. Last, but by no means least, I have given you very warm love. In return, I am entitled to your respect, if nothing else.'

'You can't *buy* respect, Daddy. I won't ask you for a thing, from now on.'

Deeply shaken and hurt, he demanded, 'How do you expect to live, for heaven's sake?'

'I'm going into the services, to help the war effort. I shan't be painting pretty-pretty pictures, but firing shells or driving a truck. Life is not art, culture and international friendship, as you've always led me to believe. Lead your life that way if you want, but keep out of mine from now on.'

'On a bleak moor in the middle of November, when the rain is thundering down, and the wind cuts like a knife, a tin hut with a concrete floor and an old iron stove at each end is not my idea of home comfort,' said a voice beside Vesta, and she turned to see a girl about her own age, with fluffy blonde hair, black-lined eyes, and astonishingly red lips. She remembered

113

glimpsing her amongst the group on the truck that had picked them all up at the railway station, but the girl had been chatting non-stop then to a funny little creature with eyes red from weeping. Vesta decided her present companion might be one of those people who become a nuisance unless discouraged, so she gave a vague smile and turned away again.

In truth, she was also acutely dismayed by her first sight of her new living quarters. She had not expected the army to provide luxury, but David had always had a room of his own in the RAF, and it had never occurred to her that she would have to sleep with nineteen others in a hut, with no personal privacy whatever. Admittedly, she was not an officer like her brother, but in the ATS they were all women, not rough and ready troops. At school she had lived in a dormitory, but each girl had had curtains to close off her bed and locker. This hump-roofed hut had windows with blackout shutters, a concrete floor, iron bedsteads – ten a side – and a wood-burning stove with a black chimney going up through the roof. Although it was alight and pushing out considerable warmth, the deafening sound of rain on the tin roof, the gloominess of the wintry day, and the lack of any colour save black and khaki made the hut seem chill and intensely desolate. Vesta thought of her pretty room at Tarrant Hall, the elegant bedroom in the London apartment, and even the room at Bayswater she had shared with Deirdre. Then she reminded herself that she had put artificiality behind her now. This was real life.

'Right, file off to right and left,' said the NCO who had brought them to the hut. 'Take a bed each. Beside the bed is a steel locker with hanging space and three drawers. All the things you have just drawn from the Quartermaster's Stores are to be kept in there, along with what you brought with you in your suitcases.' The girl's voice rose so that it could be heard above the din of the pelting rain. 'Never, at any time, are you to leave clothing or toilet articles lying about. Family photographs may be put on top of lockers, but nothing else.'

Vesta moved numbly forward with the rest and claimed a bed halfway down the hut. It had a hard straw-filled mattress covered with grey and black ticking, and at the foot was a pile of three brown blankets, a pair of coarse, bleached sheets with a matching pillowcase, and one pillow.

'Sweet dreams on this, I don't think,' said the person next to her, and Vesta realised the fuzzy blonde was to be her neighbour. In an open hut she could not have avoided her, anyway. The girl held out her hand across the bed.

'I'm Minnie. Like the mouse.'

Vesta shook her by the hand, introducing herself.

'Vesta! What kind of name is that?' exclaimed the girl.

'It's Greek.'

'Are you foreign, then?'

She shook her head, wishing she had invented a name like Ann. 'My father chose it. He likes the classics.'

'Oh,'

It was plain Minnie was none the wiser, so Vesta busied herself trying to open the great steel locker beside her bed. The handle began to turn, then stuck. Jiggling it up and down only resulted in making a terrible din that brought the NCO to her side.

'What's the trouble?'

Vesta indicated the locker. 'It's stuck.'

The girl seized the handle and jiggled it up and down to no avail. 'It's stuck,' she announced. 'We get a lot like that. Leave it for the moment, and I'll report it. What name is it?'

'Vesta.'

'We don't use first names in the ATS.'

'Sheridan.'

'Right, Sheridan, leave your things on the floor under the bed until the locker is fixed.' Clapping her hands for attention, she then called out, 'When you have put your belongings away, make up your beds. If you'll all come over here to Sheridan's place I'll show you how to do it.'

'Blimey, I've been making beds all me life,' commented a plump girl in a frock two sizes too small for her.

'Not the way we make them in the army, you haven't,' was the swift answer. 'Watch me carefully, and woe betide anyone who ends up with something that looks like an abandoned bird's nest.'

Within a few minutes, Vesta's bed was covered with sheets and blankets so tightly tucked in it seemed unlikely she would ever be able to slide into it. The NCO straightened up.

'There you are. It's quite simple. I want to see every bed in the hut looking like that when I return in half an hour to take you over to the cookhouse for your supper.' She smiled around at them all. 'In the meantime, settle in and get to know each other. Toilets and washrooms are through the door at the far end, across the covered way, and in the hut marked ablutions. You'll be sharing those facilities with the girls in Hut 49, on the far side. They are quite adequate for the numbers, but only if each of you is reasonably considerate, vacating the washroom as soon as you have finished, and leaving it as clean and tidy as you would wish to find it. One more thing. The supply of hot water is sufficient to supply all your needs, unless taps are left running. Before you leave, check that you have turned off your tap, or the girl who comes after you may have to wash in cold water.' At the sound of several sniggers, she added, 'And that girl is likely to leave her tap running next time, and force *you* to wash in icy water. You won't think it's funny then.'

Bedlam broke out the minute the NCO left. The brash and perky all had plenty to say, the shy put away their things with much noisy shutting and opening of drawers, the weepy ones all burst into tears again, bewailing the fact that they would never learn to make a bed that way, that the girl was a bitch who was enjoying every moment of their discomfort, and that they were cold, miserable and hungry.

'So are we all,' called out Minnie in a loud voice, 'but think of our lads in minesweepers patrolling the North Sea to protect our convoys. They never know when they might be torpedoed and thrown into the icy water, with little chance of being picked up. As for the bed, get that girl to make it for you first time, then sleep on the floor so's not to mess it up . . . And if you think she's a bitch, work hard and become an NCO too. There's never any problem that can't be solved, if you try.'

'What's the solution to you?' asked someone rudely.

'Stop complaining,' Vesta found herself saying. 'She can then get on with her own problems, instead of trying to sort you out.'

Minnie looked at her across the bed and gave a slow smile. 'Mmm, didn't take you for that type, somehow. What was that funny name again?'

'You can call me Vee, if you like,' she offered impulsively. Then, because her bed was already made, and she was unable to put her things in the locker, she added, 'Would you like some help with the chambermaid stuff? I could tuck in this side for you.'

'All right,' agreed Minnie,' but woe betide you if you make it look like an abandoned bird's nest.'

They both smiled and set to. The result was not perfect, but Minnie seemed pleased as she straightened up. 'Thanks. By the end of the war we might be as proficient as that girl Haines.'

'I should hope so,' said Vesta, sitting on her own bed to face the girl. 'I think it's going to last a long time, don't you?'

Minnie pushed her hair back with one hand and sighed. 'Rob says it'll go on at least as long as the last one.'

'Is Rob your brother?'

'My boyfriend. I want to get engaged, but he won't. He says

116

it isn't fair for a bloke to make promises he very likely won't be able to keep. He's probably right, but it would be nice to have something to hold on to, even for a little while.'

With a flash of intuition, Vesta asked, 'Is he on minesweepers?'

Minnie made a face. 'How did you guess? I can't help speaking up for them. Their chances of survival are pretty slim at the moment. If they're not killed in an explosion, they freeze to death in the sea.'

'My brother is in the RAF. They're all afraid of burning to death.'

'Bombers or fighters?'

'Spitfires. They gave him the DFC last month for shooting down so many Germans. But now he's got a posting to Ops; a plum job as assistant to one of the brass hats. Mummy's delighted, of course, but he hates it, judging by his letters.'

'Is your boyfriend in the RAF too?'

She felt her stomach tighten. 'No. Why didn't you join the navy?'

Twisting away to put a pile of clothes into one of her drawers, Minnie said, 'They're all rather posh and superior in the WRNS and sound like you do. I wouldn't fit in. Come to that, why didn't you join the Air Force like your brother? Is it because your boyfriend is in the army?'

'It seemed the best bet, that's all.' Bored with a conversation that led to nothing but questions about boyfriends, she said, 'I think I'll investigate the washroom.'

Once outside the far door there was a raised duckboard walkway linking Hut 48, which she had just left, to the hut marked 'Ablutions'. The roof over the walkway served no useful purpose, she decided, because the rain was driven in under it to drench anyone crossing the ten yards between huts. Quickening her steps, she pushed open the door of the other hut and entered an atmosphere of steam, shouts and squirting water. Stone-floored also, the ablutions hut had a double row of tin sinks, which emptied into channels running down the centre of the hut to a pair of large drains at the end. Half-screens shut off rows of toilets on each side of the hut, and at the far end were half a dozen crude shower cubicles. The area was full of girls in various stages of dress, trying to wash or brush their teeth at the sinks. Others were prancing about unashamedly naked in the shower area, shrieking because the water was boiling hot as it gushed from the overhead nozzles. Those at the sinks were shouting at the others to turn off the showers, because the water from the row of taps was running cold. Unfortunately, to turn off the showers it was necessary to go into the cubicles and be scalded. So the showers all continued to run at full flow, with steaming water running away by the gallon, while the girls at the sinks shivered as they splashed themselves with liquid ice. There was water everywhere: in puddles over the floor, running down the walls, and swamping the surrounds of the sinks where the girls wanted to put their holdalls and towels. But there was no water to flush the toilets, apparently. Girls were banging the doors in disgust, and walking off vowing to find another hut somehere on the camp.

Vesta retreated quickly, was pelted with rain again as she crossed the walkway, and re-entered Hut 48 to find an argument in progress over ownership of a locker. It had reached the stage of lost tempers.

'It's beside *my* bed, and *I* was here first,' said a brunette with fiery cheeks.

'It's also beside *my* bed, and *my* things are in it,' snapped the rival claimant.

'Well, you can just take them out again. That girl Haines said we have the locker to the *right* of our beds.'

'This is to the right.'

'Not when you face the wall.'

'It is when you face into the room.'

'Don't you know your bloody right from your left?'

'Don't speak to me like that, you bitch!'

Vesta walked past them to her own bed, her spirits suddenly like lead. Loneliness washed over her intensified by this bizarre change in her life. Next week she would be twenty. Up to now everything had seemed so certain, so clear-cut, so predestined. The warm glow of family love and security had kept her safely encircled, schooldays with Pat's close loyal friendship had been ordered and happy. At art school, she had believed she was branching out into a life that would continue as before, except that she would be fulfilling her creative talent professionally, and would meet a kindred spirit whom she would marry to produce another family circle like the one at Tarrant Hall. Was it the war or Felix Makoski that had broken it all apart?

Their NCO returned at that point, shouted for silence, then castigated everyone for inefficiency, sloth and untidiness. That over, she ordered everyone to put on their rain capes and form up in lines to march to the cookhouse for a supper she promised would cheer them all up.

In growing disgust, and with rain dripping from her shiny rubber cape, Vesta shuffled along beside the serving counter with her tin plate held out, watching the cooks slap mounds of mashed vegetables, differing only in colour, onto a pool of brown liquid with solid lumps in it. Dutifully taking it to a table, she sat with Minnie and the others, staring at what they told her was stew with cabbage, potatoes and swede. The real shock came when they all trooped up for pudding, and were obliged to scrape their plates into a general swill-tub that was presided over by a large woman with sharp eyes.

'Just a minute,' this guardian said, as Vesta prepared to tip away the food she had not touched. 'What's wrong with that?'

'I don't want it,' she explained.

'Why not?'

'I'm not hungry.'

'Then why did you take it?'

'I didn't. It was put on my plate without any reference to my wishes.'

The large woman looked her up and down. 'This isn't a country mansion here, you know. Your wishes are of no importance, and the sooner you realise it the better. You are no longer a single person, you're a member of a unit. That unit is part of a service designed to do a vital job in this war. Now go back and eat that dinner.'

Taking exception to her tone, Vesta said, 'When I'm given a job, you may reprimand me if I don't do it. But what I eat is my own affair.' With that she scraped her plate clean, and prepared to walk off. The NCO stopped her with her next sentence.

'Hasn't "Daddy" ever told you there are people starving in Czechoslovakia and Poland?'

Swinging round in swift bitterness, she said, 'Don't believe all those people tell you. They're pretty good liars, who have found we have sympathetic ears.'

The woman looked her over once more. 'What's your name?'

'Sheridan.'

'Right, Sheridan, as it's your first day, I'll do no more than arrange for you to give your views to the Catering Officer in the morning.'

They marched back in the rain to Hut 48, where they were instructed on how to polish their heavy shoes, clean their buttons, tie their ties, and press their thick khaki uniforms for their first inspection in the morning. While they had been at the cookhouse, someone had been in to fix Vesta's locker. It now opened, but would not shut. In the process of cleaning her shoes she dropped the tin of polish onto the bed, where it made a great brown smear on the sheet. When she finally managed to

119

take over an iron in the scramble to press uniforms, it fused. Their NCO arrived at 9.30 p.m. to switch off the lights for the night, and Vesta finally pressed her jacket and skirt in the dark at midnight, shivering in the striped flannel pyjamas they had all been given. By the light of no more than the dying glow of the stove, and with the rain still thundering on the tin roof, she pressed the creases from her new clothes, reflecting that the two silk nightdresses she had brought with her would have to be parcelled up and sent home, along with the lace-edged French knickers and matching petticoats. From now on, it would be pyjamas like David had worn as a boy, khaki interlock bloomers, woollen stockings, and heavy marching shoes. This was reality; this was what she had sought. It was proving almost as cold a shock as it had been with Felix Makoski.

The large NCO had not forgotten Vesta, as she discovered the next day when she received a summons to go to the hut housing the Catering Officer. A chilly, sleepless night had not improved Vesta's frame of mind, and she fully intended telling the woman her opinion of the food provided, having that morning shuddered at the sight of sausages and pale, greasy fried bread, floating in tomato juice for breakfast. She had drunk something they had claimed to be tea, and had forced herself to swallow a thick slice of rubbery bread spread with margarine and jam. Now she wished she had not, because it lay like a lump on her chest as she waited outside an office marked 'B. Hailey'.

A girl came out and said that Miss Hailey would see her now, and she must remember to salute as she went in.

'I haven't been shown how to do that yet,' she explained. 'I only arrived yesterday.'

The other girl looked nonplussed. 'You always salute an officer,' she insisted, and left Vesta to make what she could of that by walking off.

When she went into the austere office, however, she forgot all about saluting and uniforms. The girl behind the desk was as surprised as she.

'Good heavens, Beth, I didn't know you were in the ATS,' Vesta greeted her. 'When did you join?'

'Fancy seeing you,' exclaimed Beth Hailey. 'I heard you'd gone to art school, as you intended. Mary Haversham said she'd met you in Harrods just before last Christmas and had a long chat. How's Pat Chandler? Mary said she's apparently blissfully happy on her mother's sheep farm. Now I could imagine her in the army, but never you. What made you join?'

Still astonished at meeting one of her school friends, Vesta hedged. 'David has been flying a Spitfire over the coast all summer, and they've just given him the DFC. I thought I ought to do something too.'

'Yes, I read about your brother's DFC in the paper. He's getting his wish to emulate his famous uncle, and the propaganda people love to get hold of stuff like that to cheer us all up. Sit down,' Beth continued, indicating a chair beside her desk. 'It's time for my mid-morning tea and biscuits. I'll ask for another cup and saucer.' Picking up the telephone, she did so, then replaced the receiver, asking, 'How's your dishy father? During our last term I had a really heavy "thing" for him, you know. I'd never met anyone so good-looking and so unconcerned with the fact, besides being absolutely *brilliant*. I suppose he's young enough to be called up.'

'He won't have to fight,' Vesta said baldly, as she sat down and put out her hands to the warmth of the stove. 'He can only see a blur without those thick spectacles, and he still gets trouble with his leg in freezing weather. Besides, you know he lost two fingers from his left hand at Gallipoli, so he'd be no use in battle. They've made him a lieutenant colonel just for convenience, but he's safely behind a desk somewhere, doing translating work I should think. Meetings and conferences are his line. Nothing heroic.'

Beth Hailey looked at her curiously. 'I'm over it now. Long ago. You don't have to disillusion me.'

Vesta frowned. 'I don't understand.'

'I always thought you were proud of having such a sensational father. You enjoyed seeing us all go ga-ga over him at school. Just now, though, it sounded as if you were playing him down; dismissing him as someone rather ordinary and boring.'

The arrival of tea brought by a smart orderly saved Vesta from having to answer that, and Beth poured tea into two plain pink cups before going on.

'When I was told there was a Miss Sheridan being sent to me, I didn't connect the name with you. NCO Smithers said you were kicking up a rumpus about the food, and refused to eat any of it. She also said you were impertinent. It doesn't sound a bit like you. At school you were one of the quiet ones, always dreaming. "The Bat" was always pouncing on you for inattention.'

Vesta smiled, remembering Miss Batforth who taught Latin. 'She could never reconcile herself to the disappointment of finding I hadn't inherited Daddy's brilliance at the classics. You were top of her class instead.' Enjoying the tea, which tasted like tea, she then asked, 'You were all set to go to university... Why didn't you?'

Beth made a wry face. 'I fell very heavily for Giles, Francesca Mortimer's brother in the Life Guards, who devastated us all by turning up for Speech Day in full regalia. Do you remember? We became engaged last Christmas, just before he went overseas. I felt I wanted to be in khaki, too.'

'But why this? Catering Officer?' protested Vesta. 'You have such a good brain.'

'I also have a family who are international hoteliers, if you remember.'

'Yes. Geneva, Montreux, Rome. What connection is there with *this*? Sorry, Beth, but the food here is appalling.'

The other girl put her cup down slowly, her face serious. 'Have you heard what our troops were eating prior to Dunkirk? Can you imagine what kind of meal can be cooked in a field under bombardment?'

'We're not under bombardment here,' she pointed out.

'Only because your brother and his pals made certain we weren't. But it'll come, Vesta. One way or another, each one of us is going to be living in danger before this is over. Food is going to get shorter and shorter. Naturally you can't compare this with our continental hotels. We've had to leave the one in Rome, of course, along with the staff we had for so many years. They are not eating the way they did, either. In this camp I'm trying to do the best I can with the rations we're allowed, and with cooks who have had no more than a few weeks' training. We are not pretending to be a luxury hotel. We are a unit training girls from all walks of life to help fight a war. The men had a terrible time of it in the last one, trying to keep us out of it. We won't let that happen again.' She gave Vesta an intent look. 'Surely that's why you joined.'

Walking back across the camp, where the rain was still pouring down, Vesta felt more miserable than ever. Beth was so certain of her motives for what she was doing. Although they had sat chatting as friends and equals, the other girl had impressed on her that rank had to be observed between them in public, and went on to urge Vesta to become an officer. As she tramped through the puddles in shoes that had already raised blisters on her feet, and huddled beneath the weighty rubber cape, she tried to come to terms with the irrevocable step she had taken.

When her father had told her the truth about Felix,

something inside her had broken. The shock of what the young Pole had done to her that night had been just bearable all the time she believed the fault to be hers. While she imagined she must be somehow different from other girls, unable to enjoy what they plainly did, the wonder of Felix remained. The swift, violent love that had filled her that Christmas had been too magical to surrender, and blaming herself had allowed her to hold onto her first-love magic. The revelation that Felix had not seen his parents brutally killed, or his sisters dragged away by rapacious soldiers; that he had no family, save a schoolteacher father who still lived, was a nasty jolt. But the fact that he had a wife and baby in Poland had destroyed everything. It enabled her to see that his violation of her had been no more than a selfish need for something for which he would have to pay a prostitute. There had been no desperate love behind it, no reaching out to a girl he saw as a symbol of gentleness and compassion after horror, no search for escape from memories by taking her so totally. He had simply used her to satisfy a need his wife could not ease; used her selfishly and heartlessly. How he must have laughed at her trembling confusion over that kiss under the mistletoe, her eagerness to meet him wherever and whenever he dictated, her sympathy, her understanding... her gullibility.

Felix had used David to gain a Christmas invitation. He had used her parents for hospitality and friendship. But he had used her in the most brutal way of all. What if she had borne his child as a result? Yet it was her father she could not forgive. By taking it upon himself to investigate Felix's past, he had turned the whole thing into something degrading, unbearably sordid and self-destructive. His words had eaten away at the conviction that had salved her pride. When she had been able to see herself as some kind of sexual oddity, Felix had become even more tragically romantic. They would never have met again, but the ideal would have remained intact. The truth her father revealed had brought loathing of her own body, her femininity, her emotions and senses; it had prevented her from painting intuitively. Her canvases had begun to be covered with lurid colour, stark outlines, bitter representation. Her tutors had applauded. At last she was coming to terms with true creativity. She knew it was nonsense. She was coming to terms with shame, anger and alienation. Her father had exposed her to sordid reality. After years of distant parenthood, he had delved deeply into her life and broken it apart over tea and toast.

Hating what she put onto canvas because it spoke too clearly

123

of her bitterness, and unable to live happily at home, she had taken what she believed to be the best of the few ways out. The ATS provided a place to live and money to buy what she needed. It was now a shock to discover that the army expected something from her in return. Minnie thought she had joined to help a boyfriend; Beth Hailey thought it was to help everyone's boyfriend. How could she tell them it was merely to help herself?

They tried to have their usual Christmas that year, but it was impossible, of course. December 1940 was an extremely bleak period. With the whole of Europe and Scandinavia under the control of or allied to Germany, and Russia still believing in friendship with Hitler, Britain stood alone. Only the hope that resistance groups in occupied countries might grow strong, buoyed up the belief that they would re-enter Europe as victors. England had fought off invasion during that late summer, but was now being bombed night after night in an attempt to reduce the island and its people to a state of surrender. Britain's capital, its big industrial cities, its ports and airfields, its oil refineries were all attacked with incendiary and high-explosive bombs. Britain was aflame and breaking apart. Its people were not.

Despite rationing and absent members, most families strove to celebrate Christmas as they always had. For some, it was a time of conversion to faith, in the belief that only with God on their side could they beat Hitler. For others, it was a time of disillusionment, because He had taken from them their loved ones, or all they had worked for with pride and industry. Some bore every possible blow yet remained true to Him; some lost no more than a beloved pet animal and turned their backs on the church. In all, there was one common emotion: deep and intense hatred of their enemies. It was that hatred that united and strengthened them.

In the country things were a great deal easier than in towns. Food was more plentiful because the people produced it themselves, and the strain of nightly air raids did not affect them. The old church at Tarrant Royal had been full for the midnight service, when the Sheridans had occupied the family pew. Vesta had not been granted leave, although Chris and David had been fortunate enough to get home, and Marion had done her best to follow tradition in every way. Even in that Dorset village it was impossible to pretend nothing was different, however, as when the Chandlers arrived for

124

Christmas Day. Pat very obviously missed Vesta, and the three men were inclined to be introspective. It was left to Marion and Tessa to keep things light.

David was hard put to participate in any suggestion of festivity. Whilst on sick leave in October, he had been able to believe it would be all right when he returned to the squadron. The old stalwarts had welcomed him back too heartily; the new members had eyed him as though he were a freak. It had been all too clear everyone knew 'Sherry' Sheridan's nephew had a personal gremlin who refused to let him take his aircraft off the ground. It had been there in their careful avoidance of the subject, and in the way they studied him when they thought he could not see them. It had been there in the atmosphere that first time, as they waited at Dispersal; and it had been there as they had all run for their machines as soon as the November fog had cleared.

Eleven aircraft had risen into the sky. He had sat on the ground in the twelfth, limbs frozen, crying out silently and desperately for help as the squadron had vanished into the high cloud. His humiliation had been complete when the ground crew came to lift him from the cockpit, and found him with the tears of failure running down his cheeks.

The posting must have been one of the quickest on record. He had left the following morning while they had all been out hunting Messerschmitts, and taken up his new duties at Fighter Command headquarters. To salve his pride, he had been told his selection had been due to his extensive personal experience, which would be invaluable in advising the air vice marshal to whom he would be a personal assistant. But he knew his famous surname, plus his father's influential connections, had led to his tactful transfer to what amounted to a plum desk job.

For two months he had endured work which was completely at odds with his active nature, had tried to ignore the careful way everyone ignored his rapid transfer to administrative duties, had tried to accept the inexplicable disaster of his career. For two months he had lived the exclusive 'old boys'' existence in the select, cushioned atmosphere amidst top-ranking, often titled, men of the air. He had been lunched, dined, fussed over by men who had flown with or well remembered his Uncle Rex, and had been regaled with innumerable stories of his legendary exploits. Others had no personal acquaintance with 'Sherry' Sheridan, but knew Sir Christopher well, and told him innumerable long stories of his father's reputation as a man who had worked tirelessly for world peace. They all had one thing in common, however. None of them talked about him. It was the one subject they avoided.

For two months David had shared a headquarters with WAAFs who were perfectly groomed, well-spoken, well-connected and intensely efficient. In their immaculate uniforms, with their hair meticulously tucked into chignons or rolls above their shirt collars, and their cool, crisp mannerisms that suggested they were not to be touched by a pilot's hot sticky little hands, they hardly provided what David preferred in female guise. Feeling claustrophobic in the office life, sick of elderly men who thought he loved hearing about his father and uncle, possessed by his own sense of failure, he had longed for the breezy chumminess of a squadron Mess with its vulgar singsongs around a piano, its outrageously exaggerated tales of sexual encounters the previous night, its non-stop flow of beer, and its masculine smell of hair oil, cigarette and pipe smoke, and aero engines. Day after day he had looked from his office window and yearned to be up in the sky, hearing the voices of his comrades over the R/T as they embarked on a life or death struggle high above the earth. Cooped up physically, frustrated mentally, restricted sexually, he had gone off-duty one evening on a determined pub crawl. Gin and tonics had palled, and the urge to knock back pint after pint of frothy beer had proved too strong.

Roistering from one East End pub to another, joining in hearty renditions of 'Bless 'em All' and 'Kiss Me Goodnight, Sergeant Major', he had finally picked up a willing little bus conductress and gone with her to her dingy room for what she called 'a bit of a kiss and cuddle'. That was all it had turned out to be. Well on the way to what he desperately wanted, she had pushed her bare breasts up into his palms, blown in his ear, and whispered with a giggle, 'I've always wanted it with a Spitfire pilot, an' watch 'im dive to the attack, guns blazin'.'

Seizing up as suddenly as he did in a cockpit, he had left rapidly, slapping a pound note onto her dresser, and telling her to treat herself to a seat in the one-and-nines, where she could see Spitfire pilots doing it on the silver screen instead.

That incident had forced him to take a step which, two months before, he would never have considered doing. Using the names and reputations of his father and uncle, he had gone over the heads of his superiors to the very top, and had wangled a promise to make him operational again. He was posted to the Central Flying School as an instructor. It was not exactly what he wanted, but at least he would be flying. His first pupil had

had a lesson on how *not* to take off. Christmas leave had fortunately intervened, and he had arrived home shattered by the fact that his inability to take a machine off the ground was permanent.

Seasonal festivity was the last thing he wanted. The previous Christmas his mother had voiced her fear that things would never be the same again. How right she had been! Vesta was in the army and absent on duty. That young Pole he had impulsively invited home was dead: he had seen Makoski's name on recent casualty lists. His parents seemed strangely aloof from one another; Pat was fatter than ever; Aunt Tessa talked of nothing but Lord Woolton and his food controls . . . and he was no longer a pilot. The only one amongst them who seemed little different was Bill Chandler. Admittedly, he was quieter and made no attempt at his usual conjuring tricks, but basically he appeared to be the same man he had always been. It was that that led David to grasp at a last straw, and do what he had vehemently told his mother was out of the question and unnecessary.

On the 27th of December, traditionally the day the Sheridans spent at the Chandler's farm at Tarrant Maundle, he sought out the man he had known all his life as Uncle Bill. The Australian was some twenty years older than David's father, but he was his closest friend: a relationship that had begun between a doctor and youthful patient in a mental wing of an army hospital in 1915. Bill Chandler was a skilled neurologist specialising in traumatic amnesia: to the layman, that was a loss of memory due to shock of a physical or mental nature. To David, he was the one person likely to listen to him without being shocked, embarrassed, or dismissive.

The Chandlers had built a large home for themselves along the lines of the Outback homestead. Vastly different from the dignified character of Tarrant Hall, it was airy, full of comfort and colour, and designed to cope with muddy boots, all-weather visits to barns and outhouses, and the hand rearing of motherless lambs. It was a carefree house where regular hours could not be kept, and no one stood on ceremony. After a large lunch, the three women went to an upstairs room to discuss making clothes for children orphaned in the blitz, and David's father settled in a chair to read an article on 'battle neurosis', which had once been known as 'shell shock', which their host had written. Seeing his chance, David strolled out into the large conservatory where Bill Chandler was smoking his pipe in blissful solitude.

He turned and smiled at David. 'You've not taken to

poisoning your guts with tobacco yet, I see. But I guess you're doing it with liberal potions of beer instead.'

He was too tense and too afraid of being interrupted to lead up to it slowly. 'Uncle Bill, can I talk to you for a minute as a doctor?'

The shrewd face showed no surprise. He simply took the pipe from his mouth again and said, in an accent as broad as it had always been, 'I wondered just how long it would be before you did.'

David was immediately furious. 'So Mother has been telling you about it, has she?'

Bushy eyebrows rose. 'No one has been telling me anything, old son. I'm just a canny old bugger who can recognise when a chap has a problem. I knew you'd try your darndest to work it out for yourself rather than ask for help, because you are an independent young devil, David. No luck, eh?'

He shook his head. 'It's so bloody silly.'

'Most of the problems I deal with are, but they occur, just the same. Going to tell me about it?'

'Oh... I don't know. No one can do anything,' he said, wishing he had never started the subject.

'That's usually the point at which blokes like me are brought in,' came the dry comment.

'I'm not off my chump,' he fired up defensively.

'Did I suggest you were?'

He sighed heavily. 'No... sorry. I just don't know what can be done.'

'Maybe nothing. Tell me about it and I'll let you know.'

So, gazing from the long glass windows at the view down the valley between Wey Hill and Longbarrow Hill, where Tarrant Maundle nestled like a colour-washed dolls' village, David told his story in reluctant, apologetic sentences.

When he had finished his companion said, 'Why the hell haven't you told all this to someone long ago? The RAF have men like me on tap.'

David shrugged, suspecting it had all been a waste of time, if the only advice he was to be given was to go to the RAF nuthouse.

'It was pretty awful during that period at the end of the summer,' he explained. 'Lots of chaps just couldn't take any more, especially if they also had personal problems like children being killed in the blitz, or wives going out with other men. No one blamed them. They just lost their nerve. Hospitals are too full of physical casualties to do anything with them. They were posted to admin jobs for a rest. That's what they did

128

with me, except that I haven't lost my nerve, and I haven't got a personal problem.'

'Of course you have,' came the quiet response. 'You've grown to manhood trying to be the son of Rex Sheridan, instead of that of his brother in that sitting room, haven't you?'

'What? I... Of course I... Don't be bloody silly.'

Bill Chandler smiled. 'My God, it could be twenty-five years ago. You stand there, looking so much like him and protesting, just as he always did. I'll say to you what I said to him. If you want my help you have to be honest with yourself, as well as with me. He couldn't always do that because he had forgotten, which is why it took so long. Now, unless you're open and honest with me, I'll walk off and leave you to it.'

David knew he meant it, and said defensively, 'I've never made any secret of how I feel about him.'

'Or about Rex?'

'I... I'm not sure what you mean.'

'You can't be another Rex Sheridan, David. No man can be an exact copy of another. Even identical twins are two separate individuals.'

'I know that!'

'Then what are you trying to be?'

'I... Well, I...' he floundered, unused to being so frank with anyone on this particular subject.

'Come on, inform David Sheridan as well as me, because I don't think the young devil knows.'

Pushing his hand through his thick blond hair, he said with some awkwardness, 'He's always been my, well, my *hero*, if you like. Father thinks, like you, that I fancy myself a second "Sherry" Sheridan. That isn't true. Not strictly true,' he amended. 'When you're a boy you try to copy someone you admire, don't you? But it's more in the nature of a tribute than a belief that you are as good. If you were, he would no longer be a hero. If I've tried to copy Uncle Rex, it's more a form of hero worship than a belief that I'm a reincarnation of him. I'm not that good.' He felt his colour rising uncharacteristically, and turned to look away through the window to hide it from the other man. 'Unfortunately, everyone I met read it the wrong way, and expected me to step into his shoes. It's been a hell of a thing to live up to, but during those twelve weeks at the end of summer I did pretty well. I know it's not the thing to say, but I have all the qualities to make a damn fine fighter pilot. I proved it over and over again. I'm not afraid to go up there. I'd give anything to have another go at the Jerries. I could lead a squadron. The capability is there, without question. I have calmness, clarity of thought, and total lack of fear in combat.' He swung round then to say thickly and angrily, *'So why the hell can't I take a machine up?'*

Bill Chandler looked at him very directly. 'Because you feel you have let down "Sherry" Sheridan by shooting down one of your own boys.'

David realised then it had been a waste of time, after all. 'Look, Uncle Bill, it was an accident. My gun stuck. The same thing could have happened to Uncle Rex. It probably did at some time or other. If you're suggesting that I'm wallowing in guilt over it, you're way off course.'

'That is what you're doing, boy.'

It was said so calmly, he grew even more heated. *'I am not!* And it's not grief, either,' he added sarcastically. 'I'm terribly sorry about it, naturally, and would give anything for it not to have happened. But it did, and I've accepted it. If it had been my best friend I had killed, I might understand a subconscious reluctance to fly again. But I disliked Enright.'

The other man knocked out his pipe with a casual movement, saying, 'That's the trouble in a nutshell, David. If you had killed your best friend, all would have been well. The attitude of your comrades, their avoidance of the subject, their sidelong looks, would have been accepted by you for what they really are – the signs of acute sympathy for your bad luck. You would have grieved and appreciated their sympathy over a tragic accident. But it was well known that you and this Enright were enemies to the point of being warned by your CO, and in the state of stress and strain you were currently suffering when it happened, you convinced yourself that everyone thought you had deliberately eliminated him. Their looks became accusations, their sympathetic silence you interpreted as deliberate shunning, their consideration in leaving you alone to recover from it you took to be concerted condemnation. Worse, you convinced yourself that you had dishonoured your uncle's memory by doing something he could never have done – earned the dislike of an entire squadron. Until you can cleanse your subconscious of that belief, and redeem yourself in your own eyes, the problem will remain.'

Appalled, yet somehow seeing the sense in all that had been said, David cried, 'How will I ever redeem myself, if I can't get airborne?'

Bill Chandler's large hand fell on his shoulder and gripped it confidently, 'You'll do it some other way, lad. You're not your father's son for nothing. You've inherited his courage, like it or not.'

130

Chapter Seven

THE EVENING was turning out quite as badly as Vesta had feared and she wondered, for the fourth time, why she had allowed Minnie to talk her into it. But Minnie Turner had a persuasive bent that was hard to resist. They had become firm friends during their basic training, which was surprising in view of their vastly different backgrounds, and had subsequently been delighted to receive postings to the same camp on the east coast. They had been working as teleprinter operators for two months now. Minnie had settled into army life with gusto. Vesta was still wondering what had hit her.

It had probably been that sense of disorientation that had led to her ill-advised agreement to make a foursome for the evening with Minnie's boyfriend Rob Carter and his pal, while their ship was in at Chatham for a few days. She had also been partly influenced by Minnie's fears that she would not get Rob to herself unless someone kept his pal occupied. So there they were, in a pub, after coming from the cinema. They had seen a stirring semi-documentary about the dangerous job of keeping the seas around the British Isles free of German mines, during which Rob and his friend Mickey had roared with laughter. During the other film, a technicolour musical extravaganza with plenty of girls displaying bare legs, the two men had grown amorous. Minnie had been delighted. Vesta had jammed Mickey's hand so hard between her thigh and the metal arm rest, he had given an involuntary yell which had had all heads turning to say 'Shhh!' He had left her alone after that, but now they were in a brightly lit saloon bar with a crowd of uninhibited patrons, she was finding it difficult to be pleasant to him. He was very friendly, full of life and laughter, and with the bold kind of looks which somehow made Vesta curl up inside. Minnie's Rob was quiet and almost shy; a man of around twenty-three with a square face that suggested dependability. Vesta could well understand that he had refused to become engaged as things were. He was not the type to do anything without months of planning, and complete confidence in the outcome. If she had had to partner him that evening, all would have been well.

Squashed around a table in a corner of that smoky bar, they had to shout to each other in order to be heard above the laughter and conversation. When someone began playing 'Bless 'em All' on the piano, and a lusty chorus of inebriated singers joined in, it was impossible to be heard across the table. That isolated Vesta with the randy Mickey on one side, while Minnie and Rob gazed soulfully at each other opposite.

'Is it just me or all men you can't stand?' asked Mickey alcoholically against her ear. 'Or perhaps you prefer other girls. I've heard there's a lot of that in the ATS.'

Not sure of what he meant, Vesta tried to move further from him along the seat, and found herself hemmed in by a huge soldier wearing the turned-up hat of Australian regiments on the back of his head, and holding a quart mug of beer in each hand. Turning, he spotted her and gave a leering grin.

'Tryin' ter cuddle up? S'orlright by me, darlin'. Come to Smokey, who's miles from 'ome an' bloody lonely.' In trying to put one of his arms around her, he spilled beer in her lap, which soaked through the khaki skirt and thick stocking to her thighs.

''Ere, watch it!' cried Mickey immediately, getting to his feet. 'That's *my* girl you're annoying. You Aussies are all the same. No bloody mannners.'

'You speaking to me, mate?' queried the Australian, getting to his feet, also. 'I float blokes like you in paper boats in me bath.'

'Is that so? It's well known blokes like you never 'ave a bath,' came the swift response.

Next minute, Vesta was knocked sideways by the soldier, who lunged at Mickey, beer tankards still in his hands. Winded and frightened by such instant aggression, Vesta instinctively escaped the only way she could. Sliding down under the table, she scrambled from beneath it on her hands and knees, emerging amongst the legs of interested spectators shouting encouragement to the brawling pair. Trembling with anger she got to her feet, pulled her wet skirt into place, attempted to tuck her hair into its neat chignon, then confronted Minnie who was being drawn further into the corner by Rob.

'I'm going,' she cried above the noise. 'Don't ever ask me to make a foursome again.'

Rescuing her cap from the table that was beginning to tilt, sending their glasses sliding, she started to push her way through the excited crowd. What was she doing in a place like this? She, Vesta Sheridan of Tarrant Hall. What was happening to her life? First she had allowed herself to be violated by a married foreigner; now she had spent a terrible evening being pawed and dribbled over by a strange sailor because she had taken pity on Minnie. She was far too soft. But was that all men did? Was the ideal of love really no more than lust of the flesh in various forms?

Someone trod heavily on her toes with an army boot, which brought tears to her eyes; a Scot wearing a tammy with a green pompon asked for 'a wee kiss to cheer me up' and a painted tart said loudly that she had set two poor devils at each other's throats, then run out on both of them. Reaching the blackout screen at the pub door, Vesta jammed her cap onto her dishevelled hair and prepared to leave. But her departure was prevented by the sudden entry of two tall MPs, who must have been called by the landlord when the fighting began. Vesta stood aghast, knowing she was certain to be dragged into the affair now.

'I know another way out of here,' said a low voice beside her. 'Would you like me to show you?'

Turning quickly, she saw a man of around forty with dark hair greying at the temples, pleasant light blue eyes, and a long face that was overdue for a shave. There was something about him that suggested reliability, however, and she said quickly, 'Yes, please.'

He took her elbow in his hand, coaxed her beneath the flap of the counter, along its length, and through a door into a passageway that led to the street. Once there, she disengaged herself and prepared to leave.

'Thank you so much. I'm most grateful for your help.'

'This isn't much in your line, is it?' the man asked. 'I've been watching you since you arrived, and have reached the conclusion you are not exactly enjoying the evening.'

Warning bells began to ring very loudly, telling her she had gone from frying pan into fire. What a fool she had been to let herself be picked up by this stranger, who now felt she owed him something. His next words confirmed her suspicions.

'I imagine you're stationed at the local camp. I'm going past the main gates. Can I give you a lift in my car?'

'No, thanks,' she said swiftly, turning to go. 'There's a bus every fifteen minutes.'

He caught up with her and fell into step. With no moon to give light that evening, it was pitch black in the streets, so she was afraid to run.

'My offer is perfectly honourable,' he said in conversational tones. 'Please, don't be afraid.'

'I'm not . . . but I would prefer to go by bus,' she said tightly, still walking, and clutching her bag in case he tried to snatch it. With a sigh of relief she heard the voices of people approaching, and decided to make a voluble farewell when they drew level.

'You really don't remember me, do you?' he went on. 'You were never one of my pupils, but you surely must have seen me around the school. I remember you, even though you are hardly recognisable in uniform, and considerably out of place in that venue, Miss Sheridan.'

She was so surprised, she stopped walking, and asked the still dark shape before her, 'Who are you?'

'Gerald Bream.'

'You were at the school? Of course! Landscapes, wasn't it?'

'That's right. You remember the name, but not the face.'

Still in a whirl over the swiftness of events, she smiled apologetically to an outline who could not see her, either. 'Sorry, I didn't look too hard at you. I just wanted to get out. I suppose I panicked rather stupidly. I've left my friend in there.'

'With Rob Carter? She'll be all right with him.'

The approaching couple passed and went on with ringing footsteps and a soft laugh. No longer afraid, Vesta asked him, 'How do you know Rob? Are you friendly with everyone, Mr Bream?'

'It must seem that way to you,' he admitted in amused tones. 'I also know your father well. It was me he asked to find a place for you at the school. He showed me some of your work and I was impressed. A trifle immature, but distinctively individual.'

Lost for anything more to say, she stood silently until he asked, 'Will you accept a lift back to camp now?'

'Yes . . . yes, thank you,' she agreed, relieved that she would not have to sit on the bus with her wet skirt, to be stared at by the other passengers.

Taking her arm, he led her back the way they had come, then into the yard of the pub where a solitary car was parked. Vesta wondered how an art teacher managed to get petrol to run a car, and what he was doing at a coastal pub for the evening. A sudden wild suspicion that her father had sent him to investigate her affairs lasted no longer than a few seconds. He had found out about Felix because it was part of his job to deal with aliens. Of course he would not engage in such ridiculous nonsense. He was far too busy, and she had told him not to meddle in her life.

It was marvellous to relax in an expensive car again after so many army trucks with hard seats, and it was also marvellous to talk to someone who was not in khaki. As far as she could recall, Gerald Bream had been wearing a roll-neck pullover and a navy blue pea jacket. He settled in the driving seat and started the engine.

'I'm sorry I shan't be able to show-off my brilliance at the wheel,' he said, busily looking over his shoulder as he backed the car, 'This total blackout is death to budding race-track motorists. I'm good in daylight. You'd be impressed then, believe me.'

She smiled in the darkness. 'You don't know my brother. He takes a lot of beating. You must be an important man, Mr Bream. It's only doctors, vets and people like Daddy who are allowed to drive themselves around, these days.'

'It's an essential part of my job,' he explained, putting the car into forward gear, and setting off down the road where no more than occasional slits of light indicated other traffic passing.

After she had pondered that for a moment or two, she took it further. 'Putting two and two together, I conclude you no longer teach at the school.'

'Dear, dear, Miss Sheridan, it seems you took so little interest in me during your student days you didn't even notice I was no longer there after Christmas 'thirty-nine. I was in France during the retreat, and got out at Dunkirk. Then I spent six months with the Home Defences, before going out with the minesweepers just before last Christmas. I was on Rob Carter's ship for three months. I got to know the whole crew in that time, which is why I was surprised to see Sir Christopher Sheridan's daughter in the company of a man like Mickey Boyd tonight.'

Growing more and more intrigued, she turned to look at his silhouette. 'First you were in the army at Dunkirk, then part of the Home Guard, now the navy. What do you really do, Mr Bream? And is it *Mister* Bream, or do you have a high rank in one of the services?'

He laughed softly. 'I have a very humble rank in all three, Miss Sheridan. I am a war artist. It is my job to record on canvas the aspects of war that fighting men are too busy to notice, or which become forgotten in the passing years. War can be gentle, humane, tender, even beautiful, you know. Of

135

course, I also paint the awesome unreality of battle, the cruelty of a freezing sea as men are forced to fight for their lives, the heartrending misery of a small child wandering alone and sobbing in the midst of an air raid, but I try to concentrate on subjects that show the humanity rather than the reverse of this present state we find ourselves in, and it takes the eye of an artist to bring it forward as the main subject, with the horror as the background.'

'And you're sharing the horror?' she asked, fascinated.

'Naturally. I couldn't paint it unless I experienced it.' He swung the car round a corner that took him by surprise, and she was flung against him. As she straightened up, he went on, 'Am I correct in guessing that the dubious social event this evening was your attempt to gain experience of life? You won't get it by sitting in pubs with characters like Mickey Boyd. They see life rather like these car headlamps – through a narrow slit that eliminates turnings and side-streets, because vision is restricted.'

She sighed. 'I only came tonight because Minnie asked me to make a foursome. She's desperate to marry Rob before he gets killed, and he won't ask her because he's sure he will. I was supposed to occupy Mickey so that they could concentrate on each other.'

'You did, and they could. The aspect of this evening that should stand out in your mind is the way they sat gazing at each other while the drinking, the flirting, the boasting and the punch-ups went on around them unnoticed. I made several sketches. It'll be the perfect picture to end my series. *Home safely, the sailor gazes at the girl he dare not love.* That stuffy, smelly bar had some marvellous characters to provide the sordid background to purity of emotion. The prostitute in lurid red satin brocade that had once been someone's curtains, the brawny Australian drowning his homesickness in beer and aggression, the little dapper man with furtive eyes who has dodged call-up because of flat feet, and who deals in black market undies for anyone rich or desperate enough to buy them. And the society girl who joined up to do her bit for her country, then found herself out of her depth in the world of realities.'

She turned quickly to protest, but he said, 'Don't worry, no one will recognise you, I promise. But you recognised yourself, didn't you?'

The car rolled to a halt and Vesta realised they were outside the gates of the camp already. He switched off the engine and turned to her. All she could see of him was the gleam of his eyes.

'I apologise for bringing you straight back. I'd like to meet again in better circumstances, when you're not soaked in beer and I'm not dying for thirty-six hours non-stop sleep.' He reached into his pocket to bring out a pen and some folded paper. 'This is my number,' he added, busy scribbling. 'When you have a day off, and feel you'd like to talk to a friend of your father, give me a ring. I know a place where it's still possible to get a decent Chateaubriand, and a bottle of something special, kept for chaps like me who are prepared to do a mural or two by way of payment.' Handing her the paper, he got out, walked round to open her door and help her out, then tried to retain her hand in his. She drew it away, unwilling for physical contact.

'Don't be afraid of life,' he said softly. 'Take it by the scruff of the neck and shake it. If you can't pluck up the courage to do that, *paint* it. The good things will come shining through then, no matter how awful the background.'

In the Guard Room they stared at her damp skirt that smelled of beer, at the hole in the knee of her right stocking, and the ruined chignon beneath her cap. As the sergeant in charge gave a few pithy words expressing his opinion of her appearance which was intended to wither her into tearful insignificance, she gazed round his right arm at the biscuit tin filled with wood shavings, where a stray kitten had curled up in the warmth and security of a burly soldier's soft-heartedness. She was remembering that, not the sergeant's contempt for what he imagined she had been doing that evening, as she walked back to her hut.

The showers were not working again, so she had a quick wash in cool water, brushed her teeth, then undid all the benefits by making herself a cup of cocoa on the stove, before getting into bed with it, and sitting in the darkness hugging her knees and thinking about Gerald Bream. She had no real picture of him – in the pub she had been more intent on getting away than studying her rescuer – yet she could now see quite clearly the scene he would paint. The prostitute in old red curtains, the Australian relieving sadness with aggression, Minnie and Rob gazing at each other, even the furtive little black marketeer. She then realised it could be done in any setting and costume. It might be two Christian slaves exchanging looks of love in the lions' den, with a group of fellow victims around them; it could be Renaissance or Medieval. It could be done in oils or water colours, even monochrome. It could be a knight and his noble lady, glances meeting across an arena where jousting was about to take place. The prostitute would then be a promiscuous slave, the Australian a mysterious contender in black armour, the black marketeer a flat-footed sly pedlar of charms that did not work.

Finishing the cocoa, she slid beneath the bedclothes and put the tin cup on the floor. It was then she realised something was missing from all those versions on an original theme: the society girl who found herself out of her depth in a world of realities. There had been no obvious place for her in those mind pictures. Where did she belong? Before Felix she would surely have been the noble lady revered by the knight. Was she now the promiscuous slave? Burying her face in the pillow, she faced the fact that if she put herself into the paintings at all she would be a female eunuch.

Minnie came in half an hour later and crept about so that she would not awaken those already sleeping. When she finally got into bed, she hissed across the three feet between them, 'A fine friend you turned out to be! The boys have got jankers for the night, and I had to walk back after missing the last bus.'

'Sorry,' she whispered back.

'*Sorry!* I should have known better than to introduce Sir Bleeding Christopher's daughter to a couple of matelots. I'll get Rob to bring the ship's captain next time,' was the fierce response. Moments later, muffled sobbing came from the other bed.

Vesta made no attempt to telephone Gerald Bream. She wanted no men in her life. The meeting stayed in her mind, however, and she often thought of what he had said during the next few months, when she gradually settled into the life she had so impetuously chosen. After years of wearing good quality clothes as a young girl, then indulging her artistic flair as a student when what one wore was taken by one's fellow students to be as important as what one put onto canvas, the no-nonsense khaki uniform seemed to nullify her personality, take away individuality. As the weeks passed she realised individuality was not needed: it was teamwork that was essential now. After that, she stopped resenting the fact that they were all dressed in thick serge costumes, with shirts, ties and heavy flat shoes. She stopped rebelling against marching, taking orders from other women and the men in charge of the unit, saluting, cleaning shoes and buttons, being called Sheridan, and eating meals that had been cooked in bulk to suit all tastes and to provide the greatest nourishment from the rations.

Conditions were better than they had been during basic

training. They slept fewer to a hut, and were able to make the place homely with vases of flowers, photographs, ornaments and calendars. There were still occasional problems with the showers and toilets, but everyone now took it cheerfully in their stride, and joked about Hitler's secret weapon to undermine British womanhood. The members of Hut 4, where Vesta lived, gradually became a strange kind of family, inter-dependent and taking on inevitable rôles without realising it. A big, bluff girl called Mollie soon became 'mother', cheering them up when they were low, lending a sympathetic ear to problems, dosing them with syrup of figs when they were sluggish, rubbing them with camphorated oil when they had a chill, and filling hot water bottles to hold on their stomachs when they had a bad attack of the necessary monthly evil. Bess, who had served in her father's pub, was the clown of the group. Jean, an intense brunette who had been raised in an orphanage, could play the piano-accordian very well, and always performed at camp concerts, as well as entertaining Hut 4 whenever they felt like music. Monica, who was beautiful, was their liaison with the men on camp, and their 'agony aunt'. Minnie rallied their patriotic spirit when the news was bad, and they all wondered if the war would be lost. It was to Vesta they all turned for information. She was their encyclopaedia.

As winter turned into spring, she found the strangely assorted group in Hut 4 were better companions than her fellow students had ever been. Communal living soon dissolved poses and pretences; doing a job that was highly important did away with vanity, criticism of others, and an exaggerated sense of being on a higher plane than the rest of the world. In Hut 4 they were all equals, dressed in the same clothes, earning the same pay, governed by the same rules. They worked long hours in shifts. It was concentrated work which involved sitting at their machines to receive and send messages on everything from ration returns to vital details on moving convoys. Some days the shift would seem endless, as they passed basic lists on from various camps to headquarters. Other times, a sizzling excitement would overtake them all as the machines clattered constantly with references to a 'special consignment' or a 'priority load', moving through the unmarked roads of Britain at night for greater secrecy. One day there was a major alert, when a suspected German invasion team was spotted on the beach at East Wittering. The girls were obliged to work flat out to cope with the reports flying back and forth, and had to subdue their own rising fear as more and more confirmation came in. They all laughed heartily in relief when the 'invaders' turned out to be the local Civil Defence unit on an exercise they had neglected to report. When a final message came through from the subaltern who had led a defence platoon to counter the supposed invasion, it ended, 'Sorry girls, but thanks for splendid work. Box of chocs on its way'. They all felt ridiculously pleased with themselves. The chocolates duly arrived: a huge box with satin bows across the corners and filled with Swiss chocolates, with a note of thanks for the vital job they were doing.

They all munched the chocolates during the off-duty periods as they sat around Hut 4 darning their stockings, writing letters, or knitting socks and balaclava helmets for their boyfriends. Vesta knitted some for David. They had all fallen for the photograph she had of him, and longed to be introduced to the handsome pilot hero. All save Minnie, who was true to her Rob. He had gone to sea again without giving her the coveted ring, and she was plagued by the certainty that he would not return from this trip.

'If we had got engaged, Vee, it would mean I would have something to keep as proof of his love. Something to look at in my old age to remind me of him,' she said dolefully, after a day on which news of shipping had been bad.

'Oh, Minnie, you're killing him off mentally before anything has happened to his ship,' Vesta scolded. 'You have to believe he'll come through and that faith will probably do the trick.'

The girl gave her an old-fashioned look. 'You're not going all religious, are you? I notice you often talk about the church at home – the "family pew" and all that upper-class stuff. Don't try to convert me with ideas of "faith". God has never been anywhere near me when I most wanted Him.'

'Have you been anywhere near Him when He wanted you?'

A wry smile touched Minnie's lipsticked mouth. 'You're too clever by half, miss. But I don't think God can help, in this case. If He's got any sense, He'll keep well out of it and concentrate on the Eskimos or Pygmies for a while, until it all gets settled. Let's face it, there's British sailors and German sailors *both* asking Him to defeat their enemies and make them victorious. Even God can't sort that out. Whatever He does is bound to upset one lot, isn't it?'

Vesta laughed. 'Minnie, you're a gem! My father would find your philosophy fascinating.'

Irrepressible Minnie fluffed up her hair, saying, 'I daresay I could spare some of my valuable time for Sir Christopher, especially if your swanky good-looking brother takes after him. It'll have to be on late shift, tell him, and I'm not too keen on duck and green peas. Fish and chips'll do me, washed down with a bottle or two of Tizer.'

Vesta changed the subject abruptly. She avoided men altogether. After that disastrous evening with Mickey Boyd, she had made a firm decision and stuck to it. Men were all the same and she wanted none of them. Refusing all offers to join social outings, she was always willing to change shifts with girls who had important dates, or who desperately wanted to attend the camp dances she shunned. As her deepening friendship with Minnie led to exchange of confidences, she found herself letting rip on the subject one day when, after receiving a particularly unimpassioned letter from Rob, Minnie declared, 'I should have slept with him on his last leave. I can get him going quick enough. The reason I don't is because it seems unfair unless you mean to go all the way. I suppose he thinks I don't want to now.'

'Let him continue to think it,' advised Vesta vehemently. 'He's a nice person, Min. Don't spoil it by doing something like that.'

'Ooh, hark at the maiden aunt,' quipped Minnie. 'We don't all want to be pure and unsullied at the end of the war, when there aren't any young men left and we have to make do with grandads.' Then, seeing Vesta's face, she squeezed her hand, saying, 'Look, love, it's plain as the nose on your face some bloke's let you down. But they're not all rotten, you know. Only ninety-nine and a half per cent of them,' she finished in inimitable style. 'A girl has to look for that half per cent. When she finds it, she has to make the most of it while it lasts. I wish like anything I'd stayed the night with Rob.'

'Suppose he had made you pregnant,' Vesta pointed out stiffly.

'I'd have had something of him to keep after he goes,' came the bleak reply. 'A girl on her own without a bloke to love is like a sandwich with no filling inside it.'

Happy to be an empty sandwich, Vesta continued to avoid men as much as possible. She had to work with them, but they soon recognised that social intercourse was out where she was concerned, and left her alone. Because of that she was surprised to be told by a corporal one day to report to Miss Chalmers, their officer, because a gentleman had come to see her. Putting away the book she had been reading during her off-duty period, she put on her jacket and cap to walk over to the administrative centre. Second Subaltern Chalmers was a quiet, pleasant girl who had tried several times to persuade Vesta to take a commission, then finally accepted that she was content to be Private Sheridan doing the work she enjoyed. They were on good terms, however, and had several mutual acquaintances in civilian quarters. It was this that had prompted a summons that might not have been issued to another girl.

Although it was well into June, there was a chilly wind that made Vesta shiver slightly as she crossed the open area alongside the barrack square, and up the steps to the company office. She was told to go straight in by the sergeant in the outer office, so she knocked and entered, then received such a surprise she forgot to salute.

'*David!*'

He got up from the chair where he had been chatting with Miss Chalmers, and smiled at her. 'Hallo, Vee. How are you?'

'Fine. Whatever are you doing here?'

'I've been getting round Miss Chalmers to let you come out for a few hours with me. I think I've succeeded.'

Looking at her officer's flushed cheeks and sparkling eyes, Vesta guessed her brother had not had to try very hard for success. It was not surprising. In a uniform that was now symbolic of daring and endeavour, he looked handsome enough to sweep any girl off her feet. His thick hair shone with cleanliness, his eyes looked bluer than ever, and his square fresh-complexioned face suggested rugged dependability. Vesta suddenly saw him with new eyes. This person she had loved for twenty years, and known as a lively, humorous and loyal brother, was something entirely different to other girls. Was he ever cruel and unkind to them? Had he ever left a girl somewhere, shattered and bruised, after violating her in a cheap room smelling of kippers? Could he? Could this beloved and gentle brother do that to any girl who had fallen beneath his spell? If men were all the same, then so was he.

'Are you all right, Vee?'

She came out of her thoughts to nod. 'It's just that this is so unexpected.'

'That's why I'm prepared to give you a pass to leave camp this afternoon,' put in Miss Chalmers with a dimpled smile. 'Flight Lieutenant Sheridan is under notice of embarkation and wishes to say goodbye to you.'

Her heart sank. 'Oh, David, where are they sending you?'

'Shame on you, Private Sheridan, you should know better than to ask that, shouldn't she?' he said teasingly to Renee Chalmers, making her colour rise as he turned to face her. 'I am grateful, you know. People who say female officers are old dragons plainly haven't met you. Thanks a lot.'

142

'Have a nice time,' she said wistfully, then added, 'Get your pass from Sergeant Blane on the way out.'

Driving out from the camp beside David in a bright yellow two-seater, Vesta drew many envious glances – from girls because of David, from men because of the car.

Beginning to recover from her fey moment, she cried over the roar of the engine, 'Wherever did you get this? I thought your MG had been smashed up in that raid on your airfield, and you had neglected to insure it.'

'That's right,' he agreed, chasing the bends in the road in his usual reckless manner. 'I borrowed this one from my CO.'

'Heavens, he either has never seen the way you drive, or he's a most unusual CO,' she commented, holding her cap on with one hand and gripping the side of the car with the other.

'He's John St John Palmer,' came the clipped reply. 'His father flew in Uncle Rex's famous Arrow Squadron. Now you know why I got the car.'

'Lucky you.'

'I'd change him for Renee Chalmers any day.'

'Mmm, I guessed you two were getting on pretty well.'

'I did it all for your sake. I can't benefit from the conquest because I'm leaving at the end of the week.'

She let a few moments elapse before asking, 'Where are you being sent, David?'

He glanced quickly at her to say, 'All postings are secret, you know that.' Turning back to the road, he added, 'But it must be somewhere very warm becaue I've drawn tropical kit . . . And it must be a long way because I'm going by sea.'

'Just you?' she asked. 'Not the whole squadron?'

'Just me.'

Vesta took off her cap, as he had. It was easier than trying to hold it on all the time. They were leaving the town behind and following a road that led between orchards. Everywhere she looked there was a sea of pink and white blossoms, beneath a cool blue sky filled with small scudding white clouds. It looked so peaceful, but that was an illusion like everything else. Beauty lured one into believing it was inviolate. Into this same peaceful area each night roared the black shapes with crosses on them to destroy, maim, and kill.

'Does Mummy know you're going?'

'Not yet. I'm going down to the Hall tomorrow. I guess she'll be a bit upset.'

'Of course she'll be upset, David. She dotes on you. You will write often, won't you?'

'Haven't I always?'

'Yes,' she admitted. 'That's one of your few virtues.'

'You mean there are others?' he asked lightly.

'One or two.' After a pause, she had to say, 'What are you going to do about Daddy?'

'I've done it,' came the curt reply. 'Since there's always a slight chance that I won't come back, I thought I ought to say goodbye. I went to the apartment last evening. He wasn't there, as usual. At a conference, Sandy said.'

'So what did you do?'

'What could I do?'

'Didn't you leave a note?'

'Saying what? "Dear Father, goodbye. Yours sincerely, your son"?'

She turned on him. 'You are beastly sometimes.'

Keeping his eye on the road, he said, 'You sound like Pat. I tried to say cheerio to him. Under the circumstances I'd call it very *un*beastly of me. Anyway, I thought you were giving him the cold shoulder these days. It looked very much like it last time we were all home.'

'I'd try to say goodbye to him if I was going abroad.'

'Now we're back where we started. I tried, and he was out. Can we now drop the subject?'

She did as he asked and gazed back at the passing scene. 'Where are we going?'

'I spotted a lovely old village on the way here, with some tearooms that look just like that old photograph of the Punch and Judy in Greater Tarrant. Are you hungry?'

'Ravenous.'

'Good, so am I. I'll order the largest tea they can provide, even if it sets me back a quid. How's that for a generous brother?'

She smiled. 'Wouldn't change you for any other brother. Better the devil you know etcetera.'

'Oh, charming!'

The tea did not disappoint them. Sitting at a polished table in the bay window of an olde worlde restaurant bright with vases of over-blown tea roses, they were served with a large plate of hot buttered muffins, dainty cucumber sandwiches, and a huge Victoria sponge filled with strawberry jam and thick cream. The very young waitress with a club foot and an easy blush would have brought David the moon on a plate if he had asked for it, Vesta guessed, and she grew thoughtful again as their long conversation on her life in the ATS came to an end.

'Have you ever met a girl you really liked, David?' she asked.

He gave a puzzled frown. 'That's a funny question all of a sudden.'

'Have you?' she insisted.

'Yes. Lots of them.'

'No one in particular?'

'You sound like Mother.'

'Just now you said I sounded like Pat.'

'She's as bad. What is this fascination with how chaps feel about girls?'

'*We* are the girls.'

'Then you should be able to find out for yourselves without asking me.' As she fiddled with her knife, turning it over and back to make flashing lights on the cream-washed walls where the sun glinted through the window onto the blade, he asked, 'Are you keen on someone you met here? Don't tell me you want "Aunt Maud" to give you advice on how to find out if he feels the same about you.'

She shook her head at his knowing grin. 'I'm too busy for things like that.'

'You haven't still got a thing about Felix Makoski, have you? When we were both at home last autumn I guessed he'd bowed out rather suddenly and left you suffering the pangs of hero worship. That's all it was, Vee. He was totally unsuitable as a beau for you. We all knew that.'

'Oh, yes, totally unsuitable,' she agreed bitterly. 'He has a wife and baby in Poland. His father is a schoolteacher, still living, not a dead count. There were no mother and sisters dragged from a church by German soldiers. He lied to us all. He played on our sympathy and made fools of us, especially you, who brought him home in the first place.'

'Good God, the . . .' He drew in his breath sharply. 'Well, he won't fool anyone else. He's dead, Vee. I saw his name on the casualty lists before last Christmas. I didn't say anything to you because I thought you'd be upset. From what I heard, his squadron accounted for a number of Jerries once they were allowed up. Whatever else he was, he died fighting for Poland.'

'Well, that's where he really belonged,' she said, feeling nothing more than sympathy for a girl in a foreign country who was now a widow with a fatherless child.

'How did you find out about him?' he asked curiously.

'Daddy did some checking.'

'I see,' he said slowly. 'Is that why you've been giving him a bad time of it lately? It's a bit unfair, isn't it?'

145

She put the knife down with a sharp rap. 'Coming from you, that's rich. You haven't been decent to him for twelve years. What's so different?'

His face grew stiff. 'You're not his bastard.'

'Neither are you, you idiot.'

'Only because Grandfather and Uncle Roland got him to the altar at the end of a gun barrel. Everyone knew the reason for all the haste. Me. But in your case, he was putting himself out to protect you. He thinks a lot of you, Vee. You really ought not to be rotten to him just because he found out the truth about someone you thought you fancied. Honestly, you and Pat are as bad as each other,' he continued with a shake of his head. 'She clomps about amid the manure wearing wellingtons, and breeches that are bursting at the seams, dreaming about some man – preferably Father – offering to die for her. You read too many love stories, both of you. Men aren't like that.'

'So I've discovered,' she said with a touch of acid.

'That's no reason to blame Father.' He grinned. 'He might have saved you from the proverbial "fate worse than death" you read about in those romantic yarns.'

Touched on the raw, she hit out. 'I never thought the day would come when *you* would preach his defence to *me*.'

To her surprise, faint colour crept into his face. 'Just because I find it impossible to forgive him for what he did to Mother and me, it doesn't mean I can't see his good points – one of them being his fondness for you. He has always backed you to the hilt, and used all his influence to get you into that art school because he was certain you would justify his confidence. Instead, you threw it all up and joined the army. Dammit, Vee, you used to be as thick as thieves with him. You can't turn your back on him after all this time because he ruined your silly dreams of Felix.'

'You did it.'

'My case is different.'

'No, it isn't. You loved him for twelve years, then, just because some old fool in the village ruined *your* silly dreams, you began to hate him.'

'There's no cause for you to do the same.'

'Why? Do you hold the monopoly in hatred?'

The colour in his face deepened. 'I don't hate him.'

'You've displayed a jolly good pretence of it all these years.'

'That's not the point in question,' he said evasively. 'My feelings are of no interest to him. Yours are.'

She looked at him in amazement. 'You don't really believe that, do you? He's as fond of you as he is of me.'

146

'He didn't walk out on you.'

'You were only a baby. He was back before you were old enough to miss him.'

'Only because . . .'

'Let's leave it, David,' she said wearily. 'He's so wrapped up in his translating, or whatever it is that he does at that boring old ministry, he probably never stops to think about us, anyway. Come on, let's finish off this cake and get a jug of hot water for the teapot. We're supposed to be having a riotous afternoon out together.'

They finished their tea, and she went to the ladies' room while David paid the bill. Then they decided to walk along a pathway reached by a stile: a slim girl in khaki and a tall, broad-shouldered man in light blue, wandering through the orchards of Kent as the sun began to sink, and blackbirds poured out their hearts to each other before darkness fell to silence them. They talked about things they had done together as children, recalled family jokes and traditions, spoke of the village and characters that were the essence of life there, then of home. Inevitably, the Chandlers came into much of the conversation, and, as they reluctantly turned back after watching the sun diminish into no more than a crimson segment above the skyline, David spoke about his coming departure.

'It's through Uncle Bill that I'm going away, Vee. I asked for an overseas posting.'

Not understanding what Bill Chandler had to do with it, she asked, 'Because you want to fly again?'

'Because I can't fly.'

He went on to tell her something she found so upsetting she was glad the dusk hid the tears gathering in her eyes. Flying had been David's life from as far back as she could remember.

'Did Uncle Bill advise you to get away?' she asked, when she could.

'I interpreted his advice that way. He seemed pretty certain things wouldn't change as they were, so I thought I'd try new faces and new places. That ought to put an end to it.'

'Yes, I'm sure it will,' she agreed warmly. 'Of course it will. Uncle Bill's marvellous with those sort of problems.'

'I hope it works better than his conjuring tricks,' he said with forced lightness.

'Anything has to work better than those,' she replied equally flippantly.

They kept the mood up all the way back in the car yet, when they stood together in the blackness outside the camp gates,

Vesta suddenly flung her arms around him and burst into tears.

'Hey, what's all this?' he asked thickly. 'I thought I was the devil you knew etcetera.'

'So you are, but I've grown rather fond of you after all this time,' she said against his jacket.

Taking her upper arms, he held her away, then offered her his handkerchief. 'All the girls say that.'

Wiping her eyes she mumbled, 'You will take care, won't you?'

'Not half.'

'Write to me?'

'Haven't I always?'

'God go with you,' she said unexpectedly.

'And with you, Vee. See you at the end of the war.'

He roared away in the borrowed car, and she turned sadly into the camp just as the sirens began to wail. Another night of terror, fire and devastation in London, she thought. How did people stand it? How could a mother find her children broken and bleeding, yet carry on with the business of living? How could a man see his wife engulfed in flames within the home they had made together, yet go back to his vital job on the railways or in the factories? She remembered Gerald Bream saying, 'the good things will come shining through, no matter how awful the background'. But what could possibly shine through the holocaust created over England as soon as darkness fell?

Seeing David and talking over old times had reminded her strongly of her life prior to joining the ATS. It surprised her that that should now seem unreal, and what she was doing at present more acceptable. With even more surprise, she realised why. She had stopped taking and started giving. Instead of using the service as an escape from the disaster of Felix Makoski, she had been unconsciously drawn into the spirit of those around her. Through her job, she had become involved in other people's lives in a way she never had before. The messages that came up on her machine were from places and signallers scattered all over the country, and she passed them on to others. Yet, for a few moments, she was absolutely essential to them; she was their means of obtaining help in difficulty, reassurance during anxiety, relief in need. If, for example, she was asked to moniter the progress of a secret convoy, the messages flashing to and fro made her part of it, made her care about its safe arrival, put her in sympathy with the drivers – often young girls like herself – who were snaking their way through the countryside along dark lanes knowing the load they were carrying was highly volatile. On other occasions, when the alarm was raised over suspected enemy invaders, unexploded bombs discovered in a school playground or busy shopping centre, or the derailment of a hospital train, Vesta felt as involved in the drama as those on the spot. One one occasion, she had become so fearful for the life of a pilot who had baled out of a burning aircraft over Salisbury Plain that she had actually burst into tears of relief when, after a concentrated military search, he had been found blinded and stumbling around in circles and taken to hospital. She did not know him, she would never know him, yet she had been part of his salvation, and the experience had enriched her. Private Sheridan V.A. was a vastly different girl from Vesta Ann Sheridan of Tarrant Hall, and certainly wiser than V. Sheridan, art student and gullible fool. Six months after she had joined the ATS, she had stopped being a single person and become part of a unit. Her life was now irrevocably linked with Minnie, Jean, Bess, Monica, and Mollie, the girls of Hut 4, who had become her spiritual sisters.

Rounding the corner, she almost bumped into Renee Chalmers, who was heading towards the Officers' Mess. Peering at her in the darkness, the young subaltern said, 'Oh, it's you, Sheridan. Did you have a nice time with your brother?'

'Yes, thank you, ma'am. We drove into the country for an enormous tea. Thank you for letting me go out with him.'

'It was a rather special occasion, and your brother is very used to getting his own way, I imagine.'

Vesta smiled. 'Knowing David, he'd have promised you an enormous tea, too, if further persuasion had been needed.'

'Well, goodnight,' came the final word from the officer. 'I hope you have a quiet time on shift tonight.'

Vesta was turning away when she became paralysed by a series of sounds. First there was a concerted roar, low in the sky and approaching fast. Then came the shocking explosive echo of guns on the camp perimeter, firing simultaneously from no more than a few yards away. Next, whistles began blowing, voices shouted in alarm, and dark shapes of people began running in all directions. Still paralysed, Vesta was released from the state when a deafening thunder in the distance rocked the ground beneath her feet, and the shouts of 'Take cover' made sense.

Starting to run, panic seized her by the throat when the menace appeared to be chasing her. More thundering roars that sent shock waves through the earth below her running feet followed one after the other, getting nearer and nearer. Huge,

149

black aircraft were directly overhead now, the sound of their engines blasting her eardrums, vibrating cruelly through her head. Another, stronger series of explosions. Closer and closer to her fleeing heels. Pressure like a great wind built up to buffet her from her course. She crashed into a black, running shape.

'Get under cover, you silly bitch,' it yelled in urgent masculine tones. 'They're bombing the hell out of us.'

So saying, he caught her arm and raced her along a path to the left, his fingers deeply bruising her flesh as she was dragged at a pace that was too fast for her, until they reached a dim blue downbent light on the wall of an earth mound. Vesta was pushed so hard down the steps she stumbled, crashed onto her knees, losing her cap in the process, then found herself being pulled into the dugout by outstretched hands from within. By the low lights inside, she was vaguely aware of men and girls in khaki crowded onto the wooden seats along the sides. The smell of sour earth, sweat and stale tobacco made her feel instantly sick. She began to heave uncontrollably.

'Sit down and put your head between your legs,' commanded a clipped voice that brought instant obedience from her.

The whole place was spinning around and around. Her heart was thudding against her breast. Her knees throbbed where she had fallen on them, and she felt an uncontrollable urge to scream. A hand slid under her chin, and gently but firmly brought her head up again, the warmth of that human palm being the one reassuring thing in the whole nightmare.

'Good girl,' said that same clipped voice. 'Now suck one of these.'

A barley sugar sweet was pushed between her lips, and she sat like a slumped sack staring up at a young face with a fair moustache which she thought she should know. Letting her head slip sideways, she peered with detachment at the others there. They all looked pale, but it could have been the low lights, and all their eyes were turned upward. The ground was still reverberating with subterranean shocks. All she could think of, as fine showers of soil dropped from the roof of the shelter, was what a job it would be to get the marks from her skirt when she returned to Hut 4. It would have to be done tomorrow. She was due on duty in two hours, when the shift changed.

One of the girls began crying softly, and a man took her into his arms comfortingly. 'It's orlright, luv,' he murmured, as if to a child. 'They've gorn over now.'

The officer with the fair moustache moved cautiously out and began to mount the steps. When he failed to return, several other men went out. Their voices called in shocked tones, 'Half the ruddy camp's gone.'

Bells were ringing as fire engines and ambulances raced about the camp. The sky was a dull orange from distant flames, making it unnecessary to dim lights; the skyline was lit for miles. The guns were now silent, but whistles were blowing urgently, and there was a rising chorus of screams, moans, and hoarse shouting voices. Still hatless, Vesta walked in a daze, unable to take in what she saw. She knew about air raids. There had been pictures in the papers and on the cinema newsreels. But this was real, and it was unacceptable. She walked on, her knees protesting at every step. There was something wet on her face, and she realised it must be tears. A sudden explosion rent the air, sending bricks up into the lurid sky like a shower of child's building blocks, as one of the petrol stores went up in the path of approaching fire. Two blocks along, a clothing store began to slide out of shape before collapsing with a prolonged roar into no more than a pile of rubble.

She never reached Hut 4 because it was no longer there. Turning the corner that led to her present home, she came upon a scene she knew she would never forget. Ambulances were drawn up in a semicircle, the covers removed from their headlamps to illuminate the pile of tangled wire, wood and brick which was all that was left of the place where she and her five spiritual sisters had lived in harmony and understanding. Men were digging furiously amid the rubble, coughing and choking in the dust still rising from the debris. Appalled, Vesta watched as they brought out something that looked like a bundle of rags, and it was passed from one to the other until it was laid on a stretcher on the ground.

'Minnie,' she whispered agonisingly. 'Oh, Minnie. *No!*'

'That's five all dead,' rasped a man who appeared to be in charge. 'There's not much hope for the last one.'

'I'm the last one,' whispered Vesta with tremendous effort. 'I'm the last one. I'm the last one. *I'm the last one.*' By that time she was screaming it at the top of her voice, and faces all turned to look at this girl in torn khaki with streaks down her cheeks and dirt on her knees.

'All right, lass,' said a gentle voice beside her. 'Come over here and see Reg.'

Flinching away from the strong arm that encircled her, she stared up at a face that was familiar. It was Minnie's Rob. Whatever was he doing here? Why was he dressed in khaki? How funny it was, how hysterically funny. Minnie had been worrying all the time about Rob being killed, and the Jerries

151

had killed her instead. God was very clever. Faced with the prayers of sailors on both sides, He had solved the problem by killing Minnie. She had never thought of that solution, had she? She began to laugh, and Rob smacked her round the face. It was then she saw it was not him, after all, and began to cry instead.

Reg, whom they had wanted her to see, was in the ambulance with a white metal tray full of bottles. He had ears that stuck out, and a voice that sounded like people in American films. She sat beside him, icy cold, and shaking so much her teeth chattered. Why had God found it necessary to kill all five of her friends to solve the problem? Reg gave her something to drink, but she spilled it all down her tunic. How would she get that stain out? Where would she go to do it? What would she do it with? Everything had gone.

Then, as she stared out at that scene she realised it was not true. Caught in the beam of the vehicles' headlamps was something yellow and gold, sparkling bright against the debris of destruction. She recognised the chocolate box given to them all by a subaltern who had wanted to thank them for their help, thrown clear and miraculously intact. That box was symbolic of Minnie, Jean, Bess, Monica and Mollie . . . and Vesta Sheridan. They had been a wonderful team for a wonderful period of time. Nothing would ever eliminate that.

She drank the mixture, remembering Gerald Bream's words with clarity. If he painted this tragedy, that shining gold box would be right at the front of the picture.

Chapter Eight

'I TOLD the PM that you are amongst the most overworked men on the Home Front,' conceded Lord Moore, 'and that I am probably the biggest culprit in exploiting your extraordinary talents. I further said that he would be breaking one of the rigid rules of the game by asking you to do this.'

Chris gazed back at him steadily. 'It's not a question of asking, is it, Frank?'

'The rule that has never been broken is a rarity,' his companion went on. 'Have I ever begged favours of you without excellent cause?'

'Frequently. But I grant this is an exception. What you appear to have overlooked is that my "extraordinary talents" do not include skill at cloak and dagger activities. I am aware of what is at stake, but I'm the wong man. Subterfuge is not my game. I'm merely the referee on the sidelines.'

'Not this time, Chris. Du Vivier has to be brought over here, and you are the person most likely to succeed.'

Getting to his feet in that familiar sombre office, Chris tried to reason with the man who was asking something he regarded as preposterous.

'Two of our most experienced agents failed to bring him to England. What makes you imagine I could pull it off?'

'Because he trusts you. Because he has indicated that he will come with no one else.' A podgy fist was thumped gently on the desk. 'Think, man! He faces a highly dangerous situation. Having been a willing member of the Vichy Government from its inception, any sign that he is changing his loyalties, at a time when collaboration with the Germans is increasing, could lead to his execution. Passions are running high in France.'

'He knew that when he made his choice. I despise men who change sides when the going gets too hot.'

Frank Moore gave him a look from beneath bushy eyebrows. 'Very unforgiving, aren't you?'

'It's a family trait.'

Ignoring that, the other man went on, 'There's no proof, of course, but du Vivier maintains our agent "Bergère" intended to hand him over to a group of fanatical patriots for trial and execution, instead of bringing him to England.'

'It's possible,' agreed Chris with a frown. 'I remember "Bergère" at the school. A very secretive intense man who never smiled. However, "Milord" was vastly different. Tightly controlled with a healthy respect for blind obedience to orders. What went wrong that time?'

Lord Moore rose and went to the table holding decanters and glasses. 'An informer betrayed the network, and du Vivier had to stand by helpless while orders were issued to capture them all. Luckily, our man evaded the net and was picked up by the RAF, but it left du Vivier with a distinct mistrust of agents.' Approaching Chris with a glass of vodka in his hand, he continued his theme. 'Turncoat or no, that man has been privy to a great deal of vital information we would give anything to hear.'

'Including me?' he asked dryly.

'It's no more than a straight case of chaperoning. The people over there will do all the arranging. Your job will be to meet him and stick by his side until he gets here. There's no danger attached to it, my dear fellow.' He expelled his breath gustily. 'The PM is very grateful to you for offering your services to this vital cause.'

So it was, Chris found himself concocting his own false identity, collecting the necessary forged papers from John Frith, which proclaimed him a restorer of fine art, and preparing to go into occupied France like those he trained. Telling Frith dryly that he had no wish to be dragged from his bed by men in Gestapo uniform, for interrogation on information he himself had invented, nor did he need the services of one of the girls employed to discover if agents talked in their sleep, he was met with a typical response. Asking if Sir Christopher Bloody Sheridan imagined he was too brilliant ever to make a mistake, Frith had gone on to say that, far from sending one of the girls, he thought the test would prove more positive if a young boy undertook the task.

In a few, well-chosen sentences Chris gave his blistering opinion of men with no imagination, nothing between their ears, and an inflated sense of self-importance; who felt the world would be better off without peace, beauty and nations with widely divergent cultures. The attack would have cost him a punch on the nose, except that he declined to remove his spectacles in order to receive it. Violence was the only answer for men like Frith. Denied it, they withdrew from the lists to nurse their frustrations into something approaching hatred.

Chris glanced across the small stone-floored room at Raoul du Vivier, who was slumped in a semi-comatose condition in the chair beside the hearth, where a fitful fire gave out some warmth on a night threatened by frost. Relief filled him. After three consecutive nights of low-lying mist, which had prevented the RAF from picking them up, the Frenchman had been in such a state of nerves Chris had been obliged to administer a bromide. A coded message at the conclusion of the BBC broadcast that day had told them the operation was on for tonight, and Chris felt his Gallic companion would stand the strain of the coming hours better if artificially relaxed. In truth, the tension of the past three days had also taken its toll on him, making him jumpy, intolerant and deeply depressed. Personal experience of the work he trained others to do made it even more repugnant to someone who had devoted his life to international friendship. Lies, subterfuge, question-able loyalties, false identities, the knowledge of the price men could pay for such activities, put intolerable strain on him. This return to a country he knew and loved, to witness its people under oppression, had been heartbreaking. The reunion with a former friend who had turned into a self-centred, suspicious fugitive had been a shock.

His own words to Frank Moore had been all too true. This was not his game. He was too sensitive to accept brutality; too great a lover of beauty to see it despoiled. His personality was such that he was unable to dismiss dispassionately those things about which he could do nothing, whilst concentrating on the essential job in hand. The sight of German flags hanging in picturesque French market squares had caused protests to burn in his breast. The sound of harsh, staccato commands over loudspeakers fitted to armoured vehicles, which roamed the lanes of farming areas, was an unbearable assault on his ears. The evidence of terrified, white-faced women and children being loaded into trucks for an unknown destination had torn at his deep compassion for humanity. That Raoul du Vivier, a man whose collection of antique snuff boxes had once been his great pride and joy, could have acquiesced with such monstrous acts for so long was a cause of distress so acute, the bond of their friendship was irrevocably broken. Chris now longed for the end to this distasteful task which had been prolonged beyond expectation by the weather. Perhaps Frank

155

Moore had been right to declare there was no danger attached to it, but this delay was hatching it.

The hands of the clock crept round, whilst Chris periodically checked from the farmhouse window that the moon was still brightly shining from a clear sky. Somewhere up there, a youngster like David was risking his life to come for them. Was du Vivier worth that boy's life? Was he, himself, worth it? He held a knighthood for gossamer achievements. The first faint breath of conflict had blow them all away. He had seen the evidence in Poland, in his homeland and now here, in France. Better, surely, that one young pilot lived, rather than two mature men facing their individual failures.

The thought remained with him during the brief, tense journey from the farmhouse to the field chosen by the agent 'Felice', a young widow trained by the Free French in London, who accompanied them in the ancient car to within half a mile of the site. They walked the rest of the way cross-country, Chris and the youthful agent supporting the sleepy du Vivier until they rendezvoused with two men, who had already checked all was safe for the landing. It was a marvel of organisation and, for the first time, Chris felt something approaching gratific-ation at the evidence of successful training by his own department when the roar of an approaching aircraft was heard within two minutes of the agreed pick-up time. The agent 'Felice' flashed a torch signal and received an immediate answering signal from the aircraft, which then circled and came in to land on the runway marked by those on the ground. The downward draught blew Chris's hair across his face as the machine taxied along to the end of the field, then swung round into the wind ready to take off.

Chris propelled du Vivier towards the camouflaged aircraft, knowing speed was vital, whilst watching four dark figures climb quickly from it to melt into the shadows formed by the hedge surrounding the field. 'Felice' would take those four back with her in the car – four people coming from free England to willing danger in their homeland. Courageous souls! Pushing the Frenchman up the short ladder, Chris followed, after a brief handshake with the girl who was not much older than his own daughter. It seemed to him a gesture insufficient for the service rendered, but he had discovered that these people asked no thanks for what they did.

They were on the move almost before he had settled in the rear cockpit. A youthful, vigorous and amazingly calm voice came through the intercom from the pilot as they gained height and levelled out.

'Welcome aboard, gentlemen. Sorry about the delay, but we had some pretty duff Met. reports for the last few nights. One of our chaps tried to get over to you yesterday, but had to turn back. Couldn't see his bloody controls, much less the old terra firma.' There came a short laugh. 'Don't worry, I can see both beautifully tonight. Make youselves at home. There's a flask of coffee in that pouch to your left. Sorry it's not something stronger. Flying time around two hours ten minutes. I'll give you a shout when the jolly old white cliffs loom up.' After a short silence, he added, 'Just one thing. Apparently Jerry is mounting a big raid on London tonight, so we might have to hang around a bit before going in. I don't want to get tangled up with their operation.'

With that throwaway comment the pilot ended his speech of welcome, and pursued what was undoubtedly a frustrated ambition to be a singer with a dance band. After several impassioned songs concerning moons and Junes, he broke into a medley of those popularised by Al Jolson, who was making a comeback. Drinking the coffee in silence, Chris found himself thinking of his son, and wondering if this boy stranger who presently held their lives in his hands had a close relationship with the man who had sired him. Sharply, painfully, the truth that David could be killed at any time, with censure still in his heart, smote him anew. Was Marion right? Should he have worked unceasingly to bring about understanding with their son, instead of waiting for the boy to offer friendship when he was ready for it? Should he also have tried harder to discover the cause of Vesta's sudden animosity? He had no idea what he had done to turn such a loving daughter against him, and therein lay the worst aspect of his guilt. How could he be unaware of an action that could alienate her so totally? He poured more coffee for himself and the morose du Vivier, then hunched into his rough overcoat to pursue punishing thoughts in that dark aircraft, as it droned on, to the accompaniment of 'Nothing could be finer than to be in Carolina in the mor-or-or-ning!'

The cold was now eating into Chris's bones; the coffee had all gone. Du Vivier appeared to have fallen asleep, and the cockpit was alternating between light and darkness as drifting clouds passed over the moon.

'French coast coming up,' came the cheery voice of the pilot, who then embarked on 'Baby Face, you've got the cutest little baby face', as they flew steadily on.

All at once, the aircraft was filled with a strange rapping sound, and began to side-slip quite violently. The pilot's voice

157

broke off in mid-song to swear with fluency and imagination, as a loud roaring noise passed overhead, followed by a repeat of the rapping sound. With the aircraft performing all manner of stomach-turning manoeuvres, Chris's stunned brain told him they were being attacked. The rapping sounds were caused by bullets hitting the fuselage. Had they run into the German raiders, after all? Fear was held at bay by incredulity; the inability to believe that danger could be threatening at a time when he had believed they were safe. Again the enemy machine flashed past, guns chattering, and a sharp cry came over the intercom, followed by a string of imprecations wishing a dire fate on an enemy who risked nothing from an unarmed adversary.

Diving steeply for so long Chris feared they were about to plunge headlong into the ground, the aircraft finally pulled out no more than a few feet from an undulating silver surface he realised must be the English Channel. Their attacker appeared to have gone. Chris was severely shaken. Du Vivier was awake, wide-eyed with fright, as he clung to his seat.

'Everyone all right back there?' asked the pilot in matter-of-fact tones.

'Fine,' Chris assured him quietly.

'Sorry about that. A lone ME, who had probably lost his way, and thought he'd have sport with us. The only thing we can do is run for it. Flaming frustrating, but there it is.' After a short pause, the pilot went on, 'Don't worry about the duff engine. It'll get us there if I nurse it.'

Chris felt that whatever response he made to that would be inadequate, since it was all too audibly plain the engine was spluttering and coughing as they swayed slightly from side to side. Contact between the cockpits ceased as the youngster concentrated on trying to reach the English coast safely. There was no more singing. Chris found it additionally unnerving because he could do nothing to help the situation. What was happening up ahead? The only proof that the pilot was still there was their continuing progress, erratic though it had become. Noticing dispassionately that his Gallic companion was crossing himself in prayer, Chris concentrated on what he could see through the hood. The sea seemed dangerously close below them, and it was not the best time to remind himself he was a poor swimmer.

Despite the chill of the night, he began to sweat as the machine commenced to lurch and undulate through darkness caused by gathering cloud, which blotted out the moon for longer and longer periods. Without light it was impossible to see the water. If he could not see it, neither could the boy flying this crippled aircraft. Would they plunge into it at any minute? His pulse began thudding in his temples. He had crossed the Channel numerous times by air, yet he could not now think how long it usually took. Surely they should be over the English coast by now? Could the pilot have lost his way and be flying along the narrow waterway instead of across it? Could they possibly be going around in circles? A sudden drop in height as the engine coughed, cut out, then picked up again, had Chris sweating even more freely. How could this youngster hope to reach his destination, much less land safely? There was now an intense ache in Chris's jaw: tension had made him clench his teeth so tightly it had put the muscles of his face into spasm. It proved impossible to relax them as he continued to watch the periodic glimpses of heaving waves below, discernible only by their white spume, and to strain his eyes for the first signs of a beach or breakers against a land mass. When the pilot's voice broke into the tense silence of that tiny cockpit, he jumped nervously.

'Home in ten minutes, gentlemen. Get on the floor and put your heads between your knees *now*. It's liable to be a bit bumpy.'

It was said quietly, but there was no mistaking the strain in the voice. Joking was over. The danger was very real, and the pilot was making no attempt to hide the fact. Du Vivier looked helpless with the certainty that he was doomed, so Chris seized him and thrust him onto the floor. There, crouching beside the man the British Government thought important enough to send him to collect, Chris offered up a prayer of his own while the machine swung, lurched, and dropped in breathtaking swoops over the coastline of southern England. Through it all Chris could hear the young man guiding them in as he exchanged information with those on the ground in terse, controlled phrases.

They hit the ground with a jolt so great Chris was thrown against the side of the fuselage, and landed heavily on his shoulder almost on top of du Vivier. They careered forward with a terrible screeching of metal beneath their feet, the sound of the pilot shouting becoming no more than a faint voice in the distance. Clear thought was out of the question, and the next few minutes were no more than a jumbled impression of uncontrollable forces throwing them willy-nilly, a strong smell of burning, and intense darkness broken by flashing lights.

Bells were ringing loudly nearby when Chris realised all movement had ceased. He uncurled from his position gingerly,

159

and sat up as the hood was slid back to allow two faces to peer in.

'Are you all right, sir?'

'I think so,' he replied shakily.

'How about the other gentleman?'

Chris glanced at du Vivier. 'I think he is delighted to be in England. Simply delighted.'

They were helped out by an army of men who had manned two fire engines and an ambulance. The vehicles stood in the faint light of a clouded moon, the runway lights having been swiftly doused now they were down. Near them was the car that always collected the incoming agents with passengers and whisked them off to secret destinations. The girl in uniform stood with the door open, waiting for her distinguished passengers, but Chris left du Vivier to scramble into the car alone while he took in the scene around him. In the half-light the aircraft looked formidable, tilted on its side with one wing torn and deformed. Had he really just this minute plunged from the air to the ground in that, and survived?

Then he saw them lifting the pilot from his seat, and realised all was not well. In swift concern, he stepped across and saw his rescuer properly for the first time. With his nineteenth birthday probably still ahead of him, and a round face that hardly needed the help of a razor yet, the pilot was a slender boy with a flop of dark hair and large innocent eyes. His left trouser leg was dark with blood, which dripped steadily as they lowered him to the ground.

'Good Lord, you were hit!' exclaimed Chris sharply.

The boy managed a grin. 'Didn't want to alarm you, sir.'

'You managed to keep going against such odds?'

'Had to, really,' came the casual response. 'I'm afraid I can't swim.'

Lord Moore was considerably shaken to hear the details of a mission he had declared held no risk of danger, and protested at length that he could not be expected to anticipate German air raids, any more than he could control the weather which had delayed them in France. However, he thanked Chris for his invaluable services, and suggested he spend a few days at home before returning to work. Before catching the train to Dorset, Chris went first to his apartment to collect some things. There, he was told by Sandy that David had called to say goodbye before taking up an overseas posting, and that Marion had telephoned in a state of great agitation over a raid on Vesta's camp, hoping Chris would seek first-hand knowledge of their

160

daughter's safety. The youthful assistant had been forced to say his employer was at an important conference, and could not be disturbed.

'I rang Lord Moore, sir,' he explained, 'because I thought your son's departure overseas would be considered a strong enough reason for you to leave an imaginary conference, but he advised me to stick to the lie. However, I was able to contact General Michaels on your behalf, and reassure Lady Sheridan of Vesta's safety. David had taken her out to tea, so she was not in her quarters, which received a direct hit. Something of a lucky escape since the other five girls were killed. I thought that information was better withheld from your wife.'

Tired, with his nerves ragged from the tension of the past few days, Chris was stricken by the knowledge that David had attempted to say farewell before leaving, perhaps never to return, and Vesta could have been killed in a heavy raid. All this whilst he had been engaged in something he was forbidden to reveal to any of them. It was a sign of his exhaustion that he turned on Sandy for the first time in their association.

'I pay you to be my assistant, not to deputise for me with my family. *You* say goodbye when my son goes overseas, and *you* reassure my wife that my daughter is not dead. Small wonder they have a poor opinion of me.'

'I'm sorry, Sir Christopher. I did what I thought best.'

'Yes, yes, Sandy,' he conceded wearily. 'Forgive me. I was being very unfair.'

By the time he reached Greater Tarrant station he was hot, deeply depressed, and in need of a long undisturbed sleep. Waterloo Station had been full of men and women in uniform who reminded him of his children. Some, wearing the flashes of the Free French forces, reminded him of what he had seen over the past few days, about which he could speak to no one. All he could do was brood over the tragedy of France, and think of the courage of that young pilot who had brought them safely home. What was happening to the human race? Where had peace and love gone? Had David tried to make his peace before leaving? If Vesta had died in that raid, would love for him have died with her? Where would it all end? Had the time for beauty and gentler passions passed forever? Was there no longer such a thing as rapture such as Rex and Laura had shared? He would never feel it. At forty-four, passion was for him a thing of the past. He then realised it had died when he was twenty-one. No woman since Laura had revived it. Now it was too late, why did he suddenly yearn for an emotion he had been unaware of missing all these years? Why, after witnessing such human tragedy as there had been in France, should he feel so suddenly desperate for a relationship that would defy all the world was presently suffering? Perhaps the realisation that it could well have been his own leg shattered by enemy bullets, that it could well have been his last flight, his last moments, that made him desperate for something that had eluded him throughout his forty-four years. Life ended so swiftly. All at once, it seemed unbearably precious.

Having telephoned Marion to say he was coming, he had had to leave a message with Robson regarding the time of the train, because she was apparently somewhere on the estate talking to people whom the butler had described as 'several gentlemen from the Royal Air Force'. Thinking they must be friends of David, he had instructed Robson to tell Marion he would be with her before dinner that evening. In the event, the train had been held up on the line due to another raid, and it was well past six when he stepped onto the platform of the small rural station, where signs announcing 'Greater Tarrant' had been painted over two years before.

The flower beds edging the station platform, which had been the pride of Old Carter in Chris's youth, remained but were filled with lettuces, onions and carrots now. Old Carter had been succeeded by his grandson, Young Carter, but he had been called up, and relinquished what had become family territory to his niece, Nellie. She gave Chris a blushing smile as she took his ticket and waved the train away with her green flag.

'Good ahternoon, Sir Christopher. I knowed as you be comin' 'cos Mr Peters is outside with the pony and trap awaitin' for you. Bin 'ere some time, like, with the train bein' so late.'

'Good heavens!' said Chris. 'Peters with the trap? Where's Frampton?'

'Called up back lahst Easter, 'e be, sir. 'Er Ladyship 'ad no petrol for the car, like, so Mr Frampton went off and registered.'

'Good heavens!' said Chris again, realising how long it had been since he had been home. 'Well, I always did prefer the pony and trap. How is your uncle, Nellie?'

Her country-bloomed face beamed. 'In the desert, sir, 'e be. Can you imagine that? We got some photygraphs only lahst week, and 'e's there with a camel, and a man in a long frock, like. Funniest thing we ever see. Caused a real larf.'

Chris chuckled. 'I daresay it did.' He began walking to the white gate leading out into the lane. 'What time do you finish this evening?'

'Oh, I'll go 'ome for me tea just pahst seven when the evenin' train's gone. But I'm due back close on twelve. There's a "special" comin' through, and I got to check it, like, and signal on to Titherton Waldron that it's on its way.'

Thinking how this young country girl was helping, within her limitations, as much as the young female agents willing to face torture and death in their occupied homelands, Chris went out to greet his ageing gardener, Peters, who was ready beside the ancient trap which was his pride and joy. Rarely used in recent years, the little black and yellow carriage had been lovingly polished and maintained by Peters. He was now puffed with pride that the sleek, expensive Daimler had been reduced to a standstill through lack of petrol, whilst the old-fashioned vehicle could still run.

Saying all the right things, Chris leant back in the trap with a sigh of thankfulness. Frank Moore was right. Time seemed to have passed by this corner of Dorset. The blazing June sunshine, which had seemed so oppressive in the train, now felt wonderfully caressing as they bowled along the six miles of lanes to Tarrant Royal. He took off his cap to put on the seat beside his battledress jacket, and the briefcase containing some translating he hoped to do in the peace of his study at the Hall. The sun burnt into his face and bare arms, making him realise how much time he spent shut up in rooms these days. While he was at home, he would go riding as much as possible, and take walks with Marion and the dogs over Longbarrow Hill. He would be a fool not to take advantage of the glorious weather plus the peace and safety of the country over the next few days. Yes, he would get out into the fresh air. Maybe they would take a picnic onto Longbarrow Hill, as they used to do when the children were young. They could get Robson to set a table for two on the terrace for dinner at sunset, with the birdsong and the evening calls of the sheep as the only sounds in the blessed quietness.

Feeling the tension he had lived with for so long slowly easing to be replaced by a foolish kind of excitement, he remembered Marion saying he could be a breathtaking lover. It had been an evening such as this when he had returned, after a six-month absence, to create that night of love during which the twins had been conceived. His heart leapt with a return of the desire that had possessed him that night. He was still young and virile. Passion was not dead, surely; it had merely been slumbering. Marion would be missing David and needing comfort over both her son and daughter. He would be a breathtaking lover again. Frank Moore had also been right

163

about that. What he needed more than anything was to make love to a receptive woman. To heighten his sense of strange excitement, the smell of the briar roses in the hedgerows filled his nostrils with sweetness, and the chuckling sound of the stream that ran alongside the lane suggested a long-ago enchantment that matched the romance of that little horse-drawn carriage.

Everywhere he glanced seemed familiar, yet somehow mysteriously different. The last time he had been here, there had been Christmas frosts and holly trees in berry, a powdering of snow on the crests of the hills, and the aroma of roast goose coming from the cottages. Now, summer leaves smothered the trees, and chestnut candles were high up in the branches. Birds dashed back and forth with beaks full of food for their fledglings, and window boxes were bright with summer flowers. With cottage gardens now full of vegetables and fruit bushes, the villagers planted their beloved flowers in small boxes on their colour-washed sills. But no one could rob them of the climbing roses, wisterias, clematis and honeysuckles that rioted around doorways, and over trellis arches by garden gates. Most of the plants had been there for years and excelled themselves in glory each summer.

Over the bridge that crossed the stream and on at a spanking pace, the dainty hooves of the pony tapped a joyful tattoo as they beat on the surface of the lane. Entering Tarrant Royal, he waved gaily at those who touched their caps to him or bobbed a semblance of a curtsey. Old habits died hard in these parts, and they still respected their nominal squire. The old forge was full of activity as the blacksmith worked on repairs and the shoeing of horses, which had come into their own again now fuel was so short. The doctor's house, where Marion had been brought up, loomed on the left. But Chris's gaze was inevitably drawn the other way, to the village green, where the memorial bearing his brothers' names stood at the edge of the grass. Then there was the George and Dragon, with its oak tree reputed to be as old as the church, and the church itself, where the sun was turning the stained glass windows into winking jewels. Chris made no attempt to tell Peters to stop at the gate this evening. With what he had uppermost in his mind right then, he felt it would be out of place to salute Laura, as was his custom. Perhaps he was being quixotically foolish, but he nevertheless passed the churchyard keeping his attention on the turning ahead, which led uphill to his home.

Progress slowed as the old pony struggled with the slope, giving Chris time to take in the significance of a car with RAF

164

markings standing by his front door. Had David's friends not yet gone? He would have to send them on their way very smartly. Tonight he had promised himself things that made no allowance for guests. Peters brought the trap round beautifully to halt a few feet from the service vehicle, and Chris was so buoyed up, he vaulted over the side without waiting to open the little door to the step. He almost ran into the house, through the door that stood open, as it always did in summer, bareheaded and in shirt-sleeves rolled up past the elbows.

'Marion?' he called, heading straight for the larger sitting room.

Inside the door he pulled up short at the sight of his wife, already in smart dinner dress, entertaining three men in RAF uniform, who stood up when he entered.

'Colonel Sheridan?' asked one, looking at him with the usual air of surprise because he was not grey and bent.

'That's right.'

Marion came forward with barely a smile, and he felt quick apprehension. Was this trio anything to do with David?

'Chris, I expected you earlier,' she said. 'Dinner is practically ready. I have asked Wing Commander Molyneux, Squadron Leader Forbes and Squadron Leader Holden to stay overnight. It is so fortunate that you should have come today. It couldn't have worked out better.'

As Chris shook hands with the three men, the senior of them apologised, 'I'm not sure you'll agree with that statement of Lady Sheridan's, sir. It's very rough luck that the first evening of your leave should coincide with our call. But it will make the business easier all round, if that's any consolation.'

Conscious of looking dishevelled and extremely informal, Chris asked, 'Your visit has nothing to do with our son?'

'Nothing whatever,' came the smiling reassurance. 'Your wife has been telling us about him. A DFC, I understand. You must be very proud.'

'Yes,' said Chris, thrown off balance at the speed with which his plans were crashing down to turn to dust.

'Following in his famous uncle's footsteps, without a doubt. I had not realised, until Lady Sheridan spoke of it, that you are "Sherry" Sheridan's brother.'

'Yes, that's right,' he said again, wondering what these men wanted that required an overnight stop and the ruin of his mood.

'Chris, do go up and change,' urged Marion. 'If we wait much longer, dinner will be spoiled.'

He went, knowing the passion that had risen so quickly

during the magical drive from the station had died just as quickly. Uniforms had intruded and taken away his solitude; talk of David had taken away his wife. Youth and virility were pushed back again, into that almost forgotten side of him that had surfaced for an hour while the sun had burned his skin and fire had burned in his veins. As he went downstairs after bathing and changing into a dinner-jacket, he found the regret that swamped him was that he had not stopped at the churchyard, after all. Laura. Oh, Laura! He now felt like a traitor to her memory.

Cook had produced a dinner that had the three officers in rhapsodies of praise. Chilled consommé with a dash of sherry, fillets of fish caught in Poole harbour by Cook's brother, roast local duck with an abundance of vegetables grown at the Hall, raspberries and cream, followed by cheese from local farms. Unused to the plentiful food of country areas, the visitors grew more and more enthusiastic.

'Perhaps your cook could pass on her genius to our men, Lady Sheridan,' said Giles Holden wistfully. 'It's a long while since I've tasted such culinary delight as this.'

By that stage Chris had been told of the reason for the visit, and it sounded the death knell to his hopes for his short leave. The flying club at the far end of Longbarrow Hill was to be developed into an RAF fighter station, and the Air Ministry had commandeered Tarrant Hall for the Officers' Mess. It was the inevitable fate of large mansions – the agents' training school was another example – and Chris had known his home would have to be used for some kind of military purpose. As far back as a year ago, he and Marion had discussed the matter, and disagreed. She had suggested offering it as a hostel for children orphaned by the blitz, but Chris had drawn the line at the prospect of large numbers of youngsters running wild through valuable panelled corridors and over the lovely parquet floors, to say nothing of rendering the elegant grounds to the level of a street-corner playground. But Marion had been equally against his idea of offering it as a convalescent home for wounded officers, as it had been in the other war.

'No, Chris, please,' she had begged. 'I have to live here, and it will hold too many terrible reminders.'

So they had left the subject. Now the decision had been made for them, and it could have been worse. If David was typical, there was every chance that fighter pilots would run wild through the place, indulging in activities as frantic as orphaned children. But the grounds should be safe enough. There would be no sick and wounded to upset Marion, and maybe having youngsters in RAF uniform would make her feel closer to David.

After dinner they discussed the partition of the house, the number of the rooms, the size of the kitchens, and the probable construction of a track across the top of Longbarrow Hill for swift, direct access to the airfield. As it was getting late by then, Chris suggested that they tour the house again next morning, to discuss the final division of the accommodation. The visitors bade them goodnight and went to their respective rooms, leaving Chris alone with Marion for the first time since he had arrived home. She had been gracious but quiet during the evening, and he realised that the war was coming to Tarrant Royal again with a vengeance to destroy her beloved country peace.

He went across to her immediately, took her hands to draw her near, and said, 'Damn them for coming today, just when I have a few days' leave.' But when he bent his head to kiss her, his lips met a smooth cheek instead of her mouth. Frowning he went on, 'Don't let this upset you, my dear. We both knew it was inevitable, and we won't have to contend with the smell of anaesthetic, and bandaged men all over the lawn.'

She moved away, drawing her hands from his resolutely. 'It will hardly affect you, Chris. You are never here.'

'Most husbands are away from home, these days.'

Sitting in her favourite chair, she looked up at him with a new coolness in her eyes. 'Most men are away fighting. You are simply at your ministry in London.'

'Would you rather I was on active service?' he asked sharply. 'I thought you cried out against the idea when I first put on uniform again.'

'I did ... I do,' she agreed. 'No, Chris, you did more than enough last time.'

'So why do I detect censure in every aspect of your demeanour?' he challenged, knowing full well what the answer was.

Words rushed out in an unprecedented torrent, the force of which took him aback because it was so out of character. 'Your son has gone to a foreign battle zone. Knowing full well there is a strong chance that he might not return, he went to the apartment to offer the olive branch. You were at a meeting and couldn't be disturbed. Your son was going away, but you *couldn't be disturbed*.'

It hurt, and all he could say in defence was, 'I only discovered the fact this morning. I was very upset and gave Sandy a rocket.'

'You only discovered the fact this morning? Where have you been since last Wednesday?'

Going across to sit and face her, he tried to tell her something that was forbidden. 'I sometimes have to go away for short periods of time, for highly confidential reasons. Even Sandy has no way of reaching me then. It so happened that one of those times coincided with David's departure... and the raid on Vesta's camp. Marion, they are my children as well as yours,' he pointed out heavily.

She spread her hands in a resigned gesture. 'You have always been a part-time father, Chris. Highly confidential meetings have been a way of life for you for years.'

'Then you should be used to them,' he accused, 'and not start putting me on trial the minute I get home. I'd have given anything to have been there when David came. The long-standing misconception of me that he has had might have been banished. The chance was lost. Don't you think I deeply regret it? As for my daughter's narrow escape, words can't...' He broke off, thinking of a young girl who had also accused him of being a part-time father.

Marion leant forward to touch his hand. 'I'm sorry, Chris. We agreed never to trespass on each other's chosen way of life, never to make unreasonable demands of each other. I have kept to that agreement, haven't I? During peacetime it seemed easier, but I'm finding it more and more difficult to cope with everything alone.' She had moved forward to sit on the edge of her chair, and he noticed that a few grey hairs had appeared at her temples since Christmas. 'The estate was simple to run before the war. Clive was a level-headed, competent man who got on with his job. Now there is all the extra paperwork demanded by the Ministry of Agriculture, regular returns on yields to submit, applications and forms to fill in. He hates all that, so I do it. But he has grown crotchety over the past few months, and is forever cornering me to grumble about having too many masters. Does he work for us or the government, he wants to know, and whose land is it? So it goes on. He naturally resents men from the Ministry coming here to direct us on what to grow and where. He has become set in his ways over the years, and is finding it difficult to adjust, poor man. Unfortunately, I lose patience with him when I am up to my eyes in paperwork, and he goes off in high dudgeon, which doesn't help the general situation. Then there's the weekly meeting of the church sewing ladies. As you know, they have traditionally come to the Hall on Tuesday mornings, but the Red Cross had to change to that day for their weekly packing of parcels for prisoners of war, which is done in the old Coach House at Maundle. Some of the sewing ladies also give their services in that direction, and couldn't be in both villages at once. Tessa now plays hostess to the sewing group, though heaven knows how she manages it with her farming problems, and it means that I have to go over there for the whole day now. I go in the trap, or ride across now the Daimler is out of action. Walking takes up too much time.'

She settled back into the chair again to broach the next subject. 'I've had an awful problem with the chimneys in the west wing, where birds have been nesting in greater numbers than usual . . . and I had to get Ladbroke in to have a look at the panelling in the lower passageway. Something seems to be attacking it, Chris. Then there has been the annual business over the rabbits, only it's worse now everyone in the village is growing lettuces. Poachers are getting onto the estate from as far away as Cringe and Bethnall All Saints. They don't just bag a brace for their own benefit, they shoot them by the dozen, and sell them on the black market for a huge profit. I just don't know how to keep them off our land. They break down the fences, and cause no end of damage to the crops, then we get chastised by the Ministry for not producing our full quota.'

Chris was fighting sleep. The heavy dinner, the extra amount of alcohol he had drunk due to having guests, the long journey by train, and the lateness of the hour all made it impossible to concentrate on what Marion was saying. Passion had vanished during the requisition of his home, youth had flown under the accusations of parental neglect, ardour had cooled during details of sewing meetings, and quickened limbs had slowed to lethargy with an account of black market rabbits.

'I was used to the children being away, naturally,' she was saying, 'but wartime makes their absence a great strain. Knowing that every mother is going through the same agony, with no husband to lean on, does not lessen my personal anxiety. Sometimes I feel so alone. If I telephone you, you are never there, and I think I shall scream if I hear Sandy's calm voice saying again that you are at a conference, and can he take a message or ask you to ring back. How can I say to him that I just want reassurance from my husband, just want to hear his voice telling me that everything will be all right? How can I ask a polite assitant to tell my husband that I am reaching a point when I cannot face another form, another Red Cross parcel, another complaint from a tenant, or another night of lying awake wondering if anyone will be left alive at the end?'

She pushed her hand restlessly through her neat hair. 'I

know you must have a hundred and one important things to do, Chris, but you are not away fighting. Surely you could get home more often and take some of the strain of the estate? I suffer from the most terrible headaches. Some days I can't get up until well into the morning. Jamie Patterson has given me some tablets, but they do little good. Tessa says it's probably my eyesight, but I haven't had time to get into Dorchester to the optician. Perhaps I can now you're here. How long are you staying?'

Chris struggled up from the comatose state into which he had been sinking, lulled by the sound of her voice during an uncharacteristically long speech.

'Until the end of the week. Look, if the estate is proving too much, we'll get another man in. If you remember, I suggested it some time ago, but you insisted that you preferred to run it with just Clive Hudson, and by no means found it too much.'

'Chris, that was three years or more ago,' she cried.

'Was it?'

Getting to her feet, she sighed as she looked down at him. 'From the slant of your eyes behind those spectacles I doubt if you heard half I said to you just now. Let's get to bed.'

Lying in his bed, four feet from Marion's, where she, having swallowed three tablets to ward off her headache, was telling him about the Rector's decision to hold a memorial service for the crew of HMS Hood, of which Mr Anderson's twin sons had been members, Chris found a lump forming in his throat. He had come home seeking some sweetness in the midst of exhaustion and despair. Was it nowhere to be found? Not even with the girl with whom he had made a pact to build a future together that would override all else? Marion was slipping away from him. Or was it he who was slipping away? He fell asleep and dreamed of Vesta being parachuted into enemy territory, where she was tortured by men in the hated uniform because he had sent her off with nothing learned.

The following morning he was awakened by Robson with the tea, still feeling the need for sleep. Marion sat up with a groan, declaring that the headache had arrived, despite taking the tablets given to her by the village doctor. It was a glorious morning of hazy hillside mists, dew-trimmed cobwebs strung over the shrubs, and pure symphonies of birdsong. Chris stood in his silk pyjamas at the window while he drank his tea. The air was sweet and gentle against his face. The rose garden was at its very best now with the velvety half-open buds jewelled with dew diamonds as he gazed down on it. The heavy scent of the blooms was already rising on the hot air to charm him, and a

170

family of twittering tits rushed hither and thither as the fledglings pestered their exhausted parents for food. Raising his eyes from that enchanting sight, Chris saw a pair of squirrels chasing each other in sexual exuberance all over the widespread branches of a huge horse chestnut tree down by the pool. Sure-footed madcaps, they leapt and raced, scattering blossom and loose leaves to float to the ground.

It was so peaceful. Putting his cup and saucer on the sill he leant against the window frame with a sigh. Distantly, from the kitchen area, came the sound of clattering crockery and female chatter, as Cook and the girl who helped her (Chris could never remember her name) prepared the breakfast. The faint echo of the wireless in Robson's room joined the household serenade, which itself formed the gentle background to birdsong, the noises made by bossy cockerels and distant sheep, and the rustling of branches as squirrels played. All at once, the longing of the day before returned, and he swung round to his wife.

'Let's take the horses over Longbarrow Hill before breakfast.'

She looked back at him reproachfully. 'With this headache? Oh, Chris, I really couldn't. It promises to be a beast.'

'Sorry, I had forgotten,' he said.

'You go.'

He shook his head. It needed two for the kind of delight he had in mind. 'Take it easy there for a while, then we'll have breakfast on the terrace together. It'll be like old times.'

'We have three guests here, my dear, to discuss the taking over of our home.'

He punched the sill gently. 'Hell and damnation!'

'Chris, what's wrong?' She patted the bed. 'Come over here a minute.'

Remaining where he was, he said, 'I came home hoping to have my wife to myself, but it appears she is entertaining half the Royal Air Force, packing parcels for the Red Cross, and sewing in company with the entire population of two villages.'

She absorbed that for a moment before saying, 'There are many times when I would give anything to have my husband to myself. Last week, for instance. You haven't been home for six months, Chris. I can't sit here in a vacuum waiting for the times when you suddenly turn up.'

She looked quietly attractive in a nightdress of pale lemon silk with a v-neck and modest puff sleeves, as she sat back against the pillows with cup and saucer in her hand. They had led separate lives by mutual agreement because their personalities were so different. It had worked well; they had

171

both been contented. But that word *content* mocked him now. Why was contentment suddenly not enough? Why did the summer morning outside the window excite unbearable longings? Why did Marion's description of himself as a breathtaking lover challenge him? Why, as he looked at his wife in her neat nightgown, sipping her tea with serenity, and reproaching him for not being on hand to comfort her over their children, did he remember a day long ago when snowflakes had criss-crossed madly outside Laura's window, while she had toasted bread by the fire for him, the glorious red of her hair glowing in the flickering light from the flames?

'What is happening to us, Marion?' he asked quietly.

'Our children are now caught up in something we once experienced and we are powerless to stop it hurting them. That is what is happening to us. The only answer is to keep busy, I suppose.'

He turned back to the view from the window. Did Marion never think of him as anything other than the father of their children?

'Chris, please write to David and try to excuse your failure to meet him before he left.'

'Yes,' he murmured, back in that snow-bound room with Laura.

'And to Vesta. I detected that all was not well between you two lately. I don't think you should be off-hand with her just because she abandoned the artistic career you had set your heart on for her.'

'I don't blame her for that. Any off-handedness has been instigated by Vesta, not me. She hasn't written to me since joining the army.'

'Well, dear, I don't suppose she has much time. She is working very hard at all hours of the day.'

Before he knew it, he had put down the cup and saucer, taken up his dressing gown, and walked from the room without another word. But his intention to go riding was thwarted when, dressed in breeches and a silk shirt, he was met downstairs by his three guests, who began eulogising anew about the house and grounds. Robson, seeing that they were all gathering, asked if he could serve breakfast. Chris had no option but to say yes. Marion descended and glanced with perplexity at him, before becoming the gracious hostess.

Discussions on the forced annexation of two-thirds of their home, the conditions of the transaction, and the legal obligations towards compensation for any damage to property or grounds caused by the Royal Air Force lasted the entire

172

morning. The three men declined the offer of lunch, saying they had to push on to the site of the proposed airfield to talk to constructors due to arrive at 1.30 p.m. with plans for the erection of hangars and temporary hutted quarters for the airmen. Chris, still in his restless mood, told Robson to serve lunch on the terrace, but Marion stated her intention of foregoing the meal, in order to lie down in a darkened room in the hope of dispelling the headache which the concentrated discussion had worsened.

Alone at a table in the garden where he and his brothers had tumbled and played, Chris found his heart so heavy he left the meal practically untouched to wander, his hands in the pockets of his old flannels, through paths that revived a hundred different memories. Halting at the far end of the formal gardens by a low wall, he vividly recalled sitting there with Rex on the afternoon of his marriage to Marion, and saying desperately, 'I just don't know how I'm going to face the next sixty years,' and Rex replying, 'Try taking them one at a time. Turn what you do have to good account, and forget what might have been.'

Chris's gaze rested blindly on the deep valley below, where sheep drowsily grazed on the slopes, and the straggle of thatched roofs in the cleft between them marked the winding lane through the village. He honestly believed he had turned to good account what he had. The estate had prospered over the years between the wars – mainly thanks to Marion's management. He was respected in the world of international affairs, and had earned a knighthood in recognition of his work. He had two attractive and talented children, who were making their mark on the word as free and independent spirits. He had a wife who had been the perfect foil for his rare personality all these years. He had faced twenty-six of those sixty years he had spoken of to Rex. What now caused him to view the remaining thirty-four as a desolate journey to old age?

Robson appeared at his elbow, bringing him from his reverie. 'I am sorry to disturb you, Sir Christopher, but Lord Moore wishes to speak to you on the telephone. It appears to be a matter of some urgency.'

'Tell him I'm out riding. Anything. Take a message and say I'll ring him back this evening.'

The old butler's face looked more sorrowful than ever. 'Regretfully, I have already indicated that you are in the garden, sir.'

He sighed. 'Very well, Robson. I suppose it must be urgent for him to ring when I'm on leave.'

Setting off up the path once again, he cursed Bell for being so clever. How much more peaceful life would be without the telephone.

'Developments, as we feared, Chris,' came Frank Moore's booming voice over the line. 'Hitler has gone into Russia with over one hundred and fifty divisions, and massive air cover. Initial surprise has allowed him to sweep in so far, and fan out over so widespread an area there's no stopping him now. The Russians are in a panic. There are to be talks here, and the Poles are none too happy. I'll need you. Don't rush back this afternoon. Take the morning train. That'll give you time to do those translations I gave you yesterday.'

'Frank, I'm on leave,' he pointed out.

'Not any longer, old chap,' came the typical reply. 'Sorry, but you shouldn't be so bloody indispensable.'

The translations took him until dinner time. He had a shower, changed into his dinner jacket, then went down to join Marion, feeling jaded and lethargic. The heat had not lessened, and the evening air was undisturbed by the slightest breeze. Marion's headache was lingering. He could tell by the way a small frown marred her normally smooth brow. She was full of anxiety.

'Chris, what does this news mean?' she asked, as he poured her a glass of madeira and walked over to her with it.

'Quite a lot. Some good, some bad. Basically it indicates that Russia is certainly going to become an ally, and having German troops in the eastern sector of Europe means pressure must ease on the western front. Hitler has a large, well-equipped army, but it is not inexhaustible. The larger the area he tries to control, the weaker his campaigning ability becomes.' He stood before her chair, sipping his sherry and looking down at her. 'At this stage, there is little hope of stopping him invading any country he chooses. All we can do is wait until he has taken on far more than he can hope to control, then attack him in his weakest area.'

She looked up at him in distress. 'How long will it be before that happens?'

'Quite a long while, my dear, I'm afraid. This war is certain to last considerably longer than the last one. It's far more widespread, and his initial successes have been far more devastating. Being driven completely from Europe was the worst blow for us. We somehow have to get back into France, and with massive numbers. At present, we have no hope of that, unless the Americans decide to come into the war.'

'Will they?'

174

He shook his head. 'They are very prosaic people, not given to quixotic gestures as we are. Quite rightly, they have no wish to kill off an entire generation and beggar their country because a madman is rampaging throughout Europe. Hitler is no real threat to them.'

'He will be if he ever takes this country.'

He shook his head again. 'There's still the Atlantic. Even Hitler couldn't mount an invasion of America. No, Marion, the Americans are committed to peace, and are holding out for it. I'm the first person to approve their stand.'

She put down her glass with force. 'There are times when I find you totally inexplicable, Chris. Your son and daughter are risking their lives for their country and for freedom, yet you stand there saying you applaud the Americans for lifting no hand to help us.'

'They are,' he countered. 'Without their supplies of arms, machines and food, we would have gone under long ago. They are sending us vital convoys.'

'And lining their pockets,' she said bitterly.

He sat down beside her. 'This estate prospered from the sale of vital foodstuffs during the last war. Under Tessa's management all the money Father lost was recouped. Of course some people make a profit from war, that's inevitable. No doubt the Supermarine company is doing very well from the manufacture of the Spitfire. Do you condemn them? David certainly would not.'

'I'm not so sure.'

'Whatever does that mean?'

'Really, Chris, you know nothing of what is going on in your own family. If you concentrated a little less on the admirable qualities of the Americans, you might be aware that your son is in the deepest despair because every time he climbs into one of those Spitfires you praised, he is overtaken by involuntary paralysis and can't take it off the ground.'

Chris was shocked. 'Still?'

'Bill says it's a subconscious belief that his entire squadron thinks he shot down that poor American deliberately, because they didn't get on together. David has...' Here her voice broke, shocking him even more because she rarely cried. 'David has deliberately requested that overseas posting in the hope of solving his problem. He could have stayed here safely behind a desk, but...' Her shoulders began to heave, and she put her face in her hands. 'God knows if I shall ever see him again. If you had just talked to him! You've been through it and know what it's like. If you had made an effort to discuss it with

175

him, the problem might have gone away, or at least plagued him less.'

He sat looking at her bent figure, feeling that loneliness creeping over him again. 'If Bill couldn't give him any more help than to simply identify the cause, then David is the only one who can help himself to fly again. Don't hold me responsible for sending him away from you. You know perfectly well I am the last person he would come to for help, and he would certainly never discuss anything as personal as that in my presence.'

She looked up then and charged him wildly. 'Aren't you appalled by that admission? You are his father.'

'No, Marion, he decided at the age of twelve that he no longer wanted that relationship with me.'

'He was only a boy.'

'I was not much more when the whole affair happened, the event he can't forgive. Or thinks he can't. If you asked Bill, he'd say David's feelings for me are comparable with this flying thing. The boy himself is the only one who can put it right in his mind.'

She stood up angrily. 'How typical of you to refuse responsibility.'

Getting to his feet slowly, he faced her. 'What do you mean by that?'

'That's why he can't forgive you, Chris. Can't you see that? You ran away from us, abandoned all responsibility for your wife and son. You have been doing it ever since by involving yourself in those endless stupid committees and conventions for world peace. Do you think I haven't been aware of that?'

He stared at her, deeply shaken. 'After all these years, Marion? When we cancelled the divorce proceedings, we agreed to put the past behind us and never refer to it again.'

'It's been there, though, hasn't it? To smother it you've had your precious work; I had my wonderful children.' She brushed her cheek impatiently. 'You still have your work, but my children have gone. It would never occur to you that I have nothing left but good works in the village. I sit here day after day thinking. I'm forty-four, starting to get grey hairs and thickening hips. The miscarriage of the twins meant the end of child-bearing for me; your frequent absences meant few demands on me as a wife. Vesta has always been introverted, slightly secretive and artistic, like you. But David has been especially close. We have a bond you wouldn't understand. All the time he was here, none of the other things mattered. Now he has gone away, I'm aware of being middle-aged, bound hand

and foot by the demands of the estate, and regarded as the doyenne of philanthropic activities in the village.'

Still staring at her, he said, 'He's bound to go one day – marry and have his own family.'

'That won't be losing him. I'll gain a lovely daughter-in-law. And there'll be the grandchildren.'

'I see,' he said reflectively. 'Do I come second, third after Vesta, or way down below the lovely daughter-in-law and grandchildren in your table of affections?'

It was her turn to stare. 'That's an irrelevant question.'

'I don't think so.'

'You are my husband.'

'And?'

She took exception to his tone. 'And you are rarely here.'

'You are rarely at my side, as a wife should be. It was your decision – one which I have respected – to stay here rather than share the London apartment with me.'

'You know why. I had the children.'

'You had *David*,' he said heatedly. 'All these years it has been him you have really lived for. Even your daughter pales into insignificance beside the brightness of David. I hope to God you never lose him, because you've left yourself nothing to fall back on.'

A rustle at the door heralded Robson to announce that dinner was about to be served. They ate the meal in silence, then Marion went straight up to their room leaving Chris to brood over a quarrel that had apparently been left in abeyance for years. The sense of inevitable loneliness, increased to unbearable proportions by this revelation that his solid marriage had such deep and widening cracks, led him to start drinking as a means of dulling his emotions. It was not in his nature to indulge in this universal method of obliteration, but he sat determinedly downing large quantities of vodka as the hours wore on. Perversely, the more he drank the worse his sense of isolation grew. The distant sound of anti-aircraft fire from the direction of the coast added to the feeling of having gone around in a circle to end up where he had started.

Quite when he first became aware of the sound he was not sure, so deep in morbid reflection was he. But it grew so loud, it penetrated even the vodka-clouded muzziness of his brain, and brought him to his feet and onto the terrace to look upward in alarm. It was an incredible sight. No more than a few feet above the house, a long, dark shape was gliding through the moonlit sky to the accompaniment of a deafening roar. With clear thought suspended, he gazed at that flying shape, dark at the nose but an inferno of yellow and orange trailing flame at the rear, as it passed over his head, just missed the row of trees that marked the edge of the long driveway, and plunged beyond his view onto the village below.

Chris was already running when a deafening explosion shook the night, and vivid orange light bloomed in the sky to illuminate the stables adjoining the house, setting the horses squealing with fear. Pushing his way through the rhododendrons, he began to slither and slide down the wooded slope that provided a short cut to Tarrant Royal, his heart thudding against his ribs, and his head thick from the effects of unaccustomed heavy drinking. As he ran, he took in the direction of the fire from glimpses between the trees, and realised the aircraft could not have missed the village. The vivid glow, the sound of human shouting, came from very near by. Dear God, where had it crashed?

Out of breath, dry-mouthed, and filled with all manner of fears, Chris broke through into the lane and pounded along level ground towards the hideous spectacle of a silhouetted aircraft tail rearing up against the clear moonlight as flames leapt and roared around it. The heat from the wreckage grew, and ash flew into his eyes and throat. As he rounded the corner by the George and Dragon, he pulled up, his chest heaving from effort, and his spectacles misted by perspiration. Snatching the tortoiseshell frames from his face, he frantically polished the lenses to replace them and discover the truth of the blur, which was all he could see with the naked eye.

It was a sight he would never forget. The flaming aircraft had dived straight into the beautiful seventeenth-century church, penetrating the ancient roof to lodge there, with the tail bearing the black cross of the Luftwaffe angled upward beside the cross of Christianity on the spire. The church was alight from end to end, as if the world's supply of candles had been lit in praise of the Lord. The ancient pews, the lovingly embroidered hassocks, the altar cloths, the hymn books piled in readiness, the old plaques on the walls, the organ dating back several hundred years were all being destroyed before his eyes. There was no question of trying to rescue the enemy pilot. He was as much a part of the inferno as those who had been laid to rest there centuries before.

With a fresh rush of noise, the roof of the church collapsed, taking the German fighter with it. Flames, debris and ash flew up into the air, and those who were standing around in a state of shock, their faces still and yellowed by flames, all moved back instinctively. The shouting died away. One by one, fresh observers arrived on the scene to stand in silent awe with the rest as the fire consumed their place of worship that had stood through three centuries of a nation's life and was now vanishing in minutes by the hand of a long-standing enemy. An entire village had been saved, but its root had been lost that night.

Time went past unheeded as the church died. Chris realised he was shivering when the bright yellow and orange glare faded to no more than a dull crimson glow within the blackened shell. Only then did he move forward like a man in a daze and start to cross the singed grass of the churchyard, where ash and debris lay piled and smoking, and where the magnificent stained glass windows lay twisted, blackened and half-melted. He somehow knew, before he reached the spot, what he would find. Even in that far corner, destruction had reached out its terrible fingers. The grave itself was littered with charred remnants; of the headstone there remained nothing save a ragged foot of marble. He wandered heedlessly by the light of the clear moon until he found what he was looking for. There were just two large pieces. The rest must be somewhere amidst the rubble. With immense tenderness, he struggled to fit together the two pieces so that they made sense. But all he read was:

LAURA SHERI
Killed by enemy actio
Loving and beloved wife o
Brilliance lasts but a short wh
The afterglow remains forever

As he knelt there looking at the broken testament to a girl he could not forget, it blurred beneath his sudden, uncheckable tears.

Chapter Nine

AUGUST 1941. The war had been a reality for almost two years. Twelve months ago David had been battling in the skies above England's south-east coast, in the desperate fight to save the island from being invaded by the enemy. That battle had been won by a near miracle, and at the expense of many men's lives or minds. That battle still haunted David's dreams. It still kept him on the ground.

Yet, in Singapore, the British wallowed wealthily in the precious unreality of gin slings, weekends spent at the Yacht Club, and tea dances at Raffles Hotel. The men dressed in beautifully cut tropical suits, and went about their business in chauffeur-driven cars that were washed and polished after every journey by an entire army of 'boys'. For journeys under half a mile they sat languidly in a rickshaw, pulled by a runner in a great plaited-straw conical hat. Their offices were cooled by huge, circling fans, and blinds to lower over windows during the hottest part of the day. Work usually began by eight in the morning and ended at one in the afternoon. The more industrious occasionally returned at five to put in two hours of essential industry, but more often than not the main business of the day was conducted over sundowners on the verandah, or dinner at one of the prestigious clubs during the long slumberous evenings.

The 'memsahibs' of Singapore were roughly divided into two groups: those who were defeated by the climate and the boredom, and those who fought back by determinedly playing tennis, golf and any other energetic pastime, and filling their days with good works and social commitments. All new arrivals, especially male ones, were noted and fought over.

After a journey by sea and air, during which he had relaxed, David had arrived at the green exotic island that was a world within a world. He had acquired a deep golden tan; getting away to a fresh start had brought a return of his former breezy attitude to life. So, observers watching him disembark after the last leg of his trip saw a strikingly good-looking young officer in tropical uniform that enhanced his smooth golden skin, clear blue eyes, and thick blond hair, bleached even fairer by the sun. A physique like an athlete, a smile that began slowly and widened into a warm, slightly impertinent greeting, and the clean-cut, inbred manner of the British upper classes marked him down immediately for membership of all the right clubs, entrée into the premier houses on the island, cards of invitation for tennis parties, and as a sure candidate for the beds of those pretty enough to catch his eye.

Observers would have been astonished if they had been told the nature of the new arrival's thoughts during his first days in Singapore, and would have found it difficult to understand that he was deeply disappointed. Coming from another small island that was being blown asunder night after night, its people restricted to basic rations of essential foods, and infrequent portions of luxuries for which they had to queue with no certainty of being successful, where homes like his own were being commandeered for military purposes, David could not easily accept what he saw in Singapore. Were they so out of touch? They had letters from those at home. They always spoke of England as such, yet most of them had not seen it for years.

His biggest disappointment was professional, however. A desperate bid to master his problem had led him to use family influence to gain an overseas posting, where he hoped distance from his old squadron would be all that was needed. If Uncle Bill was right in his assertion that it was due to a subconscious belief that they all held him responsible for deliberately killing Enright, putting a whole world between them and himself would surely put things right. But the tiny airfield on the south side of Singapore was more like a private flying club than an RAF fighter squadron, as he knew it. The men manning it appeared to have succumbed to Singapore-itis.

No one had met him at the docks, and he had been rescued by a pert young girl in a green shantung dress and a topee, who had offered him a lift to his destination in her open car driven by a turbanned Sikh. Assaulted by the incredible humidity, he had gladly accepted, then been astonished by the speed with which the girl had let her hand fall, apparently unconsciously, onto his thigh, where, carried away by the enthusiasm of her verbal introduction to all they passed along the way, it moved up and down in breathtaking manner, stopping just short when his bemused mind believed she was about to undo his buttons. However, he was still fully clothed when he was deposited at the Officer's Mess, and the girl drove off after extracting a promise that he would visit her very soon for an overnight stay at her father's air-conditioned house on the north side of the island.

There was a two-day public holiday, so the Mess was deserted. He ate dinner alone, then walked out onto the verandah to stare at the small field containing open-sided sheds that served as hangars, a tiny wooden building with a verandah that was the Squadron Office, and no more than six Hurricanes – aircraft he thought inferior to his beloved Spitfire – standing neglected on the grass. He stood for a long time in the darkness of the verandah, being bitten savagely by mosquitoes, studying that distant scene, illuminated by the lamps on the corners of the flimsy sheds, sensing that he had crossed the world unnecessarily. His posting with the squadron was as a desk-bound administrator, but he had hoped to change that once he had successfully taken a machine off the ground. If the air of neglect and disuse was anything to go by, he had made one of the greatest mistakes of his life by wangling this posting. It had not been his aim to evade his problem, but to confront and overcome it.

He went to his room, had a shower, then sat in his underpants to write letters to his mother and Vesta, telling them how happy he was, and what a wonderful and interesting experience it was turning out to be. The parting from his mother had shaken him. He had not anticipated how upset she would be. Normally very self-controlled and capable, she had gone to pieces when he had kissed her at Greater Tarrant station, and clung to him in a very embarrassing manner. Her distress had put notions of guilt in his mind, and all he could do now was keep her supplied with letters that would assure her he was well and safe.

His introduction to his commanding officer was a further shock to his hopes. Squadron Leader Winterbottom was a man of middle height and built like a bull, with a round baby face, pale eyes and receding sandy coloured hair. His accent and manner betrayed coarseness. After watching David's smart salute with bemused derision, he leant back in his chair so that the buttons of his sweat-stained shirt strained across his bloated belly.

'You arrived at the wrong time, you poor bugger,' he began in friendly tones. 'There are any amount of public holidays out here, you know. What with the Malays, the Indians and the Chinks, there's hardly a week goes by without some religious celebration. Sorry you weren't met, and all that, but we always go off to the hills around this time of the year. The flaming heat gets to you after a while. You slow up, start to find your wits are addled. That's when it happens.'

'What happens?' asked David, already disliking the man.

'The rot sets in.' The pronouncement was accompanied by a gusty laugh. 'If the drink doesn't get you, the slant-eyed whores do. You'll find a list of safe drinking places and clean brothels in the Mess Rules.' He flicked an assessing glance over David's smart shorts and open-necked shirt. 'You're one of the lucky ones. You'll get all you need from colonial wives and daughters, if you play your cards right. It's easier on the pay packet – unless you prefer the superior eroticism of native girls.'

'How about station routine?' David asked doggedly. 'I've done a useful few hours in Hurricanes, but my combat flying has all been in Spitfires.'

Alan Winterbottom narrowed his eyes and reached for a blue file lying in his 'In' tray. 'Sit down, David. Let's have a chat, shall we? My dear old dad was in the last war and got the lot – gas, shells, machine guns, bayonets. I remember him coming home on leave looking like a white-faced trembling automaton.'

David faced him from the chair on the other side of the desk. 'I'm not sure what this is leading to.'

Winterbottom smiled, showing uneven teeth. 'Nephew of the great "Sherry" Sheridan, son of a titled public figure, whizz Spitfire pilot who earned the DFC during the Battle of Britain. Why would a man like that be sent to a backwater outfit like this to sit behind a desk? Sticks out a mile, doesn't it?'

Tensing, David said, 'I wasn't *sent*. I asked for this posting.'

The man nodded approval. 'Wise move. Doesn't do general morale any good to see men of your calibre crack up. This is the ideal place for you to see out the rest of the war.'

He flushed darkly with anger. 'I did not crack up. If it says that in my report, it's untrue.'

'Doesn't need to be said in the report, does it?' The CO frowned. 'Don't start getting hot under the collar, old chap, it's too flaming hot here already. Look, a DFC speaks for itself. I admire any man who holds it. But the best of us can only take so much. It's perfectly understandable, and I'm sure all the boys in the squadron feel the same. You shouldn't have any nonsense with them.'

'Oh, God... You mean they all think I'm a wreck?' he cried.

'At times they appear to be no more than large lumps of flesh running to grease, but they can put two and two together like me. So long as you're chummy, and don't try to put over the old school tie hero act, you'll get on fine with them. But I should warn you of one thing. We only have six aircraft – the parts for the rest are supposed to be on their way to us from God only knows where – and eight pilots. If you want to avoid being stripped, thrown into the Rochore Canal – an unbelievably filthy stretch of waterway – and left to run the gauntlet of Singapore women stark naked on the way back, avoid making any mention of your flying experiences. You are with the squadron as an earth-bound wallah. Remember that, and all will be well.'

The confidence that had buoyed him up from the moment the posting had come through collapsed with sickening speed. Even without the CO's strictures, a squadron with six operational aircraft and eight men squabbling over them meant death to all his hopes. The officers were a mixed bag of men from Britain and the Commonwealth with no battle experience, who all plainly believed he had lost his nerve and used influential connections to get a 'cushy number' until the end of the war. Sensing that he had gone from one group of critics to another, the feeling of desperation that had dogged him in England worsened, with the additional torments here of a punishing climate, hordes of mosquitoes, prickly heat all over his body, and the new arrival's usual introduction to dysentery. Unable to feel at ease with his fellows, he was equally unable to immerse himself in work to dull his misery. Apart from telephoning for Met. reports, and deciding which men should take up whichever of the aircraft were in working order for the twice-daily routine patrols, there was nothing else for him to do. Occasionally, one of the pilots would take a machine up-country on a social call – something David vigorously questioned until told to mind his own bloody business – and pilots from squadrons in Malaya would return the calls. For most of the time, however, the Hurricanes stood on the ground beneath the shade of the rattan roofs, or lay about in pieces while repairs were done, with the lethargy of the East.

Day after day he stood at the open window of his office and gazed at those aircraft, while he remembered the chill thrill of those three months of incredible cameraderie with youngsters like himself: the constant scrambles; the wheeling, soaring machines, the MEs on his tail, the excited voices over the R/T, the rattling guns, the elation of danger evaded; that matchless feeling of achievement coming in to land, exhausted, tattered and bloody, but triumphant. He would give anything to be doing it still, with a crowd of blaspheming, rowdy, hard-

184

drinking gods of the air. That was where he rightly belonged. He had crossed the world to prove it, and was being denied the chance. The men of the squadron squabbled enough over the machines already. If he attempted to take one up, there would be eight men jumping on him to deliver a fate worse than the Rochore Canal. But it did not stop him from gazing at those aircraft and eating his heart out.

Something approaching friendship did develop between himself and a young New Zealander, however. Ian Freemantle had been raised on a large sheep station, and often sat with a beer during the long sultry evenings, talking to David about farming in his homeland compared with England. David told him of the pedigree flock that had been built up through Tessa Chandler's experience of sheep farming in Australia in her youth. Young Pat appeared to enter the conversation a great deal, and one evening Ian said, 'She sounds like a real nice girl, with a lot of commonsense.'

David nodded. 'Except when it comes to men. She's waiting for one to come along who is prepared to die for her.'

'What's she look like?' came the inevitable question.

On the verge of saying, 'Fat and rude with health,' David stopped and really thought about the girl who was like a second sister to him. How would another fellow see her? 'She's pretty, in a straightforward, countrified way. Short hair so dark it's almost black. Plump... but goes in and out in all the right places, I suppose. I've got to admit, she has really nice eyes, an unusual silvery green like her mother's, large and very expressive.'

He fell silent for a while, gazing at the huge silver moon hanging in the sky, and thinking of Pat's father who had told him he had to sort out his problem himself.

'What wouldn't I give for someone like that here with me now,' mused his companion. 'The girls out here are nothing but tits and tattle. You can't sit and relax with them. They don't want to talk, and if you go for a stroll along the beach, they have you flat on your back with your pants down before you know what's hit you.' He sighed. 'I miss my folks, and I miss the sight of a green valley covered with bloody great woolly sheep. You can keep banana trees, flaming great palms, the stink of durians and drains. Let me return to a homestead at the back of beyond, and cool fresh air.' He sighed again. 'Do you think she'd answer if I wrote to her?'

'Who?' asked David, who had been developing a theme of his own.

'This girl Pat, with the expressive eyes.'

185

'Good Lord, I don't know. She'd be surprised... but the sheep connection might swing it. She's crazy about farming.' He sucked his lips thoughtfully, and added, 'Unfortunately, she's also crazy about my father.'

'Your father!' exclaimed Ian into the heaviness of the night. 'Is she the sugar-daddy type, then?'

'No. He's young... And he's far too good-looking to be a dry stick who wouldn't notice Dorothy Lamour if she walked past him without her sarong. Pat feels sorry for him.'

'Because he wouldn't notice Dorothy Lamour?'

David shook his head, regretting having said so much. 'Because he doesn't notice her, I expect. I'll give you her address. Perhaps you could get her mind off my old man. Send a photograph of Gary Cooper and say it's you. As you stand, I don't think you have a chance against her hero.'

'Oh, I don't know. I was the best looking guy at High School.'

'You haven't seen my father,' said David shortly. After another silence, during which they finished their beer and gazed at tropical enchantment that somehow failed to enchant them, he asked tentatively, 'If I give you Pat's address, will you do something for me?'

The youngster beside him said laconically, 'Oh yeah, here comes the payoff.'

'I want to have a shot at flying one of those Hurricanes. I've done twelve hours in them, although most of my operational flying has been done in Spits.'

'Oh no, mate,' came the instant protest. 'You want to get me a court martial, or something worse, from the lads here? Suppose you crash the flaming thing. Who'll get the comeback?'

'I won't crash,' he insisted. 'I know it's all round the squadron that I've lost my nerve, but I swear I haven't. It's just... well, it's just that I can't seem to take off.'

'Ha, ha!' came the sarcastic response. 'How the hell do you expect to fly the bloody thing, then?'

Seizing what he believed to be his one chance, he told Ian the story, leaving out no detail, including the judgement of Pat's father, which had lead to his arrival in Singapore.

'Old Winterbottom is adamant, and none of the others would let me near one of their precious machines. But if I don't get in one soon and get airborne, I'll never be able to do it,' he finished desperately. 'I've worked it all out. There's a public holiday next week. I'll assign you as duty pilot. All the rest want to go to Malacca for some kind of brass hat function.

186

With everyone away, who is to know if I go up instead of you?'

'Every bloody one if you end up in a heap at the edge of the field,' came the firm response.

'I won't. Once I take off, I swear I could knock spots off every chap in this squadron. Including you. I'm a bloody good pilot,' he claimed fervently. 'Give me the chance to get up there, and you'll see for yourself. I'd do it for you, or for any man in my position,' he added persuasively. 'Think how you'd feel to be grounded for the rest of your days, watching everyone else taking off.'

'Well... I'll give it some thought,' offered Ian reluctantly. 'I still want the address of that girl, in the meantime.'

Two days later, the New Zealander agreed to David's proposal, and was immediately nominated duty pilot for the coming holiday. It pleased the others, who were set to go to the Sultan's party in Malacca. All the same, as the week crawled slowly past, and David stared at the aircraft across the shimmering heat of the airfield, tension began to mount in him until he was almost in the condition which overcame him in a cockpit. Over and over again he pounded his brain with the philosophy of another time, another place and twelve months of rest to recover from the superhuman effort of last autumn in England. He told himself optimistically that he had forgotten what Enright had looked like, and that everything would now be all right. It was even a different model aircraft. There was nothing whatever to remind him of his humiliating failure. Yet he could think of nothing else as he sweated out the days, and lay tossing and fearful beneath his net all night.

The day before the holiday, Ian collapsed with food poisoning and was admitted to hospital. A taciturn Scot had to replace him as duty pilot, and David was just feverishly deciding to send the man on an imaginary emergency call, then take up one of the other machines during his absence, when the final blow crushed his hopes. Alan Winterbottom revealed that he was staying in Singapore over the two-day holiday, and expected David to have dinner with himself and his wife on the morrow. Their bungalow was further around the coast and entailed an overnight stop, keeping him away from the airfield during the crucial period. An invitation from a man's CO was tantamount to an order, and David had the best sleep for a long time that night, because he was so drunk he could no longer wonder when the next holiday would be, or if Ian would agree a second time to help him.

The Winterbottoms' bungalow occupied an isolated spot on the beach near a Malay fishing village. The route to it was tortuous and lonely . On arrival there, David was taken aback to find he was the only guest. When he was introduced to Rita Winterbottom, he understood the knowing grins and remarks of his fellows about initiation rites. She was the personification of every serviceman's pin-up picture, and was sizzlingly aware of the fact. In a dress of emerald Thai silk that bared one shoulder and fitted close to her superb breasts, she looked stunning as she greeted David with a smile that revealed gleaming teeth. At any other time he would have responded to the pagan attraction of long, flowing tawny hair, scarlet lips and nails, and very long tanned legs, shown generously by the deep slits in her skirt. But his current disappointment lay like a stone on his chest. He was hardly aware of her optical ravishment. Even when her feet touched his under the table during dinner, his thoughts were so black and far away, he merely moved his own to give her more room.

The evening dragged on and on, and his mood was such that he willingly accepted their lavish quantities of drink in the hope of lessening the great weight filling him. Suppose he got his CO at a weak moment and extracted a promise to let him have a go with a Hurricane? Now, while the rest of the squadron was away, was the ideal time. The man was being a friendly, generous host, treating him on equal terms. Maybe that was why he had been invited on his own; maybe Winterbottom felt the time had come to have a fresh discussion on the subject. Depression and drink was making him dozy. The little lizards that came and went on the walls seemed to have doubled in number, and the noise of cicadas outside was so loud it resembled the sound of a propeller whirling. Looking up at the ceiling, he saw that it was a propeller, whizzing round and round prior to takeoff. He was in the cockpit and everyone was watching him to see what would happen. Putting his head further back on the seat, he offered up a prayer. It was at that point that a voice suggested that it was getting late, and they thought he might like to retire. He struggled unsteadily to his feet, said goodnight as best he could, and made off for that part of the sprawling bungalow where the bedrooms were situated. He would have to tackle Winterbottom in the morning, when his head was clearer. If he rose early he might catch the man before his wife appeared. She looked the type to lie abed until late.

Although there was a circling fan and half-doors that opened onto a verandah, it was still unbearably hot in his room. After dousing himself in luke-warm water from the shower, he crawled naked beneath the mosquito net and fell asleep immediately. His dreams were of aircraft which he tried to fly, but which were chained to the ground, so that no matter how hard he pushed the control lever or revved the engine, they would not move.

He came from sleep slowly, sensing movement in his room. Then he struggled to sit up, as his blurred eyes made out the silhouette of a naked woman standing beside his bed, tawny hair falling over her white shoulders like a cape, and the glisten of her eyes and wet lips suggesting all manner of incredible things.

'Christ, what do you think you're doing?' he croaked.

She answered that by scrambling beneath his net and showing him. Going down under her assault, he was attacked in all quarters until he was in agony for her. It was definitely an initiation rite, and the rest of the squadron had plainly been through it in their time. There was no question of choice. She knew exactly what to do, when, and for how long. He had never been raped by a woman before, and there was no time to decide whether or not he enjoyed it, for it seemed to go on all night with no break for thought.

In the morning he discovered the truth. Alan Winterbottom had been down at the Malay village all night, which he frequently was, and had presented his latest juicy young officer on a plate to his wife as consolation. She had found him much to her liking, and expected him to satisfy her appetite whenever she sent a summons. It was the last straw for David, and completed his downfall. 'Sherry' Sheridan's nephew had become no more than a desk clerk and unpaid gigolo, while back in England airmen were continuing to fight and die in the sky where he rightly belonged.

By autumn 1941 it was clear that Russia was slowly going under beneath the German onslaught. Thousands upon thousands were being massacred, close on a million prisoners had been taken. So much for the friendship pact on which they had placed so much reliance! Europe, Scandinavia and the Balkans had fallen or collaborated with the Germans. The Italians were in Africa. The bombing of Britain was continuing relentlessly, some major ports and cities receiving heavy attacks night after night until it seemed nothing would be left standing. The British people had almost run out of everything in the way of luxuries. Clothes were now rationed, and so they began to look shabby as well as weary. Wine and spirits were practically unobtainable; beer was so short pubs were only open on alternate days, and then for reduced hours. Cigarettes were scarce and had to be queued for. Public canteens known as British Restaurants were erected to provide basic, filling meals off-ration to help families keep going.

Women made clothes from all manner of things: curtains, sheets, cushion-covers. Overcoats from old blankets were a common sight, and the black market value of a parachute snatched from a pilot of any nationality as he lay stunned and incapable of movement after baling-out, was astronomical. The silk made luxury underclothes for the women of an entire family, if they could get hold of one. It made all the rest bearable if one could wear silk knickers beneath a dress of dyed sheeting or the parlour curtains.

Make-up was difficult to come by, so women began making their own, often appearing in public with all manner of messy concoctions designed to produce the same effect as that achieved by American film stars, who had established the new look of bold eyebrows, thick lashes and sticky red lips. Many an ardent beau returned to his room or quarters smothered in greasy make-up that was difficult to remove. The drive for metal meant hair pins and curlers were very scarce, so women took a tip from their grandmothers, and put their hair in rags at night to acquire fashionable sausage curls.

Sacrificed along with the curlers and pins were spare keys, surplus saucepans, old kettles, empty tins, metal trinkets and garden railings, the donors being told they were helping to build another Spitfire. Coal was in short supply, which meant people had to face the cold as well as shortages in every direction. They sat indoors in their overcoats, or with eiderdowns around them, as they listened to their favourite wireless programmes, singing along with favourites like 'You Are My Sunshine' or, with typical wartime bravado, 'I Don't Want to Set the World on Fire'. They warmed their beds with bricks heated in the oven, or sat during the evening with their feet on one. When asked by the government to have no more than five inches of hot water in their baths, most people complied patriotically, the poorer families all using the same five inches. Thus, the people of Britain prepared to face the winter of 1941–2.

In Singapore David was indulging in one long round of pleasure. He filled his days with enjoyable things like women, drinking, parties, swimming and cricket, dances and the wild escapades for which young officers were famed. Fast gaining popularity with everyone including his squadron, who declared him 'a likeable sod now he has stopped playing the fallen hero', he no longer gave a damn about flying or the demands of the service. If Alan Winterbottom thought such things unimportant, and had drummed the creed into all those beneath his command, David would go along with them. There was nothing by way of duty to do in that part of the world. Why worry about what was going on elsewhere?

Having flung himself into Singapore society at the deep end, David was now much in demand by the people who mattered, and by some who did not. His good looks, his wealth and impressive background, ensured him the sweetest and juiciest fruits to be had on that tropical island, and he ate greedily. As August turned into September, then October, he crammed his days with fun and flirtation. There were dinner parties where tables groaned with every kind of exotic dish, followed by luscious fruits. After liberal amounts of wine, sinking one's teeth into the full flesh and feeling the juice run could become almost an erotic experience, when facing a ripe, luscious girl across the table doing the same thing. There were tennis parties where brown-limbed men and girls had more impact on each other than on the ball being whacked back and forth across the net. Beach picnics at the off-shore islands were held most weekends. The bronzed males showed off their physiques and strength in water sports, much to the delight of squealing, frolicking girls, who always managed to 'slip' and fall into their arms. Tea dances at Raffles were too tame for the set David had joined. Evening balls with girls in low-cut frocks and a full moon to tempt them under were more in their line.

David Sheridan was hugely popular in a very short time. He graced cricket teams with his expertise at the game, and his public school attitude towards fair play; his impeccable manners and his distinguished father listed him as indispensible to hostesses; and his increasingly golden, healthy good looks won him an endless supply of free-thinking, free-drinking girls. Flight Lieutenant Sheridan DFC was forgotten. And if he sometimes stood at the window of his office, gazing at the aircraft motionless on the field, waiting for someone to bring them to life and roar up into that incredibly blue sky, the fun-loving version of himself soon hurried him across to the Mess for a drink and oblivion.

He bought himself a fast expensive car, in which he took girls for outings up-country, which often ended in the car running short of petrol or developing a slight fault which entailed staying overnight at a Rest House, registered as Mr and Mrs Smith. It was hilarious, highly enjoyable, and totally fulfilling. All the same, he found himself visiting Rita Winterbottom whenever her husband advertised the fact that she would be

191

alone. She was like a drug that was a mixed pleasure to take but which was marvellously effective. After her brand of sexual wrestling, he slept deeply and dreamlessly. Normally he had to drink himself into slumber, but a session with Rita was equivalent to six sets of tennis, an energetic swim against the force of the breakers, or an evening of non-stop foxtrots. The more he went, the more he hated her, but she became as necessary to him as opium.

His days were so full he only remembered his family when letters arrived through a roundabout route from his mother and Vesta. Then he sat down with a good supply of beer to scribble replies full of breezy descriptions of the wonderful time he was having, omitting any mention of seduction or aircraft. The letters could have been from a civilian planter, who knew nothing of Spitfires and burning men in burning machines, enemies machine-gunning helpless parachutists ... or guns jamming to kill a comrade. There had been a letter from his father, regretting that he had been unable to see him before he left, and wishing him well in all he would be obliged to face in the coming months. He had not replied to it. What could he say? In any case, Sir Christopher Sheridan would never have the time to read it, even if he did.

He was surprised when Ian Freemantle, who was the only member of the squadron who had not been drawn into Singapore social life, said to him one day when the post had arrived, 'I've had a reply from Pat. I knew she was a nice girl when you first told me about her. It comes over strong in her letter.'

David looked up from one in which his mother wrote about the new airfield at the end of Longbarrow Hill. 'What do you want with a nice girl? The other sort are much more fun.'

The New Zealander ignored that. 'She knows a lot about sheep.'

David laughed harshly. 'Christ, don't tell me you're exchanging love-letters on the subject of white woolly things that go baa. Come out with your Uncle David one evening, and I'll show you something better than long-tailed lambs frisking about. It'll put hairs on your chest, old chap, I promise.'

Ian regarded him thoughtfully. 'She seems to think a lot of you. Sends her love to her "sort of brother". I guess she'd be disappointed if she could see how you've gone to the dogs out here.'

'You'd be wrong,' was his clipped reply. 'She thinks I'm one of the most beastly people she knows. She told me so on more than one occasion.'

'Go on the way you are, and she'll be right,' came the sharp comment.

Quick anger flooded him, as it often did these days, and he snapped, 'Mind your own bloody business. If you hadn't gone down with food poisoning just when... Oh hell, what does it matter?'

'It matters enough to make you throw everything you value to the winds, apparently. From what Pat says in this letter, you've been a pretty damn good pilot, well on the way to emulating that famous uncle of yours. Now look at you.'

On his feet in a second, David launched into his companion with bunched fists and knocked him backward in his chair. But the phlegmatic youngster had come from a country where men were fighting men when the occasion demanded, and was up and at him, charging head-down like a bull at a matador, right at his stomach, sending him staggering back against the wall with a thud that gave his head a nasty crack.

'You Kiwi bastard,' he growled, jerking himself back into the fray, throwing all his considerable weight behind the punch.

The New Zealander must have done some boxing at his school because he put up a punishing and intelligent defence as the fight took them back and forth across the verandah. By the time their colleagues had decided enough was enough, and held them immobile several feet apart, they were both bleeding from nose and mouth, and cursing roundly those who prevented them from continuing.

Even after cleaning himself up and downing several pints of beer, David could not forget what Pat had apparently written to Ian. What concern was it of hers that he had once been a pretty damn good pilot, almost as good as his famous uncle? Clenching his fists against the wall, he bowed his head between his outstretched arms, as the futility of his life swept over him once more. Damn Enright. Why had he not shot down his best friend instead, so no one would imagine he had done it deliberately? He had never had a best friend, so how could he have done? Living up to a legend had entailed being constantly one of a large group. Best friends had a habit of encouraging confidences, confessing fears of failure. He had been fool enough to confide in Ian, beg him to give him a chance in his Hurricane. Look where that had led: letters from Pat laying bare his soul to strangers.

He rang for more beer and set out to get drunk. Then he had a better idea, and took the keys of his car from the drawer. Rita would blot out everything far better, and leave no hangover. The sight of his split lip and fast-blackening eye would probably inspire her to new heights. He drove off with only one thought in mind, narrowly missing two rickshaws and another car on his way to the coast road, which would take him to Rita Winterbottom's bungalow. He laughed drunkenly. There was a misnomer if ever there was one! The road around the coast swerved and climbed, giving quick glimpses of vivid blue water, then spreads of dense green jungle. The midday sun beat down on his bare head, and sweat ran into his eyes. Even the wind rushing through his hair was hot. Accelerating in an attempt to reach her sooner, he raced round a bend so fast it felt like a swift bank in a Spitfire. The road evaporated, and he was diving low over massed tree-tops before coming in to land. He was flying again! He was airborne and back at the controls. He had done it, at last! They would all have to eat their words; retract their accusations. His uncle would be proud of him again. Then, in the middle of speaking over the R/T to Ground Control, everything went black.

It was a night flight. His experience was limited, so he was not too happy about the landing. This one was going to be a real beast, with no moon to help. What was more, the fools had forgotten to switch on the runway lights. He told them about it on the R/T but no one answered, and the lights did not come on. He shouted louder to stir them into action, expressing his opinion in good RAF language. A woman responded, and he had the grace to apologise, until it seemed he had become mixed up in someone's telephone message instead of the line to Ground Control. The woman claimed she had nothing to do with the lights and told him to lie quietly. But he had already started his descent. Out of control, he spun earthwards, trying to pull out of the fix he was in, and shouting to Control for help. A gentle voice spoke soothingly; cool hands were on his brow. Then he was given something odd to drink.

It was daylight when he opened his eyes to a curious scene. He was lying in bed in what appeared to be a small hospital ward. Two of the other five beds were occupied by European men in plaster, and a slender girl in the starched white of a nurse was talking to one of them with her back to David. He was feeling weak and very thirsty.

'I'd like a drink,' he announced in a voice that came out as a croak.

The nurse turned and came towards him. The feeling of weakness increased rapidly as he gazed up at her in a state of mesmerised incomprehension, smitten by the perfection of an oval face with a small nose and true rosebud mouth, framed by hair that was blue-black and drawn tightly into a chignon on her crown, where a fluted scrap of starched linen perched. But it was her eyes that did the most damage. Black as night, lustrous and slanting upward, they regarded him gravely.

'You had no need of lights, you see, Mr Sheridan,' she told him in a soft, lilting voice, then turned to a glass-topped trolley beside the bed to pour pale liquid into a glass. Turning back, she began to slip her arm beneath his neck. 'I will help you up to drink this. It will ease the pain.'

'I don't feel any pain,' he murmured as he discovered her proximity increased the feeling of intoxication without having drunk anything.

'You will when you move,' she warned, gently raising his head to put the glass to his lips. 'You have three cracked ribs, a severely bruised spine, and concussion.'

She was all too right, he discovered. With her arm beneath his head, her beautiful calm face hanging just above his, and her long graceful fingers just brushing his lips, he struggled against passing out and missing the wonder of her. Swallowing the liquid, he was grateful to lie back on the pillows again and just gaze at her while she straightened the sheet.

'Shall I be here long?' he asked hopefully.

'Long enough, I think.'

'Long enough for what?'

'To teach you a more serious disposition,' came the quaint reply.

He felt really ill for a week, suffering quite as much as had been predicted. The only consolation was that every day he saw the girl who created such havoc in his breast. Lying quietly, watching her move about the ward, he experienced a slow transition. This was the first beautiful girl he did not study in terms of her anatomy; this was the first beautiful girl who made him feel strangely humble. She had a wonderful dignity about the way she moved, the gestures of her long-fingered hands, the set of her head on her graceful neck. She walked with small fluid steps that suggested she was almost gliding between the beds, and her slightly accented soft voice held more nuances of expression than any female voice he could remember. Although the very nature of her work as a nurse suggested service, at no time did she appear subservient. To every patient, and every senior nurse or doctor, she displayed the same polite calmness, never raising her voice or growing flustered.

For almost a week David struggled for a description to exactly fit her. Then it came to him, as he lay watching her arranging the mosquito netting around his bed one evening.

Seeing her through the fine white mesh, it occurred to him that she looked like a bride, and he realised the quality that had proved so elusive was purity. He had never met a girl who radiated such an aura of untouched beauty.

By the end of the week he knew he was deeply attracted to her, and racked his brains for the best way to approach her. Displaying as serious a disposition as he could muster, he endeavoured to keep her beside his bed as long as possible each time she attended him. Her name was Nurse Lim, and he attemped to find out the strength of his chances when she came to give him his bromide one evening.

'Do you have another name beside Lim?' he asked quietly.

'Yes.' She measured the liquid into the medicine glass.

'May I know what it is?'

'I think it is better that you do not.'

'I can't go on calling you Nurse Lim when I take you out to dinner, can I?' he pointed out reasonably.

It plainly took her by surprise. 'Why ever would you do that, Mr Sheridan?'

'Because it would give me more pleasure than I can express,' he said with sincerity. 'I would be honoured if you would agree.'

Her almond eyes regarded him gravely. 'You are a very unusual gentleman. I have not yet decided whether or not you are a person to be believed.'

She held out the glass, and he took it, but did not swallow the contents. 'How long will it be before you do? Doctor Sanders said I can leave on Sunday. Will you know by then?'

A small frown creased her forehead. 'It is not possible for a person to judge another when he cannot move from his bed. Many gentlemen say these things to me while they are here, but it is different when they are well again. Some have wives and children. It is not nice of them, I think, to behave as they do.'

'I have no wife... and, of course, no children,' he told her warmly. 'As a matter of fact, I was feeling most dreadfully lonely before I ended up in here. Nurse Lim... Oh hell, I can't call you that when I'm trying to tell you how much I admire you. Please tell me your name.'

'Drink your medicine, sir.'

'Not until you tell me your name,' he declared. 'We may be here all night if you don't.'

She gave an involuntary smile, and he thought it was like the sun coming out. 'It is Su.'

Still holding the full glass, he said urgently, 'Please, Su, decide quickly that I am a person to be trusted. I can be very nice, you know, and I'll try very hard to cultivate a serious disposition, if you'll agree to be my friend when I leave here. It is very important to me.'

With a little nod of her head, she said, 'I will think about it, Mr Sheridan.'

'Call me David,' he told her persuasively. 'Please. I want to hear you say it.'

'It is not correct in the hospital. If I should be overheard, I should be reprimanded by the doctors.'

'Then whisper it so that you won't be overheard.'

The smile touched her face again. 'I think your disposition is not at all serious yet.'

He smiled back. 'I'm hoping you'll teach me. It may take a long time because I'm a very slow pupil.'

'You are also very slow at taking your medicine, *David*.'

Ridiculously pleased, he drank the bromide and settled back against his pillows with a sigh of contentment. As he drifted off to sleep, he dreamed of all the things they would do together.

His dreams came true one by one, and he fell deeper and deeper under the spell of the girl with the almond eyes and high standards of behaviour. She showed him the other face of her country. They wandered through the Botanical Gardens, and laughed together over the monkeys who sat and begged for bananas. They explored the bustling, odorous market where live chicks, lengths of cloth, hundred-year-old-eggs, tin bowls, gold beads and bangles, dried fish, ointments and wooden clogs all vied for space on the stalls. Su took him to a temple, where he could read his horoscope that not only foretold his future but also directed what decisions he should make. She translated the mystic Chinese characters to predict for him an early marriage to someone born in the Year of the Dragon, many sons, and great prosperity at the end of a hazardous voyage. When David laughingly asked her in which year she had been born, she refused to answer and fell quiet for a while.

When they went shortly afterwards to a tea house in some gardens, David was concerned enough to ask her what had gone wrong with the afternoon they had been enjoying so much.

With the sun flickering over her lovely face, as the leaves of a shady palm swayed in the breeze above them, she said, 'You make a joke of me. It is not a nice way to behave. I think this is how you will always be, and I cannot be so. My father and mother are dead. I am their eldest child. There are five sisters and two brothers. My aunt has made room in her house for us, but it is hard for her. Two sisters work as amah to white

197

families. The others are too small to work. My brothers can bring in no money. One is too young. The other is sick and cannot even work as a noodle boy. My nursing at the hospital earns the money to feed them. You see why such responsibility makes me serious in thought.'

Stricken, he reached across the table to take her hand. 'I know how you feel about levity. But it's not good for people to be serious all the time. It's just as important to have fun.'

'Like you, David, and drink so much you make an accident that nearly kills you? You are a rich English gentleman, and that is your way. Chinese behaviour is more dignified,' she concluded, drawing her hand away from his.

'I can be dignified,' he impressed upon her. 'I'll be so dignified from now on you won't recognise me.'

Shaking her head sadly, she said, 'No, I think it is better that we do not meet again.'

'Why?' he cried immediately. 'I'm very sorry if I upset you at the temple. Please forgive me, and give me another chance. These past two weeks have been marvellous. I was very unhappy before I met you, which was why I drank and landed myself in hospital. You *are* making me more serious, even if you think the process is rather slow. If we stop meeting, I shall go straight back to how I was. You wouldn't want that to happen, would you?' Plainly confused and unsure, she did not resist when he reached out to take her hand again. 'Su, I have grown very fond of you. I am a long way from home and from my family. Your friendship has eased my loneliness. I promise to behave exactly as you wish if you'll say we can continue to meet.'

After a brief moment of thought, she nodded. 'Yes, David, I think that you are now very serious.'

'You'll come on Saturday, as we had planned?' he asked eagerly.

Again the little nod. 'Yes, I will come. I . . . I have grown very fond of you, also.'

It was all he could wish to hear, and his commitment to her deepened. They went to see rubber being tapped, and had tea with an uncle of hers who owned a curio shop near the plantation. He was a very polite man of few words, and David detected disapproval of his niece's friendship with an Englishman. The following day, he drove Su up-country to a beach not normally frequented by Europeans. They took a picnic and ate it on a stretch of sand empty of people save themselves and some Malay fishermen. They wandered up to see what the men had caught in their nets, and it was during the walk back that David was flooded with the desire to make love to the girl who had knocked him off keel. He was not sure what to do about it. She might allow him a gentle kiss, but it would be difficult to control himself in this isolated spot, drenched by the sun, caressed by the breeze off the sea, and bombarded softly by blue-green sparkling waves.

With superhuman effort he mastered his desire on that occasion, but he knew the time would come when he could not. The monsoon season was approaching and the humidity increased. Nights were sweltering and airless, making it difficult to sleep. After his earlier sexual greed, abstinence was proving a great strain on him. Yet he had no inclination to satisfy the need with anyone else. Indeed, when he thought of Rita Winterbottom now, he experienced a feeling of self-disgust. He must have gone through a period of madness before he met Su. She had returned him to delicious sanity. He could not let her go.

Two nights later they walked together through some narrow streets in the Chinese quarter, where storytellers sat on tubs illuminated by candles in a tin, surrounded by groups of customers come to hear the old folk tales they had heard time and time again, and where letter writers carefully took down the words of the illiterate in beautiful artistic characters. It was all part of that side of Singapore David had been unaware of before meeting Su, and it had grown more and more fascinating as he shut his past from his thoughts. His broken career was sublimated by Oriental saturation. Drinking and womanising had only banished despair for short periods at a time. Su Lim and her opiate fascination banished it totally. He wallowed in folklore, temples and ancient culture. He worshipped her beauty and honoured her purity. Only feeling alive when he was with her, the time he spent at the airfield meant nothing more than hours of waiting to enter her world again. Growing quieter and more sober he felt almost numb to all feeling save his passion for her. The elusive serious disposition was near acquisition.

Breaking through onto the road that followed the coast round past the harbour, they crossed it and went to lean on the rail running parallel to the water, watching the lights of passing junks and sampans. The moon was large, reflected in the water as a great rippling light, putting enchantment into a stretch of waterway that was revealed to be one of the filthiest in the East by daylight. As they stood close together, enjoying the cool breeze from the sea, a great liner, lit from bow to stern, put to sea and sailed past them for a destination on the other side of the world – that side of the world which made impossible demands on David Sheridan. The symbolism of that ship from home put an unbearable weight of emotion in his breast, so that he could hold back no longer.

Turning to the calm girl beside him, he blurted out, 'Su, you must realise by now that I love you. I think I did the moment I opened my eyes in that hospital and saw you standing there. It has grown so strong I now need more than friendship from you. Can we go somewhere more secluded for a while?'

Her response was to look up at him with an expression he never thought to see on that lovely face. Contempt. 'I knew it all along. You are all the same. One look at a Chinese girl and you want her. The painted girls in the pleasure houses are easy. Respectable girls are more difficult, and sometimes not worth the bother. You are rich and sinful. I am surprised you lasted so long. I have seen the way girls look at you as we pass by. You could have taken any one of them. You insult me tonight, and the insult is greater because I was foolish enough to believe you had grown serious. All the time, you have just wanted a Chinese mistress.'

'No ... Oh, no,' he said in deep distress. 'You know that is untrue. Surely I have shown you the extent of my feeling for you. I want to share my life with you, make you my wife. Without you there'd be nothing. Su, I'm asking you to marry me.'

For a moment or so she stood motionless, then she put out one of her hands to catch his and take it to her cheek as a caress.

'I wished for this,' she whispered. 'You make me very happy.'

He drew her gently against him, and held her exquisite compact body at last. A feeling of relief and re-birth flooded him. The treasures of the East were all his with the winning of this girl.

Chapter Ten

BY THE start of December the situation was looking blacker than it had ever been. Britain was no longer alone, having finally gained that massive ally Russia. Certainly the Germans were now engaged on the Eastern Front, but they were sweeping victoriously towards total conquest with their troops already in the suburbs of Moscow. So the help the British had sought from the Russians had not been forthcoming, and the exhausted, hard-pressed island race was instead engaged in providing what help it could to their suffering Slavic ally. It was little enough, and Russia's universal saviour, the savage winter, had once more halted the enemy at the very gates of the city. Thousands of German soldiers, ill-equipped for such conditions, died in the frozen wastes as Napoleon's troops had done. Their great lumbering invincible tanks had been brought to a halt by frozen engines, their supplies were lost beneath snowdrifts, their aircraft were grounded, their guns were covered in ice. The German army suffered and died in a battle against an enemy that possessed a weapon more deadly than any manufactured by man.

Halfway through November the British had borne the blow of the sinking of the great aircraft carrier *Ark Royal* near Gibraltar, and it began to be feared that the coming year of 1942 might see the realisation of Hitler's dream. His control of so great a part of the world could not be wrested from him by a handful of troops, ships and aircraft. It would surely require massive armies, entire fleets of vessels, and enough bombers and fighters to fill the sky. Unless the Americans came into the war, 1942 threatened to be the year when the world became darkened by a madman's ambitions. But they struggled to maintain their neutrality whilst continuing to supply essential material help to their cousins across the Atlantic.

To give the British public a boost, and to show Hitler that the dog's tail was still wagging, massive night raids on Berlin were carried out, striking at the morale of the German civilians, who were suffering quite as much as their enemies. Food and the essentials for living were in shorter supply to them than to the British. Money, materials and foodstuffs all went to maintaining the gigantic conquering forces, and the equally gigantic losses had to be replaced at the expense of the civilians.

Winston Churchill, his ministers and advisers, his war lords, and all the people they served thrived on one hope – that Hitler's success, like an elastic band, had stretched to its absolute limit, and must either contract or snap. It was imperative to hold out until one or the other occurred. Meanwhile, it was felt that any form of sabotage, resistance, or disruption in countries already occupied would stretch the elastic tauter and tauter. Every suppy truck, every train, every storehouse or communications centre, every German soldier destroyed put intolerable strain on the enemy. In addition, every item of information on troop movements, unit strengths, the situation of airfields, anti-aircraft guns, submarine pens or bomb factories was of vital importance.

Chris found he was working more intensively than ever. The demands on agents were growing, the risks were higher, the need for secrecy was even greater after several networks had been blown by informers. Day and night, messages came in from people who were known by no more than a code word – people operating a radio transmitter in a mountain cave, a Flemish farmhouse, a Greek convent, a Yugoslavian church, a Norwegian boathouse, or even a Parisian brothel. The messages came in in a format that had to be unscrambled by experts who knew that particular agent's personal code. Once unscrambled, the messages, often in the agent's native language, had to be translated into English quickly and accurately. The replies had to be first turned into Greek, Serbo-Croat or Norwegian before the cipher people could prepare them for sending. With the establishment of innumerable networks, individual agents, and small groups on special top-secret missions, the demand on men and women with linguistic talent was enormous, and the fact that all this work was highly secret meant that those involved in it were closely watched by a special unit so highly trained only one or two people even knew of its existence. This scrutiny was not only to maintain a check on those doing the work, but also to detect any evidence of relationships being formed with questionable strangers.

Chris knew this practice must be in operation on him, but he had no idea which of his friends or associates might be detailed to keep him under close surveillance. It did not really worry him, since all he did when he had short breaks was relax in his apartment with books he loved to read, or with music. He wondered, somewhat sardonically, if he would be reported as suspicious because he enjoyed music by German composers, Hungarian dances, opera by Verdi and Puccini, and drank wine from the vineyards of his country's enemy. Even that would soon be denied him. His cellar at the apartment had always been modest, since it was easy to get what he wanted from the vintners that had once been owned by his father, and which had supplied the wealth to buy Tarrant Hall and the surrounding estate. As a favoured patron, he was still able to purchase an occasional case from them, but the bulk of their dwindling supplies was now going to the top-class hotels, which were willing to pay double the original price to obtain it for their guests. Even so, every time he opened a bottle with pleasurable anticipation, he thought of John Frith, who would not only consider it suspect of a man to enjoy drinking wine alone whilst listening to Beethoven, but would read into the act a secret liaison with the German High Command. Poor Frith! He was expert at the ruthless hard-core business of judging a person's weaknesses and breaking point, but he had no imagination. The world must be a place of black and white to him, with no hint of colour whatever.

Since his visit to Dorset in June, Chris had managed to get down once more for a weekend. Much of it had been taken up with discussions with the rector over the church, which had been so badly destroyed there was no question of services being held there. A temporary place of worship, a hut of timber from the Sheridan estate, had been erected beside it, and Chris had donated the money to provide chairs and essential church furniture. His main task, however, had been to supervise the erection of a new headstone for Laura's grave. Marion had been beside him throughout, and apparently agreed with all that he had done.

He had been saddened at the conversion of his home to an RAF Officers' Mess, and the hammering, sawing and tramping back and forth by a legion of strangers on territory he regarded as his added to his feeling that everything he held dear was changing, while he was obliged to stand by helpless to stop it.

The visit had been short, and memories of Laura had brought a return of his sexual restlessness. Marion had been a great deal happier, with no headache. Several letters had arrived from David, filled with details of the splendid time he was having in Singapore. This evidence of his enjoyment and safety took away her worries and made her world brighter.

Chris had read the letters thoughtfully. In none of the three had there been any mention of flying or, indeed, of his professional life out there. Censorship limited details, of course, but Chris detected an attempt to cover the truth, either from Marion or from the writer himself. This had worried him. His son was in a strange mental state. Any additional blow could prove fatal. Chris knew. It had happened to him.

Since the letters had brightened Marion, they had made love on that visit with mutual willingness. It had not been a magical night – the conditions had not been right for magic – but it had repaired the damage caused by the previous visit, and had been pleasantly satisfying. Nevertheless, Chris had returned to London feeling just as restless, unable to forget the occupation of his home, and the destruction of the church he loved despite the marriage he had been forced to accept within its old walls back in 1914. So long ago; such anguish of mind!

After that visit at the end of September, Chris had had little time to think of the irrevocable changes in his village. He worked extremely long hours with the espionage unit, and with Frank Moore at the Ministry. He was surprised, therefore, to be interrupted in the midst of a vital translation by a call from Lord Moore on the special emergency telephone, telling him a tricky situation had arisen.

'Sandy has been on the line,' he began briskly. 'Lady Sheridan is presently in your apartment in a state he can only describe as unreasonable desperation. She is demanding that you be fetched from the conference he has claimed you are attending, or she will walk in on it and speak to you there. You'll have to go to her, Chris. We can't have her walking into places she imagines you to be in. It sounds totally unlike Marion, but Sandy is a level-headed chap who wouldn't say she was highly volatile and liable to do anything if it wasn't true.'

'Dear God, is it Vesta?' he asked through unwilling lips.

'No. Nothing like that,' came the reassuring answer. 'Sandy says it appears to be something to do with a letter she has written. Better get over there right away, old chap.'

Requisitioning a car from the unit pool, he told the driver to put his foot down. With his head still full of Serbo-Croat phrases, sluggish from hours of concentrated study, he sat in the back of the car hunched into his greatcoat, staring out at the bleak December countryside. It would be Christmas in three weeks. The midnight service would not be the same in a wooden hut filled with collapsible chairs. David would be absent this year; maybe Vesta also. There would be just Marion and himself in a house where RAF officers cavorted about the panelled corridors, blind drunk and pawing the local tarts. It was all going – tradition, family life, the feeling of building solidly for the future.

What had put Marion in such a state? She disliked the place at the best of times. What would make her defy air raids and restrictions? Civilians travelling by train were being questioned by police on the reason for their journey and their destination. What had she given as her reason? What the hell was going on?

He jumped from the car as it drew up outside the block of apartments, and had to be called back by the driver to sign against the time of arrival on the requisition form. Then he passed the porter with no more than a nod, and took the two flights at a run, letting himself into the apartment with urgent movements. Sandy appeared at once, calm but plainly glad to see him.

'I'm sorry about this, sir, but I considered it necessary to call Lord Moore.'

'What's the problem?' he asked in swift undertones.

'Lady Sheridan telephoned first thing this morning in a state of agitation, and I had to say you were out of town. When she demanded to know where you could be reached, I offered to take a message and get you to call her. She put the receiver down very forcibly, and I shelved the matter while I did those reports you left for me. I was taken unawares when your wife turned up here soon after lunch.' He bit his lip. 'I have never seen Her Ladyship in an unreasonable mood such as this one, sir. All I have been able to deduce is that it has something to do with a letter. Mrs James has made her some tea, but... Well, I'm no expert, yet I'd say your wife is in a state of shock.'

Deeply alarmed, Chris gave Sandy his greatcoat and cap before walking into his elegant sitting room.

'Marion, this is very unexpected, my dear,' he said as easily as he could. 'Why didn't you let me know you were coming?'

She was sitting on the settee, still in her hat and coat, the tea tray before her untouched. He was shocked by her appearance. It was as if ten years had passed since they had last met, and her eyes were strangely wild.

'Would you have been here if I had?' she challenged in a monotone. 'You have never been on hand when I need you.'

Crossing swiftly to sit beside her, he tried to take her hands, but she drew them away with a movement that was instinctive rather than deliberate.

'My dear, only something exceptional would have made you arrive here like this,' he said gently. 'I have come as quickly as I could. Take off your coat, and I'll get Mrs James to bring some fresh tea. Then you can tell me what's troubling you.'

She stared at him, fighting something that threatened to overwhelm her, saying with great difficulty, 'Help me, Chris. For God's sake, help me.'

'Until you tell me what's wrong, I can do nothing,' he told her with growing alarm. 'Does it concern one of the children?'

'David.'

'Oh, God,' he murmured, already seeing his son in a ward full of men who did not know who they were.

'He's ... he's *married*.'

It was so unexpected and contrary to what he had been thinking, he could hardly take it in. 'What?'

'He was married at the end of October.'

'Good Lord. That was extremely sudden for a man like David. She must be someone very special.'

'She's ... She's *Chinese!*' she spat out with such venom he was shocked. 'My son has married a native. *Married her*, mark you. Made some little yellow-faced girl his *wife*. My son – a Sheridan – has taken a slant-eyed creature smelling of joss sticks and given her our name. They'll have babies with flat yellow faces and black hair, and wean them on rice. How can he bear to touch her? How can he ... can he ... be *intimate* with her?' Her eyes dilated with the effects of continuing shock, and her voice rose. 'My God, Chris, my wonderful, strong, golden, *clean* son has sunk to the level of the gutter and ... and surrendered his pride.'

'Marion, for heaven's sake,' he said fiercely, trying to take in all she was saying. 'Pull yourself together and stop talking such nonsense. You have worked yourself up to such a state you have no idea what you are saying.' Taking her forearms, he held her steady as she began swaying. 'Of course he hasn't surrendered his pride. Neither has he sunk to the level of the gutter. David is not a boy of eighteen, he's a man of twenty-six, well experienced, I imagine, with women. There's no doubt in my mind that if he has married a Chinese girl it is because he loves her deeply.'

'Loves her?' she whispered in anguish. 'How can he love a heathen?'

'Stop that!' he cried, shaking her angrily. 'You are behaving like one of the villagers, who think anyone born outside a thirty mile radius of Dorchester is a suspicious foreigner. I know you have constantly declined to share my pleasure in international friendship, but you have too much natural intelligence to make insulting statements about a race of people with a culture stretching back far beyond ours. Firstly, she is not a native, as

206

you declared, only inasmuch as she is a native of Singapore, where David is the foreigner. Secondly, they do not have yellow faces. That is another myth put around by the ignorant. The absence of rosy cheeks leaves them with universally pale skins, and many Chinese girls can be stunningly beautiful to Western eyes. They are fastidiously clean people, who put many Western people to shame with their beautiful manners. As to whether or not our new daughter-in-law is a heathen, we must assume that either she is already a Christian – as many of them are – or that David will ensure that she receives Christian instruction. He is not a fool, Marion. Unless she is so very beautiful she has deprived him of his wits, which is extremely unlikely in view of the bevy of beautiful girls he has attracted since puberty, he will have weighed up all the considerations before taking such a step.'

His wife's calm, pleasantly pretty face, that seemed to have aged dramatically, twisted into an expression of accusation. 'Are you saying you approve of this... this...?'

'Until I know the facts, I can't make a balanced judgement. But it appears I have more confidence in David than you have... He is also my son, Marion. If he has, by some chance, taken a disastrous step I, more than anyone, can feel for him.'

Her cheeks blazed colour. 'Are you hinting that he might have been forced to marry this girl?'

'Maybe she wanted him as much as you once wanted me,' he said softly.

She was on her feet in an instant. 'How dare you bring that up in this context! We were two children of hardly eighteen, who had no notion what we were risking. This little slut would know very well what she was after.'

He got up to face her. 'You insult your son more than the girl by believing he would consort with a slut, much less marry her, then write home to the mother he loves to announce the fact. The proof of his regard for you is that he confidently expects you to write back expressing your congratulations, and your impatience to meet the girl he has chosen from among all others to be his wife.' He reached up and turned her around to slip the heavy tweed coat from her shoulders. 'Come along, let's have some tea, my dear, and talk it over sensibly. I realise it has come as a shock, and that the circumstances are not quite what we expected, but it is his life, and he must live it as he chooses.' Turning her back to face him, he forced a smile. 'When you have shown me his letter, we'll compose a suitable reply, with our congratulations and best wishes for their future happiness.' As she stood staring at him blankly, he said, 'Please don't look

207

so shattered. It's not as if we had heard he was reported missing.'

'I put the letter and the photograph onto the fire... And I have already replied,' she told him in a distant voice. 'I told him I would never accept his wife in my home. I told him he had broken my heart, and that I never wanted to see him again.' Beginning to tremble violently, she said with a terrible sob, '*I told my son I never wanted to see him again*. Chris, you've got to get that letter back before he reads it.'

It was all he could do to keep calm. His tired brain could not seem to cope with this. Serbo-Croat or complicated diplomatic situations he could handle; his son's unexpected marriage to a Chinese girl he could not; not when his wife was hysterical and unreasonable about it.

'How can I get the letter back?' was all he could say in bewildered tones, trying to accept that Marion had burnt David's letter and photograph of the wedding with no reference to him.

'You have influence,' she claimed wildly. 'You know everyone there is to know. You have connections in all the right places. For God's sake, use them now.'

'Marion, whatever made you write such things to him?' he demanded angrily.

'I meant them.' Putting a hand up to her neck, she gripped the softly curling hair savagely. 'When I read that letter my whole life broke apart. David means everything to me. When you walked out all those years ago and Roland made me leave Tarrant Hall, it was only David that kept me sane. After you returned from Gallipoli and I saw what you had become, I transferred all I had ever felt for you to my baby. When Mike was killed, I agreed to come back to you so that David would have what was rightly his. I have devoted the remnants of my life to my beautiful son.' She swallowed and continued rather thickly, 'He grew into manhood like a young god. He had a fine, strong body, hair that was golden and shining in the sunlight, handsome features. He... he was always laughing and loving. He set his sights on the skies and won his laurels. He went into battle and came out an acknowledged hero. David made up for my youthful hurt and loss ten times over, and I revelled in what he had become.'

Chris faced her with the stunning truth dawning on him, until he could not prevent himself from bringing it into the open. 'My God, Marion, you have committed the cardinal sin of falling in love with your own son.'

Her hands, tightly clenched, moved up to her mouth as she

replied agonisingly, 'I fell in love with you when you looked as he does, and it brought me no more than shame and pain and disillusion. I knew I was safe with this brand of love.'

'But you're not,' he pointed out hollowly. 'This possessive passion has brought you all those things again.'

Her hands were clenching and unclenching convulsively now, and Chris was alarmed at the incredible tautness of her body. 'That letter took everything from me. Knowing he was with her sullied his young clean body. Thinking of their intimacy – touching, talking together, telling her his feelings and thoughts, laughing with her, giving *her* the memories that are rightly mine – thinking of that destroyed the son I knew, and degraded all I had made him. I hit back. I wrote and told him it was her or me, that he couldn't have both, and if he chose her he would cease to be my son. I drove the pony and trap all the way to Blandford to post the letter, feeling that I was underlining my words by putting the envelope into the post office with my own hand. I sat up all night hating him. Then, this morning I... I went into... his... his room, and there was his old... white rabbit sit... sitting on his bed, and his box of... of... Oh, dear God, forgive me, forgive me.'

She broke down completely, bowing her head and shoulders to indulge in racking sobs that were so full of utter despair Chris was swept by involuntary compassion. Going to her, he held her in his arms while she keened with grief. Yet, even as he comforted her, he realised that she had just confessed to an empty marriage. All she had done towards building a fond, warm relationship had been only for David's sake. There had been no love to spare for him, save as the father of her son. So what of Vesta? Had she been prized merely as a sister and companion for her son? If this was true, it was a tragedy. But the greatest victim of this all-absorbing love was David himself. She had given him life, then wrapped him around with a glittering mass of golden strands that, if broken, would turn to dross.

Marion stirred in his arms and looked up, her face ugly with stress and weeping, her hat askew on her tangled hair. 'You must stop that letter from reaching him. Swear you will. If I never saw him again, I wouldn't want to go on.'

'I can't stop the letter,' he said. 'It is somewhere along its way by now. The thing to do is write another one explaining that the news came as something of a shock, and you replied before giving yourself time to accept the situation. You now realise that you wrote things you did not mean, and are very upset in case he took them to heart.' Holding out his handkerchief to her, he added, 'He must surely be aware you might have reservations about the girl and, if I know him, he'll make allowances, being only too familiar with the stress you are suffering in these present conditions. If you write again now, and post the letter here in London, there's every chance the two will arrive together or, hopefully, the second one first.'

She pulled away from him, controlling her erratic breathing with difficulty, as she stared at him in disbelief. 'I have run your home and property all these years. I have accepted your prolonged absences and the priority claims of your brilliant career. I have never before begged you for anything, Chris. I will never do so again. Just get that letter back for me. Pick up a telephone, send a scribbled note, tell Sandy to go personally, but stop that letter leaving the country. Please, I *implore* you, don't let David read those words from me.'

He sighed heavily. 'What you're begging from me is an impossibility. I really can't ask people to sort through a mountain of letters for one addressed to my son.'

'Why not?' she cried. 'Why can't you? A word to Frank Moore, or a military order from Colonel Sheridan, and it would be done.'

'Marion, we are in the middle of a war. I could not reasonably authorise confiscation of mail leaving the country so that a search can be made for a letter from an overwrought mother. No doubt dozens of impulsive letters are written daily, and the senders would give anything to get them back.'

'They are not letters to your son!' she charged passionately. 'Do you deny that you could use all those connections you have built up over the years to get a letter stopped, if it was absolutely essential?'

'Of course I deny it,' he said with firmness. 'All those connections to which you refer are presently engaged in work that affects human lives and the fate of nations. I would not dream of expecting them to drop everything over something like this, as a favour to me.'

'But they would for something that affects human lives?'

'Well . . . yes.'

'If you specifically asked them?'

'I should imagine so.'

'This does affect human lives. Mine and David's.'

'Neither of you is likely to die if he reads that letter,' Chris protested, unable to understand her persistence.

'I shall die . . . inside.' She looked at him long and hard. 'You have resented the bond we had, I see that now. You have been jealous all these years because David cut you from his life and gave all his love to me. You want him to read that letter and cut me from his life, too.' Taking a great shuddering breath, she said, 'I'll never forgive you for this. You always were cruel, Chris, but this is the worst thing you have ever done to me.'

He stood there shattered, realising they were strangers after a lifetime of knowing each other. 'Please try to understand. You live in a world of your own down there in Tarrant Royal. To you, the war is Red Cross parcels in the church hall, filling in forms listing the produce we grow, and the house being taken over by the RAF. There's so much you don't know about, could never understand, because you haven't seen it with your own eyes. Marion, the most terrible atrocities are being committed all over the world. Compared with that, a few impulsive words in a letter are totally unimportant.'

Turning with utter weariness, she picked up her coat. 'That has always been your greatest fault, Chris. You are so concerned with what is going on in the rest of the world, you don't see the human dramas going on under your nose. You have never loved me. You have regarded your two children simply as two more members of the vast human race. I don't think you have ever cared for one single person in your life. You're too busy loving the whole world.'

He watched her prepare to leave and felt overwhelming regret. Twenty-two years of understanding and compromise gone beyond recall. A second war had come between them. Could the fragile foundation of their marriage survive this time? Did either of them now really care whether or not it did? Yet, as he looked at her tear-blotched face, he remembered her coming to him at the moment when he had lost everyone he loved, and offering to help him face the necessity of going on without them. They might never have found in each other the love they had sought, but there had been something between them that had been remarkable in its stability. He could not let her walk away in her hour of greatest need, whatever had just been said.

'I'll ring George Tyler,' he offered quietly. 'No doubt I could prevail upon him to contact his man at Singapore to have a word with David's commanding officer about incoming mail.'

She grew still, her coat half on, and looked back at him like a person exhausted after a long fight. 'Thank you.'

'Will you stop overnight? I can't do anything until later this evening.'

Letting her coat slip to the floor, she nodded as she sat down again. 'The trains are all running slow, and I hate travelling even more after dark.'

Watching her as she began pouring the tea that was now stone cold, he said with gentleness, 'This war is going to last a long time – probably longer than the last one. Have you faced the fact that you may lose him altogether?'

She looked up with an expressionless gaze. 'I have been facing *that* since September the third 1939. It's this I find so unacceptable.'

Chris never did ring George Tyler. An hour later, news came through that the Japanese had made an unprovoked attack on the American Pacific base of Pearl Harbor, destroying much of the shipping, and killing almost two thousand five hundred people. At the same time, they had attacked the British outpost of Hong Kong, and landed troops in northern Malaya. All communications with the Far East were concerned with reports of the new terrible menace, and urgent exchanges on where the Japanese might strike next. Chris was recalled immediately by Frank Moore. He left Marion looking older than ever.

In the midst of the pressures prior to Christmas, Chris made time to write to David, explaining that his mother was very tired and under considerable stress, trying to run the estate under government dictates, and having to cope with the main part of the house being used by the RAF. In consequence, her health was suffering at a time when she had the additional worry of danger to Vesta and himself at the hands of the enemy. David must try to understand that the sudden announcement of his marriage had come as something of a shock to his mother, who had naturally hoped for a less complicated union, under conditions that would have allowed her to get to know his bride, and to be present at the wedding. He concluded by saying he trusted David would forgive anything his mother had written in haste, and accept their combined congratulations and best wishes for their future. He added a welcome to his daughter-in-law, repeating the last sentiments in Cantonese, which he had obtained from a colleague as Oriental languages were not his strong point. It was all he could do about the situation, but he had his doubts whether David would ever receive his letter; or the one from Marion.

The Japanese were sweeping through the Far East, destroying all that lay before them. The British and Americans were now officially at war with them, fighting in Hong Kong, Malaya and Burma, in addition to the Philippines, losing all the way. Germany and Italy declared war on America, thus

212

bringing into the worldwide conflict a nation which had done its utmost to prevent its people from such a disaster. But, in finally gaining the massive, coveted ally, Britain had also gained a new ambitious and ruthlessly cruel enemy. On December the 10th the two vital battleships *Repulse* and *Prince of Wales* were sunk off the coast of Malaya, with tragic loss of life, thus leaving the seas in that area virtually undefended. On December the 19th Penang fell into the hands of the invader, and the local inhabitants had their awakening to the true nature of the self-proclaimed liberators of the oppressed Eastern nations. Hong Kong looked in danger of being captured at any moment, despite valiant defence from forces totally unprepared for the swiftness of the attack. In short, the winter of 1941–2 now promised to be worse than even the greatest pessimist had envisaged.

Even so, preparations went on for Christmas, with mothers fashioning toys and games for their children from all manner of things, and putting together little extras they had saved to make some kind of traditional fare for families to enjoy as a festive treat.

Having particularly requested Christmas leave, due to his concern over Marion's reaction to the new situation facing David, Chris was obliged, in return for the favour, to attend a reception three days before Christmas as a representative for Frank Moore, who was elsewhere engaged. As it was a diplomatic rather than a military affair, Chris went in evening dress and dropped his army rank. Held in the mansion of a European financier who had escaped to Britain at the start of 1940, just one jump ahead of the Germans, it was an evening that defied the gloom of the world situation.

Chris walked past piled sandbags at the entrance into a foyer overhung by glittering chandeliers, where footmen stood ready to take guests' cloaks or greatcoats. Slipping from his he trod up a curving marble staircase rich with a jewel-green carpet, and flanked by delicate pastel murals. Since he regarded the evening as an onerous duty, his mood was such that as he looked at the exquisite paintings, he could only think what John Frith would say about them – about the entire evening, come to that.

A lot of arty-tarty 'gentlemen' in penguin suits, who imagine they are winning the war with words over a glass of champers, while the real men are out there in tin hats and muddy boots getting on with the job.

Entering the first-floor salon, where men in sober black and white, or elaborate military evening dress, mingled with ladies gowned in silks and velvets, he felt bound to agree with Frith momentarily. Then his wider understanding returned to remind him that no situation in life was without its subtle shades of meaning. As British mothers were determined their children should have decorations, toys, and sweets saved from the weekly ration to celebrate Christmas, so dignitaries, exiled from a country that had gone under to one that had not, needed to pretend that nothing had changed. Closer inspection revealed that some suits were beginning to look their age, and many of the women's dresses were three years out of date. The glittering jewels and tiaras they wore were a form of defiance, touching and brave. Chris sighed. Frith had a lot to learn, but he never would.

Sizing up the other guests, Chris set out to chat to all those to whom Lord Moore would address himself if he were there. Once that duty was done, he could leave with a clear conscience. He was tired, depressed over David, and contemplating his leave with a heavy heart. There was no joy to be found at home. The RAF would undoubtedly be holding inebriated celebrations, which would make peace and quiet a thing of the past; if Vesta had leave this year, it would aggravate a situation he did not understand; and Marion's frame of mind was unpredictable. With the state of the war as bad as it could possibly be, he wanted no personal conflict to cope with and increase his depression. No, it was more than depression, he decided as he stood, glass in hand, talking in Greek to a slight acquaintance from cultural circles whom he had known before the war. At a time when many people were surrendering their lives, he was doubting the worth of his own. Had the time come once more to offer himself as a figurehead, as he had been in Gallipoli – an expendable front-runner for the people of real worth to follow in their attempt to achieve? If he pulled enough strings, he might arrange to be transferred to a front-line station. Heaven knew, he would not be missed by his family. One after the other, they had cast him off. He had numerous acquaintances – no real friends save Bill Chandler, who was probably the only person who would be deeply saddened by his loss. They had a relationship that would never be understood by people who had not been through the same experience.

'Good evening, Your Excellency... Enchantée, Madame... Your health, Vicomte... Nice to see you, Senator...' and so it went on while his thoughts were elsewhere. If he did apply for a foreign station, would Marion accuse him of running away

214

again? Would it be seen as a second deliberate desertion of his wife and family? It was pointless to weary his brain with such conjecture, anyway, because Frank Moore would never let him go. 'I'm honoured, Professor... How are you, sir?... Heard the sad news about your son, Commodore... Congratulations on your new appointment, General.'

He looked at his watch. An hour and a half of social duty should suffice. Anyone of interest to Frank Moore had been approached, and it was now permissible for him to leave. Isolated momentarily, he finished his drink, asking himself why he was anxious to return to a lonely apartment that still echoed with his wife's impassioned voice accusing him of loving the whole world to the extent of never caring for individual people. Had his life led to that? If it had, why should he feel so strongly the ache of loneliness? If there had been no caring, there would now be no sense of loss. He stood, uncharacteristically irresolute, in the midst of a noisy throng. Would it be more lonely in that elegant tasteful apartment than it was here? Suddenly, the thought of the dignified rooms that reflected his twenty years of struggle to compensate for youthful losses, filled him with strange desperation. What was the point of returning there to sit alone with his thoughts?

'Ah, my dear fellow, I thought I spotted you earlier on,' said a hearty voice to his right. 'I've been away for a while. Only returned last month. Heard your boy won a DFC. Wasn't the least surprised, of course. Always knew he'd step into his famous uncle's shoes. We all did.'

Chris turned to find a distinguished don had approached. But he saw nothing of James Bartholomew as he gazed at the woman beside him, feeling as if the ground was rocking beneath his feet and the breath had been driven from his lungs to leave him with the painful need to fill them again. She was tall and shapely, in a severe evening gown of black velvet that left her shoulders bare, and clung to her upper body before falling into fullness behind her. Ice-blue diamonds dazzled at her throat and ears, to match wonderful dark-lashed eyes that were flecked with green, in a face that was emphatically, excitingly Slavic. Glorious red hair was drawn back from high cheek-bones into a sophisticated arrangement of swathed curls. She was regarding him with an intense expression that turned his blood to ice and fire alternately, while the shock ran right through his body.

'*Laura,*' he breathed agonisingly, as he gazed back at her.

'Madame, may I present Sir Christopher Sheridan, one of

215

my distinguished associates on the boards of several cultural establishments? Chris, Madame de Martineau is not only one of the most beautiful refugees from Europe, she is one of the most talented,' said James Bartholomew in introduction.

'Sir Christopher,' she murmured in a warm accented voice, as she extended her hand.

Chris took it in his, neither shaking nor kissing it as he struggled to banish a ghost and accept reality in her stead. Words were impossible, as yet.

'Ah . . . excuse me for a moment or two,' the don put in, his attention elsewhere. 'I do have to have a word with Colonel Vilanski before he leaves, and he is showing signs of imminent flight. Look after Madame de Martineau, Chris. You'll find you have a lot in common.' He bowed and departed, leaving them in silent contemplation of each other.

After a moment or two she said quietly, 'I am full of regret that I am not she whom you first saw on turning. Any woman would be honoured to earn such passionate regard.'

As Laura finally vanished, like Giselle, from whence she had come, he managed to say, 'I beg your pardon.'

'No, it is I who should beg yours.' Gently withdrawing her hand from his clasp, she went on, 'Dr Bartholomew claims we have much in common. Shall we attempt to discover if he is right?'

Recovering from one shock, he was plunging headlong into another as he realised he had imagined passion was a thing of the past. 'By all means,' he murmured, taking in every detail once more, and wondering how she could have arrived from France without his being aware of it. Where was Monsieur de Martineau, and why was her English touched with Germanic rather than Gallic inflections? Who was this woman who had just walked into his life, and how could he ensure that she remained in it?

'Are you an artist, Sir Christopher?' she was asking.

He shook his head, trying to decide whether her eyes were blue with green flecks, or green with blue flecks. Either way, the result was devastating.

'I attempted a few water colours as a boy. My daughter is the artist of the family.'

'So, what else can it be that we share?' she mused, the very soft v-sound when she said 'what' supporting his guess that she was not French by birth. But whatever she said was enchanting to him, especially as it was accompanied by an expression of sexual recognition similar to the one he must surely be wearing.

'You have a daughter who is an artist, and a son with a DFC. I have no children, so it cannot be that. Are you, perhaps, widowed?'

He shook his head again. 'My wife runs the family estate in Dorset.'

'I see. Then you must play a musical instrument. I do not appear in concert, but I relax with my beloved piano.'

'If I attempted to play it, you would not.'

She smiled then, and his breathless feeling returned. How could he have imagined there was nothing left for him; that life offered nothing more?

'Come, Sir Christopher,' she said provocatively, 'I suspect you are being deliberately modest. If we are to discover what it is we have in common, you must confess it to me.'

'Must I?' he asked quietly. 'Do you really need a verbal statement?'

Her whole body grew very still as she gazed up at him, awareness touching her dramatically lovely features. 'I am not Laura,' she warned softly.

He drew in his breath. 'And I am not the boy I was then.'

Glancing round at the crowded salon, she turned back to him to say, 'I think we shall not be missed, do you?'

'I was about to leave, anyway.'

They moved together toward the ornate double doors, lost in a mutual glance that had already dismissed everyone else in the room. As he was on official duty for Frank Moore, Chris had a car waiting to take him home. He led her, wrapped in expensive creamy fur, down the steps to where it drew up at his signal. She gave an address in Chelsea, and the vehicle slid out from the sandbagged entrance into the pitch darkness of the streets, just as the sirens began to wail. All he could see of her by the faint light from the dashboard was an outline, and a glitter from the eyes turned to him.

'So near to Christmas,' she said softly. 'One would think the German pilots would not care to go bombing at such a time, and would instead wish to be with their families.'

'They have no choice in the matter,' he said. 'Where is your family?'

'I have no family. My mother and father have been dead for many years. My sister was tried and executed in 1939. Twelve months later, my husband was also killed.'

'You are French by marriage only, that much is obvious.'

The sweetness of her perfume wafted toward him in the confined space of the back seat as she pulled her fur closer

217

around her throat. 'You are very astute.'

'I am a linguist.'

There came a soft sigh. 'So, we at last discover a little about you.'

'You have discovered a great deal about me,' he protested. 'It is you who retains an air of mystery that is extremely challenging.'

'It is challenge that adds piquancy to life.'

'Then I must meet that challenge,' he said into the darkness.

The car drew to a halt, and the driver came round to open the door for them. The sky was already full of the heavy drone of aircraft engines, and searchlights criss-crossed in the darkness to illuminate the dark flying shadows with deadly intent. The thud of anti-aircraft guns shook the night, yet in the distance somewhere was the faint sound of a choir singing carols in defiance of it all. Chris told the driver he could go home, and the car left them standing close together, staring up at the war in the sky, that seemed too distant to affect them. It was frosty and clear, the vapour of their combined breaths mingling in the still air. How could there be enchantment in the midst of this? marvelled Chris. Yet there was.

He looked down at her. 'You're not afraid?'

'There is no longer any fear left in me.' She abandoned her study of the bombers and swinging light beams. 'And you?'

'Not for myself. Only for others.'

Turning to stand close enough for him to see the pale shape of her face, she said softly, 'I think you must now decide whether or not it would be best for you to walk away.'

'Is that what you want?'

'If I say yes?'

'I shall not believe you.'

Over in dockland there was a series of explosions as a stick of bombs hit the ground. It was closely followed by another series. Next minute, the sky over the area began to glow orange. London was burning again. As if by mutual consent, they went up the steps where she opened the main door with a key from her bag. An interior staircase led to a group of apartments, and Chris was immediately reminded of the place Rex had rented for Laura when he went to France. For a brief moment, the red-haired woman just ahead of him became another, but only for a moment. He had differentiated between the two very firmly now: Laura had never been his; never could be his.

The room was left in darkness when they entered, while she

218

walked to draw thick curtains over the windows that showed the searchlights still probing, and the distant fires. With a swish the scene was blotted out, and she switched on a table lamp near the window. Blinking in the sudden light, Chris experienced a stab of aesthetic pleasure at the sight of the elegant room decorated in shades of blue with touches of acid green, where parchment-coloured furniture was enhanced by cushions splashed with glowing red poppies, and lampshades echoed the floral theme. Then his attention was completely drawn to an illuminated niche, where a magnificent bowl on a stand winked and gleamed in the angled lights. Walking swiftly to it, he felt a rush of excitement as he drew near. It was superb, so beautiful he felt his throat constrict. Silver-rimmed and of the very finest glass, it had been exquisitely engraved with a design of water lilies and trailing ferns by the hand of a true artist. Together with the chalice he owned and kept at the apartment, it must be one of the best examples of modern glass engraving to come from one artist's skill. He was filled with envy, and the thrill of beholding perfection, as he studied it with experienced eyes.

'Do you like it?'

He swung round to find her watching him with a half-smile.

'It's the most beautiful piece by Sonja Koltay I have seen. How did you come by it?'

Her smile widened, and even from the other side of the room her eyes told him things that had no need to be said. 'How wonderful that you recognise my work on sight.'

'You...? *You* are Sonja Koltay?' he asked, knowing he had lived forty-four years for that one moment of recognition.

'Do you find it unbelievable?'

'I find this entire evening unbelievable,' he told her fervently. 'I spend a dutiful ninety minutes saying all the right things to all the right people, then find my tongue running away with me when I am presented to the one person I did not dream of meeting. For six years I have gazed at my Sonja Koltay chalice and imagined it to be the work of an ageing thickset woman, with greying black hair and dark flashing eyes.'

She moved nearer, laughing huskily with the pleasure of her surprise to him. 'You have just described Paul's Aunt Berthe.'

Everything fell suddenly into place. 'Of course! You married Paul de Martineau. I never did manage to visit him to see his porcelain collection, although Gunther Schreiber spoke of it many times.'

Her wonderful eyes widened. 'You knew Gunther?'

219

He smiled. 'Before the war I knew all the principal collectors. I also thought I knew all the artists of any importance. How wrong I was.'

'So we now discover a little more about you,' she teased, slipping from her coat to drop it onto a chair. 'You are a linguist and a connoisseur of the arts. These two things we have in common.'

His pulse quickened. 'You are also a linguist?'

'With my mixed blood, how could I not be?'

'How many?'

'Fifteen like a native. Three like a peasant,' she told him with another low laugh. 'And you?'

'A few more.' He followed her as she crossed to a cabinet, asking eagerly, 'Music?'

'The German and Hungarian composers, of course. Some Italians. The classical Russians ... and Chopin, naturally.'

'No,' he cried instinctively. 'Not Chopin, surely? So sweet, so swamped with all that fiery passion.'

Leaning back against the graceful piece of furniture, she gazed up at him challengingly. 'The notoriously cool Englishman? Is it that you dislike fiery passion, or that you dislike to admit its existence? After the look you wore when we first met, I believe I know the answer to that.'

Feeling youth, virility and happiness racing back through his veins after so long, he murmured with increasing fascination, 'I'm no Chopin.'

Turning back to the cabinet, she opened the little doors to take from it a slender bottle, which she handed to him, eyes wide with provocation. 'Tokay. I find it, like Chopin, full of brilliance and fire.' Taking up two crystal glasses, she walked to the settee before the fire, and put them onto a fine marquetry table.

Chris followed and sat beside her, pouring the Hungarian wine into the glasses before handing one to her. She took it with the hands that fashioned works of supreme beauty, and Chris picked up the other glass, feeling a strange sensation of having arrived at a destination he had been striving to reach for years.

'*Prosit!*' he said, lost in the wonder of her.

'*Prosit!*' she echoed, and they linked arms in extravagant fashion before drinking.

He had never tasted wine so heady. He gazed at her face so close to his, and so full of awareness. Then she extricated herself to lean back against the cushions and study him. The hint of sadness in those shimmering blue-green eyes excited

220

him further, as she said, 'We have experience of life, we two. We have seen that much of it can be ugly and cruel. Whatever is to be between us, let it be beautiful. Above all, let it be beautiful.'

'It will be,' he responded ardently. 'I swear it.'

Chapter Eleven

VESTA AND Pat rode side by side along Wey Hill talking non-stop. They had not seen each other for six months and, although they corresponded regularly, there still seemed to be so much news to catch up on. There was a change in their relationship, however, as they were both quick to realise. Things had happened to them both, which, for the first time in their lives, emphasised the fact that their paths had branched in different directions.

In childhood they had played and taken lessons together; at school they had continued to do so. Even when Vesta had been studying art, she had been at home for long holidays that had been spent with Pat. Now they were conscious of being separate individuals. It changed their relationship, but did nothing to weaken it. They were both turning from girls into women, and were correspondingly less giggly, less excitable, and less hasty in what they offered as an opinion.

Vesta had discovered there was a happy medium between close friendship, such as she enjoyed with Pat, and the cautious, self-conscious associations she had had with her fellow students. After the terrible shock of the raid that had killed her friends, she had learned to give just enough of herself to enjoy the company of the girls who shared her life, yet not so much that she suffered a sense of loss when they moved on. In the services one's companions were constantly changing; friends came and went according to the dictates of war. It was important to live in the present, she had discovered. She could not look back: Felix was dead, her friends were dead, her virginity was irrevocably lost. She could not look forward: there might be no brother, no parents, no friends ... no Vesta.

Communal living had done away with introversion. The vital nature of her work had made her decisive and confident. Army life had turned her from a wand-thin creature of dreams and doubts, with long flowing hair, and a gentle smile like her father's, into a brisk no-nonsense girl whose short urchin-cut hair framed a face of developing attraction, and whose body had filled out to the extent of drawing glances accompanied by wolf whistles from passing males. That was when the close observer could see the bitter twist alter the shape of her mouth, and the chin go up in a gesture of defiance. A lesson learned as brutally as hers had been was never forgotten. Pride was difficult to piece together once shattered.

There had been changes wrought in Pat, she discovered, due to the arrival of the RAF at Tarrant Hall. Aunt Tessa, whose brother Mike had been Uncle Rex's best friend in the RFC before he was also killed, had been inviting the officers to the farm for mammoth suppers, teas, or general social get-togethers to enliven their service monotony.

'I'm being wooed almost to death,' complained Pat cheerfully, as they slowed their horses to a walk after the initial canter. 'I'm getting so many cuddles now, I don't need to go on a diet. The boys are *squeezing* the extra inches away.'

Vesta laughed. 'You are a scream, Pat.'

'It's true,' she insisted. 'Don't tell me you can't see how svelte my outline has become.'

'Well, there is a difference, but it might simply be because I'm plumper that you don't appear to be so roly-poly.'

'Ha! A fine friend you are! You go off for months on end, then can't spare a single compliment for someone who is working herself to a shadow in order to feed you with your ration of lamb chops.'

'Just now you confessed to being squeezed to a shadow by the RAF. You don't deserve a compliment for that. It's downright disgusting.'

Pat gave her a wicked look. 'It's also very enjoyable.'

'Is it?' she asked hollowly.

'Not half. I'm helping the war effort by keeping up the morale of the lonely pilots.'

'Don't be a fool, Pat,' she said sharply. 'They're probably all married, and compare notes about you when they get together over several pints.'

Pat gave her a curious look. 'I'm only joking, Vee. Stop looking like a maiden aunt.'

'At least you're no longer mooning over Daddy, I suppose,' she retaliated.

They rode towards the lone tree, from where there was a marvellous view over both villages, and dismounted to stand side by side in the crisp blue December morning, looking down at the scene. The ruin of Tarrant Royal church stood out clearly, with the tail of the enemy machine still there beside the cross. The villagers had deliberately left it as a reminder of the universal destruction of war.

'I still think Uncle Chris is a wonderful person,' Pat said then. 'Look how well he's taking David's marriage, when Aunt Marion is going to pieces and looking more distraught than if he had been reported missing. She's sworn Mummy to silence over it.'

Vesta sighed. 'In view of the atrocities being committed in the Far East, I think she's very wise. The vast majority of local people would group Chinese and Japanese together, don't you think?'

'He must have gone quite mad,' declared Pat angrily. 'For as long as I can remember, he's had bevvies of adoring girls around him – I mean he's got just about everything a girl could want, hasn't he? Whatever possessed him to tie himself to such an unsuitable girl? Can you honestly imagine her as the new mistress of Tarrant Hall? The villagers would never accept her ... and can you imagine the poor little thing being happy in an environment so totally different from all she's ever known?' She looked away over the valley. 'So much for his "glamorous floosies". I never thought one of them would catch him. At least, not for a long while yet. Whatever possessed him?' she repeated hollowly.

Vesta gazed at the ruined church below, remembering how she had sat in a pew beside Felix Makoski and given no thought to suitability in the midst of attraction that had overwhelmed her. She understood what had possessed David. But it was different for a man. Surely he had not needed to marry the girl?

Vesta voiced her thoughts. 'Maybe he *had* to marry her.' As Pat's head swung round to face her again, she added, 'Like father, like son. It would explain the whole thing, wouldn't it?'

With heightened colour, Pat said reluctantly, 'I suppose so. But there's more behind this than your parents know, Vee. I haven't said anything, even to Mummy.'

Vesta frowned. 'Has David been in touch with you?'

Pat shook her head, setting her curls bobbing. 'I told you in one of my letters that I'm writing to one of the pilots in David's squadron. He's from New Zealand – a sheep farmer who's interested in our methods – and is something of a chum of David's. At least, he was before this marriage. He writes that David suddenly started running wild – drink, girls, parties night after night, and a fast car. He got in with a dubious set and grew wilder than ever. One day he flew at Ian over nothing, and they had a real punching match. Can you imagine David doing that? After the fight, he drove off more tight than sober. The car left the road, and Ian says he was lucky not to kill himself. This Chinese girl – Oh Lord, I suppose we have to call her Mrs Sheridan now,' she interpolated heavily, 'Well, this girl was his nurse in the hospital, and Ian says he appeared to change overnight. No more drinking, no parties, a very sedate car, and a passion for everything Oriental.' Her forehead wrinkled. 'Ian writes that it all seemed to stem from this business about not being able to fly any longer. I didn't understand what he meant by that.'

Vesta heard all that with tremendous compassion for her brother, remembering how he had told her at their last meeting that he had negotiated the posting in order to overcome his problem. Faint guilt flooded her. The air raid that had come right after their farewell had been such a shock, she had been occupied with her own efforts to recover, and all else had faded into the background against the struggle to get the camp operational again, and cope with signals that continued to come in to the depleted unit. To be honest, the tragic loss of her friends, the grim succession of funerals, and the nightmares that had followed, had driven from her mind what David had told her that day. Since then, his letters had been so full of descriptions of fun and frolics she had read them with only half her attention, and not a little impatience. The news of his astonishing marriage had driven away thoughts of anything else connected with his life. This reminder from Pat explained behaviour she had subconsciously condemned.

'Poor David,' she said softly. 'Oh, poor David.'

'What's it all about, Vee?' asked Pat curiously. 'What did Ian mean about not flying any more?'

'Don't you know?'

'No.'

'David told Uncle Bill all about it and asked for his advice.'

'Daddy wouldn't tell me. He wouldn't tell anyone,' said Pat in indignant defence. 'Professional confidentiality, you know.'

Vesta looked at her friend and decided that if she was getting letters about David from a man who had known him no longer than four months, an adopted sister with a lifelong fondness for him was entitled to know what everyone else appeared to know. So she went into the facts as her brother had told them, ending by saying, 'Your father says it is because he subconsciously thinks everyone believes he shot down the American deliberately. He apparently gets into a cockpit and just freezes. I know it sounds odd, Pat, but Uncle Bill told him it happens in no end of cases – not just with aircraft, but with anything a person has been doing all his life. There's nothing they can do until something occurs to break the barrier at the back of the mind.'

Pat turned and walked to the tree. She was silent for so long Vesta went to her, curious over her strange stillness. Her friend was crying.

'He's coped with it for over a year, Pat,' she said gently. 'Don't be upset. You know David. He'll overcome it. He's not Daddy's son for nothing. Perhaps this girl will do the trick.'

'I feel such a beast,' Pat mumbled. 'I've been rotten to him at times, over Uncle Rex and how he'll never be as good ... or as nice. Poor thing.' She looked at Vesta with real distress. 'Vee, flying is his *life*. It's all he has ever wanted to do. For anyone it would be absolute disaster, but for him it must be the end of the world. Everyone expects so much more from him. He's never been able to escape from the example of the great "Sherry" Sheridan, even if he wanted to. You know how he tried to live up to the legend in everything he did – the girls, the cars – I often suspected it was really just an attempt to emulate Uncle Rex in every way. When David got the DFC I was so pleased. After all, in a battle a person can't pretend to be someone else, and that medal proved David was a hero in his own right.'

Vesta smiled. 'At least he proved himself before this happened.'

'But don't you see,' Pat cried, 'He'll now feel he's letting Uncle Rex down.'

She was uncomprehending. 'Why ever should he feel that?'

'Oh, Vee, use your head! He knows what everyone will say – that "Sherry" Sheridan's nephew ran amok in a battle, and killed a fellow pilot he hated, that now he's frightened to go up in case he does it again. Of course that's what they'll say! No wonder he lost his head over this girl. She's probably the only person around just now who thinks he's wonderful just as he is.'

Vesta thought it best to leave the subject. 'I'm sure she does, and I hope she'll make him very happy. But I do think he should have kept the news to himself for a while. He must have known Mummy would take it badly.'

'Men don't think,' pronounced Pat, wiping her tears away with the back of her hand. 'I shall never understand them.'

'Since you're only twenty, you've still plenty of time to learn,' was Vesta's dry comment. 'And if you go on kissing and cuddling the RAF at the rate you claim, you'll soon be top of the class.' She turned to the horses. 'Come on, it's getting chilly. Let's go back.'

They mounted and turned the animals' heads toward Tarrant Royal again, breaking into a trot to warm themselves up. Pat looked across speculatively.

'No special man in your life, then?'

'I'm too busy,' she replied coolly. 'Besides, they come and go so much it's better not to get involved. I wrote to Minnie's Rob, you know, hoping it would help him accept her death if I told him she helped me to settle in the army, and how she cheered us all up with her warm caring personality. He didn't reply at the time, but I had a note from him last week saying he had become engaged to a girl he had known since his schooldays.'

'Perhaps he realised "now or never" courtship has to be adopted these days.'

'Minnie would be heartbroken,' she said sadly, with the bitter twist to her mouth that came too often these days.

'Not if she really loved him,' Pat pointed out. 'She'd want him to be happy.'

Vesta turned on her. 'What of *her* happiness? She defended him and his pals fiercely, and a ring would have meant so much to her. It seems to me that in this war the emphasis is on what the men need and want. Women are suffering just as much, you know. Look at Mummy, trying to run all this on her own.'

'We're doing it, too,' bridled Pat.

'But Aunt Tessa has you to help her. She doesn't have a daughter being bombed in army camps, and a son fighting on the other side of the world to worry about, in addition to the farming problems.'

They rode for a moment or two in silence, then took the short cut through the copse near the brigadier's bizarre house.

'Why didn't the RAF take over the Brig's place instead of ours?' Vesta mused aloud. 'It wouldn't matter if that was ruined by high-spirited young pilots, would it?'

'Do you think David is in danger out there, Vee?' asked Pat quietly.

Vesta shook her head. 'Shouldn't think so. If he's not flying, there's no chance of his being up in Malaya . . . and Singapore will never fall. All the men at the camp say it's unassailable, besides being the one place we'd never allow to be lost. It's too important. Mummy doesn't believe that, of course. I think she's given David up already. It's awful, Pat. She moons about in his room, looking at all his things, and making herself totally miserable. Daddy arrived home yesterday looking very buoyant, and telling her the situation is not as black as she imagines. Perhaps he knows the truth about what is going on out there. His boring old Ministry is probably in contact with Singapore.'

They stabled the horses, then walked around to the side door that was now the family entrance to the house. As they did so, they were hailed by cheerful voices from across a temporary fence, erected to keep the airmen from encroaching on the small part of the grounds reserved for the owners.

'Patsy, me girl,' called a voice with an Irish intonation. 'Come over and wish me a merry Christmas. I've a present for you.'

Without hesitation, Pat walked across with a smile. 'I thought you had leave, Paddy.'

'Cancelled, me darlin'. There's something big on, take me word for it.'

The 'present' turned out to be a comprehensive kiss on the lips under a tiny sprig of mistletoe held aloft by the kisser, a cheery robust youngster of no more than nineteen. Vesta watched Pat being embraced by Paddy and another officer with him with a feeling akin to impatience. It was all so meaningless. They probably had wives or girlfriends writing them love letters and eating their hearts out over their supposedly lonely sweethearts.

'How about some seasonal goodwill from you, honey?' called the Irishman's companion in a Canadian drawl.

Pat turned towards her with a laugh. 'That's Vesta Sheridan. You're living in her house.'

'Great,' enthused the merry Canadian. 'Come over here and let me thank you for letting us in.'

'I understand my parents had very little choice,' was her cool response, as she turned away. 'Come on, Pat, we'll be late for lunch.'

'Oh-oh, that's one cracker we won't pull, Paddy,' came the comment, loud enough for her to hear. 'She's all set for a frosty Christmas.'

With the best will in the world, it proved impossible to indulge in much merrymaking. When the two girls walked into the house, their respective parents were grouped around the wireless, taking in the shocking news that Hong Kong had that day surrendered to the Japanese, who were imprisoning Europeans, cruelly massacring Chinese and other Asians, and clearing hospitals for their own wounded by machine-gunning the patients as they lay helpless in their beds. They were all stunned. Hong Kong was special. It was a jewel in the Empire's crown. Although the population was overwhelmingly Chinese, it was a colony that was British to the core. Its surrender had

228

been unthinkable. Yet it had happened. No one appeared to notice the Christmas meal that had been prepared by Cook with dedicated pride.

Vesta was thoughtful during the meal, her mind busy with something that had been only a vague idea in her mind when she had come home for the Christmas leave. The idea was now fast turning into a resolution. Unfortunately, her best hope of realising it lay with her father. She looked at him down the table now, as he spoke of Hong Kong's unique mixture of enormous wealth and utter poverty, and the dependence of the teeming thousands of Chinese on their British masters.

'They must believe we have let them down most appallingly,' he was saying, 'although it is now apparent that the Japs have been preparing for this for some years, by placing men in all the key industries and financial departments, besides carefully noting all our military strengths and defences. It was all done openly, yet no one thought to question it or regard them with suspicion. Men like myself,' he admitted, 'who encouraged international mingling in the belief that understanding would breed peace. I have been acquainted with Japanese people who were charming and very civil. Who would have believed they were hatching up such evil?'

'You never suspect anyone of hatching up evil, Uncle Chris,' said Pat warmly.

'Then it's plainly time I started,' he said sadly. 'For too long I've seen only the beautiful things in life, and turned a blind eye to the rest. What a costly error it has proved to be.'

Vesta fought a battle within herself as she watched and listened to him. The relationship she had once had with her father would probably never be recaptured. The revulsion after Felix had been too great, and too long had passed since they had met. Constraint hung between them; constraint she felt could only be banished by her own overtures. Now she needed his help. Men used women for their ends, why should she not use men for hers? But how to set about it, that was the problem. It was solved unexpectedly soon after lunch, when she came from the room that had been allocated to her in the rearrangements of the house, and met her father as he left his room two doors along the corridor.

'Ah, I've been hoping for a moment alone with you,' he said immediately, with a smile that was almost shy. 'You won't run away, will you?'

'No, Daddy, she said awkwardly. 'Of course I won't.'

He came towards her, taking something from his pocket as he did so. For some reason that left hand with the two fingers missing affected her strongly. In the context of her recent experience, something she had always accepted took on new meaning. He had been even younger then than she was now, and had suffered as people were suffering today. Suddenly, he was a person with his own life, as apart from a father. What was he like when he was being Sir Christopher Sheridan instead of 'Daddy'?

'Apart from the cheque I sent you for your twenty-first birthday last month, I wanted to give you something special to mark the occasion of your coming of age,' he told her, still with a touch of strange shyness. 'I wouldn't risk sending it by post to your camp, and I hoped you'd have leave so that I could give it to you in person.'

Feeling even more awkward, she took the jeweller's box he held out. 'You shouldn't have. The cheque was gigantic. I'll never spend it all.'

'After the war you'll want frocks and things. Then you will.'

Opening the box carefully, she stood gazing at the contents, smitten with emotion. There was a gold chain with a circular gold disc on which was engraved, in relief, a miniature representation of Tarrant Royal church.

'It was copied from a photograph I took several years ago,' he said then. 'The artist did it to scale. I thought you'd like a reminder of what it was like. Even if they manage to rebuild it, it will never be the same, will it? Antiquity can be copied, but never retrieved.'

As she gazed down at it with a lump forming in her throat, he said quietly, 'I organised it myself... not Sandy.'

Looking up quickly, she said in wobbly tones, 'Oh Daddy, it's... it's... Trust you to think of something marvellous like this.'

'I have a rather marvellous daughter... when I can reach her.'

Even now, however, she found herself hanging back from physical contact with him, as she said sincerely, 'I'll wear it always. Providing it's out of sight under my shirt, no one will complain.'

'I'm glad you like it,' he offered, a small frown on his brow as he studied her carefully. 'How are you coping with your new life in the army?'

'It's not new,' she chided gently. 'I've been in the ATS for over a year.'

'Good Lord, I suppose you have. Yes, of course, a corporal now, aren't you? Don't you want to take a commission?'

'No, that would mean admin work. I want to do something

230

positive – a job a man would normally do.' Seizing the opportunity she asked, 'Can you spare a moment to look at something?'

'Of course. Where is it?'

'In the rumble room.' She turned to open the door and led the way in, saying, 'Even with all my things here, I can't think of it as anything other than that. Isn't it terrible having to give up more than half the house? I hate it now. How Mummy puts up with it, I don't know . . . And the men in air-force blue around all the time must remind her of David and make her unhappy.'

'Every time an aircraft goes over it must remind her of David,' he pointed out. 'You can't stop that. Now, what is this you want to show me?'

Now the moment had arrived, she was ridiculously nervous. However she took the canvas from its wrapping, and held it out to him. He took it in both hands, and again those missing fingers held her attention. What had he been like as an eighteen-year-old boy when he had made her mother pregnant? Could he ever really have behaved like Felix?

'When did you do this?' he asked intently, making her meet his eyes.

'Just after the raid on the camp. It somehow helped me over the loss of my friends. What do you think of it?' she asked anxiously.

'You already know, don't you?' he said, studying the painting further. 'It shows all your old promise has finally found direction. You didn't need my opinion, because self-assurance and determination is in every line of this. My dear girl, I can't tell you how delighted I am that you have recovered your Muse.' His eyes, such a deep blue they were almost violet, studied her through the thick lenses of his spectacles. 'You went through a period of some kind of greyness known only to you, and I am heartily thankful you have emerged into colours again. Vesta, I hope I am part of that colour.'

Avoiding that, she looked at the painting of that scene of death and destruction, where a golden chocolate box remained pure and unscathed, saying, 'I wanted you to see what I can do because I hoped you might use your influence and your acquaintance with people who matter, to help me receive commissions as a war artist. If I applied in the normal way, it would take months. A word from you would cut through the formalities so that I could start immediately. It's what I most want to do, Daddy. Will you speak to your friends on my behalf?'

She glanced back at his face, and was surprised to see that his enthusiasm appeared to have been replaced by bleakness. Surely he would not now say she was not good enough for such work? She had seen some of Gerald Bream's pictures recently, and this of hers was equal in worth, she was convinced.

'Yes, I'll see what I can do,' her father said slowly. 'Most of my acquaintances are taken up with things like the invasion of the Far East, or the possible fall of Moscow. But I daresay I could catch them during a spare five minutes.'

Sensing that she had somehow touched a sensitive spot, she said quickly, 'If it's difficult, don't give it another thought. I just mentioned it, that's all. I can go through the usual channels.'

He shook his head. 'No, I'll see what I can arrange. Hong Kong falls in spite of all we do, so why shouldn't we help our families? Maybe that's been the trouble all along. My horizons have always been too distant.'

Chris walked with Bill Chandler along the track that had been made from the Hall to Longbarrow Aerodrome for the convenience and speed of access of the pilots living in the house. It had created a great scar across the hillside that had always been famed for its beauty.

'This place grows more like a highway than a peaceful chunk of countryside,' grumbled Bill. 'Their trucks rush across here night and day; aircraft drone and roar overhead. We can even hear their bloody klaxon down in Maundle. Poor Marion is right in the middle of it. I'm amazed they haven't bundled her into one of their trucks by mistake and taken her up in a Hurricane before now.'

Chris grinned. 'Your young Pat is more likely to meet that fate, if you ask me. The lads here all look capable of taking off with her on their laps. She's highly popular with the entire squadron.'

'Good thing, too. It takes her mind off you.'

'Off me? What do you mean?'

'Silly bugger, she's been in love with you – or thought she was – for the past three years.'

'*What?*'

'It was because I knew you'd react like that that I haven't mentioned it before. You'd have started doing damn silly tricks to avoid the poor girl, and made things a bloody sight worse,' came Bill's comment in typical language and style. 'Don't look so upset, she's enjoyed it most of the time – except when you patted her cheeks and told her she was a "nice girl". That was death to young love.'

Shaken to the core, Chris said, 'You are joking, I hope.'

232

'Not over a thing like that,' Bill said seriously. 'I'm also not joking when I say that Marion is on the verge of a breakdown. It sticks out a mile to me. You'll have to do something, Chris.'

'What can I do?' he asked with asperity, still trying to accept that little Pat had been regarding him in such a light. 'Apart from getting that damned marriage dissolved, and bringing David back to live here with her, nothing will prevent it.'

'What possessed the bloody little fool to write and tell her something he must have known would break her apart?'

'For God's sake, Bill, the poor devil had plainly jumped into it in a last attempt to sort out his own life. He can't be held responsible for sorting out Marion's.'

'How about you?'

Chris looked at him swiftly. 'That's a bit below the belt, even for you. It was on your advice twenty-odd years ago that I set out to try and sort out the whole world. Look where it got me.'

'Yeah . . . Sorry, Chris. I was really looking at the complete picture. If you don't do something to fend off the inevitable, it'll be just another pressure on you. I'm no fool, mate. That bloody Ministry of yours is no more than a front for what you're really doing, these days.' He held up a hand. 'No, I don't know what it is, and I don't want to know. But I'm too wise an old cur to imagine there aren't other uses for men like you in war; uses that drive the mind to the limit. Take on another man to help Marion with all this estate work.'

'She won't have one.'

'Insist! Then use your considerable influence to get Vesta somewhere safe for the duration.'

'Good God,' he exclaimed in frustration, 'if I have anyone else asking me to beg favours from men who are nearly out of their minds trying to make critical decisions affecting the fate of the world, I swear I'll sever all connection with my connections.'

Bill put a hand on his shoulder. 'Come on, Chris, use your commonsense.'

He came to a halt with the wind whipping through his hair, and flapping the collar of his overcoat. 'All right, Bill, I'll use it. We are going to lose Malaya and Singapore. Our forces are too small, too inexperienced and too optimistic. David stands one chance in ten of surviving – maybe less than that. If we lose him, it will be the end of Marion. No amount of help with the estate or safety for Vesta will save her. Take David away and she'll have no reason to carry on.'

'Let's face that when he's gone,' said Bill gently.

'All right.' He sighed heavily. 'I'll try to get a youngster who's been invalided out, and who'll be glad of a job and some peace in the country for a while.'

'What about Vesta?'

'She has already solved that one for me. I'll look into it as soon as I get back.'

They walked on until they reached the boundary fence of the new aerodrome, where they stood looking across the blue clarity of early afternoon to where fighter aircraft stood against the breathtaking backdrop of green, softly rounded hills in a succession of ridges stretching as far as the eye could see.

Keeping his gaze on the view, Bill suddenly said, 'I remember a boy of nineteen, covered in terrible burns, bandaged like a mummy with slits for eyes, nose and mouth, and secured to the bed by bonds across his chest and iron rings around a broken leg. The most terrible thing about that boy was that he had been born only a month before, and had no idea who or where he was, or why he was in such agony from wounds that should rightly have killed him. You have fought an immensely brave battle, Chris. If you ever want anything that is in my power to give or do, just let me know.'

Dragging his thoughts away from his son, who right now was in mortal peril like that boy of nineteen Bill had mentioned, Chris turned to look at him. 'What are you really trying to say, Bill?'

'I'm trying to say that you are one hell of a man, who nevertheless is not God Almighty. Whatever it is you are doing in your spare time, let up on it somewhat. Instead of trying to solve the world's problems, study your own once in a while. I know the mind has always seemed more important to you than the body, but you're only forty-four and in your prime. Don't let it slip past you while you're worshipping at Laura's shrine. You always were a bloody romantic fool – it was all that erotic Greek poetry and suchlike you used to read – but if you don't release some of that pent-up sexual energy soon, you'll be in for trouble.'

'Is that what you were offering just now?' he asked teasingly. 'To get me a girl?'

'Get your own bloody girl,' came the typically bluff response. 'But get her soon, mate, because if Singapore falls and David goes with it, you'll have a broken marriage on your hands.'

That evening, as they all sat in the larger sitting room, which had been taken over by the RAF with the rest of that part of the house, and which now looked very spartan furnished by the government and used by careless young men, Chris let the

234

celebrations go on around him while he indulged his thoughts. The officers denied leave had organised a party to which they had felt obliged to invite their landlords, along with other wealthy residents in the area, in addition to the WAAF officers who were lodged, for propriety, at an inn on the far side of Longbarrow Hill. Chris let the others do their social best while he retired, with a glass of vodka, to the window seat.

It was only three nights ago that he had met Sonja, yet it seemed an age away. What was she doing tonight? Was she thinking of him? When would they be able to meet again? How would he endure the time until they did? One meeting, yet he knew he had found his true love, at last. Laura had been undeniably Rex's, and he had merely waited on the periphery of their passion, enchanted by something that could never be his. He would be in the centre with Sonja. She knew that as certainly as he.

They had talked well into the early hours while London had been bombed around them, both eagerly discovering that the other shared the same passions and interests. They had conversed in many languages, reminisced on countries and people they knew, argued over the relative merits of poets, authors or artists. Not once had they touched physically, yet each had been as spiritually ravished as if their bodies had entwined. When Chris had finally left, they had made no arrangements to meet again. It was impossible for him to do so, yet each knew it would happen and where it would eventually lead.

He sat in his own commandeered home that Christmas evening, filled with longing for her. He clearly heard her voice, remembering the pitch and cadences of it as she had switched from one language to another with ease equal to his own. He thought of her slender hands which created articles of superb beauty, and her eyes which could assess and study intricate patterns on glass, yet which could flash to send a man's temperature soaring. He thought of those years during which he had not known her ... years which had not been kind to her.

Sonja Koltay was the daughter of a Viennese dancer and a Hungarian nobleman, whose estate had been taken from him at the end of the last war. The Koltays had settled in Vienna with their two daughters, Sonja following her artistic skills to become highly acclaimed as a glass engraver, and her sister Hetta finding work as a secretary. The political upheaval of the thirties had led to Sandor Koltay's arrest, soon after the death of his wife after a long illness, but Sonja's sister had continued their father's political activities in secret. Then Sonja had met

Paul de Martineau, an associate of her father's, and considerably older than herself. She had married him and gone to live in his chateau in France, only to discover he was deeply involved in the same political work that had imprisoned her father, and was arranging his escape from the formidable jail. The escape had been successfully accomplished, but Sandor Koltay had been so badly treated he collapsed and died soon after gaining freedom. Hetta Koltay was arrested, tried and executed for treason. When France fell, Paul de Martineau was shot as he left his country home one morning. Friends hid Sonja until her escape to England could be arranged.

Unable to reveal that he was actively engaged in such work, Chris could not ask how she had managed to arrive without his being aware of the mission, or of her presence in England. She had simply told him that since her arrival she had continued her work, selling a great deal of it very profitably to America. Now the United States had entered the war, her professional future was uncertain. Her mixed blood had initially made her suspect, and there were some homes to which she was still refused admission. Not only was she Austro-Hungarian by birth, her maternal grandmother had been half Italian, and her paternal grandfather had been part-Russian. She had spent more than six months in an aliens' camp on arrival in England, she had told him, and only through the untiring efforts of her husband's friends had she been allowed out to continue her art.

Chris did not tell her that he had personally sent many refugees into such camps at the outbreak of the war, because his examination of their background stories had uncovered doubts and discrepancies. He had visited the camps, seen the inhabitants. The idea of the beautiful woman he had discovered that night being in such a place was unthinkable. She belonged where she was now, surrounded by elegance and richness of colour. One might as well put a Ming vase on a bric-a-brac stall as put Sonja Koltay in an aliens' camp. It made him angry just to think of it.

In the charm, delight and release of knowing what lay inevitably ahead, there was only one thing that disturbed him. Friendship with such a woman was dangerous. Frank Moore had warned him of starting an affair with one of his own staff, or one of the agents, but to embark on a close relationship with a woman of such mixed blood was like playing with dynamite. Tossing back the vodka with a defiant gesture, Chris told himself recklessly that his whole life was now dangerously volatile. He might just as well push the plunger himself, and go sky-high when he did.

236

*

Giles Elton had clearly been detailed to perform a necessary duty by taking Sir Christopher Sheridan's daughter to lunch. No one had thought to tell him that Vesta Sheridan, youthful artist, was a mere corporal in the ATS. Men of his stamp did not escort corporals in khaki uniform into a hallowed restaurant in public. It severely damaged their reputation and standing with their colleagues to be seen thus, and Mr Elton was apparently jealous of his. He was also undoubtedly in love with himself, expecting everyone to join him in the blissful state.

Vesta had disliked him from the minute they met in his hushed office. Men in general were anathema to her; this one in particular was like a red rag to a bull, she found. Tall and personable, with a confident smile, his first words had immediately riled her.

'How very unexpected! I was told you were doing your bit in uniform, but I had imagined the Red Cross or something similar. Isn't this taking things a little too far? Why on earth haven't you accepted a commission, Miss Sheridan?'

'Because I didn't choose to,' she replied coolly. 'Why haven't you, Mr Elton?'

His smile held a trace of condescension. 'Touché. But, of course, you know the answer to that.' He made it sound as if he was on such vitally important work, he could not be spared for the job of fighting the war. 'Well, I had booked a table at the Savoy, but if you feel, under the circumstances, that ...'

'The Savoy will be fine,' she assured him. 'If you mentioned that I was to be your guest, they'll probably have reserved my favourite table.'

The meeting did not improve as it progressed. Each thoroughly disliked the other. Vesta rather unusually took advantage of her father's reputation to oblige Giles to be the soul of politeness, but she had to remember that he represented a group of people on whom she depended for realisation of her ambition, and tried to keep her antagonism within bounds. His unctuous manner she treated with barely concealed humour, as they were shown to the table she had stated that she preferred to the one reserved in his name. Settling into the chair held for her by a waiter, she smiled at her companion.

'This is more secluded for a corporal. I really had no wish to be forever jumping to my feet each time an officer passed our table.'

'If you had held equal rank, there'd have been no problem,' he riposted with a forced smile. 'I fear there is little choice of menu, but I think I can promise it will be better than your normal daily fare. I think I can also promise you a tolerable wine to accompany it.'

'My grandfather made his money from wine. Did you know that?' she asked. 'When he married my grandmother, her dowry consisted of extensive vineyards in Madeira. It was revenue from these that bought the Sheridan estate, but when she died tragically young, he was so consumed with grief he shut himself up in the chateau in Madeira, abandoning his three sons and drinking his profits until, in 1914, he lost it all on the turn of a card. He then threw himself into the sea in an attempt to join the woman he loved so much. I used to think it a very romantic story when I was a young girl.'

'And how do you regard it from your present great age?' Giles asked with a supercilious smile.

'He seems pathetically weak, and very unfair to his three sons, who had to pick up the pieces and try to recoup his losses.'

Their paté arrived, and Giles remarked as he spread his triangle of toast, 'They succeeded very well, it seems.'

'It was mostly Daddy. Both my uncles were killed in the last war.'

'I understand it was also Sir Christopher who arranged your artistic education. Why did you abandon it to enter the ATS?'

'As you remarked when we met, I wanted to do my bit in uniform,' she told him, the lie reminding her of the real reason and of Felix, who had thought her fair game. 'Does all this affect my application to be a war artist?' she challenged. 'I imagined I had already been accepted. Isn't that why you have brought me out to lunch?'

He resented being hurried to the point, and frowned. 'I invited you to lunch because your father is a friend of Sir Charles, who always observes the courtesies of life. That I have been asked to deputise for Sir Charles is only due to his having a previous engagement he could not break. In most cases, official notification of your acceptance by the WAAC and details of the commission you have been given, is sent by post.'

'I'm sorry,' she said in genuine repentance. 'I apologise if I have sounded ungracious.'

'That's perfectly all right. I accept your apology,' he replied condescendingly. 'No doubt you have been obliged to adapt your behaviour to that of the kind of people with whom you are now mixing.'

'Yes, no doubt,' she agreed with an edge to her voice. 'Please tell me all I have to know.'

238

He used the arrival of the main course of braised beef as an excuse to delay telling her what she most wanted to know, then made an unwarranted ritual of the tasting and approving of the wine. Holding back her impatience, she listened to his insufferable pronouncements on the merits of various vintages, and attacked her beef in the pretence that she was sticking her fork into Giles Elton instead. Finally, he came to the point and said, with a touch of expansiveness, that her work displayed surprising flair for detail, and the Board had been quite impressed with a talent that was, as yet, only half-developed. On the evidence of her canvas, in addition to her father's personal application, she had been given an important commission for the following month of February.

Filled with delight, she ate heartily, waiting to hear the finer details of what she was to do. When he revealed them she was utterly disbelieving.

'You are, no doubt, aware that there are some titled young women in the three services – doing their bit in uniform, also,' he said with smooth condescension. 'The government wishes to make the British public aware that every class is making sacrifices for the war effort, and some of this country's most distinguished families are rolling up their sleeves and getting down to manual or dirty jobs. We have arranged for you to produce a series of paintings showing these aristocratic girls in action. Between the sixth and fourteenth of next month, we shall be sending the subjects of your pictures to a special studio to pose against a suitable background. I have been charged with the task of selecting the nature of these poses, and I think you will be impressed,' he promised with a confident smile. 'Lady Mary Hudsom changing a wheel on a truck, the Honourable Sarah Whiles at the busy switchboard of an RAF station, and Susan, Lady Mair displaying a semaphore message to an offshore ship. Rather an intelligent choice, if I do say so myself. I suggest you do your sketches of the subjects at the studio, then get your backgrounds from photographs at the War Office.' He sat back smugly. 'Providing you put some imaginative thought into it, the results should be just the ticket.'

'Mr Elton!' she cried. Then, realising she had caused eyes to turn their way, leant across the table to hiss his name instead. '*Mr Elton,* those are not war drawings, they're recruiting posters. Anyone could do that stuff for you.'

He shook his head. 'Not anyone. Don't you see that the real subtlety of this commission is that the government can also claim that the artist is the daughter of a distinguished member of one of their Ministries, who has been knighted for his services to world peace?'

More angry than ever, she cried, 'That is not in the least subtle. It simply makes Daddy look a fool. *The daughter of a champion of world peace is painting war pictures.* Read into that what subtlety you can.'

'You claimed just now they were not war pictures,' he put in silkily.

Prevented from continuing by the arrival of the waiter with the dessert trolley, Vesta sat with a storm brewing inside her. How dare this Narcissus treat her so patronisingly? Any poster artist could do what he suggested. Aristocratic girls posing with semaphore flags and spare wheels! Was that the best they could suggest? What of the chocolate box painting? Could they not see the statement she had made with that?

With a peach melba of wartime ingredients before her on the table, she returned to the attack. 'Did you see the canvas I submitted?'

'Yes. Very interesting.'

'Interesting! That scene greeted me five minutes after I emerged from the air-raid shelter. My five friends were beneath that rubble.' Realising her voice was rising again, she tried to lower it. 'If my brother had not taken me out to tea prior to leaving for Singapore, I should have been beneath it, also. *That* is war, Mr Elton, not Lady This, or the Honourable Penelope That, pretending to influence the actions of armies or navies.'

He nodded. 'Mmm, that explains the painting, of course. Unrestricted drama and morbidity. I had not realised you were under stress when you did the painting, Miss Sheridan.'

'Corporal Sheridan,' she corrected, thinking that a spell in khaki might do him a lot of good. 'I asked to be allowed to do this work because I felt I could record the truth, the human truth about war through my talent. In my own way, I hoped to do what my father has devoted most of his life to, only to see his hopes smashed. He nearly went insane, you know, during the last war. He would never speak about that experience in order to enhance peace, but I could draw and paint it so that such things would never be forgotten. I want to go out and record reality in the medium best suited to me, not produce trumped-up pictures for propaganda purposes. I want to go where the fighting is just around the next corner, or over the ridge just ahead. I want to paint the feel of war, the mood and spirit of those who know the next day might be their last. Can't you see?' she pleaded. 'I know what it is like to see a pile of debris and know my friends are under there somewhere. That is what war is.'

He drew in a long breath, and exhaled it in a long-suffering sigh. 'I can see that you have been deeply affected by a distressing experience, which has given you a desire to hit back through your painting. We all feel that, Miss Sheridan. We all suffer from air raids, rationing, the blackout, lack of little luxuries... And we would all like to hit back. But as for going where the fighting is just around the corner, or over the next ridge, oh, dear me, no.' He shook his head as if chiding a child. 'That's not women's work. We have men to do that.'

Her blood boiled. 'You don't need men, Mr Elton, you need artists. Whatever it is you males feel you have that is superior, it still only takes a hand to wield a brush... and women have two of them. I would venture to say that my two are currently more usefully employed than yours. Don't talk to me about "women's work".'

Chapter Twelve

THE TITLE Operations Controller had become a farce in that early February of 1942. There were certainly operations now, but it was impossible to control them. In an office representative of a Turkish bath, due to the overhead fan being put out of action by bombs, David fought a losing battle with chaos. Reduced to just four aircraft, one of which was presently being repaired as swiftly as the mechanics could work in the oppressive heat and constant air raids, he did his best to respond to the continuous calls for a squadron 'scramble'. How could anyone scramble three Hurricanes to meet thirty Japanese bombers with any hope of being effective? It was ludicrous for him, and suicide for the pilots. In addition, machines from other squadrons on the island were arriving haphazardly because they were either on fire, badly damaged, out of fuel, or carried a wounded pilot; or because they were unable to land at their own airfield due to bomb damage. Messages rattled in one after the other on the ancient telephone for men of squadrons not under David's control, and he had somehow to find the right person to inform.

Yet it was a situation that he understood all too well. It was like travelling back in time: familiar words, 'Bandits approaching fast from north-west, angels two-five'; men racing across the field to their aircraft, the roar of engines springing to life, the smell of fuel borne on the hot breeze, the rising machines that became no more than dots in the blue distance. The deadly silence. Then the returning dots – fewer in number; the belly-landings, the nose dives; racing ambulances and fire engines; men walking from aircraft in a staggering daze, others limping or clutching an arm pumping blood. The difference was that he was an onlooker now; just the voice at the other end of the telephone, that rang to make the heart pump faster and the nerves tighten. He stood in his sweltering office, snatching up the receiver every few minutes to take messages in clipped

242

urgent tones from Central Control, then buzzing the internal set to pass on the information to the pilots lolling around at Dispersal. From his window he could see the man answering the ringing telephone, and the sudden alertness of pilots who had been apparently inert before. When they seized their helmets and leapt from the verandah, taking the steps in one jump, to hare for their machines, David's yearning spirit was there with them. That was where he rightly belonged. His blue gaze would follow the Hurricanes up until the dots vanished, and the ache inside his breast would remain until they returned.

The air raids on the field were also something he understood well. The bombers sweeping in low over the trees to release their loads, the great trembling thuds in the earth beneath one's feet, the spouts of oil rising high into the sky; the buildings collapsing into piles of stone, the stationary aircraft flying apart or bursting into flames; men running and falling, lifeless bodies flung through the air. The shouts, the screams, the overhead din, the continuous rumbles and thuds; the smell of burning fuel, excavated earth, and sweat.

To David it was a kind of living he knew, but for others on that doomed island it was shatteringly unbelievable. Less than two months before, Singapore had been a tropical haven, untouched by the horror in the newspapers and on the wireless. Now it was a part of it. The Japanese had raced through Malaya with incredible speed. British and Commonwealth troops, drilled in standard warfare against European armies, guarded bridges, blocked roads and formed up ready to make a stand at strategic positions. The Japanese swarmed through the dense jungle bordering the roads, often dressed as the local people to avoid discovery; they advanced on bicycles along cross-country tracks, and waded through swampy rivers well away from bridges. They came up in force *behind* the strategic positions where guns and field glasses were being trained ahead, and took prisoners of those who were not even aware that they were in enemy-held territory. They landed along the coast in a series of small boats, and fanned out over wide areas away from major towns where garrisons were situated, terrorising the people in kampongs and settlements into helping them by committing atrocities before their eyes. The defending troops were bewildered, deprived of vital information, neglected by those who should have foreseen their plight, defeated by a climate and a terrain for which they were not prepared. Fighting valiantly whenever they came upon their ruthless enemy, they were nevertheless forced to fall back mile after mile, thousands of them falling into the hands of people

243

who knew refinements of humiliation and pain hitherto undreamed of in civilised warfare.

Hopelessly outnumbered and ill-equipped for the task they had to do, they might have held out in that vital Far Eastern country had they had massive air cover, or the reinforcements they had been told were on their way. The reinforcements were probably figments of someone's imagination. Ancient, sluggish fighters were ineffective against wave after wave of aircraft, flown by suicide pilots prepared to sacrifice their lives and machines in order to destroy. The RAF pilots had to carefully weigh the risks, often regretfully abandoning a chase or one-in-five chance of success in favour of returning themselves and their aircraft to fight another day.

The stresses and strains of that autumn over Britain were all repeated here, with the additional frustration for those involved of knowing the battle was being lost for want of machines and men to fly them. For the same reason Singapore was being systematically blown apart by air armadas that came and went practically unhindered. The docks and airfields were prime targets, of course, but the citizens of the island were deliberately given a taste of what lay in store by attacks on the densely populated areas of the city. Kept in ignorance of the current situation, it could no longer remain a secret from civilians, both European and Asian, when the island was suddenly flooded with weary battle-worn troops, and an almighty explosion during the night blew the causeway link with the mainland. Malaya had been lost. Now only the narrow Johore Strait separated Singapore from the enemy. Within a matter of days the Japanese had landed, declared war, then overrun territory that had been basking in tranquillity and wealth to bring death, horror and destruction beyond belief. The fighting men had risen to the occasion from their lethargy and comfort, but the civilians seemed, in the main, incredibly immune to the change in their precious colonial existence.

Alan Winterbottom, returning from a trip to the AOC in Singapore, commented on the fact as he entered David's office and flopped onto a chair.

'Singapore's done for,' he grunted. 'I know it, you know it, those poor sods going up day after day against twenty times their number know it. How is it those running the island are still calmly taking tea and fixing up weekend get-togethers for golf and yachting, as if the Japs were not just across the causeway?'

David looked at him from the map on the wall, where he had been marking in the areas just attacked and on fire. 'The easiest way of avoiding something unpleasant is to pretend it doesn't exist.'

'Unpleasant? *Unpleasant!* My God, have you heard what those filthy bastards are doing to people they capture? One story made me throw up.'

'I used the word in the context of those taking tea and fixing up a round of golf. As far as they're concerned, the causeway has been blown leaving the enemy on the mainland. Nothing more to worry about.'

'Bloody fools! I could swim across the Strait.'

'The Japs won't do that when there are boats galore lying around. They'll be over as soon as they've collected enough together.'

His CO mopped the back of his neck with his handkerchief as he studied him. 'You've been pretty damn cool throughout all this.'

'I had plenty of practice against the Jerries.'

'Mmm, yes. Tend to forget that. Couldn't have had a better man beside me over the past few weeks. Thanks.'

David turned back to his map. 'For someone who didn't have any practice, you've been pretty damn cool yourself.'

It was true. Alan Winterbottom might have run a slap-dash squadron when David first arrived, but he was very evidently a man who adapted to the prevailing situation. Since the outbreak of the war, he had been as good a squadron commander as David had known, worthy of the men serving under him who had also changed guise, like the lizards of the country, to become a tight-knit group with tenacity and purpose.

'I wasn't very cool just now when two squadron commanders were told to fly all their available aircraft to Sumatra.'

David swung round quickly. 'What?'

'S'right, I'm afraid. What we're capable of doing here is not going to stop the inevitable, and we're losing invaluable men and machines in the process. Down there in Palembang they could use both to greater effect ... until we get pushed off that island, too.'

'What about our squadron?'

The other man raised an eyebrow. 'Keep on until our you-know-whats drop off! Where are the boys now?'

'God knows,' David replied heavily. 'We got wind of thirty or more coming in, escorted by Zeros. Ian, Scotty and Jake went up an hour ago. As you'll know from your journey through the island, the raid has devastated this area,' he waved a hand over the map to indicate the maritime docks, 'and caused damage in the Naval Base. The Japs have gone, but I've had no word from our three.'

'We're getting reinforcements this evening. Seletar is closing down all operations from there. It's within range of shells from the mainland now, so their squadrons are coming here for a day or two.'

'A day or two?' queried David.

'Maybe three.' He blew out his breath resignedly. 'David, if we are still free men this time next week, I'll buy you the longest beer you've ever had.' He barked a laugh. 'Knowing what a skinflint I am, you'll see it's a safe bet I shan't have to do it.' He mopped his neck with his handkerchief again. 'By the way, I fixed a place on one of the boats leaving tomorrow for your wife.'

David left the map to come round the desk. 'About time! I've been after them every day for a fortnight only to be told there was no room. I was all set to go down today and refuse to leave the office until they allocated her a place. I don't believe they were all full. You got Rita onto a ship at almost half a day's notice.'

'Yes... well, I'm afraid it's probably because she's a Chink. Sorry... *sorry*,' he said quickly, holding up his hands defensively. 'Slip of the tongue. Can't get out of the habit. But that's maybe why... plus the fact that you took off and married her without the RAF's permission. They don't like their officers to flout them over things like that, you know.'

'Christ, we're being overrun by the enemy that rapes and tortures women for fun – and Asian or Eurasian wives of white men suffer even worse. It's no time to worry about protocol and hurt feelings,' fumed David. 'Sometimes I wonder if the human race is... Oh, what the hell! I just...'

He was interrupted by the telephone and spun round to answer it. By the time he had noted down the imminent arrival of the squadrons from Seletar and Sembawang airports, and reported that their own three aircraft had not yet returned, Alan Winterbottom was calling from the verandah for cold drinks. David quickly contacted the Mess on the internal line to organise meals and sleeping accommodation for the new arrivals, then joined his CO in time to accept a chilled lime juice from the corporal in attendance.

'Thanks for twisting arms over Su,' he said belatedly, but with sincerity.

'You'd have managed it today, no doubt,' Alan said in an off-handed manner. 'Here's mud in your eye.' He drank thirstily, then went on, as he gazed out across the pot-holed airfield, where the far line of palm trees wavered and shimmered in the heat, 'You've helped me out with Rita in the past. Felt I owed you something. Funny girl. Wrong sex, I suppose. Would have been happier as a man. I couldn't stand it night after night, like gladiators locked in combat. Began by being too exhausting, then I found it disgusted me. Malay women are gentle, you know, and full of dignity.' His voice, surprisingly, broke. 'God knows what they'll do to her. Her own people are already giving her a tough time of it – Jap propaganda against us is proving very effective in some instances. If someone points the finger at her when they get here, it doesn't bear thinking about. I tried to get her on a boat today, but they turned suddenly deaf. A Chinese wife is one thing; a Malay mistress is beyond the pale.' His hand gripping the verandah rail tightened until his knuckles were white. 'There is going to be such a debacle here, David, the shame of it will live forever. I'm as guilty as the rest, because I saw and didn't heed.'

'You'd have been a lone voice in the wilderness,' David told him quietly.

'As you were?' The other man turned to him. 'I saw you as no more than an over-privileged stud stallion, trying to impress us with your past heroics. I'm deeply sorry.'

Slightly embarrassed, David said, 'You make it sound like a dying confession.'

Pale eyes bored into his over the top of the wet glass. 'Well, it is, isn't it?'

The three Hurricanes came in eventually, Scotty full of glee because he had shot down a bomber. They all made a big thing of it in the Mess before dinner, as if it had turned the tide of the entire war, and seemed set to continue celebrating well into the night when David left for the bungalow he had rented for himself and Su near the hospital. She would be coming off duty at eight, so he would be able to tell her the good news about leaving. He had been deeply worried about her safety as the Japanese raced nearer, and had pestered his superiors for a passage on one of the ships taking women and children, and any male citizens who wished to leave. He had said nothing to her because he did not want to alarm her. Also, if he was honest, it was because he was loath to face her reaction to the idea of being parted from him.

As he drove through a darkened Singapore, now under curfew at night, he acknowledged that his marriage was not as idyllic as he had hoped. Wanting her physically, and knowing the attitude of the RAF to one of their upper-class officers taking a Chinese wife, he had requested leave and married her without applying for permission. As a fait accompli it could not be overset by the service, but it had dealt David's career a severe blow, besides inviting the cold shoulder from many quarters. Not only had he been dropped from the upper echelons of the RAF, he had been black-balled from clubs, and eradicated from the guest lists of hostesses, who felt they had been deceived by the golden boy who had turned to dross. In the strange way of society, a wealthy libertine and seducer was perfectly acceptable – until he honourably married a foreigner. He then became a blackguard.

All that had not bothered David overmuch, because he knew Su would not be happy in that society, anyway. It was the marriage itself that had proved difficult. Mad for her, he had embarked on sexual union with his usual fervour, only to find his young bride did not share it. She denied him nothing, she did anything he asked of her, more in the manner of providing a service than sharing love. Upset, he had tried to talk to her about it, but she had seemed surprised at his distress. Had she not pleased him, not fulfilled her duties as a wife? Was there something more he desired of her? When he had tried to explain sexual love as opposed to sexual satisfaction, she had told him calmly that Chinese wives were dutiful, respectful and modest. What he spoke of was more suited to the behaviour of the whores in the pleasure palaces. Did English wives do such things, she had asked, to which he had replied heatedly that he had never had an English wife, so could not tell her. Things had continued the same way, and his repeated attempts to arouse her to real passion remained unsuccessful. There was no suggestion that she found his lovemaking distasteful, but he always had to instigate it and make all the moves, while she merely acquiesced. It seemed that the air of untouched pure beauty that had captured him was also liable to defeat him.

In all other respects the marriage was satisfactory. He had rented a bungalow with a garden full of flowering shrubs, and furnished it tastefully, sparing no expense. It was peaceful and secluded, with only the sound of the golden oriole or an occasional screeching cockatoo to disturb the hot days and heavy nights. Su ran his house well. His uniform shirts and shorts were perfectly laundered and pressed. Even his underpants were ironed and folded with creases neatly down each leg. The table linen was starched and spotless; the table always meticulously set with the fine china and cutlery he had bought. His favourite foods were quickly noted; anything served to him that he hardly touched was never offered again.

In the evenings, Su liked to sit embroidering pictures on velvet with beads and silks, and David enjoyed watching her graceful movements. Yet, when he was driven to go to her and kiss her neck as she bent over her stitching, she would put aside her work, stand up, and dutifully ask if he wished to go to bed. Somehow, she always appeared to use the same tone she used to ask if he wanted a second helping of vegetables.

Yet, there was a passionate side to her nature, he had discovered. On returning home unexpectedly one day, he had found her berating the little laundry amah in a tone resembling a screech, before dealing the child a blow on the cheek with the flat of her hand. Su had appeared unperturbed by his appearance, telling him the girl had been slovenly and lazy, and therefore deserved to be chastised. It was at that point that he realised the servants had no respect for the mistress of the house, who had married a white man. The feeling extended to him, for taking a Chinese wife, and David fleetingly reflected that his father's hopes of international peace and understanding were in vain. Only then did he give any thought to the fact that his father had probably been going through much the same distress as himself over the past two years. A war of this magnitude after twenty years' work for world peace must be a tremendous blow to him – as bad as finding it impossible to take an aircraft off the ground. Why had no one appreciated the fact, and offered some consolation?

David thought of it again now as he drove home through the silent, devastated streets that had so recently been a scene of wealthy, exotic satisfaction. The loss of Singapore would be a particularly tragic disaster, humiliating because of its symbolic representation of a great nation, and unendurable for the teeming thousands who would be lost with it. How would his father feel about the news? It would surely be another nail in the coffin of his lifelong struggle. A strong sense of fellow feeling washed over him suddenly, bringing with it regret that he had left everything too late. He could at least have answered his father's letter regretting that they had been unable to say goodbye. He could have realised that one man's lost dreams – whether it be world peace or the freedom to fly – would be as painful as another's. His father never betrayed his innermost feelings, so it would not have been obvious. A small voice inside told him he would have ignored it even if it had been obvious. But surely *someone* had offered sympathy and understanding? His mother, perhaps. Yet, something told him she would have had no more notion than he that his father's reputation must have taken a hell of a beating this past couple of years. Poor devil! A worm of guilt began wriggling inside him as he then remembered Uncle Bill saying, 'You've grown to manhood trying to be the son of Rex Sheridan, instead of that of his brother.' With Pat defending him fiercely at every turn, it seemed the Chandlers had given his father more friendship and understanding than his own family. They had all been too busy with their own dreams to give a thought to his.

He turned into the wide road flanked with flame-of-the-forest trees, and headed towards the last bungalow on the right. It was too late now to write that letter. Perhaps Su would be a better ambassador than stilted words on a page. Once he put her aboard that ship, her life and safety would be in the hands of others. But she should eventually reach England and his family, as living evidence that his father's creed of international love and understanding occasionally survived. Although he had written to his mother about his marriage, enclosing a photograph of himself and Su, who had looked stunningly lovely in the ivory silk cheongsam she had worn for their wedding – he had received no reply from her, or from Vesta to whom he had sent a similar photograph. However, mail was irregular and took months to arrive – if it arrived at all. There'd be no mail now, although as prisoners of war they would doubtless be allowed to send limited messages. Such things were laid down in the Geneva Convention, along with other international rules of behaviour towards prisoners.

Parking the car beneath the bungalow, which was raised on pillars, he hoped Su would have arrived back from the hospital. On their marriage he had insisted that as his wife she should no longer work as a nurse. She had happily agreed, after he had assured her that the money she had been giving each week to her aunt for the care of her brothers and sisters would be covered by him. Her family had not come to the marriage ceremony, but had turned up, serious and in immaculate clothes, for a traditional Chinese wedding meal in a very exclusive restaurant. They had been polite, had said the correct words of traditional wedding wishes and blessings for Su to translate for her husband, and had given the usual gift of money in a small red envelope, yet David had felt no rapport with them. Su had made no attempt to bring them all together since then, and he had been happy to leave it at that. His wife visited them while he was at the airfield, and returned with greetings from them, but he had no idea where they lived, and sensed that they preferred it that way. The international friendship and understanding stopped short at integration with his wife's family.

He trod up the steps to his home, filled with mixed feelings. Su must have been aware that most of the British wives had already left, but she had made no mention of it, or of her personal feelings on the prospect of being parted from him, although this was now inevitable. As an enemy, he would be interned as a prisoner of war. Unless she left Singapore, her only chance as a Chinese non-enemy would be to hide her connection with him, for many of her own people would willingly betray her to certain terrible slaughter by men who believed East-West union to be a mortal sin of the blackest kind.

Whatever befell they were doomed to part, and he was ridiculously afraid she might betray no regret or distress over the fact. On the other hand, her characteristic calm acceptance of the inevitable would surely make the parting more bearable. Tears, vows of broken hearts, fears at the prospect of never meeting again, would only make what he was about to face more difficult for him. He had witnessed partings down on the docks, when women had walked up the gangplank leading children by the hand and blinded by tears, after being literally torn from the arms of their husbands forced to remain behind. He had seen the men, who, after cheerily waving and calling out, 'See you soon, love. Give my regards to Blighty,' had walked away around a corner to stand with shoulders heaving, while native drivers waited with impassive expressions by the sleek cars that would return them to a lonely bungalow that had witnessed love, marriage, children, and a life that had taken no account of a blood-red sunset.

Since the start of the Malayan war, Su had taken up nursing again, with David's full agreement, and she was still in her starched white dress when he entered the airy sitting room, open to whatever breeze was available, and kept cool by the shade of a huge frangipani. He went across to her immediately and took her in his arms.

'You are safe! I rang the hospital after the raid just to ensure that it hadn't been hit.'

'You, too, are safe, David,' she said softly against his chest. 'That is good. We heard so many stories at the hospital, and there were pilots and men from bombed airfields that came in all day. I kept asking for names in case one should be you.'

Kissing her temple, he murmured, 'We are the only field operational now. The other squadrons were all arriving as I left.'

'Do you leave in the morning?' she asked, drawing away from him to look up enquiringly.

'Leave?' he repeated. 'For where?'

'Sumatra. The men in the ward were talking about it. The RAF is leaving Singapore before the Japanese come over from the mainland. The island is being abandoned.'

'Nonsense,' he cried. 'That's quite untrue. Some of the boys are going down to Sumatra because they have to stop the Japs from taking it, but most of us are staying here. We wouldn't abandon Singapore.'

'The Japanese say you are. Look.' She produced from her pocket a leaflet in bad English, informing the local races that British and Australian soldiers were being secretly evacuated from the island, deserting those they had oppressed and exploited, because they were afraid to receive their just punishment from the Nippon army come to liberate the East.

Scanning it rapidly, David looked up to say, 'No one believes this, surely. The troops are still here for everyone to see.'

'But white people are leaving on every ship,' she told him in her unexcitable manner. 'Asians are being told there is no room, or quoted a fare so high they cannot afford it. Many people are angry. If there is nothing to fear, why are Europeans and Australians leaving?'

'For several reasons,' he lied quickly. 'A state of siege means the rationing of food and water, so the less people there are, the further it goes round. In addition, the troops can mount a more successful defence if civilians are reduced to a minimum.'

She backed a few steps and looked at him fearlessly. 'I always know when you are not to be believed, David, and it is so now.'

The boy came in with the chilled lime juice and soda David always had on arriving home, and conversation was halted until the Malay departed. Leaving the drink untouched, David decided to come straight to the point.

'Darling, no one knows what is going to happen here, least of all me. Anything I said would be open to disbelief. The one thing that is certain is that you will be a great deal safer elsewhere. I've managed to get you on a ship leaving tomorrow.'

The moment of truth had come, and he searched her lovely face for the signs of mixed gratitude and distress such news would surely bring. Her expression hardly changed.

'I will prepare my brothers and sisters for the journey.'

Already sensing the incredible truth, he said, 'I had the devil's own job getting a place for you. In the end, it was a word from Alan Winterbottom that swung it. You can't take your family.'

'Then I stay here,' she said unemotionally. 'I will not leave them.'

He crossed to her urgently. 'Su, you want the truth, then here it is. There is every chance we may lose Singapore. Only because of that, and because you are the wife of a British officer, have you been allocated a berth on what might be the last ship to leave. I have been pestering the RAF and the shipping companies for days to gain you this chance to get away. There is absolutely no hope of getting your family on that ship with you.'

Her black eyes looked back shrewdly. 'You have money. You could afford the fares.'

'That doesn't enter into it,' he responded, finding the unexpected situation hard to take. 'There is no room for them.'

'If they were white there would be room.'

'There are large numbers of white people staying here,' he countered angrily. 'Don't start throwing racial arguments at me at a time like this.'

'I will stay here.'

'You will leave on that ship,' he told her. 'It's fixed now.'

'I will not leave without my family,' she cried with sudden emotion.

'You are my wife,' he returned, trying to cope with this girl who had revealed passion at the worst possible time. 'I am responsible for you, not your entire family.'

'*I* am responsible for them. They must come with me.'

'*They can't go with you!*' he shouted, then realised they would be overheard by the servants, and strove to lower his voice. 'Su, this is an emergency, and you have to accept that nothing is going to be how we like it.' Taking a deep breath to steady himself, he said carefully, 'You have not once shown concern over leaving *me*. Have you realised that I shall not be travelling with you?'

'Yes, I have realised it. You said just now that the troops will not abandon the island. I have no concern for leaving you, because I shall stay.'

He shook her shoulders, digging his fingers into their sloping softness. 'You are my wife. I love you, and I am determined to protect you to the best of my ability. But I am a serving officer and bound by orders to remain here, so I shall be obliged to put you into other hands when you leave. Even so, my name and rank will continue to protect you until either I am free to join you, or my family in England is able to act on my behalf.' He drew her against him. 'I little thought when we were married that within four months we'd be obliged to part under such

253

circumstances, my darling. War brings all kinds of sadness, and we are all forced to leave those we love.'

She pulled away from him, her starched dress limp from the heat of his damp body. 'I am not under orders, as you are. I desire to remain here.'

He lost his temper. 'You are going on that ship, and that is final. I have enough to face without worrying about you.'

'Would you leave your family and sail away?' she demanded.

'I did.'

'Because you had orders,' she flung at him.

'No. I asked to come to Singapore. I left my family facing air raids, food rationing, blacked-out streets, and an enemy only a narrow waterway off – just as you will be doing.'

'I will not.'

'Have you any idea what the Japanese are doing to women like you?' he asked savagely, deciding fear was the only course left. 'If you persist in arguing, I shall be forced to tell you. Don't make me, Su. For God's sake don't make me.'

Her face registered contempt. 'So concerned, so much the English gentleman! Would you be so for any Chinese girl? Only because you desire me do you behave so well. Are you so concerned for all those in the street who will be left here? Would you protect them, also? Have no worry, I have heard what the enemy is doing. It is impossible not to hear. That is why I stay here with my sisters. If you are so afraid to speak to me of what they are doing to women, why do you not protect my sisters, and send them on the ship?'

'I can't protect every woman in Singapore,' he cried. 'I wish to God it was in my power. But if I can only save one person, I want it to be my wife.' As she stood facing him, that same expression on her face, he said desperately, 'If the RAF had been ordered to evacuate the island, you would then have had to leave your family. And if the invasion had not occurred, I should eventually have been posted back to England. You would have left them then.'

'No.'

He stared at her. 'What does that mean?'

'I have had no intention to leave Singapore. Why do you think I married you?'

'Perhaps you had better tell me,' he invited through a dry throat.

'For this *love* that you always speak of? No. Chinese girls marry for good, sensible reasons, not because they desire the body of their husband. It does not matter to you to give money to poor Chinese children to eat well, have clothes to wear, and

254

go to good school for learning to get well-paid work. You are a rich Englishman who can afford this. So I do my duty as eldest child of my family, and to help my aunt who has a great burden with her sister's children. I also do this as my duty to my dead parents. I have had no intention to leave Singapore. You have such desire for me it is easy to make you do the thing I wish. In return, I do full duty as Chinese wife. I keep house very well. I make you comfortable, and see that servants serve you well. I submit myself to your demands as husband. I please you in every way, and when you will think of leaving here, I will beg that you stay as rich planter or businessman. Then we shall all be very fortunate and happy. Now war has come to change this, and my duty to my family is greater.'

Breaking up inside, he managed to say, 'What of your duty to your husband?'

'I have ordered nice meal for you tonight. I have clean clothes ready. If you wish to go to bed, I go to bed.'

'I believed... you said you were very fond of me,' he said, hating the pleading note that had crept into his voice, yet unable to banish it.

'I am very fond of you, David. You are very kind. You have given me many things, and given money for my brothers and sisters.' For the first time, real distress overcame her. 'It was good. It worked very well. You would have stayed here, I know that, if I had asked you. But a Chinese girl learns duty, obedience and modesty. She does not learn this love that you cannot forget, and which makes you weak. You have never gained a serious disposition, as I hoped.'

Almost at the end of his tether, he said bitterly, 'If Singapore falls, I imagine my disposition will become more serious than even you could desire. I refuse to have your life on my hands, however. You said you were taught duty, obedience and modesty. The latter has been much in evidence during our short marriage. Time now to cash in on the other two. I am ordering you as a dutiful wife to leave on that ship tomorrow. Love has made me weak, you say. I am going to be strong enough to overlook all you have just said to me, and when we meet up again somewhere away from here, I'll show you just what you've taken on by marrying me.'

The following morning, even the most head-in-the-sand resident had to face facts. The Japanese were on the island and advancing across it fast. At the airfield, David was kept busy trying to control the coming and going of aircraft now concentrating on trying to repel the advance of the enemy, whilst also attempting to intercept the massive wave of bombers that continued to cause the island much loss of life and structural damage. There was a pall of smoke over the city and coast, where oil tanks had been hit and were burning fiercely. Reports flew back and forth as the troops who had been driven right down the peninsula onto the small island fought desperately to stem the invasion. The army had set up road blocks on the main highways leading from the northern part of the island. Enemy artillery, which had been smuggled across from Johore during the night, now shelled the southern sector and the vital docks, and the day was shaken by the roar of guns and the thunder of exploding bombs. The sirens wailed constantly as the sky filled with large dark aircraft yet again, and fighters dived to machine-gun those in the streets.

There were three attacks on the airfield, which, because it was the farthest south, was the only one in operation now. Still the RAF machines went up, piloted by exhausted bleary-eyed young men, sick at heart because the island could have been saved with a hundred more aircraft, or even less. There *were* less an hour later. Orders came through for two of the squadrons to take off for Palembang in Sumatra as soon as possible. The Japanese were about to land there, and the need was more urgent. As the aircraft roared up into the blue and headed toward the jungle-covered island, those left behind felt that the fall of Singapore dated from that moment.

Shortly after the departure of those aircraft, Alan Winterbottom took over from David so that he could drive out to collect Su, and take her to the docks from which the ship was due to sail at dusk. He had written several letters last night to send with his wife: one to his family, one to his banker, and one to the British representative in Java, where the ship was heading. He had given Su money to cover any expenses she would encounter, and packed into a box the gold watch his mother had given him on passing top at Cranwell, some gold cuff links that had belonged to his Uncle Rex, his DFC and the heavy signet ring engraved with his initials that Vesta had presented to him on his twenty-first birthday. He had wrapped the box and addressed it to Tarrant Hall, instructing Su that it should be given to his mother when she reached England, or handed to the British Embassy in Australia, if that was where she was advised to stay for a while. He did not see why the Japanese should have his most precious things.

The drive to his bungalow was difficult. Apart from the raids going on all around, and the shells arching overhead to explode further south amongst the docks, he was constantly halted by soldiers manning road blocks, who demanded his papers and destination. To facilitate the return, he told them he would be coming through again in thirty minutes with his wife, and that they had a boat to catch. Then he was almost there, and he felt sick. Last night had been terrible. He had tried to convince himself that the tragic times they were living through had created an impossible tug of loyalties in his beautiful gentle wife, yet he could not forget how she had looked on telling him she had married him only because he was wealthy enough to provide for her sisters and brothers, or how she had denigrated the love that had turned him into a man weak enough to do her bidding. There had been no time to talk, work out what her Oriental mind could not understand, persuade her that her first duty was to obey his decision that she must leave today. His heart had been like lead ever since. Was love truly lost? Had it ever existed . . . or had he been so determined on escape he had mistaken his own gratitude for love? Was that all they had ever shared?

Racing into the driveway, he halted the car with a spray of gravel, jumped out slamming the door, and ran up the steps into the sitting room. It was ominously quiet, as if totally deserted. On the circular carved-teak table lay the small box containing his valuables. Beside it lay the three letters he had written.

'*Su!*' he roared, charging into their bedroom.

The wardrobe that had contained her clothes was empty; the drawers of the dressing table stood open, also empty. The elaborate crystal scent spray was still on the top, but the jewel casket contained nothing. An enlargement of their wedding photograph mocked him from its silver frame. Towels had gone from the bathroom; even soap. The kitchen was deserted; the icebox bare of food. Tins had been taken from the larder, together with the cooking pots and utensils. Matches lay scattered across the stone floor where they had been spilled in haste, and left in haste. In the dining room the silver candlesticks remained along with the rest of the silver, the fine table linen, entire services of bone china, and winking crystal glasses, all in European splendour.

He crashed back into the sitting room, panting with the effort of trying to breathe in his distress. Then he spotted her work box, hanging from which was a corner of the velvet picture she had been working on earlier that week. For a moment or two he stared at it, thinking of her graceful figure bending over the work, as her slim fingers turned silks and beads into glittering dragons and peacocks. His panting grew worse, until he flung himself round and began systematically destroying everything. The china and glass he smashed in an orgy of anger and grief. Then he took an axe to the furniture, and threw all the silver into the cesspit. Returning to the bedroom, he loosened the mosquito net over the bed they had shared, let it fall out, then set it alight. The Japanese would not further his humiliation by living here.

For the next three days David lived in the Mess – or what remained of it after the constant bombing. Apart from Alan Winterbottom's initial enquiry if Su had got away on the ship all right – to which David had replied with a nod – no more mention was made of his wife or his bungalow home. The situation was too frantic for small talk, and everyone was too tense and too tired. The Japanese held so strong a hold on the island now, all hope of driving them off again had gone. The last of the Europeans, who had held onto their dream until it was almost too late, were crowding onto whichever ships remained in the harbour in a bid to escape. There was not room for them all, and many were left behind on the quays, surrounded by treasures accumulated during a lifetime in the East, still dazed by what had happened. However, no sooner did the crowded vessels put to sea than the Japanese bombers attacked them, sinking some and machine-gunning those foundering in the sea. Some of the troops were now being evacuated, leaving the rest to fight a last-stand battle in the lost campaign. Even at that stage they were being assured that reinforcements were on their way. The comments on such statements were unprintable.

At the remaining airfield, the few aircraft able to fly took off in token attacks on the enemy, returning tattered and trailing smoke without having had the slightest effect on the situation as a whole. But individual pilots accomplished feats of great daring, which showed that spirit had not died, even if the island had. Ian Freemantle proved to be one of the most unshakable and ruthless men in the air David had come across, returning time and again with his machine falling apart around him, and quiet tales of scores made or enemy patrols shot up. The least aggressive member of the squadron, he apparently became a demon once aloft. He and David drew closer during those last days in Singapore, talking about their respective homelands and families as if war did not exist. Knowing that all pilots who had aircraft to fly would leave when the word was given, David gave Ian the small box containing his most valuable and prized possessions, asking him to do his best to get it sent to his mother when he left the island. The young New Zealander offered no silly comments regarding David's certainty of coming through to give it to his mother himself, but simply accepted the charge, and promised that if it was possible he would carry it out.

Four days after Su had walked out of the bungalow to join her family at the home unknown to David, the rumour went around that a surrender was to take place within the next twelve hours. Singapore city was ablaze. The main military garrisons had been overrun and the troops taken prisoner. The Indian soldiers appeared to have largely thrown in their lot with the enemy and, in some instances, were guarding their erstwhile comrades who had been captured – and guarding them with no mercy. The wounded were killed, or, at best, left without medical attention or water in the blazing heat, like the rest of the captives.

There was only David's squadron left – three battered Hurricanes and three exhausted edgy pilots waiting to go, even though they would be travelling from frying pan to fire, for the Japanese were already in Sumatra, and possibly even Java by now. The only remaining hope of freedom was Australia, and that was two thousand miles away. Gunfire was everywhere now – the rattle of machine guns, the staccato pops of rifles, and the heavy thud of artillery. A black pall hung over the entire island, and the smell of burning oil clogged the nostrils. The telephone was out of action, and Alan Winterbottom had driven off in David's car to the only place he knew where RAF movements were still being controlled, to get orders for his men. The three pilots meanwhile decided between them that if he had not returned within the next hour, they would go. Ian sat next to David, his small bag of personal gear by his feet. 'This'll be some story to tell Pat in my next letter,' he said in his slow drawl.

'I'll say,' agreed David. 'Give her my love, won't you?'

'Sure.' He wiped his brow with the back of his hand. 'Christ, this heat gets worse.'

'I've heard it's even hotter in Sumatra,' said David conversationally, gazing at the row of palms at the far side of the field. Then his pulse leapt, and he added in a more urgent tone, 'And this is where you three get going, because that looks like Japs coming through those trees.' He jumped up shouting, 'Come on, lads, *scramble!*'

The pilots were on their feet like springs uncoiling, snatching up their bags of kit and running for the machines parked deliberately near. Yet even as they did so, from out of the sky

259

came hurtling dots as Japanese Zero fighters zoomed down on the sitting targets, raking the field with bullets that tore up the grass around the running men. Two made it to the Hurricanes and started them up, but Ian had been hit in the leg, and was clutching it as he tried to hobble on. David saw the fighters turn to come back, and ran out to help the New Zealander. Reaching Ian, he propped his own shoulder beneath the youngster's armpit, and began hurrying him towards the remaining machine. The other two were taxiing to takeoff when the Zeros streaked across once more, firing all the way. One Hurricane exploded in flames and slewed to the right, almost into the path of the other, as David watched. Then the ground around his feet began jumping as bullets thudded into it. Ian gave a sudden yell, and slumped to the ground despite his supporting arm. Bending quickly over his wounded comrade, David was aware of three things all at once. One machine was well into takeoff and roaring away to freedom, the soldiers advancing across the airfield would soon be within rifle range, and the enemy fighters had now stopped attacking for fear of hitting their own troops. On the ground Ian lay in agony, his chest a mess of blood and bone, his leg open from the knee to ankle.

'Take it up! For Christ's sake, *go!*' he urged, spewing blood with every word.

David left him there and ran for the Hurricane, knowing it would be touch and go whether he could get above the range of a rifle before the men running across the sun-baked airfield from the palms approached near enough. One leap onto the wing and then into the cockpit. No time to fasten straps. Press the starter button. Thank God, it started first time. Then the fastest, most unorthodox taxi of his life, one eye on the Japanese figures, the other on the potholes in the field.

'Come on, *come on*,' his voice urged in taut tones as he opened the throttle, expecting a Hurricane to react like a Spitfire.

It seemed he would head straight into the palms still on the ground. At least he would mow down a few Japanese as he did so. Rifles were being raised. They cracked in the still humid air. Then the ground was falling away, and the alien soldiers were growing smaller and smaller beneath him. Singapore from the air looked exactly like the maps he had been studying for the past six months. Landmarks stood out clearly to give him his bearings. Over the city hung a dark cloud. Fires were raging all over the island. The emerald jewel had become a black opal with fire in its heart. He turned southwards and headed out

260

over the sea. Only when Singapore was no more than a haze of black smoke in the distance, did he remember he could no longer take an aircraft off the ground.

Chapter Thirteen

DAVID WAS in Sumatra, a great long island covered, in the most part, by impenetrable jungle, and with a climate more humid and relentless than Singapore that bred venomous creatures. By the time he and Scotty, the other pilot who had managed to get away, overflew Palembang airfield, it had been captured by the enemy, and all RAF flights were operating from an emergency airfield in the jungle.

Their arrival brought them into contact with other men who had been in Singapore, all eager to hear about the final hours. David and Scotty had no wish to talk about it, but eventually had to report details to the senior officers in charge. Putting it into words made it seem even more tragic, and David turned in for a long sleep, only to find himself wide awake staring at the ceiling as he went over it all again. The fact that he had broken his jinx on takeoff did not seem to be the wonderful event it ought to be. The fact that he was free and not a prisoner of the Japanese, as he had expected, did not arouse jubilation in his breast. Perhaps he was no longer capable of feeling. He lay for hour after hour thinking of Su and her family somewhere in the tangle of Singapore streets, of Alan Winterbottom, almost certainly in the hands of the Japanese by now, and of Ian Freemantle dying within feet of his means of freedom. He thought of that small box containing his own most precious possessions, still in Ian's bag. He felt nothing, no sense of loss or pain, just went over all those events in his mind as the sweltering night crawled past.

His clothes had been laundered overnight, and he was given a flying helmet so that he could take part in the last-stand defence of another island. Java had already been invaded, the Celébes had been occupied, Amboina had surrendered. The first Japanese had landed on Timor, and their ships were steaming towards New Guinea. In Northern Australia, plans were afoot to move the huge herds of cattle southwards across the parched outback, to prevent such vast and vital supplies of meat falling into the hands of invaders now growing dangerously close. The enemies' successes had been so widespread and swift, it seemed possible that they would not be stopped anywhere. Even those who belived that, like Hitler, Tojo would stretch his power like an elastic band until it broke or sprang back to lash him in the face, had to acknowledge that a period of blood-red history was in the making and would never be forgotten after the world became peaceful once more.

No one questioned David's right to fly the Hurricane he had brought from Singapore, and he now felt it was his machine, even if it did still display the grinning sheep Ian had painted on the side as a sign of personal partnership with that aircraft. David felt Ian would be glad he'd got away, and was continuing to attack the enemy.

He went up in it three times that day, the last time being mid-afternoon when they were scrambled to attack a reported landing force approaching up-river to Palembang. He ran with the others and climbed into the cockpit, only momentarily thinking of that strange subconscious fear that had rendered him physically paralysed in such a situation for so long, and which had set him out on a course he had never dreamt lay ahead of him in life. At the moment, he felt in limbo; knowing the new direction awaiting him would be out of his control. His life was no longer his to arrange. He was no longer merely the nephew of the great 'Sherry' Sheridan, of whom everyone expected so much. He was one of a vast army of free men fighting tooth and claw to remain so. A great deal was expected from all of them. Personalities, backgrounds, human feelings were unimportant. David Sheridan was simply another man in another machine until destiny decided he was no longer needed. A sense of inevitability ruled him as he took the Hurricane off the ground that afternoon, and climbed with the others to head towards Palembang and the River Musi.

It was an overcast, sultry day so they kept low beneath the cloud, most of them, like David, flying with the hood back for coolness. He looked over the side at the unbroken, dense, dark green jungle stretching as far as the eye could see in every direction. It was difficult to get used to flying over such terrain after his days in Spitfires over England; no built-up areas to avoid if shot down; no English Channel full of German shipping ready to pick up a downed pilot. If a man crashed or baled out over this, it would swallow him up greedily, like exotic plants that close around anything landing on their leaves, to imprison and digest it. He shivered suddenly in the brooding, sulky skies. There was a sinister aspect about this jungle-covered island after the gaiety and colour that had once been Singapore. He did not envy the Japanese troops preparing for a long occupation there.

'There they are, lads,' came the steady voice of the leader over the R/T. 'More than enough to go round, I think. After I go in, you can each have your fun. Don't get so excited you forget to keep your eyes open for Zeros protecting this lot. And don't forget there's a hell of a lot of jungle out there just waiting for any fool who takes too many risks.'

They went down one after the other, diving onto a flotilla of small boats packed with troops, which were gliding slowly along the twisting brown waterway that cut through the jungle like a giant, bloated worm. The Japanese soldiers were defenceless sitting targets, and the first four Hurricanes raked them with bullets to such deadly effect bodies were falling into the water all around the craft by the time David went down. Still expecting his machine to react like the faster Spitfire, his dive was not as accurate as intended, and he had to skim along just above the surface for a few seconds before pressing his gun button. At some time during that strafe, it flashed through his mind that his famous uncle's last action, the one that had earned him the VC, had been the destruction of enemy boats along a waterway through dense trees. For a brief second, David felt again that approving spiritual presence in the cockpit.

Then he was up and circling for a second attack, the old skill and confidence he had had during the Battle of Britain returning with a rush, as he signalled to his nearest companion before pushing the nose down again. The dive was right on target this time, and his judgement was keen, as he pumped prolonged bursts of fire from his guns into the rows of upturned faces that flashed past beneath him. The river was now churning with spray and thrashing bodies. Some boats were sinking, some had tilted to throw the occupants into water infested with crocodiles and other horrors. The brown water was streaked with red. Pulling the nose up, he began to climb towards the large billowing clouds, when several small thuds told him all too reminiscently that he was being shot at. He would know that sound until he died. The boats must be armed with light guns. Hot on the heels of that thought came another series of thuds, then oil and glycol began spraying up over the windshield to completely obliterate his vision ahead. He had been hit, how badly he could not tell, but he knew all he could do now was try to get back before he was forced down in the jungle. Signalling to the nearest pilot that he was returning to base, he banked and set course for the clearing in the jungle. Palembang was much nearer, but he would only offer himself as a prisoner if he landed there. Flying blind was going to add to his difficulties, one of the worst being his hopes of landing safely.

Next minute, most of his difficulties were removed, leaving only one. The engine cut out and he started going down. An urgent look on both sides of his cockpit showed him that he was near enough to the coast to reach it, if the machine did not burst into flames. With luck and skill he might bring the aircraft down on the shore. From there, he could get a boat from some of the natives and try his luck at getting south of Palembang, where he had heard there were still some Dutch troops holding out. In the coming darkness there should be an even chance.

Using all the manoeuvres he could think of to propel himself to the most advantageous point, he reached the coastline only just in time to skim the top of palm trees bordering the beach, before facing the inevitable blind landing. Keeping his wheels up, he hung over the side of the cockpit to watch the line of surf breaking on his left, bracing himself for impact. It came sooner than expected, and the aircraft tipped violently sideways to nose-dive into the sea breaking on white sand. It all happened so quickly, he was hardly aware of events before he passed out on impact with the crushed metal of his cockpit.

There was intense pain in both his legs, and a roaring in his ears as he came to. When he attempted to move, he suffered even worse pain, which made him cry out. Then hands were suddenly on him, voices telling him to keep still while they extricated him. Still hazy, he registered with relief that the voices spoke in English. Australians, by the sound of it. What luck to have landed in an area still held by Allied forces. His guardian angel must have been watching over him – or the spirit of his Uncle Rex.

His rescuers pushed and pulled him in their attempt to get him out, causing gasps of agony he could not hold back. Both legs had been trapped by the crushed jagged metal, causing wounds which gushed blood with every movement. The roaring in his ears was caused by the sea foaming around the wrecked Hurricane as the tide advanced.

'All right, hold on, mate,' said a voice in his ear. 'We've got you now.'

They manhandled him over the edge of the cockpit, then carried him through the surging surf, and over the open beach to a line of trees at a very fast pace. Almost at once, the shade of the trees darkened to deep gloom due to the density of the growth. It seemed to David, who was in great pain, that his rescuers were going a very long way through what appeared to be a rough track leading into the interior. How could troops operate or set up a headquarters in the midst of such terrain? He was being carried by two burly youngsters in khaki, wearing the distinctive Australian bush hats, turned up on one side. He was on the point of asking them how much farther it was, when their way was suddenly barred by someone who materialised from the trees without a sound.

David's rescuers were big men, but this one topped them by a couple of inches. He wore similar uniform, with a sergeant's stripes on his shirt sleeves, but his expression was so hostile he could have been one of the enemy. He stood implacably, looking at his men as if David did not exist.

'You flaming stupid bastards,' he said with soft venom. 'What the hell do you think you're doing? The Nips'll have seen that thing come down, and they'll be after him. When they discover he's gone, they'll come looking, won't they? The blood on the machine'll tell them he won't get far on his own, so it'll be obvious someone's helped him. Since there isn't a kampong for miles, they'll know it's unlikely to be natives.' His lip curled. 'You brainless sods. You'll lead them straight here.'

One of his rescuers, a youngster of around twenty with thick fair eyelashes and blond hairs smothering his arms and legs, said, 'He's one of ours. We couldn't leave him there to be caught.'

'Why not? Thousands are being caught. Why not one more?'

Fighting pain David said, 'You'd know the answer to that if the one more was you, Sergeant.'

The quiet venom was turned on him. 'Look, mate, as the blokes on the ground in this war, we've got enough to do without nursemaiding pretty-boy fliers who drop out of the sky and expect special treatment. If it wasn't too risky, I'd make them take you back to that machine of yours.'

Hardly believing what he heard, David said, 'We've been out shooting up boatloads of Japs trying to land. I must have killed a dozen to help you chaps on the ground. I happen to believe that deserves some help in return. I also happen to believe my rank deserves a little respect from a sergeant.'

The Australian's mouth twisted. 'The only thing I respect is a man who proves himself to be a *real* man. You'll get no respect

266

from me just because you call blokes "cheps" in that fancy voice, and wear a coupla bars on your shoulders because you went to some fancy bloody school. I don't like Aussie officers, mate, and I don't like flaming English ones even more.'

'With that attitude rife amongst your troops, no wonder we've come to this state,' snapped David. 'You're so busy hating your allies, you've forgotten the identity of the real enemy.'

'Sarge, he's bleeding all over the place,' pointed out the other youngster holding him. 'It'll be a dead giveaway to anyone looking. Besides, he's getting bloody heavy.'

'Take me to your commander,' instructed David, fighting the faintness overtaking him once more.

'Here I am,' replied the sergeant. 'What I say goes with this bunch.'

'All right,' he said weakly. 'Just give me some bandages or something to bind my legs, and something to eat and drink, then I'll try to make my way to ... to ...'

When consciousness returned, he was lying on a pile of ferns and large, fleshy leaves in a tiny clearing. It was dark, and he was able to make out the presence of others only by the occasional gleam of whites of eyes, and the sound of subdued conversation. They gave him water to drink, a tin plate full of stew, and some slices of pineapple. His legs were now bound with strips of some kind of cloth, and the pain had been slightly reduced to a rhythmic grinding that made him sweat even more heavily. He felt terrily weak, and decided to wait until daylight before attempting a bid to set off on his own. He appeared to be with a small independent group of some kind, commanded by the sergeant, who was called Kershaw. Unless they were planning to rejoin their main unit soon, his chances of remaining with them looked slim.

They looked even slimmer when he returned to clarity four days later, following a dose of fever that left him weaker than ever. The wounds in his legs appeared to be infected, making it impossible for him to stand. He lay on his rough bed, panting with the terrible heat and pain from his wounds, while mosquitoes feasted off his flesh, and tried to work out what was going on around him. The Australian group numbered seven: five privates, a lance corporal, and Sergeant Kershaw. All except the sergeant were friendly enough, when they had time to talk to him. They came and went in pairs all through the twenty-four hours, and appeared to have stores and ammunition somewhere near, for they ate food only available in tins. David also suspected they had a radio transmitter hidden away, due to the things they said when they thought he was asleep. Until he was able to move he was dependent on them, so he did his best to show his appreciation for their help by being as undemanding and uncomplaining as possible.

During meals, they asked him about himself and his war, so he told them about escaping from Singapore at the last minute, and what the last days had been like. He also told them a little about England during the first days, and the Battle of Britain that had been touch and go for a while. He told them about Tarrant Hall, and how his home had become an RAF Officers' Mess. He also told them about Vesta in the army, and his father in a vital Ministry. When he asked them about themselves, they told him their various backgrounds in Australia, but clammed up on anything to do with the war. When David finally asked them point-blank who they were and what they were doing on Sumatra, the sergeant looked up to join in the conversation for the first time.

'That's none of your bloody business, Christopher Robin. It's beyond the understanding of blokes like you, who think you're flaming heroes because Winston Bloody Churchill said you saved Britain. There were Aussies in that lot, you know. Plenty of them. And there were Aussies in Singapore. I should know. My young kiddo brother was there – still is, far as I know – and from what I heard from some of the blokes who got away on hospital ships, the bloody English let them down. They failed to hold onto their positions when our blokes did, and surrendered at the first sign of trouble, leaving our troops in the lurch. *That's* how flaming heroic you are, mate.'

David looked up at him from his position on the ground. 'Why didn't you explain right at the start that your aggressive manner is to cover a feeling of inadequacy, because your young brother and his friends have done all the real fighting, while you have been here eating tinned ham, and peaches and cream in safety?'

Kershaw got to his feet, flushing with anger. 'You snivelling little . . .'

He was interrupted by the noisy arrival of two of the men in a state of great urgency, and swung round to swear at their careless approach.

'They've found the aircraft and they're coming this way,' panted one, a former jackaroo and tough as they came.

'It's only a small group – about a dozen. We can handle them,' said the other, the blond youngster, who was particularly interested in all David had told them about himself and England.

268

'You know the orders,' snapped Sergeant Kershaw. 'Killing them would bring others to find out where they were. This is our moment to vanish. Come on, *move!*'

With speed and skill they packed up everything lying around, and covered up any sign of human presence in the place. Then they prepared to leave. The blond private said in low tones, 'It'll take two of us to carry Dave.'

The sergeant looked over his shoulder to say, 'He's staying here. Once they find him, they'll stop looking.'

'Christ, we can't leave him. We can't do that to any bloke!'

'We've got no choice, and you know it. It's my decision. Nothing for you to worry about.'

'But ... they'll get him!'

'Then they'll be satisfied.' The big man cocked his thumb in the direction of the track, and the youngster moved off without another word. Looking at David, Kershaw said, 'If you were in my place, you'd do the same. I can't use my gun because the sound would give us away. Is that revolver of yours loaded?'

David nodded, still trying to accept that he was about to be abandoned by his allies.

'When they get here, use it.'

He was gone, and David lay watching some ants running endlessly up and down a nearby tree trunk, envying them their freedom. So he was going to end up a prisoner of war after all. Where was his guardian angel now? He drew his revolver from the webbing belt around his waist, and rolled over to prop himself against a tree to wait. His legs still felt as if knives were being stabbed into them, his body had been bitten all over by mosquitoes, and he had a five-day stubble on his face. Well, he could not have gone anywhere on foot, so perhaps this was the best solution. He would be out of the fighting now, and could get some kind of medical attention from the Red Cross people, if not his captors.

They came about fifteen minutes later, and he kept them at bay for as long as he could, to give the Australians more time to get away. But the bullets soon ran out, and they came up to him to stand around, looking down at his bandaged legs – a group of men in rough uniforms and floppy caps.

'Where you friends go?' asked one in stilted English.

'There's only me,' he answered. 'I came down in that Hurricane.'

'That five day more gone. Where you get these?' He indicated the bandages around David's legs. 'What you eat and drink?'

'We carry first-aid equipment and some supplies in our aircraft, in case we come down in places like this,' he explained

269

in casual tones. 'I'm glad you came along because I've just run out.'

'If you glad, why you fire gun?'

'I wasn't sure who you were.'

'And empty tins for food. Where they? I see nothing.'

David remained silent.

'Where you friends go?'

'I have no friends. A Hurricane only holds one.'

'I advise truth.'

'That is the truth.'

'We see.' The man nodded to two of the other Japanese, who knelt down beside his legs.

It was then that David realised Kershaw had meant he should use the revolver on himself when they came, and a feeling of utter terror rushed through him. No! His pathway through life could not lead him into this. Dear God, *no!*

The Australians followed Rod Kershaw cautiously. It could be a trap. From the cover of the trees they studied the area down by the beach with observant eyes that could spot movement almost before it came. They were highly trained, extremely valuable, and under express orders. For three days they had been nearby doing the job they had been sent to do, trying to close their ears to the periodic screams of the English officer they had been forced to abandon in order to conceal their presence. When the terrible sounds stopped, and the Japanese were observed departing, it was clear their cover was still secure. Rod Kershaw then astonished them all by going down to the beach area near the crashed Hurricane, which was being pounded by the tide. They remained expertly hidden as they listened for the sounds of stealth, and looked down at the British pilot pegged out naked in the full killing sun within reach of the high tide, which would drown him slowly if he was still alive by then. Certain there was no one else in the vicinity, the sergeant motioned the man next to him and stepped out onto the open beach. The others stood ready to cover them.

Reaching the helpless figure on the beach they stood looking down and, tough though he was, Rod Kershaw said, 'Christ, why didn't he save himself all this?'

The jackaroo levelled his gun at the forehead, where deep blue eyes gazed sightlessly at the sun.

'What the hell do you think you're doing?' rasped the senior man, knocking aside the barrel.

The young sunburnt face looked back at him defiantly. 'I left the poor bastard once. I'm not leaving him to suffer any more.'

270

'Nor am I, mate. Help me untie him and let's get going.'

'Get going?' echoed the other. 'He won't last another hour.'

'Yes, he bloody will,' came the fierce reply. 'He might be a privileged English gent and live in a flaming great mansion, but he's as good a bloke as I've ever come across. I'll get him back to his own people, alive *and* sane, or I'll have the sound of his screams in my ears for the rest of my days.'

They cut the thick vines twisted around wrists and ankles, and Rod Kershaw picked up the body as if he were cradling an infant. Once in the trees, the whole party set off silently to where they had bandages and food. None looked back at the bloodstains on the sand near the crashed Hurricane.

The shock, the stunning blow of the fall of Singapore following the loss of Hong Kong, had a devastating effect on British morale. Those glittering invincible outposts had been regarded as being almost as sacrosanct as the Royal Family. How could the sun have set so blood-red upon them? The public mood grew ugly as conflicting reports from across the world suggested mismanagement, overconfidence, lack of co-operation, and an incredible head-in-sand attitude. Why had the invaders been allowed to race through the mainland so easily? Why had the famed formidable defences on Singapore failed so lamentably? Worst of all, why, when defeat was staring them in the face, had so many troops been abandoned with no hope of getting away? Thousands had been surrendered to the vicious conquerors because no emergency evacuation plans had ever been drawn up. The native peoples might have been left to their fate, but British and Commonwealth troops would have been free to fight back. They could do nothing for the people of the Malay States from the prison cages which had been hastily thrown up to contain the vast numbers of men who must have felt betrayed by their leaders.

For the relatives of those who had been part of the Far Eastern defence forces, it was a particularly anguished period. The continuing emergency in Sumatra and Java made communications difficult. Desperately trying to stop the Japanese before the entire East was lost, military priority was frantic defence; there was no time for making lists of any kind. In any case, it was practically impossible to decide who was dead, who was a captive, or who was hiding somewhere in the vast jungle areas with little hope of eventual survival. It was not knowing which broke people's spirits quicker than anything.

Chris had had little time in which to agonise over David, due to a series of top-level meetings at which he had acted as interpreter. The Intelligence network in the Far East had collapsed and new plans had to be made. Africa was now a scene of fresh reverses with the advent of Hitler's Afrika Korps, and Chris had flown to Cairo with Frank Moore to investigate weaknesses in Intelligence links there, which, coupled with the crisis in the Pacific, was severely damaging the work of undercover agents. His work at the school had been all the more intense when he was there, but the thought of David was at the back of his mind throughout. Having been prepared for what had happened the news had not shocked him as much as the man in the street, but the strain was as great. Not only was it a blow as the father of someone caught in the tragedy, it was yet another blow to an ideal which had filled more than twenty years of his life. He sought escape at the first opportunity.

Since Christmas he had had only two chances to pursue his relationship with Sonja Koltay. He had telephoned her apartment on both evenings without success. She had returned his calls, Sandy entering them in the book as, *A lady called regarding your glass chalice*. On this evening when he had suddenly found himself free, he had rung her number, and she had invited him to dinner. Carrying an armful of roses, he took the steps two at a time and rung her bell, his heart hammering against his ribs. The cause was not the physical exertion of mounting the steps, but the fear of disappointment. Had he been so ripe for enchantment before Christmas he had seen echoes of Laura in a woman who happened to possess hair as red as hers had been? Would he see a stranger in the next moment and find another ideal flown beyond recall?

The maid admitted him, then led the way into the room with the poppy-splashed cushions, where he was stunned anew. In a loose gown of turquoise silk, embellished with multiple gold fine-chain necklets, and a heavy gold bangle on her wrist, Sonja looked even lovelier than he remembered.

Crossing the room towards him, light from the chandelier enhancing the lustrous upswept hair, she said softly, 'Roses. How absurdly romantic! I had forgotten such chivalry had been commonplace in my youth. Thank you for reminding me.'

As the maid took the flowers from the room to arrange them, Chris turned the kiss on her hand into a full-blooded embrace before he was aware of what he meant to do. He had never kissed a woman the way he then kissed her, and her response was so heady, it increased his desire to the point where he was obliged to draw away. The teasing element of her smile did nothing to ease his condition.

'The not-so-cool Englishman, it appears. I discover

272

something more of the enigmatic Sir Christopher Sheridan.'

'Enigmatic? What nonsense,' he murmured, as the maid re-entered with a tureen of soup to place on the table set for two, with a branch of candles suggesting the kind of intimacy that set him rejoicing.

Although his physical state calmed during the meal, the sensual aspects of that tête-à-tête plunged him deeper and deeper into intoxication such as he had never suspected possible. They conversed unrestrainedly on subjects ranging from triptychs to scherzos, from Budapest to Bahrain, with quicksilver changes from one language to another, until he was alight with the fire of their matching personalities. Her sweet melodious voice charmed him in whichever language she used, the graceful passionate gestures with her hands to illustrate the point she was making emphasised her Continental fascination, her expressive Slavic features revealed her feelings so clearly he felt overwhelmed at her honesty with him. All the while, her eyes teased, questioned or invited in the intimate glow of the candles.

Then, with her coffee on the lid of the piano beside his red roses, she began to play what she termed her 'after dinner pieces' for him. The intoxication became total as he sat in that room, filled with sounds that were balm to his bruised soul, watching her with growing painful hunger. The world became just that room with them the only people in it. Peace and beauty were vividly revived; gentle passions reigned. The past three months slipped gradually from his conscious thoughts, and with them the despair, apprehension and exhaustion. For years he had been searching. He had travelled the world several times over, yet still it had eluded him. The impact of this eventual discovery was so great he was forced to master threatening tears. Perfection had always moved him deeply. Only another like spirit would understand that.

Brahms played with sensitivity and understanding gave way to a brilliant passionate étude, which filled the room with cascading unbridled cadenzas, echoing the mounting desire in him. Suddenly, the showy piece ended, and she swung round on the stool for his reaction. Getting to his feet, he crossed to her, finding it almost impossible to speak through the emotion she had aroused with her music.

'I am a worshipper at your shrine,' he told her huskily. 'Your brilliance as a pianist equals that of the artist. I have been held in thrall.'

Looking at him with laughter lighting her eyes, she said provocatively, 'I played Debussy, Rachmaninov and Brahms, whom you told me you appreciate. Then I ended with Chopin, who is "too sweet and full of fiery passions". Have I won you over to him? Come, confess that I have.'

'I have fallen totally in love with you,' he said quietly.

The laughter went from her face as she stood in instinctive protest. 'No ... oh, no, my dear! I did not think you would be so foolish.'

Dismayed at her reaction, he could only ask, 'Surely you knew, you were aware that this would happen ... *had* happened?'

'I was aware there would be love between us, yes,' she declared. 'But "in love"? This is not the time for such things. "In love" means tomorrow and forever.'

'I know,' he said carefully. 'Is that so foolish?'

Moving restlessly away across the room, she said in low tones, 'How do we know there will be a tomorrow? Who can presently consider forever?' Swinging round to face him, the coldness in her eyes shocked him. 'I have seen my father and sister killed by their own countrymen. I have watched my friends being dragged from their children, never to return. My husband was shot in cold blood, and his associates risked their lives to help me to safety. Yes, I knew that first moment that there would be love between us. I asked that it would be beautiful ... not everlasting,' she finished more gently.

He crossed to her and took her hands in his. 'Would you create a work of art, then smash it because there is no room on a shelf for it? What you have created in me is there to stay. Don't attempt to drive it out.' Coaxing her to sit beside him on the settee, he went on, 'There is something I should like to tell you, which might help you to understand. Will you listen?'

His gentleness seemed to neutralise her swift change of mood, and she studied his face for a moment or two in silence, as if trying to assure herself of his sincerity. Then she gave a nod.

'Of course I will listen.'

Leaning forward with his arms along his thighs, he stared into the fire as he remembered an eighteen-year-old schoolboy coming home for the summer holidays in 1914, and he began to relate how that boy, academically brilliant and due to go to Cambridge after the vacation, had known nothing of girls because he was lost in the world of learning.

'I was unaware that the doctor's daughter, whom I had known all my life, was hopelessly attracted to the boy she imagined I was. During a thunderstorm, she deliberately

274

awoke me to sexual awareness, and was as unprepared for the outcome as I when she completed the seduction several evenings later. Her father and my eldest brother marched me to the altar, so that my child would have its rightful name and inheritance, but all I could see was the loss of my glittering career, and the sacrifice of the rest of my life for five minutes of strange pleasure. To escape the wife I hated, the baby I viewed with disgust, and the soul-destroying work I was forced to do on the estate, I walked out on them both and enlisted. Six months later, I was blown up in Gallipoli, and awoke in a hospital knowing nothing of the past, not even my name, and afraid of remembering it.

'One day, in the middle of that abyss, a man in RFC uniform walked up to announce that he was my brother Rex. It meant nothing to me, but he had brought with him a beautiful red-haired girl he said was his wife. She sang and danced at a hospital concert, and I had never seen anyone like her before. She was so gay, so vivid, so warm, and the only person visiting me who had not known me before Gallipoli. The others were always desperately trying to make me remember, and then being hurt and upset when I didn't.

'Laura was especially wonderful, because she accepted me as I was. I fell in love with her, knowing she was married to my brother. It didn't seem like treachery, because I was confined to bed, and expressed my feelings only by spending hours on drawings for her. But she pulled me through. It was for her that I worked at recovering my mental and physical powers again.'

He sighed as he remembered those long-ago years of anguish and pain. 'The day finally came when the last memory returned, and I realised the girl in the village with a three-year-old toddler was my wife, with our son. The shock was so great, I went to the one person I felt could help me hang onto my sanity.'

'Laura?'

'The beautiful actress all men adored, but who belonged solely and utterly to Rex. She made me face up to my responsibilities and try to repair my marriage. But my wife had gone through too much, also, and wanted a divorce. I was in London seeing my solicitor about it when I heard Rex had been killed. Knowing what it would do to Laura, I went to the theatre to give the news to her.' He frowned into the flames as the past became too real. 'But I didn't have to break her heart. There was an air raid and the theatre was hit. I went in to get her, but she was dead when I picked her up from the stage. I

275

carried her from the burning building and I... kissed her goodbye. From me and from Rex. That was the only time I kissed Laura.'

There was silence for a moment, then she asked quietly, 'And your wife and son?'

He turned to look at her and saw Sonja Koltay, no one else anymore. 'My wife is at home in Dorset, where we have been happy enough. My son was in Singapore when it fell – that's all I know. When he was twelve, an old man in the village told him the circumstances of his birth, and my consequent desertion of him and his mother. His immaturity led him to feel he could not forgive me. I discovered only recently that his mother has *never* forgiven me.'

They sat side by side in silence while the fire crackled and leaped, then she put her hand over his in a caress. 'Thank you for telling me all this. I realise that you have had sadness in your life, also. But, my dear, can you not see what we have been doing this evening?'

'We have been discovering each other.'

'We have been *pretending*. We see in each other a means of escape for a while. *Liebchen*, you have tonight helped me to re-create the world we once knew, which has gone forever. For a few hours we have driven away reality by bringing to life a dream we both have locked away in our hearts. Let us escape whenever we can, but let us have no illusions. Reality is still there. Think only of "now" and not "forever", I beg you.'

Taking up the hand that rested on his, he said gravely, 'Illusions flew from my window long ago. You are my reality.'

Her further response remained unspoken, for the maid entered and stood waiting. In slight abstraction, Sonja asked the girl what she wanted. Mr Alexander Matheson had telephoned to speak urgently to the gentleman visitor, the maid informed her, then retired.

'Your friends know that you are here?' asked Sonja sharply.

'Only my assistant,' he told her, wishing Sandy at the ends of the earth. 'I have to leave a number where I can be reached, night or day. He is very discreet, and would not have called unless it was extremely urgent.' Getting to his feet, he apologised. 'Forgive me for spoiling something so perfect.'

Taking up the receiver in the hallway outside he said brusquely, 'Yes, Sandy, what's the problem?'

'Air Vice Marshal Cranshaw rang two minutes ago. Will you call him back, sir?' said the well-known voice at the other end. Then, betraying only a hint of emotion, it went on, 'He indicated that it was a personal matter he felt you would want to hear immediately.'

'Yes... I see, Sandy. Thank you. I'll ring him right away.'

He dialled the number with a hand that had grown unsteady, and Charles Cranshaw answered after only three rings.

'You have some news, Charles?' he asked, in the sharp impersonal manner of one high-ranking figure to another.

'Yes, Chris, it's just come in. Thought you'd want to know, although it's uncomfirmed, as yet, of course.'

'I understand.'

'According to a Flight Lieutenant Scott of David's squadron, who is now on a hospital ship heading for India from Java, the pair of them flew out from Singapore as the Japs were crossing the airfield.'

'*Flew!* Are you certain he means David?'

'Oh yes, no doubt about that,' came the confident reply. 'Scott insists they brought out the remaining two Hurricanes and flew them to Sumatra. He goes on to say that the squadron operated over Sumatra for only two days before being ordered to Java. On the first of those days David signalled that he was in difficulties, and was last seen heading toward the coast with engine trouble.

'On their way to Java, a wrecked Hurricane was spotted on the tideline some distance from Palembang, but there was no sign of the pilot. According to people who know Sumatra, it's a jungle area barely inhabited by the natives and practically trackless.' After a momentary pause, the voice continued, 'I won't give you the customary white lie that there is every chance that he is still alive. You are a man of intelligence and will realise his hopes are very slender indeed. Thousands of our chaps have fallen into the hands of the Japanese in this Far Eastern disaster, and I think we will have little idea of their fate until we go back. I am deeply sorry, Chris. The only comfort I can sensibly offer is that if he has not survived, he might well turn out to be one of the luckier ones.'

'Well... thank you, Charles,' Chris said. 'I appreciate your friendship.'

'I have withheld the telegram, as you asked. Your wife has received no notification.'

Chris replaced the receiver and stood staring at the pattern on the gold and crimson wallpaper, seeing a blond handsome boy of twelve rushing into the room and blurting out, 'Why didn't you tell me I was a bastard?' That renunciation had not made his love for his son die. It had merely been in hibernation until revived by the warmth of understanding and forgiveness. Now it would remain in permanent half-sleep, its heartbeat growing slower and slower until it passed into mortality unnoticed. If only he had been there when the boy had come to say goodbye.

He stood for so long staring at that wallpaper, Sonja came to stand beside him in silent questioning. Swallowing painfully, he said, 'News of my son.'

'He is lost?'

'I imagine he is.'

She made no professions of sorrow, no gesture of exaggerated compassion such as taking his arm to lead him to a chair, or offering him a drink. She merely asked quietly, 'You would like to stay – not be alone tonight?'

He shook his head. 'I have something to do before I go to Dorset to tell my wife. I must leave at once.'

Greg Neave was put out at being fetched from his bed, but changed his attitude when he saw who his visitor was.

'Good Lord, old boy, don't tell me one of my people has blotted his copybook,' he exclaimed in serious tones. 'You haven't come to tell me there's a rotten apple in my barrel.'

'Nothing like that. I've come to ask for your help.'

'Surely. Take a seat,' said the thin, sharp-faced man in tartan dressing gown and slippers. 'How about a nip of something. You look a bit done in.'

'Make it a stiff one, will you?'

With glasses in hands, the two men sat in deep leather armchairs to discuss something few others knew about.

'Have you anyone in Sumatra, at present?' asked Chris, feeling the spirit warming him a little.

The other man's eyes narrowed. 'Sumatra! What's afoot?'

'My son was shot down near Palembang ten days ago.'

Greg frowned. 'It's all jungle there, you know.' He sipped his brandy. 'As it happens, I do have a couple of chaps operating there – very unsuccessfully, so far. How can anyone organise internal resistance amongst the natives when the official uniformed white defenders are being captured wholesale before their eyes? All they have managed to do so far is get advance intelligence on Jap movements out to us – not that it made any difference to the outcome, except maybe to delay it for a few days.'

'Who are they?' Chris asked.

'Far-Eastern experts. Ex-planters, the pair.'

'You mean "Buddha" and "Jade"?'

278

'That's right. I've also got "Rattan" on Java. He's had no more success than the other two.' He leant forward intently. 'I'll tell you the truth, old boy. We've heard nothing from them for a week. It seems likely they've been rumbled and executed. Or, of course, they might have ditched all their stuff and mingled with the troops in captivity, intending to break out as soon as the situation stabilises. It's total confusion out there, as I'm sure you appreciate.'

'Yes,' said Chris with a heavy sigh, 'and there's no evidence that David was killed in the crash. In some ways, it might be better if he had been. If your people do make contact again, you might ask them if they know anything.'

'Surely.' He pursed his lips thoughtfully as he studied Chris. 'Your boy came through the Battle of Britain, didn't he?'

Chris nodded. 'They gave him a DFC. Everyone expected him to be a second "Sherry", but I like to feel he proved his individual worth during those desperate months. I understand he was one of the last pilots to get away from Singapore.'

'Of course, we're not the only ones with agents there. The Australians are conducting all manner of skulduggery throughout those islands. The Dutch have never been asked for their permission – the times are too serious for the niceties of protocol – but I was told on the "need to know" basis. Didn't want to put spanners in each others' works, did we? Their Head of Operations and I are on mutual swearing terms. I'll have a word with him tomorrow, if you like.'

Chris stood up. 'I'm deeply grateful.'

His host also got to his feet. 'Don't be. The chances of being of any help are practically non-existent. I'm very sorry about your boy, Chris. We've really caught a dreadful cold over the Far East, and are likely to have the symptoms for some time yet.'

Marion was in the sitting room, still as a statue on the window seat, gazing out at the daffodils fluttering in the stiff breeze. Chris had handed his coat and cap to Robson, with the usual enquiry about Mrs Robson's health. He had tried to suggest that there was nothing especially different about his visit, but his efforts had been wasted, as was soon apparent.

'It's David, isn't it?' Marion greeted him in a flat voice, still gazing from the window. 'I've been expecting you ever since Singapore fell. Somehow I knew you'd tell me in person. I'm grateful, Chris.'

He walked across the room slowly, filled with a sudden savage decision to sell Tarrant Hall. It held too many

279

associations with death. Sitting on the window seat beside her, he realised she had become an old woman, as distant from him as any person who lived in the village.

'Did he die cleanly?' she asked in the same flat tone.

What should the answer be? All the way in the train he had striven to decide the least painful things to say. Would a profession of hope make the news more bearable? Rumours of Japanese treatment of those they had conquered were so shocking it might be better not to foster that suggestion. Should he lie and say David had been killed in action, rather than reveal that he had probably perished slowly and painfully in swamp-ridden jungle?

'Tell me the truth,' she demanded at his silence, still intent on the daffodils.

They had made a pact always to do so when they had begun rebuilding their marriage. It had proved a weak foundation, but a pact was a pact. He honoured it now.

'The telegram would have stated, "Missing presumed killed".'

She turned slowly to face him, but she could have been looking at a stone pillar, so expressionless were her eyes. 'Are you saying there is a chance he is still alive?'

'Charles Cranshaw thinks not.'

Her mouth twisted. 'Your influential friends stepping in now it's too late?'

'The situation out there is so confused,' he explained heavily. 'It's only because one of David's squadron got away on a hospital ship that we know the few facts we do have.'

He told her exactly what he had been told on the telephone the previous night, omitting the meeting he had had with Greg Neave. When he had finished, she seemed just as untouched by his words.

'What about *her*?'

'His wife? No one knows, except that this fellow Scott said he believed she had left Singapore on one of the last ships, destination uncertain. I'll attempt to gain contact with him when the ship reaches India. Some of the ships were attacked and sunk, however.'

'I hope to God she was on one of them.'

'*Marion!*'

On her feet in a sudden movement, she cried in a loud and uncontrolled voice, 'Damn your creed of international love! Damn your unbelievable pious tolerance! As God is my witness, if that creature is spared when my son is taken, I'll never enter a church again as long as I live.'

280

He got up quickly to retaliate. 'He is my son, also. Do you think this leaves me untouched? Do you think I abandoned him because he abandoned me? David was not a child of love, Marion, you know that as well as I do. He was the result of a few uncontrolled minutes between youngsters carried away on a tide of discovery. He cost me my assured future, and almost my sanity. He cost you your reputation, and three years of terrible stress that almost broke you. In spite of that – maybe because of it – we were both determined he would overcome that bad start, and shine through it to dazzle as he should. It succeeded. We found ourselves with a son on an ascending orbit and, even if I did have to stand on the periphery during the second half of his life, I still shared your pride in him. Perhaps his loss is a punishment for such inordinate pride. Perhaps, like Roland and Rex, our son had reached his zenith, and, this way, will forever remain there.'

He paused to take a deep breath. 'But we have another child, Marion, a gentle, sensitive girl born in love, who has not really begun her ascendency yet. Always in David's shadow where you were concerned, always afraid to draw too near for fear of rebuff, always believing she came second in every respect, she could be your salvation now. Something has driven her away from me – womanhood, perhaps – but if you give up on life because David is lost, you will be condemning your daughter to the same feeling of betrayal you suffered at her age. She has just lost a dear brother; she is in as much danger as he was from this war. Try to accept those few short years with your son as a precious gift, then go out and seek your daughter. For God's sake,' he finished earnestly.

'Why? What has God done for me? What has he done for any mother these last thirty years? His kingdom has ended. If you have any doubts about that, look from that hillside onto the church below,' she cried, pointing with a shaking hand to the window. 'The symbol of evil is still there. The House of God is no proof against it anymore. Everything good is being destroyed, and that creature, that heathen, destroyed David just as surely. He died with the words of my letter printed on his heart. He died believing I no longer loved him. There's nothing left, Chris. *There's nothing left.*'

The last words were made in a terrible whisper as she stood limply before him, tears rolling unheeded down her cheeks. He went to her, and held her close against him, stroking her hair as she began to moan louder and louder, until she had abandoned herself to agonised, uncontrollable sobbing.

'Twenty-seven years gone in a moment,' she cried in loud

grief. 'What was it all for? Dear God, what was it all for?'

With Robson's help, he got her upstairs and onto her bed, then he instructed the shocked servant to telephone Tarrant Maundle, where Bill Chandler was fortuitously spending a few days' leave. Warned by Chris the night before, he came immediately. His decision was swift.

'Total breakdown, as I feared. Twenty-five years ago she was a young girl. This time it has all been too much, and that damned letter haunts her. It will be a long business, Chris, and she'd be better off in a hospital for a while.'

They went downstairs so Bill could do some telephoning. Then they both had a stiff brandy. Into the silence broken only by the ticking of the clock, Bill looked at him shrewdly, saying, 'Take things easy yourself for a few weeks, old son. Tell that department of yours to go fly a kite, and relax with your music or books. You can only take so much – any man can only take so much. As for young David, I wouldn't give up on him just yet. He's your son, Chris, and you held on to life tooth and claw when you were his age. I should know. I watched every moment of your battle.'

Chapter Fourteen

THEY STOOD together beneath the overhang of the hospital entrance looking at the rain beating up off the road, as it suddenly turned into hailstones, bouncing and rolling in a frenzy of May reminders that summer was not yet here. Her father raised his arm, and a car pulled out from the rank reserved for visitors, to approach the foot of the stone steps.

'What bliss!' Vesta exclaimed. 'Trust you to get your old Ministry to lay on a car whenever you want one, Daddy.'

He smiled at her. 'I told them I was taking my daughter home to dinner. They couldn't refuse then. Ready?'

She nodded, and he took her arm to dash down the steps, where the driver was holding the door open for them. Scrambling in, she sat back breathless, brushing hailstones from her khaki tunic and pulling the cap from her short hair. Her father settled beside her and took off his thick spectacles to wipe them dry. He looked even more like David without them, and she found her throat tightening involuntarily. It still did not seem possible that she would never see her brother again. To hide her distress, she turned to gaze from the window as the car made its way through the narrow streets of the little market town, and headed towards London.

'I'm glad you wangled this forty-eight-hour pass,' he said quietly. 'We didn't have much time to talk on that last occasion, did we?'

'Not really.' She remembered that brief meeting in her company commander's office, when she had been summoned from duty and left alone with her father while he told her two pieces of bad news. She had been worried over David's safety all through the Singapore campaign, yet when it came the news had been no less shocking. She recalled so vividly the handsome tanned face smiling a goodbye that day at the camp gates, and his familiar voice saying, 'See you at the end of the war, Vee.'

It should not have been a shock to hear of her mother's breakdown, because the signs had been there at Christmas. Even so, it seemed to shut her out completely from that special relationship that had always existed between mother and son. Tears had come despite all her efforts to stop them, and she had suddenly found herself in her father's arms, grief dispelling the last of her earlier inhibitions in the drive to comfort and be comforted. He had been wonderful, a pillar of strength, despite his own sense of loss. But today she was dismayed at his appearance. Lines of strain marred his youthful good looks that he had never appeared to have been aware of, and his manner was that of a tired dispirited man. In two months he had grown sadder and quieter than ever.

Reaching out now, she took his cap from where he had lodged it over his right knee. 'Let's put that on the floor with mine and the gas masks. It's dripping all over your trousers.' Bending down to drop it by her feet, she straightened up again, forcing herself to say lightly, 'By rights, I should be in the front seat, up with the driver. Corporals are not expected to sit with august personages in the back seat.'

'Good Lord, is that what I am?' he exclaimed in his old familiar manner. 'I shall cash in on that from now on. Think what I might have achieved if I had realised it sooner.'

After a moment or two, she asked, 'How are things at home?'

'So-so. The Chandlers have been marvellous, of course. Tessa ran the place along with her own farm for almost a fortnight, until she found a most efficient woman to cope with the paperwork your mother used to do. Luckily, the government strictures on how the land should best be used have already settled into a recognised pattern which merely has to be followed month by month. The old stalwarts like Nathan Gates and Bill Rigsby don't have to be told what to do, and I understand the only serious problem is their continuing silly attitude towards the Land Army girls. Not only do they regard them as foreigners because they are not from the local area, but also as something far worse – *females*.'

'They'll never be any different,' said Vesta. 'Their lives are too narrow, and they have been living with those set attitudes for too long. But today's generation has no excuse for old-fashioned notions about women. We are doing everything in this war alongside the men. You recognise that, don't you?'

He frowned slightly.'Recognition doesn't necessarily bring approval.'

'Daddy!' she cried in protest.

'I wouldn't attempt to denigrate or undervalue the part

284

women are playing, Vesta. Take yourself, for example. But I do regret the passing of the days when they were invariably dressed in pretty things, and enjoyed being fussed over by us.'

It seemed such an astonishing speech from someone she had always imagined hardly noticed that there was a difference between sexes, she could not stop herself saying, 'Good heavens, I never thought to hear such words from you!'

He smiled with slight abstraction. 'Not suitable for the dull old Ministry? Do you know, Vesta, your Aunt Laura was one of the most determined and emancipated women I have ever come across, yet she achieved more with frills and fluttering eyelashes than a suffragette chained to railings with a placard around her neck. Don't ever scorn femininity.'

Knowing very well that she did, Vesta decided to change the subject. 'Is Pat still in the arms of the RAF? She confessed at Christmas that she no longer needed to diet because the surplus fat was being squeezed off her by a succession of swains.'

That brought a laugh from him, and she was glad her friend was not there to hear him say, 'She's such a nice girl. That sounds just her style. I've no idea what the RAF is doing with Pat, but I'm almost glad they've taken over most of the Hall because they're looking after it during this awkward period.' He hesitated, then said, 'I'm seriously considering selling the place.'

She stared at him in disbelief. 'Sell Tarrant Hall? Daddy, you *can't*. It's been in the family for years and ... and it's so heavenly there. Besides, there's Dav ...' The sentence tailed off as she realised what she had been about to say.

'I'm not sure your mother will ever want to take up the reins there again. Perhaps she'd be happier in a small cottage without all the responsibility. I have never been tempted to run the place, and when you marry you'll live with your husband.'

Ignoring that last, she pursued her protest. 'Nothing has really changed, though, has it? After the war, you won't be forced into farming so much of the land, and the estate can go back to the way it used to be. Someone could be brought in to run it – a younger man than Clive, or even a woman,' she added fiercely. 'Whatever has made you consider doing such an awful thing?'

With a sigh, he confessed, 'Too many reminders, I suppose. Nothing can be done about it yet, anyway. I had no idea you felt so strongly about the old place.'

Before she knew it, she had said, 'Daddy, you can't forget grief by selling a house. Tarrant Hall is part of us; part of the family.'

He appeared to absorb that for a few minutes, then said, 'We'll see.' With an unexpected change of topic, he went on, 'There's always the possibility that David's wife will arrive in England. That young Philip Scott has written to me from India. Did I tell you, I can't remember?'

'Yes, you wrote last week to say he knew something about the girl,' she told him with growing concern over his uncharacteristic behaviour. 'Apparently he was uncertain over the name of the ship she was on.'

'I've checked with all those that arrived safely in India or Australia. There was no Mrs Sheridan on any of them. I'm a little uncertain what to do now. She could have survived a sinking ship, and now be on one of those islands. There's no way of finding out a circumstance like that, of course. Even my friends can't help out, and the situation is somewhat tricky all round. Where is she to go? Your mother refuses to let her live at the Hall, and I can't have her at the apartment. Firstly, I'm hardly ever there, and secondly, there are so many air raids in London. It will all be so bewildering for her, at first, and how am I to explain to her why her husband's mother won't receive her? The Chinese family unit is so strong.'

'I think it's useless to worry over the problem until it becomes a fact,' she told him firmly. 'You have quite enough to cope with as it is.'

He nodded. 'How did you think your mother was today?'

'Better.'

'Than what?'

'Better than the last time I saw her.'

'Which was when?'

'A month ago. I wrote to tell you I had managed to get to the hospital one Sunday. Don't you remember?'

'I do now. Yes, I also thought there was an improvement in her general spirits today. Bill Chandler says she could go home next week, providing a nurse goes with her. What do you think?'

'I think Mummy should be asked what she would like to do. It might be too soon for her to face pilots walking around the place all the time. On the other hand, she might find comfort from being in familiar surroundings.'

'I was down there two weeks ago,' her father then said. 'I took the opportunity of removing that old white rabbit David always kept on his bed.'

'Oh, Daddy, I do think that was a mistake,' she said at once.

'Do you...? Why?'

'Because it is so much a part of David.'

'It upset your mother before.'

'Taking it away will upset her more.'

'Oh, dear. Will it?' He put his hand to his forehead wearily. 'I thought I was doing the wisest thing.'

'Don't worry about it,' she said gently. 'If Mummy does decide to go home, you can put the rabbit back before she notices. You've still got it, haven't you?'

He nodded. 'I thought she might like to have it. The little Chinese girl, I mean. They were married such a short time, and I suppose they loved each other very much. I wonder if the poor little thing has heard about David.'

Extremely concerned by now over the problems that had obviously piled up to distress him, Vesta realised her father was a very tired and troubled man. Guilt nagged at her. Until he had come to tell her about David and her mother, she had probably been an additional cause of distress to him. Perhaps it was time for her to step into the breach and practice what she now preached, time to show strength when others were at their weakest.

Picking up his cap from the floor, she held it out to him. 'We're almost at the apartment. I suggest we forget about problems that can only solve themselves, and spend the evening as we used to when I lived here. I hope Mrs James has laid on a good dinner. I have something I'd like to discuss with you while we eat it. You're the only one who would know what to advise me to do.'

'I wouldn't count on it,' he remarked ruefully. 'My advice is none too sound these days. Take the white rabbit, for instance.'

Sandy greeted them warmly, and made the only kind of compliment his nature would allow by telling Vesta she looked very fit and efficient in her smart uniform.

'You have changed a great deal since you lived here,' he added, with a faint note of regret that made her bridle.

'A change for the better, Sandy. I used to drift from day to day with no sense of purpose.'

'We probably all did that,' came the thoughtful response. 'If war does nothing good, it at least gives us a direction to follow in the certainty that we are being of some use.'

'My dear fellow,' put in her father, 'you have always been of inestimable use to me, war or no.'

Sandy smiled. 'Even on the occasions when you have cursed me roundly for reminding you of an appointment you had hoped to ignore? There were several telephone calls which need your personal attention, and quite a batch of letters. When would you prefer to deal with them?'

287

'Can't they wait until tomorrow?' Chris asked irritably.

'Not really, sir.'

'Oh, all right. I'll buzz you later.'

Vesta followed her father into the room which reflected his personality so well, enjoying the luxury of such un-military surroundings. She had grown used to bare boards, iron bedsteads, eating in a huge concrete-floored cookhouse in the company of men and women from all walks of life. This elegant, carpeted salon, furnished expensively, hung with paintings and other works of art, was of another world she had almost forgotten. Although she was finding new horizons in her present life, this room represented the roots to which she hoped to return after the war. Surely her father would not sell Tarrant Hall?

Turning to him, she asked, 'Must you work tonight, Daddy?'

Pouring himself a vodka, he replied, 'If Sandy says it won't wait, then I must. Don't worry, we'll have dinner and a nice long conversation first.' Looking across at her, he smiled. 'You haven't started on beer yet, I hope. The licentious soldiery, and so on.'

She smiled back. 'Standing there in a colonel's uniform, don't you count yourself one of the licentious soldiery?'

'Certainly not. I'm an august personage. What will you drink, Vesta?'

'Oh, nothing, thanks. I'm still like Mummy in that respect. We girls leave all the drinking to you and David. Well... we did,' she finished awkwardly. 'Look, I'll just go and tidy up before dinner, while you enjoy your vodka in peace. Won't be long.'

Escaping into the bedroom she had always occupied when staying at the apartment, she stood just inside the door for a moment or two, wondering how long it would be before it was no longer so painful to speak of David; how long it would be before he was automatically erased from the family group in thought and speech. Would the time ever come when she forgot she had ever had a brother?

With a deep sigh, she moved across the blue-carpeted room to the small integral bathroom to wash. It was so familiar, with its china soap dish, matching jars with a design of cornflowers, and pale fluffy towels. But, as she began running hot water, she noticed something very odd. The small cabinet held an assortment of razors, jars of hair cream and men's hairbrushes, together with a range of well-used toothbrushes. Even more odd was a collection of combs, dusting powders and expensive French perfumes of a quality Vesta had not seen for well over a

288

year now. Staring at them, she tried to understand their presence. Naturally, there had always been a spare comb or toothbrush for any guest who had forgotten to pack it, or who had been obliged to stay unexpectedly overnight, as there were also spare pyjamas and a dressing gown. But this array of articles suggested a great number of permanent or very frequent guests of both sexes. How very strange.

After washing, combing her hair, and applying pale pink lipstick, she went back to the sitting room ready to ask her father about the puzzle, but he was sitting in his usual chair, glass in hand, fast asleep. Stepping across Vesta took the glass gently from his fingers, and put it on the table beside him. Looking down at him she felt, for the first time, something approaching maternal love. This self-possessed man was suddenly uncertain and out of his depth in this series of domestic disasters. David was gone, and suddenly she was needed ... Now, at the precise time when she was set to follow her own course. Should she abandon it?

Full of such thoughts, she continued to gaze at her youthful father, and remembered that he had walked away from his responsibilities in 1915. David had requested an overseas posting in the hope of solving his personal problem, leaving behind his doting mother. In addition he had married a girl he must have been aware would never be accepted by her. Why, then, even though as the girl she was traditionally expected to succour the family, should she not follow her own star?

She was still debating that point when Mrs James came to announce that dinner was ready to be served. Shaken gently awake, her father was full of apologies, and went off to wash in his own bathroom. Seated at the table together, she began her soup with relish.

'You look so tired, and in no state to embark on work later tonight, Daddy. What you need is a good long sleep.'

He nodded, breaking bread abstractedly. 'Yes. If your mother does decide to return to the Hall next week, I'll attempt to get down there at the weekend to organise Robson. Mind you, it's not as easy to sleep there as it used to be. One is just getting off again after being awoken by the fighters coming in to land, when the truck with the pilots arrives at the house from Longbarrow Hill. An incredibly noisy breed, fighter pilots.'

She gave a faint smile. 'You should hear the average signalman.'

'Still enjoying that side of the army, as apart from the painting?'

Now he had given her the perfect opening, she decided it

would be foolish to ignore it. 'Yes, I enjoy it. But I'm shortly going to give it up.'

'Oh?' He drank a spoonful of soup, then added, 'Explain that announcement then.'

Putting her own spoon down, she said, 'I'm extremely grateful for your help in getting me some work as a war artist, but it hasn't turned out quite the way I thought. In February I painted three aristocratic servicewomen, in specially posed pictures intended to show the British public that class distinction doesn't apply in today's emergency. In March I went to Norfolk to do a posed study of girls surrounding a barrage balloon. Then, last month I was commissioned to make a series of small pictures of girls in army stores sorting out left and right boots to tie into pairs, packing khaki socks into boxes, and folding blankets into neat piles.'

'Very inspiring,' he commented dryly.

'Quite. Oh, Daddy, I knew you would understand,' she said with warmth. 'I did it all, much as I kicked against the traces, and they were delighted with the results. As far as I was concerned, they would have been equally as delighted with photographs of such subjects, because all I could do was record on canvas what was there to be seen. How can an artist use flair and imagination over a barrage balloon or a pair of boots?'

'Cobalt blue boots; terra cotta balloon with pink spots?' he suggested.

She giggled. 'I was tempted, but resisted it for your sake.'

He blinked through the thick spectacles. 'My dear girl, I would have been vastly taken with blue boots and pink-spotted balloons.'

'Your influential friends would have taken a dim view of it.'

'They take a dim view of almost everything, which is why they have become influential.'

Gladness filled her suddenly, and she regretted the long months during which she had voluntarily shunned the great pleasure of his company. Whatever had happened in his past, she felt certain now that he could never have behaved like Felix. She must have been mad to imagine he could have.

'Daddy, I want to paint *war*, not girls packing boots. You saw my canvas of Hut 4 after it was bombed. You said it was good, and you know why, don't you?'

He dabbed his mouth with his napkin. 'It came from the heart. When that happens, the eyes see the whole scene differently.'

'I was told there were men to paint that sort of thing.'

290

'Oh, really?' came his mild comment. 'Who made that profound statement to you?'

'Giles Elton.'

'Weren't you sufficiently adoring? He expects prayer mats to be unrolled and occupied at his door, you know.'

'Doesn't he just,' she laughed, as Mrs James brought in a salver containing a saddle of lamb, and dishes of vegetables. When the housekeeper went out again with the soup plates, Vesta sobered and said impulsively, 'It's like it used to be, isn't it? I'm very glad, Daddy.'

'So am I, Vesta. Life is too short for misunderstandings, my dear.'

Taking the plate containing meat he had cut for her, she began helping herself to vegetables. 'You know Gerald Bream is now a war artist? I met him one evening, and he gave me his number to ring him for a dinner date. I forgot all about it,' she said airily, 'but I contacted him last month and asked his advice. He gave it without hesitation.'

'He's a nice man. Gets through wives rather quickly, but otherwise very genuine,' was the considered comment. 'What was his advice?'

'Take an army commission.'

'Which you should have done at the outset. Then what?'

She frowned at the meat. 'This can't be one of the Chandlers' sheep. It's awfully tough.'

'Ho, I'll wager it beats what you get in the cookhouse.'

'It isn't that bad,' she defended gamely. 'The sausages are quite tasty.'

'*Sausages* . . . ? What are they?' he asked in mock innocence.

'I won't give you a signalman's description of them. You'd be shocked.'

'No, I wouldn't. After a lifetime of Bill Chandler's Australian epithets, nothing shocks me. Go on about Gerald Bream.'

'He maintains that once I am an officer I will be eligible for a posting as an assistant to someone at an overseas headquarters, where I might have the opportunity to freelance. That cheque you gave me for my twenty-first would cover any expenses, and Gerald said you could probably . . .' She broke off, deciding on the instant not to ask him to speak to his acquaintances on her behalf. He had enough to do already, and she had the right degree of determination to achieve it alone. 'Gerald said it would be possible to persuade whoever I worked for to give me time off for a reason like that. There'd be such opportunities for the kind of pictures I want to do – troopships arriving, local colour with the inevitable sombre khaki, tanks against a background of pyramids.'

He thought about what she had said for a moment or two, as he cut the rather tough meat. 'The theory would appear sound enough. You have Cairo in mind, have you?'

She nodded. 'The Far East is out now, and India wouldn't provide what I'm looking for.'

Putting down his knife and fork, he looked at her seriously. 'Have you really sized up all this would entail? It is not the most enchanting part of the world. Do you truly feel you are mature and experienced enough for what you propose?'

'No, Daddy, not in the least,' she said with honesty. 'But I shall be when I've done it. I've never wanted anything more in my life.'

He smiled across the table; a smile so like David's it hurt. 'That's the best reason for doing anything.'

'You're not going to try to talk me out of it, or say I'm taking on something more suited to a man?'

'Have I ever?'

She smiled affectionately. 'No, Daddy. But I won't be wearing frills, or fluttering eyelashes.'

'Ah, well, Laura did what she did best, and so will you,' he conceded, a trifle bleakly Vesta thought. 'When do you propose embarking on this scheme?'

'I already have. The board has approved my commission as from the start of June.'

'What a relief! You'll feel more at home in the back seat with august personages after that.'

They went on to speak about Cairo and the Middle East in general, her father mentioning several prominent Egyptians who would be useful contacts if she ran up against difficulties.

'I'm not sure that I can be of much help on the military side,' he confessed. 'Although I walk around dressed as a lieutenant colonel, I'm not part of the fighting set-up, as you know. If you were going there to study ancient mummies, I could lay it all on for you, but suitable secretaries for staff officers are out of my province.'

'Don't worry, Daddy. Gerald has already organised that. His brother is an aide out there. There won't be any difficulty getting a posting there, it'll be a question of when. As soon as there's a vacancy, he'll put my application forward. The waiting will be purgatory.'

Contemplating her while Mrs James cleared the main course and set before them an almond tart, a piece of cheese and some biscuits, he said as the woman departed, '*Gerald* appears to be doing an inordinate number of favours for a girl he knows only slightly. Or does he know you rather better than I thought?'

'He's a fellow artist.' She turned him from that line of questioning by asking, 'Are you going to indulge in a slice of this gorgeous gooey concoction, or stick to your usual boring cheese?'

'Oh, indubitably the boring cheese,' came his characteristic reply.

They chatted about a wide variety of subjects, then left the table to have coffee in the sitting room. Mrs James had set the tray by Vesta's chair, and she poured for them both, handing her father a cup and saucer with an apology.

'This coffee looks a bit grim, doesn't it? Won't it be heaven to get decent stuff again after the war? Remember those wonderful *brioches* we used to have for breakfast when I was here?'

He made no answer, apparently lost in the business of stirring his coffee, until he looked up with a strained expression on his features, which were half in shadow due to the shade on the carved Burmese lamp beside his chair.

'Vesta, people often speak or behave in ways easily misunderstood by those not directly involved in certain situations. Often such actions are out of character and ruled by a set of circumstances that are either intolerable or over-whelmingly irresistible. Then again, events outside a person's control might alter their whole way of life irreparably. It's too late now for me to explain to David why I did what I did when he was born, but whatever it was that made you feel you couldn't approach me must have been another of the instances to which I'm referring. I'm very glad the hurt didn't go as deeply as David's, and please bear in mind that if it ever happens again, it doesn't mean that I don't care about you.'

Feeling her throat tighten, she said, 'It wasn't you, Daddy, it was me being immature. Being in the ATS has made me grow up an awful lot.'

'Yes . . . yes, I can see that it has.'

Going across she knelt by his chair, and was distressed anew by the signs of stress on his face. 'Don't live in regret over David,' she begged softly. 'He always made such a brave show of independence where you were concerned, but I suspect it only continued so long because he was afraid of looking a fool if he abandoned it. Poor David was under such terrible pressure to live up to Uncle Rex's reputation, he could hardly make a move without fearing comparison or criticism. That made him afraid to betray anything that might be construed as weakness. He did care about you, Daddy. When he came to say goodbye to me he gave me a frightful wigging because I was being rotten to you. When I told him that was the pot calling the kettle black, he leapt to your defence, and said you didn't deserve my treatment of you.'

He put his hand over hers as it rested on the arm of the chair. 'Most of us don't deserve the treatment we sometimes get. Your mother is a case in question. She suffered a great deal in the last war, but finally pulled through with shining colours. Fate has been unkind to her, and this time it was more than her strength could sustain. Keep that in mind, Vesta.'

Her heart sank. 'Are you asking me to stay in England so that I can be near her?' she asked heavily.

He shook his head. 'No, no. But when you enthuse about going out to paint the *real* war, remember that broken-spirited mothers and wives are just as much a part of it as tanks and troops.'

June came in hot and airless. In the Far East the Japanese sweep of conquest had been halted and contained by the American Pacific forces, but in the desert Rommel was pushing the Allies back in a massive retreat to Tobruk where, finally surrounded, they had to surrender. It was one more blow for the depressed British public, who also had to cope with the prospect of a Russian surrender, and further food rationing due to severe shipping losses in the Atlantic. Air raids were still part of daily life, and new German strategy attacked the pride of the British people by destroying their heritage. Cathedral towns and places of historical architectural interest like Bath, Exeter and Canterbury were all targets. It caused a great deal of anger, but also inspired some sensations of relief in Londoners and those in garrison or dockyard towns, who had a short respite from raids.

All in all, the second half of 1942 began in a mood of depression greater than ever before. Not only were the enemies winning all the way along the line, there was hardly a family that had not suffered a loss or injury, or had not been bombed. Thousands of servicemen were in prisons all over the world, with their fate uncertain, being fed demoralising propaganda about the progress of the war and what their families at home were suffering. Wives in Britain were depressed over the absence of their menfolk at a time when they needed them most; mothers were depressed over the loss of children evacuated to the country. Women, in general, were having to work in factories, on the land, or running the essential services, besides struggling to make the ration of food last, and keep everyone decently clothed. It was inevitable that infidelities occurred, and letters from anonymous or indignant sources reached the poor caged troops in the hands of the enemy, telling them their wives or fiancées were having fun with another man. The object of such letters was mystifying. They only served to punish the helpless innocent, instead of the carefree guilty.

When the first American troops arrived in Britain, jaunty, glamorous, well-paid, and bringing with them such temptations as tinned pineapple, chocolate and nylon stockings, a new wave of unfaithfulness began. For the children who ran after these North American pied pipers, a phrase soon caught on and could be heard as they raced behind trucks, shouting, 'Got any gum, chum?' The men leaning from the backs of the trucks as they rumbled through English towns and villages, smiled broadly, and threw packets of chewing gum and chocolate to the children who had seen little of either for so long.

There was a new aggression in the air. When were the losses going to stop, the surrenders cease? When was a bid to hit back going to be made? The British public had had enough. Unless the tide turned soon, they could not guarantee their continued response to requests to tighten their belts even further. Yet it was plain to even the simplest of citizens that no attempt to re-enter Europe could be made until a few victories had occurred, and some of the huge numbers of men presently imprisoned were set free.

In Europe itself resistance was being stepped up to this end. Sabotage was being intensified, all available intelligence on German military strengths and positions was being transmitted to London, and escape routes for those breaking from internment camps, or who risked capture after being shot down, were being set up in order to get back as many men as possible to fight on.

Networks of agents, saboteurs, resistance fighters, and safe houses for escapees were being organised by any number of bodies, often without the knowledge of their equivalents elsewhere, so that occasionally work was unwittingly disrupted by rival groups working for a common end. In rare instances, agents were betrayed to the enemy by another agent who knew nothing of their identity. More and more suitable people were trained for this work, and by the second half of that year the secret units involved in this training were under greater pressure than ever before. Experienced agents, who had been

295

in the field since the start of the war, were tired and needed a rest; others, who had been identified and then escaped at the eleventh hour, knew that to go back would be dangerous, not only to themselves but also to those linked with them. These people needed somewhere to rest or hide away for a few months, and big houses all over England were being taken over by the various secret Intelligence groups for this purpose.

Chris found the perfect hideout for those handled by his unit: Brigadier Tarlestock's imitation Rhineland castle up on Wey Hill. Known locally as eccentric, and therefore avoided, the brigadier was highly delighted to have a succession of equally eccentric guests in his house. The agents were brought out of Europe by the special squadron of the RAF that had originally dropped them there, then driven straight to Tarlestock Towers by a driver, very often female, who was a member of the unit. Frequently, Chris was obliged to go there and question them: on the latest situation; why they had needed to get out quickly; how they imagined they had been detected by the Germans, and so on, before a replacement agent or an entire group could be set up.

When he was there, he naturally went across to Tarrant Hall to see Marion. The nurse had been replaced by a respectable young woman who was more of a companion, but Marion was still so preoccupied with her grief she took very little notice of her. Towards Chris she was quietly polite, but he felt she derived no benefit from his company, and he always left with a heavy heart.

There had been no news of David, either through official or undercover sources, and Chris accepted that his son was dead. Of his Chinese daughter-in-law there was no information, either, and he was worried. Painstaking enquiries of shipping lines, and those officials in Australia and India who received the refugees from Singapore, suggested that the girl had been on none of the vessels that had left during the last days, and the only Mrs Sheridan listed anywhere was the fifty-four-year-old wife of a planter from Cirencester. Yet the young pilot who had flown out with David seemed very sure the girl had been given a place on one of the ships. He knew the date it had left, but not the name of it.

Chris felt very uneasy over the affair. While he had no idea what he would do with her if she were traced, he felt an intense obligation to the girl his son had made a Sheridan, thereby bringing her into a family of which he was the head. By caring for his son's widow he might, in some way, compensate for that youthful desertion David had found unable to forgive.

His concern over Vesta was slightly different. Warmed by the renewal of the bond they had formerly enjoyed, he was also glad that she had become self-reliant and confident of her direction in life. But he was perturbed by her determination to penetrate masculine strongholds. Donning uniform and being generally accepted as a worthy substitute for men needed in the fighting lines was one thing, but she was nevertheless a female, who would be viewed as such by any males she came across. As far as he was aware, she was inexperienced in such relationships, and could very easily follow in her mother's footsteps before she realised what was happening. Approaching twenty-two, Vesta had developed into full womanhood in a most unexpected way. From a quiet introvert with a board-thin body, large dreamy eyes and a mane of flowing hair, who had swamped her personality with a code of behaviour she had believed necessary in order to be accepted by those with whom she had mixed, she had become decisive to the point of aggression, pursuing individuality with determination, and disturbingly defying the gift of a very shapely body. In addition, her face had acquired an intriguing haunting attraction, framed by a short gamine hairstyle which highlighted her eyes; eyes which gazed straight and true, but which appeared to be hiding something in their depths. Chris well believed many men would attempt to discover what it was.

With all these personal considerations at the back of his mind, he was finding the pressures of his work taking greater toll of him than ever. Tired both physically and mentally, the moment he climbed into bed his brain began turning around thoughts of his broken marriage, his dead unforgiving son, his daughter set on confronting the pitfalls of attempted equality, and a little Chinese girl somewhere in the world who bore the name of a family she could not reach. He found the voice of his eighteen-year-old self echoing again and again in his mind, as he had cried to Rex, *I just don't know how I'm going to face the next sixty years,* and his brother replying, *Try taking them one at a time.*

Each one of the years appeared to bring worse problems, more disillusionment, increasing loss. Maybe his two brothers, and Laura, had been lucky to die so young and never witness what these present years were bringing. Perhaps David was better off dead. It might have been as well if those men who had pulled the wounded Second Lieutenant Sheridan from a blazing sea at Gallipoli had left him there to burn. Anything he had achieved since was being systematically destroyed now. Perhaps Marion was right, and God's kingdom *had* ended.

Once that idea took root, he found himself lying in the darkness silently echoing her cry, *There's nothing left. Twenty-seven years gone in a moment. What was it all for?*

August brought no relief from the black tidings, save that Rommel had been halted at El Alamein and a stalemate existed between the opposing sides in the desert war. Vesta would find no troop movements or tanks against the pyramids to paint, he reflected. Another European network collapsed due to the carelessness of an overtired agent, and new people were recruited, rushed through the training, and flown over to continue the vital work. On several stifling nights Chris was shut in a cell-like room for hours, questioning and testing those preparing to risk their lives and those of others by mingling with the enemy in countries that had once been their own. On one such occasion the agent had appeared nonplussed at the questions Chris fired at her, and small wonder, since he had apparently wanted to know how long she had been in Sumatra, the name of the boat she was on, and where she had been educated in Singapore. On two separate occasions he had suddenly switched to Egyptian, from the language known to the prospective agent, apologised, then switched back to yet another unfamiliar tongue. Finally, he began the relentless interrogation of one young girl in the early hours of the morning, only to find he had forgotten the cover story he, himself, had invented for her, and could not even remember who she really was. Abandoning the session, he had gone back to his room to lie awake wondering whether Roland and Rex would hate him to sell Tarrant Hall, and whether he had been right to return David's old white rabbit, after all. Marion kept it constantly beside her. She certainly seemed to derive comfort from it, but was it delaying her recovery?

The following morning he was told to report to Frank Moore. Getting a car from the unit pool, he sat in the back seat during the drive to the City, trying not to let his hopes rise. If word of David had come through secret sources, surely Frank would have telephoned the good news rather than send an official summons to his office. Commonsense refused to prevail, however, and he entered the familiar room with barely concealed eagerness. A coffee tray was already there, which helped the suggestion that this was to be an informal meeting.

'Chris, how are you?' greeted Lord Moore, waving a hand at the chair beside the coffee table. 'Sit down, sit down.' Lowering himself into the seat on the other side of the table, he went on, 'I suppose iced coffee would be more appropriate for a day like this, but I've never cared for it cold. Must be in the eighties outside. Very tiring.'

'You haven't brought me all the way here, when we are so busy, just to discuss the weather, Frank,' Chris said impatiently. 'Get down to the reason, will you?'

'Fair enough,' came the response. 'I think we are old enough friends to have the truth between us.'

His heart sank. It did not sound like good news about David. 'By all means,' he agreed.

'John Frith has filed an urgent request to have you taken off the job. In his opinion your mental state is such that it is endangering those passing through your hands. He has detailed no less than seven instances to support his request. That is seven too many, Chris.'

It seemed too much to take in for a moment. 'I haven't been sleeping well.'

'Neither have you been working well, and in your line that can be dangerous. Frith urges that you be removed from the staff permanently on the grounds of mental instability. I think he has allowed his competence in making the request to be overshadowed by personal animosity – in its own way just as dangerous – and I believe I know you too well to give credence to his claims. I'm giving you a month's leave, Chris. Go away somewhere. Do something different. Rest that unique brain of yours. Do some sketching. Walk over the moors. Get some fresh air into your lungs. At the end of the month, I'll review the situation and make my decision.'

Chris got to his feet hardly realising that he had, and began walking from the office without another word. As he opened the door, Frank called out, 'Better leave a number where you can be reached.'

Outside, he signed off the waiting car, and began walking to his apartment through the hot streets filled with pedestrians. There was hardly a person who was not wearing a uniform of some kind, carrying the obligatory cumbersome gas mask over their shoulders. Faces were set and strained; the pace they took resigned and without joy in their step. Was each and every one of them wondering what it had all been for? His route took him past a street that had been roped off. There was not a lot of it left – the buildings along each side were mostly rubble – but the large sign at the entrance announced that there was an unexploded bomb, and somewhere along that shattered length men were risking their lives attempting to defuse it. A few more lives for the sake of a few less broken buildings. Which was more important? Was anything important any longer?

Sandy was surprised to see him, but refrained from questioning the fact. He did embark on a query about some letters that had come in, only to be silenced by Chris saying that he was on leave, and not available for anything classed as work.

'I'm taking a complete rest, Sandy,' he announced in bleak tones. 'Four whole weeks in which to relax and enjoy myself.'

'Not before time,' declared his assistant heartily. 'Dorset will be very attractive at this time of year, with summer on the wane, and autumn ready to move in.'

'Yes.'

'I'll ask Mrs James to bring you some coffee, Sir Christopher. I take it you'll wait until the afternoon train.'

'I suppose so,' he murmured. 'I'll get out of uniform before I have my coffee. Is anyone here, at present?'

Sandy nodded. 'They arrived at the usual early hour. A husband and wife, with a young woman. She is French; the couple are Belgian. Franklin brought them in. He said they'd had a dicey trip. Bit of a scramble to get off the ground before the Jerries arrived. The dispatching agent is investigating the source of an apparent tip-off, and has closed down operations from his area for the time being.'

'Wise move. When does Franklin propose moving them on?'

'Tonight, sir.'

'Fair enough. Organise that coffee, will you?'

Dressed in a lightweight grey suit, he drank his coffee in solitude, thinking about the people presently in his apartment sleeping off the tension of an escape from occupied Europe. There must have been a tip-off, or someone had made a fatal slip. The smallest mistake could cost a life in the world of espionage, and Frith had been right to take the step he had. Yet those four weeks stretched ahead of Chris like a sentence. To spend them here would be a mistake, but in Dorset all that awaited him was a house full of youngsters dressed like David, and a woman who clung to a stuffed white rabbit and had no further need of a husband. There was only one escape route, and nothing had ever seemed so beckoning, so clearly defined. Leaving the coffee half consumed, he picked up his gas mask and went from the apartment.

The maid admitted him, and left him standing in the green and blue room splashed with poppies. During those few moments of solitude he felt a strange sensation of repetition. Was he again walking out on his responsibilities? If so, there was a subtle difference this time. No one would care.

Sonja came in a guise he had not seen before. In a loose

300

smock with her hair twisted carelessly into a chignon, she looked every bit the artist, and just as irresistibly beautiful to the man hungry for her and the escape she promised.

Taking one look at his face, she went quickly into his arms and held him, saying against his shoulder, 'My dear, why have you waited so long to come to me?'

Stroking her hair with a hand that would not stop shaking, he said, 'I'm going to Scotland for four weeks. If you don't come with me, I think I may never return.'

They went up by train and stayed at a hotel in a still, quiet glen. Their days were spent on hillsides where the only company was the tough nimble highland sheep, and the eagles soaring overhead. They hired horses and followed paths across purple-clad heights, stopping at isolated inns for a lunch of thick Highland broth and mutton with home-grown vegetables, or a tea of bannocks and honey. Lying together on beds of heather during the blessed peace of those hot August days, they watched the eagles wheel in the blue freedom above and quoted poetry to each other, Chris explaining the meaning of those by Scots, whose language defeated Sonja. In breeches and silk blouse, with her hair braided around her head, she displayed another facet of her beauty to Chris, who was willingly captivated by this woman whose intellect so perfectly complemented his own. With Sonja he found a communion of mind and body that comes just once in a lifetime, if at all.

The nights brought the ultimate fulfilment. Chris realised he had been sleeping all his life, until now. On the occasion Marion had claimed he had been a breathtaking lover, he had been mentally ravishing a ghost girl who had never been his. Sonja was throbbingly, eagerly his, finding his passion more than breathtaking. They made verbal love in any language which came to mind, and he was astonished to discover that endearments he had long known, but never needed to use, came naturally when holding this woman close in his arms. He gained intense pleasure from unwinding and brushing her long, glowing hair before carrying her to the bed, where it spread out in a glory of red strands on the pillow as she gazed up at him. He loved to stroke perfumed cream into her slender feet, or to lie on the bed watching her move around the room in a delicate silk nightdress, knowing he would slip it from her the minute she came to him.

Sonja was an experienced and very sensual partner, who derived great delight in joining him in the ancient and unreliable shower to 'sculpt' what she called his Grecian lines with soap suds, worked into a lather. He could never capture her quicksilver hands before the inevitable arousal. This ravishment beneath running water was all the more erotic because she was no more than a tantalising blur without the thick lenses which brought everything into focus for him.

On the first occasion she had seen him without his spectacles, she had exclaimed immediately, 'How magnificent! So blue they are almost violet... And with the lashes of a girl. You should not hide them away, *liebchen.*'

'They're safer that way,' he had replied swiftly. Highly sensitive to the subject in the past, he found himself able to speak to her of secrets kept from others. 'My eyes once caused a young girl to seduce me at a time when neither of us thought of the consequences. Later, in Gallipoli, they drove a man into offering me love, when what I desperately needed was sanity. They're safer hidden.'

'Not with me, not with me,' she had insisted with soft passion. 'I wish very much to be seduced by them. I wish to look into them and see the boy you were then. I shall hide these lenses from you.'

'Then I shall be unable to see you clearly.'

'Perhaps *that* is safer,' she had responded with strange sadness he did not understand.

Those days with Sonja brought him the youth that had been snatched from him in 1914. They brought him incredible happiness, intellectual fulfilment, days of vigorous healthy exercise, and nights of unsuspected rapture that led to deep untroubled sleep. They also brought him the knowledge that his life was now so bound to hers he could never let her go. Yet, at the end of their third week together he found that he had to. Called to the telephone, she rejoined him at the dinner table looking very serious. Disturbed that anyone had known her whereabouts, he asked rather sharply what was wrong.

'I have to catch the overnight train to London,' she told him, in tones which suggested there was no alternative. 'I have just ordered a car to take me to the station.'

Immediate protest rose in him. 'Why, for heaven's sake? Who was that on the line?'

'Hanna.'

'Your maid dictates that you must return? I find that unacceptable.'

'Please, my dear, try not to be difficult,' she begged.

'I am trying... but the effort is proving unsuccessful.' Seeing his present happiness dissolving around him, he gazed at her in dismay. In a dress of shimmering amber, with a deep v-neck that enhanced the single topaz she wore on a gold chain, she was unbearably lovely. He had believed her his. He had believed these three weeks together had shown her that their relationship was both now *and* forever. Yet she was apparently telling him that even her 'now' was being shortened by a week – a week as precious and vital to him as breathing. The fear of losing her augmented his anger.

'What can a maid have to say that prompts an immediate return? What can be so important you can coolly bring to an end something I thought meant as much to you as it does to me?' he challenged across the table set with a coffee tray.

'I am not cool,' she responded swiftly. 'Can you truly believe that after the past three weeks?'

'I believed many things. I want to go on believing them,' he told her, aware that the only other couple in the dining room were eavesdropping on their conversation. 'Can we continue this upstairs? We appear to be performing before an audience.'

Once in their lofty room with its four-poster bed, Sonja explained that a wealthy American had recently commissioned a set of engraved goblets to take with him on his return.

'That date has been unavoidably advanced. I must work all this coming week in order to complete them,' she ended. 'I have no choice.'

'Of course you have a choice. We may not be together like this again for months. Stay with me and forget your wealthy American,' he urged.

She was already at the dressing table, taking her froth of underwear from it. 'I am an artist. I need to sell my work in order to live.'

In three strides he reached her, and pulled her round to hold her immobile. 'I'll buy the goblets. I'll give you anything you need. Stay with me for this last week.' His fingers dug into her arms. 'I need this last week. Oh God, I need *you*.'

His kiss should have left her weak and repenting, but she eventually drew away to say gently, 'Be sensible. Your words are those of an impetuous, ardent boy.'

Sensing that he had already lost her, in some inexplicable way, he grew more urgent. 'You have given me back my life over these weeks we have had together. Is your work more important than that?'

Her hand lightly touched his springy hair in a caress that was already a farewell. 'Reality has returned, *liebchen*, that is all.'

Telling her there was no joy in remaining there alone, and sick with disappointment over her relentless decision, Chris travelled back to London with her. As each mile passed, he sensed she was slipping away from him. Tense and remote, she had little to say, and he felt powerless to mend the situation. They parted outside her apartment in the early morning with the burning devastation of another night raid all around them, filling the air with the smell of smoke, and making the peaceful enchantment of the Scottish highlands seem like a fantasy. Reality had returned with a vengeance.

He walked away with his ears full of the echo of her vow that it had been as beautiful as he had promised, his steps ringing on the broken pavements in the morning quiet. Walking aimlessly, he scanned the slithering wreckage of people's homes, the cheap curtains that fluttered forlornly from windows in half-walls, the paper being chased by the wind along streets pitted and strewn with debris – remnants of love letters, treasured photographs, cuttings from ancient news-papers, all of which told the history of an ordinary family wiped out overnight. Here and there, a lone figure picked amongst the rubble, ignoring the ropes strung across to prevent access to unstable ruins. A dog sat mournfully on a street corner, waiting for an owner who would never come for him; water gushed from a fractured pipe while two tired men tried to cope with just one more impossible task. Further on, a stream of people with grey, weary faces was emerging from one of the Underground stations with all the trappings of overnight camping on hard platforms. Reality was there with a vengeance, yet Chris could not let go the memory of heather-clad hillsides where he had pledged his life in poetry; eyes that lit with laughter or passion as they gazed up at him; and a Slavic face full of sensuality, as she spoke of her art, her early life, and her love for him. Sonja was the embodiment of all his aesthetic dreams... Yet she had gone with the morning, as if that was all she had been.

The following day, the third anniversary of the outbreak of war, he travelled to Dorset, where Marion still appeared to depend on the comfort of a stuffed toy rabbit. He had dinner with the Chandlers, and Bill assured him she was making good progress. Tessa told him the harvest had been good, and she had been given permission to extend the pedigree flock of sheep. Pat was still highly popular with the pilots at Tarrant Hall, and had received a proposal of marriage. The rector of the village was considering approaching American ecclesiasti-cal bodies for financial help, and Mr Anderson at the village shop had been named as the mysterious Peeping-Tom at the collection of huts housing the Land Army girls, because he had been behaving very strangely since the death of his twin sons at sea. Mrs Robson was still suffering indifferent health, and the butler himself deplored the 'goings-on' in the main part of the house by the RAF gentlemen, who appeared unable to do anything quietly.

Life seemed to be continuing all round him, yet Chris knew his own would be in abeyance until he met Sonja again. He felt her loss so strongly that, finally, one night when the moon was a huge amber disc over Longbarrow Hill, and he stood at the window watching the dark Spitfires returning to the nearby airfield, he felt tears on his cheeks. Yet, as they multiplied to blur his vision of the moonwashed garden, he realised she had given him the release he had need so desperately, allowing him finally to mourn his lost son, the little Chinese widow, and all those whose lives had exploded on an island that had once been the emerald tip of a jewel-bright peninsula.

Chapter Fifteen

VESTA CLIMBED from the aircraft thankfully. She had discovered that her stomach and flying were incompatible when the airborne accommodation was the sweltering hold of a transport flown by a desert-happy maniac called 'Potty' Chambers, and crewed by cheery youngsters who seemed little saner. She stood in the incredible heat beside the aircraft while one of the crew, a lithe dark-haired NCO, handed her the holdall containing her things.

'You sure you're going to be all right out here?' he asked dubiously. 'It don't look no place for a lady to me.'

She smiled up at him. 'It's all right. Colonel Villiers is expecting me. Thanks for the lift.'

'You're welcome, ma'am. Now I advise you to stand well back and protect your eyes. When the cap'n revs the engines it'll kick up a deuce of a lot of sand.'

He pulled the hatch shut, and Vesta turned away. Gripping her luggage, and settling the straps of her gas mask and shoulder bag firmly, she began to walk from the makeshift airstrip where the pilot had touched down briefly in order to let her off before continuing to his destination with supplies. Although it was not yet nine o'clock in the morning, the heat was incredible, and perspiration was running down her face beneath the pith helmet she had bought in Cairo before leaving. Behind her, the aircraft was swinging round prior to takeoff with a great roar of engines and a veritable sandstorm stirred up by the propellers. Buffeted by the hot sand, Vesta dropped the grip in order to hold onto her helmet with both hands, as she bowed her head to avoid the worst of the grit in her eyes, until the machine was off the ground and climbing cumbersomely into the vivid blue of the sky. Only then did she look up and study the scene before her, screwing up her eyes in the glare.

It was far from what she had imagined, and somewhat

disconcerting. Here, right in the middle of the desert, was a cluster of green palms and the glint of sun on water. She found her first sight of an oasis, something hitherto only read about, quite exciting. It was the other aspects of the place she found disconcerting.

Apart from a small fleet of trucks, two armoured cars, and a mounted anti-aircraft gun, there appeared to be no more than a quantity of stores and a sprinkling of people moving around them. She had come to a base camp in the desert, and had expected to find a huge area filled with supplies, an armada of tanks, and an entire military community under canvas. She had come to observe desert troops returning from an offensive, or preparing to mount one. She had come to draw sunburnt, exhausted tank crews, taking a well-deserved rest before breaking out into the hostile desert again. She had come to capture the poignancy of modern warriors against the background of ancient Egypt.

Just two months after taking up the job Philip Bream had wangled for her in Cairo, she had been successful in persuading the authorities to let her come out here to make sketches for a series of paintings. Her request had been aided by the timely and coincidental need for a suitable present to be made to an influential Egyptian who had helped the Allied cause, and a word from Gerald Bream's brother had done the trick. Vesta had been charged with the task of submitting a selection of her work to be considered for the gift. The only sour note in the whole affair was that Philip Bream had expected gratitude of a kind she was not prepared to give. He was very nice, he had been extremely helpful, and she had offered to take him to dinner at Shepheard's Hotel by way of thanks, which he had unfortunately taken as an insult. It was a pity, and would create some awkwardness between them in the future, but she had set out on her own, doing what she dearly longed to do, and feeling that his male tantrums could wait for a while.

Now she was here, a sense of anti-climax washed over her. This tiny oasis settlement seemed hardly likely to provide inspiration for one picture, much less an entire series. Picking up her baggage once more, she began to walk through the soft sand towards the palm trees, thinking of the forthcoming bliss of a drink, a wash and a change of clothes after that hot flight. As she neared the area where the vehicles were parked, a man came from the shade and strolled toward her. He appeared to have a broad grin on his face.

'I haven't seen a hat like that since they stopped taking Edwardian tourists up the Nile,' he called out in a transatlantic

307

accent. Then, as he drew nearer, the grin vanished. 'Jesus, it's a woman.'

He was a big brown man, powerfully built, dressed in very brief shorts and open shirt, huge dusty boots, and khaki socks rolled down around his ankles. His skin was deeply tanned, his curly brown hair was layered with a fine dusting of sand, his eyes were equally dark, with healthy whites all the more striking against the brown face. There was a pale puckered scar across the firm muscular strength of his right thigh, his fingers were ingrained with grease, and his rugged features betrayed cynicism and a hint of ruthlessness. The violent physical impact he made on her was all the more shocking because it was twice as lethal as that inflicted by Felix Makoski on first sight. Watch out, she told herself, this man is dangerous!

'What the hell are you doing here?' he demanded, coming up to her.

She manned her defences and rolled out the cannon. 'I beg your pardon!'

Narrowing his eyes he looked her over from head to foot. 'Who are you?'

'My business is with Colonel Villiers,' she told him coolly, 'and it's obvious from your manners that you are neither an officer nor a gentleman, so you cannot be him. Perhaps you'd be civil enough to direct me to his tent.'

He put his hands on his hips, and the shirt opened further to reveal a hard brown body with dark hairs around his nipples. A very virile man, this. Her sense of danger increased.

'Villiers has gone.'

'Gone?' she echoed, dropping her grip, and fighting to disentangle the straps of her bag and gas mask which had slipped from her shoulder. 'Is he likely to be away long?'

'He's leading the spearhead sector. They'll be miles into the desert by now.' He waved his hand at the military evidence around him. 'This is the rearguard getting ready to leave.'

'Leave?' she cried in acute dismay. 'I don't understand.'

'That makes two of us. Villiers asked me to wait behind to pick up an artist coming in today from Headquarters in Cairo. He said nothing about a girl arriving.'

She looked him in the eye and said, 'I'm the artist from Headquarters in Cairo.'

'*What?*'

'Colonel Villiers gave me permission to come out and do a series of sketches here.'

'The message I got was that I was to pick up Lootenant Victor Sheridan.'

308

'Oh Lord!' she exclaimed, wiping the back of her hand across her wet forehead. 'There's obviously been a dreadful misunderstanding between Cairo and the colonel.'

'Like hell there has,' agreed the man in his rich baritone. 'So who are you?'

'Subaltern Sheridan.'

'Victor?'

'Vesta.'

'What kind of name is that?'

'The kind given by a father who was a Greek scholar,' she snapped in growing anger at his attitude. 'May I ask who you are?'

'Brad Holland. Press Corps.'

'A journalist! So you have nothing to do with the army?'

'Not on your life! I rebel against discipline.'

'That isn't difficult to believe,' she returned, furious that she had been cross-questioned by someone who had nothing to do with the military unit to which she had come. 'I'll find the senior officer and sort out the problem with him.'

As she bent to pick up her bag, he stopped her, by saying, 'To find any officer at all you'll have to catch up with the battalion. The most senior man here is a sergeant.'

Straightening up again, she sighed heavily. 'This is ridiculous! If they knew they were moving out, why didn't they contact Cairo?'

'Just like that? When orders come through to mount an attack, there are a hell of a lot more essential things to do than radio Cairo about some artist. There's a war going on out here, you know.'

'There's a war going on everywhere, Mr Holland. My brother was shot down over Sumatra in February, and five of my friends were killed before my eyes during the blitz on England last year.'

He took that in for a moment or two, then asked, 'Are you really an accredited war artist?'

'Are you really an accredited war correspondent?'

He pulled a handkerchief from the pocket of his shorts and began mopping the back of his neck as he studied her. 'Nuts have a hard resistent shell, and a soft luscious centre. You're just the reverse, I guess. But I'm sorry about your brother and your friends.'

'You didn't know them,' she said, finding it safer to stay angry. 'They were just victims of the war – a few amongst millions. Why should you feel sorry?'

'OK, have it your own way.'

They stood glowering at each other, until she said more to herself than to him, 'If I had been told about this when I landed, I could have gone on with them in that transport.'

'And if I'd been told the artist was female, I wouldn't have kicked my heels here while the rest of the boys are out there getting the action. I'm losing a hell of a lot of coverage.'

'Then we had better get going before you lose any more,' she decided. 'Colonel Villiers asked you to pick up an artist from Cairo, so that's what you'll have to do.'

He stared in disbelief. 'You're plumb crazy! That's real desert out there.'

'Well, I can't stay here, can I?' she pointed out irritably. 'I'm no happier than you over the situation, but unless you can think of an alternative we must carry out the original plan.'

He pointed to the distance. 'Have you any idea what it is like out there?'

'No, but I'm willing to find out and accept the worst. In England there was danger in simply walking down the street, Mr Holland. The days when women stayed at home with their embroidery while the men went to war have long since passed. We are doing a number of things, these days, which prove we are tougher than men imagine. If you're unaware of that you must be a very poor journalist.'

He shook his head. 'Just a poor sap who believes girls should be soft cuddlesome things with feathers for brains. But I own I'm supporting a lost cause.'

Picking up her grip with resignation, she said, 'I'll get a lift with the sergeant in one of those trucks. He can't refuse to help me, because I hold senior rank.'

As she began walking away he said, 'Have I stated that I refuse to help you?' As she turned, he shrugged. 'Villiers appointed me his deputy, so I guess I'm stuck with you. There's just one thing to get straight. I'm the boss on this trip. I've been out here eighteen months and, although no white man can be said to truly know the desert, I'm a darn sight more familiar with it than you are. I give the orders. Is that clear?'

'Perfectly. I was a corporal until four months ago. I'm used to taking orders ... and I don't rebel against discipline.'

He looked her over with resignation. 'I think I just might be out of my mind.'

'You're the best judge of that,' she replied calmly. 'There's one other thing to get straight, by the way. As Colonel Villiers' deputy, I shall expect you to behave as he would until we catch up with him.'

310

An unexpected slow grin broke out. 'OK, Vic, but until we catch up with him you won't know how he would behave. By then, it may well be too late.'

The desert was not at all what Vesta had expected. It was a lot hotter and more frightening in its isolation; less a series of undulating golden dunes than a vast area of gritty rock-strewn soil, that varied from hard-baked to shifting and treacherous, with an occasional stunted growth of camelthorn. Men had been battling back and forth over such terrain for two years. The Allies had initially raced through Libya, before the Italians had realised what had hit them in 1940: then Hitler had gone to the aid of his weak ally, and sent Rommel with his Afrika Korps to regain all the lost territory. Just four months ago, the forced surrender of Tobruk had been such a blow it had seemed the desert war was finally lost to the Allies, who had been pushed all the way back in a relentless campaign of man and machine against the terrain, killing heat, desert blindness, and the prospect of roasting alive in burning tanks.

However, they had rallied to stop Rommel at the tiny oasis of El Alamein, and now, with Montgomery confident, ruthless and with a personality that could successfully raise morale when at its lowest, the process was again in reverse. The never-ending sands were being crossed once more, with the Germans fleeing and the Allies pushing relentlessly forward through the dust raised by the columns ahead. What was it all for? Certainly not for possession of the desert. It was the vital oilfields it controlled which were the valuable prize; so valuable, thousands of lives were being given in payment.

The small rearguard column had set off by mid-morning, Brad insisting on leading it in his lightweight military truck. Vesta soon discovered why. Moving vehicles sent up clouds of dust to choke and blind anyone to the rear, so the envied position was the forward one. The trucks contained rations, ammunition and spare parts. There were two armoured vehicles with guns mounted to defend the column, and a couple of water carriers. The men were all, in marked contrast to the American, delighted to have a woman travelling with them, and had quickly provided her with a pair of goggles and an off-cut of mosquito netting to keep away the flies. Ignoring Brad's cutting remarks about her pith-helmet, Vesta wound the netting around her head and over her hat so that she looked reminiscent of ladies who had ventured forth in the very first motor cars. The goggles completed the impression of an

311

Edwardian motorist. Brad had merely grunted at the sight of her sitting in the passenger seat beside him, and murmured enigmatically, 'You'll soon learn.'

They had had several differences of opinion before setting out, due to her lack of the essential equipment for desert living. He had scoffed at the luggage she had thought suitable for an oasis camp. She had told him smartly that, had she known what would befall her, she would have come prepared, but had expected such things as bedding and eating utensils to be provided by the Officers' Mess.

'And the rest,' had been his heavily sarcastic comment on that.

The next subject for discord had been her shoes, which he declared were totally useless in sand. She had protested that she was hardly likely to be tramping about the desert like the troops, to which he had replied that she was likely to be doing a great number of things like the troops before they reached the next place where there was an airstrip, from which she could be picked up.

'Don't expect special treatment on this trip,' he warned darkly. 'Female or not, you're just an army lootenant, as you've gone to great pains to point out.'

'We pronounce it *leff*tenant, Mr Holland,' she had informed him. 'I certainly don't expect special treatment from you, since I haven't feathers for brains. But I do think this unavoidable situation could be made more acceptable if you would stop posing as Lawrence of Arabia and make the best of it, as I am trying to do.'

With a scowl, he had gone off, returning with a short stocky private carrying several pairs of boots and some thick socks for her to try. So, wearing her khaki cotton shirt and trousers, heavy laced boots with thick socks rolled around the top of them, and her Edwardian headgear, she had settled in the truck beside Brad, filled with a mixture of apprehension and excitement, and telling herself she could hold out against his dangerous attraction for four days until they reached the next airstrip.

They drove off in silence, but, five minutes later, Brad could contain himself no longer. Glancing at her as she sat beside him with all the appearance of serenity, he shook his head in resignation, 'I think I might just be out of my mind.'

'You already said that,' she told him, taking in the sobering reality of the desert now the oasis was behind them.

'You look ridiculous, you know that?'

312

'Don't look at me, then.' She smiled through the wound mosquito netting. 'I was about to add that you should keep your eyes on the road. Just how do people know which direction to take in this kind of country?'

'Sometimes there are defined tracks to follow. Otherwise, it's a case of using a compass. I suppose you would know all about that.'

She nodded. 'Covered it in our training. A lot of girls became drivers, and they wouldn't have got far without compass bearings. All the road signs and place names in England were obliterated shortly after the war began.'

They fell silent again, and Vesta's initial buoyancy began to diminish. Away from the shady palms, the true heat of the desert hit them. The vast swathe of netting around her head, plus the large pith helmet was almost suffocating her, causing sweat to roll down her face and throat to soak into the shirt already sticking to her back. Brad looked almost cool, despite the dark patches beneath his arms, and she envied him his brief shorts, loose billowing shirt and bare head. Maybe he had been right, and the netting was for when they made camp.

They were following a rough track, and the going was getting bumpy. She could see the ribbon of sand, that had been flattened by a succession of vehicles passing back and forth, running out across the stretch of wilderness to the purple horizon. Way, way off there was a dark haze that could be smoke or rising sand. The distance shimmered and danced, as heat jumped back from the surface to suggest any number of things which were not there at all. Apart from the sound of their own moving column, there was incredible sultry silence. Nothing moved, save themselves and the hot air several feet from the ground. How solitary. How bereft! In a fey moment she likened it to how she had felt when Felix had withdrawn from her and staggered to flop into a chair several feet away – forsaken, savage and barren.

'It gets at you, doesn't it?' said a quiet voice at her side, and she turned from memories of Felix to look into brown eyes containing that same beckoning fascination. 'The first time it's overwhelming, and it doesn't lessen a lot as time passes. I still feel it whenever I break into open desert from a town or oasis. The sheer immensity of it is curiously humbling.'

'I wouldn't say it has humbled you all that much.'

With eyes narrowing, he replied, 'I am a born fighter, that's why, and I recognise another when I see one. What are you fighting, Vic?'

'The war, Mr Holland,' she retorted smartly. 'And please stop using that ridiculous name. I think the joke is now exhausted.'

He drove on over a track that shook every bone in her body, sitting nonchalantly with one hand lightly on the wheel, his shirt flying in the breeze to reveal his lean bronzed body. Vesta concentrated on the view to her left.

'I guess you also know how to drive one of these trucks,' he said after a while.

'Yes.'

A few more miles passed in silence, while her craving for a drink grew, and the headgear he had scoffed at proved his point many times over. Finally, she unwound the netting and removed everything to leave her head bare. It was bliss to feel so free, with the breeze caused by their motion now ruffling her short, damp hair.

'I wondered how long it would be,' came his amused comment. 'You look a damn sight more approachable now.'

'Don't be fooled by appearances,' she advised. 'I'm not.'

'OK. I already got the message back there. You're either crazy about the Honourable Fitzroy Owen-Owen, whose principles won't allow him to make an honest woman of you while he's fighting for king and country, or some guy has hurt you so badly you're all frozen up inside.'

'Tell me about desert warfare, Mr Holland. You said you had been out here eighteen months, so you must have seen a great deal of it.'

'I'm no soldier – I also told you that,' he returned. 'And the name is Brad.'

'I didn't mean military tactics. In some ways, your job must be similar to mine. Your readers don't want statistics, they want human interest – the heart and soul of war.'

It was easy driving, which allowed him to keep his gaze on her for long periods of time. He did so now. 'You can't be much more than twenty. How come you got a job as an artist so young?'

'Influence,' she confessed. 'When you want something badly enough, you cast your scruples to the wind.'

'I'll work on that,' he murmured. 'I may get lucky.'

Ignoring that, she went on, 'My father has a great many influential acquaintances in government and cultural circles. I asked him to twist their arms on my behalf. From the start of this year, I have been fulfilling commissions at home – girls changing wheels on army trucks, or packing socks. But I wanted to paint real war, and an artist I know has a brother

314

serving in Cairo who wangled me a posting there.'

'Are you a good artist?'

'I'm an instinctive one. At school I found I couldn't adapt to being taught, so I gave it up. Unless I paint with complete freedom, I can't paint at all. I have to feel compulsion to record something on paper or canvas. The commissions I was given in England didn't touch my emotions in any way.'

'So you do have emotions?'

'Are you a good journalist, Mr Holland?' she responded smartly.

'I should be. I've been in the game for fifteen years.'

'What did you write about before the war?'

'Baseball.'

'What?'

'Baseball, politics, crime, big business. The lot.'

She was intrigued. 'You couldn't possibly be an expert at all that.'

'Like you said, readers want the heart and soul of everything. I'm pretty hot on heart and soul stuff.'

Steering him away from that line of conversation, she said, 'You still haven't told me about desert warfare.'

'No need,' he said briefly. 'You'll see for yourself soon enough.'

After being on the move for three hours, conversation was too much effort. The seat in the light truck had grown excessively hard, and her body ached all over. Her eyes were sore from the glare off the sand, she was wet, covered with a film of fine dust, and wishing she had not drunk so much tea before leaving the oasis. It posed a problem. There was no bush big enough to retire behind, and view was unrestricted for miles around. A solution would have to be found if she was to travel by this method for several days.

She need not have worried. The column halted thirty minutes later, and the ritual of desert eating unfolded before her. Jumping from their trucks, the men quickly filled empty perforated cans with sand, soaked it with petrol, then set it alight to boil water for tea. Whilst waiting, they broke open some packets of biscuits and limp, greasy processed cheese. A few minutes after climbing from his truck, the sergeant arrived before her with shyness written all over his face. His name was Kirk, a tall gangling man nearing forty, with a gravelly voice and sad blue eyes. While he made the men hop to it very smartly with his brisk manner, he was diffident in the extreme with Vesta.

'The lads and I thought you'd find things a bit hard, not

315

being used to it, miss,' he began, plainly never having dealt with a female officer before. 'So we've fixed up a sort of bathroom for you back there, where it's private. While we're getting this grub ready, p'raps you'd like to nip to the rear to wash the sand off, and so on.'

Looking down the line of parked trucks, Vesta saw that an enclosure had been contrived from stacked barrels just a few feet from the track. Relief flooded through her and she smiled at the man in real gratitude.

'How very thoughtful of you, Sergeant Kirk. I appreciate it very much.'

'No trouble, miss,' he replied, turning red. 'When you're ready you can have a nice cup o' tea.'

Taking her bag from Brad's truck she walked down the line of vehicles, then stepped off the track to her 'bathroom'. She then saw the advantages of the boots Brad insisted she should wear, as the softer sand rose up around her ankles at every step. Within the privacy of the barrels, she found a box on which had been placed a billy-can of water. Next to it was a spade. Puzzled for a moment by its presence, enlightenment then dawned. Thank heaven for the sergeant. Brad Holland would probably have relished her discomfort until she had been forced to beg his help.

Rejoining them, feeling a great deal refreshed by the water, a comb through her short hair, and liberal applications of eau de cologne, she took the mug of tea gratefully. But she had only taken one sip of the hot dark brown tea, swimming with grease from condensed milk, before she was attacked by a swarm of flies that descended on her face, neck and hands, apparently from nowhere.

'Oh,' she cried, dropping the mug in a frenzy of beating hands, as she attempted to drive them from her nostrils, eyes and ears, where they were biting into her flesh quite hard. Dancing about as if on hot coals, she found a length of netting flung over her, and realised Brad had come to her rescue. She never again made the mistake of using perfume in the middle of the desert. She also never again allowed the men to sacrifice their meagre ration of washing water to give her an entire canful, which was what Brad informed her they must have done.

He set a cracking pace which had the truck bumping and leaping over the surface. Hanging on to the sides she asked him if there was a reason for such haste, to which he replied that the area they were crossing now was a favourite hunting ground for enemy fighters, who liked to swoop from the sky to machine-gun convoys.

'Out here, we're sitting targets for aircraft. That's why everyone travels widely spaced. The Jerries can only get one truck at a time that way,' he went on. 'It has its disadvantages, of course. Where there's no obvious track it's possible for vehicles to stray off course, because their forward vision is obscured by dust. Many are the poor guys who have found the dust clearing to see Jerries going along on each side of them, and realised they had been travelling with the wrong convoy for the past hour or so.'

'Oh, surely not,' she exclaimed, certain he was joking.

'That's nothing to some stories,' he assured her. 'Tanks advance on such a wide front, the right or left flank often forges ahead out of sight of the main concentration, then the crews find that instead of chasing the enemy, Jerry tanks are coming up behind them, having been overtaken in the obscurity of the rising dust. Then there are the instances of abandoned enemy tanks or trucks being taken over by men whose own vehicles have been knocked out, only to find they get friendly waves from their opponents and bullets from their pals.' He shook his head. 'You've no idea. This is plumb crazy warfare out here.'

There did not appear to be anything humorous or crazy about the sights they came upon very shortly, and Vesta felt a sense of immense awe as each side of the track began to bear witness to the past battles. She had said she wanted the heart and soul of war, but there was a total heartlessness about black, burnt-out tanks standing in terrible isolation miles from anywhere; broken, tilting lorries with forlornly flapping canvas hoods; charred boxes from which contents had been snatched by whoever had been there months ago, and who had long since moved on; piles of blackened, sticky ashes that had once been spare tyres or boxes of rations; and the occasional desolate, broken aircraft with its nose crushed, or its frame burnt away to a skeleton. The souls of all those who had fought that battle and perished there had flown, although their mortal remains had never left the scene of their mortality. As she gazed in horror at those part skeletons, Vesta thought of her brother lost in venomous jungle to become no more than this after a few months. Her throat tightened with emotion.

'That's the aftermath of your *real* war,' said Brad. 'Is that honestly what you want to paint?'

She shook her head, thinking of Gerald Bream's addage that the good would always come shining through any situation.

317

Where was the good in this? She was still searching for an answer when they stopped for the night. The sun vanished in a veil of crimson, and it grew wonderfully chill. After vanishing into her 'bathroom' to tidy herself as best she could and don a thick pullover, she returned to the group of men sitting around the petrol-can stove to find they had set a little table for her. A box covered with folded mosquito netting looked quite romantic in the glow of the fire, beneath an enormous moon in a sky so full of stars it was almost dazzling. The problem was, Brad Holland looked even more romantic than the table, and she began to wonder about the night to come. As the sole woman with a group of more than twenty men in the midst of the desert, there was only one of whom she was afraid. Romance would end in pain and disillusionment. Oh no, she would never let any man do that to her again.

They ate bacon, sausages and beans, all with a strange smokey taste, and washed it down with strong, sweet, greasy tea. Vesta suspected all the men were on their best behaviour because she was there, and decided to retire early so that they could relax. But they seemed anxious to keep her there as long as possible by asking her about painting, the ATS and Dorset, in that order. As she answered them as fully as possible, she was conscious of Brad sitting silently a few feet away, watching and listening as she revealed too much of herself to him. Deciding to bring the conviviality to an end, she got to her feet, announcing that as the sole woman present she would undertake to wash the mess tins.

Sergeant Kirk scrambled up immediately. 'We don't wash them, miss. Water's too short for that. A handful of sand sees to it, and each man does his own. Don't we, lads?' he encouraged in significant tones, kicking the man next to him to his feet, whereupon he kicked the next man. One by one they got the message, and she bade goodnight to a line of soldiers standing stiffly to attention. Brad still lounged on the ground as she walked away in something of a dilemma. Where should she settle for the night? Something about the isolation of the area beyond that lit by the glow of the fire, combined with memories of those ghosts of battle she had seen earlier, made her uneasy about separation too far from the men. By travelling with the American, everyone had accepted that she was under his protection, and therefore his responsibility. Rather late in the day, she realised she had brought about her own predicament by insisting that he take her along, and she would have to make the best of it until they caught up with Colonel Villiers on the morrow.

318

Reaching the truck, she pulled her grip from the back seat. It would substitute for a pillow. Taking her towel from it to spread on the sand, she prepared to lie down on it when a hand fell on her arm, making her jump. Brad had come up beside her silently.

'There's no need for that,' he said brusquely. 'Give me a minute, and I'll make up a bed in the truck for you.'

'You don't have to,' she retorted, realising those stories she and Pat had read had not been in the least silly. In that huge silent desert, overhung by darkness filled with glittering stars and chill tingling air, it would be all too easy to surrender to a man of virile mystery who beckoned with every movement, every glance, every challenging word. She shivered involuntarily as he pulled a blanket from the truck to hold out to her.

'I know I don't have to do it,' he rapped out, 'and you're so darned independent, you'd probably work it out for yourself, but I'm not letting you struggle with all this after those upright soldiers of the king have given you a military send-off. We Americans are not all boneheads with no idea how to treat a lady.'

'Have I ever suggested I thought you were?' She sighed. 'The trouble is, I'm never sure whether you're being courteous or bumptious.'

'Right now, I'm asserting my status as boss,' he returned, flinging his own bag to the ground, and folding the backs of the front seats forward to make a large flat area, with the well between seats still full of his own gear. Then he spread another blanket over it.

'It's the best I can do. Sleep well,' he said, turning away.

'Where... Where will you spend the night?' she asked tentatively.

Swinging round, his teeth gleamed in the shadowed night as he gave his slow grin. 'I'll give you three guesses, Vic.'

They caught up with Headquarters in the middle of the morning. Vesta realised then why Brad had been so opposed to the idea of a woman being linked with such activities. The warlike aspects of scattered tanks, armoured cars, and desert guns impressed her deeply after the death fields they had passed on the way. Would all this look like all that in a few months hence? Already, her emotions were being engaged by the army that had been named 'The Desert Rats', and she longed to wander freely looking for the heart and soul of this armour-plated fighting force.

Brad took her straight to a light-coloured tent with an

319

extension awning, which he claimed would be Colonel Villiers' office. Vesta was happy at the prospect of being transferred to this senior officer who had agreed to her joining them – even if he had thought a male artist was arriving. Her response to the American that morning had been even more aloof. On peering cautiously over the side of the truck last night, when he had somewhat noisily settled on the sand beneath it, she had discovered him drinking from a bottle containing spirits. Catching sight of her downward tilting face, he had shrugged and murmured, 'What's a guy to do when there's a shortage of water?' She had immediately returned to the warmth of her blankets. Neither of them had mentioned the incident this morning. In fact, they had been relatively silent during the journey, and she suspected he would be as glad as she to end their forced companionship.

Their progress through the assemblage of vehicles, stores, and bare-torsoed men attracted a great deal of attention, especially when they came upon a group of four men, stark naked, washing their shorts in what smelt like petrol.

Vesta pulled up automatically, saying loudly, 'Oh, goodness!' which caused them to look up, register horror at the sight of a woman, then snatch their washing up to cover their vital areas.

Brad gripped her arm and led her past, murmuring with a hint of acid amusement, 'You wanted the heart and soul of war. I guess you just have to have the body to go with it.'

Arriving at the tent, they found two officers studying a map on a table, with a lance corporal sitting to the left of them before a radio transmitter. The man with badges denoting the rank of colonel on his shirt was heavy of build, dark-haired and clean-shaven. The captain with him had sandy hair with a trim moustache, and a good-looking face. Glancing up, he smiled in unbelieving delight. Colonel Villiers followed the direction of his gaze and swore roundly.

'What the bloody hell do you mean by bringing a woman here?' he demanded, looking straight at Brad. 'Have you taken leave of your senses, man?'

Seeming untouched by military wrath, the American said in calm tones, 'This is Lootenant Sheridan. Because I owed you a favour, you asked me to stay behind and pick up an artist you had agreed could join the unit to make some sketches. Here she is.'

As she was hatless, Vesta could not salute, so she smiled and said, 'I understand there was some mix-up with Cairo, and you were expecting a man. I'm sorry about that, sir.'

320

Ignoring her completely, Villiers roared at Brad, 'If this is a sample of your warped transatlantic humour, Holland, I must tell you you've gone too far this time. Get her out of here.'

'Sir,' put in the young captain, looking at Vesta the way a dog eyes a juicy bone, 'perhaps we should hear what the young lady has to say. After all, we are in the middle of a desert.'

'We are also in the middle of a war, Captain Peake. One that is not going all our way. I have no time for American jokes, or for stupid young women who deserve to be chained to the tent pole out of everyone's way.'

Vesta was growing angry, as she searched through her shoulder bag for all the relevant identification papers and military orders to hold out to him. 'Colonel Villiers, these will show I am Subaltern Vesta Sheridan, sent by Cairo, with your agreement, as an official war artist. My commission is to make a series of sketches with your unit for paintings intended as a gift to Mr Omar Raschid.' Because the man just stared at her, making no attempt to take the papers, she went on firmly, 'You were apparently under the impression that it was *Victor* Sheridan to whom you had agreed to play host. That is an unfortunate misunderstanding for which I can't be held responsible. So far, it is Mr Holland and myself who have suffered due to the mix-up. I have duly reported to you as senior officer here, but I promise to get in no one's way and complete my sketches before we reach the next airstrip.'

'*Sketches?*' he repeated in stupefaction. 'I'm fighting a war here, not entertaining damn silly artistic females who wouldn't know the business end of a tank from a London bus.'

From beside her, Brad said with an edge to his voice, 'Lootenant Sheridan is a commissioned army officer. Don't you think this matter should be discussed in private?'

Straightening up from his stance over the map table, the colonel snapped, 'If you are implying that I ask Corporal Galloway to leave, or that I should abandon my men in the middle of an advance by stepping away from this table for a *chat* outside, you are being abnormally thick-skulled. Get that girl out of here! I'm trying to command a fighting unit that is bogged down somewhere to the west of here where there is a larger than expected enemy armoured division.'

Vesta found herself being led away by a hand clamped around her arm, a voice murmuring in her ear, 'And you wanted me to behave like *him* until we caught them up?'

Feeling like hitting out, she controlled the impulse, and allowed Brad to take her back through the straggling camp to where they had left the truck. News of her presence had apparently spread, because grinning or disbelieving faces were peering from around piled boxes, parked vehicles, sandbags, and even from the turrets of tanks. Wolf whistles were growing into a veritable chorus.

'Sounds like someone's glad to see you,' commented Brad, letting go of her arm. 'That's your heart and soul of war – boys who've been denied the sight of a woman for months, and show their appreciation in fitting manner. You should accept the compliment.'

Shaken and upset by the predicament she was in, she said cuttingly, 'They'd whistle at anything female. That's no compliment.'

'Have you any idea how goddam terrible you look at this moment? It's a compliment, take my word for it.' His dark eyes looked searchingly into hers. 'Whoever hurt you did a hell of a good job.'

Seizing her grip from the back seat, she retaliated with, 'I thought I was crazy about the Honourable Fitzroy.'

'I ditched that theory last night,' he admitted, lounging against the vehicle.

Swinging round to face him, she prepared to leave. 'You were hardly in a state for clear thought last night. I trust you make more sober observations in your communiques. Thank you for bringing me here. I'm well aware that you put yourself out quite considerably for my sake, and I'm genuinely grateful. If I can ever help you out with anything, please don't hesitate to ask. Goodbye.'

'So long,' came his casual reply as she walked away, not having the first idea what to do now.

The solution to her problem appeared almost immediately, in company with Sergeant Kirk, whose immediate superior he turned out to be. In the standard uniform of shorts with turned-up cuffs to raise the legs to mid-thigh rather than several inches below the knee, boots with thick socks, shirt with sleeves rolled above the elbow, and cap at a jaunty angle, the young sunburnt subaltern was the equivalent of a knight in shining armour to Vesta.

'Hallo,' he greeted with a wide smile that increased the enthusiasm on his face. 'Sergeant Kirk told me you'd probably be needing a hand to settle in. I'm Peter Main.'

'I'm Vesta Sheridan,' she told him, then smiled in the direction of the NCO. 'I'm very appreciative of your thoughtfulness when you have so many other things to think of.' Turning back to the lieutenant, she added, 'You have a first-class sergeant, Mr Main.'

'You don't have to tell me that. We've been together for over a year out here, and that says a lot, believe me. Here, let me take that bag for you.' He seized her grip and put out an arm to indicate the direction they should take, saying over his shoulder, 'Righto, Sergeant, I'll look after Miss Sheridan. Come on,' he encouraged with vigour, 'we'll take a shufty at the Officer's Mess, then fix you up with accommodation.' His grin betrayed his youth. 'The other chaps'll be livid when they find out I've reached the objective and secured my position, so to speak, before they come on the scene.'

Vesta let that pass, especially as they walked back past Brad, who was talking to a man with greying hair and a French accent, but who nevertheless watched their progress from beneath half-closed lids. Peter Main was a pleasant uncomplicated youngster which, after the enigmatic American, was a great relief. But he was plainly as desert-happy as everyone else there. The Officers' Mess turned out to be four poles stuck in the sand with a canvas roof stretched between them. A long folding table stood beneath it, along with half a dozen canvas stools. A pair of old-fashioned fly-swats lay on the table.

'The usual Mess rules apply,' Peter Main announced, as if unaware of saying anything odd. 'Visitors are usually asked to pay a sub, but ladies are excused that, I should think. You won't be expected to buy the first round of drinks, either,' he added generously. 'Now I'll introduce you to the Head Steward and ensure he looks after you well. Then we'll sort out some quarters for you.'

Feeling she had strayed into a lunatic asylum, Vesta was taken to meet the sergeant who presided over the Officers' Mess, then followed her host to where a truck was parked not far away. Two men who had been playing cards on an upturned box jumped hastily to their feet as they arrived.

'Johnson, Turner, this is Miss Sheridan,' said the young officer. 'She will be joining us for the next few days. I'm billeting her in your vehicle, and making you responsible for her safety from all those chaps who, unlike you two, may try to annoy or pester her. All right?'

'Yessir,' they snapped in duet, eyes rolling to study Vesta whilst facing their subaltern.

'If you like to leave your bag here, we'll pop back to the Mess and get Sergeant Fuller to rustle up some tea and biscuits. I expect you could do with some, couldn't you?'

That night Vesta lay in the back of a truck in relative comfort,

323

thanks to the gallant generosity of the members of the Officers'
Mess, who had all contributed what they could towards
pampering the first female they had seen for months. She did
not fall asleep for some time, however. It was not easy to close
one's eyes on the magnificence of a desert night sky, with a
moon as huge and shimmery as she had ever seen, and stars so
bright above the flat wastes surrounding her it seemed there
was nothing to stop her from floating up to reach them.
Foolishly, those books so secretly read by herself and Pat at
school returned to mock her. Here in this evocative
atmosphere it was possible to believe in 'romance'. Lying
snugly between borrowed blankets offered by a group of
sunburned warriors, it seemed there might be something else
other than pain and brutishness in a room smelling of kippers.
The night was treacherously charming, and her body began to
yearn for things she had condemned since that night with Felix.
Her isolation suddenly became unbearable.

To fight it, her thoughts turned to the events of that evening,
when she had sat beneath a canvas roof to eat dinner with a
dozen men, in the pretence that there was nothing unusual in
what they were doing. It was only halfway through the meal
that Vesta had realised it was not unusual to her companions.
It had been their way of life for some months, even years. The
only difference that night, she suspected, was that they were all
neatly dressed, with hair washed and carefully combed, and
smelling overpoweringly of soap, because of her presence.
Colonel Villiers fortunately chose to eat in his own tent, as was
his custom, so the atmosphere was happy and relaxed. Much to
her surprise, she had found herself thoroughly enjoying the
company of men who were mostly from her own world, and
was pleased to answer their battery of questions about how
things had been in England when she had left in September, as
well as listening to their own anecdotes on war. They had been
'highly chuffed' to be sketched by her, and had made a great
pantomime of posing so that their best profiles were presented
to her. Only one person there had been untouched by the
general boyish hilarity, and that was Brad Holland, who had
been invited to dine with them, as the man who had saved their
female fellow officer from a 'fate worse than death' – namely
being left at the oasis to be collected by the RAF. The
American had been quiet all evening, and made inroads into a
bottle of whisky, Vesta noticed.

Now, as she lay in the midst of a sleeping camp, where those
on watch moved slowly around, rifles at the ready, waiting for
the moment when they could shake awake their relief to guard

them during the next two hours, Vesta found herself dwelling on those young men called Jimmy, Geoff, Peter, Clive and so on. Tough, hardened by desert living, they had managed to get under her guard, to touch her mentally and physically. With their eyes full of experience and shrewdness, their muscular limbs revealed by brief clothes, their deep assured voices, their ready laughter, and their flirtatious flattery, Vesta had been seduced into forgetting she had no trust in any man. Her body betrayed her resolution, and burned with longing for something she knew would only be shattered if put to the test. After two years of contempt for such feelings, they had returned in strength to show her she was still weak enough to let herself be caught in their trap. Oh, but this time she would wriggle free before being destroyed. In two more days they would have advanced far enough to reach the airstrip where she would be picked up. She could hold out against the challenge of a laconic, whisky-drinking, deadly attractive American for two more days.

She soon discovered the fatal spell of desert nights. Resolution dissolved beneath the lure of the moon and stars when a girl was dependent on a man who threatened her. Her father had suggested she should not scorn her femininity. With Brad Holland in the vicinity, how could she?

Chapter Sixteen

THEY MOVED forward the next day on the heels of the advance column, then were delayed for twenty-four hours because of a minefield through which a way had to be cleared. During the long burning daylight hours, explosions could be heard as mines were deliberately set off by those whose dangerous job it was to go ahead of the ranks to make the routes safe.

To Vesta it added to the general feeling for this kind of war, which was affecting her so strongly. Used to air raids, blackouts, rationing, searchlights criss-crossing over dark cities, beaches covered in barbed wire, and the countryside being ploughed up under government control, she now saw the conflict from an entirely new plane. Things were going well for her. Keeping clear of Colonel Villiers, she moved around, finding a wealth of inspiration for her art whether on the move or stationary; talking to the men as she did so to gain further insight into their nomadic way of life. She already had a mass of sketches from which to select the best for development, and felt a deep sense of excited confidence that she had found the ideal subject for her particular skill.

Keeping in mind Gerald Bream's dictum that good would always come shining through, Vesta had recorded in her sketch book a burly tank driver putting half his basic ration of bully beef stew onto a plate for an ugly small dog he had apparently befriended in Tobruk, and had taken around in his vehicle ever since. Other sketches included a corporal fashioning a doll from an old stores box; and a grey-haired sergeant reading a tattered copy of *Picturegoer* magazine that would inform him of all the films he was missing. There was another of the cookhouse truck, on which a wag had hung a large notice listing such delicacies as Tobruk Turnovers, Benghazi Broth, and El Alamein Eels.

Vesta found these 'Desert Rats' had an attitude towards life and a sense of humour that was peculiarly their own. They had even developed a language understood only by members of their own fraternity: a mixture of Egyptian, Libyan and various Commonwealth bastardisations. She felt thrilled to be sharing it all with them for a while, realising that the staff in Cairo were dealing on paper with a breed of men they did not really know. How would such men ever return to life in offices, factories or fields when the war ended? Surely, on still, starlit nights their spirits would return here; on wet, grey winter days they would dream of the sun that burnt down on a vast yellow emptiness, which they once crossed and re-crossed in a great armada of tracked vehicles. If she felt the spell of those great sands after only three days, how much more deeply beguiled were they?

During that period she saw little of Brad who, in company with the other correspondents, had gone up to the front for details of the action in the minefields. But he was back with the group at dusk to pound away at his typewriter, ready to hand his despatch to the pilot of the first aircraft to land at the airstrip they were nearing. Since the other newsmen had already asked her if she would undertake to carry their submissions when she left, Vesta guessed Brad would also ask the same favour when their ways parted. In truth, she wished the time would not go so fast. For all its hardships, the life of desert nomad would be bearable for a few days more. Luckily, there was safety in numbers where she was concerned, and although Peter Main's interest in her appeared rather more intense than that of the other officers, she found it possible to accept the general flattery and professions of everlasting devotion in the spirit it was all given. Just once, Brad had walked past and hesitated long enough to enquire whether she had found what she was looking for. His tone and disparaging expression suggested he still thought her presence a subject for masculine derision, so she had replied in a brief, impersonal manner that the material for the job she had been sent to do was there in abundance, and the trip was proving a great success.

With a mocking salute, he had said, 'Glad to hear it. Keep up the good work, Vic,' before walking away, leaving her feeling as if a tank had passed by missing her by inches.

The minefield had been penetrated in two wide areas. The advance troops moved forward through these safe corridors with a great number of tanks, raising tall columns of dust clearly visible to those bringing up the centre and rear. Then, halfway through the afternoon, sounds that were new to Vesta,

327

but all too familiar to those around her, began to be heard ahead. Forward movement stopped, and the desert peace was filled with the thunder of distant battle that appeared all the more sinister to her because it *was* distant.

Vesta began to feel sick as she stood beside the truck which had become home to her, watching death and destruction at long range. After the raid that had destroyed Hut 4 and half a camp around her, she had felt she could face anything. Indeed, the dangers of life in England had become an accepted part of her daily routine, as it had with others, breeding a certain carelessness that comes with familiarity and a feeling that if a bomb had your name on it, it would make no difference where you hid or how you tried to dodge it. Now, she found being a spectator – not knowing, and being prey to imagination instead – was nerve-racking in the extreme. There was nothing for her to do but watch and wonder. All around her there was a new bustle as messages began coming in on the transmitters. Men were crossing back and forth with message forms, officers were consulting and studying the area ahead with field glasses. Smiles vanished; weariness began to show through, revealing that it had been there all the time, if one had looked closely enough. Rommel had been well and truly on the run. Surely he could not turn them yet again and drive them back to El Alamein?

Vesta began remembering those spectral vehicles they had passed on the first day: the graveyard of blackened tanks and trucks; of broken, crushed aircraft; of men left unburied. When she spotted Brad Holland in a truck with several other columnists, heading for whatever was developing up with the advance troops, she could watch no longer. Was that what he was: a seeker of sensations, a ghoulish recorder of disaster and mayhem, a cynical observer of the way men humiliate and punish each other? Did he regard this with no more emotion than a report on baseball, politics, or any other subject he had covered? Would he return with what he considered a good story, rattle it off on his typewriter, then settle down to sleep with a bottle of whisky, feeling he had had a successful day? Anger at such possibilities stopped her from feeling sick. It also stopped her from worrying about what might happen to him up there in the battle area.

She did a few sketches of the new alert mood of the camp, but her heart was not in it, and she finally abandoned art for the more mundane activity of washing her clothes by the desert method of dousing them in petrol, which dried quickly and killed desert bugs. Dinner was vastly different that evening.

Those sharing the table with her were quiet and depressed. She felt an intruder for the first time. Eating her meal quickly, she left the men alone without the restriction of her presence. Huddled into her thick pullover, with a blanket around her shoulders, she sat in her truck staring into darkness.

By night, the battle seemed even worse. Quick flashes followed by thuds indicated guns firing; more vivid, prolonged brightness suggested that something had been hit. Men were dying, blown apart or slowly burning, right before her eyes – except that she could neither see them nor do anything to help their plight. David, Minnie and the girls, Felix Makoski, had all gone in different ways; yet, all gone, nevertheless. Where was the good shining through that? Suddenly she felt desperately alone and homesick. Her hand went up to finger the gold miniature of Tarrant Royal church she always wore around her neck. For eighteen years she had lived in a peaceful world, cosseted in luxury, comforted by the closeness of a loving family, confident in the security of a beautiful old home in one of the prettiest counties of England. She had had a fond successful father, a mother who had been healthy and happy, a brother with whom she had shared a close bond. Why, oh why, had she not valued it more? Thinking of her lost brother, probably dying in pain and loneliness, her broken mother, and her father whose brilliant brain seemed unable to cope with it all, she found unexpected tears standing on her cheeks.

'Can I come in?' asked a voice nearby, making her jump. Before she could answer, Brad had hauled himself into the truck beside her, saying, 'Hope I'm not queering the pitch for someone else.' He looked at her closely in the darkness, then sighed, 'This is your real war, honey. Maybe you just found out you're not as tough as you imagined.'

'What are you doing in here?' she demanded, wiping a hand quickly across her eyes.

'A hell of a lot less than I'd like to be doing, believe me.'

'Have you been drinking?'

'Sure I have. All that dust in my throat, and a shortage of water. What else is a guy to do? Here, have some.' He thrust the bottle towards her. 'Go on, it'll do you a deal of good. In more ways than one,' he added, as she hesitated.

'Whatever ideas you have you can forget,' she told him thickly.

His teeth showed white as he grinned. 'I've forgotten more ideas than you've ever had, Vic.'

'Stop using that ridiculous name!'

'Stop feeling sorry for yourself and drink up.'

She had never liked whisky. Right then, it tasted like the elixir of hope, and she swallowed more than she had intended. It made her cough, and he patted her on the back.

'Persevere, old girl,' he encouraged in his terrible mock English. 'It'll do you the most frightful amount of good.'

She tipped the bottle again and gulped. It did seem to make her feel better. Gazing across at him in the faint light, she said, 'That accent is excruciating.'

'I thought it might make you less wary of me.'

Pulling the blanket further around her shoulders, she murmured, 'It isn't your accent that makes me wary.'

Taking the bottle back, he drank from it, wiping his mouth with the back of his hand as he said, 'Want to tell me what does?'

'No, thank you.' She peered from the end of the truck. 'There are supposed to be two men called Johnson and Turner guarding me from people like you. How did you get in here?'

'I used my press pass.'

There seemed no good argument against that, so she tried something different. 'Did you get a good story?'

'Out there? I got the truth, and that's rarely a good story.'

There was a lot of sense in that statement, she felt, and asked curiously, 'What made you do this? I mean, you could've stayed in America writing about baseball and been safe, couldn't you?'

He twisted slightly, and leant back against the side of the truck. 'You asking me for the story of my life?'

'Not in the least,' she told him. 'But since you have intruded into my private quarters, you should make some effort to entertain me, don't you think?'

'OK. So once there was a handsome young Yank who had a flair for making even the dullest things appear exciting in print. One day he made something appear too exciting, and upset a very influential Congressman. The doors of every newspaper office were suddenly closed to him, and he was fool enough to retaliate. Because he was young and very angry, the novel he wrote and published was not subtle enough to disguise the true identities of his characters. The libel suit ruined him, and he quit the shores of his homeland for the civil war in Spain. After six months he realised he was on the losing side there, too, so he handed back his gun and took up his pen again. His words spoke louder than actions, for once, because he was approached and offered employment by a London press agency. He has been sitting pretty ever since.'

'So you know England,' she said accusingly.

'Sure I know England. I had an apartment in Hampstead.'
'Why didn't you say so before?'
'Did I ever get the chance?'
'I suppose not.' Feeling sleep beginning to creep over her, she murmured, 'It's possible I have misjudged you a little.'
'It's possible,' agreed his rich voice in the darkness.
'Brad... Why did you come here this evening?'
'I feel kind of responsible. I drove you here, after all.'
'Only because I made you.'
'Oh, no, no,' was his vigorous reply. 'No woman can make me do anything I don't want to do.'
She smiled, happy to know he had wanted to bring her. 'A born fighter! You said you were.'
'I said you were, too. So what happened tonight?'
Looking away across the desert to where the battle was still continuing, she realised they had been making light conversation while men had been dying.
'I weakened,' she admitted. 'But it won't happen again.'
'In that case...' She was suddenly in his arms, being kissed very thoroughly and deliberately.

Dawn had hardly broken before the wounded started coming in. The entire atmosphere around Vesta changed dramatically. Men who had been drowsing daytime hours away on previous days were now carrying stretchers, lighting cigarettes to put between the lips of men in pain, giving cups of water to those almost crazy for it, or sitting alongside injured pals to chat or read to them while they awaited medical attention. The field dressing station that had earlier dealt with cases of fever, desert sores, jaundice and dysentery now was fully occupied by the worst examples of human suffering. The medical officer and his orderlies were rushed off their feet. A canvas extension was erected to provide shade for those lying in the open, and yards of netting were draped over men whose open wounds attracted flies like vampires to feed on blood.

Vesta went immediately to offer her limited services, knowing she had no nursing experience yet feeling driven to the totally feminine task of giving comfort to those in distress. Having chatted and flirted with Robin Gaynor, the MO for several evenings, she found a vastly different man that morning. To her enquiry as to whether she could be of help, he replied tersely, 'Unless you have medical knowledge of some kind, you'll best help by keeping well away.'

Taking his advice, she had left, shaken by some of the sights. The bronzed warriors she was looking at now had been in the thick of battle, and their fight against the desert as well as the enemy had been lost. The strain of hardship, loneliness, heat and fear showed clearly on their faces, as they lay either hopelessly depressed, or savagely and uncontrollably angry. They gazed up at the canvas roof crying, not simply from pain, but for the futility of what they had been doing. Or they swore loud and long, cursing their leaders, their government and, finally, God. One caught sight of Vesta standing nearby, and roared, 'Piss off, you stupid cow. We don't want bloody drawings of this!'

Understanding how he felt, she departed. Shock made people hit out in unexpected and various ways. She had seen her own father as a disgusting stranger because of Felix; she had cursed Rob Carter because he had not given Minnie a ring for her lifeless finger. There was no way she could help these men, save through her art. They needed trained medics for their wounds; the comfort only a colleague who had faced the desert for months beside them could give. Vesta Sheridan had nothing to offer burnt and bleeding men except the ability to record their frustration, anger and sense of needless sacrifice for future generations.

Returning to her mobile home, she took block and pencils from her bag to begin work. Inspiration had never been so fast and furious. Page after page was filled with rough sketches of what she had just seen, the imprecations and curses of despair being conveyed by the men's expressions. Yet, she became aware with growing amazement, that what was coming over in such strength from the series of drawings was not in the least what she had set out to record. Overriding the frustration, anger and sacrifice was the unique comradeship of these 'Desert Rats'; the close understanding that existed between men who lived in the wilderness side by side, which seemed to shut out any outsider. Astonishingly, they appeared to have become a breed apart, like the other inhabitants of the silent sands.

Inspiration was halted suddenly when intensified activity around her broke into her absorption, and she realised men were running through the lines of stationary vehicles with unusual speed, wearing the tin hats they usually scorned. Next minute, the morning was rent with a concerted roar as the engines of a tank squadron burst into life, and the smell of petrol hung in the air all around her. Vesta jumped down from her truck and walked apprehensively to the end of the line of supply vehicles, just in time to witness the departure of those men amongst whom she had lived for the past incredible three

332

days. Lurching, lumbering forward, the tanks set off into the searing heat of the mid-morning, pennants flying, their commanders sitting atop vehicles with names like *Drake, Defiant, Dauntless* painted on their armoured sides, field glasses around their necks, and the turrets open to converse with crews inside those moving ovens. The reserves were going up to the front.

Vesta stood looking out at the departing tanks. A great bank of dust rose in their wake to float back over the camp. It descended on her, clinging to her damp skin, settling on her khaki shirt and trousers as a fine white film. Putting up a hand to shade her eyes from the glare, she looked beyond the moving column to the distant battle. The sound of gunfire seemed normal after a continuous twenty-four hours of conflict, and the smoke from burning vehicles was now so thick it was no longer possible to see even the spurts of flame which signified action. What was going on out there? What were these men she had mingled so happily with here going to meet in the heart of that black, sinister pall of battle? It frightened her.

In that moment she shamefacedly admitted to herself that in this instance she did not feel in the least equal to the men who were heading out there. They must be aware that this might be their last hour, their final sight of the sun or their fellows. They must accept that by the time the sun set this day, they might be burned, blinded or crippled for ever. How did they find the courage to go? They were not supermen, just ordinary people from all walks of life. How did they continue this month after month?

Her thoughts moved on. How had David climbed into a Spitfire time after time, knowing what might happen? He had been just a brother – a happy, generous, warm-hearted young man full of enthusiasm for flying. How had he found the courage to do what he had done? Had he been terribly afraid out there in Sumatra when he had known he would not see the next day? And what of her father? He was the gentlest man, lover of beautiful things, and champion of world friendship. How had a person with his qualities faced something as terrible as Gallipoli? She sat down slowly on the shingly ground, her gaze still on the advancing tanks, and felt incredibly humble. Women were not yet being asked to do *this*. She could not believe they ever would. A strange kind of chivalry governed even the roughest of men. Maybe an equally strange kind of gratitude governed every woman, and made her resolution weaken in the face of it. Why else would she have allowed Brad to kiss her without protest last evening? Why else would she have bidden him a soft goodnight when he departed, probably to finish off the whisky? He was out there now, recording the details of the battle, and she was glad of that truce between them. If he did not return, her conscience would not be plagued by thoughts of her ungraciousness. The physical response his kiss had aroused in her was enough to cope with, without the burden of a guilty conscience.

The day wore on towards evening, and the sense of emergency remained. Armoured vehicles with the red cross on their sides drove ceaselessly between the battle area and the rear, bringing casualties. The radio transmitters were bringing in vital details of the fighting to Colonel Villiers, then relaying it back to Command Headquarters. Food was being prepared to take out to the hungry, exhausted combatants. Vesta continued to observe and record on paper all she saw, knowing that but for an error she would never have been privileged to gain this insight to the active side of the African campaign.

When darkness fell she was the only one in the Officers' Mess. Sergeant Fulton served her, and accepted her invitation to stay and talk, but he did so with his gaze on the ambulances arriving at the dressing station, and seemed lost without the usual group of noisy precocious officers to chivvy him. Vesta felt equally lost, and wandered disconsolately through the scattering of men preparing to settle for the night, looking for something she could not identify. Was it friendship, a sense of belonging, a like spirit? Whatever it might have been, she did not find it, and eventually climbed into her truck, draped a blanket across her shoulders and sat gazing into the night, seeking the answers to many questions that had arisen over the past few days. It took some time to get around to it, but she finally realised there was just one answer to them all, and he was out there endangering his life to get a story.

With the rising of the sun, a clear picture of what was happening began to emerge. A New Zealand division on the right flank had pushed well ahead, whilst the centre had been delayed by the need to clear a minefield, and the Kiwis had then found themselves ahead of the Germans they were supposed to be pursuing. This, in turn, had led to the German tanks retreating from the New Zealanders in the same direction in which they had been advancing until halted at El Alamein. Inevitably, they ran into the Allied centre halted by the minefield, who then believed the Germans had regrouped for a new advance. For a short time chaos had reigned, with shells from the British and New Zealanders falling in each other's

334

lines. During the night the Germans had tried to break out on the left flank, but had been cut off by the reserves that had moved up. Completely boxed in, the enemy force nevertheless continued to resist, which suggested they anticipated reinforcements.

It was not long before Vesta finally found useful occupation in a situation which had formerly appeared to preclude her. The man operating the wireless station linking the camp with the battle commanders keeled over with a bout of recurring fever, and she volunteered to replace him during the remainder of that shift. The adjutant was doubtful until she assured him that she was a fully trained signals operator. Her services were then gratefully accepted. Slipping back into her old job as if she had never left it, she worked well in conditions that were trying in the extreme, receiving and sending messages in the form understood by service personnel everywhere in the world. At first, she got a few startled responses from men who were unprepared for a female voice on the line, and she smiled at such lines as, 'Christ, I've gone to heaven and didn't know it,' or 'If you're a Jerry secret weapon designed to distract me, you're succeeding, sweetheart.' But they soon accepted her. Some of the officers she had come to know over the last few days used strong language, then said, 'Sorry, Vesta. Slip of the tongue.'

Listening to the cross-talk on the battle, the urgent orders and requests for support and, occasionally, a scream followed by silence, she found her feelings of the previous day returning. This was another side of men she had not known about, and her resistence to them crumbled further. To counter-balance such violence and fear, was it any wonder they pursued the sweetness of sexual attraction so relentlessly? As the morning crawled into afternoon, and she sat with aching back and clothes wet with perspiration, she even found emotion creeping into her messages, ending with a fervent, 'Good luck' or 'Keep in touch' to encourage them, then feeling ridiculous pleasure when they replied, 'Thanks, sweetie,' or 'Righto, don't go away, will you?'

It must have been near the middle of the afternoon when her concentration was interrupted by a new sound, which she recognised immediately with a spurt of dread. Aircraft were approaching in large numbers. Men began sprinting past the tent where she sat with two runners. They were shouting, but she could hear only the voices coming through the earphones from the tank commanders. The orderlies beside her jumped up to grab their tin helmets. One put his on her head, bending down to shout beside her ear, 'Air raid, miss.'

335

They were there next minute, roaring down to rake the whole area with their guns. Vesta could hear the rattle of fire above the voices in her ears, and tried to concentrate on what was being said by men some miles off in the midst of their own attack. From the corner of her eye, she saw the sand jumping with bullets. Then all hell broke loose as trucks appeared to leap into the air in explosions of flames, boxes of stores flew into pieces that showered down onto men who had thrown themselves flat, barrels riddled with holes began spurting valuable petrol and oil. In the background came the sudden thud of their own anti-aircraft guns, and the spasmodic crack of rifle fire from those who had taken cover.

There seemed to be no more than a slight pause before the enemy aircraft were back, coming in suicidally low to avoid the artillery, and so fast it was almost impossible for men with rifles to sight them as they passed. There was the ratatat-tat of aircraft guns, and more trucks exploded with a roar of fire. Vesta just had time to register the sight of a soldier in baggy shorts and a tin hat running from his cover to snatch up the little dog standing defenceless and shivering in the open, before there was a whistle, a thud, and the wireless fell apart in front of her. Next moment, the earphones were snatched from her head, and her arm seized by one of the orderlies with her, before he dragged her from the tent. Shocked, breathless, and entirely in his hands, she found herself flung into a slit trench where others were sheltering, rifles at the ready. She landed awkwardly, and felt a sharp pain in her left ankle before she fell onto her face, hitting her cheek against the heel of a man's boot as he knelt to take aim. Struggling upright, she realised that the soldier who had given her his tin hat had been lying dead beside her as the other had pulled her from the sparking transceiver. A strange kind of chivalry, she had decided yesterday, and there was the perfect example of it.

The results of the raid were severe, but not enough to endanger the forward troops, who tightened their stranglehold on the enemy until they were left with no alternative but to surrender. German reinforcements had been non-existent; aircraft had been used as the only means of support. It had not proved sufficient, and by dusk that day the battle had been won. A great number of German tanks were now at the Allies' disposal, but there were also prisoners-of-war to be fed, provided with scarce water, and guarded. Colonel Villiers went forward to discuss the situation with the other British and New Zealand commanders. The advance would be delayed for a day or two because there were a number of casualties needing hospital-isation. So he issued his orders. A medical convoy would return to the oasis airstrip where aircraft could land to take passengers to Alexandria hospital. Vesta was to go with that convoy. Not only did she have a sprained ankle, which made her an official casualty, she was a woman, who should never have been with them in the first place.

It was a military order which Vesta had no choice but to obey. Gathering together her kit, which had luckily been in a truck that had not been hit, she was helped into the ambulance by a medical orderly, and driven back over the ground she had covered with Brad. The convoy moved night and day with a relay of drivers, reaching the oasis where she had landed five days before in less than two. During the journey, Peter Main died from his wounds, and two badly burned men lapsed into comas. As the only woman, she did all she could to cheer and comfort the men in pain, realising in doing so two indisputable things. Firstly, the mere presence of a female kept up their spirits enough to joke and flirt with her, even when suffering obviously. Secondly, if they had been attacked, each one of them would have done his utmost to protect her, regardless of his own plight.

She eventually arrived back in Cairo with her ankle bandaged and her heart bruised. Both would mend with time. When she took out her wad of sketches, however, she realised time would never erase the strange fascination of the desert, and of those men presently roaming it.

Chris lay in bed holding Sonja close against him. Outside it was snowing; he could see through the window the large flakes drifting against the glass. He had always liked snow, it brought back some happy memories. Budapest, even more beautiful draped in white; a Polish country estate; Vienna at Christmas-time, when shop windows were bright with exquisite goods, and elegant females in furs thronged the pavements, crisp with snow; Russia in winter, when trees became sculptures in ice.

Since their holiday in Scotland, they had met only once before this. Aside from his work at the espionage school, Chris had spent long hours at 'Guidons' with Frank Moore, and at high-level conferences with expatriate heads of state, all anxious to return to Europe. He had telephoned whenever he had had a few hours free, but Sonja had not been at home. She had rung several times when he had been away. Finally, they had met by accident at an official dinner party given by the Free French, and he had been forced to gaze hungrily at her whilst she smiled and chatted to other men, until he could free himself to cross to her. He had spoken in Swedish, she had replied in the same language. Fifteen minutes later, they had both left by separate doors.

He lay now at six o'clock on the morning of Christmas Eve, wanting her yet again, as his hand moved slowly over her back to explore the differing textures of soft tresses and cool, firm flesh. Her red hair spread across the paleness of his chest in a contrast of colour that heightened his pleasure. Lifting a handful of shining strands, he let them slide through his fingers, enjoying the sensation of softness caressing his skin, before his hand moved on to trace the concave curve of her waist that led to the satin rise of hips and thighs. She was Eve, Helen of Troy, Diana the Huntress. Her naked form should be depicted in oils, carved in marble, painted on china, sewn in silks, fashioned in gold, engraved on her own glass. She fulfilled him in every respect. She was perfect. 'Now' was not enough. He wanted 'forever'. How desperately he wanted that! Why was perfection so rare, so easily destroyed? A magnificent sunset was soon overcome by night, a superb symphony had only three short movements, a noble wine was contained in so small a bottle, a shooting star had only transient brilliance, a night of love consisted of no more than a clutch of marching hours.

His hand would no longer be controlled now, and it was joined by the other in an overture to returning passion, as a sense of time fleeing invaded him. Her body responded instinctively before her mind, and she sighed as he rolled over to reverse their positions, kissing her throat and breasts until, coming from sleep, she gazed up at him with misty eyes.

'Morning love is the love of youth. Take me until dawn breaks,' she whispered.

It was growing light when they finally left the bed, driven by hunger of a different kind. They stood together in the shower beneath the flow of hot water, bodies close as they kissed like lovers in the rain, reluctant to part. He stood dripping water as he wrapped a towel around her, seeing her as no more than a blur without the spectacles. Yet, when he reached for them, she caught his hand in hers.

'Not yet. Not yet. I wish to remain whoever it is you see with those uncovered eyes,' she said softly. 'Perhaps it is a young girl on a sun-washed Hungarian estate; perhaps a youthful virgin on her wedding-night. Or perhaps you see a creature of your imagination, who is all you could wish her to be. When you look through those lenses you will find a woman of thirty-eight, who has the face of great experience, and a body which is no longer charmed with youth.'

Pulling her towel-wrapped body close, he said against her temple, 'When I look through those lenses I see my whole life leap into focus from the blur it was before that evening when I turned and saw you.' Tightening his hold, he added, 'I can never let you go, you must know that. Damn your rules! When the war is over we'll go to Vienna, Budapest... anywhere you wish. So much time has already been lost, I...' He broke off as she drew away to put her fingers over his mouth.

'Make no plans. Swear no lifelong dedication. The future is so uncertain.'

Snatching up his spectacles, he put them on to look searchingly at her. 'Why this sudden change of mood? What happens to you each time I confess my lasting love?'

'I wish you would not,' she told him quietly.

Bitterness came swiftly. 'Are you saying you see our relationship merely as a form of escape from reality, as you once maintained it was? When I make love to you, do you lie there imagining you are a virgin, or a girl in a Viennese operetta? Is that what you were trying to say just now?'

'Why do you torment yourself? This *is* an escape from reality. What else can it be? You have a wife and family. I am an alien from an enemy nation, and the whole world is at war. There can be no future for us.'

He swallowed his anger to impress his next words upon her. 'If you believe that, there's no sense in anything. I once had no past. The future was all I could contemplate. I had to believe in it or go under.' Drawing her back into his arms, he rested his cheek on the top of her head. 'I have to believe in a future with you, and you must believe it too. I won't give up until you do.'

They ate breakfast of porridge and toast with coffee, Sonja in a long fleecy robe of emerald-green wool, and Chris in tweed trousers and a cashmere pullover, ready for his journey later that morning. As she poured more coffee from an elegant pot with a design of primroses, Sonja spoke about the rose bowl she was presently engraving.

'I think it is one of my best designs, and I believe I already have a purchaser for it.'

'I have told you before that I will give you any sum you need,' he put in, always hating the thought that she must earn a living by her art. 'I am a reasonably wealthy man. There is no necessity to rely on selling your work when I can very adequately provide for you.'

Shaking her head, she declared, 'I love to work... as you do at your Ministry. Such long hours you have. What is it you do that keeps you tied to your desk?'

'Tedious paperwork.'

'All night?' she asked probingly. 'I telephone from my bed and there is no reply.'

'*I* telephone and there is no reply,' he countered, steering clear of the subject.

'I go into the country to stay with friends. The air raids are troublesome, and I work better where it is quiet.'

'I go into the country,' he said semi-truthfully. 'It's unwise for an entire group of ministers to congregate under one roof in London, for obvious reasons.' He drank some coffee, then said, 'I'd give anything to stay in London over the next few days, you know that.'

Giving her characteristic little nod, she said, 'Of course. I also know that your wife needs you.'

He sighed. 'Christmas has always been such a special time for Marion, and she'll need help to get through this first one without David. With Vesta away in Egypt, I can't desert her.'

'If you did, I should not love you as I do,' came the soft reply.

Giving her a long look, he said, 'So you do admit to loving me.'

'I loved you from that first look. If I had only been Laura!'

'Laura belonged to Rex.'

'I belong to you ... For as long as we have, I belong to you.'

With a lift of his heart, he got to his feet and went to the tweed jacket hanging on the back of a chair, taking from the pocket a small package. He returned to her and held it out.

'I have a present for you to open tomorrow morning.'

Rising, she took it from him. 'Tomorrow will not do. It is your gift, and I wish to share my pleasure in it with you.'

Removing the wrappings, she sighed with delight over the small book of poems with mother-of-pearl inlaid covers and gold-edged pages, which he had gone to considerable effort and expense to buy from a collector he knew. She looked up from it with shining eyes.

'I have never before had such a gift. It is a token of love.'

'I'd give you a great deal more, if only you'd let me.'

She shook her head. 'I have your devotion. I also have something for you,' she went on, crossing to a small cabinet. 'It may explain why I love to work.'

Robbed of words, he held to the light the tall prism of glass, on one side of which was engraved a fully detailed picture of Tarrant Royal church as it used to be. The prismatic shape allowed light to reflect through the glass as if it were lit from within, showing the seventeenth-century building in perfect relief. He was so moved he could only stand holding it up to the window, where the snow outside put a brilliant light into the room.

'How did you know about this?' he asked, his throat tight.

Moving to stand beside him, she said, 'When we were in Scotland you told me of that night it was destroyed. It was clear to me that you cared very much, so I hoped to recreate it for you.'

He looked down at her, still marvelling. 'It's exact in every detail.'

Again her little nod. 'I went to Tarrant Royal.'

Strange sensations coursed through him. Sonja in Tarrant Royal! 'You went there? For what reason?'

Her anxious gaze searched his face. 'You are angry?'

'No, of course not angry.'

'You did not wish me to intrude on your life there?'

'No ... *no*,' he repeated, still shaken. 'There is no part of my life I wish to keep from you, you know that. I suppose ... Perhaps I should have liked to show it to you myself, introduce one great love to another.'

'You love this place so greatly?' came the gentle testing question.

'I ... Yes, I suppose my roots are there, despite all the travelling I have done.'

'Forgive me. I did not mean to ...'

He drew her to him, and brushed her forehead with his lips. 'There's nothing to forgive. Perhaps I couldn't bear the thought of you travelling through my childhood without me at your side. Oh God, how can I walk away from you this morning when every part of me longs to stay?'

'Because you know your wife needs your personal strength at a difficult time,' she told him, slipping her arm through his, and drawing him back to the fire. 'There is a little time before you must go for your train, however.'

Sitting beside her on the settee, he studied her work again, realising it was a very fine example of her skill. 'How could you copy what it once was?' he murmured, seeing the lovely old church in his mind's eye.

'In the little store I asked if there might be a picture, and the shop man searched in a box to find a picture postcard from before the war.'

Still finding it difficult to accept that she had wandered around his village, he could not help wondering at old Anderson's expression when Sonja Koltay pushed open the

341

door of his small shop, to ask for a postcard of Tarrant Royal church.

'Did you . . . Did you see the Hall?' he asked as casually as he could.

'Naturally I did not, my dear, although I longed to do so.' She smiled in an effort to ease the sudden tension between them. 'The Austro-Hungarian widow of a French financier murdered for his political activities, wandering through private property situated near an RAF base would, I think, be arrested by the village policeman as a suspected spy.' Her hand rested on his as it lay against his knee. 'But I did see the memorial bearing the names of your two brothers. And I visited Laura's grave in the churchyard,' she added gently. 'I had something to explain to her, you see.'

'Had you?' That news gave him even stranger sensations.

'Why is she so far in a corner, *liebchen*?'

He sighed as he remembered the newspaper headlines of the time. 'Her death, almost on the same day as Rex's, caused a sensation. They had been the darlings of a British public, which then wanted a great emotional public funeral in London. Rex would have hated that, so I did what I knew he would have wanted. After the event, the news leaked out, and we had hysterical crowds invading the churchyard to pile flowers on her grave. The villagers drove them away, and she has been peaceful there in her far corner.' He frowned in sudden sadness. 'Sheridan men invariably die away from home. My father threw himself into the sea at Madeira, Roland and Rex were blown apart somewhere in France, David has been swallowed up by the Sumatran jungle. Laura is our only link with them all; the only sacred place to visit in memory. I light a candle at her feet each Christmas. It's for all of them.'

After a moment of scrutiny, Sonja said, 'I think you still care very deeply for her.'

He nodded slowly. 'I shall always care for her . . . but it's you I love. Nothing will ever change that.'

In an attempt to make things easier for Marion, the pattern they had followed for years was changed this Christmas. Since she now refused to attend church services, Chris had sat alone through the Watchnight Service in the hut beside the wrecked church. Luckily, the hut held no family memories of past years, so he thought all the time of Sonja.

The Chandlers had invited them to the farm for the whole of the holiday, and Chris was glad to be out of the house that was hardly his own now. Even the small part they had been allowed to retain seemed cheerless, these days. Marion had always kept the rooms bright with flowers, or seasonal berries and leaves, and the dogs had romped madly about the place. Now the rooms held an air of neglect. Two of the dogs had died, not to be replaced, and the third had been adopted by the RAF officers, who made a fuss of him and took him for long walks on Longbarrow Hill. Strange how much one missed animals when they were no longer there.

So they all gathered at the farm in Tarrant Maundle, and the Chandlers had no reason not to decorate the place with holly and mistletoe. The two families were together, as usual, with the addition of a young South African pilot called Dirk, who was in love with Pat, and desperately trying to persuade her to marry him in the spring. She appeared very fond of him, but with thoughts of David's Chinese widow – who still could not be traced – in her mind, she declared herself against wartime marriages between people from different countries. They sat six around the table, Dirk wearing civilian clothes, which removed any reminders of David and the RAF, and although it was quiet in comparison with the days when the two families had joined in wild revelries, it was enjoyable enough. Chris could not help thinking of the concerts Vesta and Pat used to organise, and of Bill's terrible conjuring tricks, now things of the past for ever.

He fell to wondering what they would have done with little Su Sheridan if she had reached them from Singapore. She would have had every right to sit at this table with her husband's family, yet it would have been impossible. Marion had been unable to accept her when David was alive. Now her son was dead, there was no knowing what she might do if confronted with the girl. All in all, however, his wife appeared much improved. The white rabbit had been left at Tarrant Hall for the two days, and she joined in the conversation most of the time, even asking Dirk about his life in South Africa. But she was lifeless compared with the person she once had been, and she took no trouble with her appearance. With Chris she was polite, no more. It was that letter, of course. She would never forgive him for not trying to stop it reaching David. He wished to God he knew if it ever had. He felt Marion might come to accept his loss if she was assured her son had died unaware of the words she had written in a state of shock, denying him.

The day passed in pleasant enough style, and he was immensely grateful to the Chandlers for their help and friendship over this tricky period. The next hurdle would be David's birthday in eight days' time. He would have been twenty-eight.

When Dirk sat at the piano in the Chandlers' large modern sitting room to play some of the lighter classics and popular songs, thoughts of Sonja overwhelmed Chris. Thank God she was safe in London, not a prisoner in Europe like so many of her countrymen and women. Vesta was secure in Cairo. Marion and his closest friends were here. He was a lucky man, compared to some that night.

In the bed beside Marion's, in one of the Chandlers' guest rooms, he tossed and turned for some time after bidding his wife goodnight and switching out the light. He had not attempted to kiss her. She had made it plain that physical contact between them was no longer welcome, and he respected her wish with a sense of thankfulness. Longing for Sonja brought on by memories of their passionate night together gave him no rest, and he lay gazing out at the fresh snow falling outside the French windows, trying to cool the heat of his yearning by the sight. All it did was make him want her more: the frozen emptiness outside made him realise what his life would be like without her now.

He was awoken from fitful sleep by a figure in a woollen dressing gown, who shook his shoulder hard until he came to enough to reach for his spectacles.

'Pat! Whatever is wrong?' he murmured, looking automatically at the clock to find it was five-twenty.

'Sorry to disturb you, Uncle Chris, but there's a telephone call for you,' she whispered.

'At this hour...? Here?' he exclaimed, still drowsy.

'The caller wouldn't give his name, but he said it was important enough to wake you. I promised to fetch you right away.'

Tying the sash of his dressing gown hurriedly as he went, Chris walked barefoot to the receiver in the kitchen, where Pat had been making herself some tea.

'Sheridan here,' he said briefly.

'Chris, this is Greg Neave,' came the voice from the other end. 'I've just heard from Darwin that one of their groups has come in after months of silence. They have your boy with them. I know nothing, save that he is apparently alive. I thought you'd like to know right away. I'll be in touch when there's any more detail. Merry Christmas, old boy.'

Chris stood with the receiver still in his hand, looking at the pale yellow kitchen wall until he felt able to move. Then he replaced the receiver slowly, and turned to the girl watching him curiously.

'David has turned up in Australia,' he told her in dazed tones.

Pat put the tin of tea on the table, her face white with shock. 'Uncle Chris... *Oh, Uncle Chris*,' she murmured, then flung herself into his arms. 'He's so like you, I *knew* he'd come back.'

Chapter Seventeen

BOXING DAY in Cairo meant nothing to the local inhabitants, but Europeans crowding into the city and troops in from the desert on Christmas leave had celebrated with great gusto for the past two days. Hangovers were rife, and military policemen had had a busy time arresting those who had started brawls and fights in the numerous bars. European civilians and those on the permanent staff of military establishments had held parties, ranging from small get-togethers to full-blown official functions designed to show the flag in fitting manner.

Tobruk had been re-taken; Benghazi had fallen to the Allies. Massive British and American landings had been made in Algeria and Morocco, and these troops were pushing eastwards towards the main force battling back from defeat in a westward direction. Rommel and his Afrika Korps were now in a trap from which they could only be saved by rapid escape by sea, or by total surrender. The mood in North Africa was one of great jubilation for the Allies; the mood at home was one of renewed hope. Last Christmas the outlook could hardly have been blacker, but that longed-for victory was finally in sight. Proof that Germans could be beaten was all that was needed for morale to rise, for efforts to be renewed.

So the celebrating went on all over Cairo. Vesta sat in her room with the blinds drawn to ease the glare, and poured herself another cup of tea. Her celebrating was being done alone and quietly, but the rejoicing was no less because of it. David was alive in Australia. Fresh tears of happiness and relief welled up as she told herself the news again. It was still hard to believe. Less than an hour ago her telephone had rung, and a man announcing that he was Major Ronson from Signals told her he had received a privileged transmission from her father's Ministry, to be passed to her. At the time, she had been so overwhelmed she had said little by way of reply, and he had rung off. Now she had had a chance to think, it all seemed extremely odd. As a member of Headquarters staff, she knew the names of all those serving in Cairo, and there was no Major Ronson with Signals. Due to the time difference between London and Cairo, the message would have been sent at around six in the morning on Boxing Day. Who would have been at the Ministry to send privileged messages at that hour on such a day? Still, however the news had reached her, it was tremendous.

Vesta had received no details of David's reappearance, just that he was alive and safely in Australia. How he had got there, whether he was wounded, and what he had been doing for nine months would only be discovered later. She realised that she should have asked Major Ronson for an address in Australia, so that she could write. There was so much she should have asked the mysterious major. Yet, he would surely have told her all he knew. She must curb her impatience until receipt of the letter she knew her father would send right away with further details.

Right now, she felt tremendously homesick. This was news she felt she should share with her family. They would probably be with the Chandlers over Christmas. How pleased their great friends would be, especially Pat who felt she had been beastly to David on so many occasions. The news would bring a return of health for her mother, who might now be able to accept David's wife, when she was traced, in return for his safety. Would her faith now be restored by this semi-miracle? Oh, how she wished to be in England at that moment! Vesta prayed that David's survival would allow her father to repair the rift in his marriage, that had saddened him so much recently. She longed to see her brother, or even to write to him. But she could write to her parents, and to Pat. That would go some way to easing her frustration.

The letters written, she took a shower and washed her hair ready for the party she was going to with a group of friends that evening. Clad only in a cotton dressing gown, she was towelling her hair when there was a knock on her door. Wrapping the towel like a turban around her head, she went to open it.

'Hallo, Vic,' he said with that slow smile she had thought of so many times since leaving the desert.

Weak at the knees, she found herself breathless at the sight of him, big, brown, and plainly fighting fit just a few feet away.

'What are you doing here?'

'Taking you up on your offer,' he replied, leaning casually against the door frame. 'You did once say if there was anything I wanted I was to ask.'

Still not over the shock, she asked, 'What is it you want?'

'Tut, tut, tut,' he commented with a shake of his head. 'I thought we were past the stage of armed neutrality, and had reached something approaching fraternisation.'

'Brad, I can't stand here like this much longer. My hair is wet.'

'How long will it take to dry?'

'I . . . Why? Oh, ten minutes, or so.'

'OK. I'll see you downstairs in fifteen. Wear a frock,' he advised, as he began walking off. 'I'm taking you somewhere special where women dress up to the nines.'

'Now, just a moment!' she exploded.

'Uh, uh, you can't stand there much longer. Your hair is wet,' he reminded her. 'Fifteen minutes! If you can meet the deadline and still look gorgeous, you'll be the first woman I've met who can do it.'

He walked off along the corridor, and she flew into her room with one eye on the clock. *What a nerve!* she told herself, rubbing her hair briskly with the towel. Rushing to the wardrobe, she ignored the dress she had intended to wear and chose instead a new one of peach-coloured silk, which had a long drift of matching chiffon attached to the left shoulder with an ornate gold clip. In her petticoat, she applied pale lipstick that enhanced her sun-browned skin, and sprayed herself liberally with the expensive perfume Philip Bream had given her for Christmas.

Brushing her hair swiftly into the short style that was so convenient and cool, she then stepped into the dress, slipped her feet into gold sandals, snatched up a matching evening-bag and a heavy cream-coloured wrap, and flew to the door. There, she realised she had not put on her father's gold pendant after her shower, and she ran back to slip it over her head. *What a nerve!* she muttered to herself as she went down the wide staircase of the building commandeered by the British military for staff quarters.

Brad got to his feet at her approach. His face expressed undisguised surprise and appreciation as he looked her over from head to toe, then from toe to head again.

'Wow!'

'I'm off to a party with some friends,' she told him swiftly, saying a silent 'wow' herself now she had time to look at him properly. The white dinner jacket and dark trousers made less of a physical impact on her than the brief shorts and open shirt he wore in the desert, but he looked striking and equally irresistible in the formal clothes, with his unruly hair coaxed into neatness with a wet comb. The sense of danger he aroused in her was strong again, and despite the clothes and civilised setting, she felt the spell of the desert wash over her.

'How long have you been in Cairo?'

He looked at his watch. 'Twelve hours. I slept for ten of them.'

'How did you know where to find me?'

'I asked around for Victor Sheridan.'

'That silly joke!'

'You look some girl in a frock. Have you got rid of that darned pith-helmet?'

She could see the sand all around; feel that dry heat. 'I think it was destroyed in the raid.'

'It was probably their objective all along.' His eyes were lively with laughter. 'I heard you did pretty well with the transmitter that day.'

She shrugged. 'I'm a trained operator. Everyone but Colonel Villiers was impressed. Even that could not reconcile him to my presence in his beastly unit.'

'And to think you once directed me to behave as you were certain he would towards you!'

'Did you get your story?' she asked, changing the subject.

He put his hand beneath her elbow and began steering her toward the swing doors. 'I followed them through to Tobruk, then on to Benghazi. It was some sight when they liberated those places, I can tell you. You should have been there.' A taxi drew up at his signal, and he helped her in. 'Did you get your pictures?'

'Oh, yes,' she told him enthusiastically. 'My favourite I kept for myself. It was little Scruff – you know, that dog Trooper Braithwaite had as a pet – being snatched from his exposed position during the raid by that enormous cook who always made out he was so tough. The people here chose one of tanks against the sunset for the gift to the local celebrity, and I sent the rest to London. They seemed pleased, and bought eight of the ten. I felt no one would appreciate the dog picture the way I do.'

'I guess not.'

'Poor Peter Main died on the way back to the oasis,' she told him sadly.

'I heard. I also heard you had a duff foot.'

'Oh, that. I sprained my ankle when I fell into the trench. Hardly a wound, would you say? I also got a fearful bruise on

349

my face from hitting someone's boot as I fell. Most heroic.'

His dark eyes studied her at close quarters. 'Your face looks real good right now.'

Then she was in his arms being kissed in his thorough manner, and surfaced breathless. 'That was a bit quick off the mark, wasn't it?' she said, not sounding as indignant as she felt she ought.

'It's seven weeks since the last one. What's quick about that?'

'Do you have a ready answer for everything?' she countered tartly, rearranging her chiffon panel so that it covered a little more of her than before.

'That depends.'

'On what?'

'Who the girl is.'

'I see.' So there were other girls. Of course there were others!

'It is good to see you again, Vic,' he murmured. 'You're going to love the place I'm taking you to.'

Only then did she remember that she had fully intended going to the party with her friends.

She did love the place he took her to. Out of bounds to military personnel, it was expensive, sumptuous, and extremely romantic. Eastern-style decor consisting of lattice screens and bead curtains against a colour scheme of yellow and red made the alcoves private, almost secret. Diners ate by the light of Aladdin's lamps set on each table; the waiters wore Moroccan dress. The food was Eastern in origin, but French in presentation; the wines were international. There was an intimate dance floor, and the band had an exclusively European repertoire. As Brad was greeted like an old friend by the head waiter, the strains of a rhumba filled the restaurant, which was occupied by the cosmopolitan wealthy element of Cairo's permanent residents. The women, from dark-skinned beauties with scarlet-tipped fingers and exotic flowing gowns in vivid colours, to blonde socialites wearing Paris creations, were all *soignée*, sophisticated, and appeared supremely untouched by what was going on all over the world. The men were for the most part greying at the temples, with thickening waists and gold-filled teeth. Wealth was the common factor.

As they settled in their discreet nook Vesta studied her companion while he studied the menu. Which was the real Brad: the tough newspaperman in shorts and flapping shirt, who quenched his desert thirst with whisky; or this rugged sophisticate who mingled freely with the fleshpots of Middle Eastern society?

'Aren't you hungry?' he enquired, glancing up to catch her gaze. 'After all that bully beef stew, hard biscuit and greasy tea, I'm going to have me a royal banquet.'

'Do you come here a lot?'

'Now and then.'

'Don't you feel just a little bit the odd man out?'

He grinned. 'Not when I'm with a girl wearing a chunk of gold like you have round your neck. I recognise good stuff when I see it.' Returning to the menu, he said, 'I can recommend the chicken pilau. It's a light dish most women seem to go for.'

'Do they?' she responded serenely, deciding to choose koubbeh instead.

He ordered, then returned to the subject of her gold pendant. 'It's a very unusual design.'

'My father had it made for my coming of age. It's the church in my home village. Seventeenth century and very beautiful, until a German aircraft crashed into it. Daddy gave the jeweller a photograph he had taken several years before. It's lovely, isn't it?'

'So who is "Daddy"?' he asked, leaning back in his seat so that his face was half in shadow.

'Sir Christopher Sheridan. He's a linguist, cultural adviser, campaigner for world peace. Poor Daddy,' she reflected. 'Peace seems to have gone down the drain, culture is being ruthlessly crushed, and I suppose all he translates now is dry old bumf about blackout regulations and stirrup pumps for the masses of aliens who have arrived from Europe. When I saw him last it all seemed to be getting him down. Still, I had some marvellous news today,' she said, the excitement of it returning. 'My brother has turned up in Australia after being posted missing in the jungle for nine months. We all believed he must be dead.'

'That's great news for you. I guess he'll have one hell of a story to tell about that period.'

'I'm assuming he's all right. All they appear to know at the moment is that he's alive somewhere in Australia.'

'I'll see what I can find out. RAF, isn't he? What's his first name and rank?'

She leant forward eagerly. 'Are you really in a position to find out?'

'Could be. My syndicate has men out there. We do each other a favour now and again.'

'His name is David. He's a flight lieutenant.'

'Got it,' he said with a nod. 'But if Pete gets his story, I want twenty-five per cent of his commission for putting him on the track of it.'

Vesta felt herself tightening up. 'I thought you were... Look, David must have had a bad time for those nine months. The last thing he'll want to do is talk about it to the newspapers, even if he'd be officially allowed to. My brother is not a "story", Brad, he's a young pilot who has had an experience he probably wants to forget.'

'OK. OK. Stop getting hot under the collar,' came the clipped response. 'Here comes our banquet. Let's enjoy it.'

They began eating and she told herself that a newspaperman would only be interested in sensation, not human suffering. Disappointment ran through her. Wishing she had said nothing at all about David, she remained quiet as he made inroads into the spicy dish before him.

After a while he looked up at her. 'Still sore? If you feel that bad about it, I'll forget the whole thing.' Putting his fork down, he picked up his wine glass, saying, 'Your standards are a bit lop-sided, aren't they? You went around making sketches out there in the desert of men who haven't seen civilisation for months, sometimes years. You drew their despair, their suffering, their unique bond of fellowship, their moments of comedy. You admitted as much just a short time ago. You also told me you sold all your paintings based on what you saw. What's so different about writing it instead of painting it?'

He was right, of course. She sighed. 'Are you equally hard on all the girls you bring here?'

His smile was as intoxicating as the wine. 'They usually succumb to my charm a lot earlier than this. Why do you insist on fighting me, Vic?'

'Stop using that ridiculous name!'

They continued eating, and Vesta plied him with questions about the weeks following her departure from the desert, enquiring about the men she had come to know in that short period.

'I've never read any of your reports,' she told him. 'I'd like to.'

'I've never seen any of your pictures.'

'If that's a hint that I should ask you up to see my etchings, you'll be disappointed.'

He shook his head. 'Don't worry, I read you from the start.'

'Yes, of course, I'm mad about the Honourable Fitzroy.' The wine was relaxing her too fast, she found. Why on earth had she embarked on such an inflammable subject?

'Someone hurt you, and you can't forget him. Want to tell me about it?' he invited.

'No, thank you. Even if you were right, what possible interest would it have for you? Ah, of course,' she went on, her tongue running away with her, 'you think there may be a story in it.'

'I've already done a story about you.'

'You've *what?*'

'"Army girl takes over vital wireless set during emergency",' he quoted. '"Young artist steps into breach without turning a hair". It made good copy. How come you didn't see it?'

She was speechless for a moment, then she let rip. 'You ... you ... How *dare* you write such melodramatic rubbish?'

'Human interest, honey, same as your picture of the dog. If only you'd realise we have a great deal in common, we could abandon the preliminary sparring and get down to the vital rounds. Come on, let's dance.'

It was the worst mistake she had made all evening. He danced well, holding her far too close beneath low lights while the band played 'The Way You Look Tonight'. By the end of the dance she was weaker at the knees than before, and finding Brad Holland was still so very much the person who had driven her across miles of emptiness to join up with people who had come to mean more to her than she realised. Since returning to Cairo she had been restless and full of strange yearning. Often, at night, she had stood looking from her window at the stars – so clear in the desert sky – and had imagined herself back in that truck, wrapped in a blanket and gazing into a distance that was so quiet it seemed the world was holding its breath. She had remembered Sergeant Kirk, and the others who had made her a little bathroom of her own, and had laid a table for her in the middle of miles of sand. She had remembered the Officers' Mess, and the way members had all spruced themselves up because she was there, thrilled to have feminine company after so long. She also remembered their voices coming over the transceiver to her that morning, and her own feeling of helplessness.

For the first three weeks after her return she had spent all her free time working on the water colours, full of inspiration and knowing that what she was producing was the best work she had ever done. When it was finished, she had felt bereft. She had tried sketching parts of Cairo, even the pyramids, but her heart had not been in it. Now Brad had turned up to identify what ailed her. She wanted to be part of that desert force once

353

more. Cairo was dirty, squalid, and a backwater of the war. Her inspiration would die here.

'Brad,' she began, emboldened by the wine and semi-darkness to speak of her feelings to the one person who would best understand, 'you're wrong about me. I do realise we have a lot in common. It's you who doesn't truly appreciate the fact. You scoffed at my declaration that I wanted to paint real war, and waited to see my reaction to it with a sense of male smugness. I'll admit I got emotional one night, but I survived, didn't I? I refrained from throwing a feminine fit, and even Colonel Villiers would have to concede, under oath, that I buckled down in the emergency like any man.'

She fiddled with her coffee spoon, frowning at her thoughts. 'My paintings were good – really good – but I haven't been able to do anything worthwhile since then. They'll be taking Tripoli soon, and I'd give anything to get back there with them. All my requests have been turned down. I feel so frustrated. This is history in the making, and the opportunity to record it is being denied me.' She sighed. 'I know I probably only got the other chance because they wanted a present for old Omar, and because Villiers thought I was a man, but I thought the merit of my work might have stirred the people in London to give me a further commission.' Looking across at him, she finished, 'You're an old hand at the game. What would you advise me to do?'

'Forget it,' came his blunt response. 'You'll be banging that pretty head of yours against a wall of khaki. Villiers sent in one hell of a bombshell to this Headquarters from Tobruk, and I can tell you he conceded nothing. In fact, I'm amazed you weren't broken to the ranks, Lootenant.'

'Lefftenant,' she corrected automatically, badly shaken by his revelation. 'The spiteful misogynist *bastard!*' she said with force. 'With men like him around, why should I worry about the Germans? Oh, Brad, it's so unfair.'

'Perhaps, if you'd had a face like some beaten-up old Cadillac, and carried several hundred more pounds in weight, he'd have loved you. You just don't look anything like a man, sweetheart. No one would guess you were as tough as you are. You sure had me fooled.' As she sat staring mutinously into her coffee cup, he added softly, 'Come on, Vic, don't take it so much to heart. You'll get another chance.'

She looked up at him. 'Daddy has always said an artist should be judged on merit, not sex, and he's so right. He's so right on nearly everything, and he'd put Villiers in his place with a beautifully worded and extremely calm piece of his mind.' She gave a faint smile. 'You'd like him. You're not in the least alike, yet you've both got the same kind of balanced outlook.'

'Uh-uh,' he contradicted. 'Merit or not, I'm judging you on sex right now, and you get my top marks. Let's tango.'

They danced again, then again. The rhythm of the music grew more intoxicating as the hours passed, and Brad was so adept at Latin-American dancing, she found herself surrendering to the sensuous movements of his body in close proximity. Her resolution was vanishing like water on sand beneath the onslaught of low lights, throbbing music, and this man who had shared her unforgettable desert experience. Why not enjoy it while it lasted? He knew how far he could go, so why not let him reach those limits and have the pleasure without the final disillusioning pain?

It was well past midnight, and they were doing a slow foxtrot. Brad had been drinking whisky for some time, but seemed able to take it. Vesta was enjoying the freedom and relaxation wine had imbued in her. Her head was on his shoulder as they moved together, dreamy and contented. He smelt excitingly masculine – of warm skin, a faint whiff of alcohol, carbolic soap, his starched shirt. His body against hers was hard and hinted of strength. His soft caressing accent was gentle in her ear. His breath fanned her bare neck; his hand was splayed against her back, guiding her inexorably where he wanted her to go.

He blew gently on her short hair. 'Hey, not asleep, are you?'

She moved her head in a negative, too contented or enchanted to break the moment by looking up.

'I guess you've gotten a little tipsy,' he whispered in her ear. 'You're a darn sight easier to handle right now.'

The music ended, but they stayed gently swaying on the dance floor until he said softly, 'The party's over, sweetheart.'

She raised her head then and twisted in his encircling arm to smile up at him. 'It was a wonderful party. I nearly didn't come, but I'm glad I changed my mind.'

His mouth was so near hers he brushed the pale lips with a tantalising gesture, smiling into her eyes. 'So am I, Vic.'

They walked slowly from the floor, arms round each other, lost in mutual study until a voice broke into their togetherness.

'Brad Holland, as I live! I go right round the world, then walk in here and find you, you sonofabitch.'

The man was large, sandy haired, and semi-drunk. He was evidently a friend of Brad's from some way back in the newspaper business, because he reeled off a speech about war zones and correspondents covering the action for all manner of publications, all of whom Brad apparently knew.

Vesta leant towards Brad, saying softly, 'I'll be back in a moment,' then smiled vaguely at the robust man before making for the powder room. The girl in the mirror had flushed cheeks and badly ruffled hair, but there was an amazing glow in her eyes it was impossible to ignore.

For a while Vesta stood gazing at that girl who had changed yet again from the one who had stepped from an aircraft in an oasis, in full command of her femininity. Was it possible to surrender without humiliation? Was there joy to be had in just being a girl, for a while? Would it be different with Brad?

With the questions still unanswered, she made her way back to the restaurant, hoping Brad had managed to free himself from his old chum, who had looked set to make an evening of his reminiscences. He was still captive, however, and she stood hesitantly on the threshold of the exotic dimly-lit room. Brad had just spotted her over his friend's shoulder, when she heard the man say, in the over-loud voice of the semi-drunk, 'Ran into your wife last month in London. She looked a million dollars in the middle of all those dreary dames in uniform.'

Brad was still looking at her as she gave him one expressive, disparaging glance, before turning and walking into a waiting taxi, alone.

The train drew into Greater Tarrant station and expelled steam noisily. The trees were in full blossom behind the station building; the air was warm and gentle over the little market town, which had hardly changed with the advent of war. The tiny cinema still showed films three years after their initial release; the Assembly Rooms were still the venue for Saturday-night 'hops', although the presence of the RAF on Longbarrow Hill meant a predominance of airmen to partner the village girls, and those in the Land Army working on the surrounding farms. Even the Punch and Judy Tea Rooms managed to supply almost identical meals to those on which they had prided themselves before 1939. What was more a pot of tea, scones and jam with clotted cream, and a plate of fancy cakes was still only two-and-six. Where could anyone these days find better fare at better value?

As the train stood puffing alongside the platform, the carriage doors swung open to allow passengers to step from fusty compartments into the glorious late-May sunshine. Only three people alighted. One was a girl in the unattractive but sensible garb of the Land Army, returning from leave. Another

356

was an elderly woman of a nearby village, who had been into Bournemouth to see a specialist at the hospital about a lump in her breast, and was returning in a state of shock.

The third person was an RAF officer, who stepped down from a first-class compartment. He took longer than the others to alight, then stood looking around so long, the train had drawn out to become no more than a wisp of smoke in the distance before he began to move slowly toward the girl taking the tickets. He walked with a painful shuffle, and young Nellie Carter called out, 'Take your toime, sir. Bus doan go up to the airydrome for two hours yet.' She watched him curiously, just the same. He looked peculiar, somehow.

'Can't never fly an arioplane in thaht state, I know,' she told herself, as he made his careful way along the platform.

She had a shock as he drew nearer, and suddenly wished that the other passengers had not vanished. His face was almost as dark as an Indian's, and striped with black scars, as if someone had drawn a garden rake across his cheeks. His dark blue eyes stared as if sightless, and his hair, which she had initially thought was ash-blond, was as white as that of an old man – a skeletal old man. Frightened, she glanced round for the reassurance of another presence, but the station was now deserted. When the sinister-looking passenger held out his ticket, she was hard put not to run, for his dark-brown hand appeared to be no more than a bony claw.

'Thank you, sir,' she said as nonchalantly as she could, then went into the ticket office and locked herself in. Through the window, she watched him shuffle into the yard, then halt to look at the shower of bridal blossoms falling from the trees, as if he had never seen anything like it before. Two more awkward steps, then he stopped again to gaze back along the railway line where the lush valley was bright with pink and white campions, wild bluebells, nodding yellow cowslips, and great waving heads of yarrow. Nellie wished he would move on. She felt sorry for him, but they really should not let people like that walk around amongst everyone else.

With relief, she watched him go through the white-painted gate leading to the high street. People were passing him with overdone unconcern, then turning to gaze and whisper together. Nellie was not surprised. Still watching from the safety of the ticket office, her heart gave a lurch when the man stopped, waited motionless for a long time, then turned and looked set on coming back to the station. Trying to decide whether or not to telephone Constable Atkins, even though it was his dinner time, she thankfully noted that the disturbing stranger had thought better of it. She watched him walk haltingly to the sub-post office and try the door. That showed he was a stranger, because Miss Donkins had closed between half-past twelve and two for years. He stood leaning against the wall for a while, and Nellie let out a startled cry when the telephone in the office rang shrilly. By the time she had told Bill Cavendish that his parcel had not come in on the twelve-forty, then heard about the trouble Florrie was having with the old mangle, the man was nowhere to be seen.

'Thank 'eavens for that!' she muttered, unlocking the door and stepping out onto the platform. Next minute, she stepped back with her hand to her throat in fear. He was there, not two feet away from her.

'I'll have to use your telephone, Nellie,' he said, in such a cultured voice it sounded quite wrong for the way he looked.

How did he know her name? Unable to say anything, she merely stepped aside. Once he walked into the office, she would go for Constable Atkins. There was no train until the two twenty-nine, so he could talk as long as he liked – the longer the better, so he would still be there when she got back with Tom Atkins. The minute he vanished inside the tiny office, Nellie was off, running as fast as she could to the police office at one end of Tom's house, and praying he would be there having his dinner.

David took the little ear trumpet off the hook and waited. Betty Liddel's artificial telephone voice carolled in his ear, 'Numbah please, callah.'

'Maundle four nine.'

'Hoeld the lane. Jest putting yew threw.' A series of clicks while he said a prayer, then, 'Goe ahead, callah.'

'Hallo.'

'Hallo. Wattle Farm.'

Thank God, it was Pat. Yet he did not know how to begin.

'Hallo, are you there?' her voice asked rather impatiently.

'I'm . . . I'm at the station. I thought it would be a good idea to turn up without any fuss. Now I'm not so sure.'

There was silence from the other end, then Pat said in incredulous tones, '*David!* Oh, you idiot! Of course it wasn't a good idea. You're supposed to be on a ship somewhere between Cape Town and Southampton!' Then her calm voice broke, as she added in wobbly tones, 'Now you've made me cry, you beastly thing.'

'Can . . . Can you come?'

'Yes, of course I'll come,' she told him between sniffs. 'Trust you to turn up without giving a girl a chance to do her hair and make herself look good.'

'Just come... *Now.*'

There was a slight hesitation before she said, low-voiced, 'All right, David, I'll be there in fifteen minutes.'

'Pat,' he put in sharply.

'Yes?'

'Be prepared for... changes.'

'Yes... Yes, of course. Wait for me there.'

He sat on the white-painted seat on the platform looking at the well-loved familiar view. He had gone back and forth to school from this little station, then back and forth to Cranwell – until he had bought his first car. Over the years, he had waited here for trains with a suitcase full of new clothes for the coming term, and a tuck box filled with his favourite cakes and sweets. Later, the case had been filled with sports gear, with a cricket bat or squash racquet lashed to the side, and boots tied by the laces to the handle. At that stage, the tuck box had contained meat patties, round dairy cheeses and half a cured ham – items for a rapidly growing, healthy adolescent. Later still, the suitcase had held the coveted blue uniform, and manuals on aerodynamics. There had still been cricket bats and squash racquets, but the tuck box had been replaced by a hip flask.

Now he was sitting on that same station, unable to accept that everything looked the same as it had then. There was a sweetsmelling warm breeze blowing from across the track stretching each side of him, between meadows full of wild flowers.

Humid, suffocating heat, with no movement of air to relieve it and make breathing easier.

Butterflies were flitting haphazardly above the gentle green countryside; high aloft the skylarks were warbling joyously.

Great vicious ants swarming through the undergrowth, with snakes and other poisonous creatures; in the giant trees the raucous screeching of blue, red and green birds.

Blossom falling like gently drifting snowflakes, and clusters of wallflowers filling the noontime with heavy sweet scent in that peaceful silence.

Rain pouring down like thunder onto huge fleshy leaves, vines as thick as a man's arm to tie him down in the sun, the sickly stench of rotting swamps.

Looking back to the high street, there were people with white skins moving happily about their business, a clean neat road with shops and houses, gardens with green hedges and flowers rioting everywhere. From the baker's shop nearby wafted the delicious smell of new bread, and the air was filled with the calls of sheep to their lambs.

People with brown skins moving uneasily about their tasks, eyes filled with fear or hatred. Swampy clearings with huts on stilts, a few scrawny chickens, children who were no more than skin and bones. The wafting smell of rice cooking; the air filled with human screams.

His body was so taut he had a job to move when a voice suddenly said, 'Now come along, sir, you cahn't sit 'ere, you know. This is a railway station, and lest you've got a train ticket or platform ticket, you'll 'ave to leave the premises.'

The speaker was a little greyer, maybe fuller around the belly, but not much changed. David had known Tom Atkins all his life, yet the policeman apparently had no idea who he was addressing. Nellie Carter could be excused, perhaps, but was he so impossible to recognise? Did nothing of David Sheridan remain?

Getting to his feet, he began to make his way back along the platform to where Nellie was peering from the doorway of the ticket office.

'Can I be of some assistance to you, sir?' puffed Tom Atkins beside him. 'You goin' up to Longbarrow airfield? There's no bus until quarter three, but you bein' an officer, like, you could ring and ask someone to come for you. Is thaht what you telephoned for jest now? If so, you can wait out on the seat by the war memorial. No one minds thaht, but the station's official property, like.' He patted Nellie's hand as he passed. 'It's orlright, girl, I'll see to it now, never fear.'

Just as they left the station yard and began crossing to the war memorial in the middle of the High Street, the sound of racing hoofs heralded the arrival of a horse-drawn trap, which swept to a halt by the station. The driver was a very slim girl with long dark hair held back from her face with a dark-red band, which matched the cotton shirt tucked into well-cut jodhpurs.

It was two years since he had seen Pat, but he would know those unusual silver-green eyes anywhere. Right now they registered acute shock, and the colour drained from her face so drastically he thought she was about to faint. But she came on until they were feet from each other, the extent of the shock making her face stiff.

'Hallo, David,' she greeted with obvious emotion, yet making no attempt to touch him. 'Welcome home.'

'Thanks for coming. Especially at such short notice.'

360

'That's what friends are for.' She bit her lip as she continued to look at him with wide, fathomless eyes. 'Look, I was in the middle of lunch when you called. How about a quick cup of tea in the Punch and Judy?'

'Yes.'

'Actually, you might get something stronger from old Mr Bates, if he's around. The boys at the airfield have an arrangement with him,' she said as they walked away, leaving Tom Atkins staring in puzzlement.

'Tea will be all right,' he said.

Water, for God's sake give me water.

'Old Bates is still alive and kicking, then?'

'I'll say. He wrote to Winston Churchill complaining because they told him he was too old at eighty-eight for the Home Guard.'

'Oh.'

Pushing open the door that set a bell clanging, Pat led the way into the small parlour containing six tables, all of which were full, and continued through to the inner room where there were two tables for two, and a window nook with a tiny table before the window seat.

'Our favourite place,' she declared, going to sit rather heavily on the padded seat, the lead-paned window behind her. 'We have the place to ourselves, too.'

As he lowered himself into the arch-backed wooden chair facing her, he realised she still looked extremely white.

'Do you want anything to eat, David?' she asked as little Agnes Bates approached with pad and pencil to stand staring in disbelieving fascination at him. 'They still do those lovely sticky buns.'

'Yes . . . a sticky bun.'

It's those damn berries we ate, or the snake. That's what's tearing our guts out now.

Agnes pulled herself together and went off as if in a daze, and Pat said matter-of-factly, 'Mummy's phoning Aunt Marion.'

'Oh.'

'We couldn't have just walked in, David.'

'No.'

The tea and buns came. There were the cups, saucers and plates decorated with a heavy pattern of green and brown with pheasants, which must be as old as he was. The bun was new, of course, but he had eaten its ancestors over the last twenty-eight years. No, the last twenty-*six* years, because he had been away that long. Although he had probably not eaten sticky buns for the first two years of his life, so better make it twenty-four.

361

That was still a hell of a lot of sticky buns.

'Do you still take sugar?'

He looked up at the girl with the unusual eyes. 'It doesn't matter.'

Look, I'll drink my own urine, but no one else's, is that clear?

'David ... Why didn't you let anyone know you were here?'

'It seemed a good idea. I mean, what do you say? I'll be arriving on Tuesday. Put on your best frock and get ready to pretend you're not shocked when I walk in?'

'I don't know. I've never been in your position.' She sipped her tea. 'How did you get to England so quickly? Uncle Chris had the date the ship was due to dock. He and Aunt Marion were going to meet you there.'

'That's what I thought. I hitched a lift with the RAF from Cape Town. They brought me to a station in Hampshire this morning. I've come straight on from there.'

'Where's your luggage?'

Christ, you all look like natives! How long have you been walking around in nothing but loin-cloths?

'I haven't any.'

Her colour still had not returned as she asked quietly, 'Don't you want your sticky bun?'

He looked down at it as it sat round, brown and beautifully shiny on the partridge plate. He could not bring himself to destroy something so wonderful. 'I'll take it with me.'

'Have you had enough tea?'

When I get back I'm going to spend the first day guzzling beer non-stop. Bloody gorgeous ice-cold frothy beer. I'm not. It'll give you belly-ache, fizzing up until your guts burst open and fly all over the room. I'm going to drink gallons of tea, hot strong tea that'll bring me out in a sweat so's I won't miss this bloody heat.

'Yes, thanks.'

Pat got to her feet. 'We'll get going then, shall we?'

'Yes.' He picked up the bun with great care and wrapped it in the clean handkerchief someone had given him that morning before he had set off. Then he picked up the partridge plate and followed Pat through the outer room to the door. She stopped there to pay Mrs Bates, who was behind the desk bearing the till.

'Now, let's see, Miss Chandler,' she began, trying hard not to look at David, 'that was two teas and two buns, wasn't it?'

'And one plate,' said Pat calmly. 'How much is that altogether?'

'Oh, dear me ... Yes, well, let me see. That's ... that's two

362

teas and two buns... and one plate,' she repeated, eyes popping as she looked at the handkerchief bundle he held in the hand that resembled a talon. 'Yes, well... that's six... nine... and carry four.' She looked up and said wildly, 'That'll be two shillings and fourpence halfpenny.'

They'll take us over to Java in their boats, at a price. How much? All our shirts, Pete's boots, and the compass. What do they want with a compass, for Christ's sake? Shut up! It's cheap at the bloody price, and don't any of you say it isn't.

It was easier getting into the trap than he had expected, once he had put the bun and the plate on the seat. Having claw-like hands was an advantage: they hooked over rails and similar things to give him good leverage. Pat held the horse steady until he had settled, then jumped in beside him to set the beast going. It was called Figgy. They had named it so because it had been acquired one Christmas, and was so dappled Vesta had declared it was like the figgy pudding in the carol 'We Wish You a Merry Christmas'. So Figgy it had been from that moment on.

The high street was busy, and he realised it was because of the market in the square just past the Plough and Wheatsheaf. That meant it must be Thursday.

How the hell do I know what day it is? I don't even know the bloody month, or year. The war's probably over, and we're the only flaming stupid buggers still alive.

They were soon out of Greater Tarrant and bowling along the lane to Tarrant Royal. On both sides of the road the hedgerows were full of wild roses, and birds searching for food for their fledglings. Beyond them rose the gentle green slopes where sheep grazed, and lambs sat neatly arranged like nightdress cases, or ran back and forth with spontaneous animal joy. Further on they passed over the bridge that spanned the stream. How many times had the three of them fished for tiddlers here? The girls had carried the food, and he had gallantly brought along the nets and jam jars with string handles. They had always returned home wet through, yet the stream was not more than a foot deep at that point. How had they managed to get so wet?

Christ, I see water. Great flaming gallons of it! It's the sea. The beaut, wonderful, deep blue sea. We've made it. We've bloody made it!

They were on the outskirts of the village now, passing the swing gate that gave access to the path through the copse to Wey Hill and the brigadier's Rhineland monstrosity. Beyond that was the duck pond, the village shop and, on the left, the house his grandfather had occupied when he had been the local doctor. His mother had lived there for the first three years of his own life, while his father had been going through his own personal hell. On round the corner, past the village green with the war memorial bearing the names of Roland and Rex Sheridan, towards the George and Dragon with its great spreading oak. It all seemed to be growing shimmery and blurred.

The trap took a sudden sharp turn through the open gateway of the Lower Meadow, and slowed to a halt facing Wey Hill. Two pheasants rose in fright at their arrival, then there was silence save for the humming of bees amongst the buttercups. He sat there, fighting to stop the volcano inside him from erupting. But the boiling, gathering, explosive mass was already on its way upwards, and there seemed no way of stopping it.

'David... Oh, David, *darling*... Please don't cry,' said a voice beside him.

'It... it was all right, until I got off the train,' he confessed with great difficulty. 'It was all right... all the way to England... until I got off that train. But it's all the same... Just the same! It would have been fine if... if everything had changed. But it hasn't. It's all the bloody wonderful same... and I can't take it. Oh God, Pat, I just can't take it.'

The volcano erupted. He lay across her lap sobbing, while she stroked his hair, that had gone from gold to white since he had last been there at home.

Chapter Eighteen

DAVID FOUND things had changed, after all. The church was no more than a shell, with the tail of a German aircraft projecting from the roof to lie against the cross miraculously still there. Someone had mentioned it in a letter, but he had forgotten. Then there was his home. As Pat drove uphill on the long curving drive bordered by horse chestnut trees, he saw the great circular forecourt contained a collection of private cars and some official vehicles with RAF markings. The greater part of the Hall had been taken over as an Officers' Mess. Someone had mentioned that in a letter, too.

Two officers were in deep discussion under the raised bonnet of an ancient, lovingly kept MG as Pat drove the trap the final few yards, halting it near the side entrance normally used as access to the stables. Hearing the approach, the pair looked up and across at them. One smiled and immediately began walking over: a tall, thin dark-haired man of around twenty-four, with narrow features and sleepy eyes.

'My horoscope this morning said I'd have an unexpected romantic meeting, and here you are,' he said to Pat, before taking her in his arms and kissing her with a thoroughness that suggested he did it frequently. 'Are you all right, darling? You look rather pale.'

'I'm fine,' she told him. 'But you must expect a girl to look a little pale when she gets a telephone call from someone she thinks is on the high seas between South Africa and England, who says he's at the station waiting to be collected. Dirk, this is David. He hitched a lift and got here before we had a chance to fix up the "welcome home" sign.'

The youngster called Dirk smiled at David as he climbed with difficulty from the trap, ignoring Pat's attempt to help him.

'I'm Van Reerdon. Jolly good show on making it back,' said the South African warmly. 'Perhaps my girl can now settle

365

back to giving me her undivided attention. Ever since she heard you'd turned up Down Under, I haven't been able to do a thing with her. Females get into such a flap over things like that, don't they?'

David said the only words that came into his head. 'I hope you're comfortable in my house.'

The youngster laughed boisterously, putting his arm around Pat and holding her against his side. 'It must be hard to come on leave and find you've just gone from one squadron to another.'

'What are you flying?'

'Spits mostly. Some Hurricanes. I'll take you over one day after you've settled down, if you like. You're welcome in the Mess any time you feel like getting sloshed.' He grinned. 'As it's your house, we'll make you an honorary member.'

'Thanks.' He searched feverishly for something else to say, but he had lost the art of conversation. A man tended to run out of intelligent things to say in the jungle. The door leading into the house stood open beside him, and anything that would delay his obligation to walk through it would be welcome.

The other man's attention had turned to Pat, on whom he was looking down with an air of ownership. 'Is it still on for Saturday?'

She frowned up at him. 'Saturday?'

'My forty-eighter... A day to Falmouth, remember?'

'Oh, yes... of course.' Easing from his encircling arm, she looked at David. 'I think we should go in. Aunt Marion has been watching us from that window behind you ever since we arrived.'

'Yes,' he said, turning to the inevitable.

Over his shoulder, he heard the other man say, 'No, let him go on his own.'

'But I...'

'You're not his real sister. You've done your bit. Now let him handle this his way.'

Van Reerdon was probably right, but he would have liked Pat with him, all the same. Robson opened the door right on cue, so he must have been watching from another window, he supposed. The side entrance led into a small panelled hall where a clothes stand contained oilskins, coats, riding crops, and walking sticks. A collection of boots stood beside it. David found the combined smells of leather, rubber and floor wax unbearably familiar.

'Welcome home, Mr David,' greeted Robson with tears rolling down his cheeks. 'Mrs Robson and I prayed for your safe deliverance every night, sir, and our prayers have been answered. But the Lord saw fit to take a terrible payment from you.'

'How is Mrs Robson?' he asked automatically.

'Only fair, sir, I have to say.' He drew nearer. 'I also feel it my duty to warn you to expect changes in Her Ladyship. She has been ill, suffering from severe stress for some months. All this has been very hard on her, as I'm sure you'll understand.'

'Yes.'

'She is in the sitting room, sir.'

He could not get to the sitting room because of a partition that had been erected to shut off that part of the house. He stood staring at it in bewilderment.

'David ... We're in here,' called a gentle voice in an accent he knew so well, because he had lived with it for almost a year. Swinging round, he saw, not a dark brown emaciated man with long hair and a long beard, but a slender dark-haired woman he had known all his life. Aunt Tessa had plainly delivered the news in person rather than by telephone. They were in the small sitting room, of course.

He walked over and saw a wealth of love and sympathy in her silver-green eyes, so like her daughter's. But she merely said, 'I'll be in the garden. If it gets too much, call me.'

There was no avoiding it now. As Pat's mother walked away, he went in to face his own mother after two years' absence. She was standing in the middle of the room, wearing a smart dark green dress and an unusual amount of lipstick. It made her look like mutton dressed as lamb. Her white face had been dabbed with rouge to give an impression of rosy cheeks, but the result was almost bizarre. He felt extremely awkward about how silly she looked.

'I hitched a lift from the RAF,' he said. It was his best line so far, he felt.

The smile she gave was ghastly. He wished she had not tried so hard. 'Well, you've taken us all by surprise, darling. How are you?'

'Fine.' He swallowed and cast around wildly for something else to say. 'You look very smart.'

That was when she began to cry, standing there looking at him, with mascara running down her cheeks making black streaks across the vivid pink circles of rouge. She was shaking as she reached for him, and held him in a grip that was astonishingly strong for a woman.

'After all I said to you, you still came back to me,' she moaned. 'I should have been punished, not you, but seeing you like this is the worst punishment of all. I'm being made to pay, darling. I'm being made to pay.'

Not understanding her wild raving, he stood helplessly as she clung to him, finding it impossible to do or say anything to stop her. Through the French windows he saw Pat and Aunt Tessa making gestures to him so he put his arms around the painted stranger who used to be his mother, and they nodded their approval.

The Headman says the Nips came through here two days ago. They raped all the women, even the grannies.

His arms dropped to his sides again, and he avoided looking at the two women outside on the terrace.

Finally, the tears were all shed, and his mother pulled away, saying, 'Forgive me, darling. I meant to be so civilised.' Wiping her eyes and making the mascara run even more, she went on, 'Now you're back where you belong we can look after you. You've done enough for your country – more than enough. You'll be safe now. The summer is coming. We can go for walks across Longbarrow Hill like we used to, and ride. You'll be able to ride later on, when you're stronger. But we mustn't rush things. There's all the time in the world now, and we can just be together, letting the days pass gently.' She took hold of his left arm. 'You're *home*, David. You don't have to fight any more. We'll take care of you, give you nourishing food, plenty of sleep, and good country air. You'll be surprised how soon you forget all that and go back to being the boy you once were.' Dabbing at her nose with her wet handkerchief, she gave a little laugh. 'Here I am rattling on with all my plans, and you must be tired after your journey. I'll get Robson to bring some tea. Would you like to tidy up first?'

You stink, Dave, d'you know that? You stink so much worse than the rest of us we've all decided to forgo our ration of poisoned water so's we can clean you up enough to be socially acceptable.

'Yes, all right.'

Linking her arm through his, she began to lead him from the room. 'Luckily, the division of the house meant your room is still in our section. I intended to get it all ready and put flowers there for your arrival. You'll have to have it as it is, for now.'

They went up the rear staircase normally used by the servants. Because it spiralled fairly tightly he took a while negotiating it. The ligaments in his legs had been so badly damaged walking was still difficult. They went slowly along the corridor to the room that had once been Uncle Rex's. A room was a room. What did it matter who had used it?

His mother threw open the door saying, 'There you are, just as you left it, darling. I've kept it like that all the time you've been away. And look... Remember this?'

She held up a stuffed white rabbit. He stared at it. It reminded him of something they had come upon in a kampong soon after the Japanese had been through. The thing was lying beside what had once been its mother.'

'I'll wait downstairs, David. Come down when you're ready.' She put a hand on his arm. 'If you want Robson to help you, just ring.'

I'm sick and tired of carrying you around, Dave. I'm sick of your fever and your stinking wounds. I'm sick of trying to keep you quiet when you're delirious. But, most of all, I'm bloody sick of hearing you suggest I leave you behind. I'm getting you to Australia if it's the last thing I do. Now shut your flaming mouth!

'I won't need any help, Mother.'

He sat with a plate balanced on his knee, and a cup of tea beside him on the small table. The cup was easy because it fitted nicely into his stiffened, bent fingers, but a biscuit flat on a plate presented problems. He left it there.

His mother kept staring at his hands. She tried not to, but her eyes kept fastening in horrified fascination on them. He wished they would not. She had cleaned up her face, but had replaced the mascara and rouge with more. Aunt Tessa and Pat were still there. Three women. He had forgotten how much females talked when they got together, all about nothing. Had he really frightened little Nellie Carter at the station so much that she had gone for Tom Atkins? Had Tom really not known him? Were people so very frightened by his appearance? Had Pat only accepted him because he had been a brother to her? Had his mother put all that make-up on her face just to cover her revulsion?

'. . . don't you think, David?' came her voice now.

'Yes.' He had no idea what she had asked.

'You look tired. Are you sure you wouldn't like to lie down?'

'Sure.'

'Don't you think he might be overdoing things, Tessa? After all, he only landed at six this morning, after a long flight.'

'I'm sure he'll know when he's had enough, Marion,' came the voice in an accent that touched a chord in him.

'Well, don't be afraid to say, darling. We'll all understand.'

'Yes.'

'You're not eating anything. We can only get plain biscuits, these days, not the creams you used to like. I'll ask Robson to bring you a ham sandwich, if you'd prefer that.'

'No.'

'How about some toast?'

He shook his head.

'A slice of cake, then?'

'I'm not hungry.'

She smiled. 'You'll enjoy your dinner all the more. Cook is going to prepare something special.'

'There's no need.'

'Of course there is. Your first meal at home after two years! If we'd known you were coming we could have planned something really worthy of the occasion, but I'm sure you'll find it an improvement on all that awful rice.'

He struggled to his feet, and the plate containing the biscuit slipped to the floor. 'Oh, for Christ's sake!' he cried, looking wildly for an escape route, then making for the open French windows leading to the garden.

It was wonderful out there in the late afternoon sunshine. From the other side of the fence erected through the middle of the grounds to the rear came the sound of men's voices; masculine laughter. It was comforting. The aroma of cigarettes and pipe tobacco hung in the air, mingling with the scent of flowering almond. Flame, yellow and white azaleas stood out against the lush green hedges and were repeated in reverse in the still, clear water of the lily pond. He walked slowly until he reached the sunken garden. Looking down on it, he realised it was like looking down on a complete country from the air – forests, great green plains, masses of flowers. No venomous, stinking jungle with brown, slimy waterways; no people living in fear, no men to strip you naked and ask questions you must not answer. His mind was full of a screaming experience which had destroyed his past, and put his future in a vale of shadows.

'Hallo, David.' The voice was quiet and gentle, but it made him jump, just the same. 'Sorry, I didn't mean to startle you.'

I once looked like that, only younger, he thought dispassionately, as he studied the blond handsome man in the uniform of a lieutenant colonel, seeing him through uncovered eyes now.

'They said they'd phoned the apartment, and Sandy had said you were away.'

'I was. As luck would have it, I was on my way here. I couldn't believe it when Nellie told me at the station that you had come.'

'Oh, she's realised who that frightening fellow was, has she?'

'Was she frightened? Silly creature! They don't see much of the war down here. You'll have to make allowances for them.' He held out his hand. 'I can't put into words how marvellous it is to see you again.'

Slightly hesitantly, David offered his bent fingers for the warm clasp, then stood beside his father, looking at the azaleas. 'It's nice out here. I'd forgotten,' he murmured.

'Yes, it is. Shall we sit on the wall for a while and have a chat?'

They settled on the low wall that was warm from the sun, facing opposite ways so that it was easier to talk.

'How long have they given you before you return to duty?' his father asked quite naturally.

'Three months, initially. It depends on the medical people, really,' David told him, finding it a relief to talk about the problem. 'I want to get back as soon as possible.'

'Of course you do. They're pretty good with even the worst cases, you know.'

After a pause David asked, 'You can recommend them, can you?'

His father smiled. 'The only complaint I had was that they couldn't find a couple of spare fingers for my left hand.'

'The chap in Darwin said he thought they could do quite a lot with mine.'

'I'm sure they can. These days they seem able to put a chap back together from almost nothing. You've got a head start by still having everything intact, just a bit wonky.'

He fell silent, watching a woodlouse making its way along the path by his feet. It seemed so small. In the jungle it would be the size of a tortoise.

'Will you try for an operational posting?'

He looked up again. 'Oh, yes. They still want pilots, don't they? So long as a chap can fly a machine, they don't care what he looks like.'

His father nodded. 'That's true enough. One of the youngsters in the Mess here was burned quite badly about the face and chest last year, but he was back the moment they cleared him. You'll meet up, no doubt. He's a very nice chap. Splendid horseman. I gave him permission to use our stables any time he liked. It does us both a good turn.' He sighed. 'Longbarrow Hill is not what it used to be, you'll discover. They've made a track right across from the airfield. Bill says it grows more like a racetrack every day, the speed those trucks travel across it. One good thing is that they arrive at the Hall from the other side, through what used to be that patch of overgrown copse. They still make no end of a racket. You won't get much sleep, I'm afraid.'

'I don't get much sleep, anyway.'

'No, I imagine not. Pretty rough, was it?'

He considered that for a moment. 'No rougher than for hundreds of others – and they're still there, poor bastards.'

'We'll go back, David, there's no doubt of that.'

'We should never have lost it in the first place. It was ... It was unbelievable how fast it went under.' He remembered something then. 'I gave my personal effects to a New Zealander to send to Mother, but he was shot before he could climb into his machine. I went instead. My gold watch, Uncle Rex's cuff links, and Vesta's signet ring were in his bag. And my DFC.'

'Things go in time of war.'

'Oh, I don't grieve over it. I just thought Mother might.'

'Not when she has you.' His father stood up. 'I could do with a stiff drink. Care to join me?'

'All right.' He struggled to his feet, took another look at the woodlouse, then stepped on it hard.

They began walking slowly along the path toward the house, and his father said, 'It's proving more and more difficult to get hold of a decent bottle of wine, but I still know someone who keeps me supplied with vodka, fortunately. What's your drink, these days?'

'Water.'

They had reached the terrace near the open French window, through which he had made his stumbling escape a short while before. His father stopped and turned to him. 'Just before we go in, there's something I feel I should ask you. Have you managed to get any news of your wife? I've done all I could on your behalf, and made exhaustive enquiries in every direction I thought worth pursuing. Young Scott said you had put her on a ship, but none of the vessels that got away had any record of her.'

'She wasn't on a ship. I left her behind in Singapore. With any luck she's dead.'

'Thank God! *Oh, thank God,*' came an emotional voice from the open French window.

He turned to see his mother standing there watching them. 'There is no God ... Or, if there is, he's got a yellow face and bloody slits for eyes.'

During that summer of 1943 the tide of the war began to turn. The battle for North Africa had been won by the Anglo-

372

American troops, who then turned their attention to Sicily and Italy, with successful landings in both areas. Mussolini was captured, and the demoralised Italians signed an armistice agreement with the Allies, later declaring war against their former German allies, who then became an occupation force in Italy. In Russia, the siege of Leningrad, which had lasted sixteen months, ended with the withdrawal of German troops who finally surrendered at Stalingrad. The Red Army then began to push with renewed heart and effort, knowing that the British and Americans were gaining control of the Mediterranean areas. In the Far East, the Americans had landed on New Guinea, and the Japanese race through the islands was stopped. Australia breathed again. From Britain, massive air attacks on German industrial areas were being systematically carried out by the RAF and US air forces – including those on the Moehne and Eder dams, which were breached by the incredible 'bouncing bomb'. There were also raids on targets kept secret to all but a few top men, who had intelligence from agents concerning the development of a new deadly rocket in underground research bases.

In England there was a new feeling of hope. People began planning for the future with new confidence, anticipating the end. The flood of American troops with their drawling way of speech, their buoyant personalities, their luxury goods, their infuriating bragging, their sexual impact on lonely depressed women, and their sensational Glenn Miller – who, with his unique orchestra, had done more to keep up the spirits of war-weary people than the endless propaganda – all contributed to the general ability to sit it out just a little longer.

For David, that summer was a difficult time. He alternated between a restless drive to get back to killing people, and periods of black depression, when it would have been easy to kill himself. He was haunted by Sergeant Rod Kershaw, who had abandoned him to a relay of torturers, then gone through self-inflicted punishment in his determination to keep him alive until they could be rescued. He hated the man with raw depths of feeling, yet acknowledged a bond with the Australian that he felt would stay with him for the rest of his life, the severing of which had left him strangely bereft.

The RAF had sent him to a psychiatrist, so that he could talk the experience out of his system. But even if he had wanted to, he could not. Rod Kershaw's group had been part of a highly secret Australian unit, whose activities had to remain undercover. The fact that their initial withdrawal had been prevented by the Japanese destruction of the seaplane sent to collect them, had meant that the group itself had been forced to fall back on its own resources in order to stay alive. They had continued to operate as long as they possibly could, running from enemy patrols, hiding up in those villages that would give them shelter, and continuing with intelligence reports until the radio transceiver was damaged beyond repair. Two of the Australians had been lost – one killed by the Japanese, the other by some Javanese who had no love for white men of any kind. They might well all have been murdered by these local people whom they had initially trusted, had they not discovered their dead comrade and made a run for it. Rod Kershaw had risked his life by going back for David.

During the first few months, when the Australians' food and medical supplies had been available to nurse David back to reasonable physical strength, the memory of those three days in the hands of the Japanese had enabled him to fight for a return to a condition that would enable him to leave Kershaw and his men, and strike off on his own. But his legs had been so badly damaged he could scarcely stand, much less walk, so he had been carried around by the sergeant like a helpless child. Later, when they had all grown weak, David had only remained sane through his hatred of the man who controlled him, along with his determination to outlive Kershaw.

There had never been a farewell between them. On arrival in Darwin, David had been handed over to a major in British Intelligence; the Australians had been bundled off in a closed truck. Since then, there had hardly been a waking hour when David had not felt the abrupt severing of that bond. At night he dreamed of it, waking to the sound of his own sobs.

They worked on his hands, turning them into workable units that might allow him to fly an aircraft again. He endured the pain and rigours of the exercises in his determination that he would. The problem with his legs was more complex. They told him there would be a permanent weakness, prohibiting his taking part in the sports he loved, or any other demanding activity. Walking would become less awkward as time passed, and he was given exercises and massage to aid recovery. The marks covering his body would fade slightly, but remain as lifelong reminders of his ordeal, they stated, and he would be prone to recurring bouts of fever contracted in the jungle swamps.

In some ways he welcomed his spells at the hospital. The atmosphere was impersonal: he was just another patient. He also saw men in worse condition than himself due to crashes or burns. Yet he was the only one with snakes crawling through his mind, whose cries during the night hours were due more to nightmares than pain. The nurses offered the same dedicated compassion offered every patient. At home, his mother gave him no peace. Not only did she persist in treating him as a sick child, she silently and patiently awaited the return of the protective affection he had formerly displayed to her. Turning on her one day, he said she must have stood still while the world had gone on turning.

'Nothing will ever be the same again. Can't you see that, for Christ's sake?' he had demanded, before struggling from his chair to escape from her wounded expression.

He had taken up Van Reerdon's invitation to go across to the airfield at the end of Longbarrow Hill. It looked vastly different from the club airfield he had known so well, where he had landed with a few of his squadron as an emergency field way back in 1940. The aircraft there had interested him most. There had been innovations and developments in the Hurricanes, which were vastly more efficient machines than the ancient ones they had flown in Singapore, and he felt more at home with the Spitfires than he did at Tarrant Hall now.

'The rumour is that landings on the French coast are not far off. Then the squadron will be moving across the Channel,' Van Reerdon told him. 'The Americans will probably take over here then. How do you fancy having your ancestral home filled with Yanks chewing gum?'

'Doesn't worry me,' he had replied. 'But I'll kill any Jap who tries to go in there.'

The South African had given him an odd look. It was the same with most people. He had found the officers living in his house somewhat juvenile and artificial. The people of the village seemed like a race apart with their gossip about Anderson at the shop, their complaints about having prisoners-of-war from the camp over by Cringe forced on them to help with the farms, and their habit of sending their smaller children indoors whenever he passed. Robson seemed incredibly unreal in behaviour and attitude. David's own behaviour appeared to distress his mother constantly. She was forever giving him looks of sad concern because he swore so much, or because he was so truthful. He had upset both her and Robson by telling Mrs Robson she had been revelling in ill health for years, and that she should either get on her feet and make herself useful, or put herself out of her misery. He had caused his mother actual tears because he had thrown the stuffed white rabbit on the bonfire of garden rubbish, and because he had told the Rector he would be of far more use in a munitions factory, helping to make bombs than he was standing up each Sunday in a wooden hut, telling simple idiots someone up in the sky had their interests at heart.

When he had mentioned that the chicken leg on his dinner plate looked like monkey, but tasted sweeter, his mother had said reproachfully, 'Darling, you've been home over a month now. It's time you forgot all that.'

He had exploded into a violent attack on her. 'Forget it? I'll never forget it. For Christ's sake stop treating me like a child. You're as bad as the rest of these self-centred, complaining, fat country dwellers who think they're suffering in this war. You all make me want to throw up!'

Those scenes were always followed by periods of such blackness he either locked himself in his room, or went out on Longbarrow Hill, and stayed there until he felt he was no longer a danger to anyone. His periods at the hospital were a relief in that they got him away from home, and as his physical condition eased, he found himself able to control his intolerance and desire for violence against those around him. It did not go away; it still left him alienated from the life and people to which he had returned, but he grew strong enough to suppress it on most occasions.

There was one person, curiously enough, against whom he felt no violence, or the need to suppress anything. The man David had formerly regarded as lacking human understanding, and a dodger of responsibilities, was now the only person around him who had personal knowledge of the Far East, the Oriental races, the horror of battle, and personal physical suffering. With his father he could talk about all those things, he discovered. One evening when his father had arrived home without warning, they went for a walk together over Longbarrow Hill in the humid, stifling atmosphere before a storm. After discussing the present situation in the Far East, and the medical progress he was making, David said, 'This is the first time I've felt right since coming home.'

'Oh ... Why?' his father asked casually.

'I'm clammy and sweating.'

A faint smile lit the good-looking face. 'Funny how small things can bring a return of something completely alien in a flash. On the ship going to Gallipoli, there was a subaltern whose girlfriend had given him an entire jar of aniseed balls as a parting present. He doled them out to every man in sight. Even now, when I smell aniseed, I'm back on that ship.'

'Did you ever ... Did you ever feel that *that* was real, and this

376

here was something you couldn't accept any more?' he asked hesitantly.

His father stopped and faced him on the expanse of grass that had once been a makeshift runway for Rex Sheridan's old biplane.

'Of course I did. But I took the easy way out and conveniently forgot it all.' His brow furrowed slightly as he went on. 'I had two brothers instead of a father to confide in. You have me, and if you think I'll be of any help, go ahead.'

He looked away over the level hilltop, seeing the heavy build-up of cloud in the distance, and likening it to the violence inside his own mind. He was not sure of what to do about the offer.

'I cold-shouldered you in the past.'

'I did worse – completely disowned my own identity and that of my brothers. My mind turned them into untrustworthy strangers. When Roland was killed, I didn't grieve because I was not aware that I loved him. When I finally remembered, my tears for him seemed an almost worse betrayal of our relationship, coming as they did, several months too late. I thought you were lost, David, and believed my tears for you were also too late. Don't pass up a chance for mutual understanding now because of things in the past.'

Thrusting his misshapen hands into the pockets of his old flannels, David kept his gaze on the distant storm clouds to say, 'I understand now why you walked out on us, Mother and me.'

'Go on.'

'I married Su because she was the only beautiful sane thing in my life at the time. It was rushed because I was desperate for the release she would not give me without marriage; and because she was desperate to fulfil her obligations to her family. I got her body in return for security for her brothers and sisters.' He told his father the whole story, leaving nothing out, and finally admitting, 'I had never known the address of her family, but I made no effort to find her. When the chance to get away presented itself, I took it. Unlike you, I didn't forget her, but I feel nothing except a hope that she died quickly.'

After a moment or two, his father said, 'What if she survives?'

He turned swiftly. 'I couldn't touch her now.'

'No, I don't suppose you could.'

It seemed incredible that anyone could accept that statement so calmly, and he looked hard at the man he had once condemned. 'Are you saying you understand that?'

377

A faint smile touched that handsome face. 'I understand a lot more than you realise, David. But it's more a case of plain reasoning, surely. Although you can't bring yourself to speak of last year, I have a very good idea of what you might have experienced at the hands of Orientals. You'd not be human if it didn't give you an aversion to any Oriental person. I shouldn't worry about it. Nothing can develop until we go back to reclaim Singapore. By then, you'll have got your feelings and ideas sorted out.'

'I doubt it,' he replied bitterly.

A hand fell on his shoulder in companionship and affection, but he moved away from it. Confession was one thing; a close relationship with anyone other than Rod Kershaw was quite another.

'It'll come, David.'

'What'll come?' he challenged in harsh tones.

'Trust of others.' He turned back towards the Hall. 'Come on, we'd better make tracks before the storm breaks.' They walked slowly due to David's determination to refuse aid, and as they walked his father said conversationally, 'After Gallipoli I had severe mental problems, of course, but I was also suspicious of everyone save a little nurse I saw as a fellow victim of the sinister people surrounding me. I little knew the one soul I was reaching out to was the very one from whom I had run. Love for me as a person had died, so she was able to offer deep compassion for a disturbed invalid who did not know her.' He glanced across at David's limping figure. 'She has never stopped loving you, however, and is completely lost in this situation. You'll have to help her.'

'I've enough to do, trying to help myself.'

'I know that. I've been through it. Sometimes it's harder for those who stand and wait, David. They feel helpless and unwanted.'

'So do I, sometimes.'

'Turn to her, then.'

Finding walking an effort after a while, he gritted his teeth and pushed on. 'I think it would be better if I left home for a bit. I keep hurting her, and she seems incapable of accepting me as I am now.'

'Look for someone who will, then things will fall into place.'

He covertly watched the tall muscular figure in fawn trousers, white shirt with cravat loosely knotted at the throat, and heavy brogues, wondering whether that was an invitation rather than a piece of advice. But his father departed the following morning with no indication of when he might return, and the situation remained. With the long hot summer days stretching before him, his desire to escape the Hall led him to Tarrant Maundle and Wattle Farm. Owning to himself that Tessa Chandler's Australian accent rang more sweetly in his ears than his mother's gentle pleading tones, he was drawn more and more often to the modern well-run farm.

Aunt Tessa and Pat were too busy to fuss over him, as his mother did, and they accepted his frequent appearances at the farmhouse, riding an old gelding, or toiling up to the fields where they were working that day. Before long, he began joining in in his limited fashion, and not once did either of the two women warn him to take things easy for a while, or sit and rest. He discovered that physical work tired him enough to give him sleep with fewer dreams, and the sun-washed tranquility of that picturesque corner of Dorset gradually began to grow more real than tropical jungle. He grew used to talking to women again, words coming more naturally than they had for some time. When he felt angry or depressed and walked off to be alone, they continued with what they were doing, far too occupied to follow him or query his behaviour. It meant he came and went as the mood took him, feeling they welcomed him if he was there, but were undisturbed when he was not.

When harvest time drew near, they let him drive the tractor to free Pat for more strenuous work, and he derived enormous pleasure from being in control of a machine once more. During those hectic days, Pat and her mother ate lunch with the hands in the fields, and David sat with them on the aromatic hay, legs stretched out awkwardly, to eat lamb patties, pickled onions and fruit, feeling immensely contented.

One midday, when Aunt Tessa was spending the morning with paperwork back at the farmhouse, he sat alone with Pat in the high corner of a sloping field because the Land Army girls had gone off to collect their wages. It was wonderfully hot – the kind of heat that was dry, golden and slumberous – and he munched a hefty cheese sandwich as he looked away down the slope to the lower end where several pheasants were pecking. It was beautifully quiet without the sound of the tractor and the chatter of the girls as they worked. The sun felt pleasant on his dark brown skin; the gentle breeze ruffled his white hair and played around his throat and scarred upper chest, bared by the old shirt he wore. It had been like this before September 1939. Peace. Would he ever find it again anywhere but in this field, in this moment... With this girl?

He sat for a while with the sandwich half eaten, getting used to that last thought. Without turning to look, he could describe her. Whilst he had been away, she had become slim and immensely mature. There was no air of worldliness about her – she was dedicated to this life she led – but a strong strain of practical commonsense and honesty enabled her to comprehend things she had not personally experienced. Pat was loyal and uncomplicated. A person knew where he stood with her, even when he no longer thought of her as a sister. His father had told him to look for someone who would accept him as he was now, and that person was right here beside him.

'More tea, David?'

Angling his head toward her he nodded, holding out the thick china mug. 'It's nice here.'

'Mmm.' She poured from the large thermos. 'Vee might be having all manner of adventures in the Middle East, but I don't really envy her.'

He sipped the hot tea, leaning back contentedly against the stook. 'When you two were young, I'd have put my money on you as the one who would wander. Vee's changed a lot. We only met for a couple of hours at the airport as I passed through Cairo, and the poor girl was too upset for it to be an enjoyable meeting. But I found her surprisingly self-confident and determined. She's also grown very attractive in an elfin sort of way. I suppose some smart young staff officer will carry her off before long.'

'I'm not so sure,' came the surprising response. 'Vee hasn't much time for men. In her last letter she said she's growing bored with Cairo, and its empty life of fun and luxury. She's longing to do some more pictures. Have you seen her desert paintings?'

'Of course. I visited the gallery when I was last in London. Father said they have caused quite a stir. My favourite was the one set against a group of tanks, with the fat soldier having his hair cut by another, and the little dog with a cloth tied round his neck sitting on the box as if he was the next customer.'

Pat smiled. 'Oh yes, but I like the sunset one, with the table set in the Officers' Mess, and nothing in sight but sand and more sand. It really says something about the people who are fighting out there.' She drank some tea, then added, 'She's good. Even my layman's eye can see that. I think she'll make her name due to this war.'

He watched the pheasants in the distance, their coloured plumage bright against the pale field. 'Due to this war, you'll settle in South Africa, I take it.'

'Perhaps.'

Turning to her, he frowned slightly. 'I thought young Van Reerdon wanted to marry you.'

'I'm not sure I could leave all this,' she confessed wistfully, then gave a gentle smile. 'Don't speak as if you're an old man, David. Dirk's only four years younger than you.'

'He's a nice chap,' he pointed out.

'So are you.'

He resumed eating his sandwich, uncomfortable about that remark. 'I want to get back to flying soon. I'm tired of just hanging about like this.'

'How soon do you go before the medical board?'

'Not soon enough, I suspect. They'll let me know when.'

Pat began packing up the lunch basket. 'Ten minutes before my conscience will force me back to work. Until then I'm going to relax completely.'

With that she swung round and lay at right angles to him with her head in his lap, fidgeting about until she got comfortable. Smiling up into his face, she asked, 'You don't mind being used as a pillow, do you?'

In fact, her weight on his thighs was slightly painful, but he liked the sensation of physical contact with her too much to protest. Instead, he shook his head and said, 'Bet you've never had a pillow like me before.' She had always had very attractive eyes, and he was struck anew by the silver-green beauty of them as they gazed up at him now. It reminded him of something. 'Ian Freemantle once asked me what you looked like, and I told him you were plump, fairly pretty, but with wonderful big eyes.'

To his surprise, she turned pink in the face. 'That was very generous coming from you,' she said. 'He seemed a nice person in his letters, and so homesick for his farm in New Zealand. I received the impression that he was too gentle a person to do what he was doing. What did he look like, David?'

He thought for a few minutes, his gaze on the pheasants, then said, 'His legs were ripped to pieces and he was coughing up blood from the hole in his chest. I'm sure he died before I had even left the ground. All the same, he killed more Japs than anyone in the squadron. I wish it had been me.'

After some moments, her voice broke into his mind-pictures. 'What are you going to do after the war, David?'

'Stop here,' he found himself saying. 'I'm going to drive a tractor and watch pheasants... and eat cheese sandwiches.'

'All alone?'

He tilted his scarred face down to where she lay against his

381

legs that were no longer strong and muscular, remembering what they had done to him that had made him that way.

'Yes, all alone,' he said heavily.

The medical board declared him fit for limited duty, which did not include full operational flying. He was staying at the London apartment, and he returned to it afterwards in a black mood, staying there all the next day and night, even though his father was away, because he felt he could not face his mother's platitudes. It was there, on the second day, that he received a call from Air Vice Marshal Cranshaw's aide, asking him to go to the Ministry at noon.

'Please be prompt,' instructed the man. 'The air vice marshal has an extremely heavy programme, and time is of the essence.'

'Time is nothing when you have lived without it for nine months,' David replied.

He went at noon, however, because he liked old Cranshaw, not because his aide had insisted. September had come in gently, but David felt the chill creeping into the air. September once more. Four years ago an announcement by Chamberlain had let loose a million demons. Three years ago David had been battling in the skies above Britain to save his country and kill a man called Enright.

Who was Enright? If he had caused him to suffer hideous agony instead for three days, would he then have carried him around for months to scourge himself of guilt?

Two years ago he had been Rita Winterbottom's latest stud. One year ago... One year ago... Oh, God!

'The air vice marshal will see you now,' said a voice very loudly beside him, and David returned from thoughts of decapitated children in a jungle clearing to his present situation in a corridor of a hushed building, with a man in uniform giving him the usual odd look.

Standing up as quickly as he could manage, he walked in through the door being held open for him, and saluted the elderly officer inside. Then he shook the hand offered to him by this old friend of his father, who had flown in 'Sherry' Sheridan's famous Arrow Squadron.

'Hallo, David, take a seat. Can I offer you a drink?' he asked, going to the table where a whisky decanter stood, with a carafe.

'Thank you.'

'How do you like it? Half and half, or neat?'

'Neat water, thanks.'

There was that odd look again, but this man was older and more experienced, so he covered it quickly. Handing David a full glass of water, he sipped his own whisky as he settled behind his desk to shuffle through papers in a file. Then he glanced up with a smile,

'I understand from Wing Commander Sherwood that you were not too happy about the medical board's decision yesterday.'

'I told him I didn't want to sit at a desk, I wanted to kill the enemy as fast and comprehensively as possible. He rattled on about the mental problem.' Shifting in his chair, David added forcibly, 'I put an end to that by flying a Hurricane from Singapore, and making two sorties in it before ditching.'

'That wasn't the mental problem to which he referred, I fear. A fighter pilot has to have more than an obsession to kill, or he's a danger to himself and the rest of his squadron.'

'But the only way I can hit back is to get up there and shoot the bastards down,' he cried in protest. 'Can't he see that?'

The spare, wiry man smiled sympathetically. 'I've had my moments of wanting bloody revenge, my boy, but medical boards are there to be heeded. Their decisions can never be overturned, but . . .' his smile broadened, '. . . as I have personal acquaintance with Wing Commander Sherwood, I have persuaded him his term "limited duty" covers the flying of certain types of aircraft engaged in special duties.'

'Oh, no! Not a bloody taxi driver for VIPs!'

'In a way, yes,' came the response. 'There are other ways of hitting back at the enemy, David, apart from coming face to face with a gun. We have a squadron engaged in work for intelligence organisations. It's members must be men with extensive aerial experience and possessing outstanding cool-ness and courage in the face of danger. The work is vital and highly hazardous, and I consider you have the qualities necessary for such work. I brought you here today to offer you promotion and a place in this unique squadron. I must warn you first that, if you accept, you may tell no one the nature of the work you will be doing – not even members of your family.'

The news that he was returning to flying duty was an unwelcome shock to his mother, who protested that he should not be asked to do further service with the RAF.

'I imagined the board would proclaim you unfit and grant you a medical discharge,' she declared in great distress. 'Haven't they had their pound of flesh? Haven't they taken the

383

youth and strength from you? What more do they expect of a young man? How can you possibly fly, handicapped as you are?'

The prospect of what they had offered him was so exciting he failed to lose his temper, actually finding it possible to take her by the upper arms to say quietly, 'If Douglas Bader can fly with two tin legs, I can do it with a couple of real ones, and hams for hands.'

She drew away and stood trembling as she gazed at him. 'I can't go through it all again. All the time you were flying Spitfires I used to stand here watching the fights over by the coast, and wonder if the dots burning as they fell contained you. I was glad when you couldn't take off. *Glad,* David. When I thought you were dead, *I* wanted to die. Now I have you back, it's asking too much to put me through that agony again.' She pleaded with him. 'Haven't you had enough of suffering? Don't you feel you have sacrificed enough for your country? Don't go, David. Ask your father to get you out of it. He can't refuse to help you this time. Darling, stay here with me and get strong again. I promise not to worry and upset you if you do. *Please,* David. You are all I have.'

He walked away from her to the French window, where he stood staring out at the garden that was a blaze of shaggy chrysanthemums. 'I'm not all you have, Mother. There's Vee in Cairo, and Father. This family always seemed to split into two pairs, which worked all right before the war.' He turned carefully on his fragile legs. 'Things have happened to change that now. I blamed Father for walking out on us, and tried to compensate for what I saw as his neglect of you. Now I can understand why he went. Now I understand the hell his own actions put him through. Do you, Mother? Have you ever given a thought to his side of it? Have you really ever made an effort to be Lady Sheridan as opposed to the mother of his son, living quietly in the country instead of at his side?'

She was gazing at him in great sadness. 'Darling, if it helps to hit out at me, then do so. But when you have said all you need to say, remember that I'm the one who has always loved you.'

'If you were glad when I was unable to take off, that wasn't love,' he told her quietly. 'If you want me to sit out the rest of the war here beside you, that isn't love, either. And if you believe my life is over, apart from a stifling existence as a permanent invalid for you to cling to, then you have never loved me. I have finally come of age, Mother, and see the truth. All these years you have merely doted on the replica of a schoolboy, who turned out to be human, rather than the handsome gilded hero you had imagined. You have been turning me into *him* all these years,' he accused. 'You have been trying to fashion an image to your own design.'

Taking a deep breath, she said, 'If it is your intention to hurt me deeply, you are succeeding. Well, he has done what he set out to do. By letting that letter go through, your father has won you from me.'

Bewildered by references to a letter he did not understand, he said wearily, 'No one has won me from you. I'll be your son until the day I die. Your *son*, Mother – not a handsome, youthful copy of what you thought he was when you were a girl.'

'But you're not,' she cried in protest. 'You're not any longer.'

'No, I'm an ugly shuffling creature with broken hands. I'm also a person trying to break free. If you want to recapture that lost girlish dream, you'll have to turn back to him. If it's not already too late.'

Chapter Nineteen

DAVID WAS quickly introduced to the reasons for the particular qualities Air Vice Marshal Cranshaw had stated were necessary for the job. The squadron he had joined was engaged in ferrying agents back and forth between England and occupied Europe. To do this, he had to learn to fly an unfamiliar aircraft by night, do his own navigation with only the light from the moon to help him, and be able to land in any designated field with the guidance of nothing more than three pocket torches from the ground. He also had to be able to take off very quickly at the first sign of danger, remain level-headed if that proved impossible, make instant decisions when faced with the unexpected, destroy his aircraft and attempt to escape overland if unable to fly back, and preserve the secrecy of the identities of those men and women he carried as passengers. He was given a month in which to learn to fly a Lysander with enough skill to do the first three. The rest he had already been judged capable of, and he possessed one more skill not all the men in his new squadron had. Through schoolboy holidays abroad with his father, he spoke very good French and German.

The relief of getting back to work was so great he worked like a slave at all he had to learn. Sitting in the cockpit with the instruction manual on his lap for several hours, he studied the instruments and levers and switches until he knew where each was situated, to within inches. Then he closed his eyes and tested himself until he could put his hand on any named control with one hundred per cent accuracy. However, the actual flying of the machine caused him initial dismay, because the limitations of his hands were fully brought home to him. In the past manual control had been instinctive and effortless; now he found himself sweating when his grip seemed inadequate for a manoeuvre, then overdoing the movement of the control column to the extent of raising more sweat on his brow. After his first flight, he went for a long walk alone around the perimeter of the airfield, tense and depressed, telling himself he would never be able to fly the thing at night over enemy territory to land in a small field, without killing himself and his vital passengers. He must have been mad to think he could. His mother had more than likely been right. He was useless to the war effort now.

By the end of the first week, however, he felt as confident in the Lysander as he had been in a Spitfire. But he had not yet flown it by night, when heights were deceptive, landmarks barely visible, and landings had to be made blind. During the day prior to his first night flight he became very worked up, telling himself he would be hopeless in an emergency on enemy soil if he could get in such a state over a practice flight on home ground. Old Cranshaw had made a mistake in offering him the job. After he had completed six night flights successfully, he decided old Cranshaw had not made a mistake after all.

It was then that David discovered he had only completed the easy part of the training: he now had to do it all again simulating the real thing by landing on an unfamiliar field he had to find through his own navigation. He did it by daylight first, because the landing had to be extremely short and on the exact spot marked out by flags for him. He muffed it completely, and nearly came to grief with his wheels in a hedge on the far side of the pocket-handkerchief field. However, he managed to pull up just above the hedge, but was so badly shaken he circled for fifteen minutes before making another attempt. This time he pulled out of the descent at the last minute, realising he had gone in too high. The third time his approach was too low, and he hedge-hopped for some distance, clinging to the control column, bathed in sweat and shaking with fright. He flew back to the squadron in such a black mood, he shut himself in his room until next morning, and told the orderly he would eat his dinner up there.

The other men in the squadron were vastly different from those with whom he had served before. Strongly individual with decided views, they were all temperamentally suited to working as loners, and respected a man's solitude if he felt he needed it. David found what he wanted there: the chance to fly, to release his violence in action; and the company of others who accepted him without questions. No one tried to jolly him out of his bouts of depression; if he declined an invitation to join an outing for a binge they took 'no' for an answer and left it at that. Not once had any of them pried into his past, although he supposed they had all been acquainted with the general details of his service, and they never gave him odd looks. That no one had commented on the fact of his being 'Sherry' Sheridan's nephew, he put down to the circumstances of them all being so used to ferrying people of great note, they were unimpressed by the nephew of *anyone*. He was heartily thankful for that.

It took him almost a week before he could land successfully in the short distance demanded. On one occasion he had made an error in adjusting his tail-plane on landing which resulted in damage to the aircraft that made it necessary for a rigger to be flown in to put it right before David could fly the Lysander back.

That incident heralded another solitary night in his room. Nevertheless, when he was ready for his first attempt to land by night in a strange field, with only the guidance of three torches in the shape of an L, he did it perfectly first time. He went on to repeat the feat six times more. At the end of the month he was declared ready to go operational, after he had made two flights by night over France to find a fictional pick-up field which was merely a map-reference. He did not have to land, but he found the right place without difficulty both times. The good it did his self-confidence was enormous, and he ate with the rest of the squadron, quietly delighted with himself.

The squadron was unique in several ways, not the least being that it was only operational for the week leading up to the full moon, and the week after it. During that vital fortnight there could be as many as eight sorties, or none at all, depending on the weather. Apart from training courses with prospective agents, teaching them how to select suitable fields, and how to climb in and out of the Lysander with the greatest speed, it was possible to have a fair amount of time off during the 'dark' fortnight. That routine was perfectly suited to a man like David, and he was forced to see the wisdom of the medical board's decision.

One of the special aspects of the squadron was that its members were necessarily let into a number of secrets, including knowledge of the agents who despatched those going to Europe for specific purposes, and those men already running 'cells' in occupied areas who despatched those returning to England. These latter could be highly trained permanent agents coming back with vital intelligence, or having completed a specific mission; foreign VIPs with their families; Resistance workers endangered by pro-German informers; servicemen who had escaped from prisoner-of-war camps; or airmen who had been shot down and hidden by local people, before being passed along by one of the organisations formed to help evaders return to fight on in England. The secret information that surprised David the most was that many of the people brought back from occupied territory were taken to a reception centre at Brigadier Tarlestock's Rhineland castle on Wey Hill. Right under his nose, yet he had never suspected anything of that nature taking place in the likeable old eccentric's home. It probably took an eccentric to carry it off successfully. He would view the old boy in a different light from now on.

When at last David's CO allocated him his first operation, he experienced a return of the tension he had felt on waiting for the call to 'scramble' back in 1940. This time, he knew the time of takeoff, the destination, the code word for the operation, the pre-arranged morse signal the agent would make from the field, signifying clearance to land, and even the identities of those he must take out and collect. The tension this time was caused by the weather. Earlier in the day a car had arrived bringing two men – one English, one French – who were to be his passengers, and David was introduced to them by other members of the squadron who had taken them back and forth frequently. They were both quiet, unassuming characters whom David found difficult to associate with the dangerous work in which they were engaged. That was probably the key to their success. The key to his was going to be diligence, he decided, and he worked out his map course twice to make sure he had made no mistake. Then he spent the rest of the time leading up to takeoff worrying about Met. reports.

They were good, however, and all the other pilots told him he was a lucky dog to get away all right on his very first pick-up. All the same, he felt nervous beneath the calm veneer he displayed to his passengers as they all walked out in brilliant moonlight to the waiting Lysander. It was a very cold early November night, so he was wearing a heavy cable-patterned navy sweater, together with the prescribed mixture of service and civilian clothes necessary in case an accident trapped him in France. The RAF items would then be burnt with the Lysander; the other garments would enable him to move around as a French civilian until picked up by one of his colleagues.

Having seen his passengers safely installed in the rear cockpit, he climbed into the front one and went through the preparations for takeoff. It seemed incredible that he had once been unable to do it. There was certainly no problem now, and he made as smooth a departure as any man could wish.

Climbing into a sky moonlit so brilliantly it was almost like day, David circled once, then set course over the coast on the first leg of his flight. Once that had been done, he sat back to look at the beauty around him: a huge moon in a cold silver-blue sky, even colder silver-bright stars, great expanses of open freedom, and below him the silver-dark sea. No tangle of vine-covered trees, no sinister filthy swamps; no bloated, outsize venomous creatures; no heat, thirst and sickness; no bewildered, suspicious, terrified brown people in huts on stilts; no men in cotton uniforms and floppy caps, gouging into his flesh and hammering his fingers one by one. No Rod Kershaw controlling him, filling him with hatred, yet binding him closer and closer in a relationship no one else would understand.

The engine droned on, and David sat in his tiny world of levers and dials feeling like the only person in that night world. Then he became aware of that old feeling that the spirit of his uncle was there in the cockpit with him. This time, however, he had come along not as a mentor, but as a companion on equal terms. It was then that he realised the burden of living up to a legend had left him somewhere along the way. Was that why no one in the squadron had mentioned the link with 'Sherry' Sheridan? Did they now consider he was an aviator in his own right, dependent on no one because he had proved his worth beyond any doubt? The sensation of having a spiritual companion grew, and he felt a new bond with the hero who had seemed so far out of reach. This bond was not a dependent one; it was that of two men of the sky who understood each other exactly. He caught himself talking to the presence, welcoming him aboard and explaining the controls of an aircraft far more sophisticated than the wonderful old Nieuports and Camels his uncle had flown.

'All the same, I'll be glad of your advice when we get there,' he added. 'You've had far more experience in landing on tiny fields than I've had.'

'Can't quite understand you, skipper,' said a loud voice in his ears, making him jump.

It was the English agent in the rear, speaking through the intercom fitted so that the pilot could keep his passengers informed on what he was doing – very necessary if problems arose. Feeling rather sheepish, David replied that he had been thinking aloud.

'Are you comfortable back there?' he enquired.

'It's so bright we're playing cards,' came the reply. 'If we haven't finished when you rendezvous, circle a couple of times until we do, old chap. I've a hundred francs on it.'

The French coast arrived very quickly below, and radio communication with England ceased. They were obliged to go in low to avoid radar, and through a prescribed corridor which avoided the anti-aircraft gun emplacements, before turning onto their required course. David concentrated on the map on his knee now, glancing downward to pick up the shining ribbon that was a river, the dark area indicating woodland, pale flat stretches of heathland, the straight double lines of a railway. He had estimated that it would be two hours flying time to reach the field often used by the squadron, and claimed by them to be one of the best, chosen by a most reliable agent. The only possible hazard tonight threatened to be German night fighters. Flying without lights and camouflaged for moonlight, his only hope would be to evade them.

The engine throbbed on, taking them well over enemy territory, and David was wondering if his spiritual companion was remembering the times he had flown over the area all those years ago. This kind of thing would have been frowned on by him and his fellow cavaliers of the air. It had been a battle then between men who respected each other. Today's enemies had perpetrated such atrocities all respect had gone. David tried to explain to that presence in the cockpit with him, but it appeared he understood that things had changed and accorded no blame for what they were going out to do. He was just along for the ride.

All went well. David found his landmarks easily in the clear moonlight, and arrived over the designated field within minutes of the time given by special coded message by the BBC which would have told the agent the operation was on for that night. His heartbeat began to accelerate as he circled a short way off waiting for the exact time of rendezvous. This was the tricky point; the moment when anything could happen.

'We're over the target now,' he informed his passengers. 'As soon as I spot the correct signal, I'll be going in. Stand by to disembark.'

He was circling at around two hundred feet and could clearly see the shape of fields, the rise and fall of a small hill, a distant river, and a narrow winding lane in the vivid moonlight. Yet the area seemed totally deserted. He began to worry. Having meticulously worked out his route, checking it twice, he had followed his maps closely, finding the landmarks where he had expected them. Could he have made a mistake? No, he knew he had reached the correct rendezvous. Could the receiving agent have missed the BBC message? Most worrying of all, had the Germans discovered the waiting group? Immense disappointment flooded through him. To have got here with all the conditions so perfect, then be forced to return unsuccessful on his first operation was a failure he did not welcome. Five minutes later, he had to accept that there was no choice.

'I'm sorry, gentlemen, something appears to have gone wrong,' he told the two men in the rear. 'There's no reception committee for you. I'm turning back.'

Banking to starboard, his attention was caught by a continual flashing light about half a mile away. Turning his manoeuvre into a full circle, he took another look to make sure he was not mistaking the undulating light from distant headlamps for a torch signal. No, it was definitely morse code, signalling the correct letter for the night. Uncertain, he took a wide detour in order to get a closer look. Could he possibly have mistaken the field? Surely not. This one was very near what looked to be a small copse, and agents were instructed most emphatically not to select fields with trees at the ends from which approaches or takeoffs would be made. Despite that, the letter was being flashed again, and David had to make a swift decision. Should he attempt to go in despite the difficulties, or was the risk that the group on the ground had been taken by the Germans and forced to give the signal too great?

It was now or never, so David asked his unseen companion of the cockpit for his opinion. The answer was that risks should be taken if there was a chance of success, and that seemed to be the case now. On the instant, David reached out to flash the answering letter on his downward facing navigation light, and the L-shaped landing guide was lit immediately.

'I'm going in,' he told his passengers. 'There is a problem of some kind, so have your revolvers ready – just in case it's that kind of problem.'

Lower and lower. There were figures clearly outlined by the light from the torches now, and to his dismay he saw the surface of the field was crossed by some fairly deep ruts. However, it was too late to pull up again, so he touched down on a surface that set the aircraft bouncing and shuddering as he fought to slow and stop before he reached the torch marking the limit of the short landing area. His hands were not as good as they used to be, and he passed the light by some metres. Then he had trouble turning the Lysander round into the wind ready for takeoff, all the time expecting to hear the rattle of machine guns from hidden Germans. It remained peaceful, however, and he was aware of his passengers scrambling down the ladder from the rear cockpit as several other people stood ready to climb in. David hardly had time to think before someone jumped on the wing to shout at him over the sound of the running engine.

He could not hear the man well but, having established that he was the despatching agent well known to other members of the squadron, he demanded angrily in French what game he thought he was playing. The man, glad to hear his native tongue, apologised profusely and explained that they had been delayed by a German convoy from reaching the correct field at the specified time, and had hurriedly entered this one when they heard him circling, hoping he would see the lights from where he was.

'Our heartfelt thanks for your courage, Monsieur. One of your returning passengers had no time left. She was betrayed, and had to leave tonight, or perhaps never,' he concluded, handing David a small package as he jumped to the ground. 'Au revoir,' he shouted, giving the signal that all were aboard.

The takeoff must have ranked as his very worst. The bad surface slowed him to such an extent his wheels caught the tops of the trees at the edge of the copse as he hauled the machine off the ground, and he worried about possible damage for the next few minutes. Because of concentration on that, he momentarily forgot he was half a mile out from his carefully prepared return route, and had a bad few minutes when none of the expected landmarks appeared. By the time he had recollected and found what he was looking for, the three passengers he had picked up were chatting happily about what they planned to do when they reached the safety of England.

'Well, we made it,' he said to his uncle. 'But next time you want to take risks, bear in mind those bloody trees, will you?'

'Pardon, Monsieur?' came the voice through the intercom.

'N'important,' he returned. But it was. He had done his first lone moonlit run. He was back in business as a pilot. It would take more than a few bestial Japs to finish him! He flew on checking the ground for landmarks, and was soon over the English coast where he sensed the spiritual presence beside him departing. Thanks a lot, he said silently, assured that there was no need to say goodbye. His uncle would be back on the next trip.

David landed bang on schedule, and two cars were waiting for his passengers. As he climbed somewhat wearily from the cockpit, the woman who had been on the run from the Gestapo came to him, thanked him in quiet sincere tones for his decision to land in the unspecified field, then was whisked off in a car driven by someone from a Free French organisation for whom she worked. The two men, agents of SOE, took a little longer with their thanks, one of them saying something he did not quite take in, due to elation and the sudden onset of tiredness.

'Good Lord, is the entire Sheridan family in the espionage business?'

The man turned away to speak to one of the other pilots, who had apparently taken him over several weeks before, and David forgot the comment as he handed in his report to his CO, then accepted a mug of cocoa from the orderly, intending to take it up to bed. But the others were anxious to hear the details of his trip, so he perched on the arm of a chair while he described his sense of uncertainty when the signal came from the wrong place.

'Good thing I decided to go down,' he told them. 'The woman was on the run and desperate to get away tonight.'

'That's "Mirjana",' one of them told him. 'I took her over about three weeks ago. We all know her well. I understand she's one of the top agents for a special splinter group of the Free French which is especially secret. Don't ask me what she gets up to over there, but she's a brave woman, like all the rest. We only take 'em over, then come back. They have to stay there and take all the bloody risks. I take my hat off to each and every one of them.'

'Hear, hear!' came the chorus.

David then remembered the package given him by the agent as he had stood on the wing. Fishing it from his pocket, he held it out to his CO. 'I was given this, by the way.'

The man laughed. 'That's for you – the usual token of thanks for the pilot on these jaunts. It's a bottle of French perfume for your wife or girlfriend.'

Getting to his feet, David finished off his cocoa and put down the mug. 'I think I'll get to bed. Whoever wants the perfume can have it,' he added, putting the package on the table.

Chris read out the final sentences, then slowly closed the book and looked up. Sonja was gazing into the fire, so far away in her thoughts she was not even aware that he was now silent. Intense disappointment filled him. He had produced the official translation some years ago of this work she had stated was a favourite of hers, and he had been anxious for her opinion. It seemed her attention had not even been held by it.

Making no attempt to speak, he studied her profile gilded by the flamelight. It was one of those rare and precious occasions when he had been able to get away and she had answered his telephone call. Sonja had been working on a glass panel at the country home of a French diplomat for some weeks, and Chris had been on a brief vital trip to Washington with Frank Moore in the midst of his other work. It meant that he valued more than ever this chance to relax and refresh his brain and his body in the intellectual and sexual pursuits which so fulfilled and delighted them both. Without these meetings to re-charge him, he did not know how he would have avoided John Frith's fervent hope that he would 'go off his nut' once more. Sonja was not only the great love of his life, she was his salvation. He desperately wanted to be hers.

Leaning forward, he put the leather-bound volume on the table, then said quietly near her ear, 'Where are you?'

She twisted quickly, sadness clear in her expression. He leant back in his chair thoughtfully. She had been unusually tense during their recent lovemaking, he now realised, and her mood during the meal had been subdued. Had he failed to satisfy her for some reason? Had his energy flagged at the vital time? Was he losing her?

'Where do you go, Sonja Koltay?' he asked her uneasily. 'Who or what is it that takes you from me when I'm least prepared for it?'

A small frown creased her brow as she met his scrutiny with an honest gaze. 'I heard today that Françoise Markosa is dead. She was a dear friend from my past.' Françoise Markosa, known first to Chris as the wife of a diplomat, then as the agent 'Gladiator', had been shot along with some American airmen whilst attempting to reach Switzerland two days ago. The news had only been relayed to his office in the early hours of this morning.

'Who told you?' he asked.

'Colonel du Toit. I lunched with him today. He assured me it was true. Had you not heard?'

'No,' he lied. 'I haven't the same number of friends amongst the Free French. My acquaintance with her was only slight – I dealt mostly with her husband at the embassy – but her fame on international tennis courts had not escaped even my abysmal lack of knowledge on sporting activities. I'm sorry, so sorry. You should have told me sooner,' he chided, taking her cold hands in his.

'Will you tell me something if I ask for the truth?' she challenged, plainly not content simply to accept his comfort.

'If I am able to,' he hedged. 'But if du Toit didn't know, I doubt if I shall.'

'Will there be a landing in France soon?'

'Of course.'

'When?'

'When all the conditions are right.'

'Which conditions?'

'You must ask Churchill and Roosevelt that.'

'I have no acquaintance with them, only with Sir Christopher Sheridan, who appears to know little for all his hours at his desk.'

Disturbed by her strange mood, he retaliated. 'I know as much as anyone else that it will have to be early next year. Even the most optimistic of us accepts that it will not be a case of running up the beaches and not stopping until we reach Berlin. Our troops will have to fight every inch of the way, and progress will also depend on developments on other fronts. Things are going reasonably well for us, at present, but that situation can be reversed without warning. Look at the stalemate in Italy. The same thing could happen in France – initial surprise landings, then deadlock. The war won't end the minute we set foot in Europe.' Seeing that her eyes were surprisingly misty, he asked in quieter vein, 'Darling, what is all this about?'

Visibly fighting for control, she cried, 'When will all the killing end? For God's sake, when will it end?'

'I don't know,' he admitted, taking her in a close embrace and stroking her hair tenderly, much shaken by this evidence of a weakness she had never before betrayed. 'I have stopped asking that question and begun concentrating on making the most of those who are alive. David's return from the jungle is little short of a miracle, and although I would have willingly borne his condemnation for ever in order to spare him what he has suffered, the ordeal has brought us close again. This adult affection from him is astonishingly delightful after knowing only his childish love. He is an extremely intelligent and courageous young man. It comes through in a way that almost overwhelms me after years of animosity. Then there is my gentle daughter, who has suddenly emerged from the chrysalis to reveal that same intelligence and courage in the way she is determinedly shaping her life, in addition to claiming attention for her very individual talent as an artist. You have seen her paintings and praised them, so you must understand my pride in her.'

She nodded against his chest. 'Of course you have pride in her. She was your child of love, was she not?'

'Only in that she resulted from a night of tenderness, not, as David, from five minutes of adolescent lust. Even the twins were conceived, I see now, through no more than recognition of mutual desire. I have never had a child of love, because I have never shared it with anyone until now.'

'Nor I,' came the quiet avowal.

'But only for "now" and not "forever"?'

'You still say that, even now?' she challenged. 'Do you know Françoise Markosa was younger by three years than I? She will have no "forever".'

He put her away from him to look at her with great seriousness. 'My brothers were much younger than that when they were robbed of a future. Because of that I *had* to believe in mine and try to make it worthy of them. Darling, if we all gave up hope of life the world would come to an end. I dare to dream of some time ahead of us when we can all compensate for what is happening now.'

Her head shook in a soft negative. 'Dreams are only what they are, my dear. Regrettably, we all awake and see reality.'

It was always difficult to settle back to work after a night with Sonja, and it was even worse this time. There was an upsurge of activity concerning the German rocket stations, which were engaged in testing a new deadly pilotless bomb. With landings in Europe essential by the coming spring, production of a weapon which could devastate Britain without risking German airmen's lives, and freeing them to defend France, would be fatal. To enable British and American bombers to attack the factories making these bombs, it was essential to gain as much information as possible about the sites, rates of progress, and properties of the weapon. If it proved impossible to stop production altogether, it was vital to know how best to counter the missiles, once launched.

It was all very highly secret, with top priority for hundreds of agents operating all over the Continent. Anyone having information on 'Crossbow', as the operation was named, was picked up before any others needing to return to England. Some of the most experienced men and women, who had been operating beneath the noses of the enemy since the start of the war, were landed during moonlit periods in the hope of infiltrating these flying-bomb bases. Some had scientific training which would allow them to understand any details they might manage to see; others were explosives experts, who would seek to discover the destructive potential of the missiles.

These experienced agents, and others who were new to espionage, did not always have the degree of knowledge of the German language essential for the effectiveness of their imposture as members of the staff, or for the translation of technical documents written in German. Chris therefore found himself teaching that language to an extremely high standard to a succession of Frenchmen, Poles, Norwegians, English-men, and even one South African who planned to pose as a Dutch scientist. As November slid into December, a whole string of agents were sent out with the RAF special squadron, which picked up those returning with varying degrees of success.

It had been a surprise to Chris when David had mentioned the number of his new squadron, because he had known very well the secret nature of the work he would be doing, despite his son's description of joining a transport group. Although there was every possibility that David would discover his own involvement in the espionage network before too long, Chris had been reticent about it, feeling it was better not to rush the new relationship into the depths of a shared secret. David might take the revelation better if he heard it from other lips, particularly as he would then be aware that Chris knew more about what really happened in the Far East than he suspected.

Although it was almost a year since he had safely reached Australia, David would not speak about those long months in the jungle, even though they plainly still haunted him. Chris knew he had been captured and badly tortured before the Australians had picked him up, but had no details other than those. David allowed everyone to think his injuries had been caused by the Hurricane crash, and Chris had gone along with the pretence. Whatever had been done to David by his captors had been terrible enough to affect his attitude towards Oriental races for some time to come, if not for ever. If his Chinese wife survived the war, there would have to be a divorce for both their sakes.

A quiet word to Bill Chandler had done no good. David had avoided all Bill's skilful attempts to draw him out on the subject. All Chris could hope for now was that his son would conquer the blackness inside him with his own strength of character, which would no longer be inhibited by extreme good looks and the reputation of Rex Sheridan. If he succeeded, it would be through personality not appearances, and although he preferred to hide it, David must himself have realised he no longer needed reflected glory.

David must be playing quite a large part, in the present hectic activity between England and many small fields in France, Chris knew, and on bright moonlit nights his thoughts were with his white-haired scarred son, as much as with those he was ferrying to and from the greatest danger. Remembering the time he had gone himself to bring back Raoul du Vivier, he could imagine the dark secret flight, the skilled landing by the light of torches, the rapid unloading and re-loading, the swift takeoff with eyes peeled for signs of German vehicles racing to the spot, and the long hour or so over enemy territory before one could breathe a sigh of relief at the sight of the English coast. Most of all he recalled the calm assured manner of the youngster they had lifted from the cockpit, and his courage when wounded.

Praying nightly for David's safety, he was only thankful Vesta was back again in Cairo. A colleague had shown him a newspaper item that told of her prompt action in an emergency by taking over a wireless-receiver, and that had been the first he had known of her foray into the desert. He had felt enormously proud, but had written to her suggesting that she should not put her life at risk in order to paint the real war, since it did not discriminate between armed soldiers and very pretty talented artists. He had the two pictures declined by the people in London framed and hung on the walls of his apartment. At the time he had received them, David had been missing presumed killed, and Chris had felt that Marion would not value them in her low condition. Now he was considering taking them down to Tarrant Hall at Christmas. More than anything, he would have liked to spend the time with Sonja, but felt his first duty lay with his wife, at present. Time enough to abandon her to her beloved children and cosy village life when the war ended, and he followed his true and only love to France.

He had hoped for a meeting with Sonja before Christmas, despite the even greater pressure of work, both at the secret establishment, and with Frank Moore at 'Guidons' and the office. But, in the middle of December, there was a disaster which put a stop to all thought of time off. One of the larger cells, which had been in existence for several years with some excellent results, suddenly collapsed right at this most vital of times. An agent of charm and intellect whom everyone had trusted implicitly had been turned around by the Germans some time before, and the entire network, save two young daughters of a farmer, were captured and executed. The girls managed to arrange a moonlit pick-up by a Lysander, then were tragically killed along with the pilot when fog obliterated the south coast on their return, causing the aircraft to crash on the marshes. The entire episode was a terrible blow, and Chris had had an anxious half hour trying to trace the identity of the pilot.

It was essential to establish another network with utmost speed, due to the Allies' forthcoming plans to land in France.

When this took place, a full-scale back-up presence of agents and saboteurs was necessary. They would aid success by giving military intelligence, and by causing chaos on roads and railways to hamper the movement of German troops. Thus the gap left by the collapsed network became top priority for those attempting to fill it. By this time, the Free French, the Free Poles, and all other minority groups which had been running their own espionage activities, had decided combined efforts were more advantageous, and all suitable people were selected for a rushed programme that would get them into France two days before Christmas. If the weather prohibited actual landings, they would be dropped by parachute, if that was at all feasible.

The various units of the training establishment went into top gear for the operation. Men and women of all manner of organisations were brought together for a week of intensive instruction. They had to learn the layout of the area they had to cover, the positions of all German strongholds, the identities of known informers, the rendezvous to avoid now the cover had been blown, the details of rail movements and timetables, the code names and signs of other trusted groups, the history of towns or villages purported to be their own home towns, and their new false identities.

Chris was responsible for inventing the cover stories, and for drilling those whose national language was not French into using the local patois of the district they would be entering. In consequence, he worked at full pitch with very little sleep for about ten days in a row, along with the rest of the staff. John Frith supervised the provision of false documents, badges and other official papers the average person would be expected to have if their stories were true, and instructed the agents on the purpose of each document along with the normal procedure for obtaining one. In combined struggle for speed and complete efficiency, everyone felt tired and under stress. Chris embarked on the interrogating he always hated with more than his usual feelings of repugnance. He was tired out, and the poor devils must be apprehensive as well as weary. It seemed sadistic to burst into their rooms in the middle of the night, and drag them into a bare room to be ruthlessly questioned on a mass of detail only recently learnt under emergency conditions. It would be bad enough if it were ordinary testing, but those doing the job were told to terrify their victims into betraying themselves, if possible.

John Frith, who had to select which agent to question, then judge the person's calmness and demeanour throughout, enjoyed it. As he always said to Chris, quite rightly, 'It's useless their giving the right answers if they look as guilty as hell while doing it. They might just as well walk in and announce who they really are.'

One night, towards the end of the hectic period, Frith announced to Chris that he would be making an onslaught on the two females recruited from a very specialised French group, which had only reluctantly agreed to co-operate in the venture.

'I've been told they're so experienced we are insulting them by insisting on their joining us for training,' he said with a sneer. 'One is called "Estella" and the other is "Mirjana", so you'd better go through the stories you cooked up for them. I've a score to settle with that French bastard who scoffed at our thoroughness, so it would give me great pleasure to send one or both of them back to him as not up to our standards.'

Chris regarded him from behind his desk. 'I think that's unlikely. They are so experienced, all I had to do was concoct a cover story. They apparently speak several French dialects, know their way around this area like the backs of their hands, and are familiar with the traps newcomers can fall into. I think you are wasting valuable time by doing this with this pair – especially if you're only doing it to settle a personal score with the man who knows his own people better than you.'

The big man leant against the door frame with a cynical smile on his face. 'You always quibble at brow-beating women, don't you? It's that "English landowning gentleman" pose you try to maintain. Well, it doesn't cut any ice here. You're just a lieutenant colonel like me, and my job is to decide whom you interrogate. If they don't satisfy me with their answers, I can send them back to school or kick them out. If you don't satisfy me with your questioning, I can make you do it night after night until you get it right.'

Chris took the spectacles from his tired eyes to rub them, saying, 'Spare me the pose you try to maintain, Frith. Your idea of toughness would make a real member of the Gestapo curl up in mirth. Now give me half an hour to familiarise myself with this, then wake the poor creatures up, if you must, although a good night's sleep would probably help them far more than what you propose doing. However, I'll bully them as much as you wish, but I wager this pair won't give you the satisfaction you crave.'

Frith departed and Chris put his spectacles on again to scan the details of the cover stories he had devised for these two courageous women, who had blameless records for their activities since the fall of France. He had not had dealings with them before because they already had such fluency in languages his classes had not been necessary. Going along to the ghastly room where the interrogating was always done, he shivered on entering. The coldness was deliberate, as was the heat in summer. Sitting behind the desk, he switched on the lamps that almost blinded the victims and kept him in shadow. I am a fool, he told himself, as he always did. This procedure is designed to help save their lives, familiarise them with random surprise questioning. I know it's essential to their training, so why do I always feel like the enemy? Perhaps Frith is right and I am too squeamish. But some of the women are no older than Vesta. Imagine their risking what David went through at the hands of the Japanese!

The woman known as Estella came in looking tired but very assured, and Chris suspected at once that she had been through the real thing once, so this pretence held no fears for her. She was very good, and he found himself relaxing as the session turned into a game of matching wits, the sinister overtones forgotten. She appeared almost to enjoy the challenge, but not once did her expression betray her as he did all he could to trap her. Finally, he smiled at the plain face of an incredibly clever woman, and congratulated her before apologising for disturbing her sleep.

'If that is all which is disturbed, Monsieur, I shall be very happy,' she told him, and went out as calmly as she had entered.

'Hard luck, Frith,' Chris said over his shoulder. 'She knocked the spots off me, and I guarantee "Mirjana" will, too.'

'Don't let her knock off too many spots, or you'll be on this side of the lights,' growled John Frith.

'Who is going to interrogate me?' queried Chris with weary amusement. 'You?'

Hearing footsteps in the corridor outside, he realised the other woman was about to be flung into the freezing room, and hoped she would be as competent as her countrywoman so that he could soon get to bed. The door burst open, and the figure staggered slightly as she was given a push by the men in German uniform who had dragged her from bed. She was in a pair of shapeless winceyette pyjamas, her feet were bare, and her red hair hung loose, as he had seen it so many times. The shock was so great his heartbeat slowed, until breathing became a painful effort, as he gazed at that lovely face wearing a contemptuous expression. Now he knew why she would only

402

consider 'now'. For four years Sonja Koltay had been risking her life for a passion stronger than the one she felt for him.

They were alone together in a small room as bare and as cold as Chris now felt. He had tried to conduct the interrogation, but Sonja had recognised his voice immediately and been as shocked as he. John Frith had had his hour of revenge and relished every moment of it. A relationship based on passion between two people privy to secret information, both excellent linguists, and both having friends in countries which were presently hostile, was highly suspect. Senior men in her organisation, as well as Frank Moore, had a complete dossier on their meetings, including recordings of all they had said to each other during those rare and precious occasions they met.

Knowing their intimacy had been overheard by a relay of professional eavesdroppers had upset Sonja deeply. Chris felt angry and bitterly humiliated as he faced her, knowing the intrusion of a team of strangers had driven a wedge between them. Wearing his overcoat over her pyjamas for warmth, Sonja stood against the wall as far from him as possible; a woman he had never seen before.

'Why?' she demanded. 'Why, knowing these people would watch you, did you let it begin?'

'You were there when it began and know very well I couldn't help myself,' he replied bleakly. 'At the start . . . Yes, I suppose I faced the facts and knew it was dangerous ground. Later, I obeyed my desires and forgot all else.' He started towards her, but her expression halted him. 'Had I known what work you were doing, that they would take surveillance to such extremes . . . Dear God, surely you know I would never deliberately expose you to such . . . such . . .'

She spread her hands against the wall each side of her in a subconscious movement symbolic of entrapment, and her eyes were dark with pain as she said, 'It is unfathomable why one risks humiliation of the body with scarcely a thought, yet feels destroyed by emotional humiliation.'

'Sonja . . . *Please*,' he begged.

'You never once wore uniform in my presence. How could I guess what you did?'

'You were not meant to guess. No one was.'

'Work in a dull Ministry, you said.'

'You claimed to be no more than a working artist.'

'All those busy nights at your office desk!'

'That sudden return from Scotland! All those commissions

in the country! What a gullible fool you must have thought me,' he said in a low-voiced passion that cried out against a truth he could not accept.

'What a useless selfish creature you must have thought me.'

'You know my opinion of you.' He went to her then, but still the wild condemnation in her eyes stopped him from touching her. 'I would give up all I have for you. My love and devotion is for all time.'

Pushing away from the wall, she escaped him by walking swiftly on her bare feet to grip the back of a wooden chair in the centre of the room.

'Let us have no more declarations of undying passion to be recorded and analysed by our masters.'

Three quick strides took him behind her, where he gripped her arms fiercely. 'If it is your intention to destroy all we have been to each other, you're well on the way to succeeding.'

She remained immune to his nearness, the touch of his hands, the plea in his words, seeming as lost to him as if she had gone from the room.

'What we have been to each other cannot be destroyed because it was unreal,' she told him in flat monotones. 'We lied, we cheated, we postured. We were two people who did not exist, playing a game of pretence – pretence that we were young again in a world that was a place of beauty and kindness.'

'You asked me to make it beautiful!' he cried in protest, 'and it was not pretence but the love between us that overrode all else. Beauty and kindness *can* be found. Even in the midst of squalor or degradation they can be found, if human love and understanding are there. I've seen it in all parts of the world.'

Swinging round to face him, she said bitterly, 'You might believe even now that there was love, but certainly not understanding. My father, sister and husband all murdered, and my country occupied by a vicious tyrannical régime, yet you accepted that I could wallow in luxury with my civilian lover and do nothing to avenge them!'

'Would a uniformed lover have made any difference?' he challenged. 'Would you concede that our relationship would have been sincere if you had known from the start that I was leading a double life, training people to risk torture and death in between making love to you? Would you admit that there had been true passion between us if I had been aware of your rôle, and agonised every time you were over there avenging those murders?'

'It was an escape, that was all. You saw me as a reincarnation of Laura: a creature of all your ideals and yearnings,

404

miraculously untouched by the reality of a war which was destroying everyone else,' she charged, growing visibly moved for the first time. 'Were you blind?'

'No more than you, who apparently saw in me a reincarnation of your youthful suitors who brought you roses and their hearts on a platter,' he countered, knowing every word they were saying was driving them irrevocably apart. 'You accepted that I lost my two brothers in the last war, that my son was fighting, being captured and tortured by his enemies, and my daughter was risking her life by recording battle on canvas, while I did no more than wallow in luxurious safety with my alien mistress.'

She gazed up at him with such deep sadness it broke him apart.

'Forgive me for that. Forgive me for not being what you hoped. Most of all, forgive me for not sending you away that first evening. Reality has cut off our escape and left us with no way out.'

It snowed again that Christmas. A blizzard during Christmas Eve effectively cut Tarrant Royal off from Tarrant Maundle, so Tessa and Bill Chandler were unable to join them at the Hall. Pat was there, however, having attended the party at the Officers' Mess with Dirk, and stayed overnight in Vesta's room. David had leave, but Vesta had written that she expected to be posted back to England early in the year and would be granted leave then.

Chris lay awake in the bed next to Marion's, watching the snow flying like a cloud of feathers against the window. He had lost everything in the past, then picked up the pieces when Bill had challenged him to do so. If he lost everything this time – and Sonja *was* everything – someone else would have to pick up the pieces. He was tired of sacrifice, weary of seeing all he loved and valued trodden underfoot. Lying there at six o'clock on Christmas morning 1943 he understood why Marion had given up when she had thought David lost. Without Sonja he would never again find pleasure in music, drinking wine, studying paintings, sculptures or carvings. He would never again speak in other languages without feeling the searing pain of her loss; never visit any place they both knew well if she could not be there beside him. He would never smile again.

He twisted in the bed as he recalled her last words to him. When he had asked painfully if she really regretted not sending him away on that first evening, she had replied, 'Yes. Oh, *yes*.'

So she had gone, and he had been left with his translations and cover stories, torturing himself over the fact that he sat safely at a desk in the country while the woman he adored was doing a man's job under the noses of the enemy. He drove himself almost demented thinking of her falling into the hands of those who would do unspeakable things to her; of her dying in agonising fashion while he was powerless to help her. He had directed a deadly verbal attack on Frank Moore which severed a twenty-year-old friendship beyond repair, and had demanded that the recordings of conversations of such a deeply personal nature between himself and Sonja be immediately destroyed in his presence. This had been done, but his sense of disgust and humiliation could not be erased. His service to the Ministry and his work with the espionage unit would be merely dutiful from now on. His disillusionment was complete.

'Chris, are you awake?' came a soft voice from the other bed suddenly.

Since Marion was probably aware that his eyes were open, he thought it pointless to pretend. 'Yes.'

'It still seems to be snowing heavily. We'll be cut off for some days, I should think.'

'Very likely.'

She turned his way with a rustle of bedclothes. 'It was as deep as this on the day David was born. Do you remember?'

Would he ever forget? Roland was pitch-forked into his first delivery before he had even qualified as a doctor.

'Roland was wonderful,' she went on. 'It was a difficult birth and no one would have guessed he had never supervised one before. Daddy was full of praise when he finally got through the snow.'

The event had taken place twenty-eight years ago. Why bring the subject up now? 'Roland was always extremely competent and controlled.'

A short silence, then she said, 'If you had been present at the birth, you might have felt differently about the baby.'

'Watching a woman give birth under difficult conditions is not something an eighteen-year-old boy is likely to find fascinating – even if the baby is his,' he replied shortly. 'Try to get back to sleep.'

'Why can't you?'

'Eh?'

'You've been awake on and off for most of the night.'

'How do you know that?'

'I'm usually the only occupant of this room. When you share it I'm conscious of your movements.'

'Sorry. I'll try not to disturb you. Separate rooms might be the answer.'

Another short silence. 'With David on leave, and Pat in Vesta's room, there's nowhere else you could go. I wasn't suggesting I disliked having you here, Chris. I welcome it, as it happens. Like old times.'

'I suppose so.'

The light clicked on, and he saw the blur of a face too lacking in guile to ever pretend or deceive. This woman could never lie in moments of danger, assume unconcern in the face of brutishness, die in agony still swearing she knew nothing. Marion had always been honest, uncomplicated, and ruled by basic commonplace emotions. He had always known where he stood with her. Yet he had yearned for something different, promised long ago by Rex and Laura: a matching of two personalities that set each other afire. For Laura's headstone he had chosen the words, 'Brilliance lasts but a short while, the afterglow remains forever.' That sentiment had been as much for Rex as his wayward beautiful wife. Now Chris had found his own fiery partner, had their brilliance already ended?

'Would you like some hot milk, or a cup of tea?'

He returned from thoughts of those nights of intense passion, which had been relayed to men with earphones, eating sandwiches as they sniggered, and tried to take in what she was saying.

'No, thanks.'

'There's something on your mind, Chris,' Marion said softly. 'Would it help to talk about it?'

'I've been phenomenally busy recently, that's all.'

'Poor Chris. You look drawn and rather pale.' She sighed. 'We're both beginning to show our age, my dear.'

You are growing younger and stronger each time we meet. I should be an eager nubile girl for you, not a . . .

Not a beautiful captivating woman who fires my blood, shares my passions, and satisfies both my body and mind?

The rustle of bedclothes suggested more movement from his wife, and he could just make out the fact that she was sitting up to put on a pink woollen bed jacket.

Delightful though this silk nightgown looks moulded to that superb shape, it's even more delightful to slide it down your silken skin. Ah, La Belle Dame Sans Merci, I have been alone and palely loitering since I last held you like this. How the eavesdroppers must have curled up at that.

'We shall both be fifty in three years' time,' Marion said, shattering the image of Sonja lying naked across the bed with her glorious hair spread on the ivory silk sheets. 'The war can't last much longer, and everyone will have to start afresh. We will have to do the same, Chris, except that it will be the second time for us. I've thought a lot about it recently. The children will pursue their own futures; make their own way in the peace and prosperity of a settled world. That will leave us back where we began.'

'Oh, surely not! Too much has happened.'

'Perhaps we should start thinking about it; start planning what we shall do when the children leave.'

Would you truly give up everything for me?

You know that I would.

'I thought you would never forgive me for refusing to stop that letter.'

'David never received it. I asked him.'

'It was through no effort of mine.'

She waited for a moment or two, then pleaded softly, 'Chris, don't hide from me, please.'

With a sigh, he reached for the spectacles on the small bedside table. Marion had always accused him of hiding by removing them when he had been a bewildered nameless patient in hospital. She leapt into focus, banishing the vision of exciting Slavic features, fiery eyes and hair as red as flame. This woman in the next bed, this legal partner of his wearing a neat nightgown tied at the neck, with a pink woollen bed jacket over it, whose grey-streaked hair was slightly ruffled from the rows of curls shaped around her head, was looking at him with expectation in eyes that had only recently lost their blank look. What could she possibly expect of him after all these years?

'I said things that must have hurt you,' she began with something approaching shyness. 'But I had been unwell after the worry of David during the Battle of Britain, and the bombing of Vesta's camp. News of that impossible marriage shattered me. You are not a mother, my dear, so can't be expected to understand how I felt. But I came to you, Chris. I needed you. It was to you I turned when I was in distress. Don't hold against me forever the things I said to you then. It's very easy to cry, "I'll never forgive you" in moments of over-whelming emotion. I denied my son at that time, also, don't forget.' She held out a hand across the space between the beds. 'I have forgiven you, of course, my dear.'

He stared at her hand, and saw instead a nightmare vision of a slender graceful one that had created exquisite designs on glass, now claw-like with every finger crushed under torture.

408

Marion's arm dropped to the coverlet, and she asked thickly, 'It's not too late, is it, Chris?'

You would sacrifice your family and your career for me?

If it meant spending my life with you, yes. Yes!

Taking off the spectacles again, he said with immense bitterness, 'It was too late for us the minute I put you on your father's examination couch and robbed us both of our youth.'

Chapter Twenty

THEY STOOD on the terrace of Shepheard's Hotel in brilliant moonlight, surrounded by other merrymakers. The Egyptians, certain now of who would be the ultimate victor, welcomed the British and Americans who had celebrated non-stop for over a week. For a couple of months prior to Christmas the shops had enjoyed a roaring trade as the troops bought presents to send home. Now it was the turn of hotels and bars to benefit from the frantic attempts by those miles from their homes to pretend they did not care. At Shepheard's many of them crowded outside as midnight drew near, feeling they would somehow be closer to those at home if they stood beneath the same wide sky as 1944 arrived.

Vesta stood with Philip Bream, her partner for the evening, and thought about home. Tarrant Royal seemed like a warm and wonderful dream and, although she was geographically nearer the scene of the Nativity now, that little village nestling between gentle frost-touched green hills had somehow been closer to the notion of an inn with an adjacent stable. She had missed her home and family more this year than last. Twelve months ago there had been no David, her mother had been ill, and her father had been writing warnings not to risk her safety by going into the desert. They would all be there at Tarrant Hall now, with the Chandlers and Pat's South African, and Vesta would give anything to be there, too.

Her father would not sell Tarrant Hall now David was back. Poor David! She had seen him for a couple of hours at Cairo airport on his way home, and had felt ashamed ever since for the way she had behaved. He had looked shockingly changed, and she had been unable to hide her distress from him. When she looked at the photograph of him in his uniform when he had been awarded his wings, she still could not believe the handsome devil-may-care young man had gone forever, to be replaced by a shuffling white-haired semi-skeleton with puckered scars over his face and broken hands. He had since written that his hands were 'pretty much like they used to be' and that he had 'chucked the walking stick away', but Vesta knew his hair would never go back to that shining gold fairness, and the scars were on his face for life. David had mentioned nothing of his wife, but their father had written a brief paragraph in one of his letters, explaining that the girl had remained in Singapore, and that nothing could be done until the island was re-occupied. Her brother had returned to a transport squadron and professed to being much happier now he was back at work. Vesta thought he was pushing his luck by returning to active flying duty. Surely he could easily have secured a desk job until the war ended, even if he had conquered his problem over taking off?

She had received letters from her mother, which suggested she was a great deal better, and mentioned that she hoped it would not be long before Vesta would come home because it seemed so long since she had had the pleasure of a daughter's company. Pat had written regularly, pleased that David spent a lot of time helping them on the farm, because his new squadron only carried stores back and forth and they had periods of sitting around with nothing to do. Her friend's letters were full of village gossip, family news, and details of her Dirk and other pilots at Tarrant Hall. She had sent several photographs with names of young men who would like to correspond with the girl whose home they were occupying. Vesta had never taken up the offers. She was fully occupied with lonely officers in Cairo. So occupied, it would be a relief to get away from a host of eager suntanned Lotharios seeking a pleasant interlude during their leave. One or two had lightly touched her heart, but they always moved on. She kept that in the forefront of her mind and concentrated on the true love of her life.

The response her paintings of the desert had aroused had resulted in several commissions, so she had spent time in Alexandria, Tobruk, and the tiny El Alamein, which had now acquired everlasting fame through 'Monty' and his 'Desert Rats'. But the war in Africa was over, and she had simply painted a series of pictures which could have reflected her subject matter at any time over the peaceful years. Although she had stuck to her habit of making some small scene or object the focus of a canvas depicting large-scale activity, she had not felt personal excitement over any one of them until she had gone to El Alamein in November. There, she had been initially depressed and unable to work, spending hours with pencil and pad, doodling without any sense of inspiration. One evening, as the sun was going down, she had been so flooded with memories of that week she had spent with the tank squadron, that she had burst into tears telling herself there were only ghosts of those men left in the desert now. That had been the birth of a period of prolonged activity, resulting in a large painting that had caused such acclaim photographs of it had appeared in newspapers and magazines, which in turn had led to requests for interviews from journalists. Due to her military status, these were all handled by the army press officer in Cairo, who handed out a standard profile on Subaltern Sheridan. This had dampened the enthusiasm of those hoping for an 'exclusive', and the fuss had soon died down, leaving only two publications to print a shortened version of what they had been handed.

In one just before Christmas, however, there had been a featured article by Brad Holland, who had begun it with a reminder of his previous article on what he called 'this Jill-of-all-trades'. Claiming close friendship with the upper-class English girl, who was a trained signals operator, personal assistant to a high-ranking officer in the military Headquarters in Cairo, besides being a talented and original artist, he had then described how the girl in khaki shirt and trousers who had travelled for a week with an operational tank squadron during the great push from El Alamein, and had manned a transceiver throughout an aerial attack during which she had been injured, had later danced the night away with him in a Cairo nightclub, looking as glamorous as any woman there in an expensive peach silk evening gown.

The article had gone on to give details of her distinguished father: 'One of a vast army of men who had fought in the trenches of the last war and now lent their talents and experiences to the less dangerous but equally vital administrative jobs in government departments.' David's career was covered from his success at Cranwell to 'his courageous return to active duty'. Named as 'probably the last man to fly out of Singapore before it fell', the article had continued with a description of an ordeal 'known only to the heroic young man who endured it'. Somehow Brad had ferreted out the details of the hospital David had entered on arrival in Darwin, plus the names of doctors and nurses who had 'fought to turn a living skeleton into a man of strength again'. There was a description of Tarrant Hall where the RAF had established a squadron Mess, and the village church which had been destroyed by a German aircraft crashing into it. The article had ended with the propaganda theme, declaring that this young artistic girl was

412

the perfect example of the spirit which was winning the war for people determined to remain free.

Vesta had been absolutely furious, storming into the press officer to demand action against the man who had published the details of herself and her family so blatantly, and in such bad taste. The man's sympathy had been somewhat tempered by the strong propaganda elements of the article, but he had promised to protest most forcibly to an agency which employed the journalist in question. Two days before he had telephoned Vesta to say he had received an apology from the agency, which had stated that Mr Holland would be told of Subaltern Sheridan's displeasure when he was next able to be contacted. It had not appeased her, of course, but there was no doubt that the El Alamein painting was establishing her as an artist with a future, with or without Brad's article. Entitled 'The Mirage' it portrayed the deserted settlement together with the ghosts of troops and phantom tanks, present in that place, yet with a suggestion of having long gone. She knew it was her best work, so far, and was impatient for her posting home. Cairo had served its purpose and no longer held any attraction for her.

Standing in the moonlight on New Year's Eve, she felt 1943 had been a momentous year for her. David had returned from the dead, her mother had recovered from her breakdown, her father seemed more himself and had abandoned all thought of selling their home, and she was finding her place in the art world. What would 1944 bring? Two minutes after midnight she had her first inkling. Withdrawing from an embrace with Philip Bream, she was held at arm's length by him.

'Happy New Year, darling,' he said. 'Will you marry me some time during it?'

Caught off balance due to her thoughts of home, she replied, 'Oh, Philip, it's only just begun.'

'That's the best time to plan. We are both due for a home posting soon. We could have a June wedding in England. What do you say?'

'June is six months away.'

'It's usual to have an engaged period first,' he pointed out.

'You don't want to steal away tonight to find a willing churchman?' she asked.

'Good Lord, no! I mean... Gosh, would you? If that's what you really want... But I do think it would be more sensible to wait until we get home, darling. Your people are bound to want a traditional wedding, and my Pater and Mater would think it frightfully infra dig if we got spliced here.' He gave a laugh.

413

'They're most awfully stuffed shirt about protocol, actually. Where Gerald is concerned, they try to excuse his frequent divorces by telling themselves he's an artist, so what can one expect? But I'm pretty certain they'd insist on another ceremony in church at home. So that I could make an honest woman of you, and all that,' he finished apologetically.

'Yes, of course,' she said, a sudden flame dying. If he had swept her off to a cleric a moment ago she might have gone through with it. Thank God he had not. Regret would have come with the morning. Whilst she could not imagine this pleasant uncomplicated man flinging himself on her in a mood of frustrated patriotism and passion, seeking brutal solace from her body, neither could she imagine being with him unclothed likely to be any pleasure. She liked him a lot. He made her laugh, was attentive, courteous and well bred. Philip Bream was what others would call an excellent match for Sir Christopher Sheridan's daughter, and Vesta had no doubt life as his wife would be pleasant, socially full . . . and extremely predictable.

After his initial attempt at seduction, he had behaved himself to the extent of developing deep feelings for her. Turning a blind eye to what was certain to come, she had allowed their friendship to slide into what Cairo circles accepted as 'going steady'. It had been good; she was certain he had derived great pleasure from the friendship. Why did something which was ideal have to culminate in a proposal which, if refused, brought the whole thing to an end? More to the point, why did she persist in the idea that there must be joy to sexual union or women would have abandoned it centuries ago? Her hatred of men and their basic desires had faded to allow her enjoyment of casual embraces and spoken incitement. Yet only one man had made her shiver with anticipation when he held her, and he was married to a woman who 'looked a million dollars right in the middle of those dreary dames in uniform'.

'Aren't you happy with the way things are?' she asked, knowing it was a stupid question.

'Not in the least,' was his prompt reply. 'You know what I really want.'

'But you're prepared to wait for it until June?'

'I . . . Dash it all, darling, you've got me in a most fearfully confused state now. For a whole year you've held me off. Now I want to make the whole thing legal you're . . . Well, I'm not sure what you are suggesting.'

Sighing she said, 'Sorry, I'm being unfair. Perhaps I'm

414

suggesting we wait until we get back to England before we make any promises. This country casts spells.'

'That sounded a little reflective,' he said with more perception than he usually displayed. 'Is there someone else?'

'No.'

'Not even in the past?'

'No.'

It was his turn to sigh. 'I'll ask you the minute we reach England, then. I don't suppose two months will make any difference.'

Two months made a tremendous difference because Vesta did not go to England. Instead, she found herself ecstatically flying to Italy with a commission to do pictures of the campaign that had reached a stalemate on both fronts.

The initial landings at the toe of Italy had been followed by a race northwards when the Italians had surrendered. But Hitler had moved his armies quickly to the south, and deadlock had resulted on a line between Naples and Rome, bringing the campaign to a grinding halt on what was known as the Gustav Line. In an attempt to break it, daring landings north of the area at Anzio, only thirty miles from Rome, had been made in January. Combined British and American ships had bombarded the tiny town of Anzio until it was little more than a stretch of burning ruins along the coastline, then landing craft had put ashore massive assault forces to establish a firm beachhead. Then, an over-cautious American general had refused to advance, fearing the complete absence of German troops along the route to Rome was a lure into a trap. Little realising they could have run straight through to the ancient capital with little resistance, the troops had had to obey the order to dig in and prepare for the enemy attack. They prepared, and waited, and waited, and waited. The delighted incredulous Germans hastily brought in massive reinforcements during the lull and, when the Allies finally advanced, met them with crucifying resistance which kept them back on their beachhead.

At a time when she was organising herself for a return home, Vesta was told her journey would be via Italy, due to a special request for her to tour the area behind the lines, to do propaganda pictures of Allied troops befriending and fraternising with their former Italian enemies. The purpose was to show that surrender resulted in good treatment, property being left intact, and sufficient food for every man, woman and child. Not caring a fig for the motivation behind her commission, Vesta could hardly believe her good fortune. As a young girl she had been to Venice, Florence and Rome on one of those rare occasions when her mother had agreed to accompany the family on a holiday. Their father had obliged Vesta and David to learn basic Italian, and speak it whilst there, calling down curses from them both. Now, she was extremely thankful for his insistence. Knowing the language would make things easier all round, she felt.

Having accumulated rather a large wardrobe whilst in Cairo, she packed most of it into a trunk to be sent on to Tarrant Hall, leaving a small selection of clothes and basics to fit into her soft travelling bag for the flight in an RAF transport to Bari. Moving around by road in an area of small villages, she would need only her spare items of uniform, toilet things, and painting materials, with a frock for the occasional social evening. She intended travelling light.

The flight was so bumpy she was feeling rather sick by the time one of the crew cheerily told her they were going in to land. Dabbing her forehead with cologne once more, she prepared to endure the misery of descending through the air towards the ground, wondering how David could bear voluntarily to undergo popping ears, churning stomach and swimming head day after day. How he had ever flown a Spitfire in dives, turns and swift climbs without feeling intensely ill she could not imagine. With a jerk the undercarriage made contact, and they were soon running along the smooth tarmac toward the airport complex. Thankfully she caught up her bag, settled her cap on her head, and left the loathsome flying tube to gulp in the wonderful fresh air that improved her condition immediately.

The formalities with the military authorities were soon completed, and she passed through the large area where a mass of people, mostly men in uniform of some kind, were concerned with arriving or departing on troop-carrying aircraft. A series of trucks and other military vehicles were lined up outside, and Vesta walked through the throng toward the exit doors, feeling she was more likely to be spotted by the person from army liaison who was meeting her if she was clear of the main crowd. There were several young RAF officers eyeing her with interest, but no army subaltern with transport appeared to be waiting for her.

'Hallo, Vic.'

She turned in disbelief, her heartbeat racing. Brad was wearing the usual khaki with the press flash on his sleeve, and

416

his left arm was in a sling. He looked tired, but the old magnetism was still there.

'I suppose it is too much to hope this is one of those amazing coincidences, and you are on your way out,' she said with commendable aplomb, since she felt like a bundle of rags at the mere sight of him.

'Unlike you, I don't walk out on a date without an explanation,' he said. 'How about a cup of coffee?'

'No, thanks.'

'OK. Let's go, then.'

She stared at him. 'What does that mean?'

'Let's have some coffee and I'll tell you.'

Standing her ground she asked, 'Brad, you're not here expressly to meet me, are you?'

'Sure I am. If only you'd let me explain.'

'Let's have some coffee,' she said in resignation. 'Then I'll get in touch with Headquarters and sort it all out.'

It seemed Brad had already done that, since he was their appointed escort. 'As it was my suggestion that you should come here, they were tickled pink with my offer to look after you.' He cocked an eyebrow at her. 'Isn't that what you English officers say: *tickled pink?*'

'It was your suggestion that I come here?' she exclaimed, NAAFI cup halfway to her lips. 'What a nerve!'

'Would you sooner I had kept my mouth shut? Has a year in Cairo plus artistic acclaim over "The Mirage" changed your burning determination to paint real war?' he challenged. 'See here, I went to considerable pains to get them to bring you over, undertaking to be personally responsible for you. I am now ready to accept your gratitude for my efforts.'

'If I had known you were behind it, I'd have declined.'

The dark brown eyes studied her over the canteen table, and he wagged his head in exasperation. 'He must have hurt you a lot if you still haven't gotten over it. But do you seriously mean to let him spoil the whole of your life?'

Plonking the thick cup into the equally thick saucer, she said intensely, 'You really do have a nerve! It's well over a year since you turned up in Cairo for a few rather arrogant hours, and now you behave as if we are on good enough terms to discuss my personal affairs. In fact, we have spent no more than a total of four days in each other's company over the past eighteen months.'

His slow grin dawned. 'They were some four days!'

'You are impossible!'

'You haven't shown the slightest concern over my wound.'

'Since I imagine it was inflicted by an infuriated woman, it hardly warrants my concern.'

Watching her for a few moments while she wrestled with the situation, he said, 'Now we have the initial resistance under control, shall we get down to plans? I covered the Anzio landings, then got hit by a sniper when I went forward with some engineers clearing a minefield. I had a spell in a field hospital, by which time all action had come to a halt. I decided to do some "heart and soul" stuff on the local population – beauty surviving the desecration of battle, nature continuing whilst man does his best to destroy himself – that kind of thing. I knew it would be ideal for you, in addition to being safe, so I offered to take you around with me and ensure there was no repetition of that desert affair Villiers objected to so officially. It was a cinch. They agreed right off, and laid on a jeep for an unlimited period of time.' Finishing his coffee he said, 'I'm still ready to accept your gratitude.'

Fiddling with the spoon in her saucer, she voiced her major worry. 'Am I to assume that you and I will be on our own, travelling wherever we wish for the purpose of our work?'

'Got it first time.'

'It won't work,' she declared, trying to convince herself. 'What if we want to cover different subjects?'

'We'll fight. Where's the problem in that . . . We do it all the time.'

'I'll never find inspiration in company with you.'

'Hell, I'll have the same problem.'

'The whole scheme is ridiculous.'

He pursed his lips. 'I thought painters were prepared to suffer for their art.'

'Not that much,' she retorted.

The grin appeared again. 'Aw, come on, Vic, you know darn well what you're serving up as an argument is a lot of screwball nonsense. If you've finished your coffee, we'll get going.'

Next minute she found herself walking out beside him to the row of vehicles parked there, and up to a jeep at the rear.

'There's just one thing,' Brad explained apologetically. 'You'll have to do the driving. That's another reason they agreed to my suggestion. I told them you could handle a jeep.'

It all began to make sense then. He wanted to do some 'heart and soul' stuff, but could not get around on his own. She was expected to provide female compassion for his wounded arm, give him a steel on which to sharpen his wit, and act as his chauffeur. Controlling herself with an effort, she made the

418

resolution that, if she was to do the driving, they would go where *she* wanted to go.

'Get in,' she commanded, slipping behind the wheel, and tossing her cap onto the back seat with her bag.

Seated beside her, he said meekly, 'I'm still ready to accept your gratitude.'

'I'm very grateful.'

'You might say it with a little more warmth, even fling your arms around my neck. You see, I also had to tell them we were on pretty good terms so there'd be no problem about the nights.'

Her head swung round in fury. 'You *what*?'

Shrugging, he said, 'They're very strict about their female officers. Before they'd agree to this, I had to tell them we had plans.'

'For what? Bigamy?'

His eyes narrowed. 'So that's what bothering you, is it?'

'You have the most almighty nerve,' she fumed. 'I'll go on this "heart and soul" trip now I'm here, but it'll be on my terms. This time I'm no stranger to the country or its language, so I need no dependence on you to get the pictures I want. What's more, this time I'm in charge of the vehicle, and you are handicapped. I think that gives me every advantage.'

Leaning back in his seat, he murmured, 'Suits me, Vic.'

'And stop using that ridiculous name!' She let in the clutch and roared off, having not the slightest idea where to head first, yet suddenly feeling supremely alive.

After a week Vesta knew she was madly in love – with Italy. Totally enchanted by Mediterranean warmth, soft blue skies, villages which were an artist's gift to paint, mountains, valleys, incredibly blue sea, masses of blossom that filled the air with overpowering perfume, sloping vineyards, olive groves, and places like Amalfi, Sorrento and wonderful, wonderful Capri, she almost forgot the war. But the traffic on the roads was nearly all military, the olive groves were often sites for camps housing troops resting from the front line, and field hospitals were everywhere, with bandaged men sitting in the sunshine and waving a crutch or walking stick as they passed. There were female nurses, of course, and American Red Cross girls, in addition to the Italian women, so the business of sleeping quarters was not in the least problematical. Brad must have known that and deliberately provoked her by suggesting they would be alone together at night. It was not in the least like the desert. Living was completely civilised, with an abundance of wine, wide variety of food, and houses in which to sleep. Since the American troops had infinitely more exciting rations than the British or French, Brad always scrounged from his own countrymen, and Vesta told herself she would be growing as fat as Pat had once been if she lived for much longer on doughnuts, Chicken Maryland with sweetcorn, and flapjacks with ice-cream and maple syrup. Then there was the wine. Brad bought bottles of it wherever they went, partly to give in gratitude to his passing hosts, and partly for himself and Vesta. She drank it. How could she not when it was all part of the entire sun-kissed experience?

When she drove into villages, through narrow cobbled streets to the inevitable square with almost certainly a fountain, and spoke to the women who stood in the doorways of little colour-washed houses covered in wisteria or mimosa, Vesta found that their eyes invariably turned to the large attractive man with her. They nearly always referred to him as her husband, or very definitely her lover, and she sensed their astonishment when she asked for two separate rooms in the village. When they stayed for the night in some military settlement, Vesta was always invited to share a tent with the nurses or, if no females were there, occupied one gallantly given up by one of the officers. But even they behaved as if they took her and Brad for a pair, and they never stepped out of line with her. Soon she realised she was thinking that way, too.

Far from being unable to find inspiration in his company she worked harder than she had ever done. Sketching almost everything she saw, she had to beg him to stay put for several days at a time so that she could use her sketches for the basis of paintings. It was an artist's dream to sit in a terraced garden overlooking a valley full of almond blossom, or a tiny bay and a sapphire sea and put up an easel to do what she loved doing best, knowing it was good. Local people would come to watch over her shoulder, expecting to see a copy of the view ahead. Instead, there would be something briefly sketched a few days before, which she was now completing with her mind's eye and imagination.

Sometimes Brad sat nearby typing his reports with two fingers, the sling hanging empty until he had finished. Other times he would beg a lift with officers he knew, or other correspondents who were going up to the battle zone, and be gone all day – sometimes several days. Vesta caught herself worrying when he was away. When he returned unharmed with that slow grin, asking, 'Did you miss me, Vic?' she was always

420

angry with herself. But she worried again next time he left.

Brad always sent his reports via one of the despatch riders who raced the undulating roads on motor cycles, delivering messages which could not be relayed over normal transmitters. The reports were read by the censors, then cabled to Brad's agency in London. Vesta sent her pictures via these military messengers, also. Rolling them up, she inserted the paintings into an empty shell case for protection. They eventually found their way to Bari and were flown home with the mail. Amongst her first batch was one of wounded soldiers outside a field hospital, chasing three goats away after one big billy with a beard had seized and begun to munch the chessboard they had been using. There was another of a small bare-bottomed Italian child sitting on a low wall, on his head a German tin helmet which completely covered his face. A third was a great deal more sombre. They had visited one day a village very near the front line, which had been recently shelled, and had seen the body of a young woman sprawled in a grotesque position in a fruit orchard. Her face was serene and unmarked, still dignified in death. The attack on the village had shaken the earth so much the blossom had fallen in great showers, and on the woman's chest there had been an uncanny arrangement of pink and white blossoms that suggested a wreath. Brad declared that picture her best, but she had nightmares about it still.

It was not all art and sunshine, however. There were sudden swift air attacks from both sides of the Gustav Line, where the battle raged without ground being won. They could be driving along peaceful roads one minute, then hear the roar of aircraft overhead and be forced to stop and dive for cover in the bordering trees or a wadi, as sticks of bombs fell somewhere ahead. The target might be a column of troops, a tented camp, a strategic bridge or road. Sometimes they would drive on and encounter the devastation, sometimes it occurred behind them. Brad always insisted they went back in case there was a story. Those were the only times they argued. On one such occasion Vesta drove back reluctantly to find the German dive bombers had missed their target completely, destroying instead an innocent village. While Brad thought nothing of questioning those in a state of shock, whom he rescued from the rubble, Vesta did what she could to comfort two small children standing screaming in the ruins of a cottage, telling herself her real war was also there in the midst of paintbox villages. Coloured stucco lay everywhere, broken furniture hung from skeletons of houses, scraps of material flapped in the breeze like so many flags of disaster. Dust obscured the whole area, and it was only possible to tell where the roads had been by the remnants of cobbles. The baroque church had been split in two, the bell having been blown from the belfry to land like a lop-sided hat on the corner of the trattoria. Wine was flowing like a giant trickle of blood from the burst barrels within, and a pair of crazed dogs were lapping it up in a suicidal drinking marathon. Women and children crouched in shock against a wall, where a huge scatter of onions and red cabbages suggested there had once been a shop.

Although Vesta and Brad tried to help, once the initial shock had passed the Italians closed ranks and showed they preferred to see to their own. They thanked the two strangers who had appeared from nowhere, but their dignity was badly damaged by the strangers' presence at a time when the village had been attacked by a former ally who now derided their weakness. It was a matter of pride, which would not now allow them to accept help and kindness from former enemies. So they climbed back into the jeep, and Vesta backed it until the road was wide enough to allow her to turn. She had seen it all with shocked eyes: the dead, the dying, the terrified, the calm, the lost. She had seen it all before. Why did it seem worse today? In silence they left the scene, but she had gone no more than two hundred yards when they came upon a sight which made her cry out. A mule with its side ripped open to the bone lay beside the road, unable to die and end its own suffering. The most pitiful screaming brays came from its gaping jaws.

'Brad, oh Brad, *do* something!' she cried instinctively as they drew to a halt. 'No one will help that poor creature whilst human life is in the balance.'

He took one look at her face, then reached over to open the compartment by his seat, from which he took a revolver she had no idea he carried. Walking to the suffering animal, he shot it in the head, then walked back and got in beside her.

'We're supposed to be noncombatant, but I like to cover emergencies,' he commented as he replaced the revolver.

They remained where they were because she found herself shaking too much to drive off. Without a word he reached over to the back seat and took a bottle of whisky from his bag. Unscrewing the top he held it out.

'Take a pull at this.'

She shook her head. 'I'll never drive afterwards.'

'I'm not suggesting you drink the whole contents.' When she made no attempt to take the bottle, he said, 'You're not as tough as you make out, and this is one of the times you should let me take command. Come on, get some of this down you.'

Turning away from the sight of the dead animal she did as he asked. It was not a taste she cared for and she made an involuntary grimace. But he indicated that she should tip up the bottle again. It was strangely comforting to be bullied by him, she found. But when he got out, walked round to her side of the jeep and told her to get out, she protested.

'How can you possibly drive with that arm of yours?'

His grin seemed particularly endearing as he confessed that he could have done so for the past week. 'I thought I'd lose my driver if I let the secret out. Move over.'

As she scrambled across to the passenger seat, she muttered, 'You've got a nerve!' Then, as he settled beside her and started the engine, she asked, 'How do you know I won't go off now?'

'You've just softened up and started eating out of my hand. Now we can really get started.'

'Oh no, we can't,' she said sternly. But her head was on his shoulder when he pulled up for the night outside a hotel in a small town decked with flowers for a feast day.

The people of this town high in the mountains were already well fortified with wine by early evening on this day of celebrations, so Vesta and Brad sat in a garden to eat and watch the human cameos being played out. Sick of the everlasting khaki, she had put on a silk blouse and a full skirt of bronze-striped cotton, after washing her hair and spraying herself with expensive perfume she had bought in Naples. She told herself it was to counter-balance the grimness of the afternoon, but it could conceivably have been for Brad's benefit. The result might not be as total as Aunt Laura's frills and fluttering eyelashes her father had once mentioned, but it was a long way from the military officer in khaki on a night when all the local girls were in their best frocks. There was much kissing and cuddling amongst the young people thronging the square, and a small brass and accordion band was strolling around playing the kind of music which defied one not to dance to it. Brad appeared to be enjoying it hugely, watching the passing scene with eyes glowing darkly in the light of lanterns as he ate his pasta and washed it down with deep draughts of red wine.

'There's the true "heart and soul" stuff, Vic,' he murmured, his gaze still on the square beyond the hotel garden. 'They don't give a damn what's going on north of here. It's not their war any longer. The world is this small area high in the mountains, with a view rich people would pay a million dollars to see from their mansion windows each day. The air is clear, healthy and rarified enough to make one permanently light-headed. They know they'll never make it big, so they don't have to try. The town commissar tells them what they may or may not do; if they misbehave the padrone hears their confession and exonerates them. The church is the pivot of their lives; work is just something to do when the sun is not too hot. But life, ah, life is to be lived openly and to the full. They don't shut themselves into separate little boxes after a day spent struggling to get promotion before the other guy, worrying about the mortgage and the kids' education, eating meals out of cans in a hamburger bar on the corner of some dusty street. These people come out into the open, sit around yarning and drinking wine, dance in the street to music they know and love. They yell at each other in public marital rows, then make up just as openly. They play cards on the sidewalk, and smoke pipes without worrying about ash spilling on the carpet. They embrace as they stroll along, and invite passion with dark fiery glances that say it all. And why the hell shouldn't they? Youth is meant to call to youth. What's so goddam wrong with that?'

After a moment or two, Vesta said quietly, 'That sounded remarkably like one of two things.'

He turned quickly. 'Such as?'

'Your next article ... Or a personal protest.'

Giving a small grunt, he said, 'Wine sure loosens you up.'

'How long have you been married?' she asked, knowing it was something that needed to be discussed between them.

'I don't know ... Ten years, maybe,' was his reluctant reply, as he poured more wine into their glasses. 'Gloria could give you right down to minutes and seconds.'

'Tell me about her.'

'Why should I?'

'Look, you're the journalist, not me,' she said snappily. '*I* can't make a world scoop from what you tell me.'

'Still sore about that article?' he asked, leaning back in the chair in order to concentrate on her.

'Why did you do it?'

'You were news, and I had an exclusive on you.'

'You didn't have to print all that about Daddy, and poor David. Don't you think he suffered enough without having that nauseating rubbish splashed over the pages of a daily paper? It was a pretty rotten thing to do, Brad.'

'That's the story of my life,' he replied levelly.

'You don't care, do you?' she accused in anger.

'Not if it makes someone somewhere else care. So much of this war is accounted in multiples. If I write an article saying five thousand pilots have been shot down and crippled it makes readers say, "Gee, that's terrible," over their morning ham and eggs. If I pinpoint just one of those five thousand to show the utter tragedy, the courage involved, how it affects all those around him, how they are all under stress and pressure themselves, readers begin to understand the reality of it. They see a human life which was set in a determined productive pattern; war comes and the entire pattern is irrevocably changed. Then they start to care. Then they go out and buy war bonds, give up their precious pans and kettle for Spitfires, stop using more than five inches of water in their daily bath.' Seeing her expression, he leant forward across the table and put his hand over hers. 'Honey, there are fifty homeless kids in an orphanage. One gets featured in the press. Everyone in town wants to adopt him. It's the same principle.'

She sighed. 'I didn't tell you all that in an official interview. It was a private conversation while we were dancing.'

'Never open your heart to a newspaperman. He may print what's inside.'

'You still haven't told me about Gloria,' she said then, still finding it difficult to equate the man she had come to know with the ruthless correspondent.

'What's to tell? Gloria is my wife and enjoys making my life hell. End of exclusive.'

'No, it isn't,' she cried, determined it would not be left like that. 'Why does she hate you?'

'I don't think she does. I'm the source of too much pleasure.'

It had come to matter too deeply for her to let him fob her off with a few throwaway sophisticated remarks. 'Brad, I may end up painting your life story, but no one will recognise you in the picture. Stop evading the point. Don't you think you owe me a little honesty, at this stage?'

'What stage is that?'

Roused, she said, 'The stage when I shall get up and walk away if you continue to avoid my question. What was all that about living life openly and to the full? Practice what you preach, for once.'

Tossing back the wine, he filled his glass again. 'If I did that, you'd soon forget the guy who put ice in your veins instead of the hot blood these local girls appear to have.'

She got to her feet and walked off into the garden, where the heavy scent of mimosa filled the air. Surprisingly, she found tears in her eyes and blinked them away fiercely. All this throbbing seduction around her, plus a yearning for something elusive, which she instinctively felt could be captured under the right conditions, was making the evening too painful. He seemed to be so volatile – one minute close and endearing, the

425

next deliberately abrasive. In the desert it had been overpoweringly physical between them. Now the man within the man threatened her. The trouble was, she was uncertain of the nature of that threat. If he loved his wife it was adultery she had to fight. If the marriage was on the rocks, it was Gloria Holland who became the adversary.

Hearing movement behind her, she tensed. Yet when he took hold of her and turned her to face him, she went willingly into his arms for the kiss that changed a flirtation into a love affair. It was all she thought it could be: tender, demanding, mutually seeking and satisfying. There were no bells ringing all over the world, no dizzy plummeting in a lift, just a sensation of arriving at a destination with sighing relief. They wandered out into the festive crowd, arms around each other, living the Italian dream that made one small town the whole world. Laughing with those who were merry, kissing openly with the other lovers, singing with melodramatic gusto the songs that throbbed with emotion as these mountain people played them, and drinking wine like water. They finally returned to the hotel in the early hours of the morning. Vesta was light-headed, light-hearted and very much in love with a man she did not fully understand. Yet, when they reached her room, and he kicked the door shut before taking her in a full-blooded embrace which left her in no doubt of the state he had reached, she surfaced and backed away in the darkness.

'Goodnight, Brad,' she said with a tremendous effort.

It was very quiet for a moment or two, then he let out his breath in a gust of anger. 'Jesus, what does it take to get through to you?'

She undressed slowly after he had gone, then was drawn to her window by the sounds of the last revellers in the square. It was no real surprise to see Brad passing with a ripe laughing woman encircled by his arm, two bottles of wine in the other hand. They were lost in the charms of each other as they vanished into the darkness of one of the narrow streets leading from the square. A stranger would give him what he wanted, and he would be happy in the morning. She would yearn all night and ache with love when dawn came. But she had given herself to one married man, and had no intention of repeating her folly. He had got through to her, all right, but the message had been a warning, not an invitation to surrender.

For the next two weeks they concentrated heavily on work. Now Brad was able to drive he took off in search of news, leaving Vesta to turn her pile of sketches into suitable pictures.

426

Sometimes he was away for one night; once he was gone for three, returning to tell her he had been given the opportunity to go up to Anzio again to report on the present situation there.

'You might have let me know,' she complained.

'No time,' he replied airily. 'That's something you women never understand about this job. There's a place on a boat leaving now, and I mean *now*. How do you tell the guy willing to take you along you have to get to a phone to let some girl know where you're headed, so's she'll worry even more than if you don't ring?'

'OK,' she said, using his own idiom. 'End of subject!' But it gave her her first clue about the possible cause of discord between him and his wife.

The kissing had stopped and they were both quietly professional, treating each other with polite respect for what they were doing. Vesta's inspiration had gone for a while, and she wasted almost ten days fiddling with pictures that were no more than adequate, and gave her no satisfaction whatever. After Brad had returned from Anzio, he stayed put with her in a small town which housed some New Zealand troops, while he typed his articles with what appeared to be total concentration. However, when Vesta accepted an invitation to go into Naples with a Kiwi captain who wanted to visit a friend of his, Brad growled on her return, 'You've been a hell of a long time. What kept you?'

Full of enthusiasm, she had replied that the New Zealander's friend had turned out to be a Highlander in full regalia, who had posed for some sketches beside the ruins of Pompeii.

'I'll do a painting tomorrow,' she told him. 'It's a splendid subject. How's the article?'

'Lousy. Let's eat dinner. I'm starving.'

'Oh, did you wait for me?'

'Sure I did. I thought you'd have been back before now.'

'I would have been, but Teddy and I had dinner at a marvellous little trattoria in a village on the way back.'

'Cheers for Teddy,' he said in his best mimicry of upper-class English. 'While I eat, sit and have some wine with me.'

'Actually, I do have something of a headache. I think I'll turn in.'

'No need for the headache routine,' he told her caustically. 'All I aim to do is talk.'

That was her second clue concerning the discord between the Hollands. Gloria could not be in love with him if she invented headaches. So she washed and changed from her uniform into a cool dress, to sit and drink a little wine with him as he ate his dinner. They chatted about the course of the war and when it was likely to end. It was already May and no landing had been made on French soil. Everything had come to a standstill here in Italy, and the Far-Eastern campaign was necessarily a slow affair, due to the huge distances between the string of occupied islands.

'What'll you do when it's over, Brad?' she asked into a silence.

'What I did before it began, I guess. Once a newsman, always a newsman. I can't resist following a story. What'll you do?'

'Paint.'

'Paint what? There'll be no *real* war for you.'

She smiled faintly. 'Maybe I'll paint *real life,* instead.'

'You don't know enough about it,' he said. Then, as he leant back in his chair in the small hotel courtyard, he asked against the cheerful chatter of the other customers, 'Who was the guy who hurt you?'

Gazing into the sparkling ruby of her wine she said, 'A Polish pilot – very handsome, very brave, and very married. He's now very dead.'

'Still carrying a torch?'

Looking across at him, she said carefully, 'I think you know the answer to that. How about you? Still crazy about Gloria?'

'Not since about two weeks ago.'

'Ah, Rosa with the full curves and dark sultry eyes really got at you, did she?'

'She was a *pip,*' he riposted smartly.

'I wonder you haven't been back.'

'How can a guy repeat anything so good? That your trouble?'

'Hardly.'

'So what's wrong?' he probed, leaning forward.

'I have this allergy against men who are married.'

'You should find a cure for it. If the war continues many more years there may not be any bachelors left.'

'I'll have my art.'

'That won't keep you warm in bed.'

'Neither will a man who is in bed with his wife.'

He stood up abruptly. 'OK, Vic, you win. I guess I'm the one who has a headache.'

The following day Vesta did not do her painting of the Highlander at Pompeii because Brad received news of a fresh assault at Monte Cassino. After a brief argument about her safety, they both set off for the area. Their route took them over mountains they had visited before, where the breathtaking vistas made a mockery of the fact that they were on their way to witness a battle. The area was filled with cherry blossom and birdsong. Children washing by the roadside waved to them as they passed; wonderful white smiles in brown faces.

'What a day to die on,' said Brad suddenly. 'If I was a doomed man, I'd want to go out on a day just like this.'

'Oh no,' she protested with vigour. 'Think of lying there knowing you'd never see the sun again, or the intense blueness of a summer sky, trees in full bloom; think of never hearing a bird breaking the silence with song, or children laughing and splashing in a stream. When I die, I hope it will be a dismal winter's day, when the landscape is grey and everything else seems dead.' She looked around at the beauty of that part of Italy. 'Oh no, Brad, think of never seeing any of this again. It would make me die broken-hearted to leave on a day such as this.'

The subject of dying began to take on a more immediate relevance as they drew nearer the front line, passing through stone villages that had been reduced to little more than rubble by shells and off-target bombing by the Germans holding grimly to their positions. The survivors of these villages were stubbornly retaining their residency in tiny hovels built from the debris of their former homes. They looked at the man and girl in khaki with indifference. Friend or foe, the military invariably meant trouble of some kind, although there was little this pair could do to them now.

They soon reached a broken village set into the slope of a hill, from which they had a clear view across a plain of the utter devastation of the battlefield. Brad halted the jeep at the edge of the little settlement, where the road began to descend through vineyards. They looked across to where the great monastery, which had dominated the hill at Cassino, had been almost totally flattened by air, in the belief that the Germans would now be unable to use the cover of the building to command the uphill approaches. The theory had proved unsound. The enemy had moved into the ruins, and held the hill against all attempts to capture it. It smacked of the previous war, when thousands had died for tenure of a tiny area of complete devastation.

Right now there was another assault in progress. For some minutes they had been hearing the sounds of it; now there were the sights and smells. Each time a gun fired it emitted smoke, and special flares had been lit to lay a screen of it over the advancing troops on the slopes. Along the straight valley road wound military vehicles of every kind, and khaki figures moved in organised confusion amidst the camps that had been there for almost three months. Shells burst on the upper reaches in an attempt to silence the machine guns before the men inching their way upwards were within range; others exploded in the Allied valley positions, sent from guns that had been lobbing death over the crest of the hill for weeks on end. Overhead, the battle of opposing air forces was taking place, and the morning was further shattered by the zooming, roaring aggression of machines spitting bullets from their wings.

Vesta stared, hypnotised by this evidence of her real war. The contrast was stunning. Behind her lay beauty and golden freedom; ahead were death, hatred and fear. She had been living a romantic dream these past few weeks. This was what Brad wrote about for those who would never otherwise know what it was like. This terrible inhumanity, this locking of strangers in battle because they had no choice, this small hill which would turn decent gentle men into savages. *This* was why he had published that story about herself and David; and the parents who were suffering each in their inividual ways. This scene unfolding before her now was too immense, too bizarre, too unacceptable for those at home to take in. In order to make them feel the reality of it all, it was necessary to reduce it to *one* man firing *one* gun on *one* uphill path. Individual suffering could be mourned; mass agony was incomprehensible. Could she ever paint this? Where was the good shining through this hell across a plain? She shivered involuntarily.

Brad turned to her quickly. 'Get out! This is as far as you go. If you must make sketches of this, you'll get more than enough ideas from here. I'll pick you up on my way back.'

She scrambled to the ground, snatching her bag from the back seat, along with one of the two rugs always kept there. As he put the jeep into gear and began to move off down the sloping road, she held back her protest at what he intended doing, remembering his words on having to telephone a girl to let her know where he was going. All the same, she cried out, 'Take care... Take great care,' and received a wave in response, before he accelerated on his downward journey.

Even as he turned the first hairpin bend below her, Vesta heard a sound she immediately identified. It grew louder and louder until the ground beneath her feet began to tremble with it; a sound without a sight, as yet. Already fearful of what she could not see, her limbs turned to rubber when it was suddenly menacingly there: huge, dark, trailing flames and smoke. From behind the trees, the doomed aircraft emerged only feet from

430

the hill she was on, out of control, and hurtling towards the jeep Brad was driving. Transfixed, seeing it happen before it did, Vesta could only watch in frozen agony as the jeep swerved to the left, almost hit a tree, then swung to the right in an attempt to escape. Leaving the road, it plunged down the hillside, just as the wing of the crashing aircraft caught it and sent it somersaulting. With a deafening roar the burning machine hit the hill, and exploded in a rush of fire which quickly set the surrounding trees alight.

'Brad,' she mouthed in a terrified whisper. 'Oh, *Brad!*'

Then she was running down the sloping road towards the scene, knowing she had to be with him whatever the cost to herself. Over on Monte Cassino the battle was underway. Men were fighting face to face, one against one, inch by inch. With whole ranks falling wholesale, what did it matter if one life was taken by a cruel stroke of fate? It mattered! It mattered!

There are fifty kids in an orphanage. One is featured in the Press. Everyone wants to adopt him.

There were hundreds dying a few miles away, but this was the one she wanted to live.

The downward slope of the road made her run almost faster than she could go, threatening to throw her flat at any moment. Her heart was thudding against her ribs, and she was gasping with effort, as her legs thrust forward relentlessly in the urgent need to reach him before the fire did. Passing the roaring, flaming aircraft, she knew there must be men inside it – her own countrymen. They would have to die on this beautiful day. One must not. The trees along the lefthand side of the road were crackling and doomed as the racing fire consumed them, fanned by the breeze. Already, flames were licking out across the road, eager for the vines growing on the lower slopes. Once they caught, the conflagration would sweep downhill at speed, reducing everything in its path to ash. That thought was in her mind as she raced off the road onto soft earth. Her ankle turned and she went headlong, her face hitting the ground with a thud which brought tears to her eyes. The fall winded her further, so she was sobbing for breath by the time she reached the overturned jeep.

Brad looked to be seriously hurt as he hung over the wheel. There was blood all over his shirt, and the seat was dark with it. All she had ever heard about the dangers of moving an injured person ran through her mind, but she could not leave him to die by fire. The risk must be taken. Thinking with astonishing clarity, she snatched up the rug that had fallen from the back seat, and spread it on the ground beneath him. When she dragged him free, he would fall, and her strength would be unequal to the task of carrying him. Her only hope would be to pull him along on the rug. He bled a lot when he fell, and she told herself she had probably just killed him. But, with her eyes on the growing conflagration crossing the road no more than twenty yards away, she bent to grip the corners of the rug and start pulling.

The minutes passed. From Cassino the tumult of war rose in a crescendo as the troops inched their way up in an attempt to capture a hill where monks had formerly prayed for peace and understanding. Vesta fought her own uphill battle to beat the infant flames, before they seized the young vines and raced down to engulf her. In the sky the frenzy continued – strangers trying to kill each other over territory which was home to none of them – and still she struggled and heaved the heavy burden through the straight lines of vines. She passed the fire, which was starting to leap forward with growing ferocity, putting heat on her cheeks and drying the sweat beading there.

Only when she was well above the area where the crashed aircraft was now a blazing coffin, did she stop by the small trickling steam used as a source of irrigation, and fall gratefully beside it to drink from her cupped hands. How long she sat doing what she could for a man slowly slipping away from life, she did not know. Her shirt was stuffed into the gaping wound in his side to staunch the flow of blood, his head was cradled in her arms as she trickled water into his mouth. One or two people emerged from the broken village to walk down to the place where she sat, but they were more concerned with the destruction of the vines than they were with one more dying human.

When a staff car drew up, halted by the fire across the path, and two officers spotted her by the stream, she was hardly aware of their approach. Her hands were stained with blood, her trousers torn, her face streaked with dirt, but she was looking down at the man with her as if he were her lover.

Chapter Twenty-One

IN THE second week of May 1944 the Gustav Line dividing Italy was broken by the Allies. Monte Cassino was successfully stormed by Polish troops on the 18th. On the 4th of June the advancing army of liberation reached Rome, where cigar-smoking, gum-chewing blasphemers in khaki rode in armour-plated vehicles over ground once trod by Centurions with shields and breastplates, riding in horsed chariots.

Victorious armies change little in behaviour, however, and these modern troops accepted the acclaim of those lining the streets, then embarked on an orgy of sightseeing, intoxication, seduction and self-indulgence in the manner of those warriors of old. Two days later they celebrated again with even greater gusto. Successful landings in Normandy had put the Allies back on French soil. The beginning of the end was sensed by all. Would the war be over by Christmas – that perennial target by which all wars are hoped to end?

Vesta had been working very hard, driven by a rush of great inspiration to do some of her best work when she reached Rome. Remembering that other visit in her youth, when her father had shown her and David all the wonders of the city, she saw it now with regret that he was not with her. She wrote him several long letters, mostly concerned with her feelings about what she saw and drew, because she knew he would understand very well. To David she wrote of the military occupation of such an ancient revered city; to her mother she told of the companions who helped her find transport and accommo-dation now she no longer travelled with the members of the Press Corps. Only to Pat did she write of Brad, knowing her friend would regard it as a privileged confidence.

He was in hospital in Naples, having fought the battle to survive and won. After several massive blood transfusions he had begun to recover. Vesta had remained near him for a week, visiting every day a man who had no idea she was there. Then, because his condition had stabilised and because Rome had been occupied, she had coaxed a lift from the New Zealander who had taken her to Pompeii and gone up to Rome to work. In some obscure way, the fact that it had been Brad who had been responsible for her being in Italy inspired her to make his efforts justified by producing as much as she could. Some she threw away as sub-standard, but a great many of her sketches induced her to make further visits to venues for details. Soon, she was sending off two further shell cases containing her paintings. One fairly large picture she retained. Sticking to the style she now adopted with absolute confidence as her own, her subjects were as varied as an Italian child posing like a cherub on an ornate fountain; a GI with an organ-grinder's monkey on his shoulder being photographed by his pals for a snapshot to send home; and a young French nurse placing a handful of wild flowers on the ruins of the Cassino monastery, after the troops had moved on.

Vesta had even managed a trip to Anzio now the road from Rome was clear to the coast, and had done several pictures on what she had seen there, always finding some little amusing or moving human cameo to place against the awesome scarred background. With the passage of time, she had discovered deeper variety in Gerald Bream's addage about good shining through. Goodness came in many guises, she had discovered, and he was invariably right, even if she sometimes had to look hard for it.

Her search for the good in the midst of all else was suddenly suspended when an army order arrived, directing that she was to return to England to discuss the possibility of going to France to follow the advance into Europe, after a period of leave. The news filled her with mixed emotions. It would be marvellous to go home and see her family after almost two years. It would also be marvellous to be given the opportunity to cover the defeat of the German army, which would further her professional scope and reputation. Yet how could she bear to leave Italy when it had such a special place in her heart?

A young officer from Milwaukee drove her down to Naples. He was taking a weekend trip to see a girl he had fallen for rather heavily, and since he was of Italian descent, was all set to speak to her father about the future.

'I wish you luck, Lieutenant,' smiled Vesta when she was told of his plans.

'Call me Renzo,' he invited breezily as they left Rome, 'and we pronounce it *Loo*tenant.'

'I'll try to remember,' she promised, lost in thoughts of a

desert oasis and a brown man looking at her as if she were an apparition in that pith-helmet.

The young American was good company: cheerful, extrovert, unshakable in his belief that America was the only nation with a great future, and quite endearingly awed when she let slip that her father had a knighthood. But when he revealed to her the contents of the literature that had been issued to American troops before going to Britain, she was highly amused.

'Did you really find us unwashed through lack of soap, living on so little you could not accept an invitation without taking your own provisions, and our children without a toy in sight and suffering from malnutrition?' she asked.

He shook his head, smiling. 'I found you all darned stiff-necked, at first. Then I discovered the guys had been taking the whole thing so seriously the British thought we were patronising them, throwing our weight around by trying to help out with food parcels and things for the kids. You sure are a proud race.'

'I think our pride has taken a fearful knock over the last five years,' she told him. 'I hope your first impression was softened with further acquaintance.'

'Sure it was – once you folk realised we were often hicks who hadn't even been beyond the next state before this war, so were out of our depth and more than a little homesick.'

'My father always used to maintain that international understanding between ordinary peoples of the world would prevent wars. It's the greed or idiocy of rulers which creates the controversy, but the teeming masses which fight the battles. If the ordinary people refused to take up arms against each other, the leaders would be forced to settle their differences diplomatically, wouldn't they?'

He glanced at her as he drove. 'You spoke of your father in the past tense. Is he dead?'

'No, but I think his idealistic views are. Poor Daddy seems to have been a lone voice in the wilderness.'

Pulling up in a small cobbled square, her companion said, 'Thank God we sometimes listen to them, or the world would have come to an end long ago.' He climbed from behind the wheel and grinned. 'Since it ain't, let's go see if we can get some coffee here, shall we?'

They reached Naples in the late afternoon and parted to visit the respective loves of their lives, except that Vesta did not reveal as much to the friendly American. The hospital seemed more crowded than ever with casualties, which surprised her since there were more forward hospitals taking wounded from the continuing fierce campaign north of Rome, where the Germans were retreating only very slowly. Brad had been moved to another ward, where the sister in charge did not know Vesta.

'Mr Holland?' repeated the girl, then smiled. 'Ah, you must be his wife. We were told you would be arriving shortly.'

'I'm a friend,' Vesta corrected with difficulty, as the muscles of her face appeared to have tightened up. 'More of a professional colleague, I suppose. How is he?'

'Well enough to have my nurses covered in blushes,' was the caustic response. 'You'll find him in the end bed on the right.'

Taking a deep breath, she began walking between the beds containing wounded officers, all very interested in the girl in a crisp cotton dress of ice blue, which contrasted so well with her tanned skin. Brad's smile was still heartbreaking, but he looked drawn and showed the ravages of pain as he lay against the pillows, his open pyjama jacket revealing the bandages around his chest. His dark eyes were so full of gladness it hurt.

'Well, well, I wondered when you'd find time to visit an old buddy.'

'You've got a nerve,' she said. 'For an entire week I came with grapes and all the usual things one takes to hospital patients. You snored through every visit.'

'I never snore,' he announced, looking at her with a kind of hunger that made her weak.

'Yes, you do. I hardly slept a wink in the desert with you under the truck that night.'

'Ah, that. That was inebriated breathing, not snoring.'

She looked at the face narrowed by illness and etched with suffering, remembering every moment they had spent together. Had she made the greatest mistake of her life by sending him from her room that night in Santa Milia?

'How are you now?'

'Fine ... Just fine. Sit down. No, not there. On the bed!'

She sat on the edge of it, supremely conscious of his nearness.

'You look staggeringly beautiful,' he said in a low voice, 'and I've missed you like hell.'

'I'm flying home tomorrow,' she told him.

He gazed at her for a moment. 'You sure know how to deal out the aces.'

'Here's another. Your wife is arriving shortly.'

'I had a cable from the London office. Christ knows what's behind it. Gloria is hardly the ministering angel type.'

436

'Oh ... What type is she?'

'Very unforgiving.'

'Of what?'

His eyes narrowed thoughtfully. 'She called it infidelity.'

'What did you call it?' she asked, feeling suddenly hollow.

'You've seen the way we work,' he said with a weary gesture of his hand. 'Sometimes things get on top of you. A new place each night, some crummy room in a small town full of strangers, too much to drink, and suddenly you're so goddam lonely and haunted you need someone to ease it.'

'Like the girl at Santa Milia?'

He sighed heavily. 'That really got at you, didn't it?'

'Gloria is right. I'd call it infidelity, too.'

'With you it would have been,' came his scorching comment. 'Rosa or Lucia with the flashing eyes was purely medicinal.'

'Won't there always be a Rosa or Lucia?'

'I'm the guy who asks probing questions. You just paint real war, remember?'

Trying to recover from the inference of his earlier remark, she changed the subject. 'I've brought you a farewell present.'

'Why are you leaving?' he asked with marked heaviness of tone.

'I'm in the army and orders have arrived. After a spell of home leave, I may be sent to cover the Allied advance in France.'

'I'm sure you will. Watch yourself over there.'

'I'm sorry you missed the breakthrough and the entry into Rome,' she said, conscious of the men in the other beds watching them with interest. 'I tried to write it all down for you, but I'm an artist with paint, not words.'

He was still looking at her with that hunger. 'They told me you saved my life.'

With her defences crashing around her she said, 'You know how it is when an aircraft dives into a jeep and there's no one around but you.'

A long pause, then he said, 'It would have made a hell of an exclusive.'

She smiled shakily. 'Pity you missed it.'

He shifted against his pillows, and the movement brought his hand into contact with hers. 'Did you really come every day for a week?'

'I had nowhere else to go. The jeep was smashed up, and the troops were too busy advancing on Rome to look after me.'

'But I hope you got some good pictures to take home.'

She nodded and gave him the rolled paper she had brought

437

with her. 'This one is for you. It's done from memory and is frightfully melodramatic, but I thought it might compensate for the exclusive you didn't get.'

He unrolled it carefully and sat staring at the water colour of an aircraft on fire plunging headlong towards a jeep that was swerving into some trees. In the background there was a hill covered in the ruin of a monastery. Then he looked up at her and smiled in a way that told her she must go before she made a fool of herself.

'You're darn right, it is melodramatic ... And you know it'll never compensate for what I didn't get.'

She got to her feet, trying to force a smile. 'I really do have to go. There's all my packing, and presents to buy for the family.'

'Sure. I understand how it is,' he said, looking ridiculously romantic and helpless. 'Thanks for stopping by on your way out.'

Let me get away with dignity, she prayed. 'Take care from now on.'

'You too.'

'Well ... Goodbye, Brad.'

'So long, Vic.'

The ward was starting to shimmer as she forced herself to walk away from him; the corridors of the hospital were a complete blur by the time she reached the door. The streets of Naples could have been the streets of anywhere. Dear heaven, this was worse, far worse, than Felix. Then, she had only lost her innocence. Now she had lost her motivation.

London in the middle of June 1944 looked sad and broken – a dignified old lady, whose sparkling autumn heyday had been cruelly marred by a disease that was eating away her flesh and crippling her strength. Vesta was shocked. She had forgotten about the huge areas of devastation; the flattened spaces in the midst of historic grandeur. Almost two years in Egypt and Italy had taken from her memory the piled sandbags, the blackout, ration books, tawdry 'utility' clothes, British Restaurants, propaganda posters urging DIG FOR VICTORY or warning that CARELESS TALK COSTS LIVES. Most of all she had forgotten the white and weary faces of those who had fought a five-year battle against bombing, bereavement, deprivation, despair and surrender.

Yet, in many ways, London had changed drastically since she had left it. She could have been in New York judging by the accents and the uniforms of those thronging the streets. It was all so American: Rainbow Corner, the American Red Cross, jeeps, glamorous WAACs, gum-chewing free-and-easy soldiers wolf-whistling after girls; hamburgers, doughnuts, a mysterious substance called peanut butter; lifts being termed 'elevators' and pavements becoming 'sidewalks'; Glenn Miller and Bing Crosby; Lana Turner and Rita Hayworth. The Yanks were 'over here' with a vengeance. She smiled to herself as she remembered a young lieutenant – no, *lootenant* – who had driven her to Naples saying the British had appeared stiff-necked and proud towards their brash homesick allies. Understanding and integration appeared to be well underway now. But each and every one of those people from across the Atlantic reminded her of someone she was trying to forget – had to forget.

When she had reached London it was too late to go down to Dorset, so she went straight to the apartment. Sandy greeted her with something akin to a blush, and she wondered, with her new perception, whether he had always nursed a secret liking for her.

'I suppose it's too much to hope that Daddy is here,' she said after their initial exchange. 'That miserable old Ministry of his would never let him slip away just to see the daughter who has been out of the country for two years.'

'Actually, he's on a few days' leave at Tarrant Hall,' said Sandy as he followed her into the sitting room.

'Marvellous! He'll be there when I go down tomorrow.' She looked around with great pleasure, turning to say, 'This room so reflects his tastes and personality he seems to be here even when absent. So many beautiful things, so many reflections of his international interests, I've always loved the atmosphere of this place.' She sank into one of the chairs. 'Do you think Mrs James could manage a quick pot of tea?'

'She isn't here, I'm afraid. It's her day off. But I can make some for you.'

'I wouldn't dream of letting you,' she declared. 'I'll have a glass of wine instead.'

He smiled. 'Taken to drink, have you? You've certainly changed.'

'Have one with me. I hate drinking alone.'

'I'd love to, but could you bear to hang on for around a quarter of an hour? I was just finishing a vital report that has to go off tonight.'

She made a face. 'You and your reports! I don't know what you find to do with Daddy away so much of the time. All right, while I'm waiting I'll ring Mummy to tell her I'll be down tomorrow. She knew I was arriving some time this week, but military travel arrangements are so fluid it's impossible to be more accurate.' Getting to her feet again, she added, 'I can't believe my luck in coinciding with Daddy on leave.'

'He hasn't been too well, as it happens,' came the unwelcome information. 'Since Christmas work seems to have been getting on top of him to a disturbing degree.'

'You don't mean he's on sick leave?' she asked sharply.

'Oh, no. I think he's just very very tired. He's had a great deal of responsibility since the beginning of the war, and Lady Sheridan's breakdown when David was reported missing put extra strain on him.'

'Poor old Daddy! Good thing I'm going home. He'll cheer up when I tell him all about Rome and Naples, to say nothing of all the wonderful paintable villages I saw. Hurry up with your beastly report, Sandy. Is there anything to eat with the wine, by the way?'

'Of course. Cold pie and salad. Mrs James left it all ready.'

'Good. I'm ravenous.'

She telephoned Tarrant Hall. Her parents were delighted that she would be there the next day, and promised to send the pony and trap to Greater Tarrant station to meet the train. They both sounded lively enough, and she thought Sandy must have exaggerated her father's condition. He was certainly eager to hear all her adventures and plans. After speaking to them she had rung Pat, and they had fallen immediately into their old familiar friendship, as if two years had not passed since their last meeting. They talked so long, Sandy had finished his work and returned with a tray of food and a bottle with two glasses.

'I must go, Pat,' she said. 'Sandy is here armed with a most frightful-looking pie, some limp lettuce and a bottle of Vat Blankety Blanc, by the look of it. He's looking daggers at me for that. See you tomorrow. Come over for dinner. Oh, I suppose you'll be over to see Dirk, anyway.'

'He can wait. You're more important, Vee,' came the response that made Vesta wonder just how her friend regarded the man who wanted to marry her. Much like her own attitude to Philip Bream. She had not thought of him since leaving Cairo, and it had never occurred to her to write and tell him she was coming home. Like Pat's South African, he could wait.

What was left of the evening passed very pleasantly. She found Sandy very good company now. Perhaps he always had been, and it was she who had changed. They talked about the war, and how it would very likely not be over by Christmas because of the fierce opposition by the Germans in Normandy, which was slowing the reoccupation to a worrying degree. It was always the same – successful landings with heavy casualties, then stalemate while the opposing sides threw everything they had at each other.

'The only people who seem to have the routine down to a fine art are the Japanese,' said Sandy. 'As David would tell you if he could bring himself to speak of it.'

'How is he?' she asked sipping the Vat Blankety Blanc and comparing it unfavourably with the wine Brad had bought by the caseful.

'His hands are pretty good now, and he's put on a bit of weight. But he's still very withdrawn, poor devil. We'll probably never know the full details of what those bastards did to him during those three days.'

'What *who* did to him during *which* three days?' she asked in curiosity.

'The ... er ...' he broke off in almost embarrassed fashion. 'Those months in the jungle, I meant. There's every hope you'll see him very soon. He has an undemanding posting with Transport Command – gets a lot of time off.'

Vesta went to bed around midnight. She was tired, but talking to Sandy had delayed the moment when she was alone in the darkness and had nothing to deaden her heartache. She had drunk her full share of the wine in the hope that it would send her to sleep quickly. Once more, she had been curious about the presence in the bathroom of all manner of articles suggesting large numbers of guests. She had not asked her father about it last time; Sandy would have to solve the mystery for her in the morning. The wine certainly made her drowsy, and her thoughts of Brad were happy ones that night.

In the midst of a memory of him waving his arms and shouting imprecations at an old man leading a laden mule right through the centre of a cobbled street, she grew aware of a peculiar sound overhead. It resembled the steady loud throb of a motor cycle growing nearer and nearer, but how could it be above her, instead of in the street below? The curious noise grew louder, and it appeared to be approaching the apartment like a great purring aircraft. Completely puzzled, she threw back the sheet and left the bed to go to the window. Halfway there the sound stopped abruptly. It made no sense to her, but she turned back to the bed, deciding there would be nothing to see now. As she was on the point of settling back to sleep, there came a roar like the seven seas all breaking together on one shore, and a hurricane raced in through the bedroom window to catch up the bed and hurl it headlong into darkness, where

441

she hit something with such force it seemed her head would split open.

Pain and fear stayed with her as she lay obliquely head downward in total blackness, choking on the dust that was settling on her like fine rain. Her ears were ringing with the sound of someone calling Sandy's name, and it was some time before she realised it was her own voice, crying in a wilderness where she appeared to be the only living creature. Cold air was reaching her from somewhere above. Against her back was a slab of concrete; across her chest was some thick object, not resting on her, but preventing her from moving. All around were the fearful sounds of slithering crashing debris: a four-storey apartment building slowly collapsing. Terror rose to catch her by the throat. Death was sitting right beside her here, waiting for her to move and dislodge that unstable pile on which she was lying; waiting for some beam, some chunk of plaster, some precarious arrangement of bricks to give way under pressure and hurtle her down to be buried alive.

Carefully, with infinite slowness, she moved her fingers in an attempt to fasten them onto something more substantial than rubble or glass. There appeared to be some kind of metal bar by her left hand and, holding her breath, she gradually closed her fingers around it in a tight grip – a futile move, since the bar would go with her if the building collapsed further. But the comfort of holding something solid was considerable, as she continued to lie with the beat of her pulse shaking her whole body, wondering how long it would be before anybody arrived on the scene, and how they would know she was there.

She began to pray. Around her neck was the gold pendant of Tarrant Royal church her father had given her. The chain was pulling against her flesh, so she knew it was still there. It helped with her prayers, and the prayers helped her present sensation of loneliness and peril. An indeterminable period later, the faint sound of voices reached her from somewhere below her head, calling that help was on the way, and to keep as still as possible.

'Oh, thank you. Thank you,' she whispered to God, nevertheless thinking that, no matter how still she kept, she would still fall headlong if her rescuers shifted debris carelessly. Her danger seemed increased with help so near, and she lay in her black world wondering wildly if the Almighty was about to reverse the leniency he had shown when he had taken five members of Hut 4 instead of all six. Had her reprieve been short?

442

'Anyone there? Anyone there?' called a voice remarkably close.

'Yes, yes, I'm here.' Fine powder fell into her mouth, and she retched. 'Here I am,' she rasped in desperation lest they pass by unheeding. 'Be careful. It's all slipping.'

Tightening her hold on the metal bar, she gasped as everything shifted menacingly. 'Ooh! Are you still there?'

'I ain't going nowhere, miss, don't you fear,' said a warm, comforting voice. 'Just you 'old on 'til I reach you.'

'Yes... Yes, I will.'

'What's yer name, luv?'

'Vesta,' she said in clipped tone, as she heard bricks rumbling downward to crash a long way below in the street.

'That's pretty. Very unusual that. How old are you?'

'I'm... I think I'm twenty-four. Oh, what's that?'

'Just my pal movin' some stuff that's in our way. Twenty-four, eh. Married, are yer?'

Hanging upside down, it seemed an absurd conversation to have with a stranger. 'I... No. Not yet.'

'Got a good-lookin' boyfriend?'

'Not... not at the moment.'

'Cor, I knew this was my lucky day, luv,' came the voice from very near now. 'Ah, there you are! Right as ninepence.'

'I can't see you,' she told him nervously. 'Please be careful. This is all moving at the slightest touch.'

'Don't you worry, miss. Me and Bill've done this more times than we care to remember. All through the Blitz, and we ain't lost anyone yet.'

Suddenly there was a great rush and clatter nearby, which set her sliding head downward two feet or more before halting again against something fairly solid.

'Please, please hurry,' she begged in wobbly tones.

Silence.

'Are you still there?' she cried. 'Please, are you and Bill still there?'

'Course we are, luv,' panted the baritone voice. 'Didn't I tell you I wasn't going nowhere tonight? You lay there nice and still – quiet as a mouse – while Bill and me moves this girder.'

There was another terrifying slither above her, and she bit her lip so hard she tasted blood, every muscle tensed for the expected death plunge.

'That's better,' mumbled Bill's pal, sounding considerably closer now. 'We've just got to shift this beam across you and you'll be free.'

443

'I can't see you yet,' she whispered, fighting back the tears.

'Well, now, I ain't that much to look at,' he responded with a grunt. 'But me mum tells me I got a lovely personality.'

There was a loud crack directly beneath her, and she began sliding downward faster and faster. *I'm going!* she screamed. But hands grabbed her legs and halted her progress.

'Right, luv, I've got you safe now.' They were the most wonderful words she had ever heard. 'Bill and me's going to get you up here with us where it's clear. Then we'll pass you down the line. Just you put yourself in our hands and don't struggle. Righto, here we go.'

Slowly she was tugged upwards by her legs until a man in a rough coat caught her shoulders, and pulled her upright against him.

'Oh, thank you, thank you,' she sobbed, hanging on to him for dear life. 'Thank you, thank you.'

'It's a pleasure, luv,' said the cheery voice. 'Off you go, now. Just relax and they'll get you down ter the bottom where there's ambulances.'

'Please get Sandy,' she begged. 'Please get Sandy.'

'Never fret, we'll get everyone out, miss. See you on the Christmas tree,' he finished with a laugh.

A series of hands held her and lifted her through the blackest night she had ever known. All the voices were calm and confident, but no one appeared to have seen Sandy. She was no longer afraid; just icy cold, and so sleepy she could not keep her eyes open. They put her on a bed of some kind, all wrapped in blankets that smelled of iodine. Although she was asleep she heard the bells ringing as they raced through the streets. This had all happened before, and there should be a golden chocolate box somewhere. They did not know she was safe; that she was not beneath the rubble of Hut 4.

I'm the last one. I'm the last one. I'm the last one.

She was murmuring that when she woke after a long sleep and heard people talking all around her. The voices were dear and familiar. She lay for a moment or two just listening to them, realising that she must be in hospital somewhere because there were bandages around her head, and her right leg throbbed with pain.

'Mummy...? Daddy?'

'Hallo, dear,' said her mother in a quavering voice. 'We thought you'd never come to. How are you feeling?'

'All right... Well, tired,' she confessed.

A hand took hers. There were two fingers missing from it, and it was shaking. 'I gather you were very courageous, which is exactly what I would have expected of you, Vesta.'

'What happened, Daddy? What was it?' she asked drowsily.

'A new type of bomb which flies on its own. They drop indiscriminately wherever they happen to be when the motor cuts out. It seems . . . it seems humanity has taken another step towards total barbarism.'

She lay for a while trying to sort that information out, remembering the strange sound of an aerial motor cycle. It was a sound she would never forget. Then she asked quickly, 'What about Sandy? Is he all right?'

'No, my dear,' he told her in a broken voice. 'I'm afraid the poor fellow was killed. It must have been instantaneous.'

Immense sadness filled her, and she grew tearful very quickly. 'Oh, how terrible! Poor Sandy. We had such a nice supper together . . . although I was rather rude about Mrs James's pie and salad.'

'I'm sure you weren't, dear,' said her mother in the same quavering voice. 'Don't worry yourself about it.'

'Your lovely things, Daddy, your lovely priceless things,' she remembered then, the tears flowing faster than ever. 'You took years to collect them, now they've gone in a moment.'

After a momentary pause, he said, 'What are things compared with human life? You survived. That's what is important.'

A small voice within her suddenly questioned that statement. Surely Sandy had been more worthy of survival than she . . . And Minnie with her indomitable spirit, Peter Main who had fought so courageously in the desert and treated her with such warm courtesy; all David's friends who had fought the Battle of Britain, and those who had been lost with Singapore; the sunburned warriors roasted in blazing tanks; those who had battled time and again up the slopes of Monte Cassino, only to fall and become part of that terrible desolate hillside; the Italian girl by the roadside, with flowers resembling a wreath on her breast – even the mule with its body ripped open, which died in agony. Surely they had been more worthy of survival than a girl who painted pictures of them all to sell, and who possessed such cold pride she had given nothing of human love and understanding to those who had reached for it in a time of need.

Racked with sobs she clutched her father's hand in something approaching desperation. 'Take me home. Please just take me home.'

'I have never been able to categorise our relationship, Bill,'

445

Chris confessed as they sat with brandy after dinner in the large apartment over the London consulting room. 'You have been so many things rolled into one throughout my life – and I'm speaking of the life which began when I was nineteen. Apart from being the person responsible for saving my sanity, you've been father, brother, friend, adviser, and champion of my various causes.' He gave a taut smile. 'In fact, at one point in this war I told myself you'd be the only one to grieve at my funeral.'

Bill studied him thoughtfully. 'This is leading up to a confession of some kind. I've known you for nearly thirty years, old son, and if I really have been all those things you listed, it's high time you were grieving at *my* funeral. I'm staggered that the angels haven't called me to join them long ago.'

'It's all those ripe Australian oaths. They won't give you the wings to go with that halo until you purify your language.' He sobered swiftly to add, 'Yes, it is a confession. One I could only make to you.'

'Christ, it's that kind of confession, is it?'

'It is when I'm about to abuse our years of friendship.'

Bill dropped his bantering manner. 'Have another tot with me, then go ahead.'

With his glass re-charged Chris began. 'You have always realised that my work with the Ministry is not all I have been engaged in since the start of the war. I have enjoyed no aspect of it, and several times asked to be relieved of something I found distasteful in the extreme, aside from being the reverse of all I have worked for since 1918. My entire nature cries out against it, but my fluency in so many languages and my familiarity with so much of Europe and the rest of the world is of great value to secret organisations, and I have had to suppress my dislike for the sake of those continually risking their lives in occupied countries. We are all doing jobs we dislike, aren't we? But the inability to tell my family what I have been engaged in hasn't made life easier for me.'

'Didn't I tell you some months ago you'd crack up again if you didn't find an outlet? I believe I advocated a young redhead.'

'We met at a party,' Chris told him, 'and both of us knew immediately it was for the rest of my life.'

'*That* wasn't my advice.'

'I know. I know,' he said. 'She was extremely beautiful, cultured, multi-lingual; an artist of international repute. I was introduced as Sir Christopher, with no hint of a uniform or

446

army rank. I decided to keep things that way. My dedication to work, which was constantly condemned by my family, prevented my meeting her more than a couple of times in six months. When I happened to be free for an evening, she was often away in the country on artistic commissions. We spent several evenings together in her London apartment, both being extremely discreet for obvious reasons. We talked about art, mutual acquaintances in Europe, cities we loved, music – she is an accomplished pianist – and conversed in any number of languages for the pure pleasure of it. It was all extremely civilised,' he added, recalling the evenings they had shared before physical love.

'I was with her when I received the news that David had been lost over Sumatran jungle and presumed dead. After that I didn't see her for some months, until everything piled up to hint at the breakdown you had warned me about. They gave me a month off, and I went to her for the kind of help even you couldn't offer. We went to Scotland, and became lovers. That was when I knew I would leave Marion at the end of the war and start a new life with Sonja.'

Bill stared at him. 'Christ, you're serious, aren't you?'

'Oh, yes.' He appealed to the man who had brought him through the other war. 'Marion and I stuck at our marriage for David's sake, at first. Then for Vesta, too. It worked well enough until war intervened again. Marion had just made it crystal clear that David was her only reason for living, and I suddenly saw my life slipping away from me. Bill, how can a man betray a woman who has no love for him?'

His friend looked at him with a frown. 'Why are you telling me all this now?'

'Just before Christmas Sonja and I came face-to-face unexpectedly – I as Lieutenant Colonel Sheridan of a special unit, she as an agent of a similar unit run by the Free French. The mutual shock was so great we gave ourselves away to a man who has always disliked and resented me. It then transpired that our relationship had been monitored as highly suspect. Her apartment had been entered, and every moment we had spent together had been heard by men sitting somewhere with earphones on, and recorded for posterity.'

'*Jesus!*' Bill took in the implications of that for a moment or two. 'Had you absolutely no idea what she was doing?'

'Of course not! She was trained in subterfuge, and so was I,' he said heatedly. 'But people talk in their sleep, even if they are highly trained. We check that before sending anyone out. So they listened in on us.'

447

Bill got up, plainly disturbed by all he was hearing. 'Chris, you're breaking all the rules by telling me this now. Why?'

He got to his feet also. 'Our troops are now in France. It's only a matter of weeks before there'll be no more need for what I'm doing. I'm tired of it, Bill. Tired of being accused by my family of putting my career before my duty to them, tired of lies, tired of using the intelligence God saw fit to give me for dark and sinister purposes. My marriage is irretrievably lost, my son is scarred without and within, my daughter is shattered by all she has seen during the past five years. Sandy, who was almost like a son, has been killed by one of those terrible pilotless bombs. My London home has been reduced to rubble along with the works of art I have collected during twenty years of my life, not the least of them being two of Vesta's paintings, and a gift from Sonja which was extremely precious to me.'

Very worked up by now, he went on, 'You told me to fight back after the last war. You said it was men like me to whom the world would look to create the wonderful new future. Well, I gave twenty-one years to the task. I did what I could for the world and had it flung back in my face. I want my life to myself now.' Walking restlessly to a chair, he gripped the back of it hard. 'Marion once accused me of being so busy trying to love the whole world I had never cared for one single individual. I do now. I want her, Bill. I want my delayed youth and happiness. If I lose Sonja, not all your professional skill will save me this time.'

With a sigh, his friend sat heavily, shaking his head. 'When this war ends memorials will be going up all over the place, as they did last time. They'll be inscribed with the names of the fallen. Some will have died heroically, as Rex did; others will have died faithfully carrying out onerous duties, like Roland. Some of those named on a slab of fancy stone erected as a kind of shrine will have been mean and vicious, cowardly, even. Yet, by dying, they'll be honoured as heroes. Men like you will be expected to carry on, pick up the threads they dropped five years ago. Your brand of suffering and heroism always goes unsung, Chris.'

He was angry; angry and bitter. 'I didn't tell you this so that you could quote a lot of sentimental patriotic tripe. If you want to know about suffering and heroism ask David. He was brutally tortured by Japanese for three days because he refused to betray the whereabouts of men who were forced to abandon him to the enemy. Ask him about the agony he endured to save the lives of men who have doubtless been killed by now, anyway. Or ask Vesta how she is managing to equate her Christian faith with the orgy of pain and destruction she has recorded with her brush and high sensitivity. Around her neck she wears the gold pendant of Tarrant Royal church I gave her when she was twenty-one; refuses to take it off. After all she has been through, only unshakable courage could maintain such faith in good over evil.'

'Wearing that pendant shows faith in *you*, Chris. Don't disillusion her – not now, when it's almost over.'

Full of belligerence, Chris cried, 'I sincerely hope that's not the prelude to a speech about duty to my children. David has become his own man in a manner that makes me immensely proud of his sheer strength of character. Vesta's present disorientation is only temporary, and will probably serve to draw Marion closer to her. They'll both come through this war successfully without me.'

His old friend looked at him with something close to sadness. 'You really do mean to give up everything for Sonja, don't you?'

'There's nothing left to give up. It has all been gradually slipping away from me over the years.'

'She must be a bloody wonderful woman.'

'I've asked her to come here this evening. That's what I meant about abusing your friendship.' He walked back to pick up his glass again, feeling the need of the fiery spirit. 'You've been good enough to let me use your apartment since mine was blown apart, and I imagine it's the height of bad manners to conduct a liaison beneath the roof of my wife's best and closest friend. But the knowledge that every word we have said to each other under her roof was heard by others – even translated from several languages by complete strangers – makes it impossible to meet there again. To book a room in a hotel as Mr and Mrs Smith turns what we feel for each other into something squalid, and I know she would never agree to it. I need to be alone with her in surroundings that are neither sordid, nor reminiscent of our former times together, when we both hid secrets from each other.' He tossed back the remainder of the brandy. 'If you object to my seeing her here, you have every justification for kicking me out. I will undertake to do nothing you might view as a betrayal to Marion if you consent, however.'

'Good God, man, I don't give a damn what you do here. For Christ's sake, what do you think this place is – a monastery? I can recognise a man at the end of his tether when I see one, and

449

you've been there for months, Chris. I only wish I could help all poor sods by simply letting them go to bed with the woman they love in my apartment.'

Chris waited for Sonja in a bleak mood. When he had spoken to her on the telephone the new restraint between them had still been apparent, and she had made it quite clear that she had only contacted him because she had read of the bombing of his apartment in the newspaper. He had not known she was back in England, and had felt unbelievable relief at the sound of her voice.

Audibly upset, she had said, 'These terrible weapons. All we have been trying to do has not been enough. They have these places so well hidden it is almost impossible to find them. I am so sorry.'

Equally overwrought, he had replied, 'For heaven's sake, you can't take personal responsibility for it. Haven't you done enough already?'

'Please, let us not discuss that again,' had been her quiet response. 'We should only make each other unhappy.'

Nevertheless, she had agreed to meet him that evening, even though he sensed she was doubtful of the wisdom of it. Now the confrontation was upon him, he realised Bill's apartment was very starkly masculine, which, together with the fact that their absent host was closely associated with his past life, would not help to break down the barrier between them. Desperate to win her back, he moved about the large room, too restless to sit and wait for her arrival. By the time the doorbell rang, he was so tense he flinched at the sound, so he stood trying to gain some control before going to let her in.

They stood looking at each other as if there was nothing else in the world but that moment, and what they still felt for each other after six months of danger-filled absence. Sonja looked tense and pale, but he thought her stunningly lovely in a cream silk suit, with ropes of opalescent royal blue beads. Her hair was secured in a severe chignon banded with a royal blue Italian scarf. Paul de Martineau's heavy gold bracelet was on her right wrist. He made no attempt to touch her, and neither of them smiled a greeting.

'Thank you for coming,' he said quietly.

She walked in and glanced around the large sitting room lined with bookcases full of medical volumes, furnished without imagination, with not an ornament or picture to relieve its austere practicality. Bill Chandler was no aesthete.

450

'Where is your friend?'

'He had an evening engagement.'

'I see.'

'Won't you sit down?' Oh God, he thought as he said it, I sound like an employer about to conduct an interview instead of her lover.

She sat on a huge settee, unrelaxed and wary. He felt he should ask for a list of her qualifications, instead of confessing that life had been hell since they had been parted, that he had to win her back or go out of his mind.

She looked up at him and broke the awkwardness with a soft enquiry concerning Vesta. 'Your daughter is recovering from her ordeal?'

'She has to, like everyone else these days,' he said in clipped tones. 'Initial shock is wearing off, but it appears to have left her with a revulsion against the great talent she was given. She vows she will never paint again, claims that her muse has fled. She has courage. She is a fighter. Time will bring it back, I feel certain.' He sighed. 'I once had two beautiful talented children with the whole free world before them. Now...'

'Your son picked me up on one return,' she told him in quiet tones. 'I could not speak of it to you then, but I knew it must be he from your description of his injuries. If he was once like you then life has been cruel to him, but any man who can suffer as he undoubtedly did, then go on to pursue what he is now doing, cannot fail to be splendid. Such confidence, such cool courage to land in dangerous conditions to fetch us ... And he has your heartbreaking smile. It defies the scars. You must feel great pride in him. Your daughter will give you equal pride with her ability to ride out her present affliction. Her paintings reveal strong personality, and the true artist will never be denied the gift of creativity.'

'You are an artist,' he reminded her. 'What if you were robbed of the ability to create beauty as a result of the dangerous game you play?'

She frowned at the obvious challenge in his tone. 'Your daughter was a helpless victim. I faced the challenge willingly, knowing it was a game worth playing for even the smallest success. Against that Sonja Koltay is unimportant.'

Her words seemed to widen the gulf now between them. 'That makes me unimportant, also.'

'No, never that,' she reproved, 'but I tried to make you consider "now" rather than "forever", I agree.'

He stood looking down at her overwhelming femininity.

'You tried and failed,' he finally confessed. 'There has never been a woman who has so possessed a man the way you have possessed me.'

Leaning forward, she reached for his hands and drew him down beside her. 'I have always been honoured by your love, my dear. Let me not stand condemned by it.'

He took her hands to kiss them passionately. 'Then I must not be condemned for wanting to protect you. If you are honoured by my love, you should feel further honoured by my pain. I have known suffering of various kinds in my life, but none has been as acute as the anguish of the past months, knowing you were over there. Can you understand how your courage unmans me?' he demanded huskily. 'To sit safely behind a desk while you are risking the most fearful danger makes a mockery of every moment we have spent together.'

'No ... Oh, no,' she cried softly, her eyes dark with distress. 'How can you think this?'

'How can I not? How could any man not? Don't you see, I wanted to be all things to you.'

'But you are! You have been,' she insisted, deeply upset. 'If I have failed to show this, then how can I possess you as wholly as you say?' Her troubled gaze searched his face. 'We are experienced mature people, are we not? It cannot be that you are foolish enough to imagine a knight on a white charger.'

He thought of the manner in which he loved her, of their weeks in Scotland, their wildly romantic nights in her apartment, which had brought to life a dream he had held within him since he had pulled Laura's lifeless body from a burning theatre. He thought of impassioned words spoken in the languages of hot-blooded races, chilled wine and the fire of Liszt enchanting his senses, he thought of fulfilment of mind and body. He thought of delayed youth miraculously discovered in one glance at a party. 'Would it be so very foolish?' he asked sadly.

With matching sadness she studied his face for a moment or two, then let out a soft sigh. 'No, my dearest one, I see that with you it would not be in the least foolish.' Drawing her hands from his, she let them fall to her lap. 'So I must now tell you some things that will help you to understand and forgive me.'

'It's not you I condemn,' he told her swiftly, 'It's myself.'

'Then, that *is* unforgivably foolish. Each person has to do what is there to be done, and not be condemned for it.' She leant back against the unyielding brown leather, somehow putting a world of distance between them by doing so. 'When

452

Paul was murdered I knew it was only a matter of time before attention would turn to me. Others thought so, also, and I was offered the chance to come to England. France fell, and many people were trapped. Some felt they could better serve by remaining there; some would not leave for fear of reprisals to their families. A few felt loyalty only to their life's work, and did not care what was happening around them. For some, like myself, France was not their true homeland, and brutality from oppressors was not new. We were asked to consider work for which we were highly qualified, both by natural gifts and by our mixed blood.'

She gave a very faint smile. 'My dearest knight, I have not been for the past four years blowing up trains and setting ambushes in the forests and mountains, as you so clearly imagine. All I have done is to act as a courier to men and women anxious to reach safety, and who could not do so without aid. I have escorted from occupied countries, as well as those allied to the German cause, people of letters and learning, doctors, financiers and industrialists who felt their services should be used by those fighting a system which had become totally destructive and vile. Many of these people had been known to me or to my father. Sometimes I managed to persuade others to see the sickness in the régime they had reluctantly supported, and eventually brought them out to join us here.' Her eyes clouded momentarily. 'Sometimes it was too late, and I arrived to discover their courage had failed, or they were too ill by then to undertake such a harrowing journey. But my many languages and my familiarity with so much of Europe allowed me to bring a large number successfully to safety, where their individual talents have been especially helpful.'

Chris heard all that with his head full of pictures of trains hurtling through snowy landscapes, small buses grinding up zig-zag mountain passes, ferries crossing lakes and fjords filled with water as still as glass, and a slender red-haired woman changing nationalities at every border, where she calmly ushered her companions through heavily guarded posts and past armed guards to reach a field within range of an RAF Lysander.

Through the thickness in his throat he said, 'But you have been doing something other than that for these six months, working for us.'

'It was not so very different, my dear,' she contradicted gently. 'I lived as the person you invented for me, and moved about investigating those places photographed from the air as

453

possible sites for the new bomb. All I did was travel and report, as I have always done.' She moved her hand in a weary gesture. 'For a while it was of some use, I think, and the RAF did delay the work. But the scale of development is too great . . . and your daughter became one of the victims of our inadequacy.'

He seized her hands again. 'She was the victim of war, not anyone's inadequacy. It could have happened to her at any time during these past five years.'

'Yet it happened here in London with a weapon we worked to destroy. It was a shock to read of it in my newspaper,' she admitted in a voice that betrayed her growing emotion. 'That poor young man crushed beneath the ruins of your home I had never entered. I thought . . . I thought, what if it had been you, dead with anger still between us. Such sorrow would have been almost more than I could accept.'

'You felt that, even with the comforting evidence that I was still alive?' he cried. 'Then how do you think I have lived through these months with no news of you whatever? Frith ensured that I was told nothing by those receiving wireless relays. What do you think I have felt every day, every night, knowing we might never speak another word to each other? I have been nearly out of my mind. God forgive me, I even regretted I had not been killed along with Sandy that night.'

'No . . . Oh, my dearest one, such a terrible admission!' she cried softly in contrition. 'Please, forgive me for the things I said in anger. Forgive me for the pain I have caused you. Is it possible for you to do so?'

He nodded, almost too moved to speak. 'I could forgive you anything except the word "goodbye". Don't ever say it, darling.'

For a long moment her lovely eyes studied his face. Then she put her hand up gently to touch his thick blond hair in a caress.

'I have not been untouched by these months apart. Perhaps we did pretend and deceive because we had no choice, but now there is a chance of "forever", *liebchen*. I see there is a chance of it.'

Hardly daring to believe what she was saying, he held back from the embrace she sought. 'Are you indicating that we have a future, after all – that you will become my wife as soon as it is possible for us to marry?'

She nodded, her eyes bright with unshed tears.

'What of this dangerous work you do?'

'We are back in Europe. There is no more need of it,' she told him softly.

'You have finished with it? Your part in it is over?' he probed with growing excitement.

'It is over . . . And I am ready to be whatever you wish me to be from this moment on.'

Drawing her close against him, he buried his face in her hair, murmuring, 'You have handed me back my life. I was almost ready to abandon it.'

Chapter Twenty-Two

THEY ALL sat on the terrace to eat, because the warmth of the early July evening was too enchanting to resist. David was home, and Pat had come across to see Dirk, then accepted an invitation to dinner. The peace of the country scene was filled with birdsong, the humming of bees in flower beds presently in their full glory, and the echoing baas of sheep, but as the happy chatter went on around her, Vesta was lost in the labyrinth of her present confusion.

At the hospital they had told her to expect severe headaches from the wounds to the back of her skull. These would slowly lessen, along with the sensations of claustrophobia in enclosed spaces, caused by shock and the trauma of being buried beneath rubble for so long. They had also been reassuring about the ugly gash in her right leg, saying it would leave no more than a scar which would fade, in time. They had given no medical advice on her anguished heart and mind, because she had made no mention of them, but she tormented herself night and day with questions to which she could find no answers. There seemed no more sense to the killing of Sandy a few yards from where she had been pulled out alive, than to the bombing of Hut 4 whilst she had been fortuitously absent. Why had she twice been spared whilst others had died?

After the first reprieve she had done nothing more worthy than further her artistic career, treating those around her with smug aloofness. Why, then, should a man of sterling worth like Sandy have been crushed to death and not she? Had the Almighty some purpose for Vesta Sheridan that she had refused to recognise? Plagued by the fact that she still did not recognise it, the memory of all those who had been lost was an additional burden on her troubled spirit as she cast around in darkness for a glimmer of light to show her the way.

She was unable to find solace or peace in her art, these days. Inspiration, imagination, emotion – whichever had been her

456

motivating force – had vanished so that she felt she would never paint again.

The long summer days and nights intensified the anguish of the love she could not forget. Brad had not died on that hillside opposite Monte Cassino; she had not died in a London apartment. How could she have walked away from him that day? How could she have turned her back on the good that had come shining through that whole Italian experience? What did it matter about a woman called Gloria, or the Rosas and Lucias who crossed his path? They had found something very special in each other, and she had turned her back on it. With Brad finally out of her life, her artistic flair dead, and this inexplicable survival from a flying bomb, she expected God to indicate the new direction He had planned for her. Panic engulfed her because He did not.

Looking at those around the table now, Vesta acknowledged that, for once, Pat's commonsense could not comprehend this confusion in a lifelong friend whose path had taken her far from rural simplicity. Pat was honest, true and uncomplicated in matters of emotion. She could be no confidante in this situation. Nor, despite her determination not to repeat her mistake with David, was her mother. Trying to draw close in a way she never had before, the woman who had also spent her life devoted to country ways and pastimes was as inadequate as Pat in this matter.

To a certain extent David understood her problem, and they enjoyed relaxed companionship on a deeper level than before. After the *al fresco* meal they walked together through the dying evening to the lily pool, where they sat on the seat beneath the tree squirrels loved to explore.

'Thank heaven you're home for a few days,' she told him with a sigh, leaning back against the rustic support. 'Mummy, Robson, and even Pat painstakingly avoid mentioning what happened. I suppose they think it will upset me to talk about Sandy and the destruction of the apartment with Daddy's treasures in, but their ridiculous pretence that all's right with the world is almost unbearable. Did they do that to you when you came back?'

'Good Lord, yes... Except that they couldn't stop themselves looking at my hands, which made it even worse,' he said. 'I found them all incredibly out of touch. Except Father, of course.'

She studied him, still finding it hard to believe he had ever been a handsome golden youngster with merry blue eyes and outrageous charm.

457

'I'm so very glad you and Daddy have finally got back together. When one looks back on those years of estrangement it seems an awful waste of life, doesn't it?' Another sigh escaped her. 'Do you think we were spoiled and superficial before the war?'

'No more than anyone else. However, we'll certainly not go back to being so when this is over.'

A thrush began to sing its evening song high up in a nearby tree, and the sound was so beautiful she found herself fighting the tears that came so easily these days.

'I wish Daddy were here more often,' she confessed. 'I haven't the nerve to feel sorry for myself when he's around, too. How... How do you cope with everything, David?' she asked hesitantly. 'What is it about you and him that allows you both to fight against impossible odds – and why haven't I got it?'

His smile as he turned to her was every bit as warm and attractive as it used to be, despite the scarred face. 'You've got it, Vee, but haven't yet got around to discovering how to use it. You didn't see me when I first came home. I felt absolutely bloody, and I made sure everyone knew it. Unfortunately, they all thought it was because I resented their being whole when I was not.'

'Didn't you resent it?'

He shook his head. 'I resented their lack of appreciation of their good fortune. Poor old Robson is still unforgiving, and Mrs Robson refuses to speak to me at all since I told her to either pull herself together and do something useful, or peg out in decent manner as soon as convenient.'

That brought a laugh from her. 'How delicious! Pat said you'd become something of an *enfant terrible* since coming back from the dead.'

When he spoke next it was plain he had undergone a drastic change of mood. 'I very nearly didn't come back, Vee, and for some time after arriving here I was strongly tempted to end it all with my own hand. Then I got this new job and ... well, I saw how strongly many people are fighting for survival, and I felt ashamed.'

'Now you've made me feel ashamed,' she said emotionally. 'All I've got is a few stitches in one leg, bandages around my head, and no further inclination to paint, yet I sit and blubber for hours on end.'

His bony hand reached for hers and squeezed it. 'Everyone gets black and blue moods these days – even those who haven't followed the war around the desert and Italy, only to find it collapsing on top of them in a London apartment. These are

458

early days, and shock affects people in strange ways. You'll get over this dislike of painting, in time. Even if you don't, it's not the only career in the world. You're intelligent and quite well off. You've also matured over the last few years and turned into someone rather too disgustingly gorgeous to be a chap's sister. There are a hundred and one other things you'll be able to do with your life when the times comes, take my word for it.'

Leaning against his shoulder in gratitude she said, 'It does me so much good to talk to you. What'll you do when the war's over?'

'Run the estate,' came the instant reply.

'No more flying?'

'There'll be thousands of pilots out of work when peace comes. What few openings there'll be in civil aviation will be filled by the cream, not old crocks like me.'

'What about Uncle Rex – your ambition to equal him?'

'That was always an impossibility. He was out on his own and always will be. Anyway, we have an understanding these days. On the first day I went into action way back in 'forty, I felt him there in the cockpit with me. He was there every time, guiding me, giving me advice, telling me to watch for the one coming up on my tail. He was the veteran hero watching over the new boy. Then I shot down Enright, and he was no longer there when I climbed into a cockpit. I felt I had let him down, and we parted company for a couple of years. Then, on my first mission last October, he was suddenly there again. But he no longer takes command. We're now simply two aviators in close harmony. I . . . Well, I appear to have done enough to make him proud of me.'

Vesta heard it all with complete understanding. She knew about the spirits that wandered old battlefields; returned to the places where earthly life had ended, or where it had been lived supremely for a while. The desert had been full of them. El Alamein had revealed them to her in a painting. Yet one thing David had said puzzled her.

'I thought you were merely transporting stores now. Do they still refer to such flights as "missions"?'

'Old habits die hard,' came his easy response. 'Besides, it shoots a better line.'

She smiled. 'Yes, it does . . . And I'm glad about Uncle Rex. I always knew he'd be proud of you, you idiot. When you leave the RAF and start running the estate, do you think Uncle Roland will arrive to keep an eye on you?'

He shook his head. 'It's not the same kind of thing, Vee.'

'Has Daddy ever told you he seriously considered selling the

Hall when he thought you weren't coming back? Thank heavens you did, and stopped him from doing something so unthinkable. After all, you are the heir.'

He laughed. 'That sounds frightfully aristocratic. Pity the knighthood doesn't go with the estate. I rather fancy being Sir David.'

'Perhaps you will be one day.'

'I doubt it,' he said sobering. 'This war is proving a great leveller. We'll probably turn Communist and all become "comrades".'

'Not while there's a Royal Family... Or while there are villages like this one. We're too proud of our heritage ever to let it go. I'm sure you'll take over from Daddy as nominal squire and run the estate as it always has been.'

'We'll run it together, if you like,' he suggested. 'Teach yourself to type so that you can do the paperwork, and read all the available manuals on rearing pigs. I've had long talks with Pat about sheep. The Chandlers are planning to expand after the war, so it seems pointless to set up in competition. I plan to breed pigs, instead. You can help until you get married.'

'To whom?' she asked, growing still.

'Phil Bream, of course. He must be pretty keen to come here several times since you left hospital.'

'Yes, he's a nice man – too nice to be allowed to believe we have a future together.'

Her brother shifted his position, making her sit up to face him. 'Don't make decisions of that kind in your present state, Vee.'

'I made the decision in Cairo.'

'But he says you're unofficially engaged.'

'We're not. I don't love him.'

'In that case you'd better tell the poor blighter pretty damn quick, before he makes a bloody fool of himself,' came the reply that shook Vesta with the harshness of his tone. 'Come on, let's go indoors,' he added, pushing himself to his feet. 'It's getting too damned cold for confessions... most of which should never be made, anyway.'

Feeling bleakness return, Vesta limped up the path, thinking of the man who had made it impossible for her to love Philip Bream, and of one confession she had not made, and wished she had.

Pat stayed overnight, and David decided to ride over to the farm with her in the morning, as he often did. He was quite good on a horse now, and got in as much practice as possible.

During the moonlit periods, when the squadron was on constant standby at the South Coast airfield, he rode a horse stabled at a nearby farm whilst waiting for the night to come. It was good active exercise, infinitely preferable to sitting around growing more and more tense about the coming pick-up that night.

He had made a number of successful runs, with three dismal failures – due to unexpected fog on one night, no reception committee on another, and on the third an aborted landing, following the spotting of a pair of military trucks in a lane near the field. A message had been received late, revealing that the reception agent had gone over to the Germans to save his family from torture, and had given the welcoming signal under instructions from his new masters.

David had been staggered by the number of courageous people going in and out of France under perilous conditions – people who had been engaged in sabotage activities since the war had begun, and who must have been living on a knife edge the whole time. Many had been brutally tortured, as he had been, then escaped and unhesitatingly returned to risk further reprisals. Their courage, especially that of the very many women agents he and his fellows carried, had strengthened him to the extent that he had been able to instil confidence in his bewildered sister.

As he and Pat rode off side by side early on that July morning, he caught himself thinking of the contrasts within his present life. The other part hardly seemed credible, at the moment. Could those people he had taken over and landed in a field ten nights ago really now be wandering beneath the noses of the enemy, observing, infiltrating, noting details, operating transmitters in secret headquarters, while he lazily swayed in the saddle as he rode through a peaceful English village?

'How do you think Vee is progressing?' asked Pat.

'Eh? Oh, it's too soon to tell. One gets very extreme moods, at first. She might be quite bright and optimistic for a while, then feel like jumping from Longborrow Hill suddenly.'

'Is that how you felt, David?'

'Very often... But I think you knew that, didn't you? Much of the time you were the person who made me decide not to.'

'Was I? I'm glad,' she said in a strangely soft tone.

They headed down the drive to the lane, the sound of the horses' hooves loud in the morning air. It was a soft gentle morning with sparkles of dew on cobwebs strung over the hedgerows, and birds busy for the first worms of the day. A cloudless sky lent everything clarity of outline and colour so that the copse stood out in a medley of greens, and the distant thatched cottages were a series of pastel boxes with their prettily washed walls. Down in the village the Welsh collie, Bess, was barking at her rival, Queenie the labrador bitch, as usual, and someone was starting up a tractor with difficulty. The smell of home-baked bread hung in the air, along with that of frying bacon and potatoes. The ducks down by the pond could be heard quacking, despite their distance from Tarrant Hall, and the faint sound of the wireless in the Land Army huts announced that the girls were getting ready for their day's work.

David glanced at the girl riding beside him. She was part of all this. To Pat, life in farming areas like this corner of Dorset could hardly be bettered. What would her reaction be if he revealed the true purpose of his squadron? How would she respond if he told her the truth about his time in the East? Would she be able to accept that he was like he was today due to the bestiality of a group of Japanese soldiers, and not because of an aircraft crash? Could she ever accept that he had eaten lizards and drunk his own urine in order to stay alive? Would she ever be able to comprehend how he had felt about Rod Kershaw; how they had all felt about each other?

Conscious of his scrutiny, she turned and smiled, making him realise she was very rare and precious. There were so few people who had not known one or other of the terrors of war, and they were the ones who would help the others to forget and take up the old threads again when it was over. Pat's belief in truth, generosity, worthiness and uncomplicated relationships had never been shaken. Thank God for that. Peace could be found with a girl like her. Van Reerdon was a lucky man.

They took the short cut through the copse past Tarlestock Towers, as they always did. David was filled with admiration. No one would guess the frightful piece of architecture housed anyone other than the eccentric ex-brigadier. Then they broke out onto Wey Hill and Pat turned questioningly.

'Up to a gallop?'

He had been practising and meant to surprise her. 'If you insist.'

They were off, flying across the dew-wet turf with a thunder of hooves, the horses racing neck and neck. David was filled with pleasure at his own performance. He was not such a crock, after all. One of these days he would have a go with a cricket bat, and to hell with their gloomy predictions that he would never indulge in sport again. If that medical board could see him now they would look a set of damn fools. Pat was laughing with exhilaration beside him, her cheeks flushed with health, her dark curls bouncing around her shoulders. Slender and tanned, she looked unbearably attractive, and some of his elation melted away. The sexual urge had returned strongly in him, but no girl would want a white-haired horror with horny hands. Even prostitutes would charge twice as much to go to bed with him, he guessed, although with the light out he was sure he could hoodwink them into believing he was no different from the man he had once been. He would have to have a crack at it soon. Nights were beginning to be a problem.

Pat was reining in as she turned her horse towards the lookout point by the lone tree, where they often stopped for a breather. As she slipped from the saddle, she looked across at him, her silver-green eyes sparkling.

'I'll have to look to my laurels. You're getting far too good.'

'I always was good,' he responded immodestly. 'Far better than you, my girl.'

They let the horses graze and walked to the edge of the hill to look down on the twin villages lying like a picture-postcard view, the only scar on it being the church of Tarrant Royal. For a while they stood in silence – a girl in a cherry-red woollen shirt and stylish breeches, and a man in jodhpurs and yellow rollneck pullover, leaning against the tree trunk.

'Isn't it heavenly?' breathed Pat. 'I wouldn't exchange it for anything.'

'I thought you were going to. The South African *veld*, and all that.'

She shook her head. 'I told Dirk last night that it was over.'

'After all this time? He seemed a likeable chap.'

'He is. But I'm not in love with him.'

It did not really surprise him. He had somehow never believed she was. 'Just as well, perhaps. They don't have sheep on the *veld*, you know.'

They continued to study the view for a while, and he wondered how Van Reerdon felt about losing a girl as lovely as Pat had become. The fool should have married her long ago, before she had time to get all nostalgic about home.

'David, I've always suspected you'd prefer not to talk about it, so I've left the subject alone,' she said then, still gazing at the valley below. 'But the war *must* be over by this time next year . . . and you'll have to find out what has happened to your wife.'

He stiffened. 'You're right. I prefer not to talk about it.'

Turning she asked. 'Why?'

'That's my affair.'

'So is she, surely.'

'Not if she's dead, which is most likely.'

'Suppose she isn't?'

'She'll pick up her old life again, like us.'

'You won't bring her here?'

He shook hs head. 'She wouldn't come.'

Walking round to confront him, she asked, 'Don't you want to see her again?'

'No.'

'Why, David?'

Why? Because he knew he could not look at her – at any Oriental face – without going through a return of terror with echoes of that excruciating agony he would never forget. He gave her a hostile look. 'I don't have to answer that.'

'You must have loved her very much once.'

'What makes you think that?'

'Good heavens, you could have had any girl!' she cried with some heat. 'They were queuing up for you. Yet you choose her. Why?'

He thought about it for a moment. 'Possibly because she was the only one not in the queue. I'm not sure.'

'Didn't you think of the consequences?' She ran her hand through her curls impatiently. 'Suppose she had got away on that boat and arrived here. How do you think the poor little thing would have coped in a strange country with strange customs, and on the far side of the world from the rest of her family? Could there be a greater contrast than between the Singapore you described in your letters and Tarrant Royal? Whatever made you do it, David? You must have been mad.'

He was suddenly very angry. 'Why do any of us do what we do? Why did Father walk out on Mother and me in 1915? Why have you ditched poor Van Reerdon? And why are you so bloody concerned over a girl who made her choice two years ago and walked out on me?'

Pat stared at him. *'She walked out on you?'*

He saw the scene again, remembered burning the house down. 'She had more sense than I had. There had never been any intention on her part to come here. You're right, I was mad. But that madness has gone, Pat. Believe me, it has well and truly gone,' he told her savagely. 'Now can we forget the subject?'

She drew closer, saying in a curiously intent voice, 'No, let's follow it further... please, David.'

'Why, in God's name? It doesn't affect you in any way.'

'Of course it does. Don't you see, I said goodbye to Dirk

because I realised I've been in love with someone else all my life.'

Starting to turn away, he said, 'Shouldn't you be saying all this to my father?'

Moving round quickly to cut off his retreat, she put her hand on his arm. 'That's been the trouble all along. It was you I really loved, but I admired his personality and courage which I thought you didn't have. Now I see you had them all along. There'll never be anyone but you.'

Shaken to the core, he pushed past her to reach his horse, knowing he had to run from what she was suggesting. 'You always were a romantic fool, Pat. Girls only sacrifice themselves for wounded pilots in books. Real life is tougher than that, take my word for it. Go out and find yourself another romantic fool who is prepared to die for you, and raise sheep in your mutual paradise. I have my own plans, and they don't include any girl.'

The two friends sat on the window seat in Vesta's bedroom. The heavy showers which had persisted all day had kept them indoors when they would have preferred to be in the garden. Vesta watched the rain as it tattooed against the pane, then ran down it in crystal stripes to form a pool on the outside windowsill. David had said everyone had black and blue moods these days, and this was one of them. She had dreamed of Brad again last night, and could not shake off the feeling of loss. They had been on that hillside opposite Monte Cassino, watching the battle raging amidst the ruins of the monastery. Then Brad had been driving off in the jeep, and the flaming aircraft had appeared from nowhere to pursue his every twist and turn until he was also part of the fire. She had run to pull him free, then stood ignoring his outstretched arms, because she was afraid he would pull her into the flames where she would feel pain.

The rain outside her window symbolised the tears she could no longer shed. Since the last talk with her brother she had done no more crying, and had struggled to regain her old composure. The bandages were off her head, which helped to suggest recovery, and the healing gash in her right leg now tended to itch rather than throb. The multiple bruises which had given her such a sinister appearance had faded to no more than a pale yellow. Outwardly, she was almost back to normal. It was inner recovery that seemed far off. Confusion still filled her as she strove to find a sense of purpose again, a path to follow, a reason for her survival. Taking it further, she tried to understand the meaning of all that had happened.

For what reason had Felix Makoski entered her life? Had it been to shock her into seeking escape in the ATS? Why had she been spirited away from Hut 4 at the crucial time? Had it been planned so that she would see the chocolate box and apply to become a war artist? Why had she been sent to that very part of an immense desert where Brad was working? Why had she been shown a love that could last for eternity with a man who was already married? Why had their paths crossed again in Italy? Why had she been instrumental in saving his life, then walked away from him? Why had a flying bomb, which could have run out of power anywhere over London, fallen on the apartment during the one night she was sleeping there? And why had it killed a loyal and worthwhile person like Sandy, yet left her whole and alive? Why, why, why? The questions never stopped; were never answered. Where was the sense in it all? David maintained there were a hundred and one things she could do with her life. At the moment, she could not think of the one, much less the hundred.

'Penny for them,' said Pat suddenly, bringing her back to reality.

Before she knew it, she asked, 'Do you believe in destiny – life being mapped out from the moment one is born?'

'I've never thought about it all that deeply,' her practical friend admitted. 'I know a lot of people go around saying if a bomb has your name on it, it'll get you no matter where you are. But I think that's more a kind of comforting bravado than a belief in destiny.'

'You believe it is possible to shape one's own?'

'Unless a person is a complete nitwit, he has to. Good Lord, Vee, it's no good sitting there like a lump of flesh waiting for the Almighty to do all the work. He needs a helping hand. Take Uncle Chris, for instance. After Gallipoli he was on the path to permanent insanity, but he fought like mad against it. And look at David. How easy it would have been for him to live here like an incurable invalid, as Aunt Marion wanted, instead of being determined to fly again. They changed the course of destiny, didn't they?' Pat challenged fiercely.

'Did they? What if God gave them the strength to do what they did, because that's what He had planned for them, anyway?'

'That is an unanswerable question,' came the firm response. 'I'm sure neither of them sat around waiting for God to

466

motivate them. If that's what you're doing, Vee, you might wait a long time. He's exceptionally busy, these days.'

It touched a raw spot and Vesta hit back. 'It's easy for you to talk. Your life is serenely untroubled.'

Pat glanced away out of the window in a swift change of mood. 'No, it isn't. It's as complicated as hell. Dirk won't accept that it's over between us and keeps ringing me up. He's such a nice person. I wish he wouldn't make himself more miserable by continuing to hope I'll change my mind.'

'You'll have to pretend you're in love with someone else, that's all,' Vesta said with a trace of impatience.

'I am.'

'Good heavens, are you?' she asked in surprise. 'You told me you ended the affair because you felt you could never leave here and live in South Africa.'

'I couldn't, but that isn't the main reason.'

'Is it one of the other boys in the Mess?'

'It's David.'

She took a moment to absorb that. 'Aren't you mistaking pity for love?'

Pat shook her head vehemently. 'That's what he thinks, of course, but he's quite wrong. You maintain you are in love with Brad – irrevocably in love. Listen to how I feel about David then decide whether it's love or pity.' She leant forward and spoke softly. 'When I'm with him I don't notice the scars, his clumsy hands, his white hair that used to be so golden-blond. I never sit and dream of how he used to look. He's just David. When I'm with him everything makes sense. When we're apart I remember all he said, the expressions in his eyes, the sound of his voice, that smile which has never changed but which comes so rarely, these days. I yearn to make him so happy he'll forget all that has happened to him. I want to spend the rest of my life with him. I want to help plan the estate and raise his prize pigs. I want to have his children. I want – oh, dear heaven – I want to be all it would take to have him feel the same way about me. Vee, I think I fell in love with him years ago, but used Uncle Chris as a substitute until David grew up. Does that make any sense to you?'

It made too much sense. 'You little fool, Pat, you've made my mistake and fallen in love with a married man. Nobody ever mentions the fact these days – least of all David himself – but he has a Chinese wife in Singapore.'

'He's convinced she's dead.'

'He's *hoping* she's dead. That's not as shocking as it sounds

467

when one considers the stories of massacres and cruelties told by those who have escaped, or been freed by Americans retaking islands held by the Japanese.' She gave a small shake of her head. 'We're a good pair, aren't we? Who would have thought way back when we were silly schoolgirls that we would both end up wanting men we couldn't have?'

'Has he... Has David said anything about me to you lately?'

'Only that you've been the most tremendous help with his idea for the estate. He thinks you're very nice.'

'Oh, marvellous! I think I'm fated to go through life being regarded as no more than *very nice* by the men I fall for.' Then she went on with obvious desperation, 'What can I do to change the situation?'

'Oh, gosh, don't ask me. I'm the last person to advise on love for a married man.'

'This one happens to be your brother.'

'He's still married.'

'That doesn't lessen the longing,' the other girl said softly. 'You must know that, Vee.'

Vesta sighed. 'Just carry on being very nice until he feels he can't do without you, I suppose, if you feel there's any hope of a happy ending for you. I think it's a vain hope. Oh dear, you poor thing, not only is he tied to some girl on the far side of the world, he has always regarded you as a sister. In any case, he's bound to feel suspicious of any girl's feelings toward him now.'

After a pause Pat said, 'What about your feelings towards men?'

'Men in general, or prospective husbands?' she queried bluntly.

'How about Philip Bream?'

'Like you he's very nice.'

'Not nice enough to marry? Does he know about Brad?'

'No one knows about Brad save you.' She leaned her temple against the cold windowpane, recalling that night he had gone off with Rosa or Lucia because she had backed away from something she had feared would end the dream. 'Do you remember that Christmas at the start of the war, when we discussed "doing the necessary" and wondered what it was like? You said then that horses made the whole thing seem frightful, and you weren't sure whether the mare squealed in delight or pain.'

'Did I?' Pat's voice sounded dreamy.

'Well... have you ever done it?' she asked probingly.

'Of course not... But I came very near it on a couple of occasions with Dirk after a party. It's a terrible problem, because they do seem to get worked up very quickly, don't they?' Then it became clear Pat had drawn a conclusion. 'Gosh, Vee, you didn't with Brad, did you?'

'No . . . not him. I wish to God I had. Felix Makoski made it painful, humiliating and disgusting. I shall never know if Brad could have turned it into something wonderful.'

There was a long silence, and she guessed Pat was assimilating all that had been said as she gazed out at the thundering rain. 'The state I reached with Dirk was very exciting. He certainly knew how to make a girl weaken,' she confessed softly, before turning back to Vesta with shining eyes. 'With David it would be so wonderful I'd never want him to stop. I'm sure the mare squeals with ecstasy, Vee, and since I imagine you'd never have done it with Felix if you hadn't been crazy about him, the fault must have been with him. He couldn't possibly have cared for you. It takes two to create the magic.'

Memories of Brad came flooding back to overwhelm her with reminders of the magic they had created with a mere glance, a word, a smile. There would never be magic like it again with anyone else. What a fool she had been! Had Pat just given her the sign she had awaited? Was it too late to follow the direction she longed to take? Reaching out, she seized her friend's hand.

'Dear Pat, what would we all have done without you and your marvellous simple philosophy through the years? Like it or not, you really are *very nice*.'

The rain had stopped by the weekend, and Vesta was enjoying that Saturday because both her father and brother were at home. Life always seemed livelier when they were there. David had come the day before, and her father had turned up that mid-morning on foot, explaining that someone had given him a lift from the station to the village so he had walked up, and where was the coffee? They had eaten lunch on the terrace, the main topic of conversation being the departure of Dirk Van Reerdon's squadron, and the imminent arrival of American fliers at Longbarrow, which meant, of course, also at Tarrant Hall. After the meal David had vanished into the far regions of the estate with the man who had been employed to help Clive Hudson, and her mother had gone to lie on her bed in the hope of dispelling a headache.

Left alone with her father, Vesta asked, 'Have you heard any news regarding compensation for the apartment and its contents?'

469

'Heavens, no. Neither do I expect to for years. With half the world reduced to rubble, I shall be amazed if there is enough money available to rebuild it in my lifetime,' he said quietly. 'I'm lucky enough to have another home, and wealth enough to cope with the loss of the London place. Countless thousands have been left with nothing.'

'But it wasn't just bricks and mortar,' she protested. 'It was full of absolute treasures.'

'I know, my dear. Two of your paintings were amongst them. How can anything compensate for works of art that are lost? Like human life, no amount of money can bring them back.' He cast her a searching look. 'Neither can it restore your muse, Vesta. Only you can do that.'

The cane chair squeaked as she shifted her position. 'David has offered to let me help him breed pigs after the war.'

'David is seeking peace for a while. He'll need this house, the estate, an active outdoor life, the satisfaction of being in command of his own actions. Breeding pigs will only be an interim occupation, I feel sure, but it's an ideal start to his post-war future. On the other hand, your instinct to create won't be satisfied by beautiful bouncing piglets... And it'll be the sow and the hog doing the creating, surely?'

She smiled faintly. 'Only you could make a comment like that.'

'Is it valid or not?' he probed.

'Yes, perfectly. Anyway, there's someone far better qualified to help David than me.'

'Oh?'

'Pat wants to marry him.'

'Sensible girl, although she'll have a long wait.'

'I think she's prepared for that providing she's sure of getting him at the end of it.'

'Do you think she will?'

'Right now I imagine David feels wary of any show of emotion from people, and is happier keeping them at arms' length.'

It was a moment or two before her father asked, 'Is that how you feel – why you have turned down Philip Bream's proposal?'

Somewhat evasively she said, 'He is an excellent catch, and I'm sure my life would have been secure and ordered as his wife... but I couldn't give him the affection he deserves.'

'When you marry, do so because you simply can't help yourself, not to gain a secure and ordered life,' he advised strongly. 'Don't be afraid of waiting a while. It may not come with the first bloom of youth.'

470

She thought it strange advice from a man who had married at eighteen. Even if he was referring to his rumoured passion for Aunt Laura, he had been no older than twenty-one when he had rushed into a burning theatre to try to save her. He broke into such thoughts to continue his original theme.

'You still haven't given me an indication of what you intend to do about your future.'

Heaving a sigh, she said, 'I suppose as soon as I'm fit I'll go back to an admin posting with the ATS. If I'm no longer acting as a war artist, they're sure to draft me for general duties again.'

'I see. So the girl who has won artistic acclaim with her distinctive perception of human life, and her imagination which can conjure up humour, drama, or haunting emotions with her brushes is going to meekly sit at a desk sorting through lists of rations and replacement bootlaces,' came the comment that surprised her with its uncharacteristic anger. 'If your brother had taken that attitude he would never have emerged from that jungle alive, much less flown as an operational pilot again. I somehow always imagined you had his brand of courage, but I see I was mistaken.'

If he had struck her it would hardly have shocked her more. Staring at him in distress, she said, 'You can't compare... Daddy, you of all people ought to understand. Painting isn't something you can force yourself to do, however much courage you have.' Biting her lip, she went on, 'I'm sorry if you feel I'm letting you all down.'

'You're letting yourself down, surely,' came the chilly retort. 'Ever since you arrived back from the hospital, you have been enclosed in your private world, keeping everyone at bay in the belief that you are going through something no one else would understand. Misery is not exclusive to Vesta Sheridan.'

'I know that,' she cried, unable to believe a man she had always regarded as so gentle could be attacking her this way.

'Nor is self-pity.'

'It's not self-pity. You're wrong there... quite wrong,' she retaliated, growing angry herself. 'It's the others I'm sorry for.'

'Which others?' came the sharp question.

'The girls in Hut 4... and Sandy... and all the men in the desert and Italy. Why them and not me? What's so special about me that I have to be saved? Minnie and the girls were so full of life, and doing a vital job. So were all those men in the desert.' Rising from her chair, she looked down on her father, oblivious in her growing emotion to the peaceful garden scene, and the walls of the old house she loved. 'I saw them climb into their tanks and go out there to... to *hell*. I heard their voices over the radio; explosions after which the line went dead. I listened to their screams as they fought to escape the flames. In Italy, I saw them after a raid – old men and women, small children, maddened dogs – the dead laid in neat rows in the cobbled streets. And do you know what I did?' she asked in rising passion. 'I *drew* it all. Painted it in water colours. And I accepted money for doing it. I wasn't there in a white apron and cap with bandages for them, or making meals and carrying life-saving water to them as they lay helpless. I was making pictures of it all to sell. *That's* how worth saving I am.'

He got up slowly to stand beside her, studying her through the thick spectacles as she struggled for control of herself. 'At last, you've been able to bring it into the open. Yes, my dear, I of all people should understand. Let's talk about it, shall we?'

Taking her arm, he led her down the path which ended at the low wall enclosing the formal garden, and from which there was a view across the valley to the shattered church below. Gazing out at that view, he began speaking in his usual quiet manner.

'My brother Roland was immensely patriotic. While he would willingly have died for his country, he loved it so much he believed it was his duty to remain here and preserve all this for when the war ended. The entire village, led by your mother, began sending him white feathers. They threw him off committees, returned his donations, turned their backs when he passed, and finally formed a human barrier around the church to deny him entry. It was not that, but because I had been so severely wounded, that he did what every instinct protested against, and he served humanity as an army doctor in the trenches, gaining an MC for his gallantry in saving a dying man under fire.

'My brother Rex was a man in a million – loyal, generous, always laughing. He touched everyone he met with the warmth of his spirit. The whole world knows of his immense courage and daring. He has become a legend for youngsters to emulate.' There was a short pause as if he was remembering that red-haired merry cavalier of the air, then he went on even more quietly, 'I was a self-centred brilliant scholar who had given a village girl a child, had to marry her, then found the situation so unbearable he walked out on them both to join the army for no better reason than to get away. I was sent into battle as a mere figurehead, since there was no one else, and I only went fearlessly because I wanted to die.'

The pause this time was longer, but Vesta was so moved at hearing him speak so honestly of things that had been no more than vague stories since her youth, she was unable to break the silence of that heat-heavy summer day.

Finally he turned to ask, 'How do you think I felt when Roland and Rex were killed, whilst I survived against all odds? I believe I used the same words to Bill Chandler then as you did to me just now. "Why them and not me?" I've had to live with that ever since, Vesta, and the only way I have coped with it is to accept Bill's addage that, when the warriors have had their day, it is those with learning, culture and gentleness of heart who will put the world back on its feet.' He frowned. 'It stayed on its feet for twenty-one years, that's all. You are going to have to help resume the task at the end of this war, and I trust you do the job better than I did.'

Going into his arms, she discovered he was as emotional as she, for his hand was shaking as it stroked her short hair. 'Don't turn your back on your God-given talent, my dear,' he begged thickly. 'He did not intend us all to carry rifles, you know, and your painting will speak of this long after the sand has blown over the skeletons.'

That evening father and son walked together through the area of Tarrant Hall's graceful gardens and grounds which had been trodden by the feet of the RAF over the past few years, and which were soon to be filled with men from across the Atlantic.

'I had forgotten how extensive this was before it was divided, David. It is an imposing house, isn't it? Well worth preserving.'

David stopped beside his father and ran his glance over the rosebeds, now in full glorious colour, the graceful tumbling willows, the sloping lawns, and the distant banks of rhododendrons and azaleas.

'It looked the most beautiful place on earth when I arrived home that day. I think my decision to run the estate after the war was made then. It's strange how careless we are of the things we have until we have almost lost them.'

His father turned to smile at him. 'Rex said almost the same thing to me towards the end of his war. Having always denied any wish to run the place, he came on leave one wonderful summer weekend and decided he wanted to stay here for the rest of his life. He never would have done so, he knew that. The sky would have beckoned irresistibly, and he would have gone. Besides, Laura hated the country. "The back of beyond" she used to call Tarrant Royal.'

'Good thing Mother didn't feel that way,' he said. 'She really loves it.' The rooks were cawing noisily in the tall trees as he turned his attention back to the house itself. 'Our chaps have

473

treated it pretty well, on the whole, and I imagine the Yanks will do even better. They almost revere old places like this.'

'No doubt snapshots of Tarrant Hall will adorn dressers in houses from Milwaukee to San Francisco, and all points north and south,' said his father dryly. 'If they manage to catch Lady Sheridan in their lenses whilst cutting roses, that'll be a bonus.'

'To say nothing of the famous Sir Christopher himself,' he added with a grin. 'What'll you do when it's over, Father? Once travel gets back to normal, I suppose it will be just possible to go back and forth from here to Town. Or will you find a new London apartment?'

His father looked curiously ill at ease as he made a noncommittal remark about it being far too early to make that kind of decision. That was when David felt it was time to make his move.

'I can't say I agree with you. The war has to be over within the next few months. We're advancing so far over Europe my squadron will soon be diverted to other work, I should imagine.'

The blond head nodded. 'Transport squadrons will be fully used over there, with our strength growing with every new landing. How will you like operating in France?'

With quiet deliberation, he said, 'It'll be a hell of a sight easier having our own airfields there... And a real runway in daylight will be a welcome change from three hand torches in a moonlit field, won't it? I take it you walked over this morning from the Brig's place after questioning the people we brought in two nights ago.'

The good-looking face turned to study him. 'I wondered how long it would be before you made that discovery.'

'Why didn't you come clean as soon as I joined the squadron?'

His father smiled faintly. '"Come clean". Is that a phrase from some terrible American film?'

'You knew all I said about transporting stores was duff information,' he accused, with feeling. 'You knew what I would really be doing. I even heard you'd gone over once yourself to bring someone back. Why didn't you say as much to me, on the quiet?'

There was an apologetic shrug. 'When you arrived back in England we established a new respect for each other. I felt it might be endangered if I rushed in too quickly.'

David considered that while he looked at the man before him, still finding it hard to accept that he was not all that he had seemed to be for so long. 'I suppose you also know the truth

474

about what happened in Sumatra – who I was with and what they were doing there.'

'I know enough to be aware of my son's extreme courage,' was the quiet response. 'They don't give men medals for withstanding torture and remaining silent about vital information, but I feel sure your renowned uncle would be the first to acknowledge your equality with him.'

'He has,' David said swiftly, seeing the truth in a flash. 'He comes with me on the trips, you know, and we have complete understanding now.'

'I'm glad.'

Then, knowing it had to be said, David embarked on something he found hard to handle after so many years. Because it was difficult, and he was not the most eloquent person in the world, he blurted out the first sentence.

'I've been pretty beastly to you in the past. Some of the things I said ... well, I see they were totally unjustified. All that obvious hero worship of Uncle Rex must have made it even worse. I thought – we all thought – you were nothing more than an egghead in a safe Ministry post. Not that there's anything to be ashamed of in that, of course, but we ... I'm sure we implied that there was.' He stuck his hands in his pockets as if, with them out of the way, it would be easier. It was not. 'These past couple of years I've had to tell lies about things I've done, so I know what it's like. But no one has accused me of not caring enough, or putting my career before anything else. You've had to stand by and take all that right from the start of the war. Five years is a long time to stand accused of something that isn't true – a damn long time.'

He pulled a hand from his pocket to run it through his hair in an awkward gesture. 'Look, I know apologies always come too late in instances like this, so that's not what I'm trying to do ... at least I ...' He broke off as the right words eluded him. Then he remembered the conversation he had had with Bill Chandler when he had been desperate to fly again, and everything fell into place. He smiled. 'Uncle Bill once told me I had spent my life trying to be the son of "Sherry" Sheridan, instead of the son of his brother. I just want to say I've sorted it all out now, and I'm proud of who I am. Will you shake on it, Father?'

As if in a trance his father reached out to grip the misshapen hand so tightly it hurt. He seemed incapable of speaking, and David was astonished to see tears behind the thick spectacles. They did not suggest joy, however, but sadness.

475

Chapter Twenty-Three

THE EFFECT of the V1 Flying Bomb or 'Doodlebug' as it was dubbed, was acutely disturbing. The psychological effect of knowing the Germans could sit safely at home and complete the destruction of London was something which threatened the morale of the British people as nothing else had. They were a race which believed in sporting rules, but this weapon broke them all. The engines stopped over schools full of children, over hospitals, over institutions for the old or blind. They came over by night and day, whatever the weather. They came in their thousands until the sound of their sinister throbbing engines seemed to fill the sky continuously.

The toll of deaths and injuries rocketed. Huge areas were devastated leaving hundreds more homeless. Railways were ruptured, industry was crippled, food supplies were blown up. Just when the British were cheering the re-entry to France, which suggested the beginning of the end, they came nearer to giving in than in 1940. The RAF could not save Britain this time. The V1s came over so thick and fast the fighters could not possibly intercept them all.

It was as well that only those in certain departments and organisations knew that there was in existance a V2 – deadlier, quite silent, and with a longer range than anything so far developed. Still in the last stages of experimentation, it was vital for the Allies to advance into Europe fast enough to prevent full-scale use of such a weapon. Men from all walks of life with top scientific or engineering qualifications were recruited by intelligence units, as possible agents for spying or sabotage on the plants manufacturing the weapons.

During that month of July 1944, Chris was almost busier than he had ever been, helping to sift through prospective people with the necessary linguistic standard, then giving intensive crash courses in German to those selected who had not. The strain of high-powered work did not tell on him as it had before, however. The night he had spent with Sonja in Bill's apartment had been like an injection of fresh strength. Her pledge for their future had made their union more total and breathtaking than it had ever been. Winning her had been the most momentous event in his life.

When he had time to think, the joy she had instilled in him overrode all else to calm his weary brain, soothe his aching body, still his fears. He was able to sleep soundly when he finally reached his bed, drifting into it with thoughts of the years ahead. They would live in Vienna, perhaps, or Budapest – even somewhere on the Adriatic. She would continue to create works of art; he would concentrate on translations of literary works. They would discuss his interpretations – argue a little over them – and decide between the most literal and the more poetic versions. Their home would reflect their mutual love of the arts, and it would be filled with the music which had them both enraptured. On starry nights filled with the scent of mimosa they would sit on a sun-warmed stone terrace listening to the records of Puccini, Verdi, Debussy or Ravel. On nights when snow drifted, Sonja would thrill him with Rachmaninov, Tschaikovsky, Liszt, and even Chopin, with whom she delighted to tease him.

He might begin sketching again – a pleasure he had abandoned years ago – and maybe even attempt some water colours. There were the Greek classics he had never had time to re-read. He would take her to the Greek Islands and read them aloud to her as they lay together on a hillside. He might even show her Gallipoli. They would stand on the same cliffs, and perhaps a nineteen-year-old boy would finally find what he had gone there to seek.

During the last week of that month of July, two days after he had made a brief, somewhat unsettling visit to his home from Tarlestock Towers, he was summoned to a meeting with Frank Moore. They had no more than a working relationship now, although there was still a modicum of professional respect in it. After placing a glass of vodka at Chris's elbow, as usual, Lord Moore came to the point without preamble.

'This will be generally known within a day or so, but I'm telling you now because it is necessary to do so. On the twentieth of this month there was an attempt by a conclave of German generals to assassinate Hitler.' His brows met in a frown. 'It failed. Not only is it a tragedy because it did not rid the world of the maniac, it's a double blow in that all those who conspired in it – the moderate sensible men who are attempting to save some thousands of lives, and the devastation of

European countries through prolonged battles, by treating for peace now – are being hunted down by the SS and executed. One of them is Rommel.

'Hitler has gone over the edge with rage, and is hitting back left, right and centre. Last night he launched a non-stop attack of VIs on London in an unprecedented orgy of killing and destruction in revenge, although we took no active part in the plot. Our people knew about it, naturally, but held aloof because the conspirators were asking for peace terms we could not consider. In Paris, where an incredible misunderstanding led to the belief that the plot had succeeded, Gestapo officers were rounded up and held under arrest until the truth came out. Reprisals have been terrible; police and military officers have been slaughtered out of hand. Many have taken their own lives. Those who have gone into hiding, and a great number who tried to dissociate themselves from complicity, are being mercilessly hunted down.'

Chris heard all this with deep concentration, appreciating the widespread effects success would have had, and failure would now bring. It really did seem that good would never triumph over evil.

'It could have ended hostilities by the end of this summer,' he murmured. 'My God, think of the long-term international implications if it had come off.'

'No, don't think of them,' interjected the other man. 'Think instead how much worse it will now be. Hitler and his mad followers will have massacred all the men of reason and have a clear run. We can expect no quarter now.' He pursed his lips as he fixed Chris with a serious stare. 'Now he will be more determined than ever to exterminate us with everything he can throw at this small island. Agents we sent out recently are beginning to report back that there is even a V3 under development. Chris, if we don't reach Berlin or destroy these weapons before they're ready for us, we can lose this war even now.'

Chris stared back with a frown. 'What you mean is, there'll be none of us left to fight it, don't you?'

'More or less.'

After taking that in for a few moments while he sipped the vodka, he asked, 'Why have you asked me here? I'm no scientist or military expert, so presumably it has something to do with translating, or with some person of my acquaintance.'

Frank Moore got to his feet and thrust his hands into his pockets before starting to walk round the desk to him. 'This assassination plot has led to intense security being established

478

at all stations, borders, and road blocks. People are being stopped indiscriminately; arrested on technicalities. Movement is extremely difficult for bona fide residents. For anyone with false papers or identity it is highly dangerous.'

'Yes?' prompted Chris as Frank Moore stopped in front of him.

'It has put a bloody great spanner in our works at a vital time. One of our best people had contacted engineers working at one of the rocket bases and persuaded one to come over to us. The man is an Austrian who saw the advantages of changing sides at this point in the war. They were on their way out when this fiasco occurred. Our agent was caught in a mass swoop at a railway station leaving his passenger in a safe house, from whence he then refused to move for fear of being caught. We had to send another agent to persuade him to come in. If the weather is right, there'll be a pick-up tonight.'

Still unable to see his part in the affair Chris said, 'You need an engineer, not a linguist, surely.'

'We need both. The Austrian speaks no English; our engineer speaks nothing but. He's already waiting at Tarlestock Towers. You're to go down there this evening and stay there until the agent and passenger arrive – even if it takes all week due to bad weather. That information is top secret and needed at the very earliest opportunity. When the man arrives it'll be a matter of working non-stop until our engineer has every detail he wants.' He let out his breath gustily. 'You can have a couple of days at the Hall to catch up on your sleep after that.'

Chris got to his feet and prepared to leave. 'I'll go down on the evening train. They're not likely to reach the brigadier's place until dawn. That's if they do come tonight.' As casually as possible he asked, 'Any idea who's going over for the pick-up?'

'Young Parker, as far as I know.'

Chris nodded in relief. 'Right. What is the Austrian's name, by the way?'

'Schreibmeyer... Klaus. Don't know him, do you?'

'No. Who's bringing him out?'

Frank Moore appeared to hesitate, and something about the way he sucked in his lips made Chris repeat the question in sharp tones. 'Who is the agent, Frank?'

'"Mirjana".'

If the man had punched him in the stomach he could not have felt more sick. Swallowing, he asked, 'Whose idea was that– yours or hers?'

Lord Moore sat at his desk and drew a folder towards him as

479

he said unemotionally, 'She knows Schreibmeyer personally. We both agreed he would be more inclined to come with her than with anyone else.' Opening the folder and starting to study the contents, he added, 'This man's knowledge could save hundreds of lives. She is well aware of that. I hope you are. It is on occasions like this that you would do better to adopt John Frith's unyielding attitude to his work.'

Chris did not take the evening train to Greater Tarrant. He went, instead, in the car traditionally sent to the airfield to await the arrival of those picked up by the Lysanders. His thoughts during that drive were highly confused, and he felt a sense of inevitability; of his whole life now reaching its climax after years of struggle. For Sonja he was willing to abandon his wife, a son and daughter who were very dear to him, a valued heritage – in essence, his past, amounting to half his allotted life span. All he had asked of her was that she should keep herself safe for him. Within a month of making that pledge she had broken it.

Frank Moore had said the man she was bringing from danger could be the means of saving hundreds of lives. Colonel Petworth had said the same thing to him in Gallipoli, before sending him up a cliffside in a suicidal attempt to create a diversion from the real attack. He had been blown up; scores had been killed or maimed. The attack had been successful. Several months later, Gallipoli had been completely evacuated leaving those same cliffs to the enemy. The war had continued for three more years. Those hundreds of lives he had purportedly saved had been lost elsewhere. They always were.

What difference would one Austrian engineer make now? What point was there in the self-sacrifice of a woman who could create beauty and joy simply by existing? Sonja was wrong. Frank Moore was wrong. The whole world was wrong. It was more important for people to make each other happy while they could than for three men to huddle together in a room while formulas in German were translated into English. Someone would invent a bigger bomb next week. The war would end, and a new one would start. He wanted his one love. Dear God, how he wanted her. If it were for no more than a year, he wanted her. A month, even. Or one short wonderful week. There was no time for 'forever'; he wanted 'now'. If she returned he would claim her openly, abandon pretence and subterfuge. His time for happiness had finally come. He wanted it ... To hell with all else!

The weather was perfect for the operation. When the car

480

arrived at the old cottage used as a cover for the operations room of David's squadron, the moon was creating something approaching daylight over the airfield. Due to the short nights at that time of the year takeoff had been later than usual, so in the low-beamed cottage 'office' there were only a few people lounging sleepily in the chairs. One of them was David, the reserve pilot for that night. He stared in surprise when Chris walked in, then smiled.

He has your heartbreaking smile. It transcends the scars.

Sonja was right, and when it also lit his eyes, as it did now, his son defied the physical changes wrought by his enemies.

After shaking hands with the commanding officer Chris turned to the white-haired youngster dressed in uniform trousers, grey coarse-cloth shirt and navy blue sweater, with flying gear on the chair beside him.

'Hallo, David. Playing understudy tonight?'

'Something like that,' came the warm response. 'It's pretty bloody boring, so I'm glad you've come to perk things up. Would you like some cocoa?'

Chris made a face. 'Is that the best you chaps can manage?'

'It is when we're on duty.' Then he laughed. 'I daresay we can find something more fitting for high-ranking Intelligence bods, can't we, sir?' he asked his CO.

With a glass of vodka in his hand, Chris sat on one of the chairs, trying not to watch the hands of the clock as they crept round.

'He must be pretty important to bring you here in person,' David commented. 'We received a "Top Priority" order with this one, but thought it was because of the security purge going on over there. All we know is that this chap Schreibmeyer is part of the "Crossbow" operation. Seems a bit late to me. The V1s have been going over all night. The sound of those motors is pretty gruesome. God knows what Vee feels when she hears them.'

'Much the same way you feel when you hear certain things, I should imagine,' was his quiet response. 'What time are they due back here?'

David glanced at the clock. 'In around thirty minutes. As a matter of fact, I was thinking of turning in just as you arrived. If anything went wrong at this stage, it'd be too late to go. It'll be getting light before long.'

'Yes, it will.' Thirty minutes! Their aircraft would be over the English coast soon. What would she do when she saw him? How would she look, knowing why he was there?

'If the assassination had been successful, we'd have soon

been out of a job,' his son continued. 'Think of the war being over because of the death of just one man. If I thought I had the slightest chance of pulling it off, I'd have a go myself. Then I could get down to breeding my pigs.'

David plainly found it enjoyable to chat about information of a privileged nature to which they both had access, and he pursued the theme of what might have been possible if Hitler had been killed two days ago. As he talked, Chris listened with growing surprise. Unlike himself, his son appeared full of optimism for the future, which he had well-planned, apart from one aspect. He made no mention of a partner; someone to share his peaceful years at Tarrant Hall. Chris knew little Su Sheridan could never now console his broken son, but a man needed a woman to make sense of all he did. Another look at the clock showed him there were but ten minutes to go. He accepted another vodka, and tried to veer David from the subject of what he would do about a London home when the war ended. Now was not the time to speak of his plans.

Just when Chris realised something was wrong, he was not sure. Probably it was the behaviour of those behind him. The flight was overdue, and there had been no radio communication from the pilot, which suggested he was not even over the Channel yet. The social atmosphere changed to one of emergency. Central Control was asked if a single aircraft had been recorded approaching over the coast, or if a report of a Lysander crash had been made. The somewhat acid reply was that in the middle of a huge flock of flying bombs one aircraft was hardly obvious. Someone in the cottage said the Lysander could have collided with a V1 anywhere along its flight path. Another said it could have been shot down by their own fighters, who were attacking anything approaching through the sky from France, these days.

Chris stayed in his chair, staring into the empty glass while activity went on around him. Even David was more concerned now with the fate of his squadron colleague than discussing his plans for Tarrant Hall. Chris was too numb to discuss anything. Was this to be the end of it? Had she gone, like Laura, dedicated to a passion that precluded him? Had she ever really existed? Perhaps he had turned that night at a party and seen a ghost, after all.

'... flight aborted. Parker was hit by flak going over. He ditched in the sea and was picked up by French lobster fishermen. We're going to have another crack at it tonight.'

Chris realised David was there speaking to him, and simply echoed, 'Tonight?'

There was that smile again. 'It's five a.m., Father.'

'They're safe?' he asked urgently.

'Yes, they're tucked away somewhere, never fear. I'm off for some sleep. You'd better do the same. I'll pick 'em up in about eighteen hours from now.'

David was wrong. Ground mist developed with darkness, and the operation had to be called off for that night. Chris lived through a nightmare which he could not discuss with his son. By comparison, David seemed very relaxed during those two days, even knowing he was to do the pick-up when it was possible. He showed his father all the aspects of his present life with an eagerness almost lost on Chris, and even arranged for the hire of an extra horse so they could go riding together on that second afternoon. Although he did not appear to be aware of his father's preoccupation, Chris did catch David casting speculative looks his way now and again.

When they arrived back from the ride there was news for them. Schreibmeyer had had to be moved, due to an informer revealing the locations of safe houses in that area. He was now in such a state of nerves, convinced the Gestapo was closing in for the kill, that unless he was picked up that night there was a serious risk of his attempting suicide and his knowledge being lost. The Met. report gave the go-ahead for the operation, but since the location of the field had been changed, David went off with his maps to work out his route, leaving Chris prey to his thoughts. They drove him, after a while, to seek out the senior man with a proposition. Because the accompanying agent on this operation was a woman, she might need help with a passenger suffering from fear-hysteria. The pilot would be unable to give assistance as his essential rôle was to stay at his controls for a speedy takeoff.

'I have been over before, so am familiar with the drill,' he pointed out. 'My presence would be a calming influence on a man full of doubts over what he is doing, and worried about his personal safety with *anyone*, just now. This carries a "Top Priority" tag, and I know the reason for it. Anything which will contribute toward success should be adopted.'

The man saw the sense in what Chris proposed, and agreed. When David was told he took the news calmly – he was remarkably self-possessed these days, Chris reflected – but studied his father with a return of speculation whilst nodding his assent.

'I'll be glad to have you along,' he said warmly, 'but I can see I'll be left to my own devices on this trip. Uncle Rex will be in the back with you.'

483

They took off at eleven-thirty. For some reason, his son shook hands with him before they climbed into their respective cockpits.

'Welcome aboard,' said David, very much captain of his own aircraft. 'This should complete our reunion, don't you think? I never dreamed I'd have the pleasure of sharing this with you.'

'Nor I, David. Let's make it something to remember, shall we?'

'Righto.' As he stepped onto the wing, he called out, 'As senior in rank, Colonel Sheridan, you can have the bottle of perfume we usually get as a "thank you". You'll have to tell Mother a whopping lie about how you got it – unless you've a glamorous floosie tucked away in your stuffy old Ministry,' he added with a laugh.

Someone had lent Chris a very thick sweater, which he had on under his battledress jacket, and a pair of fur-lined boots to combat the cold encountered even on summer nights. It seemed very strange knowing his own son was flying the machine a matter of a few feet away from him, and David's voice coming over the intercom soon after increased that sense of unreality.

'What did you think of that for a smooth takeoff?'

'Top marks,' he said into the mouthpiece, gazing out at the south coast washed with moonlight.

It was an intensely exciting experience sitting up in a skyful of stars, with the beauty of a serene night wherever he looked. Below was the silver rippling sea; above, a massive moon with a clear pattern of mountains and valleys visible upon it. From the chill darkness of the cockpit, Chris gazed through the hood at the moon. Stanzas of a multitude of poems drifted through his brain. In a matter of a couple of hours Sonja would be there with him, and he would recite some of them to her. No, the Austrian would be with them, of course. Damnation! But she would be there, so that he could circle her with his arm as they flew back to their future.

'We'll go up there some day,' said a voice, bringing him from his thoughts.

'Eh?'

'The moon. We'll reach it one day, when someone invents an aircraft powerful enough.' Then David gave a soft chuckle. 'Uncle Rex disagrees. He says the necessary fuel load would make the weight impossible, and we'd never get the damn thing off the ground.' The aircraft wobbled slightly, and David apologised. 'Sorry about that. Just having a quick squint at the map. Right on course, in case you're wondering.' There was a short pause, then the voice said, 'I gather he has decided to stick with me, after all.'

'What's that?' queried Chris, still thinking of Sonja.

'Uncle Rex. He can't resist the pilot's cabin.'

After a period of companionable silence broken only by the continuous droning of the engines, David announced, 'French coast below. Are you comfortable back there?'

'Very comfortable... Apart from the hard seat, the cold, and the lack of vodka.'

His son laughed. 'There's a flask of coffee in the pouch to your left. It's really for the return journey when the passengers join you, but I won't let on if you take a swig.'

'A swig! As we're now over French soil, I think we should use the language of the country, David.'

Another chuckle. 'Lord, how I remember cursing you as a boy for making us speak like the natives.'

'That was before you cursed me for bringing you into the world.'

'Yes... yes, before then,' came the hesitant reply.

'I'm very glad I did, David.'

'So am I. In spite of everything, so am I.'

They droned on into the night, and Chris felt suddenly suspended between his past and his future, each pulling him with equal force. Forty-eight tremendous years, yet he felt they had been wasted: had achieved nothing for all the effort, the striving, the suffering. But could they just be sloughed off like the skin of a snake, to shrivel away to nothing, unwanted and of no further consequence? How much time lay ahead of him? Three score years and ten. That gave him around twenty-two more, with a new beautiful skin bearing a pattern so vivid it would dazzle. Had the thought of that dazzle blinded him to all that was already etched on the creature called Christopher Wesley Sheridan? Would it be easy to pursue ephemeral happiness and forget those who had been such a part of him? Could he walk away again as he had at the age of eighteen, this time driven by desire rather than despair? What of the vow he had made to ensure his brothers had not died in vain? He found himself sweating as indecision began to tear at his senses. Mixed images of Sonja and his family tumbled around in his brain to confuse him. It was the unnatural state of sailing through the sky above the world which brought such introspection, of course.

'Approaching target now,' came the voice over the intercom, tenser now, but still full of confidence. 'Stand by to chuck him in bodily, if necessary, Father.'

Chris's heart leapt involuntarily, and indecision fled. A few minutes and he would have her safely beside him. That new dazzling skin was partially visible already, and *how* it would dazzle. Stretching to look down he saw the French countryside clearly defined in the brightest of nights. The summer beauty of the landscape lay unblemished by battle. Foxes were out hunting, badgers roamed freely, the owls swooped in search of mice and rabbits, out eating in the moon-washed peace of the fields. Man's follies passed them by as they lived out their own defined lives. Down there Sonja was waiting,. The thought put a lump in his throat. Down there was a woman in danger; a woman he would snatch up and never allow to return. Marion would have to be told the truth, and a divorce arranged. The issue must be resolved in order to establish his right to protect the woman he loved from nights like this.

He grew aware that David was speaking again, but it was not to him. Incredibly, it appeared to be a conversation with a presence who answered for his son's ears alone. Was Rex really there with them? Could his brother be guiding and protecting David over a land he had known well from the air? Chris tried to banish such fancies.

'There's the signal,' came the voice from the front, very definitely to him now. 'I can see them waiting for us, thank God. Stand by, I'm starting the descent now.'

The engine noise increased, and there was that sensation of a force greater than nature taking hold of the aircraft as it slowed and began to return to earth. From the cockpit Chris could see the L-shape formed by the three torches, and two or three figures standing by the improvised flarepath. Lower and lower. As the trees flashed past, Chris opened the cockpit hood in readiness. He knew the drill well. They touched down with a slight bump, and ran along the uneven ground with a jolting motion, racing past the first torch and on then to the second, where David would turn into the wind ready for an immediate takeoff.

'Piece of cake,' came the confident call from the front. 'Make it snappy, Father, and I'll buy you a vodka when we get back.'

Chris found he was too tense to reply. As they drew level with the second torch he could make out the group of people waiting for the moment to climb aboard. One of them would be Sonja. The aircraft swung slowly round into the wind and came to a halt, engines still running. He was up and over the side of the cockpit, jumping the last few feet to the ground from the small metal ladder attached to the side of the fuselage. The surface was uneven, and he staggered slightly to retain his

486

balance. Then he found himself being knocked aside by a figure which made a dash for the aircraft with almost demented speed. Schreibmeyer, without a doubt.

Then Sonja came forward in a dark coat, her hair braided and wound around her head. Paled by the brilliant whiteness of the moon's light, her face clearly revealed her shock at his presence. They gripped hands during a brief exchange of glances, and she showed she understood why he was there by saying softly, 'My dearest, forgive me.'

'You know I will. You know I always will,' he replied, no longer irresolute. 'But this is the last time.'

From the corner of his eye he saw the French agent standing on the wing talking to David, and he circled Sonja with his arm to lead her the few feet to the ladder. At that moment, the night exploded with a sound he knew from long ago. The man on the wing spun round and fell to the ground, at the same time as Chris felt burning fiery pain raking his left thigh. Stifling a cry, he pushed her up the ladder with urgent hands, turning his head to see the torches shining in the other direction to show figures emerging from the line of bushes. Bullets were whistling through the air and hitting the aircraft with metallic thuds. He saw his son's pale face leaning from the cockpit, and knew there was no time for that dazzling new skin now.

'Go! For God's sake, go!' he shouted, waving his arms at David as the running men advanced across the field. Then he was punched in the back as he put a foot on the ladder, punched by something bringing red-hot pain to spread down his spine. More pain, in his leg, this time. Letting go the ladder and fighting to stay upright, he shouted again, 'Go, David, go!'

The agony tore into his side then, and he could no longer remain on his feet. Sinking down as the Lysander began to roll forward, Sonja's face was no more than a pale shape as he pitched forward onto the rutted surface of the field.

Hands seized him, pulled him over onto his back that was sticky and afire with the rawness of flesh. They shouted at him in harsh aggressive voices which made their language ugly, when it could sound lyrical. He was crying, but did not care that they saw his tears. Men such as they would never understand that he was doing so only because the lenses which gave him clear sight had fallen off, leaving the night a blur. He would willingly suffer double the agony if he could only watch that aircraft climb up amongst the stars to freedom, and set course for home. All he had was the comforting sound of the engines in his ears.

Then he realised the lenses would have been of little use to him. Darkness was closing in fast. Strangely enough, it was not the lonely sensation he had always imagined it would be. It was as if he was finally reaching that destination which had been beckoning him for years.

David sat at the controls feeling icy cold. His scarred cheeks were stiff, his brain was numb, his hand moved automatically to do what was needed. There was silence from the rear cockpit. Sitting there in the pilot's seat he felt immense and terrible isolation. That spiritual companion was no longer with him; was not making the return journey. He knew his uncle would never come with him again. He understood why, even through his grief.

Aeons passed. The English Channel appeared below, increasing the guilt of abandonment. If it had been on English soil . . . To go, leaving him in a foreign land . . . Then he realised it would not seem foreign to a man who had travelled the world, spoken its languages, understood its people, and he would be in very good company, with all those of his kinsmen who had gone before him.

Staring at the first light of morning appearing in the east, David slowly realised this was something merely delayed for almost thirty years. By rights, Christopher Sheridan should have died in 1915, but he had fought to hold onto life with an incredible sense of purpose. In the years between then and now he had enriched the world tenfold with his knowledge and understanding, he had brought new life into it to continue his hopes and dreams, and he had passed on a philosophy which nothing had shaken, and which would be taken up again when madness passed. Somehow those years of grace which had been granted him – or which he had wrested with determination – had run out. In some strange way which David barely understood at that moment, the time had come for that nineteen-year-old boy to honour his debt. There should be no guilt to be borne by anyone. It had been as inevitable as all that had happened to him in the East.

The field was clear with the light of morning when David landed and let the machine run along to the extremity of the perimeter. He carried out all the necessary procedures automatically, pulling back the hood to let in the fresh cool air. Klaus Schreibmeyer was already on the ground and hurrying towards the cottage. The ground crew were coming to take over the aircraft. The woman he knew as 'Mirjana' was standing beside the wing as he dropped down wearily to the ground. He looked at her closely, registering every detail of her face. She was deathly pale, but composed. It was that same composure displayed by all those who went back and forth risking danger to help others, and who had seen death many times. Yet her eyes betrayed her. She was suffering as much, if not more, than he was at this moment. With swift surprising insight, a half-formed suspicion crystallised into certainty, and gave him the answer to what had happened that night.

Drawing in his breath to ease the inner pain, he said slowly, 'I think my father died for you back there.'

She shook her head, replying with an effort, 'I think he died for us all... because he was that kind of man. You have his brand of courage, David. Make the rest of your life worthy of him, I beg you.'

Turning away she walked swiftly to the waiting car, leaving him to cross to his CO watching with a grave face. It seemed a great distance to go, but he reached the man eventually, having realised that the truth about his father's death could not be told, even to his mother and sister. But perhaps it was better that way.

Chapter Twenty-Four

LORD MOORE personally telephoned Tarrant Hall to break the news to Lady Sheridan that her husband had been flying to an important conference on French soil, when the aircraft had developed engine trouble and gone down in the English Channel. It was the official version of a story which could not be told, and it appeared in the newspapers two days later.

David was given immediate compassionate leave, and took the train along the south coast that morning still numbed. The chances of his being on the duty-roster for that particular flight were around five to one, and it seemed particularly cruel that he had been the man forced to leave his father to die. Yet, if one of his squadron had done so instead, would he not have accused the man evermore of treachery? That he was, indeed, dead, had been confirmed by a wireless message. Two others had been shot on the field; the third had committed suicide before he could be interrogated. There was comfort in the knowledge that his father would not suffer torture, as he himself had, but the manner of his death was so difficult to accept. Given time, acceptance *was* possible to a man who had lived through what he had experienced in the Far East – something which had broken him physically, but strengthened him inwardly – yet it would not be as easy for others, he realised.

Because of that he resolved to go across to Wattle Farm with the news rather than telephone it. His mother and Vesta were comforting each other, and he felt the truth he could not tell becoming too great a burden in their presence. It was a stormy still day, and he rode in no more than a shirt and breeches at an easy pace up through the copse and along the top of Wey Hill to Tarrant Maundle. Passing Tarlestock Towers his thoughts went automatically to the woman he had picked up, who had plainly featured strongly in his father's life. 'Mirjana' had flown with him on his very first pick-up, he remembered her clearly now. An agent, his colleagues had told him then, who had made many trips into enemy-occupied country; a woman of skill and great quiet courage. David had always imagined his father to be a man of little sexual passion, almost unaware of his good looks. Now he saw that to be a ridiculous assumption. It was surely inevitable that someone who loved beauty of words and artistry would love beauty of female form. Perhaps there had been truth in the old stories about his passion for Aunt Laura, after all.

Suddenly full of unexpressed grief, he stopped by the lone tree to dismount and stand for a while gazing down on the twin villages. All manner of thoughts and emotions ran through him as he looked at the panorama which had witnessed the youth of three Sheridan brothers. Two had made their mark and departed as very young men, leaving one to rebuild and ensure their sacrifice had not been in vain. He had fulfilled his obligation until battle madness had overtaken the world once more. Now he had joined his brothers, and David suddenly saw that the burden had passed to him. It must be not only peace he sought in returning his personal heritage to what it had once been, but a continuation of rural richness, and strength in the future. The soil of this country was precious. It had not been laid waste like that of so many European countries, and the coming years must ensure that it was made productive and remained peaceful.

By the time he swung back into the saddle he felt a great deal calmer, and two things that had troubled him deeply had been resolved. That calmness stood him in good stead when he faced Aunt Tessa. She was deeply shocked and upset by his news, but displayed her usual control as she promised to telephone Uncle Bill, who was in London.

'He will be quite shattered, David,' she declared. 'Those two had a relationship you and I will never understand. It was not as between father and son, doctor and patient, brothers, or even close friends. I believe it was a combination of all those, with the added quality brought by the fact that your father had a brilliant mind and Bill was able to see into it. The nearest I can suggest is the communion between identical twins. They spent little time together, yet, when they did meet up, it was as if time had stood still since their last meeting.'

Pat was out in the fields, so he walked in his restricted pace to the quiet hillside where she was checking the sheep. They had not met since his brutal rejection of her confession of love, but she took one look at his face and left what she was doing to go with him to the trees at the top of the field, away from the other

491

workers. He told her the official story as gently as possible, knowing she would take it badly. When he finished speaking, she turned and walked away along the line of trees, hands thrust into the pockets of her breeches, shoulders hunched, plainly fighting for control.

He went after her. 'Pat, don't walk away from me. You can cry on my shoulder, if you like.'

Her face was set and strained as she swung round to face him, coming to a halt in the shade of a tree where rabbits had a huge warren and frolicked at dawn and dusk.

'*Why him?*' she demanded thickly and unevenly. 'Why... him? After all he did... After... after coming through all that last time... Why... why should it be him?' Pulling one hand from her pocket, she clutched her dark hair at the nape of her neck as she struggled to continue. 'He was worth more than... more than...'

'I know,' he said quietly.

'*You know!*' she raged in growing passion. 'How can you know? You ignored him for years.'

'Pat, don't make it worse.'

'Make what worse? your feeling of guilt?'

'Stop that!'

Taking the two steps separating them she said in intensely passionate tones, 'You went through a damn awful time in the jungle and came back expecting everyone to understand. Well, we did, didn't we? We all sympathised. We all looked on you as a hero. We all went out of our way to make allowances. But you had lost your good looks, your intense sex appeal, so you felt sorry for yourself, became a martyr to your scars and disfigurements, went around in the self-indulgent belief that any expression of love was really pity, and any desire to share your future was really some kind of noble sacrifice in disguise.' Her hand let go of her hair, and was thrust back into her pocket again as her eyes began to sparkle with tears of rage.

'*He* went through a damn awful time in Gallipoli, but when he came back he didn't expect everyone to understand, because he had no idea who they were, or who he was. He wasn't scarred or crippled; his scars were inner ones. They lasted for two years, David. Two years of being terrifyingly alone. He was grateful for any kind of friendship, or any show of love from those around him. He had to put his past together piece by piece, and fight the threat of insanity that doing so brought him. But he did it. He... he bloody well did it,' she managed in the culmination of anger and grief. Then she added, 'If you don't abandon that stupid pride-induced isolation, and live as a

492

man worthy to be his son, it would have made more sense to rob the world of *you*.'

Swinging round she began striding away, her head thrown back to counteract building emotion, her progress wild and swerving. He watched her for a moment or two, fighting his own rising feelings, then went after her in his curious loping run until he seized her arm to halt her. She was instantly against him, holding herself to his body with arms that clung for comfort as she sobbed with total abandonment. As he stroked her hair clumsily with his bony hand, he realised that love was more than beauty and physical perfection. Love was having humility as well as pride, honesty rather than charm, compassion in addition to passion, and deep respect. Pat had offered all these to him, and he had cruelly refused them. He had turned his back on his father for years through false pride. Was he now repeating that tragic mistake by turning his back on a true love which had been there all along, unrecognised?

Her sobs had lessened, but he continued to stroke her hair as he said, 'I have been across the world, seen and done a great number of things, yet you have apparently seen more from your little corner of the world than I suspected. I have sometimes laughed at your philosophy, called it romantic nonsense.' Holding her closer, he brushed the top of her head with his lips. 'Pat, I have learned that it *is* possible for a man to love a woman enough to be prepared to die for her. If you're right about that, maybe your philosophy on life is saner than mine.' Pulling his handkerchief from his pocket, he gently wiped her wet cheeks. 'It looks as though I have so many things to do in the future, the pigs might have to wait for a while. Unless, of course, you feel like taking them on. It would mean taking me on, also, in time. There are no end of manuals on pig breeding you can read up for information, but none on men who still have a lot to learn. You'd have to work that out as you went along.' With his arm encircling her shoulders he began walking with her across the grass riddled with rabbit holes. All across the downward slope, sheep nibbled peacefully in the golden light from the sun, which was finally breaking through the sultry atmosphere. 'Will you think about it?' he asked.

Her head moved in a nod against his side as she walked. Sorrow was too immediate for happiness to leaven it. But it would, in time.

On 28th of August 1944, three days after General de Gaulle had led a liberating army of Free French troops into Paris, a memorial service for Sir Christopher Sheridan was held at

Tarrant Royal. It had been delayed for five weeks after his death, due to David's adamant refusal to use the wooden hut beside the ruin of the seventeenth-century church. He had personally organised and paid for work to remove the wreck of the German aircraft, and make the shell safe enough for people to occupy. The Rector and the people of Tarrant Royal had been astonished by the iron determination of the young man, who had never appeared to have the best of relationships with his distinguished father, but such was the esteem in which Sir Christopher had been held by them, they had backed his son to the hilt in the project. News of it had spread, and an elderly Pole claiming to have known Sir Christopher from pre-war years came to the village for the purpose of attempting to restore the organ enough to enable the hymns to be played on it. The officers and men of the American squadron now based at Longbarrow Airfield had displayed their national generosity and friendliness, by producing from their vast stores some rough pews and a number of crimson hassocks. One artistic orderly of Italian descent had melted down household candles and fashioned six altar candles with beautiful designs etched upon them. The officers at Tarrant Hall had organised a massive transparent cover as a roof for the church, but David only meant to use it if the day was wet. He wanted the sky as the roof, if at all possible.

The day dawned fine and clear. The Chandlers came to the Hall early, the two women respecting David's entreaty not to wear black for a man who had rejoiced in colour and beauty. They were dressed in frocks of deep blue and deep green, with matching hats and black gloves. Bill Chandler was in uniform, ashen-faced and still deeply upset. He undertook to escort Vesta, who appeared unable to accept that her father had gone forever, and was still unbelievably calm. She was in a dress of pale lavender with a hat of purple straw.

David's mother was different. Part of a generation brought up to respect traditional ways, she could not attend the memorial service for her husband in anything but deepest mourning. Totally uncomprehending of the death of a man, still young, who had seemed the most unlikely one to go from her life, she appeared to have lost her motivation and sense of direction. Looking to David to make all the decisions, and sitting for hours on end in the garden overlooking the green valley cradling the village, she had seemed completely detached until that morning when he went to her room to see if she was ready.

She was standing at the window on his entry, and at the

sound of his voice, her shoulders suddenly began to shake. The deluge of tears had finally come. He let her cry until she groped behind her for his comfort. When he went to her, she gripped his hand so tightly her fingers dug into the flesh taut over the crooked bones. But her gaze remained on the view from the window as she said, 'He was a part of my life almost since I was born, you know. As a small girl I used to look up to him. He was so clever, knew the answers to anything I asked. Then he grew, became taller, more muscular, strangely exciting to a young girl who had always admired him. But the cleverness I admired then isolated him from me, and I knew only one way of reaching him. That way ended by driving him away from me – from us, David. He returned a complete stranger, and, for a while, Tessa's brother Mike offered me what he never had. When Mike was killed I was lost. Then Rex and Laura went almost on the same day, and he was more lost than I with that double blow.

'At the start, I believe we felt we had something so fragile we both held back for fear of damaging it. He had valuable work to do, and I was ill-equipped to support him in it. Instead of learning to do so, I remained here looking after his home and children.' She paused for a moment, gripping his hand as if trying to hold on to her composure. 'I very foolishly tried to replace him with you, my dear. It was easy to do so, and I lived the pretence for years, little seeing what I was doing to you both.' She turned then, and looked at him with entreaty. 'You have time enough to forgive me, David. He never can.'

Fighting her tears she went on, 'When you eventually find something good, treasure it. Never leave kind words unsaid, tender gestures unmade. Never turn your back on it in false pride, or deny it because of things which have happened in the past. Never leave love and caring until it is too late.' She passed her free hand over their linked ones in a caressing gesture. 'I once . . . I once accused him of being so busy trying to love the whole world he had never cared for a single individual in his life. I see now that the whole world is made up of single individuals. If I had taken my place beside him, I might have realised it sooner.'

David stood looking at her, fighting a battle with himself. For over a month he had been trying to decide whether or not to break his silence. It was now or never. Then some instinct told him to leave things as they were. The truth would only increase his mother's sense of guilt and distress. It would also cause her to share his protest at the official lie, at the years which would have to pass before the secret could be revealed, at their inability to put his father's name on the war memorial with those of his two brothers, where it rightly belonged.

All he said was, 'It's not in the least too late, you know. The war will be over before long. There'll be the Hall to put back as it was, and the estate to re-organise. We'll start a restoration fund for the church. Vee and I don't need looking after any more, so you'll be able to devote your time to learning to love the whole world, if you want to. It'll be crying out for women like you, Mother, on welfare committees and such like. You'll carry on where Father left off five years ago, and everyone will rally round you to help.'

He took her downstairs a few minutes later to join the others, and she seemed a lot calmer when Aunt Tessa handed her a small glass of madeira. They all set out for the church on foot, as they always had in dry weather, walking in silence down the sloping driveway shaded by the horse chestnut trees until they turned into the lane leading to the village. In the distance the ducks on the pond were quacking for titbits, and one of the village dogs barked without ferocity at some passing annoyance. Birds were calling to each other from tree tops, and the occasional lazy baa from the sheep on the surrounding hills added to the sense of peacefulness. But, today there was no sound of tractors, no chatter from those working in the fields, no clattering of milk churns, no children shrieking in play. It was as if the entire village was empty.

It was apparent why when they rounded the corner. Their pace slowed instinctively, and David stared in amazement, deeply moved. The lane outside the church, the grassy verge to the gate, and the ground surrounding the ruin held a mass of people for whom there was no room inside the shell of the church itself. There were men in correct black, and women dressed in severe elegance from the city; uniforms of every description from far-flung corners of the world; the flowing robes of the Middle East, the flat faces of Orientals. There were white-haired veterans and fresh-faced youngsters. There were the bowed, the lame and the disfigured. There were statesmen, artists, linguists. And there were flowers – masses and masses of colour laid out amongst the headstones, and covering the bank behind the church like a magnificent tapestry.

'*Christ Almighty!*' exclaimed Bill Chandler in a thick voice. 'And he thought I'd be the only one to grieve at his funeral.'

'What is it?' asked Vesta faintly.

David put his hand lightly on her shoulder. 'It seems the whole world has come to honour him, Vee. The whole world.'

*

496

After the service there were so many people to speak to, so many strangers who appeared to know the man they had remembered that morning almost better than David did, it was some time before he could detach himself from the family group and cross to the red-haired woman in a vivid dress and large shady hat. She could have been dressed for a wedding. He knew why before she explained.

'He would not have wanted black.'

'I know.'

She turned to move slowly along the lane, away from the moving chattering crowd. He followed until they reached a shady area beneath the trailing branches of a willow. When she faced him again, he saw how truly beautiful she was. It made him curiously humble, for only an exceptional man could have won a woman such as she.

'I was always honoured by his love,' she told him frankly, in her faintly accented voice. 'I am equally honoured by your consideration in personally inviting me here today.'

'You were part of his life. An important part, it was tragically clear.'

Her lovely eyes seemed to be seeing more than his face as she said, 'The war took away all the beautiful things he held dear. I returned them to him for a while.'

'I think you did more than that,' he challenged.

'I loved him very deeply.' Her hand rested lightly on his arm. 'He spoke so often of you that I feel I know you. You have suffered, have witnessed bestiality and death many times. So have I. It enables us to accept his loss in a way others cannot. Naturally you must comfort your mother and sister, but if we could become friends, it would be our greatest tribute to him, David.'

He nodded. 'Yes, it would.'

'Before you consent to such a friendship, I must tell you something I have only recently learned. I am to have his child.'

As he stared at her too stunned to speak, she added, 'We have just heard the words "in death there is life", have we not? I think it is therefore not inappropriate for me to tell you this news on such a day. If you feel it is, then it will be impossible for us to be friends.'

'No . . . no,' he murmured, just realising the full implication of the revelation. 'Will you . . . I mean, can you manage?'

She smiled. 'You are so much like him. Yes, I need nothing more than your understanding and acceptance. I want his child so much, my dear. Like you, I have lost a great deal over these past years, and this will be my consolation. I have a house in

France which will be free for my return shortly. After the end comes, I will return to Vienna. May I write to you?' Holding out her hand she said, 'It may be that we shall not meet again, but I shall remember you as a very courageous young man.'

He took her hand and did something quite foreign to him. Before he thought what he was doing, he had raised it gently to kiss her fingers in an old-fashioned salute.

'The Knight on a White Charger,' she breathed with the first hint of distress. 'You are his son, without a doubt.'

When she walked away, he remained beneath the trailing willow. He would have children, but not sons to find him wanting. He wanted daughters; girls as beautiful as they could be. There was no reason for them not to be. The girl who would be their mother was lovely to look at, and his own ugliness was manmade. The Sheridan girls would put beauty and laughter back into the world. But not yet – not just yet. Meanwhile, a Sheridan without a name somewhere in Europe would have to do so until they arrived.

Vesta stood in the warmth of the sunshine, almost overcome by the perfume of the flowers surrounding her. The service had been extremely moving, the open roof letting the sound of lusty singing go straight up to the heavens. She had felt very close to her father in that ruined church, with the weight of his gold pendant around her neck.

Now she had quit the noise and chatter of the crowd, the din of their multi-lingual voices, to seek this peaceful corner of the churchyard which had meant so much to him. A multitude had come to honour him today, yet she felt her family had overlooked something vitally important. Her father had always said male Sheridans had a habit of dying in foreign lands, and Aunt Laura was their representative in the village. Vesta had come to ask her aunt to accept that responsibility for the third and last Sheridan brother – the one who had loved her without hope of love in return. Reaching out her hand, she traced the lettering on the new headstone her father had erected after the destruction of the church.

Brilliance lasts but a short while
The afterglow remains forever

Those words stood for them all, she realised.

Sinking onto the grass, she sat quietly with the distant sound of voices a mere background to her pensiveness. In the past she had visited this corner many times, had watched her parents light a candle here at Christmas, yet never had she felt such an overwhelming sense of human love as she did at that moment. It filled her empty heart, warmed the chill of loss, and gave her inner sight so that the flowers became a blaze of colour on the greatest canvas of her career which still had to be painted. Today David made the first move towards re-kindling the crusade for peace their father had been forced to abandon. Surely she could play her part in that by using the talent he had begged her to foster; by re-creating on canvas the former glory of Tarrant Royal church in dedication to his memory – surely a more fitting memorial to a man of peace than his name on a battle roll of honour.

Visions began to fill her artist's inner eye as inspiration gradually grew. Christmas, a Watchnight Service, with light streaming through the old stained glass windows onto the frosty ground outside; and over in the far corner, a single candle burning with a bright flame at the foot of a grave which represented an entire family. She would call the picture 'The Afterglow'. Swallowing the lump in her throat she told herself that it would be not only her gift of gratitude for all he had instilled in her, but also proof of her courage to accept the burden of survival in the face of others' loss, as he had.

It was a moment or two before she grew aware that someone was standing near, and looked up. It seemed a culmination of the renewed strength and hope that quiet corner had given her that he should be there. She slowly put up her hands, which he took to help her to her feet. He looked immensely tired and strained, but he was gazing at her the same way he had during their farewell in Naples.

'I went over with the troops at Normandy,' he began, keeping her hands in his. 'Since the landings I've been bogged down in some hot spots, where the mail was either very late or non-existent. Your letter only reached me two weeks ago.'

'Ah... I wondered,' she said, knowing nothing would ever end the love she felt for him.

'You wondered if I gave a damn; wondered if I'd simply tossed it away?'

'No. At least... Brad, I wasn't sure how you'd react to such a change of attitude for no apparent reason.'

'I wasn't sure myself, which is why I let time pass without doing anything positive.'

Trying to decipher his expression, she asked, 'Now you are sure?'

'Hell, no... But I read about this memorial service in a back copy of *The Times*, and passed up the chance to cover

499

De Gaulle's entry into Paris to get here today.'

Fearful of what he was trying to tell her, she fell back on the old resilient manner. 'You hardly missed an "exclusive". Every Western newsman must be witnessing the re-occupation of the French capital.'

He nodded. 'Sure they are. What I'm seeing in this village beats anything I would have scooped over there. Your father must have been quite some guy.'

'Yes... quite some guy.' All at once, the tears she had kept at bay all through the service spilled over, and she broke down.

Instantly taking her into his arms, he held her close in comfort, saying, 'I know, sweetheart, I know. Your "real" war has suddenly become far too real.'

They stood together, isolated from the crowd that was thinning with much banging of car doors and purring of expensive engines, and the sun was hot again on their heads, bared of hats during their eventual embrace. At the end of it, Brad lifted his head to say huskily, 'When you walked away from me in that hospital it was like having a limb amputated.'

'Is that why you came today?' she asked, shaken by the kiss.

'I came because I knew how much you loved your father, and I was afraid of what that loss might do to you on top of all else you've taken in this war.'

Holding her breath, she challenged him. 'It wasn't because you sensed a good story – a good piece of "heart and soul" reporting?'

'That, as well,' he admitted with complete honesty. 'I'm a newspaperman. Nothing will alter that.' Letting her absorb that for a moment or two, he went on, 'You must bear that in mind when you give your answer.'

'Answer to what?' she queried, conscious of the distant sound of the organist still playing in the shell of the church.

Brad circled her shoulders with his arm and began to lead her across the sun-warmed turf between the headstones, her purple straw hat forgotten where it lay beside Laura Sheridan's grave.

'My agency is sending me back to Italy to cover the final days of the campaign. I'd like you along with me.'

Her heart leapt as she thought of those villages, the sunshine on rioting blossoms, the simple mountain people displaying their emotions in public. Yet she stopped in her tracks to say, 'I seem to remember there was a woman called Gloria.'

'There still is. It seems she's fallen in love with the Honourable Fitzroy, who doesn't chase after "exclusives" at a moment's notice. She flew out to Naples to ask for a divorce.'

'And you agreed?'

His dark brown eyes gazed fiercely into hers. 'Are you coming with me to Italy, or not?'

'I'm coming, Brad. Of course I'm coming,' she reassured him softly. 'There is one thing I'd like to get straight between us first, however. What about Rosa or Lucia?'

'There'll be no need for either of them,' came his confident reply. 'I'll have you from now on, won't I?'

Smiling she said, 'Yes, you'll have me from now on.'

Circling her with his arm again, he guided her into the lane which lead up to Tarrant Hall, and they walked close together up the rise to her home.